The Complete Stories

ALSO BY CLARICE LISPECTOR

AVAILABLE FROM NEW DIRECTIONS

Água Viva

A Breath of Life

The Foreign Legion

The Hour of the Star

Near to the Wild Heart

The Passion According to G. H.

Selected Crônicas

Soulstorm

THE COMPLETE STORIES

Clarice Lispector

Translated from the Portuguese by Katrina Dodson

Introduction by Benjamin Moser

Edited by Benjamin Moser

A NEW DIRECTIONS BOOK

Translation copyright © 2015 by Katrina Dodson
Introduction copyright © 2015 by Benjamin Moser

Published by arrangement with the Heirs of Clarice Lispector and Agencia Literaria Carmen Balcells, Barcelona.

New Directions gratefully acknowledges the support of
MINISTÉRIO DA CULTURA
Fundação BIBLIOTECA NACIONAL

First published in cloth by New Directions in 2015
Manufactured in the United States of America
New Directions Books are printed on acid-free paper.
Design by Erik Rieselbach

Library of Congress Cataloging-in-Publication Data
Lispector, Clarice.
[Works. English]
Complete stories / Clarice Lispector ; translated by Katrina Dodson ; edited and with an introduction by Benjamin Moser.
pages cm
Includes bibliographical references.
ISBN 978-0-8112-1963-1 (alk. paper)
I. Dodson, Katrina, translator. II. Moser, Benjamin, editor. III. Title.
PQ9697.L585A2 2015
869.3'41—dc23   2015013285

10 9 8 7 6 5 4 3 2 1

New Directions Books are published for James Laughlin
by New Directions Publishing Corporation
80 Eighth Avenue. New York 10011

Contents

Glamour and Grammar by Benjamin Moser   ix

FIRST STORIES

The Triumph   3
Obsession   9
The Fever Dream   44
Jimmy and I   53
Interrupted Story   57
The Escape   63
Excerpt   68
Letters to Hermengardo   77
Gertrudes Asks For Advice   83
Another Couple of Drunks   96

FAMILY TIES

Daydream and Drunkenness of a Young Lady   105
Love   115
A Chicken   127
The Imitation of the Rose   131

Happy Birthday 151
The Smallest Woman in the World 165
The Dinner 173
Preciousness 178
Family Ties 190
Beginnings of a Fortune 200
Mystery in São Cristóvão 208
The Crime of the Mathematics Teacher 214
The Buffalo 222

THE FOREIGN LEGION

The Disasters of Sofia 235
The Sharing of Loaves 254
The Message 258
Monkeys 273
The Egg and the Chicken 276
Temptation 287
Journey to Petrópolis 290
The Solution 299
Evolution of a Myopia 302
The Fifth Story 309
A Sincere Friendship 313
The Obedient Ones 317
The Foreign Legion 323

Back of the Drawer

The Burned Sinner and the Harmonious Angels 341
Profile of Chosen Beings 354
Inaugural Address 359
Mineirinho 362

COVERT JOY

Covert Joy 369
Remnants of Carnival 373
Eat Up, My Son 377
Forgiving God 379
One Hundred Years of Forgiveness 384
A Hope 387
The Servant 390
Boy in Pen and Ink 393
A Tale of So Much Love 397
The Waters of the World 401
Involuntary Incarnation 404
Two Stories My Way 407
The First Kiss 410

WHERE WERE YOU AT NIGHT

In Search of a Dignity 415
The Departure of the Train 427
Dry Sketch of Horses 447
Where Were You at Night 455
Report on the Thing 471
Manifesto of the City 480
The Conjurings of Dona Frozina 482
That's Where I'm Going 485
The Dead Man in the Sea at Urca 487
Silence 489
A Full Afternoon 492
Such Gentleness 495
Soul Storm 497
Natural Life 500

THE VIA CRUCIS OF THE BODY

Explanation 505

Miss Algrave 507

The Body 515

Via Crucis 524

The Man Who Showed Up 529

He Drank Me Up 535

For the Time Being 539

Day After Day 542

The Sound of Footsteps 547

Before the Rio-Niterói Bridge 549

Praça Mauá 553

Pig Latin 558

Better Than to Burn 562

But It's Going to Rain 565

VISION OF SPLENDOR

Brasília 571

FINAL STORIES

Beauty and the Beast *or* The Enormous Wound 601

One Day Less 614

Appendix: The Useless Explanation 625

Translator's Note by Katrina Dodson 629

Bibliographical Note 636

Acknowledgments 644

Glamour and Grammar

"DO YOU RENOUNCE THE GLAMOUR OF EVIL," CATHOLIC
communicants are asked at Easter, "and refuse to be mastered
by sin?" The question preserves a conflation, now rare, of glamour and sorcery: glamour was a quality that confounds, shifts
shapes, invests a thing with a mysterious aura; it was, as Sir
Walter Scott wrote, "the magic power of imposing on the eye-
sight of spectators, so that the appearance of an object shall be
totally different from the reality."

The legendarily beautiful Clarice Lispector, tall and blonde,
clad in the outspoken sunglasses and chunky jewelry of a *grande
dame* of midcentury Rio, met the current definition of glamour.
She spent years as a fashion journalist and knew how to look
the part, but it is in the older sense of the word that Clarice
Lispector is glamorous: as a caster of spells, literally enchanting,
her nervous ghost haunting every branch of the Brazilian arts.

Her spell has grown unceasingly since her death. Then,
in 1977, it would have seemed exaggerated to say she was her
country's preeminent modern writer. Today, when it no longer
does, questions of artistic importance are, to a certain extent,
irrelevant. What matters is the magnetic love she inspires in

those susceptible to her. For them, Clarice is one of the great emotional experiences of their lives. But her glamour is dangerous. "Be careful with Clarice," a friend told a reader decades ago. "It's not literature. It's witchcraft."

The connection between literature and witchcraft has long been an important part of Clarice Lispector's mythology. That mythology, with a powerful boost from the internet, has developed ramifications so baroque that it might today be called a minor branch of Brazilian literature. Circulating unstoppably online is an entire shadow *oeuvre*, generally "deep" and breathing of passion. Online, too, Clarice has acquired a posthumous shadow body, as pictures of actresses portraying her are constantly reproduced in lieu of the original.

If the technology has changed its forms, the mythologizing itself is nothing new. Clarice Lispector became famous when, at the end of 1943, she published *Near to the Wild Heart*. She had just turned twenty-three, an obscure student from a poor immigrant background; her first novel had such a tremendous impact that, one journalist wrote, "we have no memory of a more sensational debut, which lifted to such prominence a name that, until shortly before, had been completely unknown." But only a few weeks after that name was becoming known, its owner departed Rio de Janeiro.

For almost two decades, she and her husband, a diplomat, lived abroad. Though she made regular visits home, she would not return definitively until 1959. In that interval, legends flourished. Her odd foreign name became a subject of speculation—one critic wondered whether it were a pseudonym—and others wondered whether she were not, in fact, a man. Taken together, the legends reflect an uneasiness, a feeling that she was something other than she seemed: "that the appearance of an object shall be totally different from the reality."

The word "appearance" must be stressed. A pretty foreign service wife, to all appearances an unthreatening pillar of the Brazilian bourgeoisie, produced a series of writings in a language so exotic that, in the words of one poet, "the foreignness of her prose" became "one of the most overwhelming facts of … the history of our language." There was something about her that was not what it seemed, a strangeness often recorded by those who encountered her writing for the first time. But it was rarely articulated as well as at the end of her life, in the middle of the military dictatorship, when she found herself being extensively vetted, and patted down physically, at Brasília airport.

"Do I look like a subversive?" she asked the security guard. The woman laughed before giving the only possible answer. "Actually," she said, "you do."

An old Scottish dictionary noted that "glamour" refers metaphorically to "female fascination." And it is an etymological curiosity that the word derives from "grammar." That word, in the middle ages, described any scholarship, but particularly occult learning: the ability to becharm, to reveal objects and lives as "totally different from the reality" of outward appearance. For a woman writer, particularly one renowned for revealing the hidden realities of visible lives through sliding, shifting syntax, the association is irresistible, and helps explain the "female fascination" Clarice Lispector has long exerted.

In these eighty-five stories, Clarice Lispector conjures, first of all, the writer herself. From adolescent promise through assured maturity to the implosion of an artist as she nears—

and summons—death, we discover the figure, greater than the sum of her individual works, who is beloved in Brazil. To speak of João Guimarães Rosa is to speak of *Grande sertão: veredas*. To speak of Machado de Assis is likewise to speak of his books, and only then of the remarkable man behind them. But to speak of Clarice Lispector is to speak of Clarice, the single name by which she is universally known: of the woman herself.

From the earliest story, published when she was nineteen, to the last, found in scratchy fragments after her death, we follow a lifetime of artistic experimentation through a vast range of styles and experiences. This literature is not for everyone: even certain highly literate Brazilians have been baffled by the cult-like fervor she inspires. But for those who instinctively understand her, the love for the person of Clarice Lispector is immediate and inexplicable. Hers is an art that makes us want to know the woman; she is a woman who makes us want to know her art. This book offers a vision of both: an unforgettable portrait, in and through her art, of that great figure, in all her tragic majesty.

Much in this book is unprecedented. For the first time in any language—including in Portuguese—all Clarice's stories are gathered in a single volume. It includes one, the first "Letter to Hermengardo," which I discovered in an archive. This unusual work offers new evidence of the importance of the Spinoza she read as a student, an influence that will echo throughout her life.

Exciting as such bibliographical landmarks are for the researcher or the biographer, something far more surprising appears when these stories are at last seen in their entirety. It is an accomplishment of whose historical significance the author herself cannot have been aware, for it could only appear retrospectively. And its force would be considerably diminished if it was an ideological expression rather than a natural outgrowth of the author's experiences.

This accomplishment lies in the second woman she conjures. If Clarice Lispector was a great artist, she was also a middle-class wife and mother. If the portrait of the extraordinary artist is fascinating, so is the portrait of the ordinary housewife whose life is the subject of this book. As the artist matures, the housewife, too, grows older. When Clarice is a defiant adolescent filled with a sense of her own potential—artistic, intellectual, sexual—so are the girls in her stories. When, in her own life, marriage and motherhood take the place of precocious childhood, her characters grow up too. When her marriage fails, when her children leave, these departures appear in her stories. When Clarice, once so gloriously beautiful, sees her body dirtied with wrinkles and fat, her characters see the same decline in theirs; and when she confronts the final unraveling of age and sickness and death, they are there beside her.

This is a record of woman's entire life, written over a woman's entire life. As such, it seems to be the first such total record written in any country. This sweeping claim requires qualifications. A wife and a mother; a bourgeois, Western, heterosexual woman's life. A woman who was not interrupted: a woman who did not start writing late, or stop for marriage or children, or succumb to drugs or suicide. A woman who, like so many male writers, began in her teens and carried on to the end. A woman who, in demographic respects, was exactly like most of her readers.

Their story had only been written in part. Before Clarice, a woman who wrote throughout her life—*about* that life—was so rare as to be previously unheard-of. The claim seems extravagant, but I have not identified any predecessors.

The qualifications are important, but even when they are dropped it is astonishing how few women had managed to create full bodies of work. Those who had were precisely the women exempted from the obstacles that kept most women from writing. These are the barriers Tillie Olsen adumbrated in her famous essay of 1962, "Silences in Literature," the barriers that led to women's being, in Olsen's calculation, "one out of twelve" writers in the twentieth century. There were exceptions, but they were exceptional in being exempted from the problems that plagued most women. "In our century as in the last," Olsen wrote, "almost all distinguished achievement has come from childless women." Edith Wharton was far from middle-class; Colette hardly lived, or wrote about, a conventional bourgeois life. Others—Gabriela Mistral, Gertrude Stein—had, like many male writers, wives of their own.

Clarice Lispector, as these stories make clear, was intimately acquainted with these barriers. Her characters struggle against ideological notions about a woman's proper role; face practical entanglements with husbands and children; worry about money; confront the private despair that leads to drinking, madness, or suicide. Like so many women writers everywhere, Clarice was ignored by publishers, agonizingly, for years on end. As even the greatest women were, she was consistently placed in a separate (lower) category by reviewers and scholars. (As late as the 1960s, Virginia Woolf herself was rarely found on syllabi.) Clarice persisted anyway, once remarking that she did not enjoy being compared to Virginia Woolf because Woolf *had* given up: "The terrible duty is to go to the end."

But her sympathy for silent and silenced women haunts these stories. The earliest, written when Clarice was in her teens and early twenties, often feature a restless girl in conflict with a man:

> Mama, before she got married, according to Aunt Emília, was a firecracker, a tempestuous redhead, with thoughts of her own about liberty and equality for women. But then along came Papa, very serious and tall, with thoughts of his own too, about ... liberty and equality for women. The trouble was in the coinciding subject matter.

If these women are sometimes crushed by imposing, fascinating men, they become more assertive as the author grows older. But it is a different kind of assertion. The strident feminism of Clarice's student years gives way to something far less explicit, and these characters no longer flaunt thoughts about "liberty and equality for women." They simply live their lives with as much dignity as they can muster. In art as in life, that is not always very much.

Many are silent. The grandmother in "Happy Birthday" surveys the petty mediocrities she has spawned with wordless revulsion. The Congolese pygmy in "The Smallest Woman in the World" has no words to express her love. The hen in "A Chicken" has no words to say that she is about to give birth — and thus cannot be killed. The adulteress in "The Burned Sinner and the Harmonious Angels" has to listen to all kinds of people talk about her. The priest admits that "I fear from this woman who is ours a word that is hers." Her husband admonishes the crowd to "beware a woman who dreams." She herself utters not a single word, and the play concludes when she is burned as a witch.

The other side of silence is speech. Today, women as writers—and women as the subjects of women writers—are so familiar that it is hard to believe that Clarice Lispector's characters or their lives ever needed to be discovered. But to see this work from the perspective of what came after is to miss its historical novelty.

Clarice was fundamentally without a tradition. She was an immigrant, and though she had the ancient European Jewish tradition behind her, that world, particularly in the tiny shtetl where she was born, was not easily adaptable to modern urban lives. And in the literature of the language she wrote, the subject of modern women no more existed than did women writers themselves.

In this respect, Portuguese was no different from any other language, and Brazil no different from any other country. Clarice was nine when Virginia Woolf asked a question she later quoted: "Who shall measure the heat and violence of the poet's heart when caught and tangled in a woman's body?" The question, Woolf believed, applied as much to women of her own day as it did to women of Shakespeare's.

This novelty explains some of the fascination and confusion early readers of "Hurricane Clarice" expressed. One imagines a similar thrill of discovery among the first readers of Dickens and Zola and Dostoevsky, when literature first cast its light on the working classes; or when gay readers first saw their lives written about sympathetically; or when colonial peoples exchanged the condescension of folklore for the higher dignity of literature. The astonishment her achievement provoked is still palpable in the yellowing scrapbooks preserving the reviews in Clarice Lispector's archives.

This achievement begs the question of how she succeeded where so many had failed: how *Clarice Lispector*—of all people—succeeded. She came from a tradition of failure, a tradition of no tradition, as a Brazilian woman writer, as a woman writer, as a woman, but perhaps most of all as a result of her own background. Her early years were so catastrophic that it is a miracle she survived them.

She was born on December 10, 1920, to a Jewish family in western Ukraine. It was a time of chaos, famine, and racial war. Her grandfather was murdered; her mother was raped; her father was exiled, penniless, to the other side of the world. The family's tattered remnants washed up in northeastern Brazil in 1922. There, her brilliant father, reduced to peddling rags, barely managed to keep his family fed; there, when Clarice was not quite nine, her mother died of her wartime injuries.

Her sister Elisa wrote that their liberal father, whose own desire to study had been thwarted by anti-Semitism, "was determined for the world to see what kind of daughters he had." With his encouragement, Clarice pursued her education far beyond the level allowed even girls far more economically advantaged. Only a couple of years after reaching the capital, Clarice, from a family clinging to the lowest rungs of the middle class, entered one of the redoubts of the elite, the National Law Faculty of the University of Brazil. There, Jews (zero) were even more rare than women (three).

Her law studies left little mark. She was already pursuing her vocation into the newsrooms of the capital, where her beauty and brilliance made a dazzling impression. She was, her boss wrote, "a smart girl, an excellent reporter, and, in contrast to almost all women, actually knows how to write." On May 25, 1940, she published her earliest known story, "The Triumph." Three months later, age fifty-five, her father died.

Before her twentieth birthday, then, Clarice was an orphan. In early 1943, she married a Catholic, unheard-of for a Jewish girl in Brazil. At the end of that year, shortly after she published her first novel, she and her husband left Rio de Janeiro. In short order, therefore, she left her family, her ethnic community, and her country. She also left her profession, journalism, in which she had a burgeoning reputation.

She found exile intolerable, and during her fifteen years abroad her tendency toward depression grew sharper. But despite its disadvantages, perhaps exile—this series of exiles— explains how she managed to write.

Her immigrant background left her less susceptible to the received ideas of Brazilian society. And in purely financial terms, her marriage was a step up. She was never rich, but as long as she was married she did not have to work on anything but writing. It is hard to imagine her creating the complex works of this period—three novels and the stories of *Family Ties*—amidst the relentless demands and meager paychecks of full-time journalism. She had two children, but she also had full-time help. This meant free hours every day: a room of her own.

This would have been the case for any Brazilian woman of the class she married into. Why, then, did so few develop their talents? Most were trapped inside the structures that blocked women everywhere: lack of education and forced motherhood topped the list. But they were also blocked by a generalized unconcern with what they might have to say, an unspoken attitude that women didn't do certain things. To be a foreigner, on the other hand, meant an exemption from the normal ways of doing things. It was a productive cultural alienation, and the other side of alienation is freedom. Clarice's experience of both resonates throughout her life.

Traditionally "female" subjects—marriage and motherhood, kids and clothes—had, of course, been treated before. They are all here. But alongside them the little dramas of women's lives gain expression, sometimes for the first time: the tedium and the covert joys of the average housewife; the young woman's delight in her beauty, and her subsequent discovery of the horrors the mirror holds: her face deformed by makeup; her body getting fat; her body growing old. Had any writer ever described a seventy-seven-year-old lady dreaming of coitus with a pop star, or an eighty-one-year-old woman masturbating? Half a century or more after they were written, many of these stories, read in an entirely different age, have lost none of their novelty, none of their power to shock.

In dance as in music, in painting as in literature, the great artist is one who uses the tiniest details—the brushstroke, the grace note, the turn of foot or phrase—to create a whole that, though made of these details, nonetheless surpasses their sum. As Clarice Lispector's reputation is more than the achievement of her individual works, so does there emerge from the portraits in these stories—short as well as long, addressing both fleeting moments and great crises—a master-narrative of human experience: of the dramas, big and small, that make up a person's life. Shortly before she died, a critic asked Clarice whether two plus two equaled five:

> For a second I was speechless. But then a darkly humor-
> ous anecdote sprang to mind: It goes like this: the psy-
> chotic says that two plus two equals five. The neurotic
> says: two plus two equals four but I just can't take it.

New subjects require new language. Part of Clarice's odd
grammar can be traced to the powerful influence of the Jewish mysticism to which she was introduced by her father. But
another part of its strangeness can be attributed to her need to
invent a tradition. As anyone who reads these stories from beginning to end will see, they are shot through by a ceaseless lin-
guistic searching, a grammatical instability, that prevents them
from being read too quickly.

The reader—not to mention the poor translator—is often tripped up by their nearly Cubist patterns. In certain late
stories, the difficulties are obvious. But many of Clarice's re-
orderings are so subtle that one not paying close attention
can easily miss them. This makes them extremely difficult to
reproduce and also explains, in part, their poetic appeal. In
"Love," for example, we read: "They were growing up, taking
their baths, demanding for themselves, misbehaved, ever more
complete moments." The sentence, like so many of Clarice's,
makes sense if read in a quick glance—and then, examined
again, slowly, begins to dissolve. In "Happy Birthday," amidst
an awkward celebration, a child verbalizes an awkward pause:
"Their mother, comma!"

In *Why This World: A Biography of Clarice Lispector*, I examined her roots in Jewish mysticism and the essentially spiritual impulse that animated her work. As the Kabbalists found
divinity by rearranging letters, repeating nonsensical words,

parsing verses, and seeking a logic other than the rational, so did Clarice Lispector. With several exceptions ("The Egg and the Chicken," "Brasília," "Dry Study of Horses"), this mystic quality, which can make her prose nearly abstract, is less visible here than in novels such as *The Passion According to G. H.* or *The Apple in the Dark*. But to see Clarice Lispector's writing as a whole is to understand the close connection between her interest in language and her interest in what—for lack of a better word—she called God.

In these stories, the divine erupts beneath carefully tended everyday lives. "She had pacified life so well," she writes in one story, "taken such care for it not to explode." When the inevitable explosions come, shifts in grammar announce them long before they explicitly appear in the plot. Laura, the bored, childless housewife in "The Imitation of the Rose," has a "painstaking taste for method"—until her grammar starts to slide.

> Carlota would be stunned to learn that they too had a private life and things they never told, but she wouldn't tell, what a shame not to be able to tell, Carlota definitely thought she was just tidy and mundane and a little annoying, and if she had to be careful not to burden other people with details, with Armando she'd sometimes relax and get pretty annoying, which didn't matter because he'd pretend to be listening without really listening to everything she was telling him, which didn't ever bother her, she understood perfectly well that her chattering tired people out a bit, but it was nice to be able to explain how she hadn't found any meat even if Armando shook his head and wasn't listening, she and the maid chatted a lot, actually she talked more than the

maid, and she was also careful not to pester the maid who sometimes held back her impatience and could get a little rude, it was her own fault because she didn't always command respect.

These signals can be much more concise, as in *The Passion According to G. H.*, when another housewife recounts the mystical shock she underwent the day before. Remembering herself as she then was, G. H. says:

I finally got up from the breakfast table, that woman.

The transformation described in the novel—then to now—yesterday to today—her to me—first person to third—is resumed in a breezy anacoluthon, the break in grammar perfectly symbolizing the break in this woman's life. Like so many of Clarice's best phrases, it is elegant precisely because it disregards the mannered conventions that are the elegance of belles lettres.

"In painting as in music and literature," Clarice Lispector wrote, "what is called abstract so often seems to me the figurative of a more delicate and difficult reality, less visible to the naked eye." The effort to supersede apparently inevitable structures animated modern art. As abstract painters sought to portray mental and emotional states without direct representation, and modern composers expanded traditional laws of harmony, Clarice undid reflexive patterns in grammar. She often had to remind readers that her "foreign" speech was not the result of her European birth or an ignorance of Portuguese. One of the most highly educated women of her generation was no more ignorant of the standard Brazilian language than Schoenberg was of the diatonic scale, or Picasso of anatomy.

Nor, needless to say, of the proper ways women presented

themselves. As a professional fashion writer, she reveled in her characters' appearances. And then she disheveled their dresses, smudged their mascara, deranged their hair, enchanting well-composed faces with the creepier glamour Sir Walter Scott described. With overturned words, she conjured an entire unknown world—conjuring, too, the unforgettable Clarice Lispector: a female Chekhov on the beaches of Guanabara.

BENJAMIN MOSER

FIRST STORIES

The Triumph
("O triunfo")

THE CLOCK STRIKES NINE. A LOUD, SONOROUS PEAL, followed by gentle chiming, an echo. Then, silence. The bright stain of sunlight lengthens little by little over the lawn. It goes climbing up the red wall of the house, making the ivy glisten in a thousand dewy lights. It finds an opening, the window. It penetrates. And suddenly takes possession of the room, slipping past the light curtains standing guard.

Luísa remains motionless, sprawled atop the tangled sheets, her hair spread out on the pillow. An arm here, another there, crucified by lassitude. The heat of the sun and its brightness fill the room. Luísa blinks. She frowns. Purses her lips. Opens her eyes, finally, and leaves them fixed on the ceiling. Little by little the day enters her body. She hears a sound of dry leaves crunching underfoot. Footsteps in the distance, tiny and hurried. A child is running out on the road, she thinks. Once more, silence. She amuses herself a moment listening to it. It is absolute, like the silence of death. Naturally since the house is remote, rather isolated. But ... what about the domestic noises of every morning? The sound of footsteps, laughter, the clattering of dishes that announce the start of the day in her house? Slowly the idea crosses her mind that she knows the reason for the silence. She pushes it away, though, stubbornly.

Suddenly her eyes widen. Luísa finds herself sitting up in bed, a shiver coursing throughout her body. She looks with her eyes, her head, her every nerve, at the other bed in the room. It's empty.

She props her pillow up vertically, leans against it, head tilting back, eyes closed.

It's true, then. She thinks back to the previous afternoon and night, the tortured, long night that followed and dragged on until dawn. He left, yesterday afternoon. He took his bags with him, the bags that just two weeks ago had come home festively covered in labels from Paris, Milan. He also took the manservant who had come with them. The silence in the house was explained. She was alone, since his departure. They had fought. She, silent, before him. He, the refined, superior intellectual, yelling, accusing her, pointing his finger at her. And that feeling she'd already experienced during their other fights: if he leaves, I'll die, I'll die. She could still hear his words.

"You, you trap me, you annihilate me! Keep your love, give it to someone who wants it, someone who has nothing better to do! Got it? Yes! Ever since I met you I haven't produced a thing! I feel tied down. Tied down by your fussing, your caresses, your excessive zeal, by you yourself! I despise you! Think about that, I despise you! I ..."

These explosions happened often. There was always the threat of his leaving. Luísa, at that word, would transform. She, so full of dignity, so ironic and sure of herself, would beg him to stay, with such pallor and madness in her face, that he'd given in every other time. And happiness would flood her, so intense and bright, that it compensated for what she'd never imagined was a humiliation, but that he'd make her see with ironic arguments, which she wouldn't even hear. This time he'd lost his temper, as he had every other time, for almost no reason. Luísa had interrupted him, he said, right when a new idea was stirring, luminous, in his brain. She'd cut off his inspiration at the very instant it was springing forth, with a silly comment about the weather, and concluding with a loathsome: "isn't it, darling?" He said he needed the proper conditions in order to produce, to continue his novel, nipped in the bud by an absolute inability to concentrate. He'd gone off somewhere to find "the atmosphere."

And the house had been left in silence. She, stuck in the bedroom, as if her entire soul had been removed from her body. Waiting, to see him reappear, his manly form framed in the doorway. She'd hear him say, his beloved broad shoulders shaking with laughter, that it was all just a joke, just an experience to insert into a page of the book.

But the silence had dragged on infinitely, punctured only by the monotonous hiss of the cicadas. The moonless night had gradually invaded the room. The cool June breeze made her shiver.

"He's gone," she thought. "He's gone." Never had this expression struck her as so full of meaning, though she'd read it many times before in romantic novels. "He's gone" wasn't that simple. She dragged around an immense void in her head and chest. If anyone were to bang on them, she imagined, they'd sound metallic. How would she live now? she suddenly asked herself, with an exaggerated calm, as if it were some neutral thing. She kept repeating and repeating: what now? She cast her eyes around the gloomy bedroom. She switched on the light, looked for his clothes, his book on the nightstand, traces of him. Nothing left behind. She got scared. "He's gone."

She'd tossed and turned in bed for hours and hours and sleep hadn't come. Toward dawn, weakened by wakefulness and pain, eyes stinging, head heavy, she fell into a semi-unconsciousness. Not even her head stopped working, images, the maddest kind, ran through her mind, barely sketched out and already fleeting.

It strikes eleven, long and leisurely. A bird lets out a piercing cry. Everything has stood still since yesterday, thinks Luísa. She's still sitting up in bed, stupidly, not knowing what to do. Her eyes fix on a marina, in cool colors. Never had she seen water give quite that impression of liquidness and movement. She'd never even noticed the painting. Suddenly, like a dart, wounding sharp and deep: "He's gone." No, it's a lie! She stands. Surely he got angry and went to sleep in the next room. She runs, pushes the door open. Empty.

She goes to the desk where he used to work, rifles feverishly through the abandoned newspapers. Maybe he's left some note, saying, for instance: "In spite of everything, I love you. I'll be back tomorrow." No, today! All she finds is a piece of paper from his notepad. She turns it over. "I've been sitting here for two solid hours and still haven't been able to focus my attention. Yet, at the same time, I'm not focusing it on anything around me. It has wings, but doesn't land anywhere. I just can't write. I just can't write. With these words I'm scratching at a wound. My mediocrity is so…" Luísa breaks off reading. What she'd always felt, only vaguely: mediocrity. She's absorbed. So he knew it, then? What an impression of weakness, of faintheartedness, on that simple piece of paper … Jorge …, she murmurs feebly. She wishes she hadn't read that confession. She leans against the wall. Silently she cries. She cries until she feels limp.

She goes to the sink and splashes her face. Sensation of coolness, release. She's waking. She perks up. Braids her hair, pins it up. Scrubs her face with soap, until her skin feels taut, shiny. She looks at herself in the mirror and resembles a schoolgirl. She tries to find her lipstick, but remembers in time that she no longer needs it.

The dining room lay in darkness, humid and stuffy. She throws open the windows. And the brightness penetrates all at once. The new air enters swiftly, touches everything, ripples the sheer curtains. Even the clock seems to strike more vigorously. Luísa halts in surprise. So much is charming about this cheerful room. About these things suddenly brightened and revived. She leans out the window. In the shadow of that line of trees, ending a long way down the red clay road ... In fact she hadn't noticed any of this. She'd always lived there with him. He was everything. He alone existed. He was gone. And things hadn't entirely lost their charm. They had a life of their own. Luísa ran her hand over her forehead, she wanted to push away her thoughts. From him she had learned the torture of ideas, plunging deeper into their slightest particulars.

She made coffee and drank it. And since she had nothing to do and was afraid of thinking, she took some clothes lying out to be washed and went to the back of the yard, where there was a large sink. She rolled up her pajama sleeves and pants and started scrubbing everything with soap. Bent over like that, moving her arms vehemently, biting her lower lip from the effort, the blood pulsing strong throughout her body, she surprised herself. She stopped, unwrinkled her brow and stood staring straight ahead. She, so spiritualized by that man's company ... She seemed to hear his ironic laugh, quoting Schopenhauer, Plato, who thought and thought ... A sweet breeze made the hairs on the back of her neck rise, dried the suds on her fingers.

Luísa finished the chore. Her whole body gave off the rough, plain scent of soap. The work had warmed her up. She looked at the large spigot, gushing clear water. She felt a wave of heat … Suddenly an idea came to her. She took off her clothes, opened the spigot all the way, and the cold water coursed over her body, making her shriek at the cold. That improvised bath made her laugh with pleasure. Her bathtub took in a marvelous view, beneath an already blazing sun. For a moment she became serious, still. The novel unfinished, the confession discovered. She became lost in thought, a wrinkle on her brow and at the corners of her lips. The confession. But the water was flowing cold down her body and noisily clamoring for her attention. A good heat was now circulating through her veins. Suddenly, she had a smile, a thought. He'd be back. He'd be back. She looked around at the perfect morning, breathing deeply and feeling, almost with pride, her heart beating steadily and full of life. A warm ray of sunshine enveloped her. She laughed. He'd be back, because she was the stronger one.

Obsession
("Obsessão")

NOW THAT THE AFFAIR IS BEHIND ME, I CAN RECOL-
lect it more serenely. I won't try to make excuses for myself. I'll
try not to point fingers. It simply happened.

I don't recall very clearly how it started. I transformed myself independently of my consciousness and when I opened my
eyes the poison was circulating through my blood irremediably, its power already ancient.

I must tell a bit about myself, before my encounter with
Daniel. Only thus can one understand the ground in which his
seeds were scattered. Though I didn't think one could entirely
comprehend why those seeds bore such sad fruit.

I was always serene and never showed the least sign of possessing those elements that Daniel brought out in me. I was
born of simple creatures, steeped in that wisdom one acquires
through experience and figures out with common sense. We
lived, from childhood until I was fourteen, in a nice house on the
outskirts of town, where I went to school, played and roamed
without a care beneath the benevolent gaze of my parents.

Until one day they discovered I was a young lady, lowered
the hem of my dress, made me wear new clothes and considered

me almost ready. I accepted the discovery and its consequences without much commotion, in the same distracted way that I studied, went out, read, and lived.

We moved to a house closer to the city, in a neighborhood whose name, along with other subsequent details, I shall suppress. There I would have the chance to meet other boys and girls, Mama said. I really did make friends quickly, with my good-natured, easygoing cheer. They thought I was adorable, and my sturdy body, my fair skin made them like me.

As for my dreams, I was so full of them at that age—those of any young girl: to get married, have children and, finally, be happy, a desire I didn't really clarify and which confusingly matched the endings of the thousand novels I'd read, without ever contaminating me with their romanticism. I only hoped that everything would be all right, though I would never be overwhelmed with satisfaction if that's how it turned out.

At nineteen I met Jaime. We got married and rented a pretty, nicely furnished apartment. We lived together for six years, without children. And I was happy. If someone asked me, I said yes, adding not without some bewilderment: "And why wouldn't I be?"

Jaime was always good to me. And I considered his not very impassioned temperament to be somehow an extension of my parents, of my former home, where I'd grown used to the privileges of an only daughter.

I lived easily. I never devoted a deeper thought to any one subject. And, as if to spare myself even more, I didn't entirely believe in the books I read. They were made just for entertainment, I thought.

Once in a while, groundless melancholy would darken my face, a dull and incomprehensible nostalgia for times never experienced would invade me. Nothing romantic, and I'd push them away as quickly as I would a useless notion unconnected to the really important things. Which ones? I didn't really define them and grouped them under the ambiguous expression "things of life." Jaime. Me. Home. Mama.

Meanwhile, the people around me carried on serenely, their foreheads smooth and unworried, in a milieu where habit had long since opened the correct paths, where facts were reasonably explained by visible causes and the most extraordinary were connected, not through mysticism but through self-serving complacency, to God. The only events that could disturb their souls were birth, marriage, death and their attendant conditions.

Or am I mistaken and could it be that, in my happy blindness, I didn't know how to peer into things more deeply? I don't know, but now I think it seems impossible for the shadowy region in every man, even the peaceful ones, not to harbor the threat of other, more terrible and suffering men.

If that vague dissatisfaction ever arose to bother me, I, without knowing how to explain it and used to giving a clear name to all things, wouldn't allow it or would attribute it to physical ailments. Furthermore, the Sunday gathering at my parents' house, together with the cousins and neighbors, whatever pleasant and lively game would quickly win me over again and set me back on the straight path, to walk again with the masses who have their eyes closed.

I realize now that it was a certain apathy, rather than peace, that turned my acts and my desires to ash. I remember how Jaime had once said, a bit emotionally:

"If only we had a child …"

I responded, carelessly:

"What for?"

A dense veil isolated me from the world and, without my knowing it, an abyss separated me from myself.

And that's how I went on until I caught typhoid fever and nearly died. My two households sprang into action and throughout nights and days of labor saved me.

Convalescence arrived to find me thin and wan, without the slightest interest in anything of the world. I hardly ate, grew irritated at the simplest words. I'd spend the day propped against the pillow, not thinking, not moving, caught in a sweet and abnormal languor. I can't say for certain whether this state more easily allowed Daniel's influence. I rather imagine that I exaggerated my infirmity to keep people around me, as when I was ill. Whenever Jaime got back from work, I'd purposely emphasize my fragility.

I hadn't meant to frighten him, but I managed to. And one day, when I'd already forgotten my "convalescent" pose, they informed me that I was to spend two months in Belo Horizonte, where the good climate and new environment would strengthen me. Argument was out of the question. Jaime took me there, on a night train. He found me a nice boardinghouse and departed, leaving me alone, with nothing to do, suddenly launched into a freedom I hadn't asked for and didn't know how to use.

Perhaps that was the start. Out of my sphere, far from the things that seemed like they'd always been there, I felt unsupported because in the end not even conventional wisdom had taken root in me, so superficially had I been living. What had kept me going until then were not convictions, but the people who held them. For the very first time they were giving me a chance to *see* with my own eyes. For the very first time they were isolating me with myself. Judging from the letters I wrote during that time and read much later, I notice that a feeling of distress had seized me. In all of them I mentioned coming home, desiring it with a certain anxiety. That is, until Daniel.

I cannot, even now, recall Daniel's face. I mean my first impressions of that physiognomy of his, altogether different from the assemblage I later got used to. Only then, unfortunately a bit too late, did I manage through daily proximity to comprehend and absorb his features. But they were different ... Of the first Daniel I've retained nothing, except the imprint.

I know that he was smiling, that's all. From time to time, some isolated feature of his comes to mind, from the former days. His long and curved fingers, those thick, wide-set brows. That's all. Because he overpowered me in a way that, if I can put it like this, almost prevented me from seeing him. I really do believe that my later anguish was intensified by this impossibility of reconstructing his appearance. So all I possessed were his words, the memory of his soul, everything that wasn't human in Daniel. And during nights of insomnia, unable to reconstruct him mentally, already exhausted by these futile attempts, I'd glimpse him as you might a shadow, huge, with shifting contours, looming oppressive yet also distant as a threat. Like a painter who bends the treetops in order to capture a gust of wind on his canvas, sending hair and skirts flying, I could only ever manage to recall him by transporting me to myself, to the version from that time. I martyred myself with accusations, despised myself and, hurt and broken-hearted, lodged him vividly inside myself.

But I must start at the beginning, to put a bit of order into this narrative of mine ...

Daniel lived in the boardinghouse where I was staying. He never approached me, nor had I ever particularly noticed him.

Until one day I heard him speak, entering suddenly into someone else's conversation, though without losing that distant manner he had, as if just emerging from a deep sleep. It was about work. Which should be no more than a means of ending immediate hunger. And, amused at scandalizing the bystanders, he added—any day now he'd abandon his own, which he'd done several times before, to live like "a good bum." A bespectacled student, after the first moment of silence and reticence that fell, coldly retorted that above all else work was a duty. "A duty in the interest of society." Daniel made some gesture, as if he couldn't be bothered to convince anyone, and granted one sentence:

"Someone's already declared there's no foundation for duty."

He left the room, leaving the student fuming. And me, surprised and amused: I had never heard anyone defy work, "such a serious obligation." Jaime and Papa's greatest revolts manifested themselves in the form of some trivial complaint. In general, I'd never recalled that you ever could not accept, could choose, could revolt ... Above all, I'd perceived in Daniel's words a disregard for convention, for "things of life" ... And it had never occurred to me, except as a slight whimsy, to wish that the world were different than it was. I recalled Jaime, always praised for "fulfilling his duties," as he said, and felt, without knowing why, safer.

Later, when I saw Daniel again, I stiffened into a cold and useless posture, since he barely noticed me, lumping me together with the rest of the boardinghouse, safeguarded. However, when I looked everyone over at dinner, I vaguely felt a certain shame in belonging to that amorphous group of men and women who had banded together in tacit agreement, stoking their indignation, united against the one who had come to disturb their comfort. I understood that Daniel scorned them and I was irritated because I too was implicated.

I wasn't used to lingering for very long over any one thought, and a subtle discontent, like an impatience, seized me. From then on, without thinking, I avoided Daniel. Whenever I saw him, I imperceptibly grew wary, eyes wide open, watchful. I think I feared he'd make one of those cutting remarks of his, because I was worried I'd agree … I mustered my dislike, defending myself from who knows what, defending Papa, Mama, Jaime and all my own people. But it was in vain. Daniel was the danger. And I was heading toward him.

Another time, I was wandering aimlessly through the empty boardinghouse, at two o'clock on a rainy afternoon, until, hearing voices in the waiting room, I went in. He was talking to a thin fellow, dressed in black. Both were smoking, speaking unhurriedly, so absorbed in their thoughts that they didn't even see me come in. I was about to retreat, but a sudden curiosity took hold of me and led me to an easy chair, at a distance from where they were sitting. After all, I justified to myself, the room belonged to the lodgers. I tried not to make a sound.

In those first few moments, to my astonishment, I understood none of what they were saying … I gradually made out a few recognizable words, among others that I'd never heard spoken aloud: terms from books. "The universality of …" "the abstract meaning of …" It must be known that I never witnessed discussions in which the subject wasn't "things" and "stories." I myself, having little imagination and little intelligence, thought strictly along the lines of my narrow reality.

His words slid over me, without penetrating. However, I sensed, singularly uncomfortable, how they hid a harmony of their own that I couldn't quite grasp … I tried not to get distracted so as not to miss any part of the magical conversation.

"Achievements kill desire," said Daniel.

"Achievements kill desire, achievements kill desire," I repeated to myself, somewhat bewildered. I drifted off and when I started paying attention again yet another brilliant and mysterious phrase had been born, disturbing me.

Now Daniel was talking about himself.

"What interests me above all is feeling, accumulating desires, filling me up with myself. Achievements open me up, leave me empty and sated."

"There's no such thing as satiety," the other one said, between exhalations from his cigarette. "Dissatisfaction returns, creating yet another desire that a normal man would try to satisfy. You're justifying its futility with some random theory. 'What matters is feeling and not doing ...' Sorry. You've failed and all you can do is assert yourself through the imagination ..."

I listened to them, numb. Not only did the conversation surprise me but, the grounds on which it was based, something far from everyday truth, but mysteriously melodic, touching upon, I sensed, other truths unknown to me. And I was also surprised to see them attack each other with unfriendly words that would have offended any other person but that they accepted indifferently, as if ... as if they didn't know the meaning of "honor," for example.

And, above all, for the very first time I, in a deep slumber until then, caught a glimpse of ideas.

The uneasiness those first conversations with Daniel produced in me arose as from a certainty of danger. One day I managed to explain to him that the thought of this danger was linked to expressions read in books with the scant attention I generally granted to everything and that now flared in my memory: "fruit of evil" ... When Daniel told me that I was speaking of the Bible, I was seized with terror of God, combined nevertheless with a strong and shameful curiosity like the kind from an addiction.

Because of all this, my story is difficult to explain, when divided into its elements. How far did my feeling for Daniel go (I use this general term because I don't know exactly what it contained) and where did my awakening to the world begin? Everything was interwoven, mixed up inside me and I couldn't specify whether my unease was desire for Daniel or yearning to seek the newly discovered world. Because I awoke simultaneously as a woman and a human.

Perhaps Daniel had acted merely as an instrument, perhaps my destiny really was the one I pursued, the destiny of those set loose upon the earth, of those who don't measure their actions according to Good and Evil, perhaps I, even without him, would have discovered myself some day, perhaps, even without him, I would have fled Jaime and his land. How can I know?

I listened to them, for nearly two hours. My staring eyes hurt and my legs, frozen in place, had fallen asleep. When Daniel looked at me. He later told me that the burst of laughter that so wounded me, to the point of making me cry, was caused by the days-long delirium he found himself in and above all by my pathetic appearance. My mouth gaping stupidly, "my foolish eyes, attesting to my animal ingenuity" … That's how Daniel spoke to me. Clawing at me with easy and colorless remarks that he tossed off but that dug into me, swift and piercing, forever.

And that's how I met Daniel. I don't recall the details that brought us closer. I only know that I was the one who sought him out. And I know that Daniel took me over gradually. He regarded me with indifference and, I imagined, would never have been drawn to my person if he hadn't found me odd and amusing. My humble approach to him was my gratitude for his favor ... How I admired him. The more I suffered his scorn, the more superior I considered him, the more I separated him from the "others."

Today I understand him. I forgive him for everything, I forgive everything in people who can't get a hold of themselves, people who ask themselves questions. People who look for reasons to live, as if life alone didn't justify itself.

Later I got to know the real Daniel, the invalid, the one who only existed, though in perpetual radiance, inside himself. Whenever he turned toward the world, now groping and spent, he realized he was helpless and, bitter, bewildered, he discovered that all he knew was how to think. One of those people who possess the earth in a second, with their eyes closed. That power he had to deplete things before getting them, that stark premonition he had of "afterward" ... Before taking the first step toward action, he had already tasted the saturation and sorrow that follow victories ...

And, as if to compensate for this impossibility of achieving anything, he, whose soul so yearned to expand, had invented yet another path suited to his inactivity, where he could expand and justify himself. To make the most of oneself, he'd repeat, is the highest and noblest human objective. To make the most of oneself would mean abandoning the possession and achievement of things in order to possess oneself, to develop one's own elements, to grow within one's own form. To make one's own music and hear it oneself ...

As if he needed a scheme like that ... Everything in him naturally reached the maximum, not by objectification, but in a state of capacity, of exalted strength, from which no one benefited and of which everyone, besides him, was ignorant. And this state was his summit. It resembled something that might precede a climax and he burned to reach it, feeling that the more he suffered, the more alive he was, more punished, nearly satisfied. It was the pain of creation, yet without the creation.

Because when everything melted away, only in his memory was there any trace.

He never let himself rest for long, despite the sterility of this struggle and no matter how exhausting it was. Soon he would once again be revolving around himself, sniffing out his nascent desires, concentrating them until they were brought to a breaking point. Whenever he managed it, he'd vibrate with hatred, beauty or love, and felt nearly compensated.

Anything was an excuse to set him off. A bird flying by, reminding him of unknown lands, breathed life into his old dream of flight. From thought to thought, unconsciously driven toward the same end, he'd reach the notion of his cowardice, revealed not only in this constant desire to flee, not to align himself with things so as not to fight for them, as in his incapacity to achieve anything, since he himself had conceived it, pitilessly dashing the humiliating good sense that kept him from flight. This duet with himself was the reflex of his essence, he discovered, and that was why it would go on all his life ... That was why it became easy to sketch out the distant, gasping, faltering future, until the implacable end— death. That alone and he would attain the goal toward which his inclination guided him: suffering.

It seems mad. However, Daniel also had his reasons. Suffering, for him, the contemplative, was the only way to live intensely ... And in the end it was for this alone that Daniel burned: to live. Only his means were strange.

He surrendered so much to the feeling he created and therefore it grew so strong that he'd eventually forget its induced and nurtured origin. He'd forget that he himself had forged it, would imbibe it, and lived from it as if from something real.

Sometimes the crisis, with nowhere to vent, became so painfully dense that, submerged in it, exhausting it, he finally longed to free himself. He would then create, so as to save himself, an opposing desire that would destroy the first. Because at those times he feared madness, felt he was ill, far from all humans, far from that ideal man who would be a serene, animalized being, with an easy and comfortable intelligence. Far from that man he could never become, whom he couldn't help but scorn, with that haughtiness gained by those who suffer. Far from that man he envied, nonetheless. When his suffering overflowed, he sought help from that kind of man who, in contrast to his own misery, seemed beautiful and perfect to him, full of a simplicity that for him, Daniel, would be heroic.

Tired of being tortured, he'd seek him out, imitate him, with a sudden thirst for peace. It was always that opposing force that he introduced in himself whenever he reached the painful extreme of his crisis. He granted himself some balance like a truce, but one that boredom soon invaded. Until, from the morbid desire to suffer anew, he would solidify this boredom, transforming it into anguish.

He lived in this cycle. Perhaps he'd permitted me to get closer during one of those times when he needed that "opposing force." I, perhaps I've already mentioned this, was the picture of health, with my restrained gestures and upright posture. And, I now know, the reason he sought to crush and humiliate me so was because he envied me. He wanted to wake me up, because he wanted me to suffer too, like a leper secretly hoping to transmit his leprosy to the healthy.

However, unsuspecting as I was, for me his very torture blurred things. Even his selfishness, even his spitefulness made him seem like a dethroned god—a genius. And besides, I already loved him.

Today, I feel sorry for Daniel. After feeling helpless, not knowing what to do with myself, with no desire to go on with the same past of tranquility and death, and not succeeding, the habit of comfort, at mastering a different future—now I realize how free Daniel was and how unhappy. Because of his past— obscure, filled with frustrated dreams—he hadn't managed to find a place in the conventional world, more or less happy, average. As for the future, he feared it too much because he was well aware of his own limits. And because, despite knowing them, he hadn't resigned himself to abandoning that enormous, undefined ambition, which, when later it had already become inhuman, was directed beyond earthly things. Failing to achieve the things right in front of him, he'd turned toward something that no one, he guessed, could ever achieve.

Strange as it seems, he suffered from unknown things, from things that, "due to a conspiracy of nature," he would never touch even for an instant with his senses, "even just to learn about its material, its color, its sex." "About its qualification in the world of perceptions and sensations," he said to me once, after I went back to him. And the greatest harm Daniel did me was awaken within me that desire that lies latent inside us all. For some people it awakens and merely poisons them, as for me and Daniel. For others it leads to laboratories, journeys, absurd experiences, to adventure. To madness.

I now know a thing or two about those who seek to feel in order to know that they are alive. I too ventured upon this dangerous journey, so paltry for our terrible anxiety. And almost always disappointing. I learned to make my soul vibrate and I know that, all the while, in the depths of one's own being, one can remain vigilant and cold, merely observing the spectacle one has granted oneself. And how often in near-boredom ...

Now I would understand it. But back then I only saw the Daniel without weaknesses, sovereign and distant, who hypnotized me. I know little about love. I only remember that I feared him and sought him.

He made me tell my life story, which I did, fearfully, choosing my words carefully so I wouldn't seem so stupid to him. Because he didn't hesitate to talk about my lack of intelligence, using the cruelest expressions. I'd tell him, obediently, small facts from the past. He'd listen, cigarette in his lips, eyes distracted. And he'd conclude by saying, in that singular way of his, a blend of the suppressed desire to laugh, of weariness, of benevolent disdain:

"Very well, quite happy ..."

I'd blush, not sure why I was furious, wounded. But I wouldn't reply.

One day I talked about Jaime and he said:

"Interesting, very normal."

Oh, the words are common, but the way they were uttered. They revolutionized me, made me ashamed of what was most hidden inside me.

"Cristina, do you know you're alive?"

"Cristina, is it good to be unconscious?"

"Cristina, there's nothing you want, is that so?"

I'd cry afterward, but I'd seek him out again, because I was starting to agree with him and secretly hoped he'd deign to initiate me into his world. And he knew just how to humiliate me. He started to dig his claws into Jaime, into all my friends, lumping them together like something contemptible. I don't know what it was that, from the start, kept me from revolting. I don't know. I only recall that for his ego it was a pleasure to dominate and I was easy.

One day, I saw him suddenly get excited, as if the inspiration struck him as both fortuitous and comic:

"Cristina, do you want me to awaken you?"

And, before I could laugh, I already saw myself nodding, in agreement.

So began the strange and revelatory outings, those days that marked me forever.

He'd have hardly condescended to look at me, he made me realize, if I hadn't decided to be transformed. As mad as it sounds, he'd repeat several times: he wanted to transform me, "to breathe into my body a little poison, that good and terrible poison" …

My education had begun.

He spoke, I listened. I learned of dark and beautiful lives, I learned of the suffering and the ecstasy of those "privileged by madness."

"Meditate on them, you, with your happy middle ground."

And I would think. The new world that Daniel's persuasive voice made me glimpse horrified me, I who had always been a docile lamb. It horrified me, yet was already pulling me in with the magnetic force of a fall …

"Get ready to feel with me. Listen to this passage with your head thrown back, eyes half-closed, lips parted …"

I'd pretend to laugh, pretend to obey as a joke, as if begging pardon from my former friends. And from myself, for accepting such a heavy yoke. Nothing, however, was more serious for me.

He, impassive, preparing me as if for a ritual, insisted, solemnly:

"More languor in your gaze … Relax your nostrils more, get them ready to absorb deeply …"

I would obey. And above all I would obey while trying not to displease him with any single thing, placing myself in his hands and begging forgiveness for not giving him more. And because he asked nothing of me, nothing that I'd hesitate any longer to offer him, I fell even further into the certainty of my inferiority and of the distance between us.

"Let yourself go even more. Let my voice be your thought."

I would listen. "For those who remain incarcerated" (not only in prisons, Daniel would interject) "tears are a part of daily experience; a day without tears is a day in which the heart has hardened, not a day in which the heart is happy." "… since the secret of life is to suffer. This truth is contained in all things."

And little by little, really, I was understanding … That slow voice ended up burning in my soul, stirring it profoundly. I had been wandering through grottos for many long years and was suddenly discovering the radiant passage to the sea … Yes, I once shouted to him barely breathing, *I was feeling*! He merely smiled, still not satisfied.

Yet it was the truth. I, so simple and primitive, who had never desired anything with intensity. I, unconscious and cheerful, "because I possessed a cheerful body" … Suddenly I was awakening: what a dark life I'd led up till then. Now … Now I was being reborn. Lively, in pain, that pain that had been lying dormant, quiet and blind in the depths of my self.

I grew nervous, agitated, but intelligent. My eyes always uneasy. I hardly slept.

Jaime came to visit, spending two days with me. When I got his telegram, I went pale. I walked as if dizzy, figuring out how to keep Daniel from seeing him. I was ashamed of Jaime.

Using the excuse that I wanted to try a hotel, I booked a

room. Jaime didn't suspect the real motive, as I expected. And this brought me closer to Daniel. I distantly yearned for my husband to react on my behalf, to snatch me from those hands. I don't know what I was afraid of.

Those were two awful days. I hated myself because I was ashamed of Jaime yet did everything possible to hide with him in places where Daniel wouldn't see us ...

When he left, finally, I, somewhere between relieved and helpless, granted myself an hour of rest, before returning to Daniel. I was trying to put off the danger, but it never occurred to me to flee.

I had faith that sometime before I left Daniel would want me.

However, news that Mama had fallen ill called me back to Rio before that day arrived. I had to leave.

I spoke with Daniel.

"One more afternoon and we may never see each other again," I ventured fearfully.

He laughed softly.

"You'll come back for sure."

I got the distinct impression that he was trying to suggest that I return, as if it were an order. He'd said to me one day: "Weak souls like yours are easily led to any kind of madness simply at a glance from strong souls like mine." However, blind as I was, I rejoiced at this thought. And, forgetting that he himself had already affirmed his indifference to me, I clung to this possibility: "If you're suggesting that I track you down one day ... isn't it because you want me?"

I asked him, trying to smile:

"Come back? Why?"

"Your education ... It's not yet complete."

I came to my senses, fell into an intense gloom that left me slack and empty for several moments. Yes, I was forced to recognize, he had never even been disturbed in the least by my presence. But, again, that coldness of his somehow excited me, built him up in my eyes. During one of those sudden exaltations that had become frequent with me, I wanted to kneel near him, abase myself, worship him. Never again, never again, I thought, frightened. I dreaded not being able to bear the pain of losing him.

"Daniel," I said to him softly.

He raised his eyes and, seeing my anguished face, narrowed them, analyzing me, comprehending me. There was a long minute of silence. I waited and trembled. I knew that this was the first truly alive moment between us, the first to link us directly. That moment suddenly cut me off from my entire past and in a singular premonition I foresaw that it would stand out like a crimson spot on the whole arc of my life.

I was waiting and as I did, all my senses on edge, I'd have wanted to freeze the whole universe, afraid that a leaf would stir, that someone would interrupt us, that my breathing, some gesture would shatter the spell of the moment, make it vanish and cast us back into the distance and into the void of words. My blood beat muffled in my wrists, in my chest, in my forehead. My hands ice-cold and clammy, almost numb. My anxiety left me extremely tense, as if on the verge of flinging myself into a maelstrom, on the verge of going mad. At a slight movement from Daniel, I nearly exploded into a scream, as if he had shaken me violently:

"And what if I come back?"

He met this phrase with displeasure, as always when "my animal intensity shocked him." He fixed his eyes on me and his features underwent a gradual transformation. I flushed. My constant concern with piercing his thoughts hadn't granted me the power to penetrate the most important ones, but I had honed my intuition for the minor ones. I knew that for Daniel to take pity on me, I would have to be ridiculous. Another person's hunger or misery moved him less than a lack of aesthetics. My hair was down, damp with sweat, falling across my flaming face and the pain, to which my physiognomy, calm for years and years, was still unaccustomed, was probably contorting my features, lending them a touch of the grotesque. At the gravest moment of my life I had become ridiculous, Daniel's punishing look told me as much.

He remained silent. And, as if at the end of a long explanation, he added, in a slow and serene voice:

"And besides, you know me far better than you'd need to live with me. I've already said too much." Pause. He lit his cigarette unhurriedly. He looked deep into my eyes and concluded with a half-smile: "I would hate you the day I had nothing more to say to you."

I'd already been so downtrodden that I wasn't hurt. It was the first time, however, that he'd openly rejected me, myself, my body, everything I had and was offering him with my eyes closed.

Terrified by my own words that dragged me along independently of my will, I proceeded with humility, trying to please him.

"Won't you at least answer my letters?"

He had an imperceptible moment of impatience. But he answered, his voice controlled, softened:

"No. Which doesn't mean you can't write me."

Before I took my leave, he kissed me. He kissed me on the lips, which didn't ease my worry. Because he was doing it for me. And I wanted him to feel pleasure, to be humanized, to be humbled.

Mama recovered quickly. And I had gone back to Jaime, for good.

I resumed my previous life. Yet I moved like a blind woman, in a kind of stupor that shook itself off only when I wrote to Daniel. I never received a word from him. I no longer expected anything. And I kept writing.

Once in a while my state worsened and every instant grew painful like a small arrow lodged in my body. I thought of fleeing, of running off to Daniel. I would fall into feverish fits that I tried in vain to control through household chores so as not to alert Jaime and the maid.

A state of lassitude would follow in which I suffered less. Yet, even during that phase, I never relaxed completely. I carefully scrutinized myself: "would it return?" I would refer to the torture with vague words, as if I could hold it off that way.

In moments of greater lucidity, I'd remember something he once told me:

"You must know how to feel, but also how to stop feeling, because if an experience is sublime it can equally become dangerous. Learn how to cast the spell and then break it. Pay attention, I'm teaching you something valuable: the magic that is the opposite of, 'open, Sesame.' The best way for a feeling to lose its perfume and stop intoxicating us is to expose it to the sun."

I had tried to think about what had happened clearly and objectively so as to reduce my feelings to a rubric, with no perfume, no subtext. It seemed vaguely like a betrayal. Of Daniel, of myself. I had tried, nevertheless. Simplifying my story in two or three words, exposing it to the sun, seemed really laughable to me, but the coolness of my thoughts didn't spread to me and it rather seemed an unknown woman with an unknown man. Oh, those two had nothing to do with the oppression that was crushing me, with that painful longing that made my eyes go blurry and troubled my mind ... And even so, I had discovered, I was afraid to free myself. "That" had grown too much inside me, leaving me full. I'd be helpless if I were ever cured. After all, what was I now, I felt, but a reflection? Were I to eradicate Daniel, I'd be a blank mirror.

I had become vibratory, strangely sensitive. I could no longer stand those agreeable afternoons with the family that once amused me so.

"Sure is hot, huh, Cristina?" said Jaime.

"I've been going over this stitch for two weeks now and I just can't get it right," said Mama.

Jaime broke in, stretching:

"Imagine that, crocheting in weather like this."

"The hard part isn't the crocheting, it's racking your brain trying to figure out that stitch," Papa replied.

Pause.

"Mercedes will end up engaged to that boy," Mama announced.

"Even as ugly as she is," Papa replied distractedly, turning the page of his newspaper.

Pause.

"The boss has now decided to use that delivery system of ..."

I would disguise my anguish and make up some excuse to step away for a moment. In the bedroom I'd bite down on my handkerchief, stifling the cries of despair that threatened my throat. I'd collapse onto the bed, my face buried in the pillow, hoping that something would happen and save me. I was starting to hate them, all of them. And I longed to abandon them, to flee that feeling that was growing by the minute, intermingled with an unbearable pity for them and for myself. As if together we were victims of the same, inevitable threat.

I'd try to reconstruct Daniel's face, feature by feature. It seemed to me that if I could remember him clearly I'd gain some kind of power over him. I'd hold my breath, tense up, press my lips together. One second ... One more second and I'd have him, gesture by gesture ... His figure was already taking shape, nebulous ... And finally, little by little, crestfallen, I'd see it vanish. I got the impression that Daniel was fleeing me, smiling. However, his presence wouldn't leave me entirely. Once, while I was with Jaime, I had felt him and blushed. I had imagined him watching us, with his calm and ironic smile:

"Well, look what we have here, a happy couple ..."

I had trembled in shame and for several days could hardly stand the sight of Jaime. I thought of Daniel, even more intensely. Lines of his stirred up a whirlwind inside me. The odd phrase would rise up and haunt me for hours and hours. "The only attitude worthy of a man is sorrow, the only attitude worthy of a man is sorrow, the only ..."

From a distance, I was starting to understand him better. I'd recall how Daniel didn't really know how to laugh. Once in a while, when I'd say something funny and if I caught him off guard, I'd see his face seem to split in two, in a grimace that contradicted those wrinkles born solely from pain and reflection. He'd look both cynical and childish, almost indecent, as if he were doing something forbidden, as if he were cheating, hiding from someone.

I couldn't bear to look at him, in those rare instants. I'd lower my head, annoyed, filled with a pity that hurt me. He really didn't know how to be happy. Maybe he'd never been taught, who knows? Always so alone, since adolescence, so far removed from the least overture of friendship. Today, without hatred, without love, with no more than indifference, how much kindness I could show him.

But back then ... Was I afraid of him? I just felt that all he'd have to do was show up, a single gesture would make me follow him forever. I used to dream of that instant, I'd imagine that, by his side, I would free myself from him. Love? I wanted to go with him, to be on the stronger side, for him to spare me, like one who seeks shelter in the arms of the enemy to stay far from his arrows. It was different than love, I was finding out: I wanted him as a thirsty person desires water, without feelings, without even wanting to be happy.

Sometimes I'd allow myself another dream, knowing it was more impossible still: he'd love me and I'd have my revenge, feeling ... No, not superior, but equal ... Because, if he wanted me, it would destroy that powerful coldness of his, his ironic and unshakable scorn that fascinated me. Until then I could never be happy. He haunted me.

Oh, I know I'm repeating myself, that I'm rambling, mixing up facts and thoughts in this short narrative. Nevertheless, it's taking me so much effort to marshal its elements and put them on paper. I've already said that I'm neither intelligent, nor cultivated. And merely suffering isn't enough.

Not speaking, with my eyes closed, something beneath my thought, deeper and stronger, apprehends what happened and, in a fleeting instant, I see it clearly. But my brain is feeble and I can't manage to transform that vivid minute into thought.

It's all true, nevertheless. And I ought to acknowledge still other, equally true feelings. Often, while thinking of him, in a slow transition, I'd see myself serving him like a slave. Yes, I'd admit, trembling and afraid: I, with a stable, conventional past, born into civilization, felt an excruciating pleasure in imagining myself at his feet, a slave … No, it wasn't love. I horrified myself: it was debasement, debasement … I'd catch myself peering in the mirror, searching for some new sign in my face, born of pain, of my vileness, and that might guide my mind toward those tumultuous instincts I still didn't want to accept. I was trying to unburden my soul, tormenting myself, whispering through clenched teeth: "Vile … despicable …" I'd answer myself, a coward: "But, my god (lowercase, as he'd taught me), I'm not guilty, I'm not guilty …" Of what? I never said exactly. Some awful and powerful thing was growing within me, some thing that paralyzed me with fright. That was all I knew.

And confusedly, faced with the memory of him, I would shrink back, unite myself with Jaime, drawing him close to me, wanting to protect us both, against him, against his power, against his smile. Because, knowing he was far away, I'd imagine him watching my days and smiling at some secret thought, the sort whose existence I could only guess at, without ever managing to penetrate its meaning. I sought, after a long while, over a year, as if to justify to myself, to Jaime and our bourgeois life, how he had taken over my soul. Those long conversations in which all I ever did was listen, that flame that lit up my eyes, that slow gaze, heavy with knowledge, beneath thick eyelids, had fascinated me, awoken in me obscure feelings, the aching desire to immerse myself in something unknown, to attain something unknown … And above all they'd awoken in me the sensation that palpitating inside my body and spirit was a deeper and more intense life than the one I was living.

At night, unable to sleep, as if speaking to someone invisible, I'd say to myself softly, defeated, "I agree, I agree that my life is comfortable and mediocre, I agree, everything I have is trivial." I felt him nod benevolently. "I can't, I can't!" I'd shout to myself, this lament containing the impossibility of no longer wanting him, of carrying on like that, of, first and foremost, following the grandiose paths he'd started to show me and where I was getting lost, puny and helpless.

I had learned of ardent lives, but had returned to my own, dull one. He had let me glimpse the sublime and insisted that I too burn in the sacred fire. I was thrashing around, with no strength. Everything I had learned from Daniel only made me realize how trivial my everyday life was and despise it. My education hadn't ended, as he'd so accurately put it.

I felt alone in the world, I tried to escape in tears. Yet my attitude in the face of suffering was still one of bewilderment.

How did I find the strength to destroy all that I had been, to hurt Jaime, to make Papa and Mama, old and tired already, so unhappy?

In the period leading up to my decision, as in certain illnesses just before death, I had moments of respite.

That day, Dora, a friend, had come over attempting to distract me from one of those headaches that I used as an excuse to surrender freely to melancholy, without being disturbed. It was a remark of hers, if I'm not mistaken, that launched me toward Daniel by other means.

"Darling, you should have heard Armando talking about music. You'd think he was talking about the best meal in the world or the most gorgeous woman. Going on and on, like he was gnawing on every little note and spitting out the bones ..."

I thought of Daniel who, on the contrary, made everything immaterial. Even the one time he'd kissed me, I had imagined it didn't involve lips. I trembled: not wanting to impoverish his memory. But another thought remained lucid and undisturbed: he used to say that the body was an accessory. No, no. One day he'd glanced with repugnance and censure at my blouse that was heaving after I'd been running to catch the bus. Revulsion, no! He'd said to me, continuing another cold thought: "You eat chocolate as if it were the most important thing in the world. You have a horrible taste for things." He ate like someone crumpling a piece of paper.

All of a sudden, I realized that a lot of people would smile at Daniel, with one of those proud and ambiguous smiles that men dedicate to one another. Perhaps I myself would have disparaged him if I weren't ill … At this thought, something rebelled inside me, strangely: Daniel …

I suddenly felt exhausted, without the strength now to go on. When the telephone rang. Jaime, I thought. It was as if I were fleeing Daniel … Ah, some help. I answered, eagerly.

"Hello, Jaime!"

"How'd you know it was me?" came his nasal, good-natured voice.

As if someone had poured cool water over my face. My nerves relaxed. Jaime, you exist. You're real. Your hands are strong, they take me in. You like chocolate too.

"Will you be long?"

"No, my girl. I called to ask if you need anything from downtown."

I struggled for another second not to scrutinize his careless sentence. Because lately I'd been comparing everything to the beautiful and profound things Daniel had told me. And I would only calm down, after I agreed with the invisible Daniel: yes, he's dull, mediocrely, incredibly happy …

"I don't need anything. But come home right away, all right? (Now, darling, before Daniel comes, before I change my mind, now!) Hello! Hello! Listen, if you want to bring me something, buy some candy … chocolate … Yes, yes. See you soon."

When Dora left, I stood in front of the mirror and fixed myself up as I hadn't done in months. But anxiety robbed my patience, left my eyes bright, my movements darting. It would be a test, the final test.

When he arrived, my agitation stopped immediately. Yes, I thought deeply relieved, I was calm, almost happy: Daniel hadn't shown up. He noticed I'd changed my hair, my nails. He kissed me, unworried. I took his hands, ran them over my cheeks, my forehead.

"What's the matter, Cristina? What happened?"

I didn't answer, but thousands of bells clanged inside me. My thoughts vibrated like a shriek: "Just this, just this: I'm going to free myself! I'm free!"

We sat on the sofa. And in the silence of the living room, I felt at peace. I thought of nothing and leaned against Jaime serenely.

"Can't we stay like this the rest of our lives?"

He laughed. Stroked my hands.

"You know? I like you better without nail polish …"

"Request granted, sir."

"That wasn't a request: it was an order …"

Then back to silence, whipping in my ears, my eyes, sapping me of strength. It was nice, tenderly nice. He ran his hands through my hair.

Then, as if a spear had pierced my back, I grew suddenly irritated on the sofa, opened my eyes, focused them, dilated, on the air …

"What happened?" asked Jaime, worried.

His hair … Yes, yes, I thought with a slight, triumphant smile, his hair was black … His eyes … Just a moment … His eyes … black too?

That same night, I decided to leave.

And suddenly, I no longer considered the matter, stopped worrying, gave Jaime a pleasant evening. I went to bed serene and slept through the night, I hadn't in a long time.

I waited for Jaime to go to work. I sent the maid home, gave her the day off. I packed a small suitcase with the essentials.

Before leaving, though, my calm suddenly evaporated. Useless, repeated movements, darting and stumbling thoughts. It seemed as if Daniel were next to me, his presence almost palpable: "These eyes of yours rendered right on the surface of your face, with a delicate brush, a touch of paint. Meticulous, light, incapable of doing good or evil …"

In a sudden burst of inspiration, I decided to leave a note for Jaime, a note that would hurt him the way Daniel would hurt him! That would trouble him, crush him. And, just for the pride of showing Daniel that I was "strong," remorseless, I wrote deliberately, trying to make myself distant and unattainable: "I'm leaving. I'm tired of living with you. If you can't understand me at least trust me: I'm telling you that I deserve to be forgiven. If you were more intelligent, I'd tell you: don't judge me, don't forgive, nobody can do that. But, for the sake of your own peace, forgive me."

Silently I took my place beside Daniel.

Gradually I took over his daily life, replaced him, like a nurse, in his movements. I looked after his books, his clothes, brightened his surroundings.

He never thanked me. He simply accepted it, as he'd accepted my companionship.

As for me, from the moment in which getting off the train I approached Daniel without being repelled, I had taken a single-minded attitude. Neither from contentment because of him, nor regret because of Jaime. Nor quite relief. It was as if I had returned to my source. As if previously they had chiseled me out of rock, cast me into life as a woman and I later returned to my true roots, like a final sigh, my eyes closed, serene, standing still for eternity.

I didn't dwell on the situation, but whenever I scrutinized it I always did so in the same way: I live with him and that's it. I stayed close to the powerful one, to the one who *knew*, that was enough for me.

Why didn't that ideal death last forever? A bit of clairvoyance, at certain moments, warned me that peace could only be fleeting. I sensed that living with Daniel wouldn't always be enough for me. And I plunged even deeper into nonexistence, granting myself respites, putting off the moment when I myself would seek life, to *discover* by myself, through my own suffering.

For the time being I would just watch him and rest.

The days passed, the months fell away one by one.

Habit settled into my existence and its guidance soon kept me busy by the minute with Daniel. Soon I no longer became enthralled, exalted, as before, when I listened to him. I had entered him. Nothing surprised me anymore.

I never smiled, I had unlearned joy. Yet I wouldn't have removed myself from his life even to be happy. I was not, nor was I unhappy. I had so incorporated myself into the situation that I no longer received stimuli and sensations that would allow me to modify it.

Only one fear disturbed my strange peace: that Daniel would send me away. Sometimes, silently mending his clothes at his side, I sensed that he was about to speak. I'd drop the sewing onto my lap, go pale and await his order:

"You can go."

And when, finally, I'd hear him tell me something or laugh at me for some reason, I'd pick the fabric back up and continue my work, fingers trembling for a few seconds.

The end, however, was near.

One day when I'd gone out early, I took longer than usual to come home, due to an accident on one of the roads. When I got to the bedroom, I found him irritated, his eyes gazing off into the distance, not replying to my "good evening." He hadn't eaten dinner yet and when I, feeling guilty, begged him to eat something, he kept up a long, willful silence and finally informed me, scrutinizing my worry with a certain pleasure: he hadn't had lunch either. I rushed to put on the coffee, while he kept up the same sullen attitude, a little childish, watching my hurried movements from the corner of his eye as I set the table.

Suddenly I opened my eyes, in shock. For the first time I was realizing that Daniel needed me! I had become necessary to the tyrant ... He, I now knew, wouldn't send me away ...

I recall that I stopped with the coffee pot in my hand, disoriented. Daniel was still gloomy, in silent protest against my accidental negligence. I smiled, a little bashfully. So ... he did need me? I didn't feel joy, but something like disappointment: well, I thought, my job is done. It frightened me, that unexpected and involuntary reflection.

I had already served out my term of slavery. Perhaps I'd go on being a slave, without rebelling, for the rest of my life. But I was serving a god ... And Daniel had gone soft, his spell was broken. He needed me! I repeated a thousand times afterward, feeling that I had received a beautiful, enormous gift, too large for my arms and for my desire. And the strangest thing is that with this impression came another, absurdly novel and powerful. I was free, I realized at last ...

How can I understand myself? Why that blind conformity at first? And afterward, the near joy of liberation? Of what matter am I made in which elements and foundations for a thousand other lives mingle but never merge? I go down every path and still none is mine. I have been sculpted into so many statues and haven't frozen into place ...

From then on, without actively deciding to, I imperceptibly neglected Daniel. And no longer accepted his dominance. I was just resigned to it.

What good is it to narrate trivial events that demonstrate my gradual progression toward intolerance and hatred? It's well-known how little it takes to transform the mood in which two people live. A slight gesture, a smile, snag like a fishhook onto a feeling coiled in the depths of calm waters and bring it to the surface, making it clamor over the others.

We went on living. And now I savored, day by day, mingled at first with the taste of triumph, the power of gazing directly upon the idol.

He noticed my transformation and, if at first he retreated in surprise at my courage, he took up the old yoke with still greater violence, prepared not to let me escape. Yet I would find my own violence. We armed ourselves and were two forces.

It was hard to breathe in the bedroom. We moved as if in the thick of danger, waiting for it to materialize and crash down on us, behind our backs. We grew cunning, seeking a thousand hidden intentions behind every word offered. We hurt each other at every turn and established victory and defeat. I grew cruel. He grew weak, showed what he was really like. There were times when he was a hair's breadth away from begging me for help, confessing to the isolation in which my freedom had left him and which, in my wake, he could no longer bear. I myself, my strength quickly flagging, sometimes wanted to reach out to him. Yet we'd gone too far and, proud, couldn't turn back. It was the struggle, now, that kept us going. Like a sick child, he grew increasingly capricious. Any word of mine was the start of a harsh quarrel. Later we discovered yet another recourse: silence. We hardly spoke.

So why didn't we separate, given that no serious ties bound us? He didn't suggest it because he'd grown used to my help and could therefore no longer live without someone to wield power over, to be a king over, since he had no other subject. And perhaps he really did love my companionship, he who'd always been so solitary. As for me—I took pleasure in hating him.

Even our new relations were invaded by habit. (I lived with Daniel for almost two years.) Now it wasn't even hatred. We were tired.

Eventually, after a week of rain that had trapped us together for days on end in the room, fraying our nerves to the limit— eventually the conclusion came.

It was a late afternoon, prematurely dark. Rain dripped monotonously outside. We'd hardly spoken that day. Daniel, his face white over the dark "scarf" of his neck, was looking out the window. Water had fogged the windowpanes; he pulled out his handkerchief and, attentively, as if this had suddenly become important, started wiping them, his movements painstaking and careful, betraying the effort it took to contain his irritation. I watched him while standing next to the sofa. The clock went on ticking in the room, heaving.

Then, as if I were continuing an argument, I said to my own surprise:

"But this can't go on ..."

He turned and I met his cold eyes, perhaps curious, definitely ironic. All my rage solidified in that moment and weighed on my chest like a stone.

"What are you laughing at?" I asked.

He kept staring at me and went back to wiping the windowpanes. Suddenly, he recovered and answered:

"At you."

I was astonished. How brave he was. I was afraid of how boldly he challenged me. I answered haltingly:

"Why?"

He leaned slightly closer and his teeth gleamed in the half-darkness. I found him terribly handsome, though the realization didn't move me.

"Why? Ah, because ... It's just that you and I ... indifferent or hateful ... An argument that has nothing really to do with us, that doesn't exhilarate us ... A disappointment."

"So why laugh at me, then?" I continued obstinately. "Aren't there two of us here?"

He wiped a droplet that had trickled onto the windowsill.

"No. You're alone. You were always alone."

Was this just a way to hurt me? I was surprised all the same, I was stunned as if I'd been robbed. My God, so ... neither of us believed anymore in whatever held us together?

"Are you afraid of the truth? We don't even feel hatred toward each other. If we did we'd almost be happy. Beings made of strong stuff. You want proof? You wouldn't kill me, because afterward you'd feel neither pleasure nor pain. You'd just think: 'what's the point?'"

I couldn't help but notice the intelligence with which he penetrated the truth. But how things were going so fast, how fast they were going! I thought.

Silence fell. The clock struck six. Back to silence.

I breathed hard, deeply. My voice came out low and heavy: "I'm leaving."

We each made a slight, quick movement, as if a struggle were about to begin. Then we looked at each other in surprise. It had been said! It had been said!

I repeated triumphantly, trembling:

"I'm leaving, Daniel." I came closer and against the pallor of his slender face, his hair looked excessively black. "Daniel"—I shook him by the arm—"I'm leaving!"

He didn't move. I then realized that my hand was clutching his arm. My declaration had opened such a gulf between us that I couldn't even bear touching him. I pulled it away with such an abrupt and sudden movement that the ashtray went flying, shattered on the floor.

I stood staring at the shards for a while. Then I lifted my head, suddenly calmed. He too had frozen, as if fascinated by the swiftness of the scene, having forgotten any mask. We looked at each other for a moment, without anger, our eyes disarmed, searching, now filled with an almost friendly curiosity, the depths of our souls, our mystery that must be the same. We averted our gaze at the same time, disturbed.

"The prisoners," Daniel said trying to lend a lighthearted, disdainful tone to the words.

That was the last moment of understanding we had together.

There was an extremely long pause, the kind that plunges us into eternity. Everything around us had stopped.

With another sigh, I came back to life.

"I'm leaving."

He didn't make a move.

I walked to the door and at the threshold stopped again. I saw his back, his dark head lifted, as if he were looking straight ahead. I repeated, my voice singularly hollow:

"I'm leaving, Daniel."

My mother had died from a heart attack, brought on by my departure. Papa had found refuge with my uncle, in the country.

Jaime took me back.

He never asked many questions. More than anything he wanted peace. We went back to our old life, though he never came completely close to me again. He sensed that I was different from him and my "lapse" frightened him, made him respect me.

As for me, I go on.

Alone now. Forever alone.

The Fever Dream
("O delírio")

THE DAY IS HOT AND NEAR ITS PEAK WHEN HE GETS
up. He looks for his slippers under the bed, groping around
with his feet, burrowing into his flannel pajamas. The sun
starts to fall across the wardrobe, reflecting the window's broad
square onto the floor.

His neck feels stiff at the nape, his movements so difficult.
His toes are some frozen, impersonal thing. And his jaw is
stuck, clenched. He goes to the sink, fills his hands with water,
drinks eagerly as it swishes around inside him as if in an empty
flask. He splashes his forehead and exhales in relief.

From the window he can see the bright and bustling street.
Boys are playing marbles in the doorway of the Mascote Bakery, a car is honking near the corner bar. Women are coming
back from the farmers' market carrying bags, sweating. Scraps
of turnip and lettuce mingle with the dirt on the narrow street.
And the sun, glaring and harsh, shining over it all.

He moves away in disgust. He turns back inside, looks at
the unmade bed, so familiar after a night of insomnia … The
Virgin Mary now stands out, distinct and commanding, in the
light of day. In the shadows, she herself a shadowy figure, it's

easier not to believe in her. He starts walking slowly, dragging his lethargic legs, lifts the sheets, pats the pillow, and slides back in, with a sigh. He's so humbled at the sight of the lively street and indifferent sun ... In his bed, in his room, eyes shut, he is king.

He burrows in deeply, as if outside it were raining, raining, and here inside some warm and silent arms were drawing him close and transforming him into a small boy, small and dead. Dead. Ah, it's the fever dream ... It's the fever dream. A very sweet light is spreading over the Earth like a perfume. The moon is slowly dissolving and a boy-sun languidly stretches his translucent arms ... Cool murmurings of pure waters that surrender themselves to the hillsides. A pair of wings dances in the rosy atmosphere. Silence, my friends. The day is about to begin.

A faraway lament comes rising along the Earth's body ... There's a bird that escapes, as always. And she, panting, suddenly tears asunder with a rumble, left with a gaping wound ... Gaping like the Atlantic Ocean and not like a wild river! She vomits gushes of mud with every shriek.

Then the sun raises its trunk erect and emerges whole, powerful, bloody. Silence, friends. My great and noble friends, ye shall witness a millennial struggle. Silence. S-s-s-s ...

From the black and broken Earth, tiny beings of pure light emerge one by one, gentle as the breath of a sleeping child, barely treading the earth with their transparent feet ... Lavender colors hover in space like butterflies. Slender flutes extend toward the heavens and fragile melodies burst in the air like bubbles. The rosy shapes keep sprouting from the wounded earth.

All of a sudden, thundering anew. Is the Earth bearing

children? The shapes dissolve in midair, scared away. Corollas wilt and colors darken. And the Earth, arms contracted in pain, splits open into fresh black fissures. A strong smell of wounded earth wafts in dense plumes of smoke.

A century of silence. And the lights reappear timidly, trembling still. From bloody and heaving grottoes, other beings are endlessly being born. The sun parts the clouds and shimmers warm shine. The flutes unfurl strident songs like gentle laughter and the creatures rehearse the most nimble of dances ... Tiny, fragrant flowers throng over the dark wounds ...

The continuously depleted Earth shrivels, shrivels in folds and wrinkles of dead flesh. The joy of the newborn beings has reached its peak and the air is pure sound. And the Earth ages rapidly ... New colors emerge from the deep gashes. The globe now spins slowly, slowly, weary. Dying. One last little being made of light is born, like a sigh. And the Earth hides.

Her children take fright ... break off from their melodies and nimble dances ... Their delicate wings flutter in midair in a confused hum.

For a moment they shimmer. Then flicker out in exhaustion and in a blind beeline plunge vertiginously into Space ...

Whose victory was it? A tiny man stands up, in the last row. He says, in an echoing, strangely lost voice:

"I can tell you who won."

Everyone shouts, suddenly furious.

"The audience won't say! The audience won't say!"

The little man is intimidated, but goes on:

"But I know! I know: it was the Earth's victory. It was her revenge, it was revenge ..."

Everyone wails. "It was revenge" comes closer and closer, reaches a violent crescendo in every ear until, gigantic, it explodes in a roaring din. And in the abrupt silence, the space is suddenly gray and dead.

He opens his eyes. The first thing he sees is a piece of white wood. Looking beyond it, he sees other planks, all alike. And in the middle of it all dangling, is a bizarre animal that gleams, gleams and sinks its long, flashing claws into his pupils, until reaching the nape of his neck. It's true that if he lowers his eyelids, the spider retracts its claws and is reduced to a red, moving speck. But it's a question of honor. The one who should leave is the monster. He points and shouts:

"Get out! You're made of gold, but get out!"

The dark girl, in a white dress, rises and says:

"You poor thing. The light's bothering you."

She turns on the light. He feels humiliated, deeply humiliated. Now what? it would be so easy to explain that it had been a light bulb ... Just to hurt him. He turns his head to the wall and starts weeping. The dark girl lets out a small cry:

"Oh don't do that, darling!"

She runs her hand over his forehead, stroking it slowly. A cool, small hand, that leaves in its wake a span of time in which there are no more thoughts. Everything would be fine if the doors weren't slamming so much. He says:

"The Earth shriveled up, girl, just shriveled up. I didn't even know there was so much light inside her ..."

"But I just turned it off ... See if you can sleep."

"You turned it off?" he tries to make her out in the darkness. "No, it went out by itself. Now all I want to know is: given the choice, would she have refused to create, if only to avoid dying?"

"Poor thing ... Oh you're so feverish. If you'd sleep you'd definitely get better."

"Later on she got her revenge. Because the creatures felt so superior, so free that they imagined they could get by without her. She always gets her revenge."

The dark girl is now running her fingers through his damp hair, sending his ideas spinning with gentle motions. He takes her by the arm, interlaces his fingers with those delicate fingers. Her palm is soft. The skin a little rough near the nails. He rests his mouth on the back of her hand and moves it every which way, meticulously, his eyes wide open in the darkness. Her hand tries to escape. He holds onto it. It stays. Her wrist. Delicate and tender, it goes tick-tick-tick. It's a little dove that he's caught. The little dove is frightened and its heart goes tick-tick-tick.

"Is this a moment?" He asks in a very loud voice. "No, not anymore. And this one? Not anymore either. All you have is the moment to come. The present is already past. Lay the cadavers of these dead moments upon the bed. Cover them with a snow-white sheet, put them in a child's coffin. They died while still children, sinless. I want adult moments! ... Miss, come here, I want to tell you a secret: miss, what should I do? Help me, for my world is shriveling ... Then what will become of my light?"

The room is so dark. Where is the Virgin Mary his aunt tucked into his suitcase, before he left? Where is she? At first he feels something moving very close to him. Then two cool lips alight on his parched mouth, gently, then more firmly. His eyes aren't stinging anymore. Now his temples stop throbbing because two moist butterflies are hovering over them. Then they fly off.

He feels good, very, very sleepy ...

"Miss ..."

He falls asleep.

Now he's on the terrace off Dona Marta's bedroom, the one that opens onto the large yard. They brought him there, laid him on a wicker lounge chair, a blanket swaddling his feet. Though he was carried there like a baby, he's worn out. He thinks that not even a fire would make him get up now. Dona Marta wipes her hands on her apron.

"Now then, my boy, how are your legs? This is my boarding-house; I'm happy you're living here, sir. But, my own business interests aside, I'd suggest you go back to the North. Only your own family could keep you to this restful routine, with regular hours for sleeping and eating ... The doctor didn't like it when I told him how you've been keeping the light on into the wee hours, reading, writing ... Not only because of the electricity, but, for Heaven's sake, that's no way to live ..."

He hardly pays attention. He can't think much, his head suddenly hollow. His eyes sink, tired.

Dona Marta winks.

"My goddaughter came to pay another little visit ..."

The girl enters. He looks at her. She gets flustered, blushes. So what happened? On his hands he feels the touch of somewhat rough skin. On his forehead ... On his lips ... He stares at her. What happened? His heart speeds up, beats hard. The girl smiles. They remain silent and feel good.

Her presence came like a gentle jolt. The melancholy is already leaving him and, lighter now, he takes pleasure in sprawling out in the chair. He thrusts his legs out, kicks off the blanket. It's not cold anymore and his head's not quite so empty. It's also true that fatigue keeps him in his seat, lethargic, in the same position. But he surrenders to it voluptuously, benevolently observing his confused desire to breathe frequently, deeply, to bare himself to the sun, to take the girl's hand.

For so long he hasn't been able to really examine himself, hasn't allowed himself a thing … He's young, after all, he's young … He smiles, out of pure joy, almost childish. Some gentle thing wells up from his chest in concentric waves and spreads throughout his body like musical swells. And the good weariness … He smiles at the girl, looks at her gratefully, lightly desires her. Why not? An escapade, yes … Dona Marta is right. And his body has its demands too.

"Did you ever visit me before?" he ventures.

She says yes. They understand one another. They smile.

He breathes more deeply still, pleased with himself. He asks excitedly:

"Do you remember when the little man in the last row stood up and said, 'I know … and …'"

He breaks off in fear. What's he saying? Mad phrases he's blurting out, unfounded … And now? They both grow serious. Now reticent, she says politely, coolly:

"Don't worry. You had a bad fever, sir, you were delirious … It's natural not to remember the fever dream … or anything else."

He looks at her in disappointment.

"Ah, the fever dream. I'm sorry, when it's over we don't know what really happened and what was a lie …"

She's now a stranger. Failure. He looks at her from behind, observes her common, delicate profile.

But that bodily languor … The heat.

"But I do remember everything," he says suddenly, determined to attempt the escapade anyway.

She gets flustered, blushes again.

"How so …?"

"Yes," he says more calmly and suddenly almost indifferently. "I remember everything."

She smiles. Little does she know, he thinks, how much this smile means to him: helping him go down a more convenient route, where more is permitted ... Perhaps Dona Marta is right and, with the gentleness of convalescence, he agrees with her. Yes, he thinks a bit reluctantly, be more human, don't worry, live. He returns the girl's gaze.

However, he doesn't feel any particular relief after deciding to pursue an easier life. On the contrary, he feels a slight impatience, an urge to steal away as if he were being pressured. He invokes a powerful thought that makes him calmly consider the idea of changing himself: one more illness like this and he might be left incapacitated.

Yet he's still uneasy, worn out in advance by what is to come. He seeks the landscape, suddenly dissatisfied, without knowing why. The terrace grows gloomy. Where is the sun? Darkness has fallen, it's cold. For a moment he feels the darkness itself inside him, a dim desire to dissolve, to disappear. He doesn't want to think, can't think. Above all, don't make any decisions right now—put it off, you coward. You're still sick.

The terrace opens onto a compact grove. In the half-light, the trees sway and moan like resigned old women. Ah, he'll sink into the chair infinitely, his legs will go to pieces, nothing will remain of him ...

The sun reappears. It drifts out from behind the cloud and emerges whole, powerful, bloody ... Its brilliance shimmers over the little wood. And now its whispering is the ever so gentle lilt of a transparent flute, extended toward the heavens ...

He sits up in the chair, a little surprised, dazzled. Frenzied thoughts suddenly collide in his head ... Yes, why not? Even the fact of the dark girl ... Is the entire fever dream rising up before his eyes? Like a painting ... Yes, yes ... He gets excited.

But what poetic material does it contain ... "The Earth is bearing children." And the dance of those beings upon the open wounds? Heat returns to his body in faint waves.

"Do me a favor," he says eagerly. "Get Dona Marta ..."

She comes.

"Will you bring me the notebook on top of my desk? And a pencil too ..."

"But ... Sir, you can't work now ... You've hardly left your bed ... You're thin, pale, you look like someone sucked all your blood ..."

He stops, suddenly pensive. And most importantly if she only knew how much effort it took him to write ... When he began, every fiber in his body stood on end, irritated and magnificent. And until he covered the paper with his jittery scrawl, until he felt that it extended him, he didn't stop, depleting himself until the very end ... "The Earth, her arms contracted in pain ..." Yes, his head's already hurting, heavy. But could he contain his light, to spare himself?

He smiles a sad smile, a little proud perhaps, apologizing to Dona Marta. To the girl, for the frustrated escapade. To himself, above all.

"No, the Earth cannot choose," he concludes ambiguously. But later she takes revenge.

Dona Marta nods. She goes to get pencil and paper.

Jimmy and I
("Eu e Jimmy")

I STILL REMEMBER JIMMY, THAT BOY WITH THE TOU-
sled chestnut hair, covering the elongated skull of a born rebel.

I remember Jimmy, his hair and his ideas. Jimmy thought
that nothing is as good as nature. That if two people like each
other the only thing to do is love each other, simple as that. That
everything else, in mankind, that gets separated from this simplicity belonging to the start of the world, is affectation, and
froth. Had those ideas sprung from another head, I wouldn't
have even put up with listening to them. But there was the excuse of Jimmy's skull and there was, above all the excuse of his
bright teeth and his clear smile of a contented animal.

Jimmy walked with his head up, his nose stuck in the air,
and, while crossing the street, would take me by the arm with
a very simple familiarity. I was unsettled. But the proof that I
was even then imbued with Jimmy's ideas and above all with his
bright smile, is that I would scold myself for being unsettled.
I'd think, unhappily, that I had evolved too much, getting separated from the prototype—animal. I'd tell myself it was pointless to blush because of an arm; nor even at an arm of clothing.
But these thoughts were diffuse and presented themselves with

the incoherence that I am now transmitting to paper. Honestly, I was just looking for an excuse to like Jimmy. And to go along with his ideas. Little by little I was adapting to his elongated head. What could I do, after all? Since I was a little girl I had seen and felt the predominance of men's ideas over women's. Mama, before she got married, according to Aunt Emília, was a firecracker, a tempestuous redhead, with thoughts of her own about liberty and equality for women. But then along came Papa, very serious and tall, with thoughts of his own too, about … liberty and equality for women. The trouble was in the co-inciding subject matter. There was a collision. And nowadays Mama sews and embroiders and sings at the piano and makes little cakes on Saturdays, all like clockwork and cheerfully. She has ideas of her own, still, but they all come down to one: a wife should always go along with her husband, as the accessory goes along with the principal (my analogy, the result of Law School classes).

Because of this and because of Jimmy, I too became, little by little, natural.

And that's how one fine day, after a hot summer night, during which I slept as much as I am writing right now (they are the antecedents to the crime), that fine day Jimmy kissed me. I had anticipated this situation, in all its variations. I was disappointed, it's true. So it's "that" after so much philosophy and buildup! But I liked it. And from then on I slept soundly; I no longer needed to dream.

I would meet Jimmy on the corner. Very simply I'd offer him my arm. And later, very simply I'd tousle his messy hair. I sensed that Jimmy was amazed at my forwardness. His lessons had produced a rare effect and the student was diligent. It was a happy time.

Later on we took exams. Here is where the actual story begins.

One of the examiners had gentle, deep eyes. His hands were quite lovely; dark.

(Jimmy was pale as a baby.) Whenever he spoke to me, his voice got mysteriously husky and warm. And I'd make an enormous effort not to close my eyes and die of joy.

There were no inner battles. I fell asleep dreaming of the examiner at six in the evening. And I was enchanted by his voice, speaking to me of ideas that were utterly un-Jimmyesque. All this suffused with twilight, in the silent, cold garden.

I was utterly happy back then. As for Jimmy he went on being tousled and with the same smile that had made me forget to tell Jimmy about the new situation.

One day, he asked me why I'd been acting so differently. I answered lightheartedly, employing terms from Hegel, heard from the mouth of my examiner. I told him that a primitive equilibrium had been disrupted and a new one had formed, with a different basis. Needless to say Jimmy didn't understand any of it, since Hegel was an item at the end of our syllabus and we never got there. I then explained to him that I was madly in love with D—— and, in a marvelous stroke of inspiration (I regretted that the examiner couldn't hear me), told him that, in this case, I was incapable of unifying the contradictory elements, making a Hegelian synthesis. The digression was useless.

Jimmy looked at me blankly and could only ask:

"What about me?"

I got irritated.

I don't know, I answered, kicking an imaginary pebble and thinking: look, figure it out for yourself! We're simple animals.

Jimmy was upset. He launched a series of insults at me, that I was no more than a woman, fickle and flighty like all the rest. And he threatened me: I'd come to regret this sudden change of heart. In vain I tried to explain myself using his theories: I liked someone and it was natural, that was all; that if I were "evolved" and "thinking" I'd have started out by making everything complicated, showing up with moral conflicts, with the foolishness of civilization, things that animals know absolutely nothing about. I spoke with a charming eloquence, all owing to the dialectical influence of the examiner (there goes Mama's idea: the woman should go along … etc.). Jimmy, pale and undone, told me and my theories to go to hell. I shouted anxiously, that those crackbrained ideas weren't mine and that, in fact, they could only have sprouted from a tousled and elongated head. He shouted, even louder still, that I hadn't understood anything he'd been explaining to me up till then so graciously: that with me everything was a waste of time. It was too much. I demanded another explanation. He told me to go to hell again.

I left in confusion. To mark the occasion, I got a bad headache. From some vestiges of civilization, remorse welled up.

My grandmother, a loveable and lucid little old lady, to whom I recounted the incident, tilted her little white head and explained to me that men have a habit of constructing certain theories for themselves and others for women. But, she added after a pause and a sigh, they forget them right when the time comes to act … I answered Granny that I, who could successfully apply Hegel's law of contradictions, hadn't understood a word she said. She laughed and explained good-naturedly:

My dear, men are a bunch of animals.

Were we back, then, at the starting point? I didn't think of it as an argument, but I felt a little consoled. I went to sleep somewhat sad. But I awoke happy, purely animal. When I opened the bedroom windows and looked out onto the cool, calm garden in the first rays of sunlight, I was certain there was nothing to do but live. Only, the change in Jimmy continued to fascinate me. It's such a good theory!

Interrupted Story
("História interrompida")

HE WAS SAD AND TALL. HE NEVER SPOKE TO ME WITH-
out making it understood that his gravest flaw lay in his tendency toward destruction. And that was why, he'd say, stroking
his black hair as if stroking the soft, hot fur of a kitten, that
was why his life amounted to a pile of shards: some shiny,
others clouded, some cheerful, others like a "piece of a wasted
hour," meaningless, some red and full, others white, but already
shattered.

I, to be honest, didn't know how to answer and regretted not
having some backup gesture, like his, of stroking his hair, to slip
out of the confusion. Nevertheless, for someone who's read a
little and thought quite a lot during nights of insomnia, it's rel-
atively easy to make up things that sound profound. I'd answer
that even by destroying he was creating: at the very least this
pile of shards to look at and talk about. Perfectly absurd. He, it
seems, thought so too, because he wouldn't reply. He'd get very
sad, looking at the ground and stroking his warm kitten.

In this way the hours passed. Sometimes I'd order a cup of
coffee, which he'd drink greedily and with plenty of sugar. And
I'd think a very funny thought: that if he really did think he went
around destroying everything, he wouldn't take such pleasure in

drinking coffee and wouldn't order more. A slight suspicion that W… was an artist, crossed my mind. To justify himself, he'd answer: one destroys everything around, but cannot destroy one's own self and desires (we have a body). Pure excuses.

One summer day I flung the window wide open. It seemed to me that the garden had entered the living room. I was twenty-two and felt nature in my every fiber. That day was beautiful. A gentle sun, as if it had risen that very instant, covered the flowers and grass. It was four in the afternoon. All around, silence.

I looked back at the room, soothed by the calm of those moments. I wanted to tell him:

"It seems to me that this is the very first hour, but afterward, no more will ever follow."

Mentally I heard him reply:

"That's merely an indefinable sentimental tendency, mixed up with modish literature, very subjectivist. From which arises this confusion of sentiments, which doesn't truly have any substance of its own, except for your psychological condition, very common in unwed young ladies your age …"

I tried to explain it to him, to resist him … Not a single argument. I turned back desolate, looked at his sad face and we were silent.

That was when I had that terrible thought: "Either I destroy him or he'll destroy me."

I had to prevent at all costs that analytical tendency, which ended up reducing the world to mere quantitative elements, from affecting me. I had to react. I wanted to see whether the grayness of his words could cloud my twenty-two years and the bright summer afternoon. I made up my mind, ready to start fighting that very moment. I turned to him, placed my hands on the windowsill, narrowed my eyes and hissed:

"This seems to me the very first hour and also the last!!"

Silence. Outside, the indifferent breeze.

He lifted his eyes to me, raised his languid hand and stroked his hair. Then he started tracing his nail over the checked pattern on the tablecloth.

I closed my eyes, let my arms drop alongside my body. My lovely and luminous twenty-two years … I ordered coffee with plenty of sugar.

After we parted ways, at the end of the avenue, I went home very slowly, chewing on a blade of grass and kicking every white pebble along the way. The sun had already set and in the colorless sky the first stars could already be seen.

I was reluctant to get home: invariably dinner, the long, empty evening with the family, a book, embroidery, and, finally, bed, sleep. I took the longest side path. The long grasses were downy and when the wind blew hard they caressed my legs.

But I was worried.

He was dark-haired and sad. And always wearing black. Oh, there was no doubt I liked him. I, so white and happy, by his side. I, in a floral dress, clipping roses, and he wearing black, no, white, reading a book. Yes, we made a lovely couple. I considered myself frivolous, doing that, imagining scenes. But I justified myself: we must please nature, adorn her. For if I would never plant jasmine next to sunflowers, how would I dare … All right, all right, what I needed to do was figure out "my situation."

For two days I thought incessantly. I wanted to find a formula that would bring him to me. I wanted to find the formula that could save him. Yes, save him. And that idea pleased me because it would justify the means I'd use to catch him. Yet everything seemed fruitless. He was a difficult man, distant, and the worst thing was that he spoke candidly of his weaknesses: where could I attack him, then, if he knew himself?

The birth of an idea is preceded by a long gestation, by a process unconscious in the person conceiving it. That's how I explain my lack of appetite during that magnificent dinner, my agitated insomnia in a bed with fresh sheets, after a busy day. At two in the morning, at last, it was born, the idea.

I sat up in bed excitedly, thinking: it came too quickly to be any good; don't get all worked up; lie down, close your eyes and wait until you calm down. I got up, though, and, barefoot so as not to wake Mira, started pacing back and forth across the room, like a businessman awaiting stock market results. Yet more and more it seemed that I'd found the solution.

Indeed, men like W—— spend their lives in search of the truth, entering the narrowest of labyrinths, reaping and destroying half the world under the pretext of eliminating errors, but when the truth rises up before their eyes it always happens unexpectedly. Perhaps because they've fallen in love with the scholarly pursuit itself, and they become like the miser who merely accumulates, accumulates, having forgotten the original goal for which he first began to accumulate. The fact is, when it came to W—— I could only achieve anything by putting him into a state of "shock."

And here's how. I'd say to him (in the blue dress that made me much blonder), my voice tender and firm, looking him in the eye:

"I've been thinking a lot about us and I've decided that the only thing left for us to do is …"

No. Simply.

"Shall we get married?"

No, no. No questions.

"W—— we're getting married."

Yes, I knew what men were like. And above all, I knew deep down what he was like. He wouldn't be able to resort to his favorite gesture. And he'd stand there frozen, amazed. Because he'd be facing the Truth … He liked me and perhaps I was the only one he hadn't managed to destroy with his analyses (I was twenty-two).

I couldn't sleep the rest of the night. I was so wide awake that Mira's snoring irritated me, and even the moon, very round, cut in half by a branch with delicate leaves, looked defective to me, swollen on one side and excessively artificial. I wanted to turn on the light, but I could already hear Mira's complaints to Mama the next day.

I awoke feeling like a girl on her wedding day. My every act was preparatory, full of purpose, like part of a ritual. I spent the morning in extreme agitation, thinking about the decor, the clothes, the flowers, phrases and dialogues. After all that, how could I make my voice tender and firm, serene and mild? If I kept on so feverishly, I'd risk greeting W—— with nervous cries: "W—— let's get married immediately, immediately." I grabbed a sheet of paper and filled it from top to bottom: "Eternity. Life. World. God. Eternity. Life. World. God. Eternity …." Those words killed the meaning of many of my feelings and left me cold for several weeks, so insignificant was I finding myself.

But in fact I didn't want to cool down: what I desired was to live the moment until I wore it out. I just needed to figure out a face that was less fiery. I sat down to a long stretch of sewing.

Calm returned little by little. And with it, a deep and thrilling certainty of love. But, I thought, there's nothing, really, nothing, for which I'd trade these coming moments! You only have a feeling like that two or three times in your life and the words hope, happiness, longing are connected to it, I discovered. And I closed my eyes and imagined him so vividly that his presence became almost real: I "felt" his hands upon mine and a slight headiness dazzled me. ("Oh, my God, forgive me, but blame it on summer, blame it on him for being so handsome and dark and on me for being so blonde!").

The idea that I was being happy filled me so much that I had to do something, perform some act of kindness, in order not to feel guilty. And what if I gave Mira my little lace collar? Yes, what's a little lace collar, even if it's pretty, in the face of … "Eternity. Life. World … Love"?

Mira is fourteen and overly excitable. That's why, when she breathlessly burst into the room and closed the door behind her, gesturing dramatically, I said:

"Have a drink of water and then tell me how the cat had thirty kittens and two black puppies."

"Clarinha said he killed himself! He shot himself in the head … Is it true, is it? It's a lie, isn't it?"

And suddenly the story splintered. It didn't even have a smooth ending. It concluded with the abruptness and lack of logic of a smack in the face.

I'm married and I have a son. I didn't name him after W——. And I don't tend to look back: I still bear in mind the punishment God gave Lot's wife. And I only wrote "this" to see whether I could find an answer to the questions that torture me, every once in a while, disturbing my peace: did the passage of W—— through the world have any meaning? did my pain have any meaning? what connects these facts to … "Eternity. Life. World. God."?

The Escape
("A fuga")

IT WAS GETTING DARK AND SHE WAS SCARED. THE rain was pouring relentlessly and the sidewalks glistened under the streetlamps. People were passing by with umbrellas, in raincoats, in a hurry, their faces weary. Cars were skidding on the wet asphalt and a horn or two sounded faintly.

She wanted to sit down on a park bench, because she actually couldn't feel the rain and didn't mind the cold. Just a little scared was all, because she still hadn't decided which way to go. The bench would be a place to rest. But the passersby were looking at her curiously so she kept going.

She was tired. She was always thinking: "But what'll happen now?" If she kept walking. That wasn't the solution. Go back home? No. She worried that some force would push her back to her point of departure. Feeling dizzy, she closed her eyes and imagined a great whirlwind emerging from "Elvira's House," violently sucking her in and depositing her by the window, book in hand, recomposing the everyday scene. She got scared. She waited for a moment when no one was coming to say with all her might: "You're not going back." She calmed down.

Now that she'd decided to leave, everything was being

reborn. If she weren't so confused, she'd have taken an infinite liking to the thought she'd had after two hours: "Well, things still exist." Yes, that discovery was simply extraordinary. She'd been married for twelve years and three hours of freedom had restored her almost entirely to herself: —the first thing to do was see if things still existed. If she were performing this same tragedy on stage, she'd pat, pinch herself to make sure she was awake. The last thing she wanted to do, though, was perform.

Joy and relief, however, weren't the only things inside her. There was also a little fear and twelve years.

She crossed the pedestrian bridge and leaned against the seawall, to gaze at the ocean. It was still raining. She'd caught the bus in Tijuca and got off at Glória. She'd already walked past the Morro da Viúva.

The ocean was churning powerfully and, when the waves broke against the rocks, the salt foam completely sprayed her. She stood for a moment wondering whether that was a deep patch, because it was getting impossible to guess: the dark, shadowy waters could be centimeters above the sand just as easily as they could be obscuring the infinite. She decided to try that game again, now that she was free. All she had to do was gaze lingeringly into the water and think about how that world was boundless. It was as if she were drowning and never touched the bottom of the sea with her feet. A heavy anguish. So then why did she seek it out?

The story about not touching the bottom of the sea was an old one, it went back to her childhood. In the chapter on the force of gravity, in elementary school, she'd invented a man with a funny disease. The force of gravity didn't work on him ... So he'd fall off the earth, and keep falling evermore, because she didn't know how to give him a destiny. Where was he falling? Later she figured it out: he kept falling, falling and got used to it, eventually learning how to eat falling, sleep falling, live falling, until he died. And would he keep falling? But right then her memory of the man didn't bother her and, on the contrary, it brought her a taste of freedom she hadn't experienced in twelve years. Because her husband had a singular feature: his mere presence made her slightest movements of thought freeze up. At first, this brought her a certain peace, since she used to tire herself out thinking about useless things, even if they amused her.

Now the rain has stopped. It's just cold and feels good. I'm not going home. Ah, yes, that is infinitely comforting. Will he be surprised? Yes, twelve years weigh on a person like pounds of lead. The days melt into one another, merge to form one whole block, a big anchor. And the person is lost. Her gaze starts evoking a deep well. Dark and silent water. Her gestures go blank and she has but one fear in life: that something will come along and transform her. She is living behind a window, peering through the glass as the rainy season covers the season of sun, then becomes summer and then the rains again. Desires are ghosts that dissolve as soon as you light the lamp of good sense. Why is it that husbands are good sense? Hers is particularly solid, good, and never wrong. The sort who only uses one brand of pencil and knows by heart what's written on the soles of his shoes. You can ask him without hesitation about the train schedule, which newspaper has the highest circulation and even in what region of the globe monkeys reproduce the fastest.

She laughs. Now she can laugh ... I used to eat falling, sleep falling, live falling. I'll look for a place to rest my feet ...

She found this thought so funny that she leaned against the wall and started laughing. A fat man stopped at a distance, staring at her. What do I do? Maybe come up and say: "Son, it's raining." No. "Son, I used to be a married woman and now I'm a woman." She started walking and forgot the fat man.

She opens her mouth and feels cool air flood it. Why did she wait so long for this renewal? Just today, after twelve centuries. She'd stepped out of the cold shower, put on some light clothes, grabbed a book. But today was different from all the afternoons of the days of all the years. It was hot and she was suffocating. She opened all the windows and doors. But no: the air was there, stagnant, solemn, heavy. Not a single breeze and the sky looming, the clouds dark, dense.

How did that happen? At first just the distress and the heat. Then something inside her began to grow. All of a sudden, in laborious, painstaking movements, she pulled the clothes off her body, ripped them apart, tore them into long strips. The air was closing in on her, constricting her. Then a loud thundering shook the house. Almost at the same time, swollen drops of warm water began falling here and there.

She stood still in the middle of the bedroom, panting. The rain fell harder. She heard its drumming on the tin roof in the yard and the shouts of the maid pulling the wash from the line. Now it was like a deluge. A cool wind was blowing through the house, stroking her hot face. She felt calmer, then. She got dressed, took all the money in the house and left.

Now she's hungry. It's been twelve years since she's felt hunger. She'll go to a restaurant. The bread is fresh, the soup is hot. She'll order a cup of coffee, a cup of strong, fragrant coffee. Ah, how beautiful and enchanting everything is. The hotel room feels foreign, the pillow is soft, the clean sheets scented. And when darkness claims the room, an enormous moon will appear, after this rain, a cool and serene moon. And she'll sleep bathed in moonlight …

Daybreak will come. She'll have the morning free to buy what she needs for the journey, because the ship departs at two in the afternoon. The sea is calm, almost no waves. The sky a violent, strident blue. The ship moves swiftly into the distance … And soon after the silence. The waters sing against its hull, liltingly, rhythmically … All around, seagulls hover, white foam escaped from the sea. Yes, all that!

But she doesn't have enough money for a trip. The tickets are too expensive. And getting soaked by all that rain left her with a piercing chill. She could very well go to a hotel. That's true. But hotels in Rio aren't appropriate for an unaccompanied lady, except the first class ones. And in those she might run into one of her husband's acquaintances, which would surely harm his business.

Oh, it's all a lie. What's the truth? Twelve years weigh like pounds of lead and the days close in on our bodies and constrict them more and more. I'm going home. I can't be mad at myself, because I'm tired. And anyway it's all just happening, I'm not provoking a thing. It's been twelve years.

She goes into her house. It's late and her husband is reading in bed. She tells him that Rosinha got sick. Didn't he get her note letting him know she'd be home late? No, he says.

She drinks a glass of warm milk because she's not hungry. She puts on some flannel pajamas, blue with white polka dots, very soft indeed. She asks her husband to turn off the light. He kisses her face and tells her to wake him at exactly seven o'clock. She promises, he turns off the light.

In the trees, a great and pure light rises.

She lies with her eyes open awhile. Then she dries her tears on the sheet, closes her eyes and gets settled in bed. She feels the moonlight fall across her slowly.

In the silence of the night, the ship moves farther and farther away.

Excerpt
("Trecho")

REALLY NOTHING HAPPENED ON THAT GRAY AFTER-
noon in April. Everything, however, foretold a big day. He had
alerted her that his arrival would constitute the great fact, the
culminating event of their lives. That's why she went into the
Bar da Avenida, sat at one of the small tables by the window,
in order to spot him, the moment he appeared on the corner.
The waiter wiped the table and asked what she'd like. Now of
all times she had no reason to be shy and afraid of committing
a *gaffe*. She was waiting for someone, she answered. He eyed
her a moment. "Do I look so forlorn that I couldn't possibly be
waiting for someone?" she told him:

"I'm waiting for a friend."

And now she knew that her voice would come out perfectly:
calm and casual. (Well it wasn't the first time she was waiting
for someone.) He rubbed at a nonexistent stain on the corner
of the small marble table and, after a calculated pause, replied,
without so much as looking at her:

"Yes, ma'am."

She settles into the narrow chair. She crosses her legs with
a certain elegance that, Cristiano himself had said, comes nat-

urally to her. She holds her purse with both hands, lets out a relaxed sigh. There. All she has to do is wait.

Flora enjoys living very much. Very much indeed. This afternoon, for instance, despite her dress pinching at the waist and her waiting in horror for the moment she'll have to stand and cross the long, narrow room in her too-tight skirt, despite all this she thinks it's nice to be sitting there, among all those people, to have coffee with little cakes, like everybody else. She feels just like when she was little and her mother would give her "real" little pans to fill with food and play "housewife."

All the little tables in the café are full. The men smoke fat cigars and the young men, stuffed into big, loose jackets, offer each other cigarettes. The women drink sodas and nibble at sweets with the daintiness of rodents, to avoid smearing their "lipstick." The heat is sweltering and the fans drone on the walls. If she hadn't been dressed in black she could have imagined herself in an African café, in Dakar or Cairo, amid handheld fans and dark men discussing illicit business dealings, for example. Amid spies even, who knows? stuffed into those Arabian sheets.

Naturally it was somewhat absurd to be playing at thinking on that afternoon of all days. Precisely when Cristiano had promised her the biggest day in the world and precisely, oh! Precisely when she was afraid nothing would happen ... simply due to Cristiano's absence ... It was absurd, but whenever "things" happened to her she would intersperse these things with perfectly pointless and meaningless thoughts. Back when Nenê was about to be born and she was in the hospital, lying down, white and scared to death, she doggedly accompanied the buzzing of a fly around a teacup and came to think, in a general way about the tumultuous lives of flies. And in fact, she'd concluded, there are great studies to be done on these tiny beings. For instance: why is it that they, with those beautiful wings, don't fly higher? Could it be that those wings were powerless or did flies lack ideals? Another question: what is the mental attitude of flies toward us? And toward the teacup, that big lake, sweetened and warm? Indeed, those problems were not unworthy of attention. We're the ones still not worthy of them.

A couple entered. The man stopped in the doorway, at length chose a spot, then made his way over there with his wife under his arm, looking fierce like someone getting ready to defend a right: "I'm paying just as much as everyone else." He sat, cast a defiant look around the room. The girl was shy and smiled at Flora, a smile of class solidarity.

Well, time is flying by. A waiter with a blond mustache heads toward Flora, acrobatically balancing a tray with a dark soda in a perspiring glass. Without asking a thing, he sets down the tray, puts the glass near her hands and moves off. But who ordered a drink, she thinks distraught. She stays still, without moving. Ah! Cristiano, come quick. It's everyone against me ... I don't want soda, I want Cristiano! I feel like crying, because today's a big day, because today's the biggest day of my life. But I'm going to stuff into some corner hidden from me (behind the door? how ridiculous) everything that torments me until Cristiano gets here. I'm going to think about something. About what? "Dear sirs, dear sirs! Here I am ready for life! Dear sirs, no one's looking at me, no one realizes I exist! Yet, dear sirs, I exist, I swear that I exist! Very much, even. Look, all of you, with that triumphant attitude, look: I can vibrate, vibrate like the taut string of a harp. I can suffer with more intensity than any of you gentlemen. I am superior. And do you know why? Because I know I exist." And what if she drank the soda? At least that woman looking at her as if she weren't there, as if she were an empty table, would see that she's doing something.

She carefully picks out a straw, unwraps it with casual movements and takes the first sip. It was better that Nenê hadn't come. The soda is very cold and Nenê wants to try everything she sees. When Cristiano comes, will he ask first about her or Nenê? Cristiano said the two of them were children, that in their group he was the only adult. But this doesn't sadden Flora much. Once, in the beginning, he'd left her sitting in a corner of the bedroom and started pacing back and forth, rubbing his chin. Then he stopped in front of her, looked at her awhile and said: "But you're a little girl!" Nevertheless, he eventually got used to it and Flora always pleased him. Also because ever since she was little she'd known how to play every role. With the Red-head boy she'd played the soldier who kills, with the downstairs neighbor girl she was a wagon driver, in high school she played the part of the Indian woman who has a flock of children, as well as a teacher, housewife, evil neighbor, beggar, cripple and greengrocer. With the Redhead she'd played soldier, forced by the circumstances, because she needed to win his admiration.

So it wasn't hard to play Cristiano's lover. And she did it so well that he, before leaving, said to her:

"You know, little girl, there's more to you than I thought. No, you're not just a little girl. You're a woman full of good sense and independence."

She enjoyed Cristiano's praise like when he'd complimented her new dress. Or when the French teacher told her: "You weel yet be *un bon poète!*" Or when her mother used to say: "When this one grows up she's going to catch them all!" Well now, of course she knew how to do lots of things and even very well. But she was in no way one of those people who became someone else just for fun or because she needed to. Flora was something else that no one had discovered yet! That was the mystery.

The soda is doing something awful to her. Her stomach is clenching in pangs of nausea. She closes her eyes a moment and sees the dark liquid churning round and round in waves, growling. And Cristiano isn't coming. She's been there an hour. If Cristiano got there right then he'd send for something bitter and the pangs of nausea would disappear. Then he'd say proudly: "I don't know what you'd do on your own. You come up with things at just the wrong moment." And why was there suddenly that taste of coffee in her mouth? She flags down the waiter. "Ice water," she orders. After the first sip, she perks up:

"What was in that soda?"

"Coffee, miss."

Ah, coffee. Ugh, it's gotten worse. The waiter peers at her with curiosity and irony:

"Are you feeling better, *mademoiselle?*"

"Certainly, I wasn't feeling anything at all."

"Drink a cup of hot coffee and that'll make it all go away," he went on resolutely.

"Bring me one, please."

"Cristiano, where are you? I am small, dear sirs, deep down I am the size of Nenê. Don't you know who Nenê is? Well she's blonde, with black eyes and Cristiano says he's never surprised to see her little face all dirty. He says that in our messy bedroom, the fresh flowers, Nenê's little face and my 'poor dear' look are inseparable. But there's something wrong with my stomach. And Cristiano's not coming. What if Cristiano doesn't come? Our landlady, dear sirs, swears it's quite common for young women with children to be abandoned. She knows of at least three cases. What are you all saying? Oh, don't smoke right now."

The waiter comes with the coffee. He has a beautiful blond mustache.

"If I were you, ma'am, I'd try to get rid of the soda. Plenty of people feel sick from coffee-flavored drinks. All you have to do is stick two fingers in the roof of your mouth. The *toilette* is on the left."

Flora returns from there humiliated and doesn't dare face the blond mustache. She leans back in the chair and feels miserably fine.

A cool breeze blows through the windows. "Declarations from Mussolini. Suicide in Leblon! Extra extra *A Noite!*" Faraway sounds of honking. Either Cristiano missed the train or he's abandoned me forever.

The café has grown familiar to her eyes. The waiters are after all a bunch of silly, very busy men. They're arranging the chairs on the bandstand, wiping the piano. Customers of another sort, the sort who after they've bathed and dined "must enjoy life while they're still young men; and what else is money for?" settle at the little tables.

"Does that mean I'm lost," Flora thinks.

She hears the start of muted drumming, rhythmic, singular and mysterious, rising from the bandstand. With growing effervescence, like little animals making bubbles in some unknown way, the rhythm intensifies. And suddenly, from the last black man in the second row, there rises a savage cry, sustained, until it dies in a sweet whimper. The mulatto in the first row twists all the way around, his instrument points into the air and responds with a hoarse, childlike "boop-boop." The drumming resembles men and women springing side to side in a religious ceremony in Africa. Suddenly, silence. The piano sings out three notes, lone and serious. Silence.

The orchestra, in gentle movements, nearly at a standstill, crouching, slips into a pianissimo "fox-blue", insinuating like a fugue.

A few couples leave intertwined.

I've been here so long, so long! Flora thinks and feels she ought to cry. That means I'm lost. She presses her hands to her forehead. What happens now? The waiter feels sorry for her and comes over to say she can wait as long as she likes. Thank you. She catches sight of herself in the mirror. But is that her over there? is that her, with the face of a scared rabbit, who's thinking and waiting? (Whose little mouth is that? Whose little eyes are those? Yours, leave me alone.) If I don't try to save myself, I'll drown. Because if Cristiano doesn't come, who will tell all these people I exist? And what if I, all of a sudden, shout for the waiter, ask for paper and pen and say: Dear sirs, I am going to write a poem! Cristiano, darling! I swear that Nenê and I are yours.

Look: Debussy was a musician-poet, but such a poet that just the title of one of his suites makes you lie down on the garden grass, arms beneath your head, and dream. Look: Bells through the leaves. Perfumes of the night … Look … a thin woman cried out at the next table, slapping the backs of her hands on the table, as if to say: "I assure you, now it's evening. Don't argue."

"Nonsense, Margarida," replied one of the men coldly, "nonsense. Come now musician-poet … Come now look …"

Flora would ask for a piece of paper and write:

"Silent trees
lost on the road.
Gentle refuge
of coolness and shadow."
Cristiano won't come. A man approaches. What is it?
"Huh?"
"I'm asking if you'd like to dance," he continues. He blinks
his nearsighted eyes in an idiotic and odd manner.
"Oh no ... Really, no ... I ..."
He keeps looking at her.
"I, honestly, I can't ... Oh, maybe later ... I'm waiting for a
friend."
He's still standing there. What to do with this castoff? My
God, my eyes.
"I can't ..."
"Please, madame, I get it," the man says offended.
And he goes away. What exactly happened, after all? I don't
know, I don't know. If I don't look down, they'll see my eyes.
Silent trees lost on the road. Oh, surely I'm not crying because
of that nearsighted man. Nor because of Cristiano who will
never come again. It's because of that sweet woman, it's because
Nenê is beautiful, beautiful, it's because those flowers have a
faraway perfume. Gentle refuge of coolness and shadow. "Dear
sirs, now of all times, when I had so much to say, I don't know
how to express myself. I'm a solemn and serious woman, dear
sirs. I have a daughter, dear sirs. I could be a good poet. I could
have anyone I wanted. I know how to play every role, dear sirs.
I could get up now and give a speech against humanity, against
life. Asking the government to create a department of abandoned and sad women, who will never again have anything to
do in the world. Asking for some urgent reform. But I cannot,

dear sirs. And that's the reason why there will never be any re-forms. Because, instead of shouting, complaining, all I feel like is crying very softly and staying still, silent. Maybe not only because of that. My skirt is short and tight. I'm not getting up from here. To make up for it I have a small handkerchief, with red polka dots, and I can very well wipe my nose without the gentlemen, who don't even know I exist, noticing."

In the doorway appears a big man, newspapers in hand. He glances around looking for someone. That man comes straight toward Flora. He presses her hand, sits. He looks at her, his eyes shining, and in confusion she hears scattered words. "My pet, poor thing … the train … Nenê … darling …"

"Nonsense Margarida, nonsense," says the man at the next table.

"Do you want anything?" Cristiano asks. "A soda?"

"Oh, no," Flora jolts awake. The waiter smiles.

Cristiano, utterly happy, squeezes her knee lightly under the table. And Flora decides that never, ever again, will she for-give Cristiano for the humiliation she's suffered. And what if he hadn't come? Ah, then all that waiting would be excused, would mean something. But, like this? Never, never. Revolt, fight, yes do it. That Flora nobody knows must, appear, at last.

"Flora, I missed you so, so much."

"My darling …" Flora says sweetly, forgetting her short tight skirt.

Letters to Hermengardo
("Cartas a Hermengardo")

My dear Hermengardo:

Today is Sunday and the city is lovely. There is no one on the streets and all the trees exist solitary and sovereign. The worries and desires and hatreds have dwindled, stretched out upon the earth, tired of existing. And at the level of my mouth all I find is the sweet, pure air of calm renunciation.

My soul, cowering all week long, feels sudden desires to sprawl out, to feel supple for a few moments, to be colored afterward with a lassitude as happy as the kind that today softens nature. I need to think for a few minutes so as to possess sweet repose thereafter.

That is why I shall speak of the passions. And I know that you will listen because I have already transmitted to you the impression and desire of Sunday. And because I tell you that I shall speak in the humble robes of a shepherd. And that makes me small and reconciles me to you.

I would like to tell you that having passions does not mean

living beautifully, but rather suffering pointlessly. That the soul was made to be guided by reason and that no one can be happy when at the mercy of the instincts. For we are animals yet we are animals disturbed by man. And if they forgive him, he is proud and demanding and never forgives their excesses.

I speak to you of the passions in terms of their quality and their effects.

In terms of their quality because whereas the body is active, the soul is contemplative by nature and, knowing nothing, contemplates so as to conclude. That is its function. And in terms of its effects, because the bow feels empty after bidding farewell to the arrow.

I tell you that there is a joy in renouncing the pain of the passions. Because to desire them is to desire pain and not contentment and those who are noble feel in themselves the necessity to sound out their capacity to burn. And I tell you that what matters is not burning ardently, what matters is repose. What matters is coming to understand oneself and life through reason, which distinguishes us from animals.

And if one day I spoke to you of "noble passions," I did not call them noble due to their nature, nor their consequences, except out of compassion for their source, the eternal void of men. Because the man disturbed by pride seeks passion as a form of finding humility. He senses (and woe to the blind) that later on humility will come and in humility lies the serenity of the flower that allows itself to sway in the breath of the breeze.

There is that hero, a man without substance who desires, in a fever, to find calm. He should not be applauded, but lamented. There is another hero, who desires only upheaval. And he is a man who could not help but go back. He is a weak man. But if you wish to call him noble, you may. Because there is also a great beauty in animals. And in any case, all that exists is beautiful, error as much as truth. It just so happens that this approach to finding beauty is the approach of one who looks down at earth from heaven and is moved by the frailties of his sons. Men, however, struggle a great deal and desire a great deal. They have no time to seek the whole. They want individual happiness.

And that is why I tell you: passion is not the way.

There exists another way, the only one.

We have reached a certain degree of consciousness of our intelligence and, knowing this to be our mark as men, have discovered that we should give our strength to it so as to attain human perfection. And by this I do not mean to say that we should stop being animals. Never shall we renounce this happiness. What we should seek is for this primitive state to rise a bit and for our pride in being rational to fall a bit until the two beings that exist in us can meet, absorb one another and form a new species in nature.

And that is why I tell you: abandon whatever destroys. Passion destroys because it dissociates. Passion arises in the body and, not comprehending it, we situate it in our souls and become disturbed.

I am explaining all this to you so that you never exalt anything that wars with the contented spirit and anything that kills itself out of love. Merely forgive them. They have yet to comprehend that in life the smile exists and that passion destroys it and transforms it into a trembling rictus, which is no longer human.

If you cannot free yourself from desiring passions, read novels and adventure stories, for that is also why writers exist.

And another thing: pass on what I have said to you to some

youth who cannot sleep at night, dreaming up new adventures for Don Quixote. Explain to him that the "ever after" of passion tastes like a stubbed-out cigarette. Ask him, on my behalf, to be a man and not a hero, because nature demands nothing of him except that he be happy and find the peace of the open glade down less painful paths.

Explain this to him and I shall be able to rest this Sunday with the necessary humility.

Now if you ask me: "How do you know these things?" I shall answer in the words of Kipling, so often quoted by my Public Law professor: "But that's another story ..."

Thank you for listening to me,
Idalina.

SECOND LETTER

My dear Hermengardo,

In truth I tell you: happily you exist. For me the existence of a creature on Earth is enough to satisfy my desire for glory, which is nothing but a profound desire for closeness. Because I was mistaken when long ago I imagined as real my former yearning to "save humanity," "*malgré*," itself. Now all I desire is another person, besides myself, to whom I can prove myself ... And by returning to Idalina I also understood how beautiful and how impossible that other dream is, that of trying to save oneself. And if it is so impossible, then why lead me to this new citadel that would now be a poor disturbed woman? I don't know. Perhaps because one must save something. Perhaps through the belated consciousness that we are the sole presence that will not leave us until death. And that is why we love and seek ourselves.

And why, so long as we exist, the world shall exist and humanity shall exist. This is how, in the end, we are connected to them.

And everything I am saying is just an arbitrary preamble to justify my fondness for giving you so much advice. Because giving advice is once more to speak about oneself. And here I am ... Yet, in the end, I can speak with a peaceful conscience. I know of nothing that grants a man as many rights as the fact that he is living.

This preamble also serves as an apology. It is because I realize, even through the sweetest words that the miracle of your breathing inspires in me, my destiny is to throw stones. Never get angry with me for that. Some are born to cast stones. And after all, (here is where my task begins) why would it be wrong to cast stones, unless because they will hit things that belong to you or to those who know how to laugh and adore and eat?

Once this point has been clarified and you allow me to throw stones, I shall speak to you of Beethoven's Fifth Symphony.

Have a seat. Stretch out your legs. Close your eyes and ears. I shall say nothing for five minutes so you can think about Beethoven's Fifth Symphony. See, and this will be more perfect still, if you manage not to think in words, but rather create a state of feeling. See if you can halt the whole whirlwind and clear a space for the Fifth Symphony. It is so beautiful.

Only thus will you have it, through silence. Understand! If I perform it for you, it will fade away, note by note. As soon as the first one is sounded, it will no longer exist. And after the second, the harmony will no longer echo. And the beginning will be the prelude to the end, as in all things. If I perform it you will hear music and that alone. Whereas there is a way to keep it paused and eternal, each note like a statue inside you.

Do not perform it, that is what you must do. Do not listen

to it and you shall possess it. Do not love and you shall have love inside you. Do not smoke your cigarette and you shall have a lit cigarette inside you. Do not listen to Beethoven's Fifth Symphony and it will never end for you.

Thus I redeem myself from casting stones, so endlessly … Thus I taught you not to kill. Erect within yourself the monument to Unsatisfied Desire. And that way things will never die, before you yourself die. Because I tell you, sadder still than casting stones is dragging corpses.

And if you cannot follow my advice, because life is always more eager than all else, if you cannot follow my advice and all the plans we made to better ourselves then go suck on some mints. They are so refreshing.

Your

Idalina

Gertrudes Asks for Advice
("Gertrudes pede um conselho")

SHE SAT DOWN IN A WAY THAT MADE HER OWN WEIGHT "iron" her wrinkled skirt. She smoothed her hair, her blouse. Now, all she could do was wait.

Outside, everything was just swell. She could see the roofs of the houses, red flowers in a window, the yellow sun streaming over everything. There was no better time than two in the afternoon.

She didn't want to wait because she'd get scared. And if she was she wouldn't make the impression she wanted on the doctor. Don't think about the discussion, don't think. Quickly make up a story, count to a thousand, think about nice things. The worst was that all she could remember was the letter she'd sent. "Dear Madame, I am seventeen years old and would like …" Idiotic, absolutely idiotic. "I'm tired of pacing back and forth. Sometimes I can't sleep, partly because I share a room with my sisters and they toss and turn too much. But the real reason I can't sleep is because I stay up thinking about things. I once decided to commit suicide, but I don't want to anymore. Can you help me? Gertrudes."

And the other letters? "I don't like anything, I am like the poets …" Oh, don't think about it. How embarrassing! Until the doctor finally wrote her, summoning her to the office. But what was she going to say, after all? Everything was so vague. And the doctor would laugh … No, no, the doctor, who took care of abandoned minors, writing advice columns in magazines, had to understand, even without her saying anything.

Today something was going to happen! Don't think 1, 2, 3, 4, 5, 6, 7 … It was no use. Once upon a time there was a blind boy who … Why blind? No, he wasn't blind. His vision was quite good in fact. Now she finally understood why God, who could do anything, created crippled, blind, wretched people. Just to pass the time. While waiting? No, God never has to wait. So what exactly does he do? He's there, even if you still believed in Him (I didn't believe in God, I'd shower right before lunch, wouldn't wear my high school uniform and had taken up smoking), even if you still believed in ghosts, there couldn't be anything appealing about eternity. If I were God I'd have already forgotten how the world began. So long ago and all those centuries still to come … Eternity has no beginning, no end. She felt a little dizzy when she tried to imagine it, and God, always everywhere, invisible, with no defined form. She laughed, remembering how she'd eagerly swallow the tales they used to tell her. She had become quite free … But that didn't mean she was happy. And that was exactly what the doctor was going to explain.

In fact, lately, Tuda hadn't been feeling well at all. Sometimes she felt a nameless anxiety, sometimes an excessive and sudden calm. She often felt like crying, which generally was no more than an urge, as though the crisis spent itself in the desire. Some days, filled with boredom, peevish and sad. Other days, languid like a cat, becoming intoxicated by the slightest occurrences. A leaf falling, a child's cry, and she'd think: another moment and I won't be able to bear such happiness. And she really couldn't bear it, though she didn't exactly know what that happiness consisted of. She would collapse into muffled sobs, unburdened, with the foggy impression that she was surrendering, who knows how or to whom.

After the tears, along with swollen eyes, came a state of gentle convalescence, of acquiescence to everything. She surprised everyone with her sweetness and transparency and, moreover, mustered a bird-like lightness. She'd hand out alms to all the poor, with the grace of someone tossing flowers.

At other times, she filled herself with strength. Her gaze became hard as steel, prickly as thorns. She felt that she "could." She'd been made to "liberate."

"Liberate" was an immense word, full of mysteries and pain. Since she'd been agreeable for days, when was she destined for that other role? Which other? Everything was mixed up and could only really be expressed by the word "liberty" and by her heavy and determined tread, in the stoic expression she adopted. At night she wouldn't fall asleep until the distant roosters started to crow. She wasn't thinking, not exactly. She daydreamed. She imagined a future in which, daring and cool, she would lead a multitude of men and women, full of faith, almost to the point of worshipping her. Later, toward the middle of the night, she would slip into a state of semi-consciousness, in which everything was good, the multitude already led, no more school, her very own room, loads of men in love with her. She'd wake up bitter, noting with repressed joy how she wasn't interested in the cake her sisters were devouring like animals, with an irritating unconcern.

She was then living her days of glory. And they reached

their peak with some thought that exalted her and plunged her into ardent mysticism: "Join a convent! Save the poor, be a nurse!" She could already imagine herself donning the black habit, her face pale, her eyes pious and humble. Her hands, those implacably flushed and broad hands, emerging, white and delicate, from long sleeves. Or else, wearing that stark white cap, with sunken hollows under her eyes from sleepless nights. Handing the doctor, silently and rapidly, the operating tools. He would look at her with admiration, real friendliness, and who knows? Love even.

But greatness was impossible in surroundings such as hers. They'd interrupt her with the most banal observations: "Have you showered yet, Tuda?" Or else, the gaze of everyone at home. A simple look, distracted, completely alien to the noble fire that burned inside her. Who could go on, she thought in dejection, amid such vulgarity?

And besides this, why didn't "things happen"? Tragedies, beautiful tragedies ...

Until she discovered the doctor. And before meeting her, she already belonged to her. At night she carried on long imaginary conversations with this stranger. During the day, she'd write her letters. Until she was summoned: they'd finally seen that she was somebody, somebody extraordinary, somebody misunderstood!

Up until the day of the appointment, Tuda was beside herself. She dwelt in an atmosphere of fever and anxiety. An adventure. Got it? An adventure.

It wouldn't be long before she went into the office. This is how it'll go: she's tall, with short hair, piercing eyes, a big chest. Kind of chubby. But at the same time resembling Diana, the Huntress, of the waiting room.

She smiles. I remain solemn.

"Good afternoon."

"Good afternoon, my child" (wouldn't this be better: Good afternoon, sister? No, people don't say that).

"I came here out of an excess of audacity, trusting in your goodness and understanding, ma'am. I'm seventeen years old and I think I'm ready to start living."

She doubted she'd have the nerve. And anyway what did the doctor, after all, even have in common with her? But, no. Something would happen. She'd offer her a job, for example. She might send her on a voyage to collect data on … on infant mortality, let's say, or on farmworkers' wages. Or she might say:

"Gertrudes, you shall play a much greater role in life. You shall …"

What? What is greatness after all? Everything comes to an end … I don't know, the doctor will tell me.

Suddenly … The young fellow scratched his ear and said, with that old air people insist on lending new and exciting facts:

"You can go in …"

Tuda crossed the room, without breathing. And found herself facing the doctor.

She was seated at her desk, surrounded by books and papers. A stranger, serious, with a life of her own, which Tuda knew nothing about.

She pretended to tidy up her desk.

"Well then?" she said afterward. "A girl named Gertrudes …" She laughed. "And what brings you to me, looking for a job?" she began, with the tact that had earned her position as a magazine advice columnist.

Diminutive, black hair curled into two coils at the nape. Her lipstick applied a little beyond her lip line, in an attempt at sensuality. Her face calm, her hands fidgety. Tuda wanted to flee.

She'd left home many years before.

The doctor went on and on, her voice slightly hoarse, her gaze unfocused. About all sorts of subjects. The latest movies, young women today, their lack of guidance, bad reading choices, who knows, lots of things. Tuda talked too. Her heart had stopped racing and the room, the doctor gradually took on a more comprehensible aspect. Tuda told a few secrets, of no importance. Her mother, for example, didn't like her going out at night, claiming she'd catch a chill. She needed to have throat surgery and constantly had a cold. But her father always said every cloud had a silver lining and that tonsils were part of the body's defenses. And also, whatever nature created had its purpose.

The doctor toyed with her pen.

"All right, now I know you more or less. In your letter you mentioned a nickname? Tudes, Tuda …"

Tuda blushed. So the stranger brought up the letters. She couldn't hear so well because she felt dizzy and her heart decided to beat right in her ears. "A difficult age … they all are … when you least expect …"

"This worrying, everything you're feeling is more or less normal, it'll pass. You're smart and you'll understand what I'm going to explain. Puberty brings about certain disruptions and…"

No, doctor, how humiliating. She was already too old for these things, what she felt was more beautiful and even …

"This will pass. You don't need to work or do anything extraordinary. If you like"— she was going to use her old trick and smiled—"if you like, get yourself a boyfriend. And then …"

She was just like Amélia, like Lídia, like everyone else, like everyone else!

The doctor was still talking. Tuda remained silent, obstinately silent. A cloud blotted out the sun and the office suddenly turned gloomy and humid. A second later, the dust motes started to float and glimmer again.

The therapist became slightly impatient. She was tired. She'd been working so hard ...

"All right? Anything else? Speak up, don't be afraid to speak up ..."

Tuda thought confusedly: I came to ask what to do with myself. But she didn't know how to sum up her condition in that question. Furthermore, she was worried about doing something eccentric and still wasn't used to herself.

The doctor had tilted her head to one side and was doodling little symmetrical lines on a piece of paper. Then she surrounded the lines with a slightly crooked circle. As always, she couldn't quite maintain the same approach for long. She was flagging and letting herself be invaded by her own thoughts. She realized it, got irritated and took out her irritation on Tuda: "So many people dying, so many 'homeless children,' so many unsolvable problems (her problems) and here was this little girl, with a family, a nice bourgeois life, inflating her own importance." She vaguely noted that this contradicted her individualist theory: "Each person is a world, each person possesses his or her own key and other people's keys don't work; you can only look at someone else's world for amusement, for some personal gain, for some other surface feeling floating by that isn't the vital one; just knowing that others feel as you do is a consolation, but not a solution." Precisely because she noted that she was contradicting herself and because a colleague's statement about female inconsistency sprang to mind and because she thought it unfair, she grew even more exasperated, wanting, angry at herself, as if to punish herself, to plunge deeper into the contradiction. A minute longer and she'd say to the girl: why don't you visit the cemetery? Vaguely, however, she noticed Tuda's dirty nails and reflected: she's still in too much turmoil to learn any lessons from the cemetery. And furthermore, she remembered her own days of dirty nails and imagined how she would have scoffed at someone who spoke to her back then about the cemetery as though about some reality.

All of a sudden, Tuda got the feeling that the doctor didn't like her. And, like that, there with that woman who had nothing to do with all these intimate matters, in that room she'd never seen and that was suddenly "a place," she thought she was dreaming. Why was she there? she asked herself startled. Everything about her mother, home, that last lunch, so peaceful, was losing its reality, and not only her confession but the inexplicable motive that brought her to the doctor seemed like a lie, a monstrous lie, that she'd gratuitously invented, just for fun ... The proof is that no one ever made use of her, as of a thing that exists. They'd say: "Tuda's dress, Tuda's classes, Tuda's tonsils ...", but they'd never say: "Tuda's unhappiness ..." She'd gone so far so fast with this lie! Now she was lost, she couldn't turn back! She'd stolen some candy and didn't want to eat it ... But the doctor would make her chew it, swallow it, as a punishment ... Ah, to slip away from that office and be alone again, without the doctor's useless and humiliating understanding.

"Look, Tuda, what I'd really like to tell you is that one day you'll have whatever it is you're now so confusedly seeking. That kind of calm that comes from knowing oneself and others. But you can't rush the arrival of that state of mind. There are things you only learn when no one teaches them. And that's how it is with life. There's even more beauty in discovering it for yourself, in spite of the suffering." The doctor felt a sudden weariness, had the impression that wrinkle #3, from her nose to her lips, had deepened. That girl was doing her harm and she wanted to be alone again. "Look, I'm sure you'll have plenty of happiness to come. Sensitive people are both unhappier and happier than others. But give it some time!" How easily banal she was, she thought without bitterness. "Go on living …"

She smiled. And suddenly Tuda felt that face digging deep into her soul. It wasn't coming from her mouth, nor from her eyes, that gaze … that divine gaze. It was like a terribly friendly shadow, hovering over the doctor. And, just then, Tuda discovered that she hadn't lied, oh, no! A joy, an urge to cry. Oh, to kneel before the doctor, bury her face in her lap, to shout: this is all I've got, this! Just tears!

The doctor was no longer smiling. She was thinking. Looking at her, there, in profile, Tuda no longer understood her. A stranger, once again. She quickly sought the other one, the divine one:

"Ma'am, why did you say: 'what I'd really like to tell you is …'? So it's not true?"

The girl was sharper than she'd thought. No, it wasn't true. The doctor knew you could spend your whole life seeking some thing beyond the mist, she also knew of the confusion that understanding oneself and others brought. She knew that the beauty of discovering life is small for those who primarily seek beauty in things. Oh, she knew a lot. But she was tired of the struggle. The office once again empty, sinking into the divan, shutting the windows—the restful darkness. Since that was her refuge, hers alone, where even he, with his calm and irritating acceptance of happiness, was an intruder!

They looked at each other and Tuda, disappointed, felt that she held a superior position to the doctor's, she was the stronger one.

The therapist hadn't noticed that she'd already betrayed herself with her eyes and added, thoughtful, her voice hesitating:

"Did I say that? I don't think so … (What did this child actually want? Who am I to be giving advice? Why didn't she just call? No, it's better that she didn't, I'm tired. Oh, if only everybody would leave me alone, that's what I want more than anything!)"

Once again everything floating in the office. There was nothing left to say. Tuda stood, her eyes moist.

"Wait," the doctor seemed to consider for an instant. "Look, why don't we make a deal? You stay in school, and don't worry too much about yourself. And when you're … let's say … twenty, yes, twenty, you'll come back …" She was sincerely excited: she felt for the girl, she'd have to help her, maybe give her a job to occupy and distract her, until she outgrew this period of maladjustment. She was so vibrant, intelligent even. "Deal? Come on, Tuda, be a good girl and agree …"

Yes, she agreed, she agreed! Everything was possible again! Ah, it was just that she couldn't speak, couldn't say how much she agreed, how much she surrendered to the doctor. Because if she spoke, she might cry, she didn't want to cry.

"But Tuda …" The divine shadow on her face. "You don't have to cry … Come on, promise that you'll be a brave little woman …" Yes, I'm going to help her. But now, the divan, oh yes, quick, plunge into it.

Tuda wiped her face with her hands.

Out on the street, everything was easier, solid and simple. She'd walked fast, fast. She didn't want—the curse of always noticing—to recall the sluggish and weary gesture with which the doctor had held out her hand. And even the faint sigh … No, no. How crazy! But little by little the thought took hold: she'd been unwanted … She flushed.

She went into an ice cream shop and bought an ice cream.

Two girls in high school uniforms went by, talking and laughing loudly. They looked at Tuda with the animosity some people feel for others and that young people still don't disguise. Tuda was alone and defeated. She thought, without linking her thought to the way the girls looked at her: what do they have to do with me? Me, who was there with the doctor, talking about deep and mysterious things? And even if they knew about the adventure, they wouldn't understand …

All of a sudden it occurred to her that after having experienced that afternoon, she couldn't go on in the same way, studying, going to the movies, hanging out with her little girl-friends, simply … She'd become distanced from everyone, even from the old Tuda … Something had unfurled inside her, her own personality that had asserted itself with the certainty that there was something in the world akin to her … She'd been taken by surprise: so she could speak of … of "that" as if it were something palpable, of her dissatisfaction that she'd hidden in shame and fear … Now … Someone had lightly touched the mysterious mists from which she'd been living for some time and suddenly they had solidified, formed a unit, existed. Until now all she had lacked was for someone to recognize her, for her to recognize herself … Everything was transforming! How? She didn't know …

She kept walking, her eyes wide open, growing ever brighter.

She was thinking: before, I was one of those people who exist, who walk around, get married, simply have children. And from now on one of those constant elements in her life would be Tuda, conscious, vigilant, always present …

Her destiny had been altered, it seemed to her. But how? Oh, not to be able to think clearly and if only the words she knew could express what she felt! A little proud, radiant, half-disappointed, she kept repeating to herself: I'm going to have another life, different from Amélia's, Mama's, Papa's … She sought a vision of her new future and could only manage to see herself walking alone over wide, unknown plains, her steps resolute, her eyes suffering, walking, walking … Where to?

She was no longer hurrying home. She possessed the kind of secret people could never share. And she herself, she thought, would only participate in everyday life with a few particles of herself, just a few, but not with the new Tuda, today's Tuda … Would she always be at the margins? … —Revelations came quickly one after another, flaring suddenly and illuminating her like little bolts of lightning. —Isolated …

She suddenly felt depressed, with no one to help her. From one moment to the next, she'd wound up alone. She hesitated, disoriented. Where's Mama? No, not Mama. Ah, to go back to the office, to seek the doctor's divine gaze, to beg her not to abandon her, because she was scared, scared!

But the doctor had her own life to live and—another revelation—nobody ever went entirely outside themselves to help … "Just" come back when you're twenty … I won't lend you a dress, I won't lend you a single thing, all you ever do is ask for things … And it wasn't even possible to be understood! "Puberty brings about certain disruptions …" "This girl isn't feeling well, João, I'll bet that her tonsils …"

"Oh, pardon me, miss ... Did I hurt you?"

She almost lost her balance from the impact. She was stunned for an instant.

"Can you see all right?" The man had pointy white teeth. "There's no need ... It was nothing ..."

The fellow walked off, a faint smile on his round face.

Opening her eyes, Tuda noticed the street in full sunlight. The strong breeze made her shiver. What a funny smile, the man's. She licked the last bit of her ice cream and since no one was watching she ate the cone (the men who make those cones have dirty hands, Tuda). She frowned. Damn! (Don't say damn, Tuda.) She'd say whatever she wanted, she'd eat all the cones in the world, she'd do exactly as she pleased.

She suddenly remembered: the doctor ... No ... No. Not even when she was twenty ... When she was twenty she'd be a woman walking across an unknown plain ... A woman! The hidden power of this word. Because after all, she thought, she ... she existed! Along with the thought came the sensation of having her own body, a body that the man had looked at, her own soul, the soul that the doctor had touched. She pressed her lips together firmly, full of sudden violence:

"What do I need any doctor for! What do I need anyone for!"

She kept walking, hurriedly, pulsating, ferocious with joy.

Another Couple of Drunks
("Mais dois bêbedos")

I WAS SURPRISED. WASN'T HE TAKING ADVANTAGE OF my good nature? Why was he acting so shrouded in mystery? He could tell me his secrets without any fear of judgment. My drunken state made me particularly inclined to benevolence and besides, after all, he was no more than a random stranger ... Why didn't he discuss his own life with the objectivity with which he'd ordered a beer from the waiter?

I refused to grant him the right to have a soul of his own, full of prejudices and love of self. One of those wrecks who, smart enough to know he was a wreck, shouldn't have lights and shadows, like me, who could tell my life story going back to the time before my grandparents had even met. I had the right to be modest and not expose myself. I was conscious, aware that I laughed, that I suffered, I'd read books on Buddhism, they'd put an epitaph on my grave when I died. And I got drunk not just for the hell of it, but for a purpose: I was somebody.

But that man who'd never venture past his narrow circle, neither especially ugly, nor especially handsome, that fugitive chin, as important as a trotting dog—what did he mean by his arrogant silence? Hadn't I asked him several questions? He was offending me. I wouldn't stand for his insolence another second, making him see that he ought to be grateful for my overtures, because otherwise I'd never know he existed. Yet he kept mute, without even getting the least bit excited about the chance to live.

That night I'd already had quite a bit to drink. I wandered from bar to bar, until, excessively happy, I was afraid I'd outdo myself: I'd grown too comfortable in my own skin. I was looking for a way to pour some of myself out, before I completely overflowed.

I dialed the phone and waited, barely breathing from impatience:

"Hello, Ema!"

"Oh, darling, at this time of night!"

I hung up. Was it a lie? The tone was true, the energy, the beauty, the love, that craving to offer up my excess were all true. The only lie was that line I thought up with so little effort.

Yet I still wasn't satisfied. Ema had a vague notion that I was different and credited everything strange I could possibly do to that account. She was so accepting of me, that I was alone when we were together. And at that moment what I was avoiding was precisely that solitude that would be too strong a drink.

I wandered the streets, thinking: I'll choose someone who never would have imagined they deserved me.

I was looking for a man or a woman. But no one particularly pleased me. They all seemed fine on their own, spinning around inside their own thoughts. Nobody needed me.

Until I saw him. Just like all the rest. But so like them that he became a type. This one, I decided, this one.

And ... there he is! Drunk on my tab and ... silent, as if he owed me nothing ...

Our movements were sluggish, the scarcely uttered words—vague, random, under the bar's dim lights that lengthened faces into shadows. Around us, a few people were playing cards, drinking, talking, in louder tones. The torpor turned people slack, with no sparks. Maybe that's why it was so hard for him to talk. But something told me he wasn't all that drunk and was keeping silent simply so he wouldn't have to acknowledge my superiority.

I drank slowly, elbows on the table, scrutinizing him. As for him—he'd slumped into his chair, feet outstretched, all the way to mine, arms flopped on the table.

"So?" I said impatiently.

He seemed to wake up, looked around and rejoined the conversation:

"So … so … nothing."

"But, sir, you were talking about your son!…"

He stared at me for a second. Then smiled:

"Ah, yes. Right, he's sick."

"What's wrong with him?"

"Angina, the pharmacist said angina."

"Who does the boy live with?"

"His mother."

"And you don't live with her?"

"What for?"

"My God … At the very least to suffer with her … Are you married to the young lady?"

"Nope, I'm not married."

"How disgraceful!" I said, though not knowing what exactly was so disgraceful. "We need to do something. Imagine if your son dies, she's left all alone …"

He wasn't moved.

"Imagine her, eyes burning, at the child's side. The child wheezing painfully, dying. He dies. His little head is contorted, his eyes are open, staring at the wall, obstinately. Everything is silent and the young lady doesn't know what to do. The boy is dead and all of a sudden she has nothing to do. She collapses onto the bed, sobbing, tearing at her clothes: 'My son, my poor son! It's death, it's death!' The household rats take fright and start to race around the room. They crawl up your son's face, still warm, gnaw at his little mouth. The woman screams and faints, for two hours. The rats visit her body too, cheerful, nimble, their tiny teeth gnawing here and there."

I got so caught up in the description that I'd forgotten the man. I looked at him suddenly and caught his mouth open, his chin resting on his chest, listening.

I smiled triumphantly.

"She wakes up from her fainting spell and doesn't even know where she is. She looks around, gets up and the rats scatter. Then she happens upon the dead boy. This time she doesn't cry. She sits in a chair, next to the little bed and stays there not thinking, not moving. Wondering why there hasn't been any news, the neighbors knock at her door. She opens it to everyone very delicately and says: 'He's better.' The neighbors come in and see that he's dead. They're afraid she doesn't know yet and prepare her for the shock, saying, 'Maybe you should call the pharmacist?' She replies: 'What for? since he's already dead.' Then everyone gets sad and tries to weep. They say: 'We have to deal with the funeral.' She replies: 'What for? since he's already dead.' They say: 'Let's call a priest.' She replies: 'What for? since he's already dead.' The neighbors are scared and think she's lost her mind. They don't know what to do. And since it's not their problem, they go off to bed.

Or maybe this is how it goes: the boy dies and she's like you, numbed of feeling, not concerned about anything. Practically in a state of ataraxia, without knowing it. Or don't you know what ataraxia is, sir?"

Resting his head on his arms, he wasn't moving. I got scared for a second. What if he was dead? I shook him forcefully and he lifted his head, barely managing to fix his bleary eyes on me. He'd fallen asleep. I glared at him furiously.

"Oh, so ..."

"What?" He drew a toothpick from the dispenser and put it in his mouth, slowly, completely drunk.

I burst into laughter.

"Are you crazy? Since you haven't eaten a thing!..."

The scene seemed so comical to me that I doubled over laughing. Tears sprang to my eyes and ran down my face. A few people turned their heads in my direction. Once I no longer felt like laughing I continued anyway. I was already thinking about something else and laughed without stopping anyway. I suddenly broke off.

"Are you making fun of me, sir? Do you think I'll leave you alone, just like that, peacefully? Let you go your merry way, even after bumping into me? Oh, never. If I have to, I'll make some confessions. There's a lot I'll tell you ... But maybe you don't get it: we're different. I suffer, inside me feelings are solidified, differentiated, they're born already labeled, self-conscious. As for you ... a nebula of a man. Maybe your great-grandson will be able to suffer more ... But it's all right: the harder the task, the more appealing, as Ema said before we got engaged. That's why I'm going to drop my fishing hook into you, sir. Maybe it'll latch onto the seed of your suffering great-grandson. Who knows?"

"Right," he said.

I leaned over the table, trying furiously to get through to him.

"Listen up, pal, the moon is way up in the sky. Aren't you scared? The helplessness that comes from nature. That moonlight, think about it, that moonlight, paler than a corpse's face, so silent and far away, that moonlight witnessed the cries of the first monsters to walk the earth, surveyed the peaceful waters after the deluges and the floods, illuminated centuries of nights and went out at dawns throughout centuries ... Think about it, my friend, that moonlight will be the same tranquil ghost when the last traces of your great-grandsons' grandsons no longer exist. Prostrate yourself before it. You've shown up for an instant and it is forever. Don't you suffer, pal? I ... I myself can't stand it. It hits me right here, in the center of my heart, having to die one day and, thousands of centuries later, undistinguished in humus, eyeless for all eternity, I, I!, for all eternity ... and the indifferent, triumphant moon, its pale hands outstretched over new men, new things, different beings. And I Dead!"—I took a deep breath. "Think about it, my friend. It's shining over the cemetery right now. The cemetery, where all lie sleeping who once were and never more shall be. There, where the slightest whisper makes the living shudder in terror and where the tranquility of the stars muffles our cries and brings terror to our eyes. There, where there are neither tears nor thoughts to express the profound misery of coming to an end."

I leaned over the table, hid my face in my hands and wept. I kept saying softly:

"I don't want to die! I don't want to die ..."

He, the man, picked at his teeth with the toothpick.

"But you haven't eaten a thing, sir," I said again, wiping my eyes.

"What?"

"'What' what?"

"Huh?"

"But, my God, 'huh' what?"

"Ah ..."

"Have you no shame, sir?"

"Me?"

"Listen, I'll tell you something else: I'd like to die while still alive, descending into my own tomb and shutting it myself, with a dull thud. And then go mad from pain in the earth's darkness. But not unconsciousness."

He still had the toothpick in his mouth.

Then I felt really good because the wine was kicking in. I took a toothpick too and held it between my fingers as if about to smoke it.

"I used to do that when I was little. And it gave me more pleasure than it does now, when I really do smoke."

"Obviously."

"The hell it's obvious ... I'm not asking for approval."

The vague words, meaningless phrases dragging along ... So good, so smooth ... Or was it drowsiness?

Suddenly, he took the toothpick from his mouth, eyes blinking, lips trembling as if about to cry, said:

FAMILY TIES
("*Laços de família*")

Daydream and Drunkenness of a Young Lady
("Devaneio e embriaguez duma rapariga")

THROUGHOUT THE ROOM IT SEEMED TO HER THE trams were crossing, making her reflection tremble. She sat combing her hair languorously before the three-way vanity, her white, strong arms bristling in the slight afternoon chill. Her eyes didn't leave themselves, the mirrors vibrated, now dark, now luminous. Outside, from an upper window, a heavy, soft thing fell to the street. Had the little ones and her husband been home, she'd have thought to blame their carelessness. Her eyes never pried themselves from her image, her comb working meditatively, her open robe revealing in the mirrors the intersecting breasts of several young ladies.

"*A Noite!*" called a paperboy into the gentle wind of the Rua do Riachuelo, and something shivered in premonition. She tossed the comb onto the vanity, singing rapturously: "who saw the lit-tle spar-row … go flying past the win-dow … it flew so far past Mi-nho!"—but, wrathful, shut herself tight as a fan.

She lay down, fanning herself impatiently with a rustling newspaper in the bedroom. She picked up her handkerchief, breathing it in as she crumpled the coarse embroidery in her reddened fingers. She went back to fanning herself, on the verge of smiling. Oh, dear, she sighed, laughing. She envisioned her bright still-young lady's smile, and smiled even more closing her eyes, fanning herself more deeply still. Oh, dear, came from the street like a butterfly.

"Good day, do you know who came looking for me here at the house?" she thought as a possible and interesting topic of conversation. "Well I don't know, who?" they asked her with a gallant smile, sorrowful eyes in one of those pale faces that so harm a person. "Why, Maria Quitéria, man!" she chirped merrily, hands by her side. "And begging your pardon, who is this young lady?" they persisted gallantly, but now without distinct features. "You!" she cut off the conversation with faint resentment, what a bore.

Oh what a succulent bedroom! she was fanning herself in Brazil. The sun caught in the blinds quivered on the wall like a Portuguese guitar. The Rua do Riachuelo rumbled under the panting weight of the trams coming from the Rua Mem de Sá. She listened curious and bored to the rattling of the china cabinet in the parlour. Impatiently, she turned onto her stomach, and as she lovingly stretched out her dainty toes, awaited her next thought with open eyes. "Finders, seekers," she chimed as if it were a popular saying, the kind that always ended up sounding like some truth. Until she fell asleep with her mouth open, her drool moistening the pillow.

She awoke only when her husband came home from work and entered the bedroom. She didn't want to have dinner or go out of her way, she fell back asleep: let the man help himself to the leftovers from lunch.

And, since the children were at their aunties' farm in Jacarepaguá, she took the opportunity to wake up feeling peculiar: murky and light in bed, one of those moods, who knows.

Her husband emerged already dressed and she didn't even know what the man had done for breakfast, and didn't even glance at his suit, whether it needed brushing, little did she care if today was his day to deal with matters downtown. But when he leaned over to kiss her, her lightness crackled like a dry leaf:

"Get away from me!"

"What's the matter with you?" her husband asks astonished, immediately attempting a more effective caress.

Obstinate, she wouldn't know how to answer, so shallow and spoiled was she that she didn't even know where to look for an answer. She lost her temper:

"Oh don't pester me! don't come prowling around like an old rooster!"

He seemed to think better of it and declared:

"Come now, young lady, you're ill."

She acquiesced, surprised, flattered. All day long she stayed in bed, listening to the house, so silent without the racket from the little ones, without the man who'd have lunch downtown today. All day long she stayed in bed. Her wrath was tenuous, ardent. She only got up to go to the lavatory, whence she returned noble, offended.

The morning became a long, drawn-out afternoon that became depthless night dawning innocently through the house.

She still in bed, peaceful, improvised. She loved ... In advance she loved the man she'd one day love. Who knows, it sometimes happened, and without guilt or any harm done to either of the two. In bed thinking, thinking, about to laugh as at a bit of gossip. Thinking, thinking. What? well, what did she know. That's how she let herself go on.

From one moment to the next, infuriated, she was on her

feet. But in the faintness of that first instant she seemed unhinged and fragile in the bedroom that was spinning, was spinning until she managed to grope her way back to bed, surprised that it might be true: "come now, woman, let's see if you really are going to get sick!" she said with misgiving. She put her hand to her forehead to see if she'd come down with fever.

That night, until she fell asleep, she fantasticized, fantasticized: for how many minutes? until she passed out: fast asleep, snoring along with her husband.

She awoke behind in the day, the potatoes still to be peeled, the little ones returning from their aunties' in the afternoon, oh I've even let myself go!, the day to get the wash done and mend the socks, oh what a trollop you've turned out to be!, she chided herself curiously and contentedly, go to the shops, don't forget the fish, behind in the day, the morning hectic with sun.

But on Saturday night they went to the tavern in the Praça Tiradentes at the invitation of that ever-so-prosperous businessman, she in that new little dress that while not quite showy was still made of top-quality fabric, the kind that would last a lifetime. Saturday night, drunk in the Praça Tiradentes, drunk but with her husband by her side to vouchsafe her, and she ceremonious around the other man, so much classier and wealthier, attempting to engage him in conversation, since she wasn't just any old village gossip and had once lived in the Capital. But it was impossible to be more hammered.

And if her husband wasn't drunk, that's because he didn't want to be disrespectful to the businessman, and, dutifully and humbly, let the other man rule the roost. Which well suited the classy occasion, but gave her one of those urges to start laughing! that scornful mocking! she looked at her husband stuffed into his new suit and thought him such a joke! It was impossible to be more hammered but without ever losing her ladylike pride. And the *vinho verde* draining from her glass.

And when she was drunk, as during a sumptuous Sunday dinner, all things that by their own natures are separate from each other—scent of olive oil on one side, man on the other, soup tureen on one side, waiter on the other—were peculiarly united by their own natures, and it all amounted to one riotous debauchery, one band of rogues.

And if her eyes were glittering and hard, if her gestures were difficult stages of finally reaching the toothpick dispenser, in fact on the inside she was even feeling quite well, she was that laden cloud gliding along effortlessly. Her swollen lips and white teeth, and the wine puffing her up. And that vanity of being drunk enabling such disdain for everything, making her ripe and round like a big cow.

Naturally she kept up the conversation. For she lacked neither subject nor talent. But the words a person spoke while drunk were like being gravid—words merely in her mouth, which had little to do with the secret center which was like a pregnancy. Oh how peculiar she felt. On Saturday night her everyday soul was lost, and how good it was to lose it, and as a sole memento from those former days her small hands, so mistreated—and here she was now with her elbows on the red-and-white checked tablecloth as if on a card table, profoundly launched into a low and revolutionizing life. And this burst of laughter? that burst of laughter coming mysteriously from her full, white throat, in response to the businessman's finesse, a burst of laughter coming from the depth of that sleep, and the depth of that assurance of one who possesses a body. Her snow-white flesh was sweet as a lobster's, the legs of a live lobster wriggling slowly in the air. And that urge to feel wicked so as to deepen the sweetness into awfulness. And that little wickedness of whoever has a body.

She kept up the conversation, and heard with curiosity what she herself was replying to the wealthy businessman who, with such good timing, had invited them out and paid for their meal. Intrigued and bewildered she heard what she herself was replying: what she said in this condition would be a good omen for the future—already she was no longer a lobster, she was a hard sign: Scorpio. Since she was born in November.

A searchlight as one sleeps that sweeps across the dawn—such was her drunkenness wandering slowly at these heights.

At the same time, what sensibility! but what sensibility! when she looked at that nicely painted picture in the restaurant, she immediately brimmed with artistic sensibility. No one could convince her that she really hadn't been born for other things. She'd always been partial to works of art.

Oh what sensibility! now not only because of the painting of grapes and pears and a dead fish glittering with scales. Her sensibility was uncomfortable without being painful, like a broken nail. And if she wanted she could allow herself the luxury of becoming even more sensitive, she could go further still: because she was protected by a situation, protected like everyone who had attained a position in life. Like someone prevented from a downfall of her own. Oh I'm so unhappy, dear Mother. If she wanted she could pour even more wine into her glass and, protected by the position she'd achieved in life, get even drunker, as long as she didn't lose her pride. And like that, drunker still, she cast her eyes around the restaurant, and oh the scorn for the dull people in the restaurant, not a single man who was a real man, who was truly sad. What scorn for the dull people in the restaurant, whereas she was swollen and heavy, she couldn't possibly be more generous. And everything in the restaurant so remote from each other as if one thing could never speak to another. Each one for himself, and God for all.

Her eyes fixed yet again on that young lady who, from the moment she'd entered, irritated her like mustard in the nose. Right when she'd entered she noticed her sitting at a table with her man, all full of hats and ostentation, blonde like a false coin, all saintly and posh—what a fancy hat she had!—bet she wasn't even married, and flaunting that saintly attitude. And with her fancy hat placed just so. Well let her make the most of that sanctimony! and she'd better not make a mess of that nobility. The most little goody two-shoes were the most depraved. And the waiter, that big dolt, serving her so attentively, the rascal: and the sallow man with her turning a blind eye to it. And that oh-so-holy saint all proud of her hat, all modest with her dainty little waist, bet she couldn't even give him, her man, a son. Oh this had nothing to do with her, honestly: from the moment she'd entered she'd felt the urge to go slap her senseless, right in her saintly blonde girlish face, that little hat-wearing aristocrat. Who didn't even have any curves, who was flat-chested. And bet you that, for all her hats, she was no more than a greengrocer passing herself off as a grande dame.

Oh, how humiliating to have come to the tavern without a hat, her head now felt naked. And that other one with her ladylike airs, pretending to be refined. I know just what you need, you little aristocrat, and your sallow man too! And if you think I'm jealous of you and your flat chest, I'll have you know that I don't give a toss, I don't give a bloody toss about your hats. Lowlife floozies like you, playing hard to get, I'll slap them senseless.

In her sacred wrath, she reached out her hand with difficulty and took a toothpick.

But at last the difficulty of getting home disappeared: she fidgeted now inside the familiar reality of her bedroom, now seated at the edge of her bed with her slipper dangling off her foot.

And, since she'd half-closed her bleary eyes, everything became flesh once more, the foot of the bed made of flesh, the window made of flesh, the suit made of flesh her husband had tossed on the chair, and everything nearly aching. And she, bigger and bigger, reeling, swollen, gigantic. If only she could get closer to herself, she'd see she was bigger still. Each of her arms could be traversed by a person, while unaware it was an arm, and you could dive into each eye and swim without knowing it was an eye. And all around everything aching a little. The things made of flesh had neuralgia. It was the little chill she'd caught while leaving the eatery.

She was sitting on the bed, subdued, skeptical.

And this was nothing yet, God only knew: she was well aware this was nothing yet. That right then things were happening to her that only later would really hurt and matter: once she returned to her normal size, her anaesthetized body would wake up throbbing and she'd pay for all that gorging and wine.

Well, since it'll happen anyway, I may as well open my eyes now, which she did, and everything became smaller and more distinct, though without any pain at all. Everything, deep down, was the same, just smaller and familiar. She was sitting quite tense on her bed, her stomach so full, absorbed, resigned, with the gentleness of someone waiting for someone else to wake up. "You overstuff yourself and I end up paying the price," she said to herself melancholically, gazing at her little white toes. She looked around, patient, obedient. Oh, words, words, bedroom objects lined up in word order, forming those murky, bothersome sentences that whoever can read, shall. Tiresome, tiresome, oh what a bore. What a pain. Oh well, woe is me, God's will be done. What could you do. Oh, I can hardly say what's happening to me. Oh well, God's will be done. And to think she'd had so much fun tonight! and to think it had been so good, and the restaurant so to her liking, sitting elegantly at the table. Table! the world screamed at her. But she didn't even respond, shrugging her shoulders with a pouty tsk-tsk, vexed, don't come pestering me with caresses; disillusioned, resigned, stuffed silly, married, content, the vague nausea.

Right then she went deaf: one of her senses was missing. She slammed her palm hard against her ear, which only made things worse: for her eardrum filled with the noise of an elevator, life suddenly sonorous and heightened in its slightest movements. It was one or the other: either she was deaf or hearing too much—she reacted to this new proposition with a mischievous and uncomfortable sensation, with a sigh of subdued satiety. To hell with it, she said softly, annihilated.

"And when at the restaurant ...," she suddenly recalled. When she'd been at the restaurant her husband's benefactor had slid a foot up against hers under the table, and above the table that face of his. Because it happened to fit or on purpose? That devil. Someone, to be honest, who was really quite interesting. She shrugged.

And when atop her full cleavage—right there in the Praça Tiradentes!, she thought shaking her head incredulously— that fly had landed on her bare skin? Oh how naughty.

Certain things were good because they were almost nauseating: that sound like an elevator in her blood, while her man was snoring beside her, her plump children piled up in the other bedroom asleep, those little scallywags. Oh what's got into me! she thought desperately. Had she eaten too much? oh what's got into me, my goodness!

It was sadness.

Her toes fiddling with her slipper. The not-so-clean floor. How lax and lazy you've turned out. Not tomorrow, because her legs wouldn't be doing so well. But the day after tomorrow just wait and see that house of hers: she'd give it a good scrub with soap and water and scrape off all that grime! just wait and see her house! she threatened wrathfully. Oh she felt so good, so rough, as if she still had milk in her breasts, so strong. When her husband's friend saw her looking so pretty and fat he immediately respected her. And when she began to feel ashamed she didn't know where to look. Oh what sadness. What can you possibly do. Seated at the edge of the bed, blinking in resignation. How well you could see the moon on these summer nights. She leaned forward ever so slightly, indifferent, resigned. The moon. How well you could see it. The high, yellow moon gliding across the sky, poor little thing. Gliding, gliding ... Up high, up high. The moon. Then the profanity exploded from her in a sudden fit of love: bitch, she said laughing.

Love

("Amor")

A LITTLE TIRED, THE GROCERIES STRETCHING OUT HER
new knit sack, Ana boarded the tram. She placed the bundle in
her lap and the tram began to move. She then settled back in
her seat trying to get comfortable, with a half-contented sigh.

Ana's children were good, something true and succulent.
They were growing up, taking their baths, demanding for
themselves, misbehaved, ever more complete moments. The
kitchen was after all spacious, the faulty stove gave off small
explosions. The heat was stifling in the apartment they were
paying off bit by bit. But the wind whipping the curtains she
herself had cut to measure reminded her that if she wanted she
could stop and wipe her brow, gazing at the calm horizon. Like
a farmhand. She had sown the seeds she had in her hand, no
others, but these alone. And trees were growing. Her brief conversation with the electric bill collector was growing, the water
in the laundry sink was growing, her children were growing,
the table with food was growing, her husband coming home
with the newspapers and smiling with hunger, the tiresome
singing of the maids in the building. Ana gave to everything,
tranquilly, her small, strong hand, her stream of life.

A certain hour of the afternoon was more dangerous. A certain hour of the afternoon the trees she had planted would laugh at her. When nothing else needed her strength, she got worried. Yet she felt more solid than ever, her body had filled out a bit and it was a sight to see her cut the fabric for the boys' shirts, the large scissors snapping on the cloth. All her vaguely artistic desire had long since been directed toward making the days fulfilled and beautiful; over time, her taste for the decorative had developed and supplanted her inner disorder. She seemed to have discovered that everything could be perfected, to each thing she could lend a harmonious appearance; life could be wrought by the hand of man.

Deep down, Ana had always needed to feel the firm root of things. And this is what a home bewilderingly had given her. Through winding paths, she had fallen into a woman's fate, with the surprise of fitting into it as if she had invented it. The man she'd married was a real man, the children she'd had were real children. Her former youth seemed as strange to her as one of life's illnesses. She had gradually emerged from it to discover that one could also live without happiness: abolishing it, she had found a legion of people, previously invisible, who lived the way a person works—with persistence, continuity, joy. What had happened to Ana before she had a home was forever out of reach: a restless exaltation so often mistaken for unbearable happiness. In exchange she had created something at last comprehensible, an adult life. That was what she had wanted and chosen.

The only thing she worried about was being careful during that dangerous hour of the afternoon, when the house was empty and needed nothing more from her, the sun high, the family members scattered to their duties. As she looked at the clean furniture, her heart would contract slightly in astonishment. But there was no room in her life for feeling tender toward her astonishment—she'd smother it with the same skill the household chores had given her. Then she'd go do the shopping or get something repaired, caring for her home and family in their absence. When she returned it would be the end of the afternoon and the children home from school needed her. In this way night would fall, with its peaceful vibration. In the morning she'd awake haloed by her calm duties. She'd find the furniture dusty and dirty again, as if repentantly come home. As for herself, she obscurely participated in the gentle black roots of the world. And nourished life anonymously. That was what she had wanted and chosen.

The tram went swaying along the tracks, heading down broad avenues. Soon a more humid breeze blew announcing, more than the end of the afternoon, the end of the unstable hour. Ana breathed deeply and a great acceptance gave her face a womanly air.

The tram would slow, then come to a halt. There was time to relax before Humaitá. That was when she looked at the man standing at the tram stop.

The difference between him and the others was that he really was stopped. Standing there, his hands reaching in front of him. He was blind.

What else could have made Ana sit up warily? Something uneasy was happening. Then she saw: the blind man was chewing gum ... A blind man was chewing gum.

Ana still had a second to think about how her brothers were coming for dinner—her heart beat violently, at intervals. Leaning forward, she stared intently at the blind man, the way we stare at things that don't see us. He was chewing gum in the dark. Without suffering, eyes open. The chewing motion made it look like he was smiling and then suddenly not smiling, smiling and not smiling—as if he had insulted her, Ana stared at him. And whoever saw her would have the impression of a woman filled with hatred. But she kept staring at him, leaning further and further forward—the tram suddenly lurched throwing her unexpectedly backward, the heavy knit sack tumbled from her lap, crashed to the floor—Ana screamed, the conductor gave the order to stop before he knew what was happening—the tram ground to a halt, the passengers looked around frightened.

Unable to move to pick up her groceries, Ana sat up, pale. A facial expression, long unused, had reemerged with difficulty, still tentative, incomprehensible. The paperboy laughed while returning her bundle. But the eggs had broken inside their newspaper wrapping. Viscous, yellow yolks dripped through the mesh. The blind man had interrupted his chewing and was reaching out his uncertain hands, trying in vain to grasp what was happening. The package of eggs had been thrown from the bag and, amid the passengers' smiles and the conductor's signal, the tram lurched back into motion.

A few seconds later nobody was looking at her. The tram rumbled along the tracks and the blind man chewing gum stayed behind forever. But the damage was done.

The knit mesh was rough between her fingers, not intimate as when she had knit it. The mesh had lost its meaning and being on a tram was a snapped thread; she didn't know what to do with the groceries on her lap. And like a strange song, the world started up again all around. The damage was done. Why? could she have forgotten there were blind people? Compassion was suffocating her, Ana breathed heavily. Even the things that existed before this event were now wary, had a more hostile, perishable aspect ... The world had become once again a distress. Several years were crashing down, the yellow yolks were running. Expelled from her own days, she sensed that the people on the street were in peril, kept afloat on the surface of the darkness by a minimal balance—and for a moment the lack of meaning left them so free they didn't know where to go. The perception of an absence of law happened so suddenly that Ana clutched the seat in front of her, as if she might fall off the tram, as if things could be reverted with the same calm they no longer held.

What she called a crisis had finally come. And its sign was the intense pleasure with which she now looked at things, suffering in alarm. The heat had become more stifling, everything had gained strength and louder voices. On the Rua Voluntários da Pátria a revolution seemed about to break out, the sewer grates were dry, the air dusty. A blind man chewing gum had plunged the world into dark voraciousness. In every strong person there was an absence of compassion for the blind man and people frightened her with the vigor they possessed. Next to her was a lady in blue, with a face. She averted her gaze, quickly. On the sidewalk, a woman shoved her son! Two lovers interlaced their fingers smiling ... And the blind man? Ana had fallen into an excruciating benevolence.

She had pacified life so well, taken such care for it not to explode. She had kept it all in serene comprehension, separated each person from the rest, clothes were clearly made to be worn and you could choose the evening movie from the newspaper—everything wrought in such a way that one day followed another. And a blind man chewing gum was shattering it all to pieces. And through this compassion there appeared to Ana a life full of sweet nausea, rising to her mouth.

Only then did she realize she was long past her stop. In

her weak state everything was hitting her with a jolt; she left the tram weak in the knees, looked around, clutching the egg-stained mesh. For a moment she couldn't get her bearings. She seemed to have stepped off into the middle of the night.

It was a long street, with high, yellow walls. Her heart pounding with fear, she sought in vain to recognize her surroundings, while the life she had discovered kept pulsating and a warmer, more mysterious wind whirled round her face. She stood there looking at the wall. At last she figured out where she was. Walking a little further along a hedge, she passed through the gates of the Botanical Garden.

She trudged down the central promenade, between the coconut palms. There was no one in the Garden. She put her packages on the ground, sat on a bench along a path and stayed there a long while.

The vastness seemed to calm her, the silence regulated her breathing. She was falling asleep inside herself.

From a distance she saw the avenue of palms where the afternoon was bright and full. But the shade of the branches covered the path.

All around were serene noises, scent of trees, little surprises among the vines. The whole Garden crushed by the ever faster instants of the afternoon. From where did that half-dream come that encircled her? Like a droning of bees and birds. Everything was strange, too gentle, too big.

A light, intimate movement startled her—she spun around. Nothing seemed to have moved. But motionless in the central avenue stood a powerful cat. Its fur was soft. Resuming its silent walk, it disappeared.

Worried, she looked around. The branches were swaying, the shadows wavering on the ground. A sparrow was pecking at the dirt. And suddenly, in distress, she seemed to have fallen into an ambush. There was a secret labor underway in the Garden that she was starting to perceive.

In the trees the fruits were black, sweet like honey. On the ground were dried pits full of circumvolutions, like little rotting brains. The bench was stained with purple juices. With intense gentleness the waters murmured. Clinging to the tree trunk were the luxuriant limbs of a spider. The cruelty of the world was tranquil. The murder was deep. And death was not what we thought.

While imaginary—it was a world to sink one's teeth into, a world of voluminous dahlias and tulips. The trunks were crisscrossed by leafy parasites, their embrace was soft, sticky. Like the revulsion that precedes a surrender—it was fascinating, the woman was nauseated, and it was fascinating.

The trees were laden, the world was so rich it was rotting. When Ana thought how there were children and grown men going hungry, the nausea rose to her throat, as if she were pregnant and abandoned. The moral of the Garden was something else. Now that the blind man had led her to it, she trembled upon the first steps of a sparkling, shadowy world, where giant water lilies floated monstrous. The little flowers scattered through the grass didn't look yellow or rosy to her, but the color of bad gold and scarlet. The decomposition was deep, perfumed ... But all the heavy things, she saw with her head encircled by a swarm of insects, sent by the most exquisite life in the world. The breeze insinuated itself among the flowers. Ana sensed rather than smelled its sweetish scent ... The Garden was so pretty that she was afraid of Hell.

It was nearly evening now and everything seemed full, heavy, a squirrel leaped in the shadows. Beneath her feet the earth was soft, Ana inhaled it with delight. It was fascinating, and she felt nauseated.

But when she remembered the children, toward whom she was now guilty, she stood with a cry of pain. She grabbed her bag, went down the dark path, reached the promenade. She was nearly running—and she saw the Garden all around, with its haughty impersonality. She rattled the locked gates, rattled them gripping the rough wood. The guard appeared, shocked not to have seen her.

Until she reached the door of her building, she seemed on the verge of a disaster. She ran to the elevator clutching the mesh sack, her soul pounding in her chest—what was happening? Her compassion for the blind man was as violent as an agony, but the world seemed to be hers, dirty, perishable, hers. She opened her front door. The living room was large, square, the doorknobs were gleaming spotlessly, the window-panes gleaming, the lamp gleaming—what new land was this? And for an instant the wholesome life she had led up till now seemed like a morally insane way to live. The boy who ran to her was a being with long legs and a face just like hers, who ran up and hugged her. She clutched him tightly, in alarm. She protected herself trembling. Because life was in peril. She loved the world, loved what had been created—she loved with nausea. The same way she'd always been fascinated by oysters, with that vaguely sick feeling she always got when nearing the truth, warning her. She embraced her son, nearly to the point of hurting him. As if she had learned of an evil—the blind man or the lovely Botanical Garden?—she clung to him, whom she loved more than anything. She had been touched by the demon of faith. Life is horrible, she said to him softly, ravenous. What would she do if she heeded the call of the blind man? She would go alone … There were places poor and rich that needed her. She needed them … I'm scared, she said. She felt the child's delicate ribs between her arms, heard his frightened sobbing. Mama, the boy called. She held him away from her, looked at that face, her heart cringed. Don't let Mama forget you, she told him. As soon as the child felt her embrace loosen, he broke free and fled to the bedroom door, looking at her from greater safety. It was the worst look she had ever received. The blood rushed to her face, warming it.

She let herself fall into a chair, her fingers still gripping the mesh sack. What was she ashamed of?

There was no escape. The days she had forged had ruptured the crust and the water was pouring out. She was facing the oyster. And there was no way not to look at it. What was she ashamed of? That it was no longer compassion, it wasn't just compassion: her heart had filled with the worst desire to live.

She no longer knew whether she was on the side of the blind man or the dense plants. The man had gradually receded into the distance and in torture she seemed to have gone over to the side of whoever had wounded his eyes. The Botanical Garden, tranquil and tall, was revealing this to her. In horror she was discovering that she belonged to the strong part of the world—and what name should she give her violent mercy? She would have to kiss the leper, since she would never be just his sister. A blind man led me to the worst in myself, she thought in alarm. She felt banished because no pauper would drink water from her ardent hands. Ah! it was easier to be a saint than a person! By God, hadn't it been real, the compassion that had fathomed the deepest waters of her heart? But it was the compassion of a lion.

Humiliated, she knew the blind man would prefer a poorer

love. And, trembling, she also knew why. The life of the Botanical Garden was calling her as a werewolf is called by the moonlight. Oh! but she loved the blind man! she thought with moist eyes. Yet this wasn't the feeling you'd go to church with. I'm scared, she said alone in the living room. She got up and went to the kitchen to help the maid with dinner.

But life made her shiver, like a chill. She heard the school bell, distant and constant. The little horror of the dust threading together the underside of the oven, where she discovered the little spider. Carrying the vase to change its water—there was the horror of the flower surrendering languid and sickening to her hands. The same secret labor was underway there in the kitchen. Near the trash can, she crushed the ant with her foot. The little murder of the ant. The tiny body trembled. The water droplets were dripping into the stagnant water in the laundry sink. The summer beetles. The horror of the inexpressive beetles. All around was a silent, slow, persistent life. Horror, horror. She paced back and forth across the kitchen, slicing the steaks, stirring the sauce. Round her head, circling, round the light, the mosquitoes of a sweltering night. A night on which compassion was raw as bad love. Between her two breasts sweat slid down. Faith was breaking her, the heat of the stove stung her eyes.

Then her husband arrived, her brothers and their wives arrived, her brothers' children arrived.

They ate dinner with all the windows open, on the ninth floor. An airplane went shuddering past, threatening in the heat of the sky. Though made with few eggs, the dinner was good. Her children stayed up too, playing on the rug with the others. It was summer, it would be pointless to send them to bed. Ana was a little pale and laughed softly with the others.

After dinner, at last, the first cooler breeze came in through the windows. They sat around the table, the family. Worn out from the day, glad not to disagree, so ready not to find fault. They laughed at everything, with kind and human hearts. The children were growing up admirably around them. And as if it were a butterfly, Ana caught the instant between her fingers before it was never hers again.

Later, when everyone had gone and the children were already in bed, she was a brute woman looking out the window. The city was asleep and hot. Would whatever the blind man had unleashed fit into her days? How many years would it take for her to grow old again? The slightest movement and she'd trample one of the children. But with a lover's mischief, she seemed to accept that out of the flower emerged the mosquito, that the giant water lilies floated on the darkness of the lake. The blind man dangled among the fruits of the Botanical Garden.

If that was the oven exploding, the whole house would already be on fire! she thought rushing into the kitchen and finding her husband in front of the spilled coffee.

"What happened?!" she screamed vibrating all over.

He jumped at his wife's fright. And suddenly laughed in comprehension:

"It was nothing," he said, "I'm just clumsy." He looked tired, bags under his eyes.

But encountering Ana's strange face, he peered at her with greater attention. Then he drew her close, in a swift caress.

"I don't want anything to happen to you, ever!" she said.

"At least let the oven explode at me," he answered smiling.

She stayed limp in his arms. This afternoon something tranquil had burst, and a humorous, sad tone was hanging over the house. "Time for bed," he said, "it's late." In a gesture that wasn't his, but that seemed natural, he held his wife's hand, taking her along without looking back, removing her from the danger of living.

The dizziness of benevolence was over.

And, if she had passed through love and its hell, she was now combing her hair before the mirror, for an instant with no world at all in her heart. Before going to bed, as if putting out a candle, she blew out the little flame of the day.

A Chicken

("Uma galinha")

SHE WAS A SUNDAY CHICKEN. STILL ALIVE BECAUSE IT wasn't yet nine in the morning.

She seemed calm. Since Saturday she'd been huddling in a corner of the kitchen. She looked at no one, no one looked at her. Even when they selected her, feeling up her intimate parts indifferently, they couldn't tell whether she was fat or skinny. No one would ever guess she had a yearning.

So it came as a surprise when they saw her flap her wings made for brief flight, puff up her chest and, in two or three bursts, reach the terrace railing. For a second she wavered—long enough for the cook to cry out—and soon was on the neighbor's terrace, from which, in another awkward flight, she reached a roof. There she stood like an out of place ornament, hesitating on one foot, then the other. The family was urgently summoned and in dismay saw their lunch by a chimney. The man of the house, recalling the dual need to engage sporadically in some kind of sport and to have lunch, gleefully donned a pair of swim trunks and decided to follow in the chicken's path: with cautious leaps he reached the roof where she, hesitant and trembling, was urgently determining a further route.

The chase intensified. From rooftop to rooftop they covered more than a block. Ill-adapted to a wilder struggle for life, the chicken had to decide for herself which way to go, without any help from her race. The boy, however, was a dormant hunter. And inconsequential as the prey was, the rallying cry had sounded.

Alone in the world, without father or mother, she ran, panting, mute, focused. At times, mid-escape, she'd flutter breathlessly on the eave of a roof and while the boy went stumbling across other roofs she'd have time to gather herself for a moment. And then she seemed so free.

Stupid, timid and free. Not victorious as an escaping rooster would have been. What was it in her guts that made her a being? The chicken is a being. It's true you couldn't count on her for anything. Even she didn't count on herself for anything, as the rooster believes in his comb. Her sole advantage was that there were so many chickens that whenever one died another emerged that very instant as alike as if it were the same.

Finally, on one of her pauses to revel in her escape, the boy reached her. Amid cries and feathers, she was caught. Then carried triumphantly by one wing across the rooftops and placed on the kitchen floor with a certain violence. Still dizzy, she shook herself a little, clucking hoarsely and uncertainly.

That's when it happened. Completely frantic the chicken laid an egg. Surprised, exhausted. Perhaps it was premature. But right after, born as she was for maternity, she looked like an old, experienced mother. She sat on the egg and stayed there, breathing, her eyes buttoning up and unbuttoning. Her heart, so small on a plate, made her feathers rise and fall, filling with warmth a thing that would never be more than an egg. The little girl was the only one nearby and watched everything in terror. Yet as soon as she managed to tear herself away, she pried herself off the floor and ran shouting:

"Mama, Mama, don't kill the chicken anymore, she laid an egg! she cares about us!"

Everyone ran back into the kitchen and wordlessly surrounded the youthful new mother. Warming her offspring, she was neither gentle nor standoffish, neither cheerful nor sad, she was nothing, she was a chicken. Which wouldn't suggest any special feeling. The father, the mother and the daughter had been staring for quite some time, without thinking anything in particular. No one had ever petted a chicken's head before. The father finally made up his mind somewhat abruptly:

"If you have this chicken killed I'll never eat chicken again for the rest of my life!"

"Me neither!" vowed the girl ardently.

The mother, tired, shrugged.

Unconscious of the life she had been granted, the chicken began living with the family. The girl, coming home from school, would fling her binder down without missing a beat in her dash to the kitchen. Occasionally the father would recall: "And to think I made her run in that condition!" The chicken had become queen of the house. Everyone, except her, knew it. She carried on between the kitchen and the back terrace, employing her twin talents: apathy and alarm.

But whenever everyone in the house was quiet and seemed to have forgotten her, she would fill up with a little courage, vestiges of the great escape—and roam the tiled patio, her body following her head, pausing as if in a field, though her little head gave her away: vibratory and bobbing rapidly, the ancient fright of her species long since turned mechanical.

Every once in a while, though increasingly rarely, the chicken would again recall the figure she had cut against the air on the edge of the roof, about to proclaim herself. That's when she'd fill her lungs with the kitchen's sullied air and, even if females were given to crowing, wouldn't crow but would feel much happier. Though not even then would the expression change on her empty head. Fleeing, resting, giving birth or pecking corn—it was a chicken's head, the same one designed at the start of the centuries.

Until one day they killed her, ate her and years went by.

The Imitation of the Rose
("A imitação da rosa")

BEFORE ARMANDO GOT HOME FROM WORK THE HOUSE
had better be tidy and she already in her brown dress so she
could tend to her husband while he got dressed, and then
they'd leave calmly, arm in arm like the old days. How long
since they had done that?

But now that she was "well" again, they'd take the bus, she
gazing out the window like a wife, her arm in his, and then
they'd have dinner with Carlota and João, reclining comfortably in their chairs. How long since she had seen Armando
at last recline comfortably and have a conversation with a
man? A man's peace lay in forgetting about his wife, discussing the latest headlines with another man. Meanwhile she'd
chat with Carlota about women's stuff, giving in to Carlota's
authoritative and practical benevolence, receiving again at last
her friend's inattention and vague disdain, her natural bluntness, and no more of that perplexed and overly curious affection—and at last seeing Armando forget about his wife. And
she herself, at last, returning gratefully to insignificance. Like
a cat who stayed out all night and, as if nothing had happened,
finds a saucer of milk waiting without a word. People were

luckily helping her feel she was now "well." Without looking at her, they were actively helping her forget, pretending they themselves had forgotten as if they'd read the same label on the same medicine bottle. Or they really had forgotten, who knows. How long since she had seen Armando at last recline with abandon, forget about her? And as for her?

Breaking off from tidying the vanity, Laura looked at herself in the mirror: and as for her, how long had it been? Her face held a domestic charm, her hair was pinned back behind her large, pale ears. Her brown eyes, brown hair, her tawny, smooth skin, all this lent her no longer youthful face a modest, womanly air. Would anyone happen to see, in that tiniest point of surprise lodged in the depths of her eyes, would anyone see in that tiniest offended speck the lack of the children she'd never had?

With her meticulous penchant for method—the same that compelled her as a student to copy the lesson's main points in perfect handwriting without understanding them—with her penchant for method, now taken back up, she was planning to tidy the house before the maid's day off so that, once Maria was gone, she wouldn't have to do anything else, except 1) calmly get dressed; 2) wait for Armando ready to go; 3) what was three? Right. That's exactly what she'd do. And she'd put on the brown dress with the cream lace collar. Already showered. Back at Sacré Coeur she'd been tidy and clean, with a penchant for personal hygiene and a certain horror of messiness. Which never made Carlota, already back then a bit original, admire her. Their reactions had always been different. Carlota ambitious and laughing heartily: she, Laura, a little slow, and as it were careful always to stay slow; Carlota not seeing the danger in anything. And she ever cautious. When they'd been assigned to read the *Imitation of Christ*, she'd read it with a fool's ardor without understanding but, God forgive her, she'd felt that whoever imitated Christ would be lost — lost in the light, but dangerously lost. Christ was the worst temptation. And Carlota hadn't even wanted to read it, she lied to the nun saying she had. Right. She'd put on the brown dress with the real lace collar.

But when she saw the time she remembered, with a jolt that made her lift her hand to her chest, that she'd forgotten to drink her glass of milk.

She went to the kitchen and, as if in her carelessness she'd guiltily betrayed Armando and her devoted friends, while still at the refrigerator she drank the first sips with an anxious slowing, concentrating on each sip faithfully as if making amends to them all and repenting. Since the doctor had said: "Drink milk between meals, avoid an empty stomach because it causes anxiety" — so, even without the threat of anxiety, she drank it without a fuss sip by sip, day after day, without fail, obeying with her eyes closed, with a slight ardor for not discerning the slightest skepticism in herself. The awkward thing was that the doctor seemed to contradict himself when, while giving a precise order that she wished to follow with a convert's zeal, he'd also said: "Let yourself go, take it easy, don't strain yourself to make it work — forget all about what happened and everything will fall back into place naturally." And he patted her on the back, which flattered her and made her blush with pleasure. But in her humble opinion one order seemed to cancel the other, as if they'd asked her to eat flour and whistle at the same time. To combine them she'd recently resorted to a trick: that glass of milk that had ended up gaining a secret power, every sip of which contained the near-taste of a word and renewed that firm pat on the back, she'd take that glass of milk into the living room, where she'd sit "very naturally," pretending not to care at all, "not straining herself" — and thereby cleverly carrying out the second order. "It doesn't matter if I gain weight," she thought, looks had never been the point.

She sat on the sofa like a guest in her own house that, so recently regained, tidy and cool, evoked the tranquility of someone else's house. Which was so satisfying: unlike Carlota, who had made of her home something akin to herself, Laura took such pleasure in making her house an impersonal thing; somehow perfect for being impersonal.

Oh how good it was to be back, really back, she smiled in satisfaction. Holding the nearly empty glass, she closed her eyes with a sigh of pleasant fatigue. She'd ironed Armando's shirts, drawn up methodical lists for the next day, minutely calculated how much she'd spent at the market that morning, hadn't stopped in fact for even a second. Oh how good it was to be tired again.

If a perfect person from the planet Mars landed and discovered that Earthlings got tired and grew old, that person would feel pity and astonishment. Without ever understanding what was good about being human, in feeling tired, in giving out daily; only the initiated would comprehend this subtlety of defectiveness and this refinement of life.

And she'd finally returned from the perfection of the planet Mars. She, who had never cherished any ambition besides being a man's wife, was gratefully reencountering the part of her that gave out daily. With her eyes shut she sighed in appreciation. How long since she had got tired? But now every day she felt nearly exhausted and had ironed, for example, Armando's shirts, she'd always enjoyed ironing and, modesty aside, had a knack for it. And then she'd be exhausted as a reward. No longer that alert lack of fatigue. No longer that empty and wakeful and horribly marvelous speck inside her. No longer that terrible independence. No longer the monstrous and simple ease of not sleeping—day or night—which in its discreet way had made her suddenly superhuman compared to a tired and perplexed husband. He, with that bad breath he got whenever he went mute with worry, which gave her a pungent compassion, yes, even within her wakeful perfection, compassion and love, she superhuman and tranquil in her gleaming isolation, and he, whenever he'd come to visit timidly bearing apples and grapes that the nurse would eat with a shrug, he paying formal visits like a boyfriend, with his unfortunate bad breath and stiff smile, straining heroically to comprehend, he who had received her from a father and a priest, and had no idea what to do with this girl from Tijuca who had unexpectedly, as a tranquil boat bursts into sail on the waters, become superhuman.

Now, no more of this. Never again. Oh, it had just been a bout of weakness; genius was the worst temptation. But afterward she'd returned so completely that she'd even had to start being careful again not to wear people down with her old penchant for detail. She clearly remembered her classmates at Sacré Coeur saying to her: "You've told it a thousand times!" she recalled with an embarrassed smile. She'd returned so completely: now she got tired every day, every day her face would sag at dusk, and then night would take on its former purpose, it wasn't just the perfect starlit night. And everything lined up harmoniously. And, as with everyone else, each day wore her out; like everyone else, human and perishable. No longer that perfection, no longer that youth. No longer that thing that one day had spread brightly, like a cancer, to her soul.

She opened her sleep-laden eyes, feeling the nice solid glass in her hands, but closed them again with a comfortable smile of fatigue, bathing like some nouveau riche in all her particles, in that familiar and slightly nauseating water. Yes, slightly nauseating; what did it matter, since she too was a bit nauseating, she was well aware. But her husband didn't think so, and so what did it matter, since thank God she didn't live in an environment that required her to be more clever and interesting, and she'd even freed herself from high school, which had so awkwardly demanded that she stay alert. What did it matter. In fatigue — she'd ironed Armando's shirts, not to mention she'd gone to the farmers' market that morning and lingered there so long, with that pleasure she took in making the most of things — in fatigue there was a nice place for her, the discreet and dulled place from which, so embarrassingly for herself and everyone else, she had once emerged. But, as she kept saying, thank God, she'd returned.

And if she sought with greater faith and love, she would find within her fatigue that even better place called sleep. She sighed with pleasure, in a moment of spiteful mischief tempted to go along with that warm exhalation that was her already somnolent breathing, tempted to doze off for a second. "Just a second, just one little second!" she begged herself, flattered to be so drowsy, begging pleadingly, as if begging a man, which Armando had always liked.

But she didn't really have time to sleep now, not even for a quick nap — she thought vainly and with false modesty, she was such a busy person! She'd always envied people who said "I didn't have time" and now she was once again such a busy person: they were going to Carlota's for dinner and everything had to be orderly and ready, it was her first dinner party since coming back and she didn't want to be late, she had to be ready when ... right, I've already said it a thousand times, she thought sheepishly. Once was enough to say: "I don't want to be late"—since that reason sufficed: if she had never been able to bear without the utmost mortification being a nuisance to anyone, then now, more than ever, she shouldn't ... No, there wasn't the slightest doubt: she didn't have time to sleep. What she ought to do, familiarly slipping into that intimate wealth of routine—and it hurt her that Carlota scoffed at her penchant for routine—what she ought to do was 1) wait till the maid was ready; 2) give her money to get meat in the morning, rump roast; how could she explain that the difficulty of finding quality meat really was a good topic of conversation, but if Carlota found out she'd scoff at her; 3) start meticulously showering and getting dressed, fully surrendering to the pleasure of making the most of her time. That brown dress complemented her eyes and its little cream lace collar gave her a childlike quality, like an old-fashioned boy. And, back to the nocturnal peace of Tijuca—no longer that blinding light from those coiffed and perky nurses leaving for their day off after tossing her like a helpless chicken into the abyss of insulin— back to the nocturnal peace of Tijuca, back to her real life: she'd go arm-in-arm with Armando, walking slowly to the bus stop, with those short, thick thighs packed into that girdle making her a "woman of distinction"; but whenever, upset, she told Armando it was because of an ovarian insufficiency, he, who took pride in his wife's thighs, replied rather cheekily: "What would I get out of marrying a ballerina?" that was how he replied. You'd never guess, but Armando could sometimes be really naughty, you'd never guess. Once in a while they said the same thing. She explained that it was because of an ovarian insufficiency. So then he'd say: "What would I get out of marrying a ballerina?" He could be really shameless sometimes, you'd never guess. Carlota would be astonished to learn that they too had a private life and things they never told, but she wouldn't tell, what a shame not to be able to tell, Carlota definitely thought she was just uptight and mundane and a little annoying, and if she had to be careful not to bother other people with details, with Armando she'd sometimes relax and get pretty annoying, which didn't matter because he'd pretend to be listening without really listening to everything she was telling him, which didn't hurt her feelings, she understood perfectly well that her chatter tired people out a bit, but it was nice to be able to explain how she hadn't found any meat even if Armando shook his head and wasn't listening, she and the maid chatted a lot, actually she talked more than the maid, and she was also careful not to pester the maid who sometimes held back her impatience and could get a little rude, it was her own fault because she didn't always command respect.

But, as she was saying, her arm in his, she so short and he tall and slim, but he was healthy thank God, and she a brunette. She was a brunette as she obscurely believed a wife ought to be. To have black or blonde hair was an excess to which she, in her desire to do everything right, had never aspired. Therefore, as for green eyes, it seemed to her that having green eyes would be like keeping certain things from her husband. Not that Carlota exactly gave her reason to gossip, but she, Laura—who if given the chance would defend her fervently, but never got the chance—she, Laura, grudgingly had to agree that her friend had a peculiar and funny way of dealing with her husband, oh not that she acted "as if they were equals," as people were doing nowadays, but you know what I mean. And Carlota was even a bit original, she'd even mentioned this once to Armando and Armando had agreed but hadn't thought it mattered much. But, as she was saying, dressed in brown with her little collar … —this daydream was filling her with the same pleasure she got from tidying drawers, sometimes she'd even mess them up just to be able to tidy them again.

She opened her eyes, and as if the room had dozed off instead of her, it seemed refreshed and relaxed with its brushed armchairs and the curtains that had shrunk in the last wash, like pants that were too short while the person stood comically peering down at his legs. Oh how nice it was to see everything tidy and dusted again, everything cleaned by her own skillful hands, and so silent, and with a vase full of flowers, like a waiting room. She'd always found waiting rooms lovely, so courteous, so impersonal. How rich normal life was, she who had returned from extravagance at last. Even a vase of flowers. She looked at it.

"Oh they're so lovely," her heart exclaimed suddenly a bit childish. They were small wild roses she'd bought at the farmers' market that morning, partly because the man had been so insistent, partly out of daring. She'd arranged them in the vase that very morning, while drinking her sacred ten o'clock glass of milk.

Yet bathed in the light of this room the roses stood in all their complete and tranquil beauty.

I've never seen such pretty roses, she thought with curiosity. And as if she hadn't just had that exact thought, vaguely aware that she'd just had that exact thought and quickly glossing over the awkwardness of realizing she was being a little tedious, she thought in a further stage of surprise: "Honestly, I've never seen such pretty roses." She looked at them attentively. But her attention couldn't remain mere attention for long, it soon was transformed into gentle pleasure, and she couldn't manage to keep analyzing the roses, she had to interrupt herself with the same exclamation of submissive curiosity: they're so lovely.

They were some perfect roses, several on the same stem. At some point they'd climbed over one another with nimble eagerness but then, once the game was over, they had tranquilly stopped moving. They were some roses so perfect in their smallness, not entirely in bloom, and their pinkish hue was nearly white. They even look fake! she said in surprise. They might look white if they were completely open but, with their central petals curled into buds, their color was concentrated and, as inside an earlobe, you could feel the redness coursing through them. They're so lovely, thought Laura surprised.

But without knowing why, she was a little embarrassed, a little disturbed. Oh, not too much, it was just that extreme beauty made her uncomfortable.

She heard the maid's footsteps on the kitchen tile and could tell from the hollow sound that she was wearing heels; so she must be ready to leave. Then Laura had a somewhat original idea: why not ask Maria to stop by Carlota's and leave her the roses as a present?

And also because that extreme beauty made her uncomfortable. Uncomfortable? It was a risk. Oh, no, why would it be a risk? They just made her uncomfortable, they were a warning, oh no, why would they be a warning? Maria would give Carlota the roses.

"Dona Laura sent them," Maria would say.

She smiled thoughtfully: Carlota would think it odd that Laura, who could bring the roses herself, since she wanted to give them as a present, sent them with the maid before dinner.

Not to mention she'd find it amusing to get roses, she'd think it "refined" ...

"There's no need for things like that between us, Laura!" her friend would say with that slightly rude bluntness, and Laura would exclaim in a muffled cry of rapture:

"Oh no! no! It's not because you invited us to dinner! it's just that the roses were so lovely I decided on a whim to give them to you!"

Yes, if when the time came she could find a way and got the nerve, that's exactly what she'd say. How was it again that she'd say it? she mustn't forget: she'd say—"Oh no!" etc. And Carlota would be surprised by the delicacy of Laura's feelings, no one would ever imagine that Laura too had her little ideas. In this imaginary and agreeable scene that made her smile beatifically, she called herself "Laura," as if referring to a third person. A third person full of that gentle and crackling and grateful and tranquil faith, Laura, the one with the little real-lace collar, discreetly dressed, Armando's wife, finally an Armando who no longer needed to force himself to pay attention to all of her chattering about the maid and meat, who no longer needed to think about his wife, like a man who is happy, like a man who isn't married to a ballerina.

"I couldn't help but send you the roses," Laura would say, that third person so, so very ... And giving the roses was nearly as lovely as the roses themselves.

And indeed she'd be rid of them.

And what indeed would happen then? Ah, yes: as she was saying, Carlota surprised by that Laura who was neither intelligent nor good but who also had her secret feelings. And Armando? Armando would look at her with a healthy dose of astonishment—since you can't forget there's no possible way for him to know that the maid brought the roses this afternoon!—Armando would look fondly on the whims of his little woman, and that night they'd sleep together.

And she'd have forgotten the roses and their beauty.

No, she thought suddenly vaguely forewarned. She must watch out for other people's alarmed stares. She must never again give cause for alarm, especially with everything still so recent. And most important of all was sparing everyone from suffering the least bit of doubt. And never again cause other people to fuss over her—never again that awful thing where everyone stared at her mutely, and her right there in front of everyone. No whims.

But at the same time she saw the empty glass of milk in her hand and also thought: "he" said not to strain myself to make it work, not to worry about acting a certain way just to prove that I'm already …

"Maria," she then said upon hearing the maid's footsteps again. And when Maria approached, she said impetuously and defiantly: "Could you stop by Dona Carlota's and leave these roses for her? Say it like this: 'Dona Carlota, Dona Laura sent these.' Say it like this: 'Dona Carlota …'"

"Got it, got it," said the maid patiently.

Laura went to find an old piece of tissue paper. Then she carefully took the roses out of the vase, so lovely and tranquil, with their delicate and deadly thorns. She wanted to give the arrangement an artistic touch. And at the same time be rid of them. And she could get dressed and move on with her day. When she gathered the moist little roses into a bouquet, she extended the hand holding them, looked at them from a distance, tilting her head and narrowing her eyes for an impartial and severe judgment.

And when she looked at them, she saw the roses.

And then, stubborn, gentle, she coaxed inwardly: don't give away the roses, they're lovely.

A second later, still very gentle, the thought intensified slightly, almost tantalizing: don't give them away, they're yours. Laura gasped a little: because things were never hers.

But these roses were. Rosy, small, perfect: hers. She looked at them in disbelief: they were beautiful and hers. If she managed to think further, she'd think: hers like nothing else had ever been.

And she could even keep them since she'd already shed that initial discomfort that made her vaguely avoid looking at the roses too much.

Why give them away, then? lovely and you're giving them away? After all when you happen upon a good thing, you just go and give it away? After all if they were hers, she coaxed persuasively without finding any argument besides the one that, with repetition, seemed increasingly convincing and simple. They wouldn't last long—so why give them away while they were still alive? The pleasure of having them didn't pose much of a risk— she deluded herself—after all, whether or not she wanted them, she'd have to give them up soon enough, and then she'd never think of them again since they'd be dead—they wouldn't last long, so why give them away? The fact that they didn't last long seemed to remove her guilt about keeping them, according to the obscure logic of a woman who sins. After all you could see they wouldn't last long (it would be quick, free from danger). And besides—she argued in a final and triumphant rejection of guilt—by no means had she been the one who'd wanted to buy them, the vendor kept insisting and she always got so flustered when people put her on the spot, she hadn't been the one who'd wanted to buy them, she was in no way to blame whatsoever. She looked at them entranced, thoughtful, profound.

And, honestly, I've never seen anything more perfect in all my life.

Fine, but now she'd already spoken to Maria and there was no way to turn back. So was it too late?, she got scared, seeing the little roses waiting impassively in her own hand. If she wanted, it wouldn't be too late ... She could tell Maria: "Listen Maria, I've decided to take the roses over myself when I go to dinner!" And, of course, she wouldn't take them ... And Maria would never have to know. And, before changing clothes, she'd sit on the sofa for a second, just a second, to look at them. And to look at those roses' tranquil detachment. Yes, since, having done the deed, you might as well take advantage of it, wouldn't it be silly to take the blame without reaping the rewards. That's exactly what she'd do.

But with the unwrapped roses in her hand she waited. She wasn't putting them back in the vase, she wasn't calling Maria. She knew why. Because she ought to give them away. Oh she knew why.

And also because a pretty thing was meant for giving or receiving, not just having. And, above all, never just for "being." Above all one should never be the pretty thing. A pretty thing lacked the gesture of giving. One should never keep a pretty thing, just like that, as if stowed inside the perfect silence of the heart. (Although, if she didn't give away the roses, no one in the world would ever know that she'd planned to give them away, who would ever find out? it was horribly easy and doable to keep them, since who would ever find out? and they'd be hers, and that would be the end of it and no one would mention it again ...)

So? and so? she wondered vaguely worried.

So, no. What she ought to do was wrap them up and send them off, without any enjoyment now; wrap them up and, disappointed, send them off; and in astonishment be rid of them. Also because a person must have some consistency, her thinking ought to have some continuity: if she'd spontaneously decided to hand them over to Carlota, she should stick to her decision and give them away. Because no one changed their mind from one moment to the next.

But anyone can have regrets! she suddenly rebelled. Since it was only the moment I picked the roses up that I realized how beautiful I thought they were, for the very first time in fact, when I picked them up, that's when I realized they were beautiful. Or just before? (And besides they were hers). And besides the doctor himself had patted her on the back and said: "Don't strain to pretend you're well, ma'am, because you *are* well," and then that firm pat on the back. That's why, then, she didn't have to be consistent, she didn't have to prove anything to anyone and she'd keep the roses. (And besides — besides they were hers).

"Are they ready?" asked Maria.

"Yes," said Laura caught by surprise.

She looked at them, so mute in her hand. Impersonal in their extreme beauty. In their extreme, perfect rose tranquility. That last resort: the flower. That final perfection: luminous tranquility.

Like an addict, she looked with faint greed at the roses' tantalizing perfection, with her mouth slightly dry she looked at them.

Until, slow, austere, she wrapped the stems and thorns in the tissue paper. She had been so absorbed that only when she held out the finished bouquet did she realize that Maria was no longer in the room—and she was left alone with her heroic sacrifice. Vaguely afflicted, she looked at them, remote at the end of her outstretched arm—and her mouth grew still more parched, that envy, that desire. But they're mine, she said with enormous timidity.

When Maria returned and took the bouquet, in a fleeting instant of greed Laura pulled her hand away keeping the roses one second longer—they're lovely and they're mine, it's the first thing that's lovely and mine! plus it was that man who insisted, it wasn't me who went looking for them! fate wanted it this way! oh just this once! just this once and I swear never again! (She could at least take one rose for herself, no more than that: one rose for herself. And only she would know, and then never again oh, she promised herself that never again would she let herself be tempted by perfection, never again!)

And the next second, without any transition at all, without any obstacle at all—the roses were in the maid's hand, they were no longer hers, like a letter already slipped into the mailbox! no more chances to take it back or cross anything out! it was no use crying: that's not what I meant! She was left empty-handed but her obstinate and resentful heart was still saying: "you can catch Maria on the stairs, you know perfectly well you can, and snatch the roses from her hand and steal them." Because taking them now would be stealing. Stealing something that was hers? Since that's what someone who felt no pity for others would do: steal something that was rightfully hers! Oh, have mercy, dear God. You can take it all back, she insisted furiously. And then the front door slammed.

Then the front door slammed.

Then slowly she sat calmly on the sofa. Without leaning back. Just to rest. No, she wasn't angry, oh not at all. But that offended speck in the depths of her eyes had grown larger and more pensive. She looked at the vase. "Where are my roses," she then said very calmly.

And she missed the roses. They had left a bright space inside her. Remove an object from a clean table and from the even cleaner mark it leaves you can see that dust had been surrounding it. The roses had left a dustless, sleepless space inside her. In her heart, that rose she could at least have taken for herself without hurting anyone in the world, was missing. Like some greater lack.

In fact, like the lack. An absence that was entering her like a brightness. And the dust was also disappearing from around the mark the roses left. The center of her fatigue was opening in an expanding circle. As if she hadn't ironed a single one of Armando's shirts. And in the clear space the roses were missed. "Where are my roses," she wailed without pain while smoothing the pleats in her skirt.

Like when you squeeze lemon into black tea and the black tea starts brightening all over. Her fatigue was gradually brightening. Without any fatigue whatsoever, incidentally. The way a firefly lights up. Since she was no longer tired, she'd get up and get dressed. It was time to start.

But, her lips dry, she tried for a second to imitate the roses inside herself. It wasn't even hard.

It was all the better that she wasn't tired. That way she'd go to dinner even more refreshed. Why not pin that cameo onto her little real-lace collar? that the major had brought back from the war in Italy. It would set off her neckline so nicely. When she was ready she'd hear the sound of Armando's key in the door. She needed to get dressed. But it was still early. He'd be caught in traffic. It was still afternoon. A very pretty afternoon.

Incidentally it was no longer afternoon.

It was night. From the street rose the first sounds of the darkness and the first lights.

Incidentally the key familiarly penetrated the keyhole.

Armando would open the door. He'd switch the light on. And suddenly in the doorframe the expectant face that he constantly tried to mask but couldn't suppress would be bared. Then his bated breath would finally transform into a smile of great unburdening. That embarrassed smile of relief that he'd never suspected she noticed. That relief they had probably, with a pat on the back, advised her poor husband to conceal. But which, for his wife's guilt-ridden heart, had been daily reward for at last having given back to that man the possibility of joy and peace, sanctified by the hand of an austere priest who only allowed beings a humble joy and not the imitation of Christ.

The key turned in the lock, the shadowy and hurried figure entered, light violently flooded the room.

And right in the doorway he froze with that panting and suddenly paralyzed look as if he'd run for miles so as not to get home too late. She was going to smile. So he could at last wipe that anxious suspense off his face, which always came mingled with the childish triumph of getting home in time to find her there boring, nice and diligent, and his wife. She was going to smile so he'd once again know that there would never again be any danger of his getting home too late. She was going to smile to teach him sweetly to believe in her. It was no use advising them never to mention the subject: they didn't talk about it but had worked out a language of facial expressions in which fear and trust were conveyed, and question and answer were mutely telegraphed. She was going to smile. It was taking a while but she was going to smile.

Calm and gentle, she said:

"It's back, Armando. It's back."

As if he would never understand, his face twisted into a dubious smile. His primary task at the moment was trying to catch his breath after sprinting up the stairs, since he'd triumphantly avoided getting home late, since there she was smiling at him. As if he'd never understand.

"What's back," he finally asked in a blank tone of voice.

But, as he was trying never to understand, the man's progressively stiffening face had already understood, though not a single feature had altered. His primary task was to stall for time and concentrate on catching his breath. Which suddenly was no longer hard to do. For unexpectedly he realized in horror that both the living room and his wife were calm and unhurried. With even further misgiving, like someone who bursts into laughter after getting the joke, he nonetheless insisted on keeping his face contorted, from which he watched her warily, almost her enemy. And from which he was starting to no longer help noticing how she was sitting with her hands crossed on her lap, with the serenity of a lit-up firefly.

In her brown-eyed and innocent gaze the proud embarrassment of not having been able to resist.

"What's back," he said suddenly harsh.

"I couldn't help it," she said, and her final compassion for the man was in her voice, that final plea for forgiveness already mingled with the haughtiness of a solitude almost perfect now. I couldn't help it, she repeated surrendering to him in relief the compassion she had struggled to hold onto until he got home. "It was because of the roses," she said modestly.

As if holding still for a snapshot of that instant, he kept that same detached face, as if the photographer had wanted only his face and not his soul. He opened his mouth and for an instant his face involuntarily took on that expression of comic indifference he'd used to hide his mortification when asking his boss for a raise. The next second, he averted his eyes in shame at the indecency of his wife who, blossoming and serene, was sitting there.

But suddenly the tension fell away. His shoulders sagged, his features gave way and a great heaviness relaxed him. He looked at her older now, curious.

She was sitting there in her little housedress. He knew she'd done what she could to avoid becoming luminous and unattainable. Timidly and with respect, he was looking at her. He'd grown older, weary, curious. But he didn't have a single word to say. From the open doorway he saw his wife on the sofa without leaning back, once again alert and tranquil, as if on a train. That had already departed.

Happy Birthday
("Feliz aniversário")

THE FAMILY BEGAN ARRIVING IN WAVES. THE ONES
from Olaria were all dressed up because the visit also meant
an outing in Copacabana. The daughter-in-law from Olaria
showed up in navy blue, glittering with "pailletés" and draping that camouflaged her ungirdled belly. Her husband didn't
come for obvious reasons: he didn't want to see his siblings.
But he'd sent his wife so as not to sever all ties—and she came
in her best dress to show that she didn't need any of them,
along with her three children: two girls with already budding
breasts, infantilized in pink ruffles and starched petticoats, and
the boy sheepish in his new suit and tie.

Since Zilda—the daughter with whom the birthday girl
lived—had placed chairs side-by-side along the walls, as at a
party where there's going to be dancing, the daughter-in-law
from Olaria, after greeting the members of the household with
a stony expression, plunked herself down in one of the chairs
and fell silent, lips pursed, maintaining her offended stance. "I
came to avoid not coming," she'd said to Zilda, and then had
sat feeling offended. The two little misses in pink and the boy,
sallow and with their hair neatly combed, didn't really know

how to behave and stood beside their mother, impressed by her navy blue dress and the "pailletés."

Then the daughter-in-law from Ipanema came with two grandsons and the nanny. Her husband would come later. And since Zilda—the only girl among six brothers and the only one who, it had been decided years ago, had the space and time to take in the birthday girl—and since Zilda was in the kitchen with the maid putting the finishing touches on the croquettes and sandwiches, that left: the stuck-up daughter-in-law from Olaria with her anxious-hearted children by her side; the daughter-in-law from Ipanema in the opposite row of chairs pretending to deal with the baby to avoid facing her sister-in-law from Olaria; the idle, uniformed nanny, her mouth hanging open.

And at the head of the large table the birthday girl who was turning eighty-nine today.

Zilda, the lady of the house, had set the table early, covered it with colorful paper napkins and birthday-themed paper cups, scattered balloons drifting along the ceiling on some of which was written "Happy Birthday!", on others "Feliz Aniversário!". At the center she'd placed the enormous frosted cake. To move things along, she'd decorated the table right after lunch, pushed the chairs against the wall, sent the boys out to play at the neighbor's so they wouldn't mess up the table.

And, to move things along, she'd dressed the birthday girl right after lunch. Since then she'd fastened that pendant around her neck and pinned on her brooch, sprayed her with a little perfume to cover that musty smell of hers—seated her at the table. And since two o'clock the birthday girl had been sitting at the head of the long empty table, rigid in the silent room.

Occasionally aware of the colorful napkins. Looking curiously when a passing car made the odd balloon tremble. And occasionally that mute anguish: whenever she watched, fascinated and powerless, the buzzing of a fly around the cake.

Until four o'clock when the daughter-in-law from Olaria arrived followed by the one from Ipanema.

Just when the daughter-in-law from Ipanema thought she couldn't bear another second of being seated directly across from her sister-in-law from Olaria—who brimming with past offenses saw no reason to stop glaring defiantly at the daughter-in-law from Ipanema—at last José and his family arrived. And as soon as they all kissed the room started filling with people greeting each other loudly as if they'd all been waiting below for the right moment to, in the rush of being late, stride up the three flights of stairs, talking, dragging along startled children, crowding into the room—and kicking off the party.

The birthday girl's facial muscles no longer expressed her, so no one could tell whether she was in a good mood. Placed at the head was what she was. She amounted to a large, thin, powerless and dark-haired old woman. She looked hollow.

"Eighty-nine years old, yes sir!" said José, the eldest now that Jonga had died. "Eighty-nine years old, yes ma'am!" he said rubbing his hands in public admiration and as an imperceptible signal to everyone.

Everyone broke off attentively and looked over at the birthday girl in a more official manner. Some shook their heads in awe as if she'd set a record. Each year conquered by the birthday girl was a vague step forward for the whole family. "Yes sir!" a few said smiling shyly.

"Eighty-nine years old!" echoed Manoel, who was José's business partner. "Just a little bean sprout!" he said joking and nervous, and everyone laughed except his wife.

The old woman showed no expression.

Some hadn't brought her a present. Others brought a soap dish, a cotton slip, a costume jewelry brooch, a little potted cactus—nothing, nothing that the lady of the house could use for herself or her children, nothing that the birthday girl herself could really use and thereby save money for the lady of the house: she put away the presents, bitter, sarcastic.

"Eighty-nine years old!" repeated Manoel nervously, looking at his wife.

The old woman showed no expression.

And so, as if everyone had received the final proof that there was no point making any effort, with a shrug as if they were with a deaf woman, they kept the party going by themselves, eating the first ham sandwiches more as a show of enthusiasm than out of hunger, making as if they were all starving to death. The punch was served, Zilda was sweating, not a single sister-in-law was really helping, the hot grease from the croquettes gave off the smell of a picnic; and with their backs turned to the birthday girl, who couldn't eat fried food, they laughed nervously. And Cordélia? Cordélia, the youngest daughter-in-law, seated, smiling.

"No sir!" José replied with mock severity, "no shop talk today!"

"Right, right!" Manoel quickly backed down, darting a look at his wife whose ears pricked up from a distance.

"No shop talk," José boomed, "today is for Mother!"

At the head of the already messy table, the cups dirtied, only the cake intact—she was the mother. The birthday girl blinked.

And by the time the table was filthy, the mothers irritated at the racket their children were making, while the grandmothers were leaning back complacently in their chairs, that was when they turned off the useless hallway light so as to light the candle on the cake, a big candle with a small piece of paper stuck to it on which was written "89." But no one praised Zilda's idea, and she wondered anxiously if they thought she was trying to save candles—nobody recalling that nobody had contributed so much as a box of matches for the party food that she, Zilda, was serving like a slave, her feet exhausted and her heart in revolt. Then they lit the candle. And then José, the leader, sang with great gusto, galvanizing the most hesitant or surprised ones with an authoritarian stare, "come on! all together now!"—and they all suddenly joined in singing loud as soldiers. Roused by the voices, Cordélia looked on breathlessly. Since they hadn't coordinated ahead of time, some sang in Portuguese and others in English. Then they tried to correct it: and the ones who'd been singing in English switched to Portuguese, and the ones who'd been singing in Portuguese switched to singing very softly in English.

While they were singing, the birthday girl, in the glow of the lit candle, meditated as though by the fireside.

They picked the youngest great-grandchild who, propped in his encouraging mother's lap, blew out the candle in a single breath full of saliva! For an instant they applauded the unexpected power of the boy who, astonished and exultant, looked around at everyone in rapture. The lady of the house was waiting with her finger poised on the hallway switch—and turned on the light.

"Long live Mama!"

"Long live Grandma!"

"Long live Dona Anita," said the neighbor who had shown up.

"Happy Birthday!" shouted the grandchildren who studied English at the Bennett School.

A few hands were still clapping.

The birthday girl was staring at the large, dry, extinguished cake.

"Cut the cake, Grandma!" said the mother of four, "she should be the one to cut it!" she asserted uncertainly to everyone, in an intimate and scheming manner. And, since they all approved happily and curiously, she suddenly became impetuous: "cut the cake, Grandma!"

And suddenly the old woman grabbed the knife. And without hesitation, as if in hesitating for a moment she might fall over, she cut the first slice with a murderer's thrust.

"So strong," the daughter-in-law from Ipanema murmured, and it wasn't clear whether she was shocked or pleasantly surprised. She was a little horrified.

"A year ago she could still climb these stairs better than me," said Zilda bitterly.

With the first slice cut, as though the first shovelful of dirt had been dug, they all closed in with their plates in hand, elbowing each other in feigned excitement, each going after his own little shovelful.

Soon enough the slices were divided among the little plates, in a silence full of commotion. The younger children, their mouths hidden by the table and their eyes at its level, watched the distribution with mute intensity. Raisins rolled out of the cake amid dry crumbs. The anguished children saw the raisins being wasted, intently watching them drop.

And when they went over to see, wouldn't you know the birthday girl was already devouring her last bite?

And so to speak the party was over.

Cordélia looked at everyone absently, smiling.

"I already told you: no shop talk today!" José replied beaming.

"Right, right!" Manoel backed down placatingly without glancing at his wife who didn't take her eyes off him. "You're right," Manoel tried to smile and a convulsion passed rapidly over the muscles of his face.

"Today is for Mother!" José said.

At the head of the table, the tablecloth stained with Coca-Cola, the cake in ruins, she was the mother. The birthday girl blinked.

There they were milling about boisterously, laughing, her family. And she was the mother of them all. And what if she suddenly got up, as a corpse rises slowly and imposes muteness and terror upon the living, the birthday girl stiffened in her chair, sitting up taller. She was the mother of them all. And since her pendant was suffocating her, she was the mother of them all and, powerless in her chair, she despised them all. And looked at them blinking. All those children and grandchildren and great-grandchildren of hers who were no more than the flesh of her knee, she thought suddenly as if spitting. Rodrigo, her seven-year-old grandson, was the only one who was the flesh of her heart, Rodrigo, with that tough little face, virile and tousled. Where's Rodrigo? Rodrigo with the drowsy, conceited gaze in that ardent and confused little head. That one would turn out to be a man. But, blinking, she looked at the others, the birthday girl. Oh how despicable those failed lives. How?! how could someone as strong as she have given birth to those dimwitted beings, with their slack arms and anxious faces? She, the strong one, who had married at the proper hour and time a good man whom, obediently and independently, she respected; whom she respected and who gave her children and repaid her for giving birth and honored her recovery time. The trunk was sound. But it had borne these sour and unfortunate fruits, lacking even the capacity for real joy. How could she have given birth to those frivolous, weak, self-indulgent beings? The resentment rumbled in her empty chest. A bunch of communists, that's what they were; communists. She glared at them with her old woman's ire. They looked like rats jostling each other, her family. Irrepressible, she turned her head and with unsuspected force spit on the ground.

"Mama!" cried the lady of the house, mortified. "What's going on, Mama!" she cried utterly mortified, and didn't even want to look at the others, she knew those good-for-nothings were exchanging triumphant glances as if it was up to her to make the old woman behave, and it wouldn't be long before they were claiming she didn't bathe their mother anymore, they'd never understand the sacrifice she was making. "Mama, what's going on!" she said softly, in anguish. "You've never done this before!" she added loudly so everyone would hear, she wanted to join the others' shock, when the cock crows for the third time you shall renounce your mother. But her enormous humiliation was soothed when she realized they were shaking their heads as if they agreed that the old woman was now no more than a child.

"Lately she's been spitting," she ended up confessing apologetically to everyone.

Everyone looked at the birthday girl, commiserating, respectful, in silence.

They looked like rats jostling each other, her family. The boys, though grown—probably already in their fifties, for all I know!—the boys still retained some of their handsome features. But those wives they had chosen! And the wives her grandchildren—weaker and more sour still—had chosen. All vain with slender legs, and those fake necklaces for women who when it comes down to it can't take the heat, those wimpy women who married off their sons poorly, who didn't know how to put a maid in her place, and all their ears dripping with jewelry—none, none of it real gold! Rage was suffocating her.

"Give me a glass of wine!" she said.

Silence fell suddenly, everyone with a glass frozen in their hand.

"Granny darling, won't it make you sick?" the short, plump little granddaughter ventured cautiously.

"To hell with Granny darling!" the birthday girl exploded bitterly. "The devil take you, you pack of sissies, cuckolds and whores! give me a glass of wine, Dorothy!" she ordered.

Dorothy didn't know what to do, she looked around at everyone in a comical plea for help. But, like detached and unassailable masks, suddenly not a single face showed any expression. The party interrupted, half-eaten sandwiches in their hands, some dry piece stuck in their mouths, bulging their cheeks with the worst timing. They'd all gone blind, deaf and dumb, croquettes in their hands. And they stared impassively.

Forsaken, amused, Dorothy gave her the wine: slyly just two fingertips' worth in the glass. Expressionless, at the ready, they all awaited the storm.

But not only did the birthday girl not explode at the miserable splash of wine Dorothy had given her but she didn't even touch the glass.

Her gaze was fixed, silent. As if nothing had happened.

Everyone exchanged polite glances, smiling blindly, abstractedly as if a dog had peed in the room. Stoically, the voices and laughter started back up. The daughter-in-law from Olaria, who had experienced her first moment in unison with the others just when the tragedy triumphantly seemed about to be unleashed, had to retreat alone to her severity, without even the solidarity of her three children who were now mingling traitorously with the others. From her reclusive chair, she critically appraised those shapeless dresses, without any draping, their obsession with pairing a black dress with pearls, which was anything but stylish, cheap was all it was. Eyeing from afar those meagerly buttered sandwiches. She hadn't helped herself to a thing, not a thing! She'd only had one of each, just to taste.

And so to speak, once again the party was over.

People graciously remained seated. Some with their attention turned inward, waiting for something to say. Others vacant and expectant, with amiable smiles, stomachs full of that junk that didn't nourish but got rid of hunger. The children, already out of control, shrieked rambunctiously. Some already had filthy faces; the other, younger ones, were already wet; the afternoon was fading rapidly. And Cordélia, Cordélia looked on absently, with a dazed smile, bearing her secret in solitude. What's the matter with her? someone asked with a negligent curiosity, head gesturing at her from afar, but no one answered. They turned on the remaining lights to hasten the tranquility of the night, the children were starting to bicker. But the lights were fainter than the faint tension of the afternoon. And the twilight of Copacabana, unyielding, meanwhile kept expanding and penetrating the windows like a weight.

"I have to go," one of the daughters-in-law said, disturbed, standing and brushing the crumbs off her skirt. Several others rose smiling.

The birthday girl received a cautious kiss from each of them as if her so unfamiliar skin were a trap. And, impassive, blinking, she took in those deliberately incoherent words they said to her attempting to give a final thrust of enthusiasm to something that was no more than the past: night had now fallen almost completely. The light in the room then seemed yellower and richer, the people older. The children were already hysterical.

"Does she think the cake takes the place of dinner," the old woman wondered in the depths of herself.

But no one could have guessed what she was thinking. And for those who looked at her once more from the doorway, the birthday girl was only what she appeared to be: seated at the head of the filthy table, her hand clenched on the tablecloth as though grasping a scepter, and with that muteness that was her last word. Fist clenched on the table, never again would she be only what she was thinking. Her appearance had finally surpassed her and, going beyond her, was serenely becoming gigantic. Cordélia stared at her in alarm. The mute and severe fist on the table was telling the unhappy daughter-in-law she irremediably loved perhaps for the last time: You must know. You must know. That life is short. That life is short.

Yet she didn't repeat it anymore. Because truth was a glimpse. Cordélia stared at her in terror. And, for the very last time, she never repeated it — while Rodrigo, the birthday girl's grandson, tugged at Cordélia's hand, tugged at the hand of that guilty, bewildered and desperate mother who once more looked back imploring old age to give one more sign that a woman should, in a heartrending impulse, finally cling to her last chance and live. Once more Cordélia wanted to look.

But when she looked again — the birthday girl was an old woman at the head of the table.

The glimpse had passed. And dragged onward by Rodrigo's patient and insistent hand the daughter-in-law followed him in alarm.

"Not everyone has the privilege and the honor to gather

around their mother," José cleared his throat recalling that Jonga had been the one who gave speeches.

"Their mother, comma!" his niece laughed softly, and the slowest cousin laughed without getting it.

"We have," Manoel said dispiritedly, no longer looking at his wife. "We have this great privilege," he said distractedly wiping his moist palms.

But that wasn't it at all, merely the distress of farewells, never knowing just what to say, José expecting from himself with perseverance and confidence the next line of the speech. Which didn't come. Which didn't come. Which didn't come. The others were waiting. How he missed Jonga at times like this—José wiped his brow with his handkerchief—how he missed Jonga at times like this! He'd also been the only one whom the old woman had always approved of and respected, and this gave Jonga so much self-assurance. And when he died, the old woman never spoke of him again, placing a wall between his death and the others. She'd forgotten him perhaps. But she hadn't forgotten that same firm and piercing gaze she'd always directed at the other children, always causing them to avert their eyes. A mother's love was hard to bear: José wiped his brow, heroic, smiling.

And suddenly the line came:

"See you next year!" José suddenly exclaimed mischievously, finding, thus, just like that, the right turn of phrase: a lucky hint! "See you next year, eh?" he repeated afraid he hadn't been understood.

He looked at her, proud of the cunning old woman who always slyly managed to live another year.

"Next year we'll meet again around the birthday cake!" her son Manoel further clarified, improving on his business partner's wit. "See you next year, Mama! and around the birthday cake!" he said in thorough explanation, right in her ear, while looking obligingly at José. And the old woman suddenly let out a weak cackle, understanding the allusion.

Then she opened her mouth and said:

"Sure."

Excited that it had gone so unexpectedly well, José shouted at her with emotion, grateful, his eyes moist:

"We'll see each other next year, Mama!"

"I'm not deaf!" said the birthday girl gruffly, affectionately.

Her children looked at each other laughing, embarrassed, happy. It had worked out.

The kids went off in good spirits, their appetites ruined. The daughter-in-law from Olaria vengefully cuffed her son, too cheerful and no longer wearing his tie. The stairs were difficult, dark, it was unbelievable to insist on living in such a cramped building that would have to be demolished any day now, and while being evicted Zilda would still cause trouble and want to push the old woman onto the daughters-in-law— reaching the last step, the guests relievedly found themselves in the cool calm of the street. It was nighttime, yes. With its first shiver.

Goodbye, see you soon, we have to get together. Stop by sometime, they said quickly. Some managed to look the others in the eye with unflinching cordiality. Some buttoned up their children's coats, looking at the sky for some hint of the weather. Everyone obscurely feeling that when saying goodbye you could maybe, now without the threat of commitment, be nice and say that extra word—which word? they didn't know exactly, and looked at each other smiling, mute. It was an instant that was begging to come alive. But that was dead. They started going their separate ways, walking with their backs slightly turned, unsure how to break away from their relatives without being abrupt.

"See you next year!" José repeated the lucky hint, waving with effusive vigor, his thinning, white hair fluttering. He really was fat, they thought, he'd better watch his heart. "See you next year!" José boomed, eloquent and grand, and his height seemed it might crumble. But those already a ways off didn't know whether to laugh loudly for him to hear or if it was enough to smile even in the darkness. More than a few thought that luckily the hint contained more than just a joke and that not until next year would they have to gather around the birthday cake; while others, already farther off in the darkness of the street, wondered whether the old woman would hang on for another year of Zilda's nerves and impatience, but honestly there was nothing they could do about it. "Ninety years old at the very least," thought the daughter-in-law from Ipanema melancholically. "To make it to a nice, round age," she thought dreamily.

Meanwhile, up above, atop the stairs and contingencies, the birthday girl was seated at the head of the table, erect, definitive, greater than herself. What if there's no dinner tonight, she mused. Death was her mystery.

The Smallest Woman in the World
("A menor mulher do mundo")

IN THE DEPTHS OF EQUATORIAL AFRICA THE FRENCH explorer Marcel Pretre, hunter and man of the world, came upon a pygmy tribe of surprising smallness. He was all the more surprised, then, when informed that an even smaller people existed beyond forests and distances. So deeper still he plunged.

In the Central Congo he indeed discovered the smallest pygmies in the world. And—like a box within a box, within a box—among the smallest pygmies in the world was the smallest of the smallest pygmies in the world, obeying perhaps the need Nature sometimes has to outdo herself.

Amid mosquitoes and trees warm with moisture, amid the rich leaves of the laziest green, Marcel Pretre came face-to-face with a woman who stood eighteen inches tall, full-grown, black, silent. "Dark as a monkey," he would inform the press, and that she lived in the top of a tree with her little consort. In the tepid, wild mists, which swell the fruits early and make them taste almost intolerably sweet, she was pregnant.

There she stood, then, the smallest woman in the world. For an instant, in the drone of the heat, it was as if the Frenchman had unexpectedly arrived at the last conclusion. Undoubtedly, it was only because he wasn't insane, that his soul neither fainted nor lost control. Sensing an immediate need for order, and to give a name to whatever exists, he dubbed her Little Flower. And, in order to classify her among the recognizable realities, he quickly set about collecting data on her.

Her race is gradually being exterminated. Few human examples remain of this species which, if not for the cunning danger of Africa, would be a dispersed people. Aside from disease, infectious vapors from the waters, insufficient food and roving beasts, the greatest risk facing the scant Likoualas are the savage Bantus, a threat that surrounds them in the silent air as on the morning of battle. The Bantus hunt them with nets, as they do monkeys. And eat them. Just like that: they hunt them with nets and Eat them. That tiny race of people, always retreating and retreating, eventually took up residence in the heart of Africa, where the lucky explorer would discover them. For strategic defense, they live in the tallest trees. From which the women descend to cook corn, grind cassava and gather vegetables; the men, to hunt. When a child is born, he is granted his freedom almost immediately. It's true that often the child won't enjoy this freedom for very long among wild beasts. But then it's true that, at the very least, no one will lament that, for so short a life, the labor was long. For even the language the child learns is short and simple, strictly essential. The Likoualas use few names, referring to things with gestures and animal sounds. In terms of spiritual advancement, they have a drum. While they dance to the sound of the drum, a little male stands guard against the Bantus, who will come from no one knows where.

It was, therefore, thus, that the explorer discovered, standing there at his feet, the smallest human thing in existence.

His heart beat because no emerald is as rare. Neither are the teachings of the sages of India as rare. Neither has the richest man in the world ever laid eyes on so much strange grace. Right there was a woman the gluttony of the most exquisite dream could never have imagined. That was when the explorer declared, shyly and with a delicacy of feeling of which his wife would never have judged him capable:

"You are Little Flower."

At that moment Little Flower scratched herself where a person doesn't scratch. The explorer—as if receiving the highest prize for chastity to which a man, who had always been so idealistic, dared aspire—the explorer, seasoned as he was, averted his eyes.

Little Flower's photograph was published in the color supplement of the Sunday papers, where she fit life-size. Wrapped in a cloth, with her belly far along. Her nose flat, her face black, eyes sunken, feet splayed. She resembled a dog.

That Sunday, in an apartment, a woman, seeing Little Flower's picture in the open newspaper, didn't want to look a second time "because it pains me so."

In another apartment a lady felt such perverse tenderness for the African woman's smallness that—prevention being better than cure—no one should ever leave Little Flower alone with the lady's tenderness. Who knows to what darkness of love affection can lead. The lady was disturbed for a day, one might say seized with longing. Besides it was spring, a dangerous benevolence was in the air.

In another house a five-year-old girl, seeing the picture and hearing the commentary, became alarmed. In that household of adults, this girl had up till now been the smallest of human beings. And, if that was the source of the best caresses, it was also the source of this first fear of love's tyranny. Little Flower's existence led the girl to feel—with a vagueness that only years and years later, for very different reasons, would solidify into thought—led her to feel, in a first flash of wisdom, that "misfortune has no limit."

In another house, amid the rite of spring, the young bride-to-be experienced an ecstasy of compassion:

"Mama, look at her little picture, poor little thing! just look how sad she is!"

"But," said the mother, firm and defeated and proud, "but it's the sadness of an animal, not human sadness."

"Oh! Mama," said the girl discouraged.

It was in another house that a clever boy had a clever idea:

"Mama, what if I put that little African lady on Paulinho's bed while he's sleeping? when he wakes up, he'll be so scared, right! he'll scream, when he sees her sitting on the bed! And then we could play so much with her! we could make her our toy, right!"

His mother was at that moment curling her hair in front of the bathroom mirror, and she recalled something a cook had told her about her time at the orphanage. Having no dolls to play with, and maternity already pulsating terribly in the hearts of those orphans, the sly little girls had concealed another girl's death from the nun. They hid the corpse in a wardrobe until the nun left, and played with the dead girl, giving her baths and little snacks, punishing her just so they could kiss her afterward, consoling her. This is what the mother recalled in the bathroom, and she lowered her pendulous hands, full of hairpins. And considered the cruel necessity of loving. She considered the malignity of our desire to be happy. Considered the ferocity with which we want to play. And how many times we will kill out of love. Then she looked at her clever son as if looking at a dangerous stranger. And she felt horror at her own soul that, more than her body, had engendered that being fit for life and happiness. That is how she looked, with careful attention and an uncomfortable pride, at that boy already missing his two front teeth, evolution, evolution in action, a tooth falling out to make way for one better for biting. "I'm going to buy him a new suit," she decided looking at him deep in thought. Obstinately she dressed her gap-toothed son in nice clothes, obstinately wanting him to be squeaky clean, as if cleanliness would emphasize a calming superficiality, obstinately perfecting the courteous side of beauty. Obstinately distancing herself, and distancing him, from something that ought to be "dark like a monkey." Then, looking in the bathroom mirror, the mother made a deliberately refined and polite smile, placing, between that face of hers with its abstract lines and Little Flower's crude face, the insurmountable distance of millennia. But, after years of practice, she knew this would be one of those Sundays on which she'd have to conceal from herself the anxiety, the dream, and millennia lost.

In another house, beside a wall, they were engaged in the excited task of measuring Little Flower's eighteen inches with a ruler. And that was where, delighted, they gasped in shock: she was even smaller than the keenest imagination could conceive. In each family member's heart arose, nostalgic, the desire to have that tiny and indomitable thing for himself, that thing spared from being eaten, that permanent source of charity. The family's eager soul wanted to devote itself. And, really, who hasn't ever wished to possess a human being for one's very own? Which, to be sure, wouldn't always be convenient, there are times when you don't want to have feelings:

"I bet if she lived here, it would lead to fighting," said the father seated in his armchair, definitively turning the page of his newspaper. "In this house everything leads to fighting."

"There you go again, José, always pessimistic," said the mother.

"Mama, have you thought about how tiny her little baby would be?" the eldest daughter, age thirteen, said ardently.

The father stirred behind his newspaper.

"It must be the smallest black baby in the world," replied the mother, oozing with pleasure. "Just imagine her serving dinner here at home! and with that enormous little belly!"

"Enough of this chatter!" the father growled.

"But you must admit," said the mother unexpectedly offended, "that we're talking about a rare thing. You're the one being insensitive."

And the rare thing herself?

Meanwhile, in Africa, the rare thing herself held in her heart—who knows, maybe it was black too, since a Nature that's erred once can no longer be trusted—meanwhile the rare thing herself harbored in her heart something rarer still, like the secret of the secret itself: a tiny child. Methodically the explorer peered closely at the little belly of the smallest full-grown human being. In that instant the explorer, for the first time since he'd met her, instead of feeling curiosity or exaltation or triumph or the scientific spirit, the explorer felt distress.

Because the smallest woman in the world was laughing.

She was laughing, warm, warm. Little Flower was delighting in life. The rare thing herself was having the ineffable sensation of not yet having been eaten. Not having been eaten was something that, at other times, gave her the agile impulse to leap from branch to branch. But, in this moment of tranquility, amidst the dense leaves of the Central Congo, she wasn't putting that impulse into action—and the impulse had become concentrated entirely in the smallness of the rare thing herself. And so she was laughing. It was a laugh that only one who doesn't speak, laughs. That laugh, the embarrassed explorer couldn't manage to classify. And she kept enjoying her own soft laughter, she who wasn't being devoured. Not being devoured is the most perfect of feelings. Not being devoured is the secret goal of an entire life. So long as she wasn't being eaten, her bestial laughter was as delicate as joy is delicate. The explorer was confounded.

Second of all, if the rare thing herself was laughing, it was because, within her smallness, a great darkness had sprung into motion.

It was that the rare thing herself felt her breast warmed with what might be called Love. She loved that yellow explorer. If she knew how to speak and told him she loved him, he'd puff up with vanity. Vanity that would shrivel when she added that she also loved the explorer's ring very much and that she loved the explorer's boots very much. And when he deflated in disappointment, Little Flower wouldn't understand why. For, not in the slightest, would her love for the explorer—one might even say her "profound love," because, having no other resources, she was reduced to profundity—for not in the slightest would her profound love for the explorer be devalued by the fact that she also loved his boots. There's an old mistake about the word love, and, if many children have been born of this mistake, countless others have missed their only instant of being born merely due to a susceptibility that demands you be mine, mine! that you like me, and not my money. But in the humidity of the forest there are no such cruel refinements, and love is not being eaten, love is thinking a boot is pretty, love is liking that rare color of a man who isn't black, love is laughing with the love of a ring that sparkles. Little Flower blinked with love, and laughed warm, tiny, pregnant, warm.

The explorer tried to smile back at her, without knowing exactly to what abyss his smile responded, and then got flustered as only a big man gets flustered. He pretended to adjust his explorer helmet, blushing bashfully. He turned a lovely color, his own, a greenish pink, like that of a lime at dawn. He must have been sour.

It was probably while adjusting his symbolic helmet that the explorer pulled himself together, severely regained the discipline of work, and recommenced taking notes. He'd learned some of the few words spoken by the tribe, and how to interpret their signals. He could already ask questions.

Little Flower answered "yes." That it was very good to have a tree to live in, her own, her very own. For—and this she didn't say, but her eyes went so dark that they said it—for it is good to possess, good to possess, good to possess. The explorer blinked several times.

Marcel Pretre had several difficult moments with himself. But at least he kept busy by taking lots of notes. Those who didn't take notes had to deal with themselves as best they could:

"Because look,"—suddenly declared an old woman shutting the newspaper decisively—"because look, all I'll say is this: God knows what He's doing."

The Dinner
("O jantar")

HE CAME INTO THE RESTAURANT LATE. HE HAD CER-
tainly just been occupied with very important business. He
might have been around sixty, was tall and corpulent, with
white hair, bushy eyebrows and powerful hands. On one finger the ring of his might. He sat down, ample and solid.

I lost sight of him and while eating went back to observing
the slim woman in the hat. She was laughing with her mouth
full and her dark eyes sparkled.

Just as I raised my fork to my mouth, I looked over at him.
There he sat with his eyes closed chewing his bread vigorously
and mechanically, both fists clenched on the table. I kept eating
and staring. The "garçon" was setting dishes on the tablecloth.
But the old man kept his eyes shut. At one of the waiter's live-
lier gestures he opened them so abruptly that this same movement was conveyed to his large hands and a fork dropped. The
"garçon" whispered friendly words while stooping down to retrieve it; he didn't respond. Because now awakened, he was suddenly turning his meat over, examining it vehemently, the tip of
his tongue peeking out—he pressed on the steak with the back
of his fork, nearly sniffed it, his mouth working in anticipation.
And he began slicing it with a gratuitously vigorous movement

of his whole body. Soon after he was lifting a bite to a certain level of his face and, as if he had to snatch it in mid-flight, gobbled it with a jerk of his head. I looked down at my plate. When I stared at him again, he was immersed in the full glory of his dinner, chewing with his mouth open, running his tongue over his teeth, his gaze fixed on the ceiling light. I was just about to slice my meat again, when I saw him stop entirely.

And as if he couldn't stand it anymore—what?—he quickly grabs his napkin and presses it against his eye sockets with his hairy hands. I paused watchfully. His body was having trouble breathing, it was growing. He finally takes the napkin off his eyes and gazes numbly into the distance. He breathes while opening and shutting his eyelids excessively, wipes his eyes carefully and slowly chews the remaining food in his mouth.

A second later, however, he's recomposed and hardened, he spears a forkful of salad with his whole body and eats hunched over, his chin active, the oil moistening his lips. He breaks off for a second, wipes his eyes again, shakes his head briefly— and another forkful of lettuce with meat is snatched in mid-air. He says to the passing "garçon":

"This isn't the wine I told you to bring."

The very voice I'd been expecting of him: a voice that allows no possibility for rebuttal by which I saw that no one could ever do anything for him. Except obey.

The "garçon" left courteously holding the bottle.

But now the old man freezes again as if his chest were constricted and obstructed. His violent power quakes imprisoned. He waits. Until hunger seems to assault him and he starts chewing hungrily again, frowning. I was the one eating slowly, slightly nauseated without knowing why, participating in I didn't know what. Suddenly he's trembling all over, lifting the napkin to his eyes and pressing them with a brutality that transfixes me … I drop my fork on the plate with a certain decisiveness, I myself experiencing an unbearable tightness in my throat, furious, broken into submission. But the old man doesn't let the napkin linger on his eyes. This time, when he pulls it off unhurriedly, his pupils are extremely sweet and tired, and before he wipes his face—I've seen it. I've seen the tear.

I hunch over my meat, lost. When I finally manage to look at him from the depths of my pale face, I see that he too has hunched over with his elbows propped on the table, head in his hands. And he just couldn't stand it anymore. His bushy eyebrows were furrowed. The food must have got stuck right below his throat in the harshness of his emotion, for when he managed to go on he made a terrible gesture of effort to swallow and ran the napkin over his forehead. I couldn't take it anymore, the meat on my plate was raw, I was the one who couldn't take it anymore. Yet he—he was eating.

The "garçon" brought the bottle in a bucket of ice. I noted everything, indiscriminately: it was a different bottle, the waiter in coattails, the light haloing Pluto's robust head that was now stirring with curiosity, gluttonous and intent. For an instant the "garçon" blocks my view of the old man and I see only the black wings of coattails: hovering over the table, he was pouring red wine into the glass and waiting with fervent eyes—because here was a guaranteed big tipper, one of those old men who are still at the center of the world and of power. The aggrandized old man took a confident sip, put the glass down and bitterly consulted the taste in his mouth. He smacked his lips together, clucked his tongue in disgust as if what was good was intolerable. I waited, the "garçon" waited, both leaning forward in suspense. Finally, he made a grimace of approval. The waiter bowed his shining head in subjection to this thanks, departed bowing, and I sighed in relief.

Now he was mingling the meat with sips of wine in that large mouth and his false teeth chomped heavily as I spied on him in vain. Nothing else was happening. The restaurant seemed to radiate with redoubled force under the clinking of glasses and cutlery; in the hard, brilliant corona of the room the murmurs ebbed and flowed in soft waves, the woman in the big hat smiling with her eyes half-closed, so slim and beautiful, the "garçon" slowly pouring wine into the glass. But now he gestures.

With his heavy, hairy hand, its palm so fatefully etched with lines, he makes a thinking gesture. He says in pantomime as much as he can, and I, I don't understand. And as if he could no longer stand it—he put the fork down on his plate. This time you've really been caught, old man. He sits there breathing, done, noisy. Then he grabs his wine glass and drinks with his eyes closed, in resounding resurrection. My eyes sting and the brightness is loud, persistent. I am seized by the heaving ecstasy of nausea. Everything seems big and dangerous to me. The increasingly beautiful slim woman trembles, solemn, under the lights.

He's finished. His face empties of expression. He closes his eyes, stretches out his jaw. I try to seize this moment, in which he no longer possesses his own face, to see at last. But it's no use. The grand appearance that I see is unknown, majestic, cruel and blind. What I want to see directly, through the venerable elder's extraordinary strength, doesn't exist in this instant. He doesn't want it to.

Dessert comes, some kind of mousse, and I am surprised by the decadence of his choice. He eats slowly, takes a spoonful and watches the sticky liquid drip. He ingests it all, however, grimaces and, enlarged, well-fed, pushes the plate away. Then, no longer hungry, the great horse rests his head on his hand.

The first clearer sign appears. The old devourer of children is thinking in his depths. Blanching I watch him lift his napkin to his mouth. I imagine hearing a sob. We both sit in silence at the center of the room. Perhaps he's eaten too quickly. Because, in spite of everything, you haven't lost your hunger, have you!, I goaded him with irony, rage and exhaustion. But he was falling to pieces in plain sight. His features now sunken and demented, he swung his head from side to side, from side to side no longer restraining himself, lips compressed, eyes shut, rocking back and forth—the patriarch was crying inside. My anger was choking me. I saw him put his glasses on and age by several years. As he counted his change, he clicked his teeth while jutting out his chin, surrendering for an instant to the sweetness of old age. As for me, so intent on him had I been, that I hadn't seen him take out his money to pay, nor examine the bill, and I hadn't noticed the "garçon" returning with the change.

At last he took off his glasses, clicked his teeth, wiped his eyes while grimacing needlessly and painfully. He ran his square hand through his white hair, smoothing it powerfully. He stood holding the table's edge with vigorous hands. And now, free of anything to lean on, he seems weaker, though still enormous and still capable of stabbing any one of us. With nothing for me to do about it, he puts on his hat caressing his tie in the mirror. He crosses the luminous shape of the room, disappears.

But I am still a man.

Whenever they betrayed or murdered me, whenever someone leaves forever, or I lost the best of what I still had, or when I found out that I am going to die—I do not eat. I am not yet this power, this structure, this ruin. I push away the plate, reject meat and its blood.

Preciousness
("Preciosidade")

(for Mafalda)

EARLY IN THE MORNING IT WAS ALWAYS THE SAME thing renewed: waking up. Which was languorous, unfurling, vast. Vastly she'd open her eyes.

She was fifteen years old and not pretty. But inside her scrawniness, the nearly majestic vastness in which she moved as within a meditation. And inside the haziness something precious. That never sprawled, never got involved, never got contaminated. That was intense as a jewel. Her.

She awoke before everyone else, since to get to school she'd have to catch a bus and a tram, which would take her an hour. Which would give her an hour. Of daydreaming keen as a crime. The morning wind violating the window and her face until her lips grew stiff, frozen. Then she'd smile. As if smiling were a goal in itself. All this would happen if she were lucky enough for "no one to look at her."

When she awoke at dawn—gone that instant of vastness in which she fully unwound—she'd dress in a hurry, trick herself into thinking there wasn't time for a shower, and her sleeping family had never guessed how few she actually took. Under the glare of the dining room light, she'd gulp down the coffee that the maid, scratching herself in the kitchen darkness, had warmed up. She hardly touched the bread that butter never softened. Her mouth fresh from fasting, books tucked under her arm, she'd finally open the door, cross the threshold of the house's insipid warmth, dashing into the frosty fruition of the morning. Then she'd no longer hurry.

She had to traverse the long, deserted street before reaching the main avenue, at the end of which a bus would emerge careening through the fog, its headlights still on at the stoplight. In the wintry June wind, her mysterious, authoritative and perfect act was to raise her arm—and already from a distance the shuddering bus would start contorting itself in obedience to the arrogance of her body, the representative of a supreme power, from a distance the bus would grow uncertain and lumbering, lumbering and advancing, increasingly solid—until it screeched to a halt right in her face amid fumes and heat, heat and fumes. Then she'd board, solemn as a missionary because of all the laborers on the bus who "might say something to her." Those men who were no longer young. But she was afraid of young men too, afraid of boys too. Afraid they "might say something" to her, that they'd look at her too long. In the seriousness of her closed mouth was this great supplication: for them to respect her. More than that. As if she'd taken vows, she must be venerated, and, while inwardly her heart beat with fear, she too venerated herself, she, the guardian of a rhythm. If they looked at her, she grew stiff and doleful. What spared her was that the men didn't see her. Though something inside her, as the age of sixteen was approaching amid fumes and heat, something was intensely surprised—and this surprised a few men. As if someone had tapped them on the shoulder. A shadow perhaps. On the ground the looming shadow of a girl without a man, an indeterminate, crystallizable element that took part in the monotonous geometry of great public cere- monies. As if they'd been tapped on the shoulder. They looked and never saw her. She cast more of a shadow than she existed.

On the bus the laborers were silent, holding their lunch boxes, sleep still on their faces. She felt ashamed at not trust- ing them, tired as they were. But until she forgot them, the dis- comfort. Because they "knew." And since she knew too, hence her discomfort. They all knew the same thing. Her father knew too. An old man begging for change knew. The wealth distributed, and the silence.

Then, marching like a soldier, she'd cross—unscathed— the Largo da Lapa, where it was day. By now the battle was nearly won. She'd choose a row on the tram that was empty if possible or, with luck, sit next to some reassuring woman with a bundle of laundry on her lap, for example—and that was the first truce. She'd still have to face the long hallway at school where her classmates would be standing around chat- ting, and where the heels of her shoes would make a noise that her tense legs couldn't hold back as if she wished in vain to make her heart stop beating, shoes that danced of their own accord. A vague silence would descend over the young men who sensed perhaps, beneath her disguise, that she was one of the devout. She'd pass by the ranks of classmates growing, and they wouldn't know what to think or what to say about her. The noise her shoes made was ugly. She was betraying her own secret with wooden heels. If the hallway went on any lon- ger, it would be as if she'd forgotten her destiny and she'd break into a run with her hands over her ears. All the shoes she had were sturdy. As if they were still the same ones they'd solemnly slipped on her feet at birth. She'd walk the length of the interminable hallway as if mired in the silence of the trenches, and in her face was something so fierce—and haughty too, because of her shadow—that no one said a thing to her. Forbidding, she prevented them from thinking.

Until, at last, the classroom. Where suddenly everything became unimportant and faster and lighter, where her face had some freckles, her hair fell into her eyes, and where she was treated like a boy. Where she was intelligent. The sly profession. She seemed to have done her homework. Her curiosity gave her more information than answers ever did. She'd sense, tasting in her mouth the citric flavor of heroic pains, she'd sense the fascinated revulsion her thinking head inspired in her classmates, who, once more, didn't know what to say about her. The big faker was getting smarter and smarter. She'd learned how to think. The necessary sacrifice: that way "no one had the nerve."

Sometimes, while the teacher was talking, she, intense, hazy, would make symmetrical lines in her notebook. If a line, which had to be both strong and delicate, strayed outside the imaginary circle it was supposed to fit inside, everything would collapse: she'd concentrate absently, guided by eagerness for the ideal. Sometimes, instead of lines, she'd draw stars, stars, stars, so many and so high that she'd emerge from this annunciatory work exhausted, raising a barely awake head.

The way home was so plagued by hunger that impatience and hatred gnawed at her heart. On the way back it looked like a different city: across the Largo da Lapa hundreds of people reverberating with hunger seemed to have forgotten and, if reminded, would gnash their teeth. The sun outlined every man in black charcoal. Her own shadow was a black pole. At this hour that required greater caution, she was protected by a kind of ugliness that hunger accentuated, her features darkened by the adrenaline that darkened the flesh of hunted animals. In the empty house, the whole family away at work, she'd shout at the maid who wouldn't even respond. She'd eat like a centaur. Her face close to the plate, her hair nearly in the food.

"So skinny, but you sure can wolf it down," the clever maid would say.

"Go to hell," she'd shout gloomily.

In the empty house, alone with the maid, she no longer marched like a soldier, since she no longer needed to be careful. But she missed the battle on the streets. The melancholy of freedom, with the horizon still so far off. She'd given herself to the horizon. But this nostalgia for the present. The apprenticeship of patience, the vow of waiting. From which she might never manage to free herself. The afternoon stretching out interminably and, until everyone came home for dinner and with relief she could become a daughter, it was the heat, the book opened and then shut, an intuition, the heat: she sat with her head in her hands, hopeless. When she was ten, she recalled, a boy with a crush on her had thrown a dead rat at her. Disgusting! she'd yelled pale with indignation. It had been an experience. She'd never told anyone. With her head in her hands, sitting. She'd say fifteen times over: I am vigorous, I am vigorous, I am vigorous—then realize that she was only paying attention to the count. Compensating with quantity, she'd say one more time: I am vigorous, sixteen. And now she was no longer at the mercy of anyone. Despondent because, vigorous, free, she was no longer at their mercy. She had lost her faith. She went to talk with the maid, ancient priestess. They understood one another. Both barefoot, standing in the kitchen, steam from the stove. She had lost her faith, but, on the verge of grace, she sought in the maid only what was already lost, not what she had gained. So she'd act distracted and, chatting, avoid the subject. "She thinks that at my age I ought to know more than I do and might try to teach me something," she thought, head in her hands, shielding her ignorance as she would a body. There were elements she lacked, but she didn't want them from someone who'd already forgotten them. The great waiting played a part. Inside the vastness, plotting.

All that, yes. Prolonged, weary, the exasperation. But at dawn the next day, like a slow ostrich straightening itself out, she was waking up. She awoke to the same intact mystery, opening her eyes she was the princess of the intact mystery.

As if the factory whistle had already blown, she dressed in a hurry, downed her coffee in one gulp. Opened the front door.

And then she stopped hurrying. The great immolation of the streets. Cunning, alert, an Apache woman. Part of the crude rhythm of a ritual.

It was an even colder, darker morning than the others, she shivered inside her sweater. The white haziness made the end of the street invisible. Everything was cottony, you couldn't even hear the sound of a bus passing on the avenue. She was heading toward the unforeseeable of the street. The houses were sleeping behind closed doors. The gardens rigid with cold. In the dark air, more than in the sky, in the middle of the street a star. A great ice star that hadn't yet returned, tentative in the air, damp, formless. Surprised in its delay, it swelled roundly in hesitation. She looked at the nearby star. She walked alone through the bombarded city.

No, she was not alone. Eyes frowning in disbelief at the far end of her street, inside the mist, she saw two men. Two young men approaching. She looked around as if she could have had the wrong street or city. But her timing was off by minutes:

she'd left home before the star and the two men had time to vanish. Her heart took fright.

Her initial impulse, when realizing her mistake, was to re-trace her steps and go back home until they had passed:"they're going to look at me, I know it, there's no one else for them to look at and they're going to stare at me!" But how could she turn back and flee, if she had been born for adversity. Since all her slow preparation had an unknown destiny that she, out of de-votion, must obey. How could she retreat, and then never again forget the shame of having waited miserably behind a door?

And anyway maybe there wasn't any danger. They wouldn't have the nerve to say anything because she'd stride firmly past, jaw set, with her Spanish rhythm.

Legs heroic, she kept walking. The closer she got, the closer they got too—so that they were all getting closer, the street shrinking bit by bit. The shoes of the two young men mingled with the sound of her own, it was awful to hear. It was relent-less to hear. Either their shoes were hollow or the sidewalk was hollow. The paving stones sounded a warning. All was echo and she heard, unable to prevent it, the silence of the siege being broadcast through the neighborhood streets, and she saw, unable to prevent it, that the front doors were shut even tighter. Even the star had retreated. In the newly arisen pallor of the dark, the street left to those three. She walked, listened to the men, since she couldn't look at them yet needed to know about them. She listened to them and was surprised by her own nerve in pressing on. But it wasn't nerve. It was her gift. And the great vocation for a destiny. She kept on, suffering in obedience. If she managed to think about something else she wouldn't hear their shoes. Nor whatever they might say. Nor the silence with which their paths would cross.

With abrupt rigidity she looked at them. When she least expected to, betraying her vow of secrecy, she glimpsed them. Were they smiling? No, they were somber.

She shouldn't have seen. Because, by seeing, she for an instant risked becoming an individual, and so did they. That's what it seemed she'd been warned against: as long as she operated in a classical world, as long as she was impersonal, she'd be a daughter of the gods, aided by whatever must be done. Yet, having seen whatever it is that eyes, upon seeing, diminish, she risked being a she-herself that tradition couldn't support. For an instant she hesitated completely, having lost her way. But it was too late to retreat. The only way it wouldn't be too late was if she ran. But running would be like going astray at every step, and losing the rhythm that still sustained her, the rhythm that was her sole talisman, which had been delivered unto her at the edge of the world where one must be alone—at the edge of the world where all memories were wiped out, and all that remained as an incomprehensible souvenir was the blind talisman, a rhythm she was destined to copy, performing it for the consummation of the world. Not her own. If she ran, this order would be altered. And she'd never be forgiven the worst thing of all: haste. And even when you flee they give chase, these are things everyone knows.

Rigid, catechistic, not altering for a second the slow pace at which she advanced, she advanced. "They're going to look at me, I know it!" But she struggled, out of some instinct from a past life, not to signal her fear to them. She sensed that fear unleashed things. It would be swift, painless. For just a fraction of a second they'd cross paths, swiftly, instantaneously, thanks to her advantage that she was moving ahead while they approached in an opposite movement, reducing the instant to its bare essence—to revealing the first of the seven mysteries that were so secret that only one thing was known about them: the number seven. Make them not say anything, make them just think, I'll let them think. It would be swift, and a second after the transposition she'd declare in wonder, dashing down streets further and further on: it barely hurt at all. But what happened next had no explanation.

What happened next were four difficult hands, four hands that didn't know what they wanted, four errant hands belonging to people who lacked the vocation, four hands that touched her so unexpectedly that she did the best thing she could have in the realm of movement: she got paralyzed. They, whose predestined role consisted only of passing near the darkness of her fear, and then the first of the seven mysteries would be revealed; they who represented only the horizon of a single approaching footstep, they hadn't understood their designated function and, with the individuality of the fearful, had attacked. It was less than a fraction of a second on the tranquil street. In a fraction of a second they touched her as if entitled to all the seven mysteries. All of which she preserved, and she became more larval, and seven years further behind.

She didn't look at them because her face was turned serenely toward the nothing.

But from the haste with which they hurt her she could tell they were more scared than she was. So scared that they weren't even there anymore. They were running. "They were scared she would scream and the front doors would open one by one," she reasoned, they didn't know you don't scream.

She stood there, listening in tranquil madness to their fleeing shoes. Either the sidewalk was hollow or their shoes were hollow or she herself was hollow. In the hollow sound of their shoes she listened intently to their fear. The sound rang distinctly off the paving stones as if they were banging on the door incessantly and she was waiting for them to go away. So distinctly on the bareness of the stone that the tap dance didn't seem to be fading into the distance: it was right there at her feet, like a victory dance. Standing there, she had nothing to hold her up except her ears.

The sonority wasn't fading, their distance was conveyed to her by the ever-more-precise hurrying of heels. Their heels no longer echoed off the stone, they echoed in the air like ever-more-delicate castanets. Then she realized she hadn't heard a noise in a while.

And, brought back by the breeze, silence and an empty street.

Until that instant she'd kept quiet, standing in the middle of the sidewalk. Then, as if passing through several stages of the same immobility, she stood still. After a while, she sighed. And in another stage, she stayed still. Next she moved her head, and then stood even more deeply still.

Then she retreated slowly over to a wall, hunched, very slowly, as if her arm were broken, until all her weight slumped against the wall, where she became inscribed. And then she stayed still. The important thing is not to move, she thought distantly, not to move. After a while, she had probably told herself this: now move your legs a little but very slowly. Since, very slowly, she moved her legs. After which, she sighed and kept quiet while glancing around. It was still dark.

Then morning came.

Slowly she gathered her books strewn on the ground. Further off lay her open notebook. When she bent to retrieve it, she saw the large, curved handwriting that until this morning had been hers.

Then she left. Without knowing how she had filled the time, except with footsteps and footsteps, she got to school over two hours late. Since she hadn't been thinking about anything, she didn't know how much time had passed. The presence of her Latin teacher made her realize with polite surprise that third period had already begun.

"What happened to you?" whispered the girl at the next desk.

"Why?"

"You're pale. Are you getting sick?"

"No," she said so loudly that several classmates looked at her. She got up and said very loudly:

"Excuse me."

She went to the restroom. Where, facing the great silence of the tiles, she shrieked piercingly, supersonically: "I'm alone in the world! Nobody's ever going to help me, nobody's ever going to love me! I'm alone in the world!"

There she was missing her third class too, sitting on the long bench in the restroom, across from several sinks. "It's okay, later I'll just copy the main points, I'll borrow someone's notes to copy at home—I'm alone in the world!" she interrupted herself pounding her fist several times on the bench. The sound of those four shoes suddenly started up again like a light swift rain. A blind sound, nothing bouncing off the gleaming tiles. Just the distinctness of each shoe that never got entangled with the other shoe. Like nuts falling. All she could do was wait the way you wait for someone to stop banging on the door. Then they stopped.

When she went to the mirror to wet her hair, she was so ugly.

She possessed so little, and they had touched it.

She was so ugly and precious.

She was pale, her features grown delicate. Her hands, dampening her hair, still stained with yesterday's ink. "I need to take better care of myself," she thought. She didn't know how. The truth is that more and more she knew how even less. Her nose stuck out like a snout poking through the fence.

She returned to the bench and sat there quietly, with a snout. "A person is nothing." "No," she shot back in mild protest, "don't say that," she thought with kindness and melancholy. "A person is something," she said just to be nice.

But at dinner life took an urgent and hysterical turn:

"I need new shoes! mine make too much noise, a woman can't walk in wooden heels, they attract too much attention! Nobody ever gets me anything! Nobody ever gets me anything!"—and she was so frantic and sputtering that no one had the nerve to tell her she wouldn't be getting them. All they said was:

"You aren't a woman and all heels are made of wood."

Until, just as a person gets fat, she stopped, without knowing how it happened, being precious. There's an obscure law that makes one protect the egg until the chick is born, a firebird.

And she got the new shoes.

Family Ties
("Os laços de família")

THE WOMAN AND HER MOTHER FINALLY SQUEEZED
into the taxi that was taking them to the station. The mother
kept counting and recounting the two suitcases trying to convince herself that both were in the car. The daughter, with her
dark eyes, whose slightly cross-eyed quality gave them a constant glimmer of derision and detachment—watched.

"I haven't forgotten anything?" the mother was asking for
the third time.

"No, no, you haven't forgotten anything," the daughter answered in amusement, patiently.

That somewhat comic scene between her mother and her
husband still lingered in her mind, when it came time to say
goodbye. For the entire two weeks of the old woman's visit, the
two could barely stand each other; their good-mornings and
good-afternoons constantly struck a note of cautious tact that
made her want to laugh. But right when saying goodbye, before
getting into the taxi, her mother had transformed into a model
mother-in-law and her husband had become the good son-in-
law. "Forgive any misspoken words," the old lady had said, and
Catarina, taking some joy in it, had seen Antônio fumble with

the suitcases in his hands, stammering—flustered at being the good son-in-law. "If I laugh, they'll think I'm mad," Catarina had thought, frowning. "Whoever marries off a son loses a son, whoever marries off a daughter gains a son," her mother had added, and Antônio took advantage of having the flu to cough. Catarina, standing there, had mischievously observed her husband whose self-assurance gave way to a diminutive, dark-haired man, forced to be a son to that tiny graying woman … Just then her urge to laugh intensified. Luckily she never actually had to laugh whenever she got the urge: her eyes took on a sly, restrained look, went even more cross-eyed—and her laughter came out through her eyes. Being able to laugh always hurt a little. But she couldn't help it: ever since she was little she'd laughed through her eyes, she'd always been cross-eyed.

"I'll say it again, that boy is too skinny," her mother declared while bracing herself against the jolting of the car. And though Antônio wasn't there, she adopted the same combative, accusatory tone she used with him. So much that one night Antônio had lost his temper: "It's not my fault, Severina!" He called his mother-in-law Severina, since before the wedding he'd envisioned them as a modern mother- and son-in-law. Starting from her mother's first visit to the couple, the word Severina had turned leaden in her husband's mouth, and so, now, the fact that he used her first name hadn't stopped … —Catarina would look at them and laugh.

"The boy's always been skinny, Mama," she replied.

The taxi drove on monotonously.

"Skinny and anxious," added the old lady decisively.

"Skinny and anxious," Catarina agreed patiently.

He was an anxious, distracted boy. During his grandmother's visit he'd become even more remote, slept poorly, was upset by the old woman's excessive affection and loving pinches. Antônio, who'd never been particularly worried about his son's sensitivity, had begun dropping hints to his mother-in-law, "to protect a child" ...

"I haven't forgotten anything ..." her mother started up again, when the car suddenly braked, launching them into each other and sending their suitcases flying. Oh! oh!, shouted her mother as if faced with some irremediable disaster, "oh!" she said shaking her head in surprise, suddenly older and pitiable. And Catarina?

Catarina looked at her mother, and mother looked at daughter, and had some disaster also befallen Catarina? her eyes blinked in surprise, she quickly righted the suitcases and her purse, trying to remedy the catastrophe as fast as possible. Because something had indeed happened, there was no point hiding it: Catarina had been launched into Severina, into a long forgotten bodily intimacy, going back to the age when one has a father and mother. Though they'd never really hugged or kissed. With her father, yes, Catarina had always been more of a friend. Whenever her mother would fill their plates making them overeat, the two would wink at each other conspiratorially and her mother never even noticed. But after colliding in the taxi and after regaining their composure, they had nothing to talk about—why weren't they already at the station?

"I haven't forgotten anything," her mother asked in a resigned voice.

Catarina no longer wished to look at her or answer.

"Take your gloves!" she said as she picked them up off the ground.

"Oh! oh! my gloves!" her mother exclaimed, flustered.

They only really looked at each other once the suitcases

were deposited on the train, after they'd exchanged kisses: her mother's head appeared at the window.

Catarina then saw that her mother had aged and that her eyes were glistening.

The train wasn't leaving and they waited with nothing to say. The mother pulled a mirror from her purse and studied herself in her new hat, bought at the same milliner's where her daughter went. She gazed at herself while making an excessively severe expression that didn't lack in self-admiration. Her daughter watched in amusement. No one but me can love you, thought the woman laughing through her eyes; and the weight of that responsibility left the taste of blood in her mouth. As if "mother and daughter" were life and abhorrence. No, you couldn't say she loved her mother. Her mother pained her, that was all. The old woman had slipped the mirror back into her purse, and was smiling steadily at her. Her worn and still quite clever face looked like it was struggling to make a certain impression on the people around her, in which her hat played a role. The station bell suddenly rang, there was a general movement of anxiousness, several people broke into a run thinking the train was already leaving: Mama! the woman said. Catarina! the old woman said. They gaped at each other, the suitcase on a porter's head blocked their view and a young man rushing past grabbed Catarina's arm in passing, jerking the collar of her dress off-kilter. When they could see each other again, Catarina was on the verge of asking if she'd forgotten anything ...

"... I haven't forgotten anything?" her mother asked.

Catarina also had the feeling they'd forgotten something, and they looked at each other at a loss — for if they really had forgotten something, it was too late now. A woman dragged a

child along, the child wailed, the station bell resounded again
... Mama, said the woman. What was it they'd forgotten to say
to each other? and now it was too late. It struck her that one day
they should have said something like: "I am your mother, Catarina." And she should have answered: "And I am your daughter."

"Don't sit in the draft!" Catarina called.

"Come now, girl, I'm not a child," said her mother, never taking her attention off her own appearance. Her freckled hand,
slightly tremulous, was delicately arranging the brim of her
hat and Catarina suddenly wanted to ask whether she'd been
happy with her father:

"Give my best to Auntie!" she shouted.

"Yes, of course!"

"Mama," said Catarina because a lengthy whistle was heard
and the wheels were already turning amid the smoke.

"Catarina!" the old woman called, her mouth open and her
eyes astonished, and at the first lurch her daughter saw her
raise her hands to her hat: it had fallen over her nose, covering
everything but her new dentures. The train was already moving and Catarina waved. Her mother's face disappeared for
an instant and immediately reappeared hatless, her loosened
bun spilling in white locks over her shoulders like the hair of
a maiden—her face was downcast and unsmiling, perhaps no
longer even seeing her daughter in the distance.

Amid the smoke Catarina began heading back, frowning,
with that mischievous look of the cross-eyed. Without her
mother's company, she had regained her firm stride: it was
easier alone. A few men looked at her, she was sweet, a little
heavyset. She walked serenely, dressed in a modern style, her
short hair dyed "mahogany." And things had worked out in
such a way that painful love seemed like happiness to her—

everything around her was so alive and tender, the dirty street, the old trams, orange peels—strength flowed back and forth through her heart in weighty abundance. She was very pretty just then, so elegant; in step with her time and the city where she'd been born as if she had chosen it. In her cross-eyed look anyone could sense the enjoyment this woman took in the things of the world. She stared at other people boldly, trying to fasten onto those mutable figures her pleasure that was still damp with tears for her mother. She veered out of the way of oncoming cars, managed to sidestep the line for the bus, glancing around ironically; nothing could stop this little woman whose hips swayed as she walked from climbing one more mysterious step in her days.

The elevator hummed in the beachfront heat. She opened the door to her apartment while using her other hand to free herself of her little hat; she seemed poised to reap the largess of the whole world, the path opened by the mother who was burning in her chest. Antônio barely looked up from his book. Saturday afternoon had always been "his," and, as soon as Severina had left, he gladly reclaimed it, seated at his desk.

"Did 'she' leave?"

"Yes she did," answered Catarina while pushing open the door to her son's room. Ah, yes, there was the boy, she thought in sudden relief. Her son. Skinny and anxious. Ever since he could walk he'd been steady on his feet; but nearing the age of four he still spoke as if he didn't know what verbs were: he'd confirm things coldly, not linking them. There he sat fiddling with his wet towel, exact and remote. The woman felt a pleasant warmth and would have liked to capture the boy forever in that moment; she pulled the towel from his hands disapprovingly: that boy! But the boy gazed indifferently into the air, communicating with himself. He was always distracted. No one had ever really managed to hold his attention. His mother shook out the towel and her body blocked the room from his view: "Mama," said the boy. Catarina spun around. It was the first time he'd said "Mama" in that tone of voice and without asking for anything. It had been more than a confirmation: Mama! The woman kept shaking the towel violently and wondered if there was anyone she could tell what happened, but she couldn't think of anyone who'd understand what she couldn't explain. She smoothed the towel vigorously before hanging it to dry. Maybe she could explain, if she changed the way it happened. She'd explain that her son had said: "Mama, who is God." No, maybe: "Mama, boy wants God." Maybe. The truth would only fit into symbols, they'd only accept it through symbols. Her eyes smiling at her necessary lie, and above all at her own foolishness, fleeing from Severina, the woman unexpectedly laughed aloud at the boy, not just with her eyes: her whole body burst into laughter, a burst casing, and a harshness emerging as hoarseness. Ugly, the boy then said peering at her.

"Let's go for a walk!" she replied blushing and taking him by the hand.

She passed through the living room, informing her husband without breaking stride: "We're going out!" and slammed the apartment door.

Antônio hardly had time to look up from his book—and in surprise saw that the living room was already empty. Catarina! he called, but he could already hear the sound of the descending elevator. Where did they go? he wondered nervously, coughing and blowing his nose. Because Saturday was his, but he wanted his wife and his son at home while he enjoyed his Saturday. Catarina! he called irritably though he knew she could no longer hear him. He got up, went to the window and a second later spotted his wife and son on the sidewalk.

The pair had stopped, the woman perhaps deciding which way to go. And suddenly marching off.

Why was she walking so briskly, holding the child's hand? through the window he saw his wife gripping the child's hand tightly and walking swiftly, her eyes staring straight ahead; and, even without seeing it, the man could tell that her jaw was set. The child, with who-knew-what obscure comprehension, was also staring straight ahead, startled and unsuspecting. Seen from above, the two figures lost their familiar perspective, seemingly flattened to the ground and darkened against the light of the sea. The child's hair was fluttering ...

The husband repeated his question to himself, which, though cloaked in the innocence of an everyday expression, worried him: where are they going? He nervously watched his wife lead the child and feared that just now when both were beyond his reach she would transmit to their son ... but what exactly? "Catarina," he thought, "Catarina, this child is still innocent!" Just when does a mother, holding a child tight, impart to him this prison of love that would forever fall heavily on the future man. Later on her son, a man now, alone, would stand before this very window, drumming his fingers against this windowpane; trapped. Forced to answer to a dead person. Who could ever know just when a mother passes this legacy to her son. And with what somber pleasure. Mother and son now understanding each other inside the shared mystery. Afterward no one would know from what black roots a man's freedom is nourished. "Catarina," he thought enraged, "that child is innocent!" Yet they'd disappeared somewhere along the beach. The shared mystery.

"But what about me? what about me?" he asked fearfully. They had gone off alone. And he had stayed behind. "With his Saturday." And his flu. In that tidy apartment, where "everything ran smoothly." What if his wife was fleeing with their son from that living room with its well-adjusted light, from the tasteful furniture, the curtains and the paintings? that was what he'd given her. An engineer's apartment. And he knew that if his wife enjoyed the situation of having a youthful husband with a promising future—she also disparaged it, with those deceitful eyes, fleeing with their anxious, skinny son. The man got worried. Since he couldn't provide her anything but: more success. And since he knew that she'd help him achieve it and would hate whatever they accomplished. That was how this calm, thirty-two-year-old woman was, who never really spoke, as if she'd been alive forever. Their relationship was so peaceful. Sometimes he tried to humiliate her, he'd barge into their bedroom while she was changing because he knew she detested being seen naked. Why did he need to humiliate her? yet he was well aware that she would only ever belong to a man as long as she had her pride. But he had grown used to this way of making her feminine: he'd humiliate her with tenderness, and soon enough she'd smile—without resentment? Maybe this had given rise to the peaceful nature of their relationship, and those muted conversations that created a homey environment for their child. Or would he sometimes get irritable? Sometimes the boy would get irritable, stomping his feet, screaming from nightmares. What had this vibrant little creature been born from, if not from all that he and his wife had cut from their everyday life. They lived so peacefully that, if they brushed up against a moment of joy, they'd exchange rapid, almost ironic, glances, and both would say with their eyes: let's not waste it, let's not use it up frivolously. As if they'd been alive forever.

But he had spotted her from the window, seen her striding swiftly holding hands with their son, and said to himself: she's savoring a moment of joy—alone. He had felt frustrated because for a while now he hadn't been able to live unless with her. And she still managed to savor her moments—alone. For example, what had his wife been up to on the way from the train to the apartment? not that he had any suspicions but he felt uneasy.

The last light of the afternoon was heavy and beat down solemnly on the objects. The dry sands crackled. The whole day had been under this threat of radiating. Which just then, without exploding, nonetheless, grew increasingly deafening and droned on in the building's ceaseless elevator. Whenever Catarina returned they'd have dinner while swatting at the moths. The boy would cry out after first falling asleep, Catarina would interrupt dinner for a moment … and wouldn't the elevator let up for even a second?! No, the elevator wouldn't let up for a second.

"After dinner we'll go to the movies," the man decided. Because after the movies it would be night at last, and this day would shatter with the waves on the crags of Arpoador.

Beginnings of a Fortune
("Começos de uma Fortuna")

IT WAS ONE OF THOSE MORNINGS THAT SEEM TO HANG in the air. And that are most akin to the idea we have of time.

The veranda doors stood open but the cool air had frozen outside and nothing was coming in from the garden, as if any overflow would break the harmony. Only a few glistening flies had penetrated the dining room and were hovering over the sugar bowl. At that hour, not all of Tijuca was awake. "If I had money ..." thought Artur, and a desire to amass wealth, to tranquilly possess, gave his face a detached and contemplative look.

"I'm not a gambler."

"Cut that nonsense out," his mother replied. "Don't start again with this money talk."

Actually he didn't feel like initiating any pressing conversations that might lead to solutions. A bit of the mortification from the previous night's dinner conversation about his allowance, his father mixing authority with understanding and his mother mixing understanding with basic principles—a bit of the previous night's mortification demanded, nevertheless, further discussion. It just seemed pointless to try to muster yesterday's urgency. Every night, sleep seemed to answer all his needs. And in the morning, unlike the adults who awake dark and unshaven, he got up ever more fresh-faced. Tousled, but different from his father's disarray, which suggested that things had befallen him in the night. His mother would also emerge from their bedroom a little disheveled and still dreamy, as if the bitterness of sleep had given her satisfaction. Until they'd had breakfast, all were irritable or pensive, including the maid. It wasn't the right time to ask for anything. But for him, establishing his authority in the morning was a peacemaking necessity: whenever he awoke he felt he had to recuperate the previous days. So thoroughly did sleep sever his moorings, every night.

"I'm not a gambler or a big spender."

"Artur," said his highly exasperated mother, "I've got my hands full with my own worries!"

"What worries?" he asked curiously.

His mother looked at him as dryly as if he were a stranger. Still he was much more related to her than his father was, who, so to speak, had joined the family. She pursed her lips.

"Everyone has worries, dear," she corrected herself, thereby shifting into a new relational mode, somewhere between maternal and instructive.

And from that point on his mother had taken the day in hand. The kind of individuality with which she'd awoken had dissipated and Artur now could count on her. Ever since he could remember, they either accepted him or reduced him to being merely himself. When he was little they used to play with him, tossing him up in the air, smothering him with kisses—and then all of a sudden they'd become "individuals"—they'd put him down, saying kindly but already intangible: "all done now," and he'd go on vibrating with caresses, with so many bursts of laughter still to let out. Then he'd get cranky, kicking at one thing or another, seething with a rage that, nonetheless, would give way just then to delight, sheer delight, if they only wanted it.

"Eat up, Artur," his mother concluded and now once more he could count on her. Just like that he grew younger and more misbehaved:

"I've got worries of my own but nobody cares. Whenever I say I need money it's like I'm asking to go out gambling or drinking!"

"So now, mister, you admit it might be for gambling or drinking?" said his father striding into the room and making his way toward the head of the table. "Well, well! That's some nerve!"

He hadn't counted on his father coming home. Disoriented, but used to it, he began:

"But Papa!" his voice cracking in a protest that didn't quite manage to be indignant. Counterbalancing things, his mother was already won over, calmly stirring her milk into her coffee, indifferent to a discussion that seemed to amount to little more than a few extra flies. She waved them off the sugar bowl with a languid hand.

"Time to get going," his father cut him off. Artur turned to his mother. But she was buttering her bread, pleasurably absorbed. She'd escaped again. She'd say yes to everything, without paying any attention.

Shutting the front door, he again had the impression that they were constantly handing him over to life. That's how the street seemed to greet him. "When I've got my own wife and kids I'll ring the doorbell here and visit and it'll all be different," he thought.

Life outside the house was something else entirely. Besides the difference in light—as if only by leaving could he tell what the weather was really like and what course things had taken in the night—besides the difference in light, there was the difference in his manner. When he was little his mother would say: "outside the house he's a sweetie, at home he's a devil." Even now, passing through the little gate, he'd become visibly younger and at the same time less childish, more sensitive and above all with not much to say. But with a tame interest. He wasn't the type who struck up conversations, but if someone asked him as they did now: "Sonny, what side of the street is the church on?" he'd grow gently animated, tilt his long neck downward, since everyone was shorter than he; and answer engagedly, as if this entailed an exchange of courtesies and a source of curiosity. He watched intently as the old lady turned the corner in the direction of the church, patiently responsible for her route.

"But money is made to be spent and you know on what," Carlinhos told him fervently.

"I want it to buy stuff," he answered somewhat vaguely.

"A little bicycle?" Carlinhos scoffed with a laugh, flushed with mischief.

Artur laughed grimly, unamused.

Seated at his desk, he waited for the teacher to rise. Clearing his throat, a preface to the start of class, was the usual signal for the students to sit further back in their chairs, open their eyes attentively and think about nothing. "Nothing," came Artur's flustered reply to the teacher who was interrogating him with irritation. "Nothing" vaguely referred to prior conversations, to hardly definitive decisions about a movie that afternoon, to—to money. He *needed* money. But in class, forced to sit still and free from any responsibility, any desire was based on idleness.

"So you couldn't tell right away that Glorinha wanted

to be invited to the movies?" Carlinhos said, and they both looked curiously at the girl who was walking away clutching her binder. Thoughtful, Artur kept walking next to his friend, looking at the stones on the ground.

"If you don't have enough money for two tickets, I'll cover you, you can pay me back later."

Apparently, as soon as he got money he'd be forced to use it for a thousand things.

"But then I'll have to pay you back and I already owe Antônio's brother," he replied evasively.

"So what? what's wrong with that!" his friend reasoned, practical and vehement.

"So what," he thought with restrained fury, "so what, apparently, as soon as you get money everybody comes around wanting to use it, which explains how people lose their money."

"Apparently," he said diverting his anger from his friend, "apparently all you need are a few measly cruzeiros for a woman to sniff it out right away and fall all over you."

They both laughed. After that he felt happier, more confident. Above all less oppressed by his circumstances.

But later it was already noon and every desire was becoming more brittle and harder to stand. All through lunch he deliberated bitterly over whether to go into debt and he felt like a broken man.

"Either he's studying too hard or he doesn't eat enough in the morning," his mother said. "The fact is that he wakes up in a good mood but then comes back for lunch with that pale face. Right away his features look strained, that's the first sign."

"Oh it's nothing, it's just how the day wears on people," his father said affably.

Looking at himself in the hallway mirror before leaving, he

really did look just like one of those working fellows, tired and boyish. He smiled without moving his lips, contented in the depths of his eyes. But at the entrance to the theater he couldn't help borrowing from Carlinhos, because there was Glorinha with a girlfriend.

"Do you guys want to sit in the front or the middle?" Glorinha was asking.

At that, Carlinhos paid for the friend's ticket while Artur covertly took the money for Glorinha's ticket.

"Apparently, the movies are ruined," he said to Carlinhos in passing. He immediately regretted doing so, since his schoolmate hardly heard him, focused on the girl. There was no need to cut himself down in the eyes of his friend, for whom going to the movies just meant getting somewhere with a girl.

As it turned out the movies were only ruined at first. His body soon relaxed, he forgot all about the presence beside him and started watching the movie. It was only near the middle that he became aware of Glorinha and with a sudden start stole a glance at her. He was somewhat surprised to realize she wasn't quite the gold digger he'd taken her for: there was Glorinha leaning forward, mouth open in concentration. Relieved, he leaned back in his seat.

Later on, though, he wondered whether he had in fact been used. And his anguish was so intense that he stopped in front of a window display with a horrified expression. His heart pounded like a fist. Beyond his startled face, floating in the glass of the window, were assorted pans and kitchen utensils that he looked at with a certain familiarity. "Apparently, I've been had," he concluded and couldn't quite superimpose his rage over Glorinha's blameless profile. The girl's very innocence gradually became her worst fault: "So she was using me, using me, and then she just sat there all smug watching the movie?" His eyes filled with tears. "Ingrate," he thought in a poorly chosen word of accusation. Since the word was a token of complaint rather than of anger, he got a little confused and his anger subsided. Now it seemed to him, considered from the outside and leaving out personal preference, that in this case she should have paid for her own ticket.

But sitting before his closed books and notes, his gloomy expression cleared up.

He no longer heard doors slamming, the neighbor's piano, his mother talking on the phone. There was a great silence in his room, as in a vault. And the waning afternoon seemed like morning. He was far away, far away, like a giant who could be outside with just his fingers inside the room and leave them absorbed in twirling a pencil around and around. Sometimes his breathing became labored like an old man's. Most of the time, though, his face barely grazed the bedroom air.

"I already did my homework!" he shouted to his mother who was asking about the sound of the water. Carefully washing his feet in the bathtub, he thought about how Glorinha's friend was better than Glorinha. He hadn't even tried to see whether Carlinhos had "taken advantage" of her. At this thought, he hurried out of the tub and paused before the sink mirror. Until the tiles chilled his wet feet.

No! he didn't want to have to justify himself to Carlinhos and no one was going to tell him how to spend the money he'd get, and Carlinhos could go ahead and think he was spending it on bicycles, but so what if he was? and what if he never, but never, wanted to spend his money? and he just got richer and richer?... what's the big deal, you wanna fight? so you think that ...

"… maybe you're just too wrapped up in your own thoughts," his mother said interrupting him, "but at least eat your dinner and say something every once in a while."

Then he, in a sudden return to his paternal home:

"First you say we're not supposed to talk at the dinner table, then you want me to talk, then you say we're not supposed to talk with our mouths full, then …"

"Watch how you speak to your mother," said his father without severity.

"Papa," asked Artur meekly, frowning, "Papa, what are promissory notes?"

"Apparently," said his father with pleasure, "Apparently high school's useless."

"Have some more potatoes, Artur," his mother tried in vain to pull the two men toward her.

"Promissory notes," his father began while pushing his plate away, "work like this: let's say you have a debt to pay."

Mystery in São Cristóvão
("Mistério em São Cristóvão")

ONE MAY EVENING — THE HYACINTHS RIGID AGAINST the windowpane—the dining room in a home was illuminated and tranquil.

Around the table, frozen for an instant, sat the father, the mother, the grandmother, three children and a skinny girl of nineteen. The perfumed night air of São Cristóvão wasn't dangerous, but the way the people banded together inside their home made anything beyond the family circle hazardous on a cool May evening. There was nothing special about the gathering: they had just finished dinner and were chatting around the table, mosquitoes circling the light. What made the scene particularly sumptuous, and each person's face so blooming, was that after so many years this family's progress had at last become nearly palpable: for one May evening, after dinner, just look at how the children have been going to school every day, the father keeps up his business, the mother has worked throughout years of childbirth and in the home, the girl is finding her balance in the delicateness of her age, and the grandmother has reached a certain status. Without realizing this, the family gazed happily around the room, watching over that rare moment in May and its abundance.

Afterward they each went to their rooms. The old woman stretched out groaning benevolently. The father and mother, after locking up, lay down deep in thought and fell asleep. The three children, choosing the most awkward positions, fell asleep in three beds as if on three trapezes. The girl, in her cotton nightgown, opened her bedroom window and breathed in the whole garden with dissatisfaction and happiness. Unsettled by the fragrant humidity, she lay down promising herself a brand new outlook for the next day that would shake up the hyacinths and make the fruits tremble on their branches—in the midst of her meditation she fell asleep.

Hours passed. And when the silence was twinkling in the fireflies—the children suspended in sleep, the grandmother mulling over a difficult dream, the parents worn out, the girl asleep in the midst of her meditation—a house on the corner opened and from it emerged three masked individuals.

One was tall and had on the head of a rooster. Another was fat and had dressed as a bull. And the third, who was younger, for lack of a better idea, had disguised himself as a lord from olden times and put on a devil mask, through which his innocent eyes showed. The masked trio crossed the street in silence.

When they passed the family's darkened home, the one going as a rooster and who came up with nearly all the group's ideas, stopped and said:

"Look what we have here."

His comrades, made patient by the torture of their masks, looked and saw a house and a garden. Feeling elegant and miserable, they waited resignedly for him to finish his thought. Finally the rooster added:

"We could go pick hyacinths."

The other two didn't reply. They'd taken advantage of the

delay to examine themselves despondently and try to find a way to breathe more easily inside their masks.

"A hyacinth for each of us to pin on our costumes," the rooster concluded.

The bull got riled up at the idea of yet another decoration to have to protect at the party. But, after a moment in which the three seemed to think deeply about the decision, without actually thinking about anything at all—the rooster went ahead, shimmied over the railing and set foot on the forbidden land of the garden. The bull followed with some difficulty. The third, despite some hesitation, in a single bound found himself right in the middle of the hyacinths, with a dull thud that stopped the trio dead in their tracks: holding their breath, the rooster, the bull and the devil lord peered into the darkness. But the house went on among shadows and frogs. And, in the perfume-choked garden, the hyacinths trembled unaffected.

Then the rooster pushed ahead. He could have picked the hyacinth right by his hand. The bigger ones, however, rising near a window—tall, stiff, fragile—shimmered calling out to him. The rooster headed toward them on tiptoe, and the bull and the lord went along. The silence was watching them.

Yet no sooner had he broken the largest hyacinth's stalk than the rooster stopped cold. The other two stopped with a sigh that plunged them into sleep.

From behind the dark glass of the window a white face was staring at them.

The rooster had frozen in the act of breaking off the hyacinth. The bull had halted with his hands still raised. The lord, bloodless under his mask, had regressed back to childhood and its terror. The face behind the window stared.

None of the four would ever know who was punishing

whom. The hyacinths ever whiter in the darkness. Paralyzed, they peered at each other.

The simple approach of four masks on that May evening seemed to have reverberated through hollow recesses, and others, and still others that, if not for that instant in the garden, would forever remain within this perfume in the air and within the immanence of four natures that fate had singled out, designating time and place—the same precise fate of a falling star. These four, coming from reality, had fallen into the possibilities afoot on a May evening in São Cristóvão. Every moist plant, every pebble, the croaking frogs, were taking advantage of the silent confusion to better position themselves—everything in the dark was mute approach. Having fallen into the ambush, they looked at each other in terror: the nature of things had been cast into relief and the four figures peered at each other with outstretched wings. A rooster, a bull, the devil and a girl's face had unleashed the wonder of the garden ... That was when the huge May moon appeared.

It was a stroke of danger for the four visages. So risky that, without a sound, four mute visions retreated without taking their eyes off each other, fearing that the moment they no longer held each other's gaze remote new territories would be ravaged, and that, after the silent collapse, only the hyacinths would remain—masters of the garden's treasure. No specter saw any other vanish because all withdrew at the same time, lingeringly, on tiptoe. No sooner, however, had the magic circle of four been broken, freed from the mutual surveillance, than the constellation broke apart in terror: three shadowy forms sprang like cats over the garden railing, and another, bristling and enlarged, backed up to the threshold of a doorway, from which, with a scream, it broke into a run.

The three masked gentlemen who, thanks to the rooster's disastrous idea, had been planning to surprise everyone at a dance happening such a long time after Carnival, were a big hit at the party already in full swing. The music broke off and those still intertwined on the dance floor saw, amid laughter, the three breathless, masked figures lurking like vagrants in the doorway. Finally, after several tries, the revelers had to abandon their wish to crown them kings of the party because, fearful, the three refused to split up: a tall one, a fat one and a young one, a fat one, a young one and a tall one, imbalance and union, their faces speechless under three masks that swung about on their own.

Meanwhile, all the lights had come on in the hyacinth house. The girl was sitting in the living room. The grandmother, her white hair braided, held the glass of water, the mother smoothed the daughter's dark hair, while the father searched the entire house. The girl couldn't explain a thing: she seemed to have said it all in her scream. It was clear that her face had become smaller—the entire painstaking construction of her age had come undone, she was a little girl once more. But in her visage rejuvenated by more than one phase, there had appeared, to the family's horror, a white hair among those framing her face. Since she kept looking toward the window, they left her sitting there to rest, and, candlesticks in hand, shivering with cold in their nightgowns, set off on an expedition through the garden.

Soon the candles spread out dancing through the darkness. Ivy shrank from the sudden light, illuminated frogs hopped between feet, fruits were gilded for an instant among the leaves. The garden, roused from dreaming, sometimes grew larger sometimes winked out; somnambulant butterflies fluttered past. Finally the old woman, keen expert on the flower beds, pointed out the only visible sign in the elusive garden: the hyacinth still alive on its broken stalk … So it was true: something had happened. They returned, turned all the lights on in the house and spent the rest of the night in wait.

Only the three children slept more soundly still.

The girl gradually recovered her true age. She was the only one not constantly peering around. But the others, who hadn't seen a thing, grew watchful and uneasy. And since progress in that family was the fragile product of many precautions and a handful of lies, everything came undone and had to be remade almost from scratch: the grandmother once again quick to take offense, the father and mother fatigued, the children intolerable, the entire household seeming to hope that once more the breeze of plenty would blow one night after dinner. Which just might happen some other May evening.

The Crime of the Mathematics Teacher
("O crime do professor de matemática")

WHEN THE MAN REACHED THE HIGHEST HILL, THE bells were ringing in the city below. Only the uneven rooftops were in sight. Nearby was the lone tree on the plateau. The man was standing there holding a heavy sack.

He looked down below with nearsighted eyes. The Catholics were entering the church slow and tiny, and he strained to hear the scattered voices of the children dispersed throughout the square. But despite the morning's clearness the sounds barely reached the high plain. He also saw the river that appeared motionless from above, and thought: it's Sunday. In the distance he saw the highest mountain with its dry slopes. It wasn't cold but he drew his sport coat around him more snugly. At last he carefully laid the sack on the ground. He took off his glasses maybe to breathe better since, while holding his glasses, he breathed very deeply. Sunlight hit his lenses, which sent out piercing signals. Without his glasses, his eyes blinked brightly, almost youthful, unfamiliar. He put his glasses back on, became a middle-aged man and picked up the sack again: it was heavy as if made of stone, he thought. He squinted trying to make out the river's current, tilting his head to catch any noises: the river was at a standstill and only the hardier sound of a single voice reached those heights for an instant—yes, he was quite alone. The cool air was inhospitable, since he'd been living in a warmer city. The branches of the lone tree on the plateau swayed. He looked at it. He was biding his time. Until he decided there was no reason to wait any longer.

And nevertheless he waited. His glasses must have been bothering him because he took them off again, breathed deeply and tucked them into his pocket.

He then opened the sack, peered partway into it. Next he put his bony hand inside and started pulling out the dead dog. His whole being was focused solely on that important hand and he kept his eyes deeply shut as he pulled. When he opened them, the air was even brighter and the joyful bells pealed once more summoning the faithful to the solace of punishment.

The unknown dog was out in the open.

Then he set to work methodically. He picked up the stiff, black dog, laid it in a depression in the ground. But, as if he'd already done too much, he put on his glasses, sat beside the dog and started surveying the landscape.

He saw very clearly, and with a certain futility the deserted plateau. But he noted precisely that when seated he could no longer glimpse the town below. He breathed again. He reached back into the sack and pulled out the shovel. And considered which site to choose. Maybe under the tree. He caught himself musing that he'd bury this dog under the tree. But if it were the other one, the real dog, he'd actually bury it where he himself would like to be buried if he were dead: at the very center of the plateau, facing the sun with empty eyes. So, since the unknown dog was standing in for the "other" one, he wanted it, for the greater perfection of the act, to get exactly what the other would. There was no confusion whatsoever in the man's head. He coldly understood himself, no loose ends.

Soon, being excessively scrupulous, he became highly absorbed in rigorously trying to determine the middle of the plateau. It wasn't easy because the lone tree stood on one side and, marking a false center, divided the plain asymmetrically. Faced with this obstacle the man admitted: "I didn't need to bury him at the center, I'd have also buried the other one, let's say, right where I'm standing this very second." Because it was a question of granting the event the fatefulness of chance, the sign of an external and obvious occurrence—similar to the children in the square and the Catholics entering the church—it was a question of rendering the fact as visible as possible on the surface of the world beneath the heavens. It was a question of exposing himself and exposing a fact, and not allowing the intimate and unpunished form of a thought.

At the idea of burying the dog where he was standing that very moment—the man recoiled with an agility that his small and singularly heavy body wouldn't allow. Because it seemed to him that beneath his feet the outline of the dog's grave had been drawn.

So he began digging right there, his shovel rhythmic. Sometimes he'd pause to take his glasses off and put them back on. He was sweating grievously. He didn't dig very deep but not because he wanted to save his energy. He didn't dig very deep because he thought lucidly: "if it were for the real dog, I'd dig a shallow hole, I'd bury him close to the surface." He thought that near the surface of the earth the dog wouldn't be deprived of its senses.

Finally he dropped the shovel, gently lifted the unknown dog and placed it in the grave.

What a strange face that dog had. When, with a start he'd come upon the dead dog on a street corner, the idea of burying it had made his heart so heavy and surprised, that he hadn't even noticed that stiff muzzle and crusted drool. It was a strange and objective dog.

The dog came up slightly higher than the hole he had dug and after being covered with dirt it would be a barely discernible mound on the plateau. That was exactly how he wanted it. He covered the dog with dirt and smoothed it over with his hands, feeling its shape under his palms intently and with pleasure as if he were petting it several times. The dog was now merely a feature of the terrain.

Then the man stood, brushed the dirt off his hands, and didn't give the grave another look. He thought with a certain pleasure: I think I've done everything. He gave a deep sigh, and an innocent smile of liberation. Yes, he'd done everything. His crime had been punished and he was free.

And now he could think freely about the real dog. He immediately started thinking about the real dog, which he'd avoided doing up till now. The real dog that even now must be wandering bewilderedly through the streets of the other town, sniffing all over that city where he no longer had a master.

He then started to think with some trouble about the real dog as if he were trying to think with some trouble about his real life. The fact that the dog was far away in that other city troubled the task, though longing brought him closer to its memory.

"While I was making you in my image, you were making me in yours," he thought then with the aid of longing. "I gave you the name José to give you a name that would also serve as your soul. And you—how can I ever know what name you gave me? How much more you loved me than I loved you," he reflected curiously.

"We understood each other too well, you with the human name I gave you, I with the name you gave me that you never spoke except with your insistent gaze," thought the man smiling tenderly, now free to reminisce as he pleased.

"I remember you when you were little," he thought amused, "so small, cute and weak, wagging your tail, looking at me, and I unexpectedly finding in you a new form of having my soul. But, from then on, every day you were already starting to be a dog one could abandon. Meanwhile, our games were getting dangerous from so much understanding," the man recalled in satisfaction, "you ended up biting me and growling, I ended up hurling a book at you and laughing. But who knows what that fake laugh of mine meant. Every day you were a dog one could abandon."

"And how you sniffed at the streets!" thought the man laughing a little, "you really didn't leave a single stone unsniffed … That was your childish side. Or was it your true calling as a dog? and the rest was just playing at being mine? Because you were indomitable. And, calmly wagging your tail, you seemed to reject silently the name I'd given you. Ah, yes, you were indomitable: I didn't want you to eat meat so you wouldn't get ferocious, but one day you leaped onto the table and, as the children happily shouted, snatched the meat and, with a ferocity that doesn't come from what you eat, you stared at me mute and indomitable with the meat in your mouth. Because, though you were mine, you never yielded to me even a little of your past or your nature. And, worried, I started to understand that you didn't demand that I give up anything of mine to love you, and this started to bother me. It was at the endpoint of the stubborn reality of our two natures that you expected us to understand each other. My ferocity and yours shouldn't be exchanged out of sweetness: that was what you taught me little by little, and that too was starting to weigh on me. By not asking anything of me, you asked too much. From yourself, you demanded that you be a dog. From me, you demanded that I be a man. And I, I pretended as best I could. Sometimes, sitting back on your paws in front of me, how you'd stare at me! So I'd look at the ceiling, cough, pretend not to notice, examine my nails. But nothing affected you: you went on staring at me. Who were you going to tell? Pretend—I'd tell myself—quick pretend you're someone else, give a false interview, pet him, throw him a bone—but nothing distracted you: you went on staring at me. What a fool I was. I shuddered in horror, when you were the innocent one: if I turned around and suddenly showed you my true face, and, bristling, hurt, you'd drag yourself over to the door forever wounded. Oh, every day you were a dog one could abandon. One could choose to. But you, trusting, wagged your tail.

"Sometimes, touched by your perceptiveness, I'd manage to see your particular anguish in you. Not the anguish of being a dog which was your only possible form. But the anguish of existing so perfectly that it was becoming an unbearable joy: then you'd leap and lick my face with a freely given love and a certain threat of hatred as if I were the one who, through friendship, had exposed you. I'm pretty sure now I wasn't the one who had a dog. You were the one who had a person.

"But you possessed a person so powerful that he could choose: and so he abandoned you. With relief he abandoned you. With relief, yes, since you demanded—with the serene and simple incomprehension of one who is a heroic dog—that I be a man. He abandoned you with an excuse the whole household approved of: since how could I move house with all that baggage and family, and on top of that a dog, while adjusting to a new high school and a new city, and on top of that a dog? 'Who there's no room for,' said Marta being practical. 'Who'll bother the other passengers,' reasoned my mother-in-law without knowing that I'd already thought of excuses, and the children cried, and I looked neither at them nor at you, José. But you and I alone know that I abandoned you because you were the constant possibility of the crime never committed. The possibility that I would sin which, in the concealment of my eyes, was already a sin. So I sinned right away to be guilty right away. And this crime stands in for the greater crime that I wouldn't have the nerve to commit," thought the man ever more lucidly.

"There are so many ways to be guilty and lose yourself forever and betray yourself and not face yourself. I chose to hurt a dog," thought the man. "Because I knew that would be a lesser crime and that no one goes to Hell for abandoning a dog that trusted a man. Because I knew that crime wasn't punishable."

As he sat on the plateau, his mathematical head was cool and intelligent. Only now did he seem to comprehend, in all his icy plenitude, that what he'd done to the dog was truly unpunished and everlasting. For they hadn't yet invented a punishment for the great concealed crimes and for the profound betrayals.

A man might yet outsmart the Last Judgment. No one condemned him for this crime. Not even the Church. "They're all my accomplices, José. I'd have to go door to door and beg them to accuse me and punish me: they'd all slam the door on me with suddenly hardened faces. No one condemns me for this crime. Not even you, José, would condemn me. For all I'd have to do, powerful as I am, is decide to call you—and, emerging from your abandonment in the streets, in one leap you'd lick my cheek with joy and forgiveness. I'd turn the other cheek for you to kiss."

The man took off his glasses, sighed, put them back on.

He looked at the covered grave. Where he had buried an unknown dog in tribute to the abandoned dog, attempting at last to repay the debt that distressingly no one was demanding. Attempting to punish himself with an act of kindness and be freed of his crime. The way someone gives alms in order at last to eat the cake for which another went without bread.

But as if José, the abandoned dog, demanded much more from him than this lie; as if he were demanding that he, in a final push, be a man—and as a man take responsibility for his crime—he looked at the grave where he had buried his weakness and his condition.

And now, more mathematically still, he sought a way not to have punished himself. He shouldn't be consoled. He coolly sought a way to destroy the false burial of the unknown dog. He crouched then, and, solemn, calm, with simple movements—unburied the dog. The dark dog at last appeared whole, unfamiliar with dirt in its eyelashes, its eyes open and glazed over. And thus the mathematics teacher renewed his crime forever. The man then looked around and to the heavens beseeching a witness to what he had done. And as if that still weren't enough, he started descending the slopes toward the bosom of his family.

The Buffalo
("O búfalo")

BUT IT WAS SPRING. EVEN THE LION LICKED THE LION-ess's smooth forehead. Both animals blond. The woman averted her eyes from the cage, where the hot smell alone recalled the carnage she'd come looking for at the Zoological Gardens. Then the lion paced calmly, mane flowing, and the lioness slowly recomposed the head of a sphinx upon her outstretched paws. "But this is love, it's love again," railed the woman trying to locate her own hatred but it was spring and two lions had been in love. Fists in her coat pockets, she looked around, surrounded by the cages, caged by the shut cages. She kept walking. Her eyes were so focused on searching that her vision sometimes darkened into a kind of sleep, and then she'd recompose herself as in the coolness of a pit.

But the giraffe was a virgin with freshly shorn braids. With the mindless innocence of large and nimble and guiltless things. The woman in the brown coat averted her eyes, feeling sick, sick. Unable—in front of the perching aerial giraffe, in front of that silent wingless bird—unable to locate inside herself the spot where her sickness was the worst, the sickest spot, the spot of hatred, she who had gone to the Zoological

Gardens to get sick. But not in front of the giraffe that was more landscape than being. Not in front of that flesh that had become distracted in its height and remoteness, the nearly verdant giraffe. She was searching for other animals, trying to learn from them how to hate. The hippopotamus, the moist hippopotamus. That plump roll of flesh, rounded and mute flesh awaiting some other plump and mute flesh. No. For there was such humble love in remaining just flesh, such sweet martyrdom in not knowing how to think.

But it was spring, and, tightening the fist in her coat pocket, she'd kill those monkeys levitating in their cage, monkeys happy as weeds, monkeys leaping about gently, the female monkey with her resigned, loving gaze, and the other female suckling her young. She'd kill them with fifteen dry bullets: the woman's teeth clenched until her jaw ached. The nakedness of the monkeys. The world that saw no danger in being naked. She'd kill the nakedness of the monkeys. One monkey stared back at her as he gripped the bars, his emaciated arms outstretched in a crucifix, his bare chest exposed without pride. But she wouldn't aim at his chest, she'd shoot the monkey between the eyes, she'd shoot between those eyes that were staring at her without blinking. Suddenly the woman averted her face: because the monkey's pupils were covered with a gelatinous white veil, in his eyes the sweetness of sickness, he was an old monkey—the woman averted her face, trapping between her teeth a feeling she hadn't come looking for, she quickened her step, even so, turned her head in alarm back toward the monkey with its arms outstretched: he kept staring straight ahead. "Oh no, not this," she thought. And as she fled, she said: "God, teach me only how to hate."

"I hate you," she said to a man whose only crime was not

loving her. "I hate you," she said in a rush. But she didn't even know how you were supposed to do it. How did you dig in the earth until locating that black water, how did you open a passage through the hard earth and never reach yourself? She roamed the zoo amid mothers and children. But the elephant withstood his own weight. That whole elephant endowed with the capacity to crush with a mere foot. But he didn't crush anything. That power that nevertheless would tamely let itself be led to a circus, a children's elephant. And his eyes, with an old man's benevolence, trapped inside that hulking, inherited flesh. The oriental elephant. And the oriental spring too, and everything being born, everything flowing downstream.

The woman then tried the camel. The camel in rags, humpbacked, chewing at himself, absorbed in the process of getting to know his food. She felt weak and tired, she'd hardly eaten in two days. The camel's large, dusty eyelashes above eyes dedicated to the patience of an internal craft. Patience, patience, patience, was all she was finding in this windblown spring. Tears filled the woman's eyes, tears that didn't spill over, trapped inside the patience of her inherited flesh. The camel's dusty odor was all that arose from this encounter she had come for: for dry hatred, not for tears. She approached the bars of the pen, inhaled the dust of that old carpet where ashen blood flowed, sought its impure tepidness, pleasure ran down her back into the distress, but still not the distress she'd come looking for. In her stomach the urge to kill convulsed in hunger pangs. But not the camel in ragged burlap. "Dear God, who shall be my mate in this world?"

So she went alone to have her violence. In the zoo's small amusement park she waited meditatively in the line of lovers for her turn on the roller coaster.

And there she was sitting now, quiet in her brown coat. Her seat stopped for now, the roller-coaster machinery stopped for now. Separate from everyone in her seat, she looked like she was sitting in a Church. Her lowered eyes saw the ground between the tracks. The ground where simply out of love—love, love, not love!—where out of pure love weeds sprouted between the tracks in a light green so dizzying that she had to avert her eyes in tormented temptation. The breeze made the hair rise on the back of her neck, she shivered refusing it, in temptation refusing, it was always so much easier to love.

But all of a sudden came that lurch of the guts, that halting of a heart caught by surprise in midair, that fright, the triumphant fury with which her seat hurtled her into the nothing and immediately swept her up like a rag doll, skirts flying, the deep resentment with which she became mechanical, her body automatically joyful—the girlfriends' shrieks!—her gaze wounded by that enormous surprise, that offense, "they were having their way with her," that enormous offense—the girlfriends' shrieks!—the enormous bewilderment at finding herself spasmodically frolicking, they were having their way with her, her pure whiteness suddenly exposed. How many minutes? the minutes of an extended scream of a train rounding the bend, and the joy of another plunge through the air insulting her like a kick, her dancing erratically in the wind, dancing frantically, whether or not she wanted it her body shook like someone laughing, that sensation of laughing to death, the sudden death of someone who had neglected to shred all those papers in the drawer, not other people's death, her own, always her own. She who could have taken advantage of the others screaming to let out her own howl of lament, she forgot herself, all she felt was fright.

And now this silence, sudden too. They'd come back to earth, the machinery once again completely stopped.

Pale, kicked out of a Church, she looked at the stationary earth from which she'd departed and back to which she'd been delivered. She straightened out her skirts primly. She didn't look at anyone. Contrite as on that day when in the middle of everyone the entire contents of her purse had spilled onto the ground and everything that was valuable while lying secretly in her purse, once exposed in the dust of the street, revealed the pettiness of a private life of precautions: face powder, receipt, fountain pen, her retrieving from the curb the scaffolding of her life. She rose from her seat stunned as if shaking off a collision. Though no one was paying attention, she smoothed her skirt again, did what she could so no one would notice how weak and disgraced she was, haughtily protecting her broken bones. But the sky was spinning in her empty stomach; the earth, rising and falling before her eyes, remained distant for a few moments, the earth that is always so troublesome. For a moment the woman wanted, in mutely sobbing fatigue, to reach out her hand to the troublesome earth: her hand reached out like that of a crippled beggar. But as if she had swallowed the void, her heart stunned.

Was that it? That was it. Of the violence, that was it.

She headed back toward the animals. The ordeal of the roller coaster had left her subdued. She didn't make it much further: she had to rest her forehead against the bars of a cage, exhausted, her breath coming quick and shallow. From inside the cage the coati looked at her. She looked at him. Not a single word exchanged. She could never hate that coati who looked at her with the silence of an inquiring body. Disturbed, she averted her eyes from the coati's simplicity. The curious coati asking her a question the way a child asks. And she averting her eyes, concealing from him her deadly mission. Her forehead was pressed against the bars so firmly that for an instant it looked like she was the caged one and a free coati was examining her.

The cage was always on the side she was: she let out a moan that seemed to come from the soles of her feet. After that another moan.

Then, born from her womb, it rose again, beseeching, in a swelling wave, that urge to kill—her eyes welled up grateful and black in a near-happiness, it wasn't hatred yet, for the time being just the tormented urge to hate like a desire, the promise of cruel blossoming, a torment like love, the urge to hate promising itself sacred blood and triumph, the spurned female had become spiritualized through her great hope. But where, where to find the animal that would teach her to have her own hatred? the hatred that was hers by right but that lay excruciatingly out of reach? where could she learn to hate so as not to die of love? And from whom? The world of spring, the world of beasts that in spring Christianize themselves with paws that claw but do not wound … oh no more of this world! no more of this perfume, of this weary panting, no more of this forgiveness in everything that will die one day as if made to surrender. Never forgiveness, if that woman forgave one more time, even just once, her life would be lost—she let out a hoarse, brief moan, the coati gave a start—caged in she looked around, and since she wasn't the kind of person people paid attention to, she crouched down like an old solitary assassin, a child ran past without noticing her.

Then she started walking again, smaller now, tough, fists once again braced in her pockets, the undercover assassin, and

227

everything was caught in her chest. In her chest that knew only how to give up, knew only how to withstand, knew only how to beg forgiveness, knew only how to forgive, that had only learned how to have the sweetness of unhappiness, and learned only how to love, love, love. Imagining that she might never experience the hatred of which her forgiveness had always been made, this caused her heart to moan indecently, she began walking so fast that she seemed to have found a sudden destiny. She was almost running, her shoes throwing her off balance, and giving her a physical fragility that once again reduced her to the imprisoned female, her steps mechanically assumed the beseeching despair of the frail, she who was nothing more than a frail woman herself. But, if she could take off her shoes, could she avoid the joy of walking barefoot? how could you not love the ground on which you walk? She moaned again, stopped before the bars of an enclosure, pressed her hot face against the iron's rusty coolness. Eyes deeply shut she tried to bury her face between the hardness of the railings, her face attempted an impossible passage through the narrow bars, just as before when she'd seen the newborn monkey seek in the blindness of hunger the female's breast. A fleeting comfort came from how the bars seemed to hate her while opposing her with the resistance of frozen iron.

She opened her eyes slowly. Her eyes coming from their own darkness couldn't see a thing in the afternoon's faint light. She stood there breathing. Gradually she started to make things out again, gradually shapes began solidifying, she was tired, crushed by the sweetness of tiredness. Her head tilted inquiringly toward the budding trees, her eyes saw the small white clouds. Without hope, she heard the lightness of a stream. She lowered her head again and stood gazing at the buffalo in the distance. Inside in a brown coat, breathing without interest, no one interested in her, she interested in no one.

A certain peace at last. The breeze ruffling the hair on her forehead as if brushing the hair of someone who had just died, whose forehead was still damp with sweat. Gazing detachedly at that great dry plot surrounded by tall railings, the buffalo plot. The black buffalo was standing still at the far end of that plot. Then he paced in the distance on his narrow haunches, his dense haunches. His neck thicker than his tensed flanks. Seen straight on, his large head was broader than his body, blocking the rest from view, like a severed head. And on his head those horns. At a distance he slowly paced with his torso. He was a black buffalo. So black that from afar his face looked featureless. Atop his blackness the erect stark whiteness of his horns.

The woman might have left but the silence felt good in the waning afternoon.

And in the silence of the paddock, those meandering steps, the dry dust beneath those dry hooves. At a distance, in the midst of his calm pacing, the black buffalo looked at her for an instant. The next instant, the woman again saw only the hard muscle of his body. Maybe he hadn't looked at her. She couldn't tell, since all she could discern of that shadowy head were its outlines. But once more he seemed to have either seen or sensed her.

The woman raised her head a little, retracted it slightly in misgiving. Body motionless, head back, she waited.

And once more the buffalo seemed to notice her.

As if she couldn't stand feeling what she had felt, she suddenly averted her face and looked at a tree. Her heart didn't beat in her chest, her heart was beating hollowly somewhere between her stomach and intestines.

The buffalo made another slow loop. The dust. The woman clenched her teeth, her whole face ached a little.

The buffalo with his constricted torso. In the luminous dusk he was a body blackened with tranquil rage, the woman sighed slowly. A white thing had spread out inside her, white as paper, fragile as paper, intense as a whiteness. Death droned in her ears. The buffalo's renewed pacing brought her back to herself and, with another long sigh, she returned to the surface. She didn't know where she'd been. She was standing, very feeble, just emerged from that white and remote thing where she'd been.

And from where she looked back at the buffalo.

The buffalo larger now. The black buffalo. Ah, she said suddenly with a pang. The buffalo with his back turned to her, standing still. The woman's whitened face didn't know how to call him. Ah! she said provoking him. Ah! she said. Her face was covered in deathly whiteness, her suddenly gaunt face held purity and veneration. Ah! she goaded him through clenched teeth. But with his back turned, the buffalo completely still.

She picked up a rock off the ground and hurled it into the paddock. The torso's stillness, quieted down even blacker: the rock rolled away uselessly.

Ah! she said shaking the bars. That white thing was spreading inside her, viscous like a kind of saliva. The buffalo with his back turned.

Ah, she said. But this time because inside her at last was flowing a first trickle of black blood.

The first instant was one of pain. As if the world had convulsed for this blood to flow. She stood there, listening to that first bitter oil drip as in a grotto, the spurned female. Her strength was still trapped between the bars, but something incomprehensible and burning, ultimately incomprehensible, was happening, a thing like a joy tasted in her mouth. Then the buffalo turned toward her.

The buffalo turned, stood still, and faced her from afar.

I love you, she then said with hatred to the man whose great unpunishable crime was not wanting her. I hate you, she said beseeching the buffalo's love.

Provoked at last, the enormous buffalo approached unhurriedly.

He approached, the dust rose. The woman waited with her arms hanging alongside her coat. Slowly he approached. She didn't take a single step back. Until he reached the railings and stopped there. There stood the buffalo and the woman, face to face. She didn't look at his face, or his mouth, or his horns. She looked him in the eye.

And the buffalo's eyes, his eyes looked her in the eye. And such a deep pallor was exchanged that the woman fell into a drowsy torpor. Standing, in a deep sleep. Small red eyes were looking at her. The eyes of the buffalo. The woman was dazed in surprise, slowly shaking her head. The calm buffalo. Slowly the woman was shaking her head, astonished by the hatred with which the buffalo, tranquil with hatred, was looking at her. Nearly absolved, shaking an incredulous head, her mouth slightly open. Innocent, curious, plunging deeper and deeper into those eyes staring unhurriedly at her, simple, with a drowsy sigh, neither wanting nor able to flee, trapped in this mutual murder. Trapped as if her hand were forever stuck to the dagger she herself had thrust. Trapped, as she slid spellbound down the railing. In such slow dizziness that just before her body gently crumpled the woman saw the whole sky and a buffalo.

THE FOREIGN LEGION

("A legião estrangeira")

The Disasters of Sofia
("Os desastres de Sofia")

WHATEVER HIS PREVIOUS JOB HAD BEEN, HE HAD LEFT it behind, changed careers, and onerously moved on to teaching primary school: that was all we knew of him.

The teacher was fat, big and silent, with hunched shoulders. Instead of a lump in his throat, he had hunched shoulders. He wore a sport coat that was too short, rimless glasses, with a gold wire perched on his broad Roman nose. And I was attracted to him. Not in love, but attracted by his silence and the restrained impatience with which he taught us and which, feeling offended, I had sensed. I started acting up in class. I'd talk really loudly, pester my classmates, disrupt the lesson with wisecracks, until he'd say, reddening:

"Quiet down, young lady, or I'll send you out of the classroom."

Wounded, triumphant, I'd answer defiantly: go ahead! He wouldn't do it, since that would mean obeying me. But I exasperated him so much that it had become painful for me to be the object of hatred for that man whom in some way I loved. I didn't love him like the woman I would one day be, I loved him like a child who clumsily tries to protect an adult, with the fury of one who has yet to be a coward and sees a strong man with such stooped shoulders. He irritated me. At night, before I fell asleep, he irritated me. I had recently turned nine, a tough age like the unbroken stem of a begonia. I goaded him, and whenever I succeeded in aggravating him I'd taste, in the glory of martyrdom, the unbearable acidity of the begonia when crushed between the teeth; and I'd bite my nails, exultant. In the morning, as I passed through the school gates, walking along all pure with my milky coffee and scrubbed face, it was a shock to bump into, in flesh and blood, the man who had made me fantasize for an abysmal minute before falling asleep. On the surface of time it had only lasted a minute, but in its depths it was ancient centuries of the darkest sweetness. In the morning—as if I hadn't counted on the actual existence of the person who had unleashed my black dreams of love—in the morning, face to face with that big man in his short jacket, in a collision I was launched into shame, bewilderment and frightening hope. Hope was my greatest sin.

Each day renewed the meager struggle I had initiated for that man's salvation. I wished for his well-being, and in return he hated me. Bruised, I became his demon and torment, symbol of the hell it must have been for him to teach that giggling, uninterested class. It had become an already-terrible pleasure, not leaving him in peace. The game, as always, fascinated me. Unaware that I was obeying old traditions, but with a wisdom that the evil are born with—those evil ones who bite their nails in alarm—, unaware that I was obeying one of the most common occurrences in the world, I was playing the prostitute and he the saint. No, maybe that wasn't it. Words precede and surpass me, they tempt and alter me, and if I am not careful it will be too late: things will be said without my having said them. Or, at the very least, that wasn't the only thing. My entanglement comes from how a carpet is made of so many threads that I can't resign myself to following just one; my ensnarement comes from how one story is made of many stories. And I can't even tell them all—a more truthful word could from echo to echo cause my highest glaciers to crumble down the precipice. Therefore, then, I'll no longer mention the maelstrom within me when I'd fantasize before falling asleep. Or else even I'll end up thinking it was that gentle vortex alone that propelled me toward him, forgetting my desperate renunciation. I had become his seductress, a duty no one had imposed on me. It was regrettable that the task of saving him through temptation had fallen into my wayward hands, since of all the adults and children from that time I was probably the least suitable. "That's not a flower you want to sniff," as our maid used to say. But it was as if, alone with a mountaineer paralyzed with terror of the precipice, I, no matter how clumsy I was, couldn't help but try to help him climb down. The teacher had suffered the misfortune of being stranded alone at his deserted outpost with the most ill-advised person of all. Risky as it was on my side, I had to drag him over to it, since the side he was on was fatal. That's what I was doing, as an annoying child tugs a grown-up by the hem of his jacket. He wouldn't turn around, wouldn't ask what I wanted, and would pull himself free with a jerk. I kept pulling him by the jacket, my only tool was persistence. And of all this the only thing he noticed was that I was ripping his pockets. It's true that not even I really knew what I was doing, my life with the teacher was invisible. But I felt that my role was evil and dangerous: I was propelled by voraciousness for a real life that was being delayed, and worse than being inept, I also enjoyed ripping his pockets. Only God would forgive what I was because

237

only He knew of what He had made me and to what end. I let myself, then, be His matter. Being the matter of God was my only goodness. And the source of a nascent mysticism. Not mysticism for Him, but for His matter, for raw life filled with pleasure: I was a worshipper. I accepted the vastness of which I knew nothing and entrusted it with everything of myself, with secrets of the confessional. Could it be for the sake of the darknesses of ignorance that I was seducing the teacher? and with the ardor of a nun in her cell. A cheerful and monstrous nun, alas. And I couldn't even brag about it: all of us in the class were just as monstrous and gentle, eager matter of God.

But if his fat, hunched shoulders and his tight short jacket had an effect on me, my bursts of laughter only managed to make him, as he pretended with great effort to forget about me, tense up even more from all that self-restraint. The antipathy that man felt for me was so strong that I hated myself. Until my laughter started definitively replacing my impossible tact.

As for learning, I learned nothing during those lessons. I was already too caught up in the game of making him unhappy. Enduring my long legs and always worn-out shoes with brazen bitterness, humiliated at not being a flower, and above all tortured by an enormous childhood that I feared would never end—I made him unhappier still and I would haughtily toss my sole treasure: the straight hair that I planned to beautify some day with a perm and that, bearing the future in mind, I'd already practiced tossing. As for studying, I never studied, trusting in my always successful idleness that the teacher took as yet another provocation from that hateful girl. He was wrong about that. The truth is that I didn't have time to study. My joys kept me busy, being alert took days and days; there were the storybooks that I read, while passionately biting my nails down to the quick, in my first ecstasies of sorrow, a refinement I'd already discovered; there were boys I had chosen and who hadn't chosen me, I wasted hours suffering because they were unattainable, and even more hours suffering by accepting them with tenderness, since the man was my King of Creation; there was the hopeful threat of sin, I kept busy with fear while waiting; not to mention that I was permanently busy wanting and not wanting to be what I was, I couldn't decide which me, every me was impossible; having been born meant being full of mistakes to correct. No, it wasn't to annoy the teacher that I didn't study; all I had time for was growing up. Which I was doing all over, with an awkwardness that seemed more the result of a mathematical error: my legs didn't go with my eyes, and my mouth was emotional while my fidgety hands would get dirty — in my haste I was growing up without knowing in what direction. The fact that a picture from that time shows me, to the contrary, to be a well-grounded girl, wild and gentle, with thoughtful eyes beneath thick bangs, this real picture doesn't contradict me, all it does is reveal a ghostly stranger that I wouldn't understand even if I were her mother. Only much later, after having settled into my body and feeling fundamentally more assured, could I venture out and study a bit; previously, however, I couldn't risk learning, I didn't want to disrupt myself — I was intuitively careful with what I was, since I didn't know what I was, and I vainly cultivated the integrity of innocence. It's too bad the teacher never saw what I unexpectedly became four years later: at thirteen, my hands clean, freshly bathed, all nice and composed, he would have seen me standing there like a Christmas decoration on the balcony of a house. But, instead of him, it was an ex-classmate walking by who yelled my name, without realizing that I was no longer a kid on the street but a respectable young lady whose name could no longer be hollered over city sidewalks. "What is it?" I inquired of the interloper with utmost coldness. That's when I received the shouted news that the teacher had died that morning. And pale, eyes wide open, I had looked down at the dizzying street at my feet. My composure cracked like a broken doll's.

Going back four years again. Maybe it was because of everything I've mentioned, mixed up and all together, that I wrote the composition the teacher had assigned, the point at which this story unravels and others begin. Or it was just that I was in a hurry to finish the assignment however I could so I could go play in the park.

"I'm going to tell a story," he said, "and you're all going to write it down. But using your own words. When you're finished you don't have to wait for the bell, you can just go straight to recess."

The story he told: a very poor man dreamed he had found some treasure and became very rich; when he woke up, he readied his pack and set out in search of the treasure; he wandered all over the world, on and on without ever finding the treasure; worn out, he returned to his poor, poor little house; and since he had nothing to eat, he began to plant things in his poor yard; so much did he plant, so much did he harvest, so much did he begin to sell, that he ended up becoming very rich.

I listened with an air of contempt, conspicuously playing with my pen, as if wanting to make clear that I wasn't taken in by his stories and that I knew full well who he was. He told the story without once looking at me. It's because, in my awkward way of loving him and in the enjoyment I took in harassing him, I also hounded him with my gaze: I responded to everything he said with a simple, direct gaze, for which no one in their right mind could blame me. It was a gaze I made quite limpid and angelic, very open, like the gaze of purity upon crime. And I always provoked the same result: disturbed, he'd avoid my eyes, start stammering. Which filled me with a power that cursed me. And with compassion. Which in turn irritated me. It irritated me that he would force a lousy kid to understand a man.

It was almost ten in the morning, soon the recess bell would ring. That school of mine, which rented a building in a city park, had the biggest playground I had ever seen. It was as lovely for me as it would have been for a squirrel or a horse. It had scattered trees, extensive rolling hills and a sweeping lawn. It was endless. Everything there was big and spread out, made for a girl's long legs, with a place for piled-up bricks and wood of unknown origin, for bushes with sour begonias that we used to eat, for sun and shade where the bees made honey. It contained an immense open space. And we'd done it all: we had already rolled down every hill, whispered intensely behind every pile of bricks, tasted various flowers, and on every trunk we had carved the date, sweet ugly names and hearts pierced with arrows; boys and girls made their honey there.

I was nearing the end of my composition and the scent of those hidden shadows was already calling to me. I hurried. Since I knew only how "to use my own words," writing was simple. What also made me hurry was the desire to be the first to walk across the classroom—the teacher had ended up quarantining me at the last desk—and insolently turn in my composition, thereby demonstrating my quickness, a quality I felt to be essential for living and that, I was sure, the teacher couldn't help but admire.

I turned in my notebook and he took it without even looking at me. Feeling wronged, with no praise for my speed, I went skipping off to the big park.

The story that I'd transcribed in my own words was exactly like the one he had told. Only, around that time I was just beginning to "spell out the moral of the story," which, if it earned me reverence, would later threaten to stifle me with rigidity. With a certain flourish, then, I'd added the final sentences. Sentences that hours later I would keep reading and rereading to see what was so powerful about them that they had finally provoked the man in a way I myself hadn't yet managed. The thing the teacher had probably wished to imply in his sad story is that hard work was the only way to make a fortune. But flippantly I had ended with the opposite moral: something about the treasure that remains hidden, that lies where you least expect it, that all you have to do is find, I think I talked about dirty yards full of treasure. I don't remember anymore, I don't know if that was exactly it. I can't possibly imagine with what childish words I could have revealed a simple sentiment that becomes a complicated thought. I suppose that, by arbitrarily contradicting the story's real meaning, I was somehow already promising myself in writing that leisure, more than work, would grant me the great free rewards, the only kind to which I aspired. It may also be that even back then the theme of my life was already unreasonable hope, and that I'd already begun my great stubbornness: I'd give away everything that was mine for free, but I wanted everything to be given to me for free. Unlike the workingman in the story, in my composition I shrugged off all duties and emerged free and poor, and with a treasure in hand.

I went to recess, where I was left alone with the useless

prize of having been the first, scratching at the dirt, waiting impatiently for the kids who were gradually coming out of the classroom.

In the midst of our rowdy games I decided to go look in my desk for something I don't recall, to show the park caretaker, my friend and protector. Dripping with sweat, flushed with an irrepressible happiness that would have got me spanked at home—I flew toward the classroom, sprinted through it, and so carelessly that I didn't see the teacher leafing through the notebooks piled on his desk. Already holding the thing I had gone to get, and starting to race back out—only then did my gaze stumble on the man.

Alone at his post: he was looking at me.

It was the first time we'd come face to face, by ourselves. He was looking at me. My steps, meandering, almost halted.

For the very first time I was alone with him, without the whispered support of the class, without the admiration my daring provoked. I tried to smile, feeling the blood rise to my face. A bead of sweat ran down my forehead. He was looking at me. His gaze was a soft, heavy paw upon me. But though the paw was gentle, it completely paralyzed me like a cat unhurriedly pinning the mouse's tail. The bead of sweat went sliding down my nose and mouth, splitting my smile down the middle. That was it: with an expressionless gaze, he was looking at me. I started backing up against the wall, eyes lowered, all of me hanging onto my smile, the sole feature of a face that had already lost its shape. I'd never noticed how long the classroom was; only now, at the slow pace of fear, did I see its actual size. Not even my lack of time had let me notice up till then how austere and high the walls were; and hard, I could feel the hard wall on my palms. In a nightmare, in which smiling played a role,

I hardly believed I'd ever get anywhere near the door—from which point I'd run, oh how I'd run! to hide among my peers, the children. Besides concentrating on my smile, my meticulous zeal was bent on not making a sound with my feet, thus adhering to the intimate nature of a danger of which I knew nothing further. It was with a shudder that a sense of myself came to me as suddenly as in a mirror: a humid thing backed against the wall, slowly moving on tiptoe, and with a gradually intensifying smile. My smile had crystallized the room in silence, and even the noises coming from the park slid around outside the silence. I finally reached the door, and my imprudent heart started beating too loudly, at the risk of awakening the gigantic world that slept.

That's when I heard my name.

Suddenly nailed to the ground, mouth dry, there I stood with my back to him lacking the courage to turn around. The breeze coming in through the door had just dried the sweat on my body. I turned slowly, containing within my clenched fists the impulse to run.

At the sound of my name the room had been dehypnotized.

And very slowly I saw the whole entire teacher. Very slowly I saw that the teacher was very big and very ugly, and that he was the man of my life. The new and great fear. Small, sleepwalking, alone, facing the thing to which my inescapable freedom had finally led me. My smile, all that was left of a face, had also gone out. I was two leaden feet on the floor and a heart so empty that it seemed to be dying of thirst. There I stood, out of the man's reach. My heart was dying of thirst, yes. My heart was dying of thirst.

Calm as if about to kill in cold blood, he said:

"Come closer ..."

How is it that a man takes revenge?

The globe that I myself had thrown at him was about to come back and strike me in the face, one that, even still, I didn't recognize. I was about to be struck again by a reality that wouldn't have existed if I hadn't recklessly figured it out and thus given it life. To what extent was that man, that heap of compact sadness, also a heap of rage? But my past was now too late. A stoic repentance kept my head held high. For the first time, ignorance, which up to that point had been my greatest guide, abandoned me. My father was at work, my mother had died months before. I was the only I.

"… Take your notebook …," he added.

Surprise made me suddenly look at him. So that was it!? The unexpected relief was almost more shocking than my previous alarm. I stepped forward, reached out my hand while stammering.

But the teacher didn't move and didn't hand over the notebook.

To my sudden torment, without taking his eyes off me, he started slowly removing his glasses. And he looked at me with naked eyes that had so many lashes. I had never seen his eyes that, with their innumerable eyelashes, looked like two sweet cockroaches. He was looking at me. And I hadn't learned how to exist in front of a man. I hid it by looking at the ceiling, the ground, the walls, and kept my hand outstretched because I didn't know how to withdraw it. He was looking at me mildly, curiously, his eyes disheveled as if he had just awoken. Would he crush me with an unexpected hand? Or demand that I kneel and beg forgiveness. My sliver of hope was that he hadn't found out what I had done, just as I myself no longer knew, in fact I had never known.

"How did the idea of the treasure in disguise occur to you?"

"What treasure?" I murmured idiotically.

We went on staring at each other in silence.

"Oh, the treasure!" I blurted suddenly without even understanding, anxious to admit any fault whatsoever, begging him for my punishment to consist solely of suffering forever from guilt, for eternal torture to be my sentence, but never this unknown life.

"The treasure that's hidden where you least expect it. That all you have to do is find? Who told you that?"

The man's lost his mind, I thought, because what did the treasure have to do with any of this? Stunned, uncomprehending, and moving from one unexpected thing to the next, I still foresaw some less dangerous terrain. In all my racing around I'd learned to pick myself up after falling even when I was limping, and I quickly regained my composure: "It was my composition about the treasure! so that must have been my mistake!" Weak, and though treading carefully on this new and slippery reassurance, I had still picked myself up enough from my fall to be able to toss, in an imitation of my former arrogance, my future wavy hair:

"No one really ...," I answered trailing off. "I made it up myself," I said trembling, but already starting to sparkle again.

If I'd been relieved to have finally found something concrete to deal with, I was nevertheless starting to become aware of something much worse. His sudden lack of anger. I looked at him intrigued, out of the corner of my eyes. And gradually with extreme suspicion. His lack of anger had started to scare me, there were new threats I didn't understand. That gaze that never left me—and devoid of rage ... Bewildered, and in exchange for nothing, I had lost my enemy and sustenance. I looked at him in surprise. What did he want from me? He was embarrassing me. And his gaze devoid of anger had started to bother me more than the violence I'd been fearing. A small dread, all cold and sweaty, was overtaking me. Slowly, so he wouldn't notice, I backed up until I hit the wall, and then my head backed up until it had nowhere else to go. From the wall onto which I had completely mounted myself, I looked at him furtively.

And my stomach filled with a nauseous liquid. I can't explain it.

I was a very odd girl and, going pale, I saw it. Bristling, about to vomit, though to this day I don't know for sure what I saw. But I know I saw it. I saw deep as into a mouth, in a flash I saw the abyss of the world. What I saw was as anonymous as a belly opened up for an intestinal operation. I saw some thing forming on his face—the already petrified distress was fighting its way up to his skin, I saw the grimace slowly hesitating and bursting through a crust—but this thing that in mute catastrophe was being uprooted, this thing so little resembled a smile as if a liver or a foot were trying to smile, I don't know. Whatever I saw, I saw at such close range that I don't know what I saw. As if my curious eye were glued to the keyhole and in shock came upon another eye looking back at me from the other side. I saw inside an eye. Which was as incomprehensible as an eye. An eye opened up with its moving jelly. With its organic tears. An eye cries all by itself, an eye laughs all by itself. Until the man's effort reached a peak of full awareness, and in a childish victory he showed, a pearl plucked from his open belly—that he was smiling. I saw a man with entrails smiling. I could see his extreme worry about getting it wrong, the diligence of the slow student, the clumsiness as if he'd suddenly become left-handed. Without understanding, I knew I was being asked to accept this offering from him and his open belly, and to accept the weight of this man. My back was desperately pushing against the wall, I shrank away—it was too soon for me to see all that. It was too soon for me to see how life is born. Life being born was so much bloodier than dying. Dying is uninterrupted. But seeing inert material slowly trying to loom up like one of the living-dead ... Seeing hope terrified me, seeing life tied my stomach in knots. They were asking too much of my bravery simply because I was brave, they were asking for my strength simply because I was strong. "But what about me?" I shouted ten years later because of lost love, "who will ever see my weakness!" I looked at him in surprise, and never ever figured out what I saw, what I had seen could blind the curious.

Then he said, using for the first time the smile he had learned:

"Your composition about the treasure is so lovely. The treasure that you just have to discover. You ..." he didn't add anything for a moment. He scrutinized me gently, indiscreetly, as intimately as if he were my heart. "You're a very funny girl," he finally said.

It was the first real shame in my life. I lowered my eyes, unable to hold the defenseless gaze of that man I had wronged.

Yes, I got the impression that, despite his anger, he had somehow trusted me, and therefore I had wronged him with the fib about the treasure. Back then I thought everything made up was a lie, and only the tormented awareness of sinning redeemed me from this vice. I lowered my eyes in shame. I preferred his former rage, which had helped me in my struggle against myself, since it crowned my methods with failure and might end up setting me straight some day: what I didn't want was this gratitude that was not only my worst punishment, because I didn't deserve it, as much as it also encouraged my wayward life that I so feared, living waywardly attracted me. I very much wanted to tell him that treasure can't be found just anywhere. But, as I looked at him, I lost my nerve: I didn't have the courage to disillusion him. I was already used to protecting other people's joy, that of my father, for example, who was less wary than I. But how hard it was for me to swallow whole this joy I'd so irresponsibly caused! He seemed like a beggar thanking someone for a plate of food without noticing he'd been given rotten meat. The blood had risen to my face, so hot now that I thought my eyes were bloodshot, while he, probably mistaken again, must have thought his compliment had made me blush with pleasure. That same night all this would be transformed into an uncontrollable attack of vomiting that kept all the lights on in my house.

"You," he then repeated slowly as if gradually admitting in wonder something that had sprung to his lips by accident. "You're a very funny girl, you know? You're a silly little thing ..." he said putting on that smile again like a boy sleeping with his new shoes on. He didn't even know he was ugly when he smiled. Trusting, he let me see his ugliness, which was the most innocent part of him.

I had to swallow it as best I could, the way he offended me by believing in me, I had to swallow my compassion for him, my shame at myself, "fool!" I could have shouted at him, "I made up that whole story about the treasure in disguise, it's just stuff for little girls!" I was very aware of being a child, which explained all my serious flaws, and had put so much faith in growing up one day—and that big man had let himself be fooled by a naughty little girl. He was killing my faith in adults for the first time: he too, a man, believed, as I did, in big lies ...

… And suddenly, my heart beating with disappointment, I couldn't stand it a second longer—without taking my notebook I ran out to the park, hand over my mouth as if someone had smashed my teeth. Hand over my mouth, horrified, I went running, running to never ever stop, the profound prayer isn't the one that asks, the most profound prayer is the one that no longer asks—I went running, running in such fright.

In my impurity I'd placed my hope for redemption in adults. The need to believe in my future goodness made me venerate grown-ups, whom I had made in my own image, but in an image of myself purified at last by the penitence of growing up, liberated at last from the dirty soul of a little girl. And now the teacher was destroying all that, and destroying my love for him and for myself. My salvation would be impossible: that man was also me. My bitter idol who had unwittingly fallen into the lures of a mixed-up impure child, and who had meekly let himself be led by my diabolical innocence … Hand clamped over my mouth, I ran through the dust of the park.

When I finally realized that I was far out of the teacher's vicinity, I exhaustedly reined in my gallop, and nearly collapsing leaned all my weight against a tree trunk, breathing heavily, breathing. There I stood panting and with my eyes shut, tasting the trunk's dusty bitterness, my fingers running over and over the rough carving of a heart with an arrow. And suddenly, squeezing my eyes further shut, I moaned while understanding a bit more: could he mean that … that I was a treasure in disguise? The treasure where you least expect it … Oh no, no, poor little thing, poor thing that King of Creation, that was why he had needed … what? what had he needed? … to have transformed even me into a treasure.

I still had a lot more running inside me, I forced my dry

throat to catch its breath, and angrily shoving the tree trunk I started running again toward the end of the world.

But I still hadn't spotted the shadowy end of the park, and my steps grew sluggish, excessively tired. I couldn't go any further. Maybe it was fatigue, but I was giving in. My steps were slowing down and the foliage of the trees was slowly swaying. My steps were a bit dazzled. Hesitantly I came to a halt, the trees swirling high above. For an entirely strange sweetness was wearing out my heart. Intimidated, I hesitated. I was alone in the grass, barely standing, with nothing to lean on, hand on my weary chest like a virgin annunciate. And from fatigue of that first gentleness a finally humble head that from a distance may have resembled a woman's. The grove swayed back, and forth. "You're a very funny girl, you're a silly little thing," he'd said. It was like a love.

No, I wasn't funny. Without even realizing it, I was very serious. No, I wasn't a silly little thing, reality was my destiny, and that was the thing in me that pained others. And, for God's sake, I wasn't a treasure. But if I had already discovered in myself all the eager venom that we're born with and that gnaws away at life—only in that instant of honey and flowers was I discovering how I healed others: whoever loved me, that was how I would cure whoever was pained for my sake. I was dark ignorance with its hungers and laughter, with its little deaths feeding my inevitable life—how could I help it? I already knew that I was inevitable. But if I was good for nothing, at that moment I was all that man had. He would have to love at least once, not loving a person—through a person. And I alone had been there. Though this was his sole advantage: having no one but me, and forced to start off by loving something evil, he had begun by doing something few ever managed. It would be too easy to desire something clean; ugliness was what was unattainable through love, loving the impure was our deepest nostalgia. Through me, someone hard to love, he had received, with great compassion for himself, the thing of which we are made. Did I understand all this? No. And I don't know what I understood back then. But it was as if I'd seen for an instant in the teacher, with terrified fascination, the world—and even now I still don't know what I saw, only that forevermore and in a single second I saw—just like that I had understood us, and I'll never know what I understood. I'll never know what I understand. Whatever I understood in the park was, with a shock of sweetness, understood through my ignorance. Ignorance that while standing there—in a painless solitude, no less than what the trees felt—I was completely recovering, ignorance and its incomprehensible truth. There I was, the too-clever girl, and it turned out that everything worthless in me was worth something to God and men. Everything worthless in me was my treasure.

Like a virgin annunciate, yes. For him to let me make him smile at least, with that he had announced me. He had just transformed me into something more than the King of Creation: he had made me the wife of the King of Creation. Because it had fallen to me of all people, with all my claws and dreams, to pluck the barbed arrow from his heart. In a flash it became clear why I'd been born with rough hands, and why I'd been born without recoiling when faced with pain. Why do you have those long nails? To wrest you from death and pluck out your deadly thorns, answers the wolf of man. Why do you have that cruel, hungering mouth? To bite you and blow so I don't hurt you too much, my love, since I must hurt you, I am the inevitable wolf because life was given me. Why do you have those hands that sting and clutch? So we can hold hands, for I need it so much, so much, so much—howled the wolves, and they looked fearfully at their own claws before snuggling atop each other to love and fall asleep.

... And that was how in the big park of the school I slowly started learning how to be loved, bearing the sacrifice of not deserving it, just to soothe the pain of one who doesn't love. No, that was only one reason. Since the others lead to other stories. In some of them it was from my heart that other claws full of hard love plucked the barbed arrow, and without recoiling from my scream.

The Sharing of Loaves
("A repartição dos pães")

IT WAS SATURDAY AND WE HAD BEEN INVITED TO THE
obligatory luncheon. But we all liked Saturday too much to
waste it on people we didn't want to be with. We'd all been
happy once and marked by desire. Me, I wanted everything.
And there we were, trapped, as if our train had derailed and
we were forced to spend the night with strangers. No one there
wanted me, I wanted no one. As for my Saturday—swaying
outside the window in acacias and shadows—I preferred, instead of squandering it, to grasp it in my tight fist, where I
crumpled it like a handkerchief. While waiting for lunch, we
drank without pleasure, to the health of resentment: tomorrow would already be Sunday. I don't want to spend it with
you, said our arid stares, and we slowly exhaled the smoke
from our dry cigarettes. Our greediness not to have to share
Saturday was progressively gnawing at us and closing in like
rust, until any joy whatsoever would have been an insult to
greater joy.

The hostess was the only one who didn't seem to be saving
up her Saturday to use on a Thursday night. She, nonetheless,
whose heart had already known other Saturdays. How had she

forgotten that people desire more and more? She wasn't even the least impatient with this disparate, dreamy bunch, who were resigned to the fact that all there was to do at her house was wait, as for the departure of the first train, any train—anything except staying in that empty station, except having to rein in the horse that would run, its heart pounding, toward others, other horses.

We finally went into the living room for a lunch that lacked the blessing of hunger. And that was when in surprise we happened upon the table. It couldn't possibly be for us ...

It was a table laid for men of good will. Who could be the actual expected guests who hadn't come? But it really was for us. So that woman gave away her best to just anyone? And contentedly washed the feet of the first stranger. Embarrassed, we stared.

The table had been spread with a solemn abundance. Piled on the white tablecloth were stalks of wheat. And red apples, enormous yellow carrots, plump tomatoes nearly bursting their skin, watery-green chayote, pineapples malignant in their savagery, calm and orangey oranges, gherkins spiky like porcupines, cucumbers wrapped taut round their watery flesh, hollow red peppers that stung our eyes—all entangled with strands and strands of corn silk, reddish as near a mouth. And all those grapes. They were the deepest shade of purple grape and could hardly wait for the moment they'd be crushed. And they didn't care who crushed them. The tomatoes were plump to please no one: for the air, for the plump air. Saturday was for whoever showed up. And the orange would sweeten the tongue of whoever arrived first. Alongside the plate of every undeserving guest, the woman who washed the feet of strangers had placed—without even singling us out, without even loving us—a stalk of wheat or a bunch of spicy radishes or a red slice of watermelon with its cheerful seeds. All cut through with the Spanish tartness the limes suggested. In the jugs was milk, as if it had crossed the desert bluffs with the goats. Wine, nearly black from being so thoroughly pressed, trembled in earthen vessels. Everything before us. Everything unsullied by twisted human desire. Everything the way it is, not the way we wanted it. Simply existing, and whole. Just like a field exists. Just like the mountains. Just like men and women, and not us, the greedy ones. Just like a Saturday. Just as it simply exists. It exists.

In the name of nothing, it was time to eat. In the name of no one, it was good. Without any dreams. And we were slowly rising to the day, slowly becoming anonymous, growing, adults, to the level of possible life. Then, like rustic noblemen, we accepted the food.

There was no holocaust: it all wanted to be eaten as badly as we wanted to eat it. Saving nothing for the next day, there and then I made an offering of what I was feeling to what was making me feel. It was a way of living that I hadn't paid in advance with the suffering of waiting, a hunger born when the mouth is already nearing the food. Because now we were hungry, a complete hunger that encompassed everything down to the crumbs. Whoever was drinking wine, kept an eye on the milk. Whoever slowly drank the milk, tasted the wine someone else was drinking. Outside, God in the acacias. Which existed. We kept eating. As if watering a horse. The carved meat was doled out. The geniality was crude and rural. No one spoke ill of anyone because no one spoke well of anyone. It was a harvest gathering, and there was a truce. We kept eating. Like a horde of living beings, we gradually covered the earth.

Busy like people who plow for their existence, and plant, and harvest, and kill, and live, and die, and eat. I ate with the honesty of someone who doesn't betray the things he eats: I ate that food and not its name. Never was God so taken by what He is. The food was saying crudely, happily, austerely: eat, eat and share. All that belonged to me, it was my father's table. I ate without tenderness, I ate without the passion of piety. And without offering myself to hope. I ate without longing. And I really did deserve that food. Because I cannot always be my brother's keeper, and I cannot be my own any longer, oh I don't want myself any longer. And I don't want to shape life since existence already exists. It exists like some ground over which we all advance. Without a word of love. Without a word. But your pleasure understands mine. We are strong and we eat. Bread is love among strangers.

The Message
("A mensagem")

AT FIRST, WHEN THE GIRL SAID SHE FELT ANGUISH, the boy was so surprised that he blushed and quickly changed the subject to disguise the quickening of his heart.

Yet for a long time now—since he was young—he had boldly outgrown the childish oversimplification of discussing events in terms of "coincidence." Or rather—having *evolved* substantially and no longer believing in them—he considered the expression "coincidence" just another play on words and yet another ruse.

Thus, excitedly swallowing the involuntary joy that the truly shocking coincidence that she too felt anguish had provoked in him—he found himself talking to her about his own anguish, and with a girl of all people! he who from a woman's heart had only ever received a mother's kiss.

He found himself talking to her, harshly concealing the wonder of finally being able to talk about things that really mattered; and with a girl of all people! They also discussed books, barely able to conceal their urgency to catch up on everything they had never talked about before. Even so, certain words were never exchanged between them. In this case not because the term was yet another trap *the others* set to fool young people. But from embarrassment. Because he wouldn't have the nerve to say everything, though she, because she felt anguish, was trustworthy. He'd never even mention a *mission*, though this most perfect term, which he in a manner of speaking had created, burned in his mouth, anxious to be uttered.

Naturally, the fact that she too suffered had simplified the way you were supposed to treat a girl, because it granted her a masculine quality. He started treating her like a buddy.

She herself also started flaunting her own anguish with a haloed modesty, like a new sex. Being hybrids—not yet settling on an individual way of walking, and not yet possessing a defined handwriting, copying the lesson's main points in a different hand each day—being hybrids they sought each other out, barely concealing their seriousness. Every once in a while, he still felt that incredulous acceptance of the coincidence: that he, such an original, had found someone who spoke his language! Over time they came to an agreement. All she had to do was say, like a code word, "I had a terrible afternoon yesterday," for him to know austerely that she suffered the same way he did. There was sadness, pride and daring between them.

Until even the word anguish started to wither, showing how spoken language lied. (They hoped to write some day.) The word anguish started acquiring that tone *the others* used, and eventually became a source of slight hostility between them. Whenever he was suffering, he would consider it a faux pas for her to speak of anguish. "I'm already *over* that word," he was always *over* everything before she was, only afterward did the girl ever catch up to him.

And she eventually got tired of being the sole anguished woman in his eyes. Though it gave her an intellectual quality, she was also wary of that kind of misjudgment. Since they both wanted, more than anything, to be *authentic*. She, for example, didn't want any mistakes even if they were in her favor, she wanted the *truth*, bad as it might be. Anyhow, sometimes it was all the better if it were "bad as it might be." Above all the girl had already started taking no pleasure in being awarded the title of man whenever she showed the slightest hint ... of being a person. While this flattered her, it offended her a bit: it was as if he were surprised that she was competent, precisely because he didn't think she was. Still, if they weren't careful, the fact that she was a woman could suddenly come up. They were careful.

Yet, naturally, there was confusion, no possibility of explaining, and that meant time was passing. Entire months.

And though the hostility between them grew progressively more intense, like hands that come close but never clasp, they couldn't help seeking each other out. And that was because— if in the mouths of *the others* being called "young" was an insult—between them "being young" was their mutual secret, and their same irremediable curse. They couldn't help seeking each other out because, despite their hostility—with the repulsion that members of the opposite sex feel when they don't desire one another—, despite their hostility, they believed in one another's sincerity, *versus* everyone else's big lie. Neither offended heart forgave everyone else's lies. They were sincere. And, not being petty, they overlooked the fact that they were good at lying—as if the main thing was solely the sincerity of the imagination. So they kept seeking each other out, vaguely proud of being different from *the others*, so different that they weren't even in love. Those *others* who did nothing but live. Vaguely aware that something rang false in their relationship. Like homosexuals of the opposite sex, and with no possibility of uniting, as one, their separate misfortunes. All they agreed on was the sole point that united them: the error in the world and their tacit certainty that if they didn't save it they'd be traitors. As for love, they weren't in love, of course. She'd even told him about her recent crush on a teacher. He'd even managed to tell her—since she was like a man to him—, he'd even managed to tell her, with a coldness that unexpectedly shattered into a horrible pounding of his heart, that a guy has to take care of "certain problems," if he wants his head clear in order to think. He was sixteen, and she, seventeen. That he, with severity, occasionally took care of certain problems, was something not even his father knew.

The thing is, once they'd found the secret part of themselves in each other, the temptation and the hope arrived, of one day reaching the greatest. The greatest what?

What, after all, did they want? They didn't know, and were using each other like people clinging to smaller rocks until all by themselves they can scale a big one, the difficult and impossible one; they were using each other to rehearse for the initiation; they were using each other impatiently, practicing the beating of their wings until they finally—each alone and freed—could take wing in that great solitary flight that also meant farewell to each other. Was that it? They needed each other temporarily, each annoyed at the other for being clumsy, each blaming the other for not being experienced. They failed at every encounter, as if disillusioned in bed. What, after all, did they want? They wanted to learn. Learn what? they were an incompetent pair. Oh, they couldn't say they were unhappy without feeling ashamed, because they knew there were people who were starving; they'd eat with appetite and shame. Unhappy? How? if in fact they were touching, for no reason, some extreme of happiness as if the world were shaken and a thousand fruits fell from that immense tree. Unhappy? if they were bodies coursing with blood like flowers in the sun. How? if they were forever propped on their own weak legs, tumultuous, free, miraculously standing, her legs shaven, his indeterminate but ending in size 44 shoes. How could beings like this ever be unhappy?

They were very unhappy. Weary, expectant, they sought each other out, forcing a continuation of the initial and casual comprehension that was never repeated—and without even loving one another. The ideal was suffocating them, time was uselessly passing, urgency was calling them—they didn't know where they were going, and the path was calling them. Each was asking a lot of the other, but both had the same neediness, and neither would ever have sought an older partner to teach them, because they weren't crazy enough to surrender for no good reason to the ready-made world.

One possible way they might still have saved themselves would be the thing they never would have called *poetry*. In fact, what was poetry anyway, that embarrassing word? Could it be meeting when, by coincidence, a sudden rain fell over the city? Or perhaps, while having sodas together, they both looked simultaneously at a passing woman's face? or even running into each other on that old night of moon and wind? But they'd both already been born by the time the word poetry was being published with the greatest shamelessness in the Sunday paper. Poetry was the word older people used. And their wariness was enormous, like that of animals. Whom instinct alerts: that one day they will be hunted. They had been fooled far too many times to start believing now. And, hunting them would have required utmost caution, lots of tracking and fast-talking, and an even more cautious tenderness—tenderness that wouldn't offend them—in order to, catching them off guard, capture them in the net. And, more cautiously still to avoid tipping them off, leading them slyly into the world of addicts, into the ready-made world; since that was the role of adults and spies. From having been tricked for so long, prideful from their own bitterness, they felt an aversion to words, especially when a word—like poetry—was so clever that it almost expressed something, and only then really showed how little it expressed. They both felt, in fact, an aversion to most words, which hardly facilitated communication, since they still hadn't invented better words: they were constantly at odds, stubborn rivals. Poetry? Oh, how they detested it. As if it were sex. They also thought *the others* wanted to hunt them not for sex, but for *normality*. They were fearful, scientific, exhausted by experience. As for the word experience, yes, they'd talk about it without shame and without explaining it: indeed the term was always changing its meaning. *Experience* also sometimes got mixed up with *message*. They used both words without deepening their meaning much.

Anyhow, they weren't deepening anything, as if there weren't time, as if there were too many things to discuss. Without realizing that they didn't have a single idea to discuss.

Well, it wasn't just that, and it wasn't that simple. It wasn't just that: meanwhile time was passing, mixed up, vast, fragmented, and at the heart of time there was a shock and that hatred toward the world that no one could convince them was desperate love and compassion, and they had the skeptical wisdom of the ancient Chinese, a wisdom that could suddenly break down exposing two faces that got upset because they couldn't sit naturally in an ice cream parlor: then everything would break apart, suddenly revealing two imposters. Time was passing, not a single thing was discussed, and never, never did they understand each other as perfectly as that first time when she'd said she felt *anguish* and, miraculously, he'd said he felt it too, and that horrible pact had been formed. And never, never did anything happen to finish off at last the blindness with which they were reaching out their hands and that would ready them for the destiny that impatiently awaited them, and made them finally bid farewell forever.

Perhaps they were as ready to break free of each other as a drop of water about to fall, and were just waiting for something symbolizing the fullness of *anguish* in order to go their separate ways. Perhaps, ripe as a drop of water, they had sparked the event of which I am about to tell.

The vague event surrounding the old house only came into existence because they were ready for it. It was just an old, empty house. But they had a life that was poor and anxious as if they would never grow old, as if nothing would ever happen to them — and so the house became an event. They'd come from the last class of the year. They had taken the bus, gotten off, and started walking. As always, their pace was somewhere between fast and separate, then suddenly slowing down, never falling into step, uneasy with each other's presence. It was an *awful* day for both, right before summer vacation. The last class left them with no future and nothing tying them down, each contemptuous of what their families had in store for them at home in terms of future and love and incomprehension. With no next day and nothing tying them down, they were worse off than ever, mute, eyes wide open.

That afternoon the girl's teeth were clenched, she was glaring at everything with resentment or ardor, as if seeking in the wind, in the dust and in her own extreme poverty of spirit something else to provoke her rage.

And the boy, on that street whose name they didn't even

know, the boy bore little resemblance to the Man of Creation. The day was pale, and the little boy even paler still, involuntarily boyish, windblown, forced to live. Nevertheless he was mild and indeterminate, as if any pain whatsoever would only make him more boyish, unlike her, who was feeling aggressive. Unformed as they were, anything was possible for them, their qualities were even sometimes interchangeable: she became mannish, and he possessed the almost lowly sweetness of a woman. Several times he almost took his leave, but, vague and empty as he was, he didn't know what to do once he got home, as if the end of school had severed his last link. So he walked on, mute, behind her, following with a meek helplessness. Only a seventh sense of minimal listening to the world kept him going, connecting him in obscure promise to the next day. No, they weren't exactly neurotic and—despite what they vindictively thought about each other in moments of barely contained hostility—it doesn't seem that psychoanalysis would have fixed them completely. Or maybe it would.

It was one of those streets that let out onto the São João Batista cemetery, with its dry dust, loose stones and black men lingering in the doorways of corner bars.

They walked down a potholed sidewalk so narrow they could hardly fit. She made a movement—he thought she was going to cross the street and took a step to follow her—she turned around without knowing which side he was on—he hung back seeking her. In that sliver of a second in which they worriedly looked for each other, they simultaneously turned their backs to the buses—and stood facing the house, their searching still on their faces.

Perhaps everything happened because their searching stayed on their faces. Or perhaps from the fact that the house was right on the sidewalk and stood so "close." They hardly had room to look at it, crowded as they were on the narrow sidewalk, caught between the threatening movement of the buses and the absolutely serene stillness of the house. No, it wasn't that it had been bombarded: but it was a broken house, as a child would say. It was big, wide and tall like the multi-storied houses of old Rio. A big rooted house.

With an inquiry much greater than the question on their faces, they had recklessly turned around at the same time, and the house stood as close as if, coming out of nowhere, a sudden wall had risen before their eyes. Behind them the buses, before them the house—there was no way for them not to be there. If they backed away they'd be hit by the buses, if they stepped forward they'd hit the monstrous house. They'd been captured.

The house was tall, and close, they couldn't look at it without having to tilt their heads up childishly, which suddenly made them very small and transformed the house into a mansion. It was as if nothing had ever been so close to them. The house must have had a color. And whatever the original color of the window frames had been, they were now merely old and solid. Shrunken, they widened their eyes in astonishment: the house was *anguished.*

The house was anguish and calm. As no word had ever been. It was a building that weighed on the chests of the two kids. A two-storied house like someone raising a hand to his throat. Who? who had built it, erecting that ugliness stone by stone, that cathedral of solidified fear?! Or had it been time that embedded itself in single walls and given them that strangled look, the silence of a tranquil hanged corpse? The house was strong as a boxer dog without a neck. And having your head directly connected to your shoulders was anguish. They looked at the house like children facing a stairway.

At last both had unexpectedly reached the goal and stood before the sphinx. Openmouthed, in the extreme union of fear and respect and pallor, before that truth. Naked anguish had leaped up and stood facing them—not even familiar like the word they'd grown accustomed to using. Just a thick, crude house with no neck, just that ancient power.

I am the thing itself you were seeking at last, the big house said.

And the funniest thing is that I don't have any secrets at all, the big house also said.

The girl looked on sleepily. As for the boy, his seventh sense snagged on the building's innermost part and he felt the slightest tug of a response at the end of the line. He barely moved, fearful of frightening off his own watchfulness. The girl had become anchored in her alarm, afraid to emerge from it into the terror of a discovery. At their slightest word, the house would collapse. Their silence left the old house intact. Yet, if at first they were forced to look at it, now, even if someone informed them that they were free to escape, they would have stayed there, trapped by fascination and horror. Staring at that thing erected so long before they were born, that ages-old thing that was already bereft of meaning, that thing from the past. But what about the future?! Oh God, give us our future! The eyeless house, with the power of a blind man. And if it had eyes, they were the empty, round eyes of a statue. Dear God, don't let us be the children of this empty past, deliver us unto the future. They wanted to be someone's children. But not of this hardened, inevitable carcass, they didn't understand the past: oh deliver us from the past, let us fulfill our difficult duty. For freedom wasn't what the two children wanted, they really wanted to be persuaded and subjugated and led—but it would have to be by something more powerful than the great power that was pounding in their chests.

The young lady suddenly averted her face, I'm so unhappy, I've always been so unhappy, school's over, everything's over!—because in her eagerness she was ungrateful for a childhood that had probably been happy. The girl suddenly averted her face with a kind of grunt.

As for the boy, he quickly lost his footing in the vagueness as if mired without a thought. That was also because of the afternoon light: it was a livid light unmarked by the hour of day. The boy's face was greenish and calm, and now he was getting no help whatsoever from the words of *the others*: just as he had rashly hoped he would one day manage. Only, he hadn't counted on the misery there was in being unable to express.

Green and nauseated, they didn't know how to express. The house symbolized some thing they could never attain, even after a lifetime spent seeking expression. Seeking expression, be it for an entire life, would be an amusement in itself, bitter and bewildered, but an amusement, and it would be a diversion that would gradually distance them from the dangerous truth—and save them. They, of all people, who, in their desperate cunning to survive, had already invented a future for themselves: both would be writers, and with a determination as obstinate as if expressing a soul would stifle it once and for all. And if it weren't stifled, that would be a way of merely knowing that you were lying in the solitude of your own heart.

Whereas the house from the past wasn't something they could play around with. Now, so much smaller than it, they felt they'd only been playing at being youthful and suffering and sharing the *message*. Now, alarmed, they finally had what they'd been dangerously and imprudently asking for: they were two youths who really were lost. As their elders would say: "They were getting what they deserved." And they were as guilty as guilty children, as guilty as criminals are innocent. Ah, if only they could yet pacify the world they'd exacerbated, reassuring it: "we were just kidding! we're impostors!" But it was too late. "Surrender unconditionally and make yourself a part of me for I am the past"—their future life told them. And, for God's sake, in whose name could anyone insist on hoping that the future belonged to them? who?! but who cared to dispel the mystery for them, and without lying? was there anyone working to that end? This time, struck mute as they were, it wouldn't even occur to them to blame society.

The young lady had suddenly turned her face away with a grunt, some kind of sob or cough.

"Just like a woman to start crying at a time like this," he thought from the depths of his perdition, not knowing what he meant by "a time like this." But this was the first solid thing he'd found for himself. Grabbing this first plank, he could bob up to the surface, and as always before the girl. He recovered first, and saw a house standing there with a "For Rent" sign. He heard the bus behind him, saw an empty house, and beside him the girl with a pained face, trying to hide it from the now-awakened man: she for some reason was trying to hide her face.

Still hesitant, he waited politely for her to regain her composure. He waited hesitantly, yes, but a man. Skinny and irreparably boyish, yes, but a man. A man's body was that solid thing that always let him bounce back. Every so often, whenever he really needed to, he became a man. Then, with an unsure hand, he stiffly lit a cigarette, as if he were *the others*, rescuing himself with the gestures the Masonic brotherhood of men had given him as a crutch and a direction. And as for her?

But the girl emerged from all this smeared with lipstick,

her rouge a little smudged, and adorned with a blue necklace. Plumage that a moment before had belonged to a situation and a future, but now it was as if she hadn't washed her face before going to bed and had woken up with the indecent traces of a previous orgy. For she, every so often, was a woman.

With a comforting cynicism, the boy looked at her curiously. And saw that she was no more than a girl.

"I'm just going to stay here," he told her then, taking his leave haughtily, he who no longer even had to be home by a certain time and was feeling the house key in his pocket.

While saying goodbye, they, who never shook hands because it would be conventional, shook hands, for she, flustered at her bad timing in having breasts and a necklace, she had awkwardly reached hers out. The contact between the two clammy hands groping each other without love embarrassed the boy like a shameful operation, he blushed. And she, wearing lipstick and rouge, tried to disguise her own embellished nakedness. She was nothing, and walked away as if a thousand eyes were following her, flighty in her humility at having a condition that could be labeled.

Seeing her walk away, he examined her incredulously, with amused interest: "could a woman really know what anguish is?" And his doubt made him feel very strong. "No, women were good for something else, that you couldn't deny." And what he needed was a male friend. Yes, a loyal male friend. He then felt clean and candid, with nothing to hide, loyal like a man. From any tremor of the earth, he'd emerge with a free forward movement, with the same proud negligence that makes a horse neigh. Whereas she left with her back to the wall like an intruder, nearly a mother already to the children she'd some day have, her body anticipating its submission, sacred and impure body about to bear. The boy looked at her, amazed at having been tricked by the girl for so long, and almost smiled, almost beat the wings he had just grown. I am a man, his sex told him in obscure victory. From every struggle or rest, he'd emerge still more of a man, being a man was even nourished by that wind that was now dragging dust down the lanes of the São João Batista cemetery. The same dusty wind that made that other being, the female, curl up wounded, as if no covering would ever protect her nakedness, that wind in the streets.

The boy saw her walk away, following her with pornographic and curious eyes that didn't spare a single humble detail of the girl. The girl who suddenly broke into a desperate run so as not to miss the bus ...

Alarmed, fascinated, the boy saw her running like a madwoman so as not to miss the bus, intrigued he saw her climbing onto the bus like a monkey in a short skirt. The fake cigarette fell from his hand ...

Something uncomfortable had thrown him off balance. What was it? A moment of great wariness was coming over him. But what was it?! Urgently, disturbingly: what was it? He'd seen her run so nimbly even if the girl's heart, he easily guessed, were faint. And he'd seen her, all full of powerless love for humanity, climb like a monkey onto the bus—and then saw her sit quiet and polite, fixing her blouse as she waited for the bus to leave ... Could that be it? But what about that could fill him with mistrustful wariness? Maybe the fact that she started running for no reason, since the bus wasn't leaving, so there was time ... She didn't even need to run ... But what about all that made him prick up his ears in anguished listening, in the deafness of someone who will never hear the explanation?

He had just been born a man. But, as soon as he owned up

271

to his birthright, he was also owning up to that weight on his chest; as soon as he owned up to his glory, a fathomless experience was giving him his first future wrinkle. Ignorant, uneasy, as soon as he owned up to his masculinity, a new eager hunger was arising, an aching thing like a man who never cries. Could he be experiencing his first fear that something was impossible? The girl was a zero on that waiting bus, and yet, man that he now was, the boy suddenly needed to lean on that nothing, on that girl. And not even to lean on her on equal terms, not even to lean on her in order to concede … But, stuck in his manly kingdom, he needed her. For what? so he could remember some stipulation? so that she or some other woman wouldn't let him go too far and get lost? so that he might feel with a jolt, as he was feeling now, that there was the possibility of error? He needed her hungrily so he wouldn't forget that they were made of the same flesh, that poor flesh from which, by climbing onto the bus like a monkey, she seemed to have made a fateful path. What! but what after all is happening to me? he thought fearfully.

Nothing. Nothing, and you shouldn't make too much of it, it was just an instant of weakness and hesitation, that's all, there wasn't any danger.

Just an instant of weakness and hesitation. But within that system of hard last judgment, which doesn't allow even a second of disbelief or else the ideal collapses, he stared in a daze at the long street—and now everything was ruined and dried up as if his mouth were full of dust. Now and finally alone, he was defenseless and at the mercy of the hasty lie with which *the others* were trying to teach him to be a man. But what about the message?! the message had crumbled in the dust that the wind was dragging toward the gutter. Mama, he said.

Monkeys
("Macacos")

THAT FIRST TIME WE HAD A MARMOSET IN THE HOUSE
was around New Year's. We had no running water and no maid,
people were lining up to buy meat, the summer heat had exploded—and that was when, silent with bewilderment, I saw
the present come into the house, already eating a banana, already examining everything with great speed and a long tail.
He seemed more like a big monkey not yet fully grown, he had
tremendous potential. He'd climb the laundry hanging on the
clothes line, from where he'd holler like a sailor, and toss banana peels wherever they fell. And I was exhausted. Whenever
I'd forget and wander absentmindedly into the laundry room,
the big shock: that cheerful man was there. My youngest son
knew, before I did, that I would get rid of that gorilla: "And what
if I promise that one day the monkey's going to get sick and
die, will you let him stay? and what if you knew that sooner or
later he'll fall out the window anyway and die down there?" My
feelings made me avert my gaze. The little-big monkey's happy
and filthy lack of awareness made me responsible for his destiny, since he himself wouldn't take the blame. A girlfriend understood of what bitterness my acquiescence was made, what

crimes fed into my dreamy manner, and crudely saved me: some boys from the favela showed up in a happy commotion, took away the laughing man, and for the lackluster New Year I at least got a monkey-free house.

A year later, I'd just been feeling a surge of joy, when right there in Copacabana I spotted the crowd. A man was selling little monkeys. I thought of the boys, of the joys they gave me for free, unrelated to the worries they also gave me for free, I imagined a circle of joy: "Whoever gets this must pass it on," and on and on, like a chain reaction running up a trail of gunpowder. And right on the spot I bought the one whose name would be Lisette.

She nearly fit in my hand. She was wearing the skirt, earrings, necklace and bracelet of a Bahian woman. And she had the air of an immigrant who lands still dressed in her country's traditional clothing. There was also an immigrant quality in her wide eyes.

As for this one, she was a miniature woman. She spent three days with us. She was so delicately built. And so incredibly sweet. More than just her eyes, her gaze was wide. At every movement, her earrings would tremble; her skirt was always neat, her red necklace shiny. She slept a lot, but was sober and tired when it came to eating. Her rare caresses were just light bites that left no mark.

On the third day we were in the laundry room admiring Lisette and the way she was ours. "A little too gentle," I thought, missing my gorilla. And suddenly my heart replied very sternly: "But that's not sweetness. It's death." The harshness of the message left me speechless. Then I told the boys: "Lisette is dying." Looking at her, I then realized how far our love had gone. I rolled up Lisette in a napkin, went with the boys to the nearest emergency room, where the doctor couldn't see us because he was performing an urgent procedure on a dog. Another taxi—Lisette thinks we're on an outing, Mama—another hospital. There they gave her oxygen.

And with that breath of life, a Lisette we didn't know was suddenly revealed. Her eyes were much less wide, more secretive, more laughing, and her protruding and ordinary face had a certain ironic superiority; a little more oxygen, and she felt like saying that she could hardly stand being a monkey; she was indeed, and had a lot to say. Soon, however, she succumbed once more, exhausted. More oxygen and this time a serum injection to whose prick she reacted with an angry little swipe, her bracelet tinkling. The nurse smiled: "Lisette, dear, calm down!"

The diagnosis: she wasn't going to make it, unless she had oxygen nearby and, even then, it was unlikely. "Don't buy monkeys on the street," he scolded me shaking his head, "sometimes they're already sick." No, you had to buy a good monkey, to know where it came from, for at least five years of guaranteed love, you had to know what it had or hadn't done, as if you were getting married. I talked it over with the boys for a moment. Then I said to the nurse: "Sir, you've taken quite a liking to Lisette. So if you let her spend a couple days near the oxygen, and she gets better, she's yours." But he thought about it. "Lisette is pretty!" I implored. "She's beautiful," he agreed, thoughtful. Then he sighed and said: "If I cure Lisette, she's yours." We left, with an empty napkin.

The next day they called, and I told the boys that Lisette had died. My youngest asked me: "Do you think she died wearing her earrings?" I said yes. A week later my eldest said to me: "You look so much like Lisette!" "I like you too," I replied.

The Egg and the Chicken
("O ovo e a galinha")

IN THE MORNING IN THE KITCHEN ON THE TABLE I SEE
the egg.

I look at the egg with a single gaze. Immediately I perceive
that one cannot be seeing an egg. Seeing an egg never remains
in the present: as soon as I see an egg it already becomes having seen an egg three millennia ago. —At the very instant of
seeing the egg it is the memory of an egg. —The egg can only
be seen by one who has already seen it. —When one sees the
egg it is too late: an egg seen is an egg lost. —Seeing the egg
is the promise of one day eventually seeing the egg. —A brief
and indivisible glance; if indeed there is thought; there is none;
there is the egg. —Looking is the necessary instrument that,
once used, I shall discard. I shall keep the egg. —The egg has
no itself. Individually it does not exist.

Seeing the egg is impossible: the egg is supervisible just as
there are supersonic sounds. No one can see the egg. Does the
dog see the egg? Only machines see the egg. The construction
crane sees the egg. —When I was ancient an egg landed on my
shoulder. —Love for the egg cannot be felt either. Love for the
egg is supersensible. We do not know that we love the egg. —

When I was ancient I was keeper of the egg and I would tread lightly to avoid upending the egg's silence. When I died, they removed the egg from me with care. It was still alive. —Only one who saw the world would see the egg. Like the world, the egg is obvious.

The egg no longer exists. Like the light of an already-dead star, the egg properly speaking no longer exists. —You are perfect, egg. You are white. —To you I dedicate the beginning. To you I dedicate the first time.

To the egg I dedicate the Chinese nation.

The egg is a suspended thing. It has never landed. When it lands, it is not what has landed. It was a thing under the egg. —I look at the egg in the kitchen with superficial attention so as not to break it. I take the utmost care not to understand it. Since it is impossible to understand, I know that if I understand it this is because I am making an error. Understanding is the proof of making an error. Understanding it is not the way to see it. —Never thinking about the egg is a way to have seen it. —I wonder, do I know of the egg? I almost certainly do. Thus: I exist, therefore I know. —What I don't know about the egg is what really matters. What I don't know about the egg gives me the egg properly speaking. —The Moon is inhabited by eggs.

The egg is an exteriorization. To have a shell is to surrender. —The egg denudes the kitchen. It turns the table into a slanted plane. The egg exposes. —Whoever plunges deeper into an egg, whoever sees more than the surface of the egg, is after something else: that person is hungry.

An egg is the soul of the chicken. The awkward chicken. The sure egg. The frightened chicken. The sure egg. Like a paused projectile. For an egg is an egg in space. An egg upon blue. —I love you, egg. I love you as a thing doesn't even know it loves another thing. —I do not touch it. The aura of my fingers is what sees the egg. I do not touch it. —But to dedicate myself to the vision of the egg would be to die to the world, and I need the yolk and the white. —The egg sees me. Does the egg idealize me? Does the egg meditate me? No, the egg merely sees me. It is exempt from the understanding that wounds. —The egg has never struggled. It is a gift. —The egg is invisible to the naked eye. From one egg to another one arrives at God, who is invisible to the naked eye. —The egg could have been a triangle that rolled for so long in space that it became oval. —Is the egg basically a vessel? Could it have been the first vessel sculpted by the Etruscans? No. The egg originated in Macedonia. There it was calculated, fruit of the most arduous spontaneity. In the sands of Macedonia a man holding a stick drew it. And then erased it with his bare foot.

An egg is a thing that must be careful. That's why the chicken is the egg's disguise. The chicken exists so that the egg can traverse the ages. That's what a mother is for. —The egg is constantly persecuted for being too ahead of its time. —An egg, for now, will always be revolutionary. —It lives inside the chicken to avoid being called white. The egg really is white. But it cannot be called white. Not because that harms it, but people who call the egg white, those people die to life. Calling something white that is white can destroy humanity. Once a man was accused of being what he was, and he was called That Man. They weren't lying: He was. But to this day we still haven't recovered, one after the next. The general law for us to stay alive: one can say "a pretty face," but whoever says "the face," dies; for having exhausted the topic.

Over time, the egg became a chicken egg. It is not. But, once it was adopted, it took that name. —One should say "the chicken's egg." If one merely says "the egg," the topic is exhausted, and the world becomes naked. —When it comes to the egg, the danger lies in discovering what might be called beauty, that is, its veracity. The veracity of the egg is not verisimilar. If they find out, they might want to force it to become rectangular. The danger is not for the egg, it wouldn't become rectangular. (Our guarantee is that it is unable: being unable is the egg's great strength: its grandiosity comes from the greatness of being unable, which radiates from it like a not-wanting.) But whoever struggles to make it rectangular would be losing his own life. The egg puts us, therefore, in danger. Our advantage is that the egg is invisible. And as for the initiates, the initiates disguise the egg.

As for the chicken's body, the chicken's body is the greatest proof that the egg does not exist. All you have to do is look at the chicken to make it obvious that the egg cannot possibly exist.

And what about the chicken? The egg is the chicken's great sacrifice. The egg is the cross the chicken bears in life. The egg is the chicken's unattainable dream. The chicken loves the egg. She doesn't know the egg exists. If she knew she had an egg inside her, would she save herself? If she knew she had the egg inside her, she would lose her state of being a chicken. Being a chicken is the chicken's survival. Surviving is salvation. For living doesn't seem to exist. Living leads to death. So what the chicken does is be permanently surviving. Surviving is what's called keeping up the struggle against life that is deadly. That's what being a chicken is. The chicken looks embarrassed.

The chicken must not know she has an egg. Or else she would save herself as a chicken, which is no guarantee either, but she would lose the egg. So she doesn't know. The chicken exists so that the egg can use the chicken. She was only meant to be fulfilled, but she liked it. The chicken's undoing comes from this: liking wasn't part of being born. To like being alive hurts. —As for which came first, it was the egg that found the chicken. The chicken was not even summoned. The chicken is directly singled out. —The chicken lives as if in a dream. She has no sense of reality. All the chicken's fright comes because they're always interrupting her reverie. The chicken is a sound sleep. —The chicken suffers from an unknown ailment. The chicken's unknown ailment is the egg. —She doesn't know how to explain herself: "I know that the error is inside me," she calls her life an error, "I don't know what I feel anymore," etc.

"Etc., etc., etc.," is what the chicken clucks all day long. The chicken has plenty of inner life. To be honest, the only thing the chicken really has is inner life. Our vision of her inner life is what we call "chicken." The chicken's inner life consists of acting as if she understands. At the slightest threat she screams bloody murder like a maniac. All this so the egg won't break inside her. An egg that breaks inside the chicken is like blood.

The chicken looks at the horizon. As if it were from the line of the horizon that an egg is coming. Beyond being a mode of transport for the egg, the chicken is silly, idle and myopic. How could the chicken understand herself if she is the contradiction of an egg? The egg is still the same one that originated in Macedonia. The chicken is always the most modern of tragedies. She is always pointlessly current. And she keeps being redrawn. The most suitable form for a chicken has yet to be found. While my neighbor talks on the phone he redraws the chicken with an absentminded pencil. But there's nothing to be done for the chicken: part of her nature is not to be of use to herself. Given, however, that her destiny is more important than she is, and given that her destiny is the egg, her personal life does not concern us.

Inside herself the chicken doesn't recognize the egg, but neither does she recognize it outside herself. When the chicken sees the egg she thinks she's dealing with something impossible. And with her heart beating, with her heart beating so, she doesn't recognize it.

Suddenly I look at the egg in the kitchen and all I see in it is food. I don't recognize it, and my heart beats. The metamorphosis is happening inside me: I start not to be able to discern the egg anymore. Beyond every particular egg, beyond every egg that's eaten, the egg does not exist. I can now no longer believe in an egg. More and more I lack the strength to believe, I am dying, farewell, I looked at an egg too long and it started putting me to sleep.

The chicken who didn't want to sacrifice her life. The one who chose wanting to be "happy." The one who didn't notice that, if she spent her life designing the egg inside herself as in an illuminated manuscript, she would be good for something. The one who didn't know how to lose herself. The one who thought she had chicken feathers to cover her because she had precious skin, not understanding that the feathers were meant exclusively for helping her along as she carried the egg, because intense suffering might harm the egg. The one who thought pleasure was a gift to her, not realizing that it was meant to keep her completely distracted while the egg was being formed. The one who didn't know "I" is just one of those words you draw while talking on the phone, a mere attempt to find a better shape. The one who thought "I" means having a one-self. The chickens who harm the egg are those that are a ceaseless "I." In them, the "I" is so constant that they can no longer utter the word "egg." But, who knows, maybe that's exactly what the egg was in need of. For if they weren't so distracted, if they paid attention to the great life forming inside them, they would get in the way of the egg.

I started talking about the chicken and for a while now I have no longer been talking about the chicken. But I'm still talking about the egg.

And thus I don't understand the egg. I only understand a broken egg: I crack it on the frying pan. In this indirect way I give myself to the egg's existence: my sacrifice is reducing myself to my personal life. I turned my pleasure and my pain into my hidden destiny. And having only one's own life is, for those who have already seen the egg, a sacrifice. Like the ones who, in a convent, sweep the floor and do the laundry, serving without the glory of a higher purpose, my job is to live out my pleasures and my pains. I must have the modesty to live.

I pick up another egg in the kitchen, I break its shell and shape. And from this precise moment there was never an egg. It is absolutely essential that I be a busy and distracted person. I am necessarily one of those people who refuse. I belong to that Masonic society of those who once saw the egg and refused it as a way to protect it. We are the ones who abstain from destroying, and by doing so are consumed. We, undercover agents dispersed among less revealing duties, we sometimes recognize each other. By a certain way of looking, by a way of shaking hands, we recognize each other and call this love. And then our disguise is unnecessary: though we don't speak, neither do we lie, though we don't speak the truth, neither must we dissemble any longer. Love is when we are allowed to participate a bit more. Few want love, because love is the great disillusionment with all the rest. And few can bear losing the rest of their illusions. There are people who would volunteer for love, thinking love will enrich their personal lives. On the contrary: love is ultimately poverty. Love is not having. Moreover love is the disillusionment of what you thought was love. And it's no prize, that's why it doesn't make people vain, love is no prize, it's a status granted exclusively to people who, without it, would defile the egg with their personal suffering. That doesn't make love an honorable exception; it is granted precisely to those bad agents, those who would ruin everything if they weren't allowed to guess at things vaguely.

All the agents are granted several advantages so that the egg may form. It is no cause for envy since, even certain statuses, worse than other people's, are merely the ideal conditions for the egg. As for the agents' pleasure, they also receive it without pride. They austerely experience all pleasures: it is even our sacrifice so that the egg may form. Upon us has been imposed, as well, a nature entirely prone to much pleasure. Which makes it easier. At the very least it makes pleasure less arduous.

There are cases of agents committing suicide: they find the minimal instructions they have received insufficient, and feel unsupported. There was the case of the agent who publicly revealed himself as an agent because he found not being understood intolerable, and could no longer stand not being respected by others: he was fatally run over as he was leaving a restaurant. There was another who didn't even have to be eliminated: he was slowly consumed by his own rebellion, his rebellion came when he discovered that the two or three instructions he had received included no explanation whatsoever. There was another, eliminated too, because he thought "the truth should be bravely spoken," and started first of all to seek it out; they say he died in the name of the truth, but in fact he was just making the truth harder with his innocence; his seeming bravery was foolhardiness, and his desire for loyalty was naive, he hadn't understood that being loyal isn't so tidy, being loyal means being disloyal to everything else. Those extreme cases of death aren't caused by cruelty. It's because there's a job, let's call it cosmic, to be done, and individual cases unfortunately cannot be taken into consideration. For those who succumb and become individuals there are institutions, charity, comprehension that doesn't distinguish motives, in a word our human life.

The eggs crackle in the frying pan, and lost in a dream I make breakfast. Lacking any sense of reality, I shout for the children who sprout from various beds, drag the chairs out and eat, and the work of the breaking day begins, shouted and laughed and eaten, white and yolk, merriment amid fighting, the day that is our salt and we are the day's salt, living is extremely tolerable, living keeps us busy and distracts us, living makes us laugh.

And it makes me smile in my mystery. My mystery is that being merely a means, and not an end, has given me the most mischievous of freedoms: I'm no fool and I make the most of things. Even to the point of wronging others so much that, frankly. The fake job they have given me to disguise my true purpose, since I make the most of this fake job and turn it into my real one; this includes the money they give me as a daily allowance to ease my life so that the egg may form, since I have used this money for other purposes, diverting the funds, I recently bought stock in Brahma beer and am rich. All this I still call having the necessary modesty to live. And also the time they have granted me, and that they grant us just so that in this honorable leisure the egg may form, well I have used this time for illicit pleasures and illicit pains, completely forgetting the egg. That is my simplicity.

Or is that exactly what they want to happen to me, precisely so the egg can carry out its mission? Is it freedom or am I being controlled? Because I keep noticing how every error of mine has been put to use. My rebellion is that for them I am nothing, I am merely valuable: they take care of me from one second to the next, with the most absolute lack of love; I am merely valuable. With the money they give me, I have taken to drinking lately. Abuse of trust? But it's because nobody knows how it feels inside for someone whose job consists of pretending that she is betraying, and who ends up believing in her own betrayal. Whose job consists of forgetting every day. Someone of whom apparent dishonor is required. Not even my mirror still reflects a face that is mine. Either I am an agent, or it really is betrayal.

Yet I sleep the sleep of the righteous because I know that my futile life doesn't interfere with the march of great time. On the contrary: it seems that I am required to be extremely futile, I'm even required to sleep like one of the righteous. They want me busy and distracted, and they don't care how. Because, with my misguided attention and grave foolishness, I could interfere with whatever is carried out through me. It's because I myself, I properly speaking, all I have really been good for is interfering. What tells me that I might be an agent is the idea that my destiny surpasses me: at least they really did have to let me guess that, I was one of those people who would do their job badly if they couldn't guess at least a little; they made me forget what they had let me guess, but I still had the vague notion that my destiny surpasses me, and that I am an instrument of their work. But in any case all I could be was an instrument, since the work couldn't really be mine. I have already tried to set myself up on my own and it didn't work out; my hand trembles to this day. Had I kept at it any longer I would have damaged my health forever. Since then, ever since that thwarted experiment, I have tried to consider things this way: that much has already been given me, that they have granted me everything that might be granted; and that other agents, far superior to me, have also worked solely for something they did not know. And with the same minimal instructions. Much has already been given me; this, for example: every once in a while, with my heart beating at the privilege, I at least know that I am not recognizing anything! with my heart beating from emotion, I at least do not understand! with my heart beating from trust, I at least do not know.

But what about the egg? This is one of their ploys: while I was talking about the egg, I had forgotten the egg. "Talk, talk!" they instructed me. And the egg is fully protected by all those words. Keep talking, is one of the instructions, I am so tired.

Out of devotion to the egg, I forgot it. My necessary forgetting. My self-serving forgetting. Because the egg is an evasion. In the face of my possessive adoration it could retreat and never again return. But if it is forgotten. If I make the sacrifice of living only my life and of forgetting it. If the egg becomes impossible. Then—free, delicate, with no message for me—perhaps one last time it will move from space over to this window that I have always left open. And at dawn it will descend into our building. Serene all the way to the kitchen. Illuminating it with my pallor.

Temptation
("Tentação")

SHE WAS SOBBING. AND AS IF THE TWO O'CLOCK GLARE weren't enough, she had red hair.

On the empty street the cobblestones were vibrating with heat—the little girl's head was aflame. Sitting on the front steps of her house, she endured. Nobody on the street, just one person waiting in vain at the tram stop. And as if her submissive and patient gaze weren't enough, her sobs kept interrupting her, making her chin slip off the hand it was resting on in resignation. What could you do about a sobbing redhaired girl? We looked at each other wordlessly, dejection to dejection. On the deserted street not a sign of the tram. In a land of dark-haired people, being a redhead was an involuntary rebellion. What did it matter if one day in the future her emblem would make her insolently hold erect the head of a woman. For now she was sitting on a shimmering doorstep, at two o'clock. What saved her was an old purse, with a torn strap. She clutched it with a long-familiar conjugal love, pressing it against her knees.

That was when her other half in this world approached, a brother in Grajaú. The possibility of communication appeared at the scorching angle of the street corner, accompanied by a lady, and incarnated in the form of a dog. It was a basset hound, beautiful and miserable, sweet inside its fate. It was a red-haired basset hound.

There he came trotting, ahead of his owner, stretching his body out. Unsuspecting, nonchalant, dog.

The girl widened her eyes in amazement. Mildly alerted, the dog stopped in front of her. His tongue quivered. They looked at each other.

Of all the beings suited to become the owner of another being, there sat the girl who had come into this world to have that dog. He growled gently, without barking. She looked at him from under her hair, fascinated, solemn. How much time passed? A big sob jangled her. He didn't even tremble. She overcame her sobs and kept staring at him.

Both had short, red hair.

What did they say to each other? Nobody knows. All we know is they communicated rapidly, since there was no time. We also know that without speaking they were asking for each other. They were asking for each other urgently, bashfully, surprised.

Amid so much vague impossibility and so much sun, here was the solution for the red child. And amid so many streets to be trotted down, so many bigger dogs, so many dry gutters—there sat a little girl, as if she were flesh of his ginger flesh. They stared at each other deeply, immersed, absent from Grajaú. Another second and the suspended dream would shatter, yielding perhaps to the seriousness with which they asked for one another.

But both were already committed.

She to her impossible childhood, the center of the innocence that would only open once she was a woman. He, to his imprisoned nature.

His owner waited impatiently beneath her parasol. The red-haired basset finally pried himself away from the girl and went off sleepwalking. She sat there in shock, holding the event in her hands, in a muteness that neither her father nor mother would understand. She followed him with black eyes that could hardly believe it, hunched over her purse and knees, until she saw him round the other corner.

But he was stronger than she. He didn't look back once.

Journey to Petrópolis
("Viagem a Petrópolis")

SHE WAS A WITHERED LITTLE OLD LADY WHO, SWEET
and stubborn, didn't seem to understand that she was alone in
the world. Her eyes were always tearing up, her hands rested
on her dull black dress, an old document of her life. On the
now-stiff fabric were little bread crumbs stuck on by the drool
that was now resurfacing, recalling the cradle. There was a
yellowish stain, from an egg she'd eaten two weeks before.
And marks from the places where she slept. She always found
somewhere to sleep, at someone or other's house. Whenever
they asked her name, she'd say in a voice purified by frailty and
countless years of good manners:

"Missy."

People would smile. Pleased at sparking their interest, she'd
explain:

"My name, my real name, is Margarida."

Her body was small, dark, though she'd been tall and fair.
She'd had a father, mother, husband, two children. All had died
one after the other. Only she remained, with her rheumy, expectant eyes nearly covered by a velvety white film. Whenever
anyone gave her money it was very little, since she was small

and really didn't need to eat much. Whenever they gave her a bed to sleep in they gave her a hard, narrow one because Margarida was gradually losing mass. Nor did she offer much thanks: she'd smile and nod.

Nowadays she was sleeping, no one remembered why, in a room behind a big house, on a broad, tree-lined street in Botafogo. The family thought Missy was quaint but forgot her most of the time. It was because she was also a mysterious old lady. She rose at the crack of dawn, made up her dwarf's bed and darted out nimbly as if the house were on fire. Nobody knew where she went. One day one of the girls of the house asked her what she was doing. She answered with a pleasant smile:

"Strolling around."

They thought it quaint that an old lady, living off charity, would stroll around. But it was true. Missy was born in Maranhão, where she had always lived. She'd come to Rio not long before, with a very nice lady who'd been planning to put her in a nursing home, but it didn't work out: the lady went to Minas and gave Missy some money to set herself up in Rio. And the old woman strolled around getting to know the city. All you had to do anyhow was sit on a park bench and you'd already be seeing Rio de Janeiro.

Her life was going along smoothly, when one day the family from the Botafogo house was surprised that she'd been in their house so long, and thought it was too much. In a way they were right. Everyone there was very busy, every so often weddings, parties, engagements, visits came up. And whenever they rushed busily past the old lady, they'd start as if they'd been interrupted, accosted with a swipe on the shoulder: "hey!" In particular one of the girls of the house felt an irritated distress, the old lady annoyed her for no reason. In particular her permanent

smile, though the girl understood it was just an inoffensive rictus. Perhaps because they didn't have time, no one brought it
up. But as soon as someone thought of sending her to Petrópolis, to their German sister-in-law's house, there came a more
enthusiastic consensus than an old lady could have provoked.

So, when the son of the house took his girlfriend and two
sisters for a weekend in Petrópolis, they brought the old lady
along in the car.

Why didn't Missy sleep the night before? At the idea of a
trip, in her stiff body her heart lost its rust, all dry and skipping
a beat, as if she'd swallowed a large pill without water. There
were moments when she couldn't even breathe. She talked all
night long, sometimes loudly. Her excitement about the promised outing and the change in her life suddenly cleared up some
of her ideas. She remembered things that a few days before she'd
have sworn never existed. Starting with her son who was run
over, killed by a tram in Maranhão—if he had lived amid the
traffic of Rio de Janeiro, then he'd really have been run over. She
remembered her son's hair, his clothing. She remembered the
teacup Maria Rosa had broken and how she'd yelled at Maria
Rosa. If she had known her daughter would die in childbirth, of
course she wouldn't have needed to yell. And she remembered
her husband. She could only recall her husband in shirtsleeves.
But that couldn't be, she was sure he went to the office in his
clerk uniform, he'd go to parties in a sport coat, not to mention
that he couldn't have gone to the funerals of his son and daughter in shirtsleeves. Searching for her husband's sport coat tired
the old lady out further as she tossed and turned lightly in bed.
Suddenly she discovered that the mattress was hard.

"What a hard mattress," she said very loudly in the middle
of the night.

What happened is that all her senses had returned. Parts of her body she hadn't been aware of in a long time were now clamoring for her attention. And all of a sudden—oh what raging hunger! Hallucinating, she got up, unfastened her little bundle, took out a stale piece of buttered bread she had secretly kept for two days. She ate the bread like a rat, scratching up the places in her mouth that had only gums until they bled. And thanks to the food, she felt increasingly reinvigorated. She managed, though fleetingly, to catch a vision of her husband saying goodbye on his way to work. Only after the memory vanished did she notice she'd forgotten to check whether he was in shirtsleeves. She lay down again, scratching her searing body all over. She spent the rest of the night in this pattern of seeing for an instant and then not managing to see anymore. Near dawn she fell asleep.

And for the very first time she had to be roused. While it was still dark, the girl came to get her, kerchief tied around her head and suitcase already in hand. Unexpectedly Missy asked for a few seconds to comb her hair. Her tremulous hands held the broken comb. She combed her hair, combed her hair. She'd never been the kind of woman who went out without first combing her hair thoroughly.

When she finally approached the car, the young man and the girls were surprised by her cheerful manner and sprightly step. "She's healthier than I am!" the young man joked. The thought occurred to the girl of the house: "And to think I was even feeling sorry for her."

Missy sat by the car window, a little cramped by the two sisters crowded onto the same backseat. She didn't say anything, smiling. But when the car jerked into motion, launching her backward, she felt pain in her chest. It wasn't just from joy, it was tearing at her. The young man turned around:

"Don't get sick, Granny!"

The girls laughed, especially the one who'd sat in front, the one who occasionally leaned her head on the young man's shoulder. Out of politeness, the old lady wanted to answer, but couldn't. She wanted to smile, she couldn't. She looked at everyone, teary-eyed, which the others already knew didn't mean she was crying. Something in her face somewhat deadened the joy the girl of the house felt and lent her a stubborn expression.

It was quite a lovely journey.

The girls were pleased, Missy had started smiling again. And, though her heart was racing, everything was better. They drove past a cemetery, past a grocery store, tree, two women, a soldier, cat! signs—everything swallowed up by speed.

When Missy awoke she no longer knew where she was. The highway was now in broad daylight: it was narrow and dangerous. The old lady's mouth stung, her frozen feet and hands were growing distant from the rest of her body. The girls were talking, the one in front had rested her head on the young man's shoulder. Their belongings were constantly tumbling down.

Then Missy's head started working. Her husband appeared to her in a sport coat—I found it, I found it! the sport coat had been on a hanger the whole time. She remembered the name of Maria Rosa's friend, the one who lived across the street: Elvira, and Elvira's mother was even crippled. The memories nearly wrenched a shout from her. Then she moved her lips slowly and murmured a few words.

The girls were talking:

"Well, thank you very much, I won't accept a present like that!"

That's when Missy finally started not to understand. What was she doing in the car? how had she met her husband and where? how did Maria Rosa and Rafael's mother, their very own mother, end up in a car with these people? A moment later she was used to it again.

The young man said to his sisters:

"I think it's better not to park in front, to avoid gossip. She'll get out of the car, we'll show her where it is, she'll go by herself and tell them she's supposed to stay."

One of the girls of the house felt uneasy: she worried that her brother, being dense like a typical man, would say too much in front of his girlfriend. They didn't visit their brother in Petrópolis anymore, and saw their sister-in-law even less.

"Right," she broke in just before he said too much. "Look, Missy, go down that alley and you can't miss it: at the red-brick house, you ask for Arnaldo, my brother, okay? Arnaldo. Say you couldn't stay with us anymore, say there's room at Arnaldo's and you could even look after their boy sometimes, okay ..."

Missy got out of the car, and for a while kept standing there but floating dizzily above wheels. The cool wind blew her long skirt between her legs.

Arnaldo wasn't home. Missy entered the alcove where the lady of the house, with a dust rag tied around her head, was having breakfast. A blond boy—surely the one Missy was supposed to look after—was seated in front of a plate of tomatoes and onions and eating drowsily, while his white, freckled legs were swinging under the table. The German woman filled his dish with oatmeal, pushed buttered toast across the table to him. The flies were buzzing. Missy felt faint. If she drank some hot coffee maybe the chill in her body would go away.

The German woman examined her silently every so often: she hadn't believed the story about her sister-in-law's suggestion, though "from them" anything was possible. But maybe the old lady had heard the address from someone, maybe even on a tram, by chance, that sometimes happened, all you had to do was open the newspaper and see the things that went on. It was just that the story wasn't very convincing, and the old lady had a sly look, she didn't even hide her smile. Best not to leave her alone in the alcove with the cupboard full of new dishes.

"First I have to eat breakfast," she told her. "After my husband gets home, we'll see what can be done."

Missy didn't understand very well, because the woman spoke like a foreigner. But she understood that she was to stay seated. The smell of coffee gave her a craving, and a dizziness that darkened the whole room. Her lips stung drily and her heart beat completely independently. Coffee, coffee, she looked on, smiling and tearing up. At her feet the dog was gnawing at its own paw, growling. The maid, also somewhat foreign, tall, with a very slender neck and large breasts, the maid brought a plate of soft white cheese. Wordlessly, the mother smashed a hunk of cheese onto the toast and pushed it over to her son's side of the table. The boy ate it all and, with his belly sticking out, grabbed a toothpick and stood:

"Mother, gimme a hundred cruzeiros."

"No. For what?"

"Chocolate."

"No. Sunday's not till tomorrow."

A flicker of light lit up Missy: Sunday? what was she doing in that house on the eve of the Sabbath? She could never have guessed. But she'd be pleased to look after that boy. She'd always liked blond children: all blond boys looked like the Baby Jesus. What was she doing in that house? They kept making her move from one side to the other for no reason, but she'd tell about everything, they'd see. She smiled sheepishly: she wouldn't tell on them at all, since what she really wanted was coffee.

The lady of the house shouted toward another room, and the indifferent maid brought out a bowl, filled with dark mush. Foreigners sure ate a lot in the morning, Missy had witnessed as much in Maranhão. The lady of the house, with her no-nonsense manner, because foreigners in Petrópolis were just as serious as they were in Maranhão, the lady of the house took a spoonful of white cheese, mashed it with her fork and mixed it into the mush. Honestly, it really was foreign slop. She then started eating, absorbed, with the same look of distaste foreigners in Maranhão have. Missy watched. The dog growled at its fleas.

Finally Arnaldo appeared in full sunlight, the crystal cabinet sparkling. He wasn't blond. He spoke with his wife in a hushed voice, and after a drawn-out discussion informed Missy firmly and carefully: "It's just not possible, there's just no room here."

And since the old lady didn't object and kept on smiling, he said it louder:

"There's just no room, okay?"

But Missy remained seated. Arnaldo half gestured. He looked at the two women in the room and got a vague sense of the comic nature of the contrast. His wife taut and ruddy. And past her the old lady shriveled and dark, with folds of dry wrinkles hanging from her shoulders. Faced with the old lady's mischievous smile, he lost his patience:

"And I'm very busy now! I'll give you some money and you take the train to Rio, okay? go back to my mother's house, and when you get there say: Arnaldo's house isn't an old folks' home, okay? there's no room here. Say this: Arnaldo's house isn't an old folks' home, okay!"

Missy took the money and headed for the door. When Arnaldo was just sitting down to eat, Missy reappeared:

"Thank you, may God help you."

Out on the street, she thought once more of Maria Rosa, Rafael, her husband. She didn't miss them the slightest bit. But she remembered. She headed for the highway, getting farther and farther from the station. She smiled as if playing a trick on somebody: instead of heading back right away, she'd take a little stroll first. A man walked by. Then a very odd and utterly unimportant thing was illuminated: when she was still a woman, men. She couldn't manage to get an exact image of the men's faces, but she saw herself in light-colored blouses with long hair. Her thirst returned, burning her throat. The sun flamed, sparkling on every white pebble. The Petrópolis highway is quite lovely.

At the wet black stone fountain, right on the highway, a barefoot black woman was filling a can of water.

Missy stood still, watching. Then she saw the black woman cup her hands and drink.

Once the highway was empty again, Missy darted out as if emerging from a hiding place and stole up to the fountain. The rivulets of water ran icily into her sleeves up to her elbows, tiny droplets glistened, caught in her hair.

Her thirst quenched, stunned, she kept strolling, eyes widened, focused on the violent churning of the heavy water inside her stomach, awakening little reflexes throughout the rest of her body like lights.

The highway climbed quite a bit. The highway was lovelier than Rio de Janeiro, and climbed quite a bit. Missy sat on a rock beside a tree, to admire it all. The sky was incredibly high, without a cloud. And there were many little birds flying from the chasm toward the highway. The sun-bleached highway extended along a green chasm. Then, since she was tired, the old lady rested her head on the trunk of the tree and died.

The Solution
("A solução")

HER NAME WAS ALMIRA AND SHE'D GROWN TOO FAT.
Alice was her best friend. At least that's what she told everyone
woefully, wanting her own vehemence to compensate for the
lack of friendship the other woman devoted to her.

Alice was pensive and smiled without hearing her, typing
away.

The more nonexistent Alice's friendship was, the more
Almira's grew. Alice had an oval, velvety face. Almira's nose
was always shiny. Almira's face held an eagerness she'd never
thought to hide: the same she felt for food, her most direct
contact with the world.

Why Alice put up with Almira, no one understood. The
two were typists and coworkers, which didn't explain it. The
two ate lunch together, which didn't explain it. They left the
office at the same time and waited for the bus in the same
line. Almira always looking after Alice. The latter, distant and
dreamy, letting herself be adored. Alice was small and delicate.
Almira had a very wide face, sallow and shiny: her lipstick
never stayed on, she was the sort who ate off her lipstick without meaning to.

"I just loved that show on Ministry of Education Radio," Almira would say trying somehow to please. But Alice took everything as if it were her due, including the Ministry of Education opera.

Only Almira's nature was delicate. With that whole big fat body, she could spend a sleepless night over having spoken a poorly chosen word. And a piece of chocolate could suddenly turn bitter in her mouth at the thought that she'd been unfair. What she never lacked was chocolate in her purse, and alarm at what she might have done. Not out of kindness. It might have been feeble nerves in a feeble body.

On the morning of the day it happened, Almira left for work in a rush, still chewing on a piece of bread. When she reached the office, she looked over at Alice's desk and didn't see her. An hour later she showed up with bloodshot eyes. She didn't want to explain or answer Almira's nervous questions. Almira was practically crying over her typewriter.

Finally, at lunchtime, she begged Alice to have lunch with her, her treat.

It was precisely during lunch that the incident occurred.

Almira kept wanting to know why Alice had shown up late and with bloodshot eyes. Dejected, Alice barely replied. Almira ate eagerly and kept pressing the issue, her eyes welling with tears.

"You fatso!" Alice said suddenly, pale with rage. "Can't you just leave me alone?!"

Almira gagged on her food, tried to speak, started stammering. From Alice's soft lips had come words that couldn't go down with the food in Almira G. de Almeida's throat.

"You're a pest and a busybody," Alice exploded again. "So you want to know what happened, do you? Okay I'll tell you,

you pest: what happened is that Zequinha took off for Porto Alegre and he's not coming back! happy now, fatso?"

Indeed Almira seemed to have grown even fatter in those last few seconds, and with food still stuck in her mouth.

That was when Almira started to snap out of it. And, as if she were a skinny girl, she took her fork and stabbed it into Alice's neck. The restaurant, according to the newspaper, rose as one. But the fat woman, even after the deed was done, remained seated staring at the ground, not even looking at the other woman's blood.

Alice went to the emergency room, which she left with bandages and her eyes still bulging in fright. Almira was arrested in flagrante.

A few observant people remarked that there'd always been something off about that friendship. Others, friends of the family, recounted how Almira's grandmother, Dona Altamiranda, had been a very strange woman. No one remembered that elephants, according to experts on the subject, are extremely sensitive creatures, even on their thick feet.

In prison Almira behaved in a docile and cheerful manner, melancholy perhaps, but cheerful all the same. She did favors for her companions. At last, she had companions. She was responsible for the laundry, and got along very well with the guards, who occasionally snuck her a chocolate bar. Just like for a circus elephant.

Evolution of a Myopia
("Evolução de uma miopia")

IF HE WAS CLEVER, HE DIDN'T KNOW IT. BEING CLEVER or not depended on the instability of other people. Sometimes what he said would suddenly spark in the adults a satisfied and knowing look. Satisfied, because they had kept secret the fact that they found him clever and didn't coddle him; knowing, because they were more aware of what he'd said than he himself was. That's why, then, whenever he was considered clever, he also got the uneasy feeling of being unaware: something had escaped him. The key to his cleverness also escaped him. Since at times, trying to imitate himself, he'd say things sure to provoke that swift move on the checkerboard again, since he had the impression of an automatic mechanism on the part of his family members: as soon as he said something clever, all the adults would glance at each other, with a clearly suppressed smile on their lips, a smile suggested only by their eyes, "oh how we'd smile right now, if we weren't such good teachers" — and, as in a square dance in a Western movie, they'd have each somehow switched partners and places. In sum, they understood each other, his family members; and they understood each other at his expense. Besides understanding each other at his expense, they misunderstood each other permanently, but as a new kind of square dance: even when misunderstanding each other, he felt they were beholden to the rules of a game, as if they'd agreed to misunderstand.

Sometimes, then, he'd try to reproduce his own best lines, the ones that had provoked a move on the checkerboard. It wasn't exactly to reproduce his past success, nor was it exactly to provoke the silent moves of the family. But rather an attempt to possess the key to his "cleverness." In this attempt to discover laws and causes, however, he was failing. And, whenever he repeated a good line, this time the others met it distractedly. His eyes blinking with curiosity, at the onset of his myopia, he'd wonder why he had managed to move his family once, and not again. Was his cleverness judged according to other people's lack of discipline?

Later, when he substituted the instability of other people with his own, he entered a state of conscious instability. When he became a man, he maintained the habit of blinking suddenly at his own thought, while also wrinkling his nose, which made his glasses slip—expressing in this twitch his attempt to substitute the judgment of other people with his own, in an attempt to deepen his own perplexity. But he was a boy with a knack for statics: he'd always been able to keep his perplexity as perplexity, without its being transformed into another sentiment.

That he didn't hold his own key, he'd grown used to knowing this while still a boy, and he'd start blinking so rapidly that, when his nose wrinkled, it would make his glasses slip. That nobody held the key, was something he gradually discovered without disappointment, his calm myopia demanding progressively stronger lenses.

Strange as it might seem, it was precisely due to this state of permanent uncertainty and due to his premature acceptance that nobody held the key—it was through all this that he grew up normally, and while living in serene curiosity. Patient and curious. A little nervous, they said, referring to the tic with his glasses. But "nervous" was the name the family had been giving to the instability of the family's own judgment. Another name that the instability of the adults gave him was "well-behaved," and "easy." Thereby giving a name not to what he was, but to the varying needs of those moments.

Now and then, in his extraordinary bespectacled calm, something happened inside him that was shining and a bit convulsive like an inspiration.

It happened, for example, when they told him that in a week he would spend a whole day at a cousin's house. This cousin was married, didn't have children and adored them. "A whole day" included lunch, a snack, dinner, and coming home half-asleep. And as for the cousin, the cousin meant extra love, with its unexpected advantages and an incalculable eagerness—and all this would allow special requests to be considered. At her house, everything that he was would have a guaranteed value for a whole day. Over there love, more easily stable because it was just for a day, wouldn't leave any margin for instabilities of judgment: for a whole day, he'd be judged as the same boy.

During the week preceding "the whole day," he started off trying to decide whether to act naturally with his cousin. He attempted to decide whether to say something clever as soon as he arrived—with the result that he'd be judged clever for the whole day. Or whether, as soon as he arrived, he'd do something she would judge "well-behaved," which would make him the well-behaved boy for the whole day. Having the possibility of choosing what he would be and, for the first time throughout a long day, made him adjust his glasses constantly.

Gradually, during the preceding week, the sphere of possibilities kept expanding. And, with his ability to handle confusion—he was meticulous and calm when it came to confusion—he ended up learning that he could arbitrarily decide to be a clown for a whole day, for example. Or that he could spend the day in a very sad mood, if he so decided. What put him at ease was knowing that his cousin, with her childless love and especially with her lack of experience in dealing with children, would accept whichever way he decided that she should judge him. What also helped was knowing that nothing he was that day would really change him. Because prematurely—being a precocious child—he was superior to other people's instability and to his own. Somehow he floated above his own myopia and that of others. Which gave him a lot of freedom. At times merely the freedom of a calm incredulity. Even when he became a man, with extremely thick glasses, he never managed to become aware of this kind of superiority he had over himself.

The week preceding the visit to his cousin was one of constant anticipation. Sometimes his stomach would clench apprehensively: because in that house with no kids he'd be completely at the mercy of a woman's indiscriminating love. "Indiscriminating love" represented a threatening stability: it would be permanent, and would surely result in a single way of judging, and that was stability. Stability, even back then, meant danger to him: if other people made a mistake in their first pass at stability, the mistake would become permanent, without the advantage of instability, which is that of a possible correction.

Something else that worried him beforehand was what he'd do for the whole day at his cousin's house, besides eating and being loved. Well, there was always the solution of being able to go to the bathroom every once in a while, which would make the time pass more quickly. But, having some experience at being loved, it embarrassed him in advance that his cousin, a stranger to him, would regard his trips to the bathroom with infinite affection. In general the mechanism of his life had become a reason for tenderness. Well, it was also true that, as for going to the bathroom, the solution might be not going to the bathroom at all. But that would not only be, for a whole day, impossible so much as—since he didn't want to be judged as "a boy who doesn't go to the bathroom"—it offered no advantage either. His cousin, stabilized by her permanent desire for children, would be led, by his not going to the bathroom, down the wrong track of great love.

During the week that preceded "the whole day," it wasn't that he was suffering due to his own vacillation. Because the step most people never manage to take was one he'd already taken: he'd accepted uncertainty, and was dealing with the components of uncertainty with the concentration of someone peering through the lens of a microscope.

As, during the week, these lightly convulsive inspirations followed one another, they gradually started changing in stature. He abandoned the problem of deciding which elements to offer his cousin so she in turn could temporarily grant him the certainty of "who he was." He abandoned these musings and started wanting to determine ahead of time how his cousin's house would smell, how big the little yard was where he'd play, what drawers he'd open while she wasn't looking. And finally he took up the matter of the cousin herself. How should he handle the love his cousin had for him?

However, he had neglected one detail: his cousin had a gold tooth, on the left side.

And that—when he finally entered his cousin's house—
that was what in a single instant threw his entire anticipated
structure off balance.

The rest of the day might have been called horrible, if the
boy was inclined to put things in terms of horrible or not horrible. Or it could have been called "dazzling," if he were the type
to expect that things are or not.

There was that gold tooth, which he hadn't counted on. But,
with the sense of security he found in the idea of a permanent
unpredictability, so much that he even wore glasses, he didn't
become insecure because he encountered right from the start
something he hadn't counted on.

After that the surprise of his cousin's love. It turned out his
cousin's love started off being obvious, unlike what he'd imagined. She'd greeted him with a naturalness that insulted him
at first, but that soon after no longer did. She said right away
that she was going to clean the house and that he could go
off and play. Which gave the boy, out of the blue, a whole day,
empty and full of sun.

At some point, wiping his glasses, he attempted, though
with a certain detachment, a stroke of cleverness and made
an observation about the plants in the yard. Since whenever
he made an observation aloud, he was judged very observant.
But his cool observation about the plants got the reply: "um-
hmm" between sweeps of the floor. So he went to the bathroom where he decided that, since everything had failed, he'd
play at "not being judged": for a whole day he wouldn't be anything, he simply wouldn't be. And he yanked open the door
with a surge of freedom.

But as the sun climbed higher, the more the delicate pressure of his cousin's love started to make itself felt. And by the
time he realized it, he was beloved. At lunchtime, the food

was pure love, misguided and stable: under the doting eyes of his cousin, he adapted with curiosity to the strange taste of that food, maybe it was a different brand of oil, he adapted to a woman's love, a new love that didn't resemble the love of the other adults: it was a love begging to be fulfilled, since his cousin had missed out on pregnancy, already itself a fulfillment of maternal love. But it was a love without the prior pregnancy. It was a love begging, *a posteriori*, for conception. In short, impossible love.

For the whole day love demanding a past to redeem the present and future. For the whole day, without a word, her demanding of him to have been born from her womb. His cousin wanted nothing from him, except that. She wanted from the boy with glasses not to be a childless woman. On that day, thus, he met with one of the rare forms of stability: the stability of unrealizable desire. The stability of the unattainable ideal. For the first time, he, a being devoted to moderation, for the first time he felt attracted to immoderation: attraction to the impossible extreme. In a word, to the impossible. And for the first time he then felt love for passion.

And it was as if his myopia had disappeared and he was seeing the world clearly. The deepest and simplest glimpse he had of the kind of universe he would live in and inhabit. Not a mental glimpse. It was only as if he'd taken off his glasses, and myopia itself is what made him see. Maybe that had been when he picked up a lifelong habit: whenever his confusion grew and he could barely see, he'd take off his glasses under the pretext of wiping them and, without his glasses, fix his interlocutor with the reverberating stare of a blind man.

The Fifth Story

("A quinta história")

THIS STORY COULD BE CALLED "THE STATUES." AN-
other possible name is "The Murder." And also "How to Kill
Cockroaches." So I will tell at least three stories, all true because they don't contradict each other. Though a single story,
they would be a thousand and one, were I given a thousand
and one nights.

The first, "How to Kill Cockroaches," begins like this: I
was complaining about cockroaches. A lady overheard me.
She gave me this recipe for killing them. I was to mix equal
parts sugar, flour and plaster. The flour and sugar would attract them, the plaster would dry up their insides. That's what
I did. They died.

The other story is actually the first one and is called "The
Murder." It begins like this: I was complaining about cockroaches. A lady overheard me. The recipe follows. And then
comes the murder. The truth is that I was only complaining
about cockroaches in the abstract, since they weren't even
mine: they belonged to the ground floor and would crawl up
the building's pipes to our home. Only once I prepared the mixture did they become mine too. In our name, then, I began to

measure and weigh the ingredients with a slightly more intense concentration. A vague resentment had overtaken me, a sense of outrage. By day the cockroaches were invisible and no one would believe in the secret curse that gnawed at such a peaceful home. But if they, like secret curses, slept during the day, there I was preparing their evening poison. Meticulous, ardent, I concocted the elixir for drawn-out death. An excited fear and my own secret curse guided me. Now I icily wanted just one thing: to kill every cockroach in existence. Cockroaches crawl up the pipes while we, worn out, dream. And now the recipe was ready, so white. As if for cockroaches as clever as I was, I expertly spread the powder until it looked more like something from nature. From my bed, in the silence of the apartment, I imagined them crawling one by one up to the laundry room where the darkness was sleeping, just one towel alert on the clothesline. I awoke hours later with a start when I realized how late it was. It was already dawn. I crossed the kitchen. There they were on the laundry-room floor, hard, huge. During the night I had killed. In our name, day was breaking. Up in the favela a rooster crowed.

The third story that now begins is the one about the "Statues." It begins by saying that I had been complaining about cockroaches. Then comes the same lady. It keeps going up to the point where, near dawn, I awake and still sleepy cross the kitchen. Even sleepier than I is the room from the perspective of its tile floor. And in the darkness of dawn, a purplish glow that distances everything, I discern at my feet shadows and white forms: dozens of statues scattered, rigid. The cockroaches that have hardened from the inside out. Some, belly up. Others, in the middle of a gesture never to be completed. In the mouths of some a bit of the white food. I am the first witness of daybreak in Pompeii. I know how this last night went, I know of the orgy in the dark. Inside some of them the plaster will have hardened as slowly as during some vital process, and they, with increasingly arduous movements, will have greedily intensified the night's joys, trying to escape their own insides. Until they turn to stone, in innocent shock, and with such, such a look of wounded reproach. Others—suddenly assaulted by their own core, without even the slightest inkling that some internal mold was being petrified!—these suddenly crystallize, the way a word is cut off in the mouth: it's you I ... They who, taking the name of love in vain, kept singing through the summer night. Whereas that one there, the one whose brown antenna is smeared with white, must have figured out too late that it had been mummified precisely for not having known how to make use of things with the gratuitous charm of being in vain: "because I looked too deep inside myself! because I looked too deep inside ..."—from my cold, human height I look at the destruction of a world. Day breaks. The occasional antenna of a dead cockroach quivers drily in the breeze. From the previous story the rooster crows.

The fourth narrative inaugurates a new era at home. It begins as we know: I was complaining about cockroaches. It goes up to the moment I see the plaster monuments. Dead, yes. But I look toward the pipes, from where this very night a slow and living population will renew itself in single file. So would I renew the lethal sugar every night? like someone who can no longer sleep without the eagerness of a rite. And every dawn lead myself to the pavilion with the compulsion of greeting the statues that my sweaty night has been erecting. I trembled with wicked pleasure at the vision of that double life of a sorceress. And I also trembled at the sign of plaster drying: the compulsion to live that would burst my internal mold. A harsh instant of choosing between two paths that, I thought, are bidding each other farewell, and sure that either choice would be a sacrifice: me or my soul. I chose. And today I secretly boast in my heart a plaque of virtue: "This house has been disinfested."

The fifth story is called "Leibniz and the Transcendence of Love in Polynesia." It begins like this: I was complaining about cockroaches.

A Sincere Friendship
("Uma amizade sincera")

NOT THAT WE WERE FRIENDS FROM WAY BACK. WE only met in our last year of school. From then on we were together all the time. We had both been in need of a friend for so long that there was nothing we didn't confide to each other. We reached the point of friendship at which we could no longer keep a thought to ourselves: one would soon call the other, making plans to meet right away. After the conversation, we felt as happy as if we had given ourselves to each other as presents. This state of constant communication reached such a level of exaltation that, the day neither of us had anything to confide, we searched with some distress for something to talk about. Only, the topic had to be serious, because not just anything would contain the vehemence of a sincerity experienced for the first time.

Right around that time came the first signs of disturbance between us. Sometimes one would call the other, we'd meet, and have nothing to say. We were very young and didn't know how to sit quietly. At first, when we started running out of topics, we tried talking about people. But we were well aware that we were already adulterating the nucleus of our friendship. Trying to talk about our respective girlfriends was also out of the question, since a man didn't talk about his loves. We tried sitting quietly—but we'd get worried soon after parting ways.

My solitude, upon returning from these outings, was great and arid. I started reading books just to be able to talk about them. But a sincere friendship called for the purest sincerity. Seeking this, I began to feel empty. Our outings were getting ever more disappointing. My sincere poverty was gradually being revealed. He too, I knew, had reached the impasse of himself.

That's when, since my family had moved to São Paulo, and he was living alone, because his family was from Piauí, that's when I invited him to move into our apartment, which had remained in my care. What a tumult of the soul. Ecstatic, we arranged our books and records, setting up an environment perfect for friendship. After everything was ready—there we were at home, at a loss, mute, filled solely with friendship.

We wanted so badly to save each other. Friendship is the stuff of salvation.

But we'd already gone over every problem, already studied every possibility. All we had was that thing we'd sought thirstily until at last finding it: a sincere friendship. The only way, we knew, and how bitterly we knew it, to emerge from the solitude a spirit feels in the body.

But how synthetic this friendship revealed itself to us. As if we wanted to disseminate through a lengthy speech a truism that a single word would exhaust. Our friendship was as unsolvable as the sum of two numbers: it was pointless trying to explore for more than a second the certainty that two and three make five.

We tried to throw a few wild parties at the apartment, but not only did the neighbors complain as it was no use.

If only we could have at least done each other favors. But no opportunity came up, nor did we believe in giving proof of a friendship that didn't need any. The most we could do was what we did: know that we were friends. Which wasn't enough to fill the days, especially the long holidays.

The real trouble dates from these holidays.

He, to whom I could offer nothing but my sincerity, he started becoming an accusation of my poverty. Moreover, our solitude when side by side, listening to music or reading, was much greater than when alone. And, more than greater, uncomfortable. There was no peace. Heading to our own rooms afterward, in relief we wouldn't even look at each other.

It's true there was a break in the course of things, a truce that gave us more hope than there was actually room for. It happened when my friend had a little dispute with City Hall. Not that it was a serious issue, but we made it one to put it to better use. Because by that time we'd already fallen into the habit of doing favors. I went around enthusiastically to the offices of family acquaintances, pulling strings on my friend's behalf. And when it came time for the paperwork, I ran all over the city—I can say in good conscience that not a single signature was notarized without my intervention.

During that time we'd meet at home in the evenings, exhausted and excited: we'd recount the day's exploits, plan our next line of attack. We didn't really delve into what was happening, it was enough that it had the makings of friendship. I thought I understood why couples gave each other presents, why the husband makes a point of comforting his wife, and she toils at making him food, why the mother goes overboard when caring for her child. It was, incidentally, during this time that, with a bit of sacrifice, I gave a little gold brooch to the woman who's now my wife. Only much later did I understand that being there is also giving.

Once the trouble with City Hall was over—let the record show, by the way, that we won—we went on side by side, without finding that word that would yield the soul. Yield the soul? but after all, who wants to yield his soul? Of all things.

After all, what did we want? Nothing. We were worn out, disillusioned.

Under the pretext of a vacation with my family, we parted ways. Incidentally he was also going to Piauí. A heartfelt handshake was our farewell at the airport. We knew we wouldn't see each other again, except by chance. More: that we didn't want to see each other again. And we also knew that we were friends. Sincere friends.

The Obedient Ones
("Os obedientes")

IT WAS A SIMPLE SITUATION, A FACT TO MENTION AND forget.

But if you're imprudent enough to linger an instant longer than you should, a foot sinks in and you're involved. From the instant we venture into it, it's no longer one more fact to tell, we begin to lack the words that would not betray it. At that point, we're in too deep, the fact is no longer a fact and becomes merely its dispersed repercussion. Which, if overly stunted, will one day explode as it did on this Sunday afternoon, when it hasn't rained for weeks and when, like today, beauty desiccated persists nonetheless as beauty. Before which I grow solemn as before a grave. At that point, what has happened to the initial fact? it became this afternoon. Without knowing how to handle it, I hesitate to be aggressive or to retreat a bit wounded. The initial fact is suspended in the sunlit dust of this Sunday—until they call me to the phone and in a single bound I go gratefully to lick the hand of the one who loves me and sets me free.

Chronologically the situation was thus: a man and a woman were married.

Merely by noting this fact, my foot has sunk in. I have been forced to think about something. Even if I said nothing else, and concluded the story by establishing this, I'd have already got involved in my most unknowable thoughts. It would already be as if I had seen, black outline on a white background, a man and a woman. And on that white background my eyes would be riveted with quite enough to see, for every word has its shadow.

That man and that woman began—without the least intention of going too far, and perhaps spurred by some need people have—they began trying to live more intensely. In search of the destiny that precedes us? and toward which instinct wants to lead us? instinct?!

The attempt to live more intensely led them, in turn, into a kind of constant verifying of revenue and expenditures, trying to weigh what was and wasn't important. They did this in their own way: awkwardly and lacking experience, modestly. They groped along. In a compulsion they both discovered too late in life, each for their own part tried constantly to distinguish what was from what wasn't essential, that is, they would never have used the word *essential*, which didn't belong to their milieu. But the vague, almost embarrassed effort they made came to nothing: the plot eluded them daily. It was only, for example, in looking back at the day that they got the impression of having—somehow and so to speak behind their backs, and thus it didn't count—the impression of having lived. But by then it was night, they put on their slippers and it was night.

All this never quite created a circumstance for the couple. In other words, something they each could tell even themselves when turning over in bed toward one side and, for a second before falling asleep, lay awake with their eyes open. And people need so badly to tell their own story. They didn't have anything to tell. With a sigh of comfort, they'd close their eyes and sleep fitfully. And whenever they calculated the balance of their lives, they couldn't even reckon this attempt to live more intensely, and deduct it, as with income tax. A balance that they gradually started to calculate more frequently, even without the technical equipment of a terminology suited to thoughts. If it was a circumstance, it never managed to become a circumstance for ostensible living.

But that wasn't the only way it happened. In fact they were also calm because "not guiding," "not inventing," "not erring," was for them, far beyond a habit, a point of honor they had tacitly adopted. They would have never considered disobeying.

They had the proud conviction that came from their noble consciousness of being two people among millions of equals. "Being an equal" had been the role that suited them, and the task that fell to them. The pair, distinguished, solemn, gratefully and civic-mindedly lived up to the trust that their equals had placed in them. They belonged to a caste. The role they played, with some emotion and with dignity, was of anonymous people, children of God, as in a club.

It was perhaps strictly due to the insistent passage of time that all this had started, nevertheless, becoming daily, daily, daily. Sometimes breathless. (The man as much as the woman had already entered the critical age.) They'd open the windows and remark on how hot it was. Without exactly living in tedium, it was if they never got any news. Tedium, anyhow, was part of a life of honest feelings.

Yet, ultimately, since all this was incomprehensible to them, and far, far over their heads, and if expressed in words they wouldn't recognize it — all this, taken together and considered as already past, resembled that irremediable life. To which they submitted with a silence of the masses and with that slightly wounded look possessed by men of goodwill. It resembled the irremediable life God wanted us for.

An irremediable life, but not a concrete one. In fact it was a life of dreams. Sometimes, when speaking of some eccentric, they'd say with the benevolence one class bears another: "Ah, he leads the life of a poet." It might be said, taking advantage of the few words known about the couple, it might be said that they led, minus the extravagance, the life of a bad poet: a life of dreams.

No, that's not true. It wasn't a life of dreams, since that had never guided them. But of unreality. Despite moments when suddenly, for some reason or other, they sank into reality. And then they felt they had touched the bottom somewhere beyond which no one could go.

As, for example, whenever the husband got home earlier than usual and his wife hadn't yet returned from some errand or visit. For the husband a flow was then interrupted. He'd carefully sit down to read the paper, immersed in a silence so quiet that even a dead person beside him would have broken it. He feigning with severe honesty a minute absorption in the newspaper, his ears pricked. Just then the husband would touch the bottom with surprised feet. He couldn't stay that way for long, without the risk of drowning, because touching the bottom also means having water over your head. Thus were his concrete moments. Which made him, logical and sensible as he was, break away quickly. He'd quickly break away, though curiously against his will, since his wife's absence was such a promise of dangerous pleasure that he got a taste of what disobedience would be like. He'd break away against his will but without arguing, obeying what was expected of him. He wasn't a deserter who would betray the trust of the others. Besides, if that's what reality was like, there was no way of living in or off it.

As for the wife, she touched reality more often, since she had more leisure and less of what are called facts, such as coworkers, a crowded bus, administrative terms. She'd sit down to mend clothes, and little by little along came reality. The sensation of sitting there mending clothes was intolerable while it lasted. The sudden manner in which the *i* was dotted, that way of fitting entirely into whatever existed and of everything remaining so distinctly whatever it was—was intolerable. But, once it faded, it was as if the wife had drunk of a possible future. Gradually this woman's future was turning into something she brought into the present, something meditative and secret.

It was surprising how untouched they were, for example, by politics, by changes in government, by developments in general, though they sometimes discussed these matters too, like everyone else. Indeed, they were such reserved people that they would have been surprised, flattered, if anyone ever told them they were reserved. They would have never imagined that's what it was called. They might have understood better if told: "you symbolize our military reserve." A few acquaintances said of them, after it all happened: they were good people. And there was nothing else to say, since they were.

There was nothing else to say. They lacked the weight of a grave error, which so often just happens to be what opens a door. At some point they'd taken something very seriously. They were obedient.

Not just out of submissiveness: as in a sonnet, it was obedience from love of symmetry. Symmetry was their possible art.

How each came to the conclusion that, alone, without the other, they'd live more—would be a long arc to reconstruct, and a pointless undertaking, since plenty of people have arrived at the same point from all over.

The wife, beneath this continual fantasy, not only rashly arrived at this conclusion but she transformed her life into something broader and more bewildered, richer, and even superstitious. Each thing seemed to signal another, all was symbolic, and even had a touch of spiritualism within the bounds of what Catholicism would allow. Not only did she rashly move on to this but — provoked exclusively by the fact of being a woman — she began to think that another man would save her. Which wasn't altogether absurd. She knew it wasn't. Being half right confused her, plunged her into reflection.

The husband, influenced by the milieu of afflicted masculinity in which he lived, and by his own as well, which was shy but effective, started to think that life would be many love affairs.

Dreamy, they began to suffer dreamily, it was heroic to bear. Quiet about their own fleeting visions, disagreeing over the best time to have dinner, one serving as a sacrifice for the other, love is sacrifice.

Thus we arrive at the day on which, long since engulfed in dreams, the woman, taking a bite of an apple, felt one of her front teeth crack. Still holding the apple and looking at herself too closely in the bathroom mirror — and thus losing all perspective — she saw a pale, middle-aged face, with a cracked tooth, and her own eyes ... Touching the bottom, and with the water already up to her neck, fifty-something years old, without a note, instead of going to the dentist, she threw herself out the apartment window, a person toward whom such gratitude could be felt, that military reserve and pillar of our disobedience.

As for him, once the riverbed ran dry and with no water left to drown in, he walked along the bottom without looking at the ground, briskly as if using a cane. With the riverbed unexpectedly dry, he walked bewildered and out of danger along the bottom with the nimbleness of someone about to fall on his face.

The Foreign Legion
("A legião estrangeira")

IF ANYONE ASKED ME ABOUT OFÉLIA AND HER PAR-
ents, I'd have answered with the decorum of honesty: I hardly
knew them. Before the same jury I'd answer: I hardly know
myself—and to every face in the jury I'd say with the same
clear-eyed look of someone hypnotized into obedience: I
hardly know you. Yet sometimes I awake from a long slumber
and I meekly turn to the delicate abyss of disorder.

I am trying to talk about that family that disappeared years
ago without leaving a trace in me, and of whom all I've retained
is an image tinged green by distance. My unexpected consent
to know was provoked today by the fact that a chick turned
up in the house. It was brought by a hand that wanted the
pleasure of giving me something born. As soon as we released
the chick, its charm took us by surprise. Tomorrow is Christmas, but the moment of silence I await all year came a day
before Christ's birth. A thing peeping on its own rouses that
ever so gentle curiosity that beside a manger is worship. Well,
well, said my husband, and now look at that. He'd felt too big.
Dirty, mouths open, the boys approached. I, feeling a bit daring, was happy. The chick, it kept peeping. But Christmas

is tomorrow, my older boy said bashfully. We were smiling helplessly, curious.

Yet feelings are the water of an instant. Soon—as the same water is already different when the sun turns it clear, and different when it gets riled up trying to bite a stone, and different over a submerged foot—soon our faces no longer held only aura and illumination. Surrounding the woeful chick, we were kind and anxious. With my husband, kindness makes him gruff and severe, which we're used to; he crucifies himself a bit. In the boys, who are more solemn, kindness is a kind of ardor. With me, kindness intimidates. In a little while the same water was different, and we watched with strained looks, tangled in our clumsiness at being good. And, the water different still, gradually our faces held the responsibility of a yearning, hearts heavy with a love that was no longer free. What also threw us off was the chick's fear of us; there we were, and none of us deserved to be in the presence of a chick; with every peep, it scattered us back. With every peep, it reduced us to doing nothing. The steadiness of its fright accused us of a frivolous joy that by then was no longer even joy, it was vexation. The chick's moment had passed, and it, ever more urgently, was expelling us without letting us go. We, the adults, had already shut down our feelings. But in the boys there was a silent indignation, and their accusation was that we were doing nothing for the chick or for humanity. With us, father and mother, the increasingly endless peeping had already led to an embarrassed resignation: that's just how things are. But we had never told the boys this, we were ashamed; and we'd been putting off indefinitely the moment to call them and explain clearly that's how things are. It got harder every time, the silence would grow, and they'd slightly push away the eagerness with which we wanted to offer them, in exchange, love.

Since we'd never discussed these things, now we had to hide from them all the more the smiling that ultimately came over us at the desperate peeping from that beak, smiling as if it were up to us to bless the fact that this was just how things are, and we had newly blessed them.

The chick, it kept peeping. On the polished table it didn't venture a step, a movement, it peeped inwardly. I didn't even know where there was room for all that terror in a thing made only of feathers. Feathers covering what? a half dozen bones that had come together weakly for what? for the peeping of a terror. In silence, respecting the impossibility of understanding ourselves, respecting the boys' revolt against us, in silence we watched without much patience. It was impossible to offer it that reassuring word that would make it not be afraid, to console a thing frightened because it was born. How could we promise it would get used to things? A father and mother, we knew how fleeting the chick's life would be. It knew as well, in that way that living things know: through profound fright.

And meanwhile, the chick full of grace, brief and yellow thing. I wanted for it too to feel the grace of its life, just as we'd been asked to, that being who was a joy for others, not for itself. For it to feel that it was gratuitous, not even necessary—one chick has to be useless—it had been born only for the glory of God, thus it was the joy of men. Yet wanting the chick to be happy just because we loved it was loving our own love. I also knew that only a mother can resolve birth, and ours was the love of those who rejoice in loving: I was caught up in the grace of having been allowed to love, bells, bells ringing because I know how to worship. But the chick was trembling, a thing of terror, not beauty.

The youngest boy couldn't bear it any longer:

"Do you want to be its mother?"

I said yes, startled. I was the envoy dispatched to that thing that didn't understand my only language: I was loving without being loved. The mission could fail, and the eyes of four boys awaited with the intransigence of hope my first effective gesture of love. I retreated a little, smiling in total solitude, looked at my family, wanting them to smile. A man and four boys were staring at me, incredulous and trusting. I was the woman of the house, the granary. Why this impassiveness from the five of them, I didn't get it. How often I must have failed to cause, in my moment of shyness, them to be looking at me. I tried to isolate myself from the challenge of the five men so that I too would put hope in myself and remember what love is like. I opened my mouth, about to tell them the truth: I don't know how.

But what if a woman came to me at night. What if she were holding her son in her lap. And said: heal my son. I'd say: how is it done? She'd answer: heal my son. I'd say: I don't know how either. She'd reply: heal my son. So then—so then because I don't know how to do anything and because I don't remember anything and because it is night—so then I reach out my hand and save a child. Because it is night, because I am alone in someone else's night, because this silence is too great for me, because I have two hands in order to sacrifice the better one and because I have no choice.

So I reached out my hand and picked up the chick.

In that moment I saw Ofélia again. And in that moment I remembered that I had borne witness to a little girl.

Later I remembered how the neighbor, Ofélia's mother, was dusky like a Hindu. She had purplish circles under her eyes that greatly heightened her beauty and gave her an air of fatigue that made men give her a second look. One day, on a bench in the square, while the children were playing, she'd told me with that head of hers, obstinate as someone gazing at the desert: "I've always wanted to take a cake-decorating class." I recalled that her husband—dusky too, as if they'd chosen each other for the dryness of their color—wished to move up in life through his business interests: hotel management or even ownership, I never quite understood. Which gave him a stiff politeness. Whenever we were forced into more prolonged contact in the elevator, he'd accept our exchange of words in a tone of arrogance he brought from greater struggles. By the time we reached the tenth floor, the humility his coldness forced on me had already calmed him somewhat; perhaps he arrived home more satisfied. As for Ofélia's mother, she was afraid that our living on the same floor would create some kind of intimacy and, without knowing that I too kept to myself, avoided me. Our only moment of intimacy had occurred on that park bench, where, with the dark circles under her eyes and her thin mouth, she'd talked about decorating cakes. I hadn't known how to respond and ended up saying, so she'd know I liked her, that I'd enjoy that cake class. That single moment in common distanced us even more, for fear of an abuse of understanding. Ofélia's mother even turned rude in the elevator: the next day I was holding one of the boys by the hand, the elevator was slowly descending, and I, oppressed by the silence that, with the other woman there, was strengthening—said in a pleasant voice that I also immediately found repugnant:

"We're on our way to his grandmother's."

And she, to my shock:

"I didn't ask you anything, I never stick my nose in my neighbors' business."

"Well," I said softly.

Which, right there in the elevator, made me think that I was paying for having been her confidante for a minute on the park bench. Which, in turn, made me think she might have figured that she'd confided more than she actually had. Which, in turn, made me wonder whether she hadn't in fact told me more than either of us realized. As the elevator kept descending and stopping, I reconstructed her insistent and dreamy look on the park bench—and looked with new eyes at the haughty beauty of Ofélia's mother. "I won't tell anyone you want to decorate cakes," I thought glancing at her.

The father aggressive, the mother keeping to herself. An imperious family. They treated me as if I already lived in their future hotel and were offended that I hadn't paid. Above all they treated me as if I neither believed, nor could they prove who they were. And who were they? I wondered sometimes. Why that slap imprinted on their faces, why that exiled dynasty? And they so failed to forgive me that I acted unforgiven: if I ran into them on the street, beyond my circumscribed sector, it took me by surprise, caught red-handed: I'd stand aside to let them pass, give them the right of way—all three, dusky and dressed up, would walk by as if on their way to mass, that family that lived under the sign of some pride or concealed martyrdom, purple-hued like passion flowers. An ancient family, that one.

But our contact happened through the daughter. She was an extremely beautiful little girl, with long, stiff curls, Ofélia, with dark circles under her eyes just like her mother's, the same purplish gums, the same thin mouth like a slit. But this one, the mouth, spoke. It led to her showing up at my place.

She'd ring the doorbell, I'd open the peephole, not see anything, hear a resolute voice:

"It's me, Ofélia Maria dos Santos Aguiar."

Disheartened, I'd open the door. Ofélia would come in. The visit was for me, since back then my two boys were too young for her drawn-out wisdom. I was grown up and busy, but the visit was for me: with an entirely inward focus, as if there were time enough for everything, she'd carefully lift her ruffled skirt, sit down, arrange her ruffles—and only then look at me. As for me, then in the process of transcribing the office records, I'd work and listen. As for Ofélia, she'd give me advice. She had a clear opinion about everything. Everything I did was a bit wrong, in her opinion. She'd say "in my opinion" in an offended tone, as if I should have asked her advice and, since I didn't, she gave it. With her eight haughty and experienced years, she'd say that in her opinion I wasn't raising the boys properly; because give boys an inch and they'll take miles. Never mix bananas and milk. It's deadly. But of course you do whatever you like, ma'am; to each his own. It was too late to be in your bathrobe; her mother changed clothes as soon as she got out of bed, but everyone ends up leading the life they want to live. If I explained that it was because I hadn't yet showered, Ofélia wouldn't say anything, watching me intently. Somewhat gently, then, somewhat patiently, she'd add that it was too late not to have showered. I never got the last word. What last word could I offer when she'd tell me: vegetable pies don't have a top crust. One afternoon at a bakery I found myself unexpectedly confronted with the pointless truth: there with no top crust was a row of vegetable pies. "I told you so," I heard as if she were right there. With her curls and ruffles, with her firm delicacy, she brought an inquisition into the still-messy living room. What mattered was that she also talked a lot of non-sense, which, in my despondency, made me smile hopelessly.

The worst part of the inquisition was the silence. I'd lift my eyes from the typewriter and have no idea how long Ofélia had been silently watching me. What about me could possibly attract that little girl? I wondered in exasperation. Once, after her long silence, she calmly told me: ma'am, you're weird. And I, struck squarely in my unsheltered face—of all things in the face that, being our insides, is such a sensitive thing—I, struck squarely, thought angrily: I'll bet it's that weirdness that brings you around. She who was completely sheltered, and had a sheltered mother, and a sheltered father.

I still preferred, anyhow, advice and criticism. What was less tolerable was her habit of using the word *therefore* to connect clauses in an unerring concatenation. She told me that I had bought too many vegetables at the market—therefore—they wouldn't fit in that small refrigerator and—therefore—they'd wilt before the next market day. Days later I stood looking at the wilted vegetables. Therefore, yes. Another time she had noticed fewer vegetables scattered on the kitchen table, I who had covertly obeyed. Ofélia stared, stared. She seemed on the verge of not saying anything. I stood waiting, combative, mute. Ofélia remarked in an even tone:

"That's not enough to last until the next market day."

The vegetables ran out halfway through the week. How does she know? I wondered curiously. "Therefore" could have been the answer. Why did I never, ever know? Why did she know everything, why was the earth so familiar to her, and I unsheltered? Therefore? Therefore.

One time Ofélia made a mistake. Geography—she said sitting across from me with her fingers clasped in her lap—is a way of studying. It wasn't exactly a mistake, it was more of a slightly cross-eyed thought—but for me it held the charm of a fall, and before the moment faded, I inwardly told her: that's exactly how it's done, just like that! keep going slowly like that, and one day it'll be easier or harder for you, but that's how it is, keep making mistakes, very, very slowly.

One morning, in mid-discussion, she informed me authoritatively: "I'm going home to check on something but I'll be right back." I ventured: "If you're really busy, you don't have to come back." Ofélia stared at me mute, inquisitive. "There goes a very unlikeable little girl," I thought very clearly so she could see the entire statement exposed on my face. She kept staring. A stare in which—with surprise and sorrow—I saw faithfulness, patient trust in me and the silence of someone who never spoke. When had I thrown her a bone to make her mutely follow me for the rest of her life? I looked away. She sighed calmly. And said even more resolutely: "I'll be right back." What does she want?—I got worked up—why do I attract people who don't even like me?

Once, when Ofélia was sitting there, someone rang the doorbell. I went to answer it and found Ofélia's mother. There she stood, protective, demanding:

"Is Ofélia Maria there by any chance?"

"She is," I excused myself as if I had kidnapped her.

"Don't do this anymore," she said to Ofélia in a voice directed at me; then she turned to me and, suddenly offended: "Sorry for the inconvenience."

"Not at all, this little girl is so clever."

Her mother looked at me in mild surprise—but suspicion flickered in her eyes. And in them I read: what do you want from her?

"I've already told Ofélia Maria she's not allowed to bother you," she said now with open distrust. And firmly grabbing the girl's hand to take her away, she seemed to be defending her against me. With a feeling of decadence, I peered through the peephole I cracked open without a sound: there they went down the hallway to their apartment, the mother covering her daughter with lovingly murmured scolding, the daughter impassive with her curls and ruffles bobbing. Closing the peephole I realized I hadn't yet changed clothes and, therefore, had been witnessed in that state by the mother who changed clothes as soon as she got out of bed. I thought somewhat unapologetically: well, now the mother looks down on me, therefore I'm rid of that girl ever coming back.

But she kept coming back. I was too attractive to that child. I had plenty of flaws for her advice, I was fertile ground for her to cultivate her severity, I'd already become the realm of that slave of mine: she kept coming back, lifting her ruffles, sitting down.

On that occasion, because it was almost Easter, the market was full of chicks, and I brought one home for the boys. We played with it, then it stayed in the kitchen, the boys went outside. Later Ofélia showed up for a visit. I was typing away, distractedly giving in every so often. The girl's steady voice, the voice of someone reciting by heart, was making me a little dizzy, slipping in among the written words; she kept talking, kept talking.

That's when it struck me that everything had suddenly stopped. Sensing a lack of torture, I looked at her hazily. Ofélia Maria was holding her head erect, her curls completely still.

"What's that," she said.

"That what?"

"That!" she said unwavering.

"That?"

We would have been stuck indefinitely in a round of "that?" and "that!" if not for the exceptional will of that child, who, without a word, solely through the extreme authority of her stare, compelled me to hear what she herself was hearing. In the rapt silence she had forced on me, I finally heard the faint peeping of the chick in the kitchen.

"It's the chick."

"Chick?" she said, extremely suspicious.

"I bought a chick," I replied in resignation.

"A chick!" she repeated as if I'd insulted her.

"A chick."

And we would have been stuck there. If not for a certain something I saw and that I'd never seen before.

What was it? But, whatever it was, it was no longer there. A chick had twinkled for a second in her eyes and submerged into them never to have existed. And the shadow had fallen. A deep shadow across the land. From the instant her trembling mouth had been on the verge of involuntarily thinking "I want one too," from that instant the darkness had gathered in the depths of her eyes in a retractable desire that, if anyone touched her, would shut even tighter like the leaves of a bashful mimosa. And would shrink before the impossible, the impossible that came close and, in temptation, had almost been hers: the darkness in her eyes flickered like a gold coin. A certain mischief then passed over her face—if I hadn't been there, out of mischief, she'd have stolen anything. In those eyes blinking with dissimulated wisdom, in her eyes that great propensity for plunder. She glanced at me, and it was envy, you have everything, and reproach, since we're not the same and I have a chick, and covetousness — she wanted me for herself. Slowly I started leaning into the back of my chair, her envy that bared my poverty, and turned my poverty pensive; if I hadn't been there, she'd have stolen my poverty too; she wanted everything. After the covetous tremor faded, the darkness in her eyes suffered in full: I hadn't just exposed her to an unsheltered face, I had now exposed her to the best thing in the world: a chick. Without seeing me, her hot eyes stared at me in an intense abstraction that placed itself in intimate contact with my intimate self. Something was happening that I couldn't manage to understand with the naked eye. And once more the desire came back. This time her eyes grew anguished as if there was nothing they could do with the rest of her body that was independently pulling away. And they grew even wider, alarmed at the physical force of the decomposition happening inside her. Her delicate mouth became a little childish, a bruised purple. She looked at the ceiling — the circles under her eyes gave her an air of supreme martyrdom. Without moving, I was looking at her. I knew about the high incidence of infant mortality. In her case I got swept up in the great question: is it worthwhile? I don't know, my increasing stillness told her, but that's how it is. There, faced with my silence, she was giving herself over to the process, and if she asked me the great question, it would have to go unanswered. She had to give herself — for nothing. That's how it would have to be. And for nothing. She was clinging to something inside herself, not wanting it. But I was waiting. I knew that we are the thing that must happen. I could only help her in silence. And, dazzled by misunderstanding, I heard a heart beating inside me that wasn't mine. Before my fascinated eyes, right there before me, like an ectoplasm, she was being transformed into a child.

Not without pain. In silence I was seeing the pain of her difficult joy. The slow fury of a snail. She ran her tongue slowly over her thin lips. (Help me, said her body in its arduous bifurcation. I'm helping, my immobility answered.) The slow agony. She was swelling all over, slowly being deformed. There were moments her eyes became all lashes, with the eagerness of an egg. And her mouth had a trembling hunger. She was nearly smiling then, as if laid out on an operating table saying it didn't hurt that badly. She didn't lose sight of me: there were the footprints she didn't see, someone had already walked through there, and she guessed that I had walked a lot. More and more she was being deformed, nearly identical to herself. Do I risk it? do I let myself feel?, she was asking inside herself. Yes, she answered herself through me.

And my first yes intoxicated me. Yes, my silence repeated to hers, yes. As when my son was born I said to him: yes. I had the audacity to say yes to Ofélia, who knew that we can also die in childhood without anyone noticing. Yes, I repeated intoxicated, because there is no greater danger: when you go, you go together, you yourself will always be there: that, that is what you will take along into whatever you shall be.

The agony of her birth. Until then I had never seen courage. The courage to be something other than what one is, to give birth to oneself, and to leave one's former body on the ground. And without having answered to anyone about whether it was worthwhile. "I," her fluid-soaked body was trying to say. Her nuptials with herself.

Ofélia asked slowly, wary of what was happening to her:

"Is it a chick?"

I didn't look at her.

"Yes, it's a chick."

From the kitchen came the faint peeping. We sat in silence as if Jesus had been born. Ofélia was breathing, breathing.

"A little chick?" she confirmed doubtfully.

"Yes, a little chick," I said guiding her carefully toward life.

"Oh, a little chick," she said, considering it.

"A little chick," I said without being hard on her.

For several minutes now I had found myself facing a child. The metamorphosis had occurred.

"It's in the kitchen."

"In the kitchen?" she repeated pretending not to understand.

"In the kitchen," I repeated authoritatively for the first time, without adding anything else.

"Oh, in the kitchen," Ofélia said in a very fake voice and looked up at the ceiling.

But she was suffering. Somewhat ashamed I finally realized that I was taking my revenge. She was suffering, pretending, looking at the ceiling. That mouth, those circles under her eyes.

"You can go in the kitchen and play with the chick."

"Me ... ?" she asked, playing dumb.

"But only if you want to."

I know I should have ordered her to, so as to avoid exposing her to the humiliation of wanting to so badly. I know I shouldn't have given her the choice, and then she'd have the excuse of being forced to obey. But right then it wasn't out of revenge that I was giving her the torment of freedom. It was because that step, that step too she had to take on her own. On her own and now. She herself would have to go to the mountain. Why — I was confusing myself — why am I trying to breathe my life into her purple mouth? why am I giving her breath? how dare I breathe into her, if I myself ... — just so she can walk, I am giving her these arduous steps? I breathe my life into her just so that one day, exhausted, she for an instant can feel that the mountain went to her?

It would be my right. But I had no choice. It was an emergency as if the girl's lips were turning more and more purple.

"Only go see the little chick if you want to," I then repeated with the extreme severity of someone saving another.

We sat face to face, dissimilar, bodies separate from each other; only hostility united us. I was harsh and inert in my chair so that the girl would cause herself pain inside another being, firm so she would struggle inside of me; getting stronger the more that Ofélia needed to hate me and needed me to resist the suffering of her hatred. I cannot live this for you—my coldness said to her. Her struggle was happening ever closer and inside me, as if that individual who at birth had been extraordinarily endowed with strength were drinking of my weakness. By using me she was hurting me with her strength; she was clawing at me while trying to cling to my smooth walls. Finally her voice resounded in soft and slow anger:

"I guess I'll go see the chick in the kitchen."

"Go ahead," I said slowly.

She took her time, trying to maintain the dignity in her back.

She came back from the kitchen immediately—she was amazed, unabashed, showing the chick in her hand, and with a bewilderment in her eyes that wholly questioned me:

"It's a little chick!" she said.

She looked at it in her outstretched hand, looked at me, then looked back at her hand—and suddenly filled with an anxiousness and worry that automatically drew me into anxiousness and worry.

"But it's a little chick!" she said, and reproach immediately flickered in her eyes as if I hadn't told her who was peeping.

I laughed. Ofélia looked at me, outraged. And suddenly—

suddenly she laughed. We both burst into laughter then, a bit shrill.

After we'd laughed, Ofélia put the chick on the floor to let it walk around. If it ran, she ran after it, she seemed to let it be autonomous just so she could miss it; but if it cowered, she'd rush to protect it, sorry that it was under her control, "poor thing, he's mine"; and whenever she held it, her hand was crooked with care — it was love, yes, tortured love. He's really small, therefore you have to be really careful, we can't pet him because it's really dangerous; don't let them pick him up whenever they want, you can do what you like, ma'am, but corn's too big for his little open beak; because he's so fragile, poor thing, so young, therefore you can't let your sons pet him; only I know how he likes to be petted; he keeps on slipping, therefore the kitchen floor isn't the right place for a little chick.

For quite some time I'd been trying to go back to typing in an attempt to make up for all that lost time and with Ofélia lulling me, and gradually talking only to the little chick, and loving with love. For the first time she'd dropped me, she was no longer me. I looked at her, all golden as she was, and the chick all golden, and the two of them humming like distaff and spindle. And my freedom at last, and without a rupture; farewell, and I was smiling with nostalgia.

Much later I realized that Ofélia was talking to me.

"I think — I think I'm going to put him in the kitchen."

"Go ahead."

I didn't see when she left, I didn't see when she returned. At some point, by chance and distractedly, I sensed how long things had been quiet. I looked at her for an instant. She was seated, fingers clasped on her lap. Without knowing exactly why, I looked at her a second time:

"What is it?"

"Me ... ?"

"Are you feeling sick?"

"Me ... ?"

"Do you want to go to the bathroom?"

"Me ... ?"

I gave up, went back to the typewriter. A while later I heard her voice:

"I'm going to have to go home."

"All right."

"If you let me, ma'am."

I looked at her in surprise:

"Well, if you want to ..."

"Then," she said, "then I'm going."

She left walking slowly, shut the door without a sound. I kept staring at the closed door. You're the weird one, I thought. I went back to work.

But I couldn't make it past the same sentence. Okay—I thought impatiently looking at my watch—and what is it now? I sat there interrogating myself halfheartedly, seeking within myself for what could be interrupting me. When I was about to give up, I recalled an extremely still face: Ofélia. Something not quite an idea flashed through my head which, at the unexpected thought, tilted to better hear what I was sensing. Slowly I pushed the typewriter away. Reluctant, I slowly moved the chairs out of my way. Until I paused slowly at the kitchen door. On the floor was the dead chick. Ofélia! I called in an impulse for the girl who had fled.

From an infinite distance I saw the floor. Ofélia, I tried in vain to bridge the distance to the speechless girl's heart. Oh, don't be so afraid! sometimes we kill out of love, but I swear that some day we forget, I swear! we don't love very well, listen, I repeated as if I could reach her before, giving up on serving the truth, she'd haughtily serve the nothing. I who hadn't remembered to warn her that without fear there was the world. But I swear that is what breathing is. I was very tired, I sat on the kitchen stool.

Where I am now, slowly beating the batter for tomorrow's cake. Sitting, as if for all these years I've been waiting patiently in the kitchen. Under the table, today's chick trembles. The yellow is the same, the beak is the same. As we are promised on Easter, in December he will return. Ofélia is the one who didn't return: she grew up. She went off to become the Hindu princess her tribe awaited in the desert.

BACK OF THE DRAWER
(Fundo de gaveta)

The Burned Sinner and the Harmonious Angels
("A pecadora queimada e os anjos harmoniosos")

INVISIBLE ANGELS: BEHOLD US NEARLY HERE, COMING down the long path that exists before you all. But we are not tired, such a road does not require strength and, were it to require vigor, not even that of your prayers would lift us. Dizziness alone is what makes us whirl round shouting with the leaves until the opening of a birth. Is dizziness all it takes, as far as we know? if men hesitate over men, angels know nothing of angels, the world is wide and may whatever is be blessed. We are not tired, our feet have never been washed. Screeching at this next diversion, we came so as to suffer what must be suffered, we who have yet to be touched, we who have yet to be boy and girl. Behold us in the web of true tragedy, from which we shall extricate our primary form. When we open our eyes to become those who are born, we shall remember nothing: babbling children we shall be and we shall wield your very weapons. Blind on the path that precedes footsteps, blind shall we push onward when we are born with eyes that already see. Nor do we know what we have come to. All we need is the conviction that what is to be done shall be done: an angel's fall is a direction. Our true beginning precedes the visible beginning, and our true end will follow the visible end. Harmony, terrible harmony, is our only prior destiny.

Priest: In love for the Lord I have not lost my way, always secure in Thy day as in Thy night. And this simple woman lost her way for so little, and lost her nature, and behold her possessing nothing more and, now pure, whatever remains to her they will yet burn. The strange paths. She sealed her fate with a single sin to which she surrendered entirely, and behold her on the threshold of being saved. Every humble path is a path: crude sin is a path, ignorance of the commandments is a path, lust is a path. The only thing not a path was my premature joy at taking, as a guide and so easily, the sacred path. The only thing not a path was my presumption of being saved halfway through. Lord, grant me the grace to sin. It weighs heavily, the lack of temptation in which thou hast left me. Where are the water and fire through which I never passed? Lord, grant me the grace to sin. This candle I was, burning in Thy name, was always burning in the light and I saw nothing. Yet, ah hope that will open the doors of Thy violent heaven to me: now I see that, if thou hast not made of me the torch that will blaze, at least thou hast made the one who fans the flames. Ah hope, in which I can still see my pride in being chosen: in guilt I beat my breast, and with joy that I would like to mortify I say: the Lord sought me out to sin more than she who sinned, and at last I shall seal my tragedy. For it was my wrathful word that Thou didst employ so I might perform, more than the sin, the sin of punishing the sin. So that I might descend so far beneath my dangerous peace that the total darkness—where neither candelabras nor papal purple exist and not even the symbol of the Cross—the total darkness might be Thee. "The darkness shall not blind thee," it was said in the Psalms.

People: For days we have gone hungry and here we are in search of food.

Enter sinner and two guards.

Priest: "She took her delight in the slavery of the senses," by the sign of the Holy Cross.

People: Behold her, behold her, and behold her.

Sleepy child: Behold her.

Woman of the people: Behold her, she who erred, she who in order to sin required two men and one priest and one people.

1st guard: We are the guardians of our homeland. We suffocate in airless peace, and of the last war we have already forgotten even the bugles. Our beloved King distributes us to posts of extreme responsibility, but in keeping useless watch we have nearly put to sleep our virility. Created to die in glory, behold us ashamedly living.

2nd guard: We are the guardians of a lord, whose domain seems rather confusing to us: sometimes extending to the borders established by habit and use, and our spears then rise at the cries of the heralds. At other times this domain penetrates into lands where there exists a much older law. So behold us this time guarding something that on its own will always be guarded, by the people and by fate. Under this sky of strangled tranquility, bread may be lacking, but the mystery of achievement never will. For what are we imaginarily watching over? if not the destiny of a heart.

1st guard: How your last words recall the longed-for thundering of a cannon. What desire to keep watch at last over a smaller world, where our spears deal the death-blow to whatever is going to die. But here we are guarding a woman who in a manner of speaking has already been set afire of her own accord.

Invisible angels: Set afire by harmony, bloody sweet harmony, which is our prior destiny.

Enter the Husband.

People: Behold the husband, he who was betrayed.

Husband: Behold her, she who will be burned by my wrath. Who spoke through me, giving me such fatal power? I was the one who incited the word of the priest and gathered this troop of people and roused the spears of the guards, and granted this public square such an aspect of glory that crumbles its walls. Ah still-beloved wife, I would like to be relieved of this invasion. I dreamed of being alone with you and reminding you of our past joy. Leave her alone with me, for since yesterday I live and do not live, leave her alone with me. Before you all — strangers to my former happiness and to my present wretchedness — I can no longer see in this woman she who was and was not mine, nor in our past celebration she who was and was not ours, nor can I taste the bitterness that is mine and mine alone. What will happen to this heart of mine that no longer recognizes the offspring of its Vengeance? Ah remorse: I should have brandished the dagger with my own hand, and then I would have known that, as the one betrayed, I took vengeance myself. But this spectacle no longer belongs to my world, and this woman, whom I took in modesty, I lose to the sound of trumpets. Leave me alone with the sinner. I want to regain my former love, and then be filled with hatred, and then murder her myself, and then worship her again, and then never forget her, leave me alone with the sinner. I want to take possession of my disgrace and my vengeance and my loss, and you are all preventing me from being lord of this fire, leave me alone with the sinner.

Priest: Many years has it been since a saint was born. Many years has it been since a child prophesied from the cradle.

Many years has it been since the blind man has seen, the leper was cured, ah what a barren time. We exist beneath the burden of such a mystery to be revealed that at the first sign, in a bolt of lightning, Thy hoped-for miracle must be sealed.

1st guard: Everyone speaks and no one listens.

2nd guard: Everyone is alone with the guilty woman.

Enter the Lover.

1st guard: The comedy is complete: behold the lover, I am overjoyed.

People: Behold the lover, behold the lover and behold the lover.

Sleepy child: Behold the lover.

Lover: Irony that makes me laugh not: to call lover he who burned with love, to call lover he who lost it. No, not the lover. But the lover betrayed.

People: We do not understand, we do not understand and we do not understand.

Lover: Because this woman who in my arms deceived her husband, in the arms of her husband deceived the one deceiving him.

People: So then she hid her lover from her husband, and her husband from her lover? Behold the sin of sins.

Lover: But I laugh not and for a moment I do not suffer. I now open the eyes I have kept closed out of pridefulness, and I ask of you: who? who is this foreign woman, who is this solitary woman for whom one heart was not enough.

Husband: She is the one for whom I would bring back brocades and precious stones from my travels, and for whom all my commerce of value had become a commerce of love.

Lover: For in her candid joy she would come to me so singularly mine that I never would have guessed she was coming from a home.

Husband: There was no jewel she did not covet, and for her the bareness of her neck did not choke. Nothing existed that I did not give her, since for a humble and weary traveler peace is in his wife.

Priest: "A man's foes shall be they of his own household."

Husband: But in the transparency of a diamond she was already foreseeing the arrival of a lover. He who tells you this is one who has tasted venom: beware a woman who dreams.

Lover: Ah wretched woman, for she dreamed beside me too. What more therefore did she want? who is this foreign woman?

Priest: She is the one to whom on holy days I would offer in vain words of Virtue that might with a thousand cloaks have covered her nakedness.

Woman of the people: All these words have strange meanings. Who is this woman who sinned and seems instead to receive praise for her sin?

Lover: She is that unrevealed woman whom only pain revealed to my eyes. For the first time, I love. I love you.

Husband: She is that woman whom sin belatedly proclaimed to me. For the first time I love you, and not my peace.

People: She is that woman who in truth gave herself to no one, and now is completely ours.

Invisible angels: For harmony is terrible.

People: We do not understand, we do not understand and etc.

Invisible angels: Even here on this side of the edge of the world we hardly understand, much less you, the starving, and you, the sated. May the generative sentence be enough for you: what must be done shall be done, this is the one perfect principle.

People: We do not understand, we are hungry and we are hungry.

1st guard: This tiresome people, if summoned to a feast or a funeral, might just sing ...

People: ... we are hungry.

2nd guard: They always lay the same trap that consists of a single chant ...

People: ... we are hungry.

Priest: Do not interrupt with your hunger, rather be calm, for yours shall be the Kingdom of Heaven.

People: Where we shall eat, and eat and eat, and get so fat that through the eye of a needle at last and at last we shall not pass.

Priest: What did this people come to do? and wherefore did the husband, the lover, and the guards come? For alone with me, this woman would be set afire.

Lover: What did this people come to do? Alone with me, she would love again, again would she sin, repent again—and thus in a single instant Love would again be fulfilled, the thing that carries its own dagger and end. I would recall to you those messages at nightfall ... The impatient horse would wait, the lamp on the terrace ... And then ... ah earth, thy fields at day-break, a certain window that already in the dark was starting to dawn. And the wine that I in joy would then sip, until sinking with drunken tears into gloom. (Ah then it is true that even in happiness I already sought in tears to know the foretaste of misfortune.)

Invisible angels: The foretaste of terrible harmony.

Sleepy child: She is smiling.

People: She is smiling, she is smiling and she is smiling.

Husband: And her eyes glisten damply as in a glory ...

Woman of the people: In the end how does it come to pass

that this woman about to be burned is already becoming her own story?

People: What is this woman smiling at?

Priest: Perhaps she is thinking that, alone, she would already have been set afire.

People: What is this woman smiling at.

1st and 2nd guards: At sin.

Invisible angels: At harmony, harmony, harmony that tarries not.

Lover: You smile, inaccessible, and the first burst of wrath seizes me. Remember how in the alcove where I met you your smile was different, and the way your eyes glistened, your only tears. Through what strange grace did abject sin transfigure you into this woman who smiles filled with silence?

Husband: Impotent fury: behold her smiling, yet more absent from me than when she belonged to another. Why has this people heard me so much more than my words wished to be heard? Ah cruel mechanism I unleashed with my wounded laments. For I have rendered her unattainable even before she dies. The incitement for the burning was mine, but the victory will not be: it now belongs to the people, to the priest, to the guards. For you, wretches, cannot hide that it is upon my misery that you shall live in the end.

Lover: You smile because you used me so that even while alive you might yet blaze in the fire.

Husband: Hear me once more, wife … (How strange it is, perhaps she heard, but it is I who can no longer find the former words. Doubt that now exceeds bounds: when was it I and when was it not I? I was the one who loved her, but who is this person being avenged? He who in me was speaking until now, fell silent as soon as he achieved his aims. What is happening for me not to recognize the former face of my love? Perhaps she heard me, but speaking has ended for me.)

Invisible angels: Remove your hands from your face, husband. He who was no longer is, the opening of the curtains has revealed: that you are the lowliest, lowliest, lowliest wheel of the terrible, terrible harmony.

Lover: I thought I had lived, but she was the one who was living me. I was lived.

Husband: How can I recognize you, if you are smiling utterly sanctified? These chaste arms are not the arms that deceivingly embraced me. And could this hair be the same that I used to let down? I have interrupted you all, and the one who says so is the same who incited you. For I see an error and I see a crime, a monstrous upheaval: behold, the woman sinned with one body, and you burn another.

Priest: But "Lord, thou art always the same."

1st guard: All regret what is too late to regret, and disagree for the sake of disagreeing, knowing full well they came here to kill.

2nd guard: Behold at last the moment that will grant us the taste of war.

Priest: Behold the moment when, by the grace of the Lord, I shall sin with the sinner, I shall blaze with the sinner, and in the infernos to which I shall descend with her, by Thy name shall be saved.

Invisible angels: Behold the moment has arrived. Already we feel a difficulty of dawn. We are on the threshold of our initial form. It must be good to be born.

People: May she who is about to die speak.

Priest: Leave her be. I fear from this woman who is ours a word that is hers.

People: May she who is about to die speak.

Lover: Leave her be. Don't you see how alone she is.

People: May she speak, may she speak and may she speak.

Invisible angels: May she not speak … may she not speak … since we hardly need her …

People: May she speak, may she speak and may etc.

Priest: Take her death as her word.

People: We do not understand, we do not understand and we do not understand.

1st and 2nd guards: Get ye away, for the fire may spread and through ye garments set all the city ablaze.

People: This fire was already ours, and the whole city burns.

1st and 2nd guards: Behold the first radiant light. Long live our King.

People: Under the sign of the Salamander.

1st and 2nd guards: Under the sign of the Salamander.

Invisible angels: Under the sign of the Salamander …

1stand 2nd guards: See the great light. Long live our King.

People: Well then hurrah, hurrah and hurrah.

Invisible angels: Ah …

Priest: Ave Maria, how far shall I descend?, "though I have nothing for which to be reproached, that is not enough to absolve me," "Lord deliver me from my need," pray, pray …

Invisible angels: … tremble, tremble, a plague of angels now darkens the horizon …

Lover: Woe is me who am not burned. I exist under the sign of the same fate but my tragedy will never blaze.

Angels being born: How good to be born. Look what a sweet earth, what sweet and perfect harmony … From what is fulfilled we are born. In the spheres where we used to alight it was easy not to live and to be the free shadow of a child. But on this earth where there is sea and foam, and fire and smoke, there exists a law prior to the law and still prior to the law, and that gives form to the form to the form. How easy it was to be an angel. But on this night of fire what furious, turbulent and abashed desire to be boy and girl.

Husband: She sinned with one body and they set fire to another. I was hurt in one soul, and behold I am taking vengeance in another.

People: What a beautiful tawny color burnt flesh has.

Priest: But not even the color is hers any longer. It is from the Flame. Ah how purification blazes. At last, I suffer.

People: We do not understand, we do not understand and we are hungry for roast meat.

Husband: With my cloak I might still smother the fire on your garments!

Lover: Not even her death does he understand, he who shared with me the woman who belonged to no one.

Priest: How I suffer. But "ye have not yet resisted unto blood."

Husband: If with my cloak I were to smother your garments ...

Lover: You could, yes. But understand: would she have the strength to extend over a long life the pure fire of an instant?

Priest: Behold, she who will become ashes and dust. Ah, "verily thou art a God that hidest thyself."

1st guard: I tell ye, she burns faster than a heathen.

Priest: "And the world passeth away, and the lust thereof."

2nd guard: I tell ye, the smoke is such that I can hardly see the body.

Husband: I can hardly see the body of what I was.

Priest: Praised be the name of the Lord, "Thy grace suffices me," "I counsel thee to buy of me gold tried in the fire," was spoken at the Apocalypse, praised be the name of the Lord.

People: Well amen, amen and amen.

Priest: "She took her delight in the slavery of the senses."

Husband: She was no more than a common, common, common woman.

Lover: Ah she was sweet and common. You were so very mine and common.

Priest: I suffer.

Lover: For me and for her began something that forever must be.

The newborn angels: Good morning!

Priest: "Waiting for the day of eternal brightness to rise and the shadows of the symbols to disperse."

1st and 2nd guards: All speak and none listen.

Priest: It is a melodious uproar: I already hear the angels of the dying.

The newborn angels: Good morning, good morning and good morning. And already we do not understand, we do not understand and we do not understand.

Husband: Cursed be, if you think you have freed yourself from me and that I have freed myself from you. Beneath the weight of brutal attraction, you shall not leave my orbit and I shall not leave yours, and with nausea we shall spin, until you overtake my orbit and I overtake yours, and in a superhuman hatred we shall be one.

Priest: The beauty of a night without passion. What abundance, what consolation. "Great and unfathomable are His works."

1st and 2nd guards: Just as in war, when evil is committed to the flames, the good is not what remains …

The newborn angels: ... we are born.

People: We do not understand and we do not understand.

Husband: I shall return now to the dead woman's house. For there is my former wife, awaiting me in her empty necklaces.

Priest: The silence of a night without sin ... What brightness, what harmony.

Sleepy child: Mother, what has happened?

The newborn angels: Mama, what has happened?

Women of the people: My children, it went like this: etc. etc. and etc.

Member of the people: Forgive them, they believe in fatality and are therefore fatal themselves.

Profile of Chosen Beings
("Perfil de sêres eleitos")

HE WAS A BEING WHO CHOSE. AMONG THE THOUSAND things he might have been, he had gone along choosing himself. In work for which he wore glasses, discerning whatever he could and using his damp hands to grope at whatever he couldn't see, the being kept choosing and therefore would indirectly choose himself. Bit by bit he had gathered himself into being. He kept separating, separating. In relative liberty, if one discounted the furtive determinism that had acted discreetly without naming itself. Discounting this furtive determinism, the being chose himself freely. What guided him was the desire to discover his own determinism, and to make an effort to follow it, since the true line is very faded, the others are more visible. He kept separating, separating. He would separate the so-called wheat from the chaff, and the best, the best the being ate. Sometimes he ate the worst. The difficult choice was to eat the worst. He separated dangers from the great danger, and it was the great danger that the being, though afraid, would keep. Just to measure by fear the weight of things. He pushed away all the lesser truths that he never ended up learning. He wanted the truths that were hard to take. Since he ignored the lesser truths, the being seemed shrouded in mystery; since he was ignorant, he was a mysterious being. He had also become: an ignorant savant; a naive sage; forgetful but well aware; an honest fake; an absentminded contemplative; nostalgic for what he had neglected to learn; wistful for what he had definitively lost; and courageous because it was already too late. All this, paradoxically, gave the being the wholesome joy of the peasant who only deals with the basics, though he has no clue what movie is currently playing. And all this gave him the involuntary austerity that all vital work gives. Choosing and gathering had no proper start or end time, indeed it lasted a lifetime.

All this, paradoxically, increasingly gave the being the kind of profound joy that needs to be revealed, displayed, and communicated. In this communication the being was helped by his innate gift for liking. And this was something he hadn't even gathered or chosen, it was a gift indeed. He liked the deep joy of others, through his innate gift he discovered the joy of others. Through his gift, he could also discover the solitude that other people had in relation to their own deepest joy. The being, also through his gift, knew how to play. And from birth he knew that gestures, without wounding through offense, transmitted the liking he felt for others. Without even feeling that he was using his gift, the being expressed himself; he would give, without realizing when he was giving, he would love without realizing that this was called love. His gift, in fact, was like the lack of a shirt on a happy man: since the being was very poor and didn't have anything to give, the being would give himself. He would give himself in silence, and give what he had gathered of himself, like someone calling others over so they can see too. All this discreetly, for he was a shy being. It was also discreetly that the being saw in others what others had gathered of themselves; the being knew how difficult it was to find the faded line of one's own destiny, how difficult it was to be careful not to lose sight of it, to go over it with pencil, erring, erasing, getting it right.

That was how the mistake came to surround the being. The others believed almost simplemindedly that they were seeing a static and fixed reality, and viewed the being as you view a picture. A very rich picture. They didn't understand that for the being, pulling himself together, had been a labor of paring down and not of wealth. And, by mistake, the being was chosen. By mistake the being was loved. But feeling loved would mean recognizing oneself in this love. And that being was loved as if he were another being: as if he were a chosen being. The being shed the tears of a statue who at night on the square weeps without moving atop his marble horse. Falsely loved, the being ached all over. But whoever had chosen him wasn't giving him a hand to get off the horse of hard silver, nor did they want to mount the horse of heavy gold. Aching stone was what the being felt while breaking to pieces alone in the square. Meanwhile, the beings who had chosen him slept. In fear? but they slept. Never had the darkness been greater in the square. Until dawn came. The rhythm of the earth was so generous that dawn came. But at night, when night fell, it grew dark again. The square enlarged again. And again, those who had chosen him slept. In fear, perhaps, but they slept. Were they afraid because they thought they would have to live in the square? They didn't know that the square had merely been the being's place of work. But that, in order to wander, he didn't want a square. Those who slept didn't know that the square had meant war for the chosen being, and that the war had been intended precisely to conquer what lay beyond the square. They thought, those who slept, that the chosen being, wherever he went, would throw open a square the way someone unrolls a canvas to paint on. They didn't know that the canvas, for the chosen being, had merely been the way to survey on a map the world where the chosen being wished to go. The being had been preparing his whole life to be suitable for what lay beyond the square. It's true that the being, upon feeling as ready as someone bathed in oils and perfumes, the chosen being had seen that there hadn't been any time left to learn how to smile. But it's true that this didn't bother the being, since it was at the same time his great expectation: the being had left an entire land to be granted him by whoever wanted to grant it. The calculation of the being's dream had been to remain deliberately incomplete.

But something had gone wrong. When the being caught sight of himself in the picture the others had taken of him, he was humbled in astonishment at what the others had made of him. They had made of him, no more, no less, than a chosen being; that is, they had besieged him. How to undo the mistake? To simplify things and save time, they had photographed the being. And now they no longer referred to the being, they referred to the photograph. All they had to do really was open the drawer and pull out the picture. Anyone, in fact, could get a copy. It was cheap, in fact.

Whenever people said to the being: I love you (but what about me? what about me? why not me too? why just my picture?), the being would get upset because he couldn't even at least thank them: there was nothing to thank. And he didn't complain, since he knew that the others weren't making the mistake out of ill will, the others had given themselves to a photograph, and people don't joke around: they have a lot to lose. And they couldn't risk it: it was the photograph, or nothing. The being, for the sake of kindness, sometimes tried to imitate the photograph in order to validate what the others possessed, that is, the photograph. But he couldn't remain at the simplified height of the picture. And sometimes he got all mixed up: he hadn't learned to copy the picture, and had forgotten what he was like without it. So that, as they say of the laughing clown, the being sometimes wept beneath his whitewashed painting of a court jester.

Then the chosen being undertook a covert operation to destroy the photograph. He did or said things so counter to the photograph that it would bristle in the drawer. In the hopes of becoming more current than his own image, and causing it to be substituted by something less: by the being himself. But what happened? What happened was that everything the being did just ended up retouching the picture. The being had become a mere contributor. And an inevitable contributor: it no longer mattered what the contributor gave, it no longer mattered that the contributor didn't give at all, everything, even dying, embellished the photograph.

And so it went. Until, profoundly disillusioned in his sincerest aspirations, the chosen being died as people die. He ended up making a great effort to get off the stone horse by himself, fell several times, but finally learned how to walk around by himself. And, as they say, never had the land seemed so beautiful to him. He recognized that this was precisely the land for which he had prepared himself: he hadn't been mistaken, then, the treasure map held the right directions. Walking around, the being touched everything, and with a smile. The being had learned all by himself how to smile. One fine day, ...

Inaugural Address
("Discurso de inauguração")

... THE FUTURE THAT WE ARE INAUGURATING HERE IS a metallic line. It is something deliberately stripped down. Of all we have lived only this line shall remain. It is the result of the mathematical calculation of insecurity: the more it is purified, the less risk it will run, the metallic line does not run the same risk as the line of flesh. Only the metallic line will not feed the vultures. Our metallic line holds no possibility of rot. It is a line guaranteed to be eternal. We, the ones who are here right now, initiate it with the intention that it be eternal. We want a metallic line because from beginning to end it is made of the same metal. We do not know with much certainty whether this line will be strong enough to save, but it is strong enough to endure. To endure on its own, as our creation. Tests have yet to be made to see whether the line bows under the weight of the first soul that hangs from it, as over the abysses of Hell.

What is this line like? It is slippery and cylindrical. And like a strand of hair, though ever so fine, has room to be hollow — like this our line is empty. It is deserted inside. But we, who are here, have a fondness and a nostalgia for deserted things as if

we had already been disappointed by blood. We shall leave it
hollow so the future may fill it. We who, out of vitality, might
have filled it with ourselves, we abstain. Thus shall all of you
be our survival, but without us: this mission of ours is a suicide
mission. The eternal metallic line, product of us all gathered
here now, that eternal metallic line is our crime against today
and also our purest effort. We launch it into space, we launch
it from our umbilical cord, and this thrust is for eternity. The
hidden intention is that, by thrusting it, our body too—bound
to it by the umbilical cord—our body too will be wrenched
from the ground of today and thrust into space. This is our
hope, this is our patience. This is our calculation of eternity.
The mission is suicidal: we have volunteered ourselves for the
future. We are businessmen who need not money, but our own
posterity. What we have taken for ourselves from the present
has in no way used up eternity. We have loved, but this does
not use up the future, for we have loved exclusively in the style
of today, what one day will be mere flesh for the vultures; we
have also eaten bread with butter, which also does not steal
from the future, for bread with butter is merely our simple fil-
ial pleasure; and at Christmas we have gathered with our families. But none of this harms the eternal line, which is our true
enterprise. We are the artists of this enterprise and we make
the sacrifice as a bargain: our sacrifice is the most lucrative
investment. Once in a while, also without using up eternity,
we surrender to passion. But we can calmly take this for ourselves from the present, since in the future we shall be merely
the dead elders of others. We shall not do as our own dead
elders who left us, as inheritance and burden, flesh and soul,
and both unfinished. Not us. Defeated by centuries of passion,
defeated by a love that has been in vain, defeated by a dishon-

esty that has borne no fruit—we have invested in honesty as being more lucrative and we have created a line of the sincerest metal. We shall bequeath a hard and solid skeleton that contains the void. As within the narrow hollow space of a strand of hair, for those to come it will be arduous to get inside the metallic line. We, who inaugurate it now, know that to enter our metallic line will be the narrow doorway for those to come.

As for ourselves, just as our children find us strange, the eternal metallic line will find us strange and be ashamed of us, the ones who built it. We are nonetheless aware that this is a suicide mission of survival. We, the artists of this great enterprise, know that the work of art does not understand us. And that living is a suicide mission.

Mineirinho

YES, I SUPPOSE IT IS IN MYSELF, AS ONE OF THE REP-resentatives of us, that I should seek the reasons why the death of a thug is hurting. And why it does me more good to count the thirteen gunshots that killed Mineirinho rather than his crimes. I asked my cook what she thought about it. I saw in her face the slight convulsion of a conflict, the distress of not understanding what one feels, of having to betray contradictory feelings because one cannot reconcile them. Indisputable facts, but indisputable revolt as well, the violent compassion of revolt. Feeling divided by one's own confusion about being unable to forget that Mineirinho was dangerous and had already killed too many; and still we wanted him to live. The cook grew slightly guarded, seeing me perhaps as an avenging justice. Somewhat angry at me, who was prying into her soul, she answered coldly: "It's no use saying what I feel. Who doesn't know Mineirinho was a criminal? But I'm sure he was saved and is already in heaven." I answered, "more than lots of people who haven't killed anyone."

Why? For the first law, the one that protects the irreplaceable body and life, is thou shalt not kill. It is my greatest assurance: that way they won't kill me, because I don't want to die, and that way they won't let me kill, because having killed would be darkness for me.

This is the law. But there is something that, if it makes me hear the first and the second gunshots with the relief of safety, at the third puts me on the alert, at the fourth unsettles me, the fifth and the sixth cover me in shame, the seventh and eighth I hear with my heart pounding in horror, at the ninth and tenth my mouth is quivering, at the eleventh I say God's name in fright, at the twelfth I call my brother. The thirteenth shot murders me—because I am the other. Because I want to be the other.

That justice that watches over my sleep, I repudiate it, humiliated that I need it. Meanwhile I sleep and falsely save myself. We, the essential phonies. For my house to function, I demand as my primary duty that I be a phony, that I not exercise my revolt and my love, both set aside. If I am not a phony, my house trembles. I must have forgotten that beneath the house is the land, the ground upon which a new house might be erected. Meanwhile we sleep and falsely save ourselves. Until thirteen gunshots wake us up, and in horror I plead too late—twenty-eight years after Mineirinho was born—that in killing this cornered man, they do not kill him in us. Because I know that he is my error. And out of a whole lifetime, by God, sometimes the only thing that saves a person is error, and I know that we shall not be saved so long as our error is not precious to us. My error is my mirror, where I see what in silence I made of a man. My error is the way I saw life opening up in his flesh and I was aghast, and I saw the substance of life, placenta and blood, the living mud. In Mineirinho my way of living burst. How could I not love him, if he lived up till the thirteenth gunshot the very thing that I had been sleeping? His frightened violence. His innocent violence—not in its consequences, but innocent in itself as that of a son whose father neglected him. Everything that was violence in him is furtive in us, and we avoid each other's gaze so as not to run the risk of understanding each other. So that the house won't tremble. The violence bursting in Mineirinho that only another man's hand, the hand of hope, resting on his stunned and wounded head, could appease and make his startled eyes lift and at last fill with tears. Only after a man is found inert on the ground, without his cap or shoes, do I see that I forgot to tell him: me too.

I don't want this house. I want a justice that would have given a chance to something pure and full of helplessness in Mineirinho—that thing that moves mountains and is the same as what made him love a woman "like a madman," and the same that led him through a doorway so narrow that it slashes into nakedness; it is a thing in us as intense and transparent as a dangerous gram of radium, that thing is a grain of life that if trampled is transformed into something threatening—into trampled love; that thing, which in Mineirinho became a knife, it is the same thing in me that makes me offer another man water, not because I have water, but because, I too, know what thirst is; and I too, who have not lost my way, have experienced perdition. Prior justice, that would not make me ashamed. It was past time for us, with or without irony, to be more divine; if we can guess what God's benevolence might be it is because we guess at benevolence in ourselves, whatever sees the man before he succumbs to the sickness of crime. I go on, nevertheless, waiting for God to be the father, when I know that one man can be father to another. And I go on living in my weak house. That house, whose protective door I lock so tightly, that house won't withstand the first gale that will send a locked door flying through the air. But it is standing, and Mineirinho lived rage on my behalf, while I was calm. He was gunned down in his disoriented strength, while a god fabricated at the last second hastily blesses my composed wrongdoing and my stupefied justice: what upholds the walls of my house is the certainty that I shall always vindicate myself, my friends won't vindicate me, but my enemies who are my accomplices, they will greet me; what upholds me is knowing that I shall always fabricate a god in the image of whatever I need in order to sleep peacefully, and that others will furtively pretend that we are all in the right and that there is nothing to be done. All this, yes, for we are the essential phonies, bastions of some thing. And above all trying not to understand.

Because the one who understands disrupts. There is something in us that would disrupt everything—a thing that understands. That thing that stays silent before the man without his cap or shoes, and to get them he robbed and killed; and stays silent before Saint George of gold and diamonds. That very serious thing in me grows more serious still when faced with the man felled by machine guns. Is that thing the killer inside me? No, it is the despair inside us. Like madmen, we know him, that dead man in whom the gram of radium caught fire. But only like madmen, and not phonies, do we know him. It is as a madman that I enter a life that so often has no doorway, and as a madman that I comprehend things dangerous to comprehend, and only as a madman do I feel deep love, that is confirmed when I see that the radium will radiate regardless, if not through trust, hope and love, then miserably through the sick courage of destruction. If I weren't mad, I'd be eight hundred policemen with eight hundred machine guns, and this would be my honorableness.

Until a slightly madder justice came along. One that would take into account that we all must speak for a man driven to despair because in him human speech has already failed, he is already so mute that only a brute incoherent cry serves as signal. A prior justice that would recall how our great struggle is that of fear, and that a man who kills many does so because he was very much afraid. Above all a justice that would examine itself, and see that all of us, living mud, are dark, and that is why not even one man's wrongdoing can be surrendered to another man's wrongdoing: so that this other man cannot commit, freely and with approbation, the crime of gunning someone down. A justice that does not forget that we are all dangerous, and that the moment that the deliverer of justice kills, he is no longer protecting us or trying to eliminate a criminal, he is committing his own personal crime, one long held inside him. At the moment he kills a criminal—in that instant an innocent is killed. No, it's not that I want the sublime, nor for things to turn into words to make me sleep peacefully, a combination of forgiveness, of vague charity, we who seek shelter in the abstract.

What I want is much rougher and more difficult: I want the land.

COVERT JOY
("*Felicidade clandestina*")

Covert Joy
("Felicidade clandestina")

SHE WAS FAT, SHORT, FRECKLED, AND HAD REDDISH, excessively frizzy hair. She had a huge bust, while the rest of us were still flat-chested. As if that weren't enough, she'd fill both pockets of her blouse, over her bust, with candy. But she had what any child devourer of stories would wish for: a father who owned a bookstore.

She didn't take much advantage of it. And we even less: even for birthdays, instead of at least a cheap little book, she'd present us with a postcard from her father's shop. Even worse, it would be a view of Recife itself, where we lived, with the bridges we'd seen countless times. On the back she'd write in elaborately curlicued script words like "birthday" and "thinking of you."

But what a talent she had for cruelty. She was pure vengeance, sucking noisily on her candy. How that girl must have hated us, we who were unforgivably pretty, slender, tall, with flowing hair. She performed her sadism on me with calm ferocity. In my eagerness to read, I didn't even notice the humiliations to which she subjected me: I kept begging her to lend me the books she wasn't reading.

Until the momentous day came for her to start performing a kind of Chinese torture on me. As if in passing, she informed me that she owned *The Shenanigans of Little Miss Snub-Nose*, by Monteiro Lobato.

It was a thick book, my God, it was a book you could live with, eating it, sleeping it. And completely beyond my means. She told me to stop by her house the next day and she'd lend it to me.

Up until the next day I was transformed into the very hope of joy itself: I wasn't living, I was swimming slowly in a gentle sea, the waves carrying me to and fro.

The next day I went to her house, literally running. She didn't live above a shop like me, but rather in a whole house. She didn't ask me in. Looking me right in the eye, she said she'd lent the book to another girl, and that I should come back the next day. Mouth agape, I left slowly, but soon enough hope completely took over again and I started back down the street skipping, which was my strange way of moving through the streets of Recife. This time I didn't even fall: the promise of the book guided me, the next day would come, the next days would later become the rest of my life, love for the world awaited me, I went skipping through the streets as usual and didn't fall once.

But things didn't simply end there. The secret plan of the bookseller's daughter was serene and diabolical. The next day, there I stood at her front door, with a smile and my heart beating. Only to hear her calm reply: the book hadn't been returned yet, and I should come back the next day. Little did I know how later on, over the course of my life, the drama of "the next day" with her would repeat itself with my heart beating.

And so it went. For how long? I don't know. She knew it

would be for an indefinite time, until the bile oozed completely out of her thick body. I had already started to guess that she'd chosen me to suffer, sometimes I guess things. But, in actually guessing things, I sometimes accept them: as if whoever wants to make me suffer damn well needs me to.

For how long? I'd go to her house daily, without missing a single day. Sometimes she'd say: well I had the book yesterday afternoon, but you didn't come till this morning, so I lent it to another girl. And I, who didn't usually get dark circles under my eyes, felt those dark circles deepening under my astonished eyes.

Until one day, when I was at her front door, listening humbly and silently to her refusal, her mother appeared. She must have been wondering about the mute, daily appearance of that girl at her front door. She asked us to explain. There was a silent commotion, interrupted by words that didn't clarify much. The lady found it increasingly strange that she wasn't understanding. Until that good mother understood. She turned to her daughter and with enormous surprise exclaimed: But that book never left the house and you didn't even want to read it!

And the worst thing for that woman wasn't realizing what was going on. It must have been the horrified realization of the kind of daughter she had. She eyed us in silence: the power of perversity in the daughter she didn't know and the little blond girl standing at the door, exhausted, out in the wind of the streets of Recife. That was when, finally regaining her composure, she said to her daughter firmly and calmly: you're going to lend that book right this minute. And to me: "And you can keep that book for as long as you like." Do you understand? It was worth more than giving me the book: "for as long as I liked" is all that a person, big or small, could ever dare wish for.

How can I explain what happened next? I was stunned, and just like that the book was in my hand. I don't think I said a thing. I took the book. No, I didn't go skipping off as usual. I walked away very slowly. I know that I was holding the thick book with both hands, clutching it against my chest. As for how long it took to get home, that doesn't really matter either. My chest was hot, my heart thoughtful.

When I got home, I didn't start reading. I pretended not to have it, just so later on I could feel the shock of having it. Hours later I opened it, read a few wondrous lines, closed it again, wandered around the house, stalled even more by eating some bread and butter, pretended not to know where I had put the book, found it, opened it for a few seconds. I kept inventing the most contrived obstacles for that covert thing that was joy. Joy would always be covert for me. I must have already sensed it. Oh how I took my time! I was living in the clouds ... There was pride and shame inside me. I was a delicate queen.

Sometimes I'd sit in the hammock, swinging with the book open on my lap, not touching it, in the purest ecstasy.

I was no longer a girl with a book: I was a woman with her lover.

Remnants of Carnival
("Restos do Carnaval")

NO, NOT THIS PAST CARNIVAL. BUT I DON'T KNOW why this one transported me back to my childhood and those Ash Wednesdays on the dead streets where the remains of streamers and confetti fluttered. The occasional devout woman with a veil covering her head would be heading to church, crossing the street left so incredibly empty after Carnival. Until the next year. And when the celebration was fast approaching, what could explain the inner tumult that came over me? As if the budding world were finally opening into a big scarlet rose. As if the streets and squares of Recife were finally explaining why they'd been made. As if human voices were finally singing the capacity for pleasure that was kept secret in me. Carnival was mine, mine.

However, in reality, I barely participated at all. I had never been to a children's ball, they'd never dressed me up in costume. To make up for it, they'd let me stay up until eleven in the front stairwell of the house where we lived, eagerly watching others have fun. I'd get two precious things that I saved up greedily so they'd last all three days: some party spray and a bag of confetti. Ah, it's getting hard to write. Because I'm feeling how my heart is going to darken as I realize how, even barely joining in on the merriment, I thirsted so much that even next to nothing made me a happy little girl.

And the masks? I was afraid but it was a vital and necessary fear for it went along with my deepest suspicion that the human face was also a kind of mask. In my front stairwell, if someone in a mask spoke to me, I'd suddenly come into indispensable contact with my inner world, which was made not only of elves and enchanted princes, but of people with their mystery. Even my fright at the people in masks, then, was essential for me.

They didn't dress me up: with all the worry about my sick mother, no one at home could spare a thought for a child's Carnival. But I'd ask one of my sisters to curl that straight hair of mine that I so hated and then I'd take pride in having wavy hair for at least three days a year. During those three days, moreover, my sister gave in to my intense dream of being a young lady—I could hardly wait to leave behind a vulnerable childhood—and she painted my lips with bright lipstick, putting rouge on my cheeks too. Then I felt pretty and feminine, I was no longer a kid.

But there was one Carnival that was different from the rest. So miraculous that I couldn't quite believe so much had been granted me, I, who had long since learned to ask for little. What happened was that a friend's mother had decided to dress up her daughter and the costume pattern was named the *Rose*. To make it she bought sheets and sheets of pink crepe paper, from which, I suppose, she planned to imitate the petals of a flower. Mouth agape, I watched the costume gradually taking shape and being created. Though the crepe paper didn't remotely resemble petals, I solemnly believed it was one of the most beautiful costumes I had ever seen.

That's when simply by chance the unexpected happened: there was leftover crepe paper, and quite a bit. And my friend's mother—perhaps heeding my mute appeal, the mute despair of my envy, or perhaps out of sheer kindness, since there was leftover paper—decided to make me a *rose* costume too with the remaining materials. So for that Carnival, for the first time in my life I would get what I had always wanted: I would be something other than myself.

Even the preparations left me dizzy with joy. I had never felt so busy: down to the last detail, my friend and I planned everything out, we'd wear slips under our costumes, so if it rained and the costume melted away at least we'd still be somewhat dressed—the very idea of a sudden downpour that would leave us, in our eight-year-old feminine modesty, wearing slips on the street, made us die of anticipated shame—but oh! God would help us! it wouldn't rain! As for the fact that my costume existed solely thanks to the other girl's leftovers, I swallowed, with some pain, my pride, which had always been fierce, and I humbly accepted the handout destiny was offering me.

But why did precisely that Carnival, the only one in costume, have to be so melancholy? Early Sunday morning I already had my hair in curlers, so the waves would hold longer. But the minutes weren't passing, because I was so anxious. Finally, finally! three in the afternoon arrived: careful not to tear the paper, I dressed up as a *rose*.

Many things much worse than these have happened to me, that I've forgiven. Yet I still can't even understand this one now: is a toss of the dice for a *destiny* irrational? It's merciless. When I was all dressed in the crepe paper and ready, with my hair still in curlers and not yet wearing lipstick or rouge—my mother's health suddenly took a turn for the worse, an abrupt upheaval broke out at home, and they sent me quickly to buy medicine at the pharmacy. I ran off dressed as a *rose*—but my still-bare face wasn't wearing the young-lady mask that would have covered my utterly exposed childish life—I ran and ran, bewildered, alarmed, amid streamers, confetti and shouts of Carnival. Other people's merriment stunned me.

When hours later the atmosphere at home calmed down, my sister did my hair and makeup. But something had died inside me. And, as in the stories I'd read about fairies who were always casting and breaking spells, the spell on me had been broken; I was no longer a *rose*, I was once again just a little girl. I went out to the street and standing there I wasn't a flower, I was a pensive clown with scarlet lips. In my hunger to feel ecstasy, I'd sometimes started to cheer up but in remorse I'd recall my mother's grave condition and once again I'd die.

Only hours later did salvation come. And if I quickly clung to it, that's because I so badly needed to be saved. A boy of twelve or so, which for me meant a young man, this very handsome boy stopped before me and, in a combination of tenderness, crudeness, playfulness and sensuality, he covered my hair, straight by now, with confetti: for an instant we stood face to face, smiling, without speaking. And then I, a little woman of eight, felt for the rest of the night that someone had finally recognized me: I was, indeed, a rose.

Eat Up, My Son
("Come, meu filho")

"THE WORLD SEEMS FLAT BUT I KNOW IT'S NOT. KNOW why it seems flat? 'Cause, whenever we look, the sky's above, never below, never to the side. I know the world's round 'cause people say so, but it would only seem round if we looked and sometimes the sky was below. I know it's round, but to me it's flat, but Ronaldo only knows that the world is round, it doesn't seem flat to him."

"..."

"'Cause I've been to lots of countries and I saw how in the United States the sky's above too, that's why the world seems totally straight to me. But Ronaldo's never been out of Brazil and he might think the sky's above only here, that it's not flat in other places, that it's only flat in Brazil, that in other places he hasn't seen it gets rounder. When people tell him stuff, he just believes them, things don't even have to make sense. Do you like bowls or plates, Mama?"

"Bow ...—plates, I mean."

"Me too. It seems like bowls can fit more, but it's just on the bottom, with plates everything gets spread out so you can see everything you've got right away. Don't cucumbers seem *inreal?*"

"Unreal."

"Why do you think?"

"That's how you say it."

"No, why did you also think that cucumbers seem *inreal*? Me too. You look at them and you can see part of the other side, it's got the exact same pattern all over, it's cold in your mouth, it sounds kind of like glass when you chew it. Don't you think it seems like someone invented cucumbers?"

"It does."

"Where did they invent beans and rice?"

"Here."

"Or at that Arabian place, like Pedrinho said about something else?"

"Here."

"At the Sorveteria Gatão the ice cream tastes good because it tastes just like the color. Does meat taste like meat to you?"

"Sometimes."

"Yeah right! I bet: does it taste like the meat hanging in the butcher's shop?!"

"No."

"And not even like the meat we're talking about. It doesn't taste like when you say meat has vitamins."

"Don't talk so much, eat up."

"But you're giving me that look, but it's not to make me eat, it's because you're liking me so much, did I guess it?"

"You guessed it. Eat up, Paulinho."

"That's all you ever think about. I was talking a lot so you wouldn't only think about food, but you just can't forget about it."

Forgiving God
("Perdoando Deus")

I WAS WALKING ALONG DOWN AVENIDA COPACABANA
and looking distractedly at buildings, patches of sea, people,
not thinking about anything. I still hadn't noticed that I wasn't
actually distracted, my guard was just down, I was being something quite rare: free. I saw everything, and at random. I was
gradually starting to notice that I was noticing things. My freedom then grew slightly more intense, without ceasing to be
freedom. It wasn't a *tour du propriétaire*, none of it was mine,
nor did I want it to be. But I seemed to feel satisfied with what
I saw.

I then had a feeling I've never heard of before. Out of pure
affection, I felt I was the mother of God, I was the Earth, the
world. Out of pure affection, really, without any arrogance or
glory, without the least sense of superiority or equality, I was,
out of affection, the mother of whatever exists. I also discovered that if all this "really was" what I was feeling—and not
a potentially mistaken feeling—that God without pride or
pettiness would let someone show affection toward Him, and
with no obligation to me. The intimacy with which I felt affection would be acceptable to Him. The feeling was new to me,

but quite assured, and it hadn't occurred before only because it couldn't have existed. I know that we love whatever is God. With serious love, solemn love, respect, fear, and reverence. But I'd never heard of maternal affection for Him. And as my affection for a son doesn't reduce him, it even expands him, in this way, being mother of the world was my merely free love.

And that was when I almost stepped on a huge dead rat. In less than a second I was bristling from the terror of living, in less than a second I was shattering in panic, and doing my best to rein in my deepest scream. Nearly running in fright, blind in the midst of all those people, I wound up on the next block leaning on a pole, violently shutting my eyes, which no longer wanted to see. But the image stuck to my eyelids: a big red-haired rat, with an enormous tail, its feet crushed, and dead, still, tawny. My boundless fear of rats.

Trembling all over, I managed to keep on living. Utterly bewildered I kept walking, my mouth made childish with surprise. I tried to sever the connection between the two facts: what I'd felt minutes earlier and the rat. But it was no use. At least contiguity linked them. The two facts illogically had one nexus. It shocked me that a rat had been my counterpart. And suddenly revolt seized me: so couldn't I surrender heedlessly to love? What was God trying to remind me of? I'm not someone who needs to be reminded that inside everything is blood. Not only do I not forget the blood inside but I allow and desire it, I am too much blood to forget blood, and for me the spiritual word has no meaning, and neither does the earthly word. There was no need to throw a rat in my bare naked face. Not right then. What could easily have been taken into account was the terror that has hounded me and made me delirious since childhood, rats have mocked me, in the past of the world rats have devoured me quickly and furiously. So that's how it was?, with me roaming through the world not asking for a thing, not needing a thing, loving out of pure, innocent love, and God shows me his rat? God's coarseness hurt and insulted me, God was a brute. As I walked with my heart closed off, my disappointment was as inconsolable as disappointment was only when I was a child. I kept walking, trying to forget. But the only thing that occurred to me was revenge. But what sort of revenge could I wreak on an All-Powerful God, on a God who even with a crushed rat could crush me? My vulnerability of a solitary creature. In my craving for revenge I couldn't even face Him, since I didn't know wherein He most resided, in what thing He most likely resided, and would I, glaring angrily at this thing, would I see Him? in the rat? in that window? in the stones on the ground? Inside me is where He no longer was. Inside me is where I no longer saw Him.

Then the revenge of the weak occurred to me: ah, that's how it is? then I won't keep any secret, and I'm going to tell. I know it's low to enter Someone's private life, and then to tell his secrets, but I'm going to tell—don't tell, strictly out of affection don't tell, keep the things He's ashamed of to yourself—but I'm going to tell, yes, I'm going to tell everyone what happened to me, he won't get away with it this time, just for this, I'll tell what He did, I'll ruin His reputation.

... but who knows, maybe it happened because the world too is a rat, and I had thought I was ready for the rat too. Because I imagined myself stronger. Because I was making an incorrect mathematical calculation about love: I thought that, in adding up everything I understood, I loved. I didn't know that, adding up everything you don't understand is the way to truly love. Because I, just from having felt affection, thought that loving is easy. It's because I didn't want solemn love, not understanding that solemnity ritualizes incomprehension and transforms it into an offering. And also because I've always tended to fight a lot, fighting is my way of doing things. It's because I always try to handle things my way. It's because I still don't know how to give in. It's because deep down I want to love the thing I would love—and not what is. It's because I'm still not myself, and so the punishment is loving a world that's not itself. It's also because I offend myself for no reason. It's because I might need to be told brutally, since I'm so stubborn. It's because I'm so possessive and therefore was asked with some irony if I'd also like a rat for myself. It's because I can only be mother of all things once I can pick up a rat with my hand. I know I'll never be able to pick up a rat without dying my worst death. So, then, let me resort to the *Magnificat* that chants blindly about whatever is not known or seen. And let me resort to the formalism that pushes me away. Because formalism hasn't wounded my simplicity, but my pride, since it's through the pride of being born that I feel so intimate with the world, but this world that I nevertheless extracted from myself with a mute scream. Because the rat exists as much as I do, and perhaps neither I nor the rat are meant to be seen by our own selves, distance makes us equal. Perhaps I have to accept above all else this nature of mine that desires the death of a rat. Perhaps I consider myself too refined just because I haven't committed my crimes. Just because I've restrained my crimes, I think I'm made of innocent love. Perhaps I cannot look at the rat as long as I don't look without outrage upon this soul of mine that is merely restrained. Perhaps I must call "world" this way I have of being a bit of everything. How can I love the greatness of the world if I cannot love the extent of my nature? As long as I imagine that "God" is good just because I am bad, I won't be loving anything: that will merely be my way of denouncing myself. I, who without even at least searching myself thoroughly, have already chosen to love my opposite, and I want to call my opposite God. I, who will never get used to myself, was hoping the world wouldn't scandalize me. Because I, who only ever got myself to submit to me, since I am so much more inexorable than I, I was hoping to compensate myself for me with an earth less violent than I. Because as long as I love a God just because I don't want myself, I'll be a loaded die, and the game of my greater life won't be played. As long as I invent God, He doesn't exist.

One Hundred Years of Forgiveness
("Cem anos de perdão")

IF YOU'VE NEVER STOLEN ANYTHING YOU WON'T UN-
derstand me. And if you've never stolen roses, then you can
never understand me. I, as a child, used to steal roses.

In Recife there were countless streets, rich people's streets,
lined with mansions set amid extensive gardens. A little friend
and I would often play at deciding whose mansions they were.
"That white one's mine." "No, I already said the white ones are
mine." "But that one's not all white, it's got green windows."
Sometimes we'd halt for a long time, our faces pressed to the
wrought-iron fence, staring.

That's how it started. During one of those games of "that's
my house," we stopped before one that looked like a small cas-
tle. Behind it you could see an immense orchard. And, in the
front, in well-tended beds, the flowers were planted.

Yes, but standing apart in its bed was a single rose, only
partway open and bright pink. I was dumbstruck, staring in
admiration at that proud rose that wasn't even a fully formed
woman yet. And then it happened: from the bottom of my
heart, I wanted that rose for myself. I wanted it, oh how I
wanted it. And there was no way to get it. If the gardener had

been around, I'd have asked for the rose, though I knew he'd have kicked us out the way they do with street kids. There was no gardener in sight, nobody. And the windows, because of the sun, were shuttered. It was a street where no trams passed and cars rarely ever appeared. In between my silence and the rose's, was my desire to possess it as my very own. I wanted to be able to pluck it. I wanted to sniff it until I felt my vision go dark from so much heady perfume.

And then I couldn't take it any longer. The plan formed in me instantaneously, full of passion. Yet, like the good schemer I was, I coolly devised a plan with my little playmate, explaining her role: to keep watch on the windows or for the gardener's still-possible approach, to watch out for the odd passerby on the street. Meanwhile, I slowly opened the slightly rusty gate, already anticipating the slight creaking. I cracked it just enough for my slender girlish body to slip past. And, treading lightly but quickly, I walked over the gravel surrounding the flower beds. The time it took to reach the rose was a century of my heart pounding.

Then I'm standing before it at last. I stop for a second, dangerously, because up close it's even more beautiful. Finally I start to break its stem, scratching myself on its thorns, and sucking the blood off my fingers.

And, all of a sudden—it's completely in my hand. The dash back to the gate also had to be noiseless. I slipped through the gate I had left cracked open, clasping the rose. And then both pale, the rose and I, we literally ran away from the house.

What was I doing with the rose? I was doing this: it was mine.

I took it home, put it in a glass of water, where it stood magnificent, its petals thick and velvety, in several shades of pale pink. Its color grew more concentrated at the center and its heart looked almost red.

It felt so good.

It felt so good that I simply began stealing roses. The process was always the same: the girl on the lookout, while I went in, broke off the stem and fled with the rose in my hand. Always with my heart pounding and always with that glory that no one could take away from me.

I used to steal pitanga berries too. There was a Presbyterian church near my house, surrounded by a tall, green hedge so dense that it blocked the church from view. I never managed to catch sight of it, except for one corner of the roof. The hedge was a pitanga shrub. But pitangas are fruits that hide: I couldn't see a single one. Then, looking around first to make sure no one was coming, I stuck my hand between the iron bars, plunged it into the hedge and groped around until my fingers felt the moisture of the tiny fruit. Several times in my haste, I smashed an overripe pitanga with my fingers, which ended up looking bloodstained. I picked several that I ate right there, even a few that were too green, which I tossed aside.

No one ever found out. I don't regret it: rose and pitanga thieves get one hundred years of forgiveness. It's the pitangas themselves, for example, that beg to be picked, instead of ripening and dying on the branch, virgins.

A Hope
("Uma esperança")

RIGHT HERE AT HOME A HOPE LANDED. NOT THE CLAS-
sic kind that so often proves illusory, though even still it always
sustains us. But the other kind, very concrete and green: the
cricket.*

There came a muffled cry from one of my sons:

"A hope! and on the wall right over your chair!" His excitement also unites the two kinds of hope, he's already old enough
for that. The surprise was mostly mine: a hope is a secret thing
and usually lands right on me, without anyone's knowing, and
not above my head on a wall. A minor fuss: but it was undeni-
able, there it was, and as skinny and green as could be.

"It hardly has a body," I complained.

"All it has is a soul," my son explained and, since children
are a surprise to us, I realized in surprise that he was talking
about both kinds of hope.

It was walking slowly on the threads of its long legs, among
the pictures on the wall. Three times it stubbornly attempted
to find a way out between two pictures, three times it had to
backtrack. It was a slow learner.

---

* *Esperança* means both "hope" and "cricket."

"It's pretty dumb," the boy remarked.

"Don't I know it," I answered somewhat tragically.

"Now it's looking for a different way, look, poor thing, how it's hesitating."

"I know, that's just how it goes."

"It seems like hopes don't have eyes, Mama, it uses its antennae."

"I know," I went on, unhappier still.

There we sat, for I don't know how long, looking. Keeping watch as they kept watch over the first sparks in the hearth in Greece or Rome so that the fire wouldn't go out.

"It forgot it can fly, Mama, and it thinks all it can do is walk slowly like that."

It really was walking slowly—could it be hurt? Ah no, if it were it would be bleeding, that's how it's always been with me.

That was when, catching a whiff of a world that's edible, out from behind a picture came a spider. Not a spider, but it struck me as "the" spider. Walking along its invisible web, it seemed to glide softly through the air. It wanted the hope. But we wanted it too and, oh! God, we wanted less than to eat it. My son went to get the broom. I said weakly, confused, not knowing whether the time had unfortunately come to lose this hope:

"It's just that we're not supposed to kill spiders, I've heard they're good luck ..."

"But it'll pulverize the hope!" the boy answered fiercely.

"I need to speak to the maid about dusting behind the pictures," I said, sensing that the statement was out of place and catching a certain weariness in my voice. Then I daydreamed a little about how I'd be curt and mysterious with the maid: I'd only say: would you please clear the way for any hope.

The boy, once the spider was dead, made a pun, on the cricket and our hope. My other son, who was watching television, heard it and laughed with pleasure. There was no doubt: hope had alighted in our home, soul and body.

But how lovely the hope is: it alights more than it lives, it's a little green skeleton, and so delicately formed that it explains why I, who like catching things, never tried to catch it.

Once, incidentally, I remember now, a hope much smaller than this one, landed on my arm. I didn't feel a thing, light as it was, I only noticed its presence when I saw it. I grew bashful at its delicateness. I didn't move my arm and thought: "Now what? what should I do?" I did nothing. I held extremely still as if a flower had sprung up inside me. I no longer remember what happened next. And, I think nothing happened.

The Servant
("A criada")

HER NAME WAS EREMITA.* SHE WAS NINETEEN. A CON-
fident face, a few pimples. Where was her beauty? There was
beauty in that body that was neither ugly nor pretty, in that
face in which a sweetness eager for greater sweetnesses was its
sign of life.

As for beauty, I don't know. There may not have been any,
though indefinite features attract as water attracts. There was,
indeed, living substance, nails, flesh, teeth, a mixture of re-
sistances and weaknesses, constituting a vague presence that
nonetheless immediately solidified into an inquisitive and readily helpful head, as soon as someone uttered a name: Eremita.
Her brown eyes were untranslatable, at odds with her whole
face. As independent as if they'd been planted in the flesh of
an arm, and were peering at us from there—open, moist. She
was made entirely of a sweetness bordering on tears.

Sometimes she'd answer with a servant's ill-breeding.
She'd been like that since childhood, she explained. Not that
it stemmed from her character. For there was nothing hard
about her spirit, no perceptible law. "I got scared," she'd say

* "Hermit."

naturally. "It made me hungry," she'd say, and whatever she said was always indisputable, who knows why. "He respects me a lot," she'd say of her fiancé and, though it was a borrowed and conventional expression, whoever heard it entered a delicate world of animals and birds, where all respected each other. "I'm embarrassed," she'd say, and smile, entangled in her own shadows. If her hunger was for bread—which she ate quickly as if it could be taken away—her fear was of thunder, her embarrassment was of speaking. She was kind, honest. "God forbid, right?" she'd say absently.

Because she had her absent moments. Her face would get lost in an impersonal and unwrinkled sorrow. A sorrow more ancient than her spirit. Her eyes would pause, vacant; I'd even say a bit harsh. Whoever was next to her suffered and could do nothing. Except wait.

Because she was devoted to something, that mysterious infant. No one would have dared touch her right then. You'd wait a little solemnly, heart constricted, keeping an eye on her. There was nothing you could do for her except hope for the danger to pass. Until in an unhurried movement, almost a sigh, she'd rouse herself as a newborn goat rises on its legs. She had returned from her repose in sorrow.

She would return, you couldn't say richer, but more reassured after having drunk from some unknown fount. What you could see is that the fount must have been ancient and pure. Yes, there was depth in her. But no one would find a thing if they descended into her depths—except depth itself, as in the dark you find the dark. It's possible that, if someone pressed ahead, they'd find, after walking miles through the shadows, the hint of a path, guided perhaps by a beating of wings, by some trace of an animal. And—suddenly—the forest.

Ah, so that must have been her mystery: she had discovered

a trail into the forest. Surely that was where she went during her absences. Returning with her eyes filled with gentleness and ignorance, eyes made whole. An ignorance so vast that inside it all the world's wisdom could be contained and lost.

That was Eremita. Who, if she rose to the surface with everything she had found in the forest, would be burned at the stake. But what she had seen — on what roots she had gnawed, on what thorns she had bled, in what waters she had bathed her feet, what golden darkness held the light that had shrouded her — she didn't speak of all this because she didn't know about it: perceived in a single glance, too fleeting to be anything but a mystery.

Thus, whenever she emerged, she was a maid. Who was constantly being summoned from the darkness of her trail for lesser duties, to do the laundry, wipe the floor, serve someone or other.

But would she really serve? For if anyone paid attention they'd see that she did the laundry — in the sun; that she wiped the floor — wet from the rain; that she hung the sheets — in the wind. She found ways to serve much more remotely, and other gods. Always with the wholeness of spirit she had brought back from the forest. Without a thought: just a body moving calmly, a face full of a gentle hope that no one can give and no one can take away.

The only sign of the danger through which she had passed was her furtive way of eating bread. In all else she was serene. Even when she pocketed the money her mistress had forgotten on the table, even when she took her fiancé supplies wrapped in a discreet bundle. Pilfering was something else she'd learned in her forests.

Boy in Pen and Ink
("Menino a bico de pena")

HOW CAN YOU EVER KNOW A LITTLE BOY? TO KNOW him I have to wait until he deteriorates, and only then will he be within reach. There he is, a dot in the infinite. No one will ever know his today. Not even he himself. As for me, I look, and it's no use: I can't manage to understand something that's solely in the present, completely in the present. What I do know about him is his setting: the little boy is the one whose first teeth have just started coming in and the same one who'll go on to be a doctor or a carpenter. Meanwhile—there he is sitting on the ground, made of a reality that I must call vegetative to understand. Thirty thousand of these boys sitting on the ground, might they have the chance to construct another world, one that takes into account the memory of the absolute present to which we once belonged? There would be strength in numbers. There he sits, starting all over again but for his own future protection, with no true chance of really getting started.

I don't know how to sketch the boy. I know it's impossible to sketch him in charcoal, for even pen and ink bleed on the paper beyond the incredibly fine line of extreme presentness in which he lives. One day we'll domesticate him into a human, and then we can sketch him. Since that's what we did with ourselves and with God. The boy himself will aid in his domestication: he's diligent and cooperates. He cooperates without knowing that this aid we seek of him goes toward his self-sacrifice. Lately he's even been practicing a lot. And that's how he'll keep progressing until, little by little—through the necessary goodness with which we save ourselves—he'll go from present time to routine time, from meditation to expression, from existence to life. Making the great sacrifice of not going mad. I haven't gone mad out of solidarity with the thousands of us who, so as to construct what's possible, have also sacrificed the truth that would be a kind of madness.

Yet for now he's sitting on the floor, immersed in a profound emptiness.

From the kitchen his mother checks on him: are you sitting still over there? Summoned to work, the boy struggles to get up. He wobbles on his legs, his full attention turned inward: all his balance is internal. Now that he's managed this, his full attention turns outward: he observes what the act of getting up has provoked. For standing brings all sorts of consequences: the ground shifts uncertainly, a chair looms over him, the wall delimits him. And on the wall there's the portrait of *The Little Boy*. It's hard to look at the portrait high up there without leaning on a piece of furniture, he hasn't practiced this yet. But here's where his very difficulty gives him something to lean on: what keeps him standing is precisely focusing on the portrait high up there, looking hoists him like a crane. But he makes a mistake: he blinks. Blinking cuts him off for a fraction of a second from the portrait propping him up. He loses his balance—in a single complete motion, he falls into sitting. From his lips, slightly parted from the force of life, clear drool slides and drips onto the floor. He looks at the droplet up close, as if it were an ant. His arm rises, extends in an arduous, multi-stage mechanism. And suddenly, as if to pin down something ineffable, with unexpected violence he flattens the drool with the palm of his hand. He blinks, waits. Finally, once the time it takes to wait for things has passed, he carefully unclamps his hand and looks at the fruit of experience on the floorboards. The floor is empty. In another abrupt stage, he looks at his hand: so the drop of drool is stuck to his palm. Now he knows this too. Then, eyes wide open, he licks the drool that belongs to the boy. He thinks very loudly: boy.

"Who's that you're calling?" asks his mother from the kitchen.

With effort and kindness he looks around the living room, looks for whomever his mother says he's calling, turns and falls backward. While crying, he sees the room distorted and re-fracted by his tears, its white mass expanding until reaching him—Mother! absorbs him with strong arms, and now the boy is high in the air, deep in the warmth and goodness. The ceiling is closer, now; the table, below. And, since he's too tired to go on, his pupils start rolling back until they plunge into the horizon of his eyes. He shuts them on the last image, the bars of his crib. He falls asleep exhausted and serene.

The moisture has dried up in his mouth. The fly knocks against the windowpane. The boy's sleep is streaked with brightness and heat, his sleep vibrates in the air. Until, in a sud-den nightmare, one of the words he's learned occurs to him: he shudders violently, opens his eyes. And in terror sees only this: the hot, bright emptiness of the air, without his mother. What he's thinking bursts into sobs throughout the whole house. While crying, he begins to recognize himself, transforming into something his mother will recognize. He nearly collapses into sobs, urgently he must transform into a thing that can be seen and heard or else he'll be left alone, he must transform into something comprehensible or else no one will understand him, or else no one will go to his silence no one will know him if he doesn't speak and explain, I'll do whatever it takes to belong to others and for others to be mine, I'll give up my real happiness that would only bring abandonment, and I'll be like everyone else, I strike this bargain to be loved, it's absolutely magical to cry in exchange for: a mother.

Until the familiar sound comes through the door and the boy, mute with interest in what a boy's power can provoke, stops crying: mother. A mother is: not dying. And his security is knowing there is a world to be betrayed and sold out, and that will sell him out.

It's mother, yes it's mother holding a diaper. As soon as he sees the diaper, he starts crying again.

"Look you're all wet!"

The news shocks him, his curiosity starts up again, but now it's a comfortable and assured curiosity. He looks blindly at his own wetness, in another stage he looks at his mother. But suddenly he tenses up again and listens with his whole body, his heart beating heavily in his belly: beep beep! he recognizes it suddenly in a shriek of victory and terror—the boy has just recognized it!

"That's it!" his mother says proudly, "that's it, my darling, it's beep beep that went by in the street just now, I'm going to tell Papa what you've learned, that's exactly how you say it: beep beep, my darling!" says his mother tugging at him from bottom to top and then from top to bottom, lifting him by the legs, leaning him back, tugging at him again from bottom to top. In every position the boy keeps his eyes wide open. They're dry as the fresh diaper.

A Tale of So Much Love
("Uma história de tanto amor")

ONCE UPON A TIME THERE WAS A LITTLE GIRL WHO observed chickens so closely that she got to know their souls and innermost yearnings. The chicken is anxious, whereas the rooster suffers a near-human anguish: he lacks a true love in that harem of his, and moreover has to keep watch all night long so as not to miss the first of the most distant daybreaks and to crow as sonorously as possible. It is his duty and his art. Back to the chickens, the little girl had two of her very own. One was named Pedrina and the other Petronilha.

Whenever the girl thought that one had a sick liver, she'd sniff under their wings, with a nurse's directness, considering it the primary symptom of illness, for the smell of a live chicken is no laughing matter. Then she'd ask her aunt for some medicine. And her aunt would say: "There's absolutely nothing wrong with your liver." Then, being very close to this favorite aunt, she explained to her who the medicine was for. The girl thought it wise to give as much to Pedrina as to Petronilha to avoid mysterious contagions. It was almost pointless to give them medicine because Pedrina and Petronilha continued to spend all day pecking at the ground and eating the junk that hurt their livers. And the smell under their wings was precisely that foul odor. It didn't occur to her to put deodorant on them because in Minas Gerais where they lived people didn't use it just as they didn't wear underclothes made of nylon but of muslin. Her aunt went on giving her the medicine, a dark liquid that the girl suspected was water with a few drops of coffee—and then came the hell of trying to pry open the chickens' beaks to give them something that would cure them of being chickens. The girl hadn't yet understood that people can't be cured of being people and chickens of being chickens: people as well as chickens possess sorrows and greatness (the chicken's is laying a perfectly formed white egg) inherent to their own species. The girl lived in the countryside and there weren't any pharmacies nearby to advise her.

Another hellish difficulty came whenever the girl thought Pedrina and Petronilha were too skinny beneath their ruffled feathers, though they ate all day long. The girl hadn't understood that fattening them up would hasten their destiny on the dinner table. And she'd start in again on the hardest task of all: prying open their beaks. The girl became a great intuitive expert on chickens in that immense yard in Minas Gerais. And when she grew up she was surprised to discover that chicken was slang for something else.* Not realizing the comic seriousness the whole thing took on:

"But the rooster's the one who gets worked up, who wants it! The chickens don't really do anything! and it goes by so fast you hardly notice! The rooster's the one who's always trying to love one of them and can't!"

One day the family decided to take the little girl to spend the

* A loose woman.

day at a relative's house, far away from home. And when the girl returned, she who in life had been Petronilha was no more. Her aunt told her:

"We ate Petronilha."

The girl was a creature with a great capacity for loving: a chicken can't return the love you give yet the girl kept loving it without expecting to be reciprocated. When she found out what happened to Petronilha she began hating everyone in the house, except for her mother who didn't like chicken and the servants who ate beef or oxtail. As for her father, well, she could hardly look at him: he was the one who liked chicken most of all. Her mother noticed all this and explained things to her.

"When people eat animals, the animals become more like people, since they end up inside us. We're the only ones in the house who don't have Petronilha inside us. It's too bad."

Pedrina, secretly the girl's favorite, dropped dead of natural causes, for she'd always been a fragile thing. The girl, seeing Pedrina trembling in a yard being scorched by the sun, bundled her in a dark cloth and after she was all bundled up, put her on top of one of those big brick ovens they have on ranches in Minas Gerais. Everyone warned her she was hastening Pedrina's death, but the girl was stubborn and placed the swaddled Pedrina on top of the hot bricks anyway. The next morning when Pedrina began the day stiff from being so dead, only then was the girl, amid endless tears, convinced she had hastened the death of that dear being.

When she was a little older, the girl got a chicken named Eponina.

Her love for Eponina: this time it was a more realistic love and not romantic; it was the love of someone who has suffered from love before. And when it came Eponina's turn to be eaten, the girl not only knew but also considered it the inevitable fate of whoever is born a chicken. Chickens seem to have a pre-science about their own fate and they never learn to love either their owners or the rooster. A chicken is alone in the world.

But the girl hadn't forgotten what her mother had said about eating beloved animals: she ate more of Eponina than the rest of the family, she ate without appetite, but with a near-physical pleasure because now she knew this was how Eponina would be incorporated into her and become more hers than in life. They had cooked Eponina in a blood sauce. So the girl, in a pagan ritual transmitted to her from body to body through the centuries, ate her flesh and drank her blood. During this meal she was jealous of whoever else was eating Eponina too. The girl was a being made to love until she grew into a young woman and there were men.

The Waters of the World
("As águas do mundo")

THERE IT IS, THE SEA, THE MOST UNINTELLIGIBLE OF
non-human existences. And here is the woman, standing on
the beach, the most unintelligible of living beings. As a human
being she once posed a question about herself, becoming the
most unintelligible of living beings. She and the sea.

Their mysteries could only meet if one surrendered to the
other: the surrender of two unknowable worlds made with
the trust by which two understandings would surrender to
each other.

She looks at the sea, that's what she can do. It is only cut off
for her by the line of the horizon, that is, by her human incapacity to see the Earth's curvature.

It is six in the morning. There is only a free dog hesitating on the beach, a black dog. Why is a dog so free? Because
it is the living mystery that doesn't wonder about itself. The
woman hesitates because she's about to go in.

Her body soothes itself with its own slightness compared
to the vastness of the sea because it's her body's slightness that
lets her stay warm and it's this slightness that makes her a poor
and free person, with her portion of a dog's freedom on the

sands. That body will enter the limitless cold that roars without rage in the silence of six o'clock. The woman doesn't know it: but she's fulfilling a courage. With the beach empty at this morning hour, she doesn't have the example of other humans who transform the entry into the sea into a simple lighthearted game of living. She is alone. The salty sea is not alone because it's salty and vast, and this is an achievement. Right then she knows herself even less than she knows the sea. Her courage comes from not knowing herself, but going ahead nevertheless. Not knowing yourself is inevitable, and not knowing yourself demands courage.

She goes in. The salt water is cold enough to make her legs shiver in a ritual. But an inevitable joy—joy is an inevitability—has already seized her, though smiling doesn't even occur to her. On the contrary, she is very serious. The smell is of a heady sea air that awakens her most dormant age-old slumbers. And now she is alert, even without thinking, as a hunter is alert without thinking. The woman is now a compact and a light and a sharp one—and cuts a path through the iciness that, liquid, opposes her, yet lets her in, as in love when opposition can be a request.

The slow journey fortifies her secret courage. And suddenly she lets herself be covered by the first wave. The salt, iodine, everything liquid, blind her for a few instants, streaming all over—surprised standing up, fertilized.

Now the cold becomes frigid. Moving ahead, she splits the sea down the middle. She no longer needs courage, now already ancient in the ritual. She lowers her head into the shine of the sea, and then lifts out the hair that emerges streaming over her salty eyes that are stinging. She plays with her hand in the water, leisurely, her hair in the sun almost immediately stiffens with salt. With cupped hands she does what she's always done in the sea, and with the pride of people who never explain even to themselves: with cupped hands filled with water, she drinks in great, good gulps.

And that was what she'd been missing: the sea inside her like the thick liquid of a man. Now she's entirely equal to herself. Her nourished throat constricts from the salt, her eyes redden from the salt dried by the sun, the gentle waves slap against her and retreat for she is a compact embankment.

She dives again, again drinks more water, no longer greedy for she doesn't need more. She is the lover who knows she'll have everything all over again. The sun rises higher and makes her bristle as it dries her, she dives again: she is ever less greedy and less sharp. Now she knows what she wants. She wants to stand still inside the sea. So she does. As against the sides of a ship, the water slaps, retreats, slaps. The woman receives no transmissions. She doesn't need communication.

Afterward she walks in the water back to the beach. She's not walking on the water—ah she'd never do that since they walked on water millennia ago—but no one can keep her from: walking in the water. Sometimes the sea resists her, powerfully dragging her backward, but then the woman's prow pushes ahead a bit harder and tougher.

And now she steps onto the sand. She knows she is glistening with water, and salt and sun. Even if she forgets a few minutes from now, she can never lose all this. And she knows in some obscure way that her streaming hair is that of a castaway. Because she knows—she knows she has created a danger. A danger as ancient as the human being.

Involuntary Incarnation
("Encarnação involuntária")

SOMETIMES, WHEN I SEE SOMEONE I'VE NEVER SEEN before, and have some time to observe that person, I incarnate myself in the other person and thus take a great step toward knowing who it is. And this intrusion into a person, whoever it may be, never ends in self-accusation: once I incarnate myself in someone else, I understand her motives and forgive. I must be careful not to incarnate myself into a dangerous and attractive life, and thus not want to return to myself.

One day, on the airplane … "Oh, my God," I pleaded, "not this, I don't want to be that missionary!"

But it was no use. I knew that three hours in her presence would make me a missionary for several days. Her missionary gauntness and extremely polished refinement had already claimed me. I succumb with curiosity, some wonder and advance weariness to the life I'm going to experience living for a few days. And with some apprehension, from a practical standpoint: I've been way too busy lately with my own responsibilities and pleasures to withstand the burden of this life unknown to me—but whose evangelical tension I'm already starting to feel. Right there on the plane I notice that I've already started walking like a lay saint: then I understand how patient the missionary is, how she effaces herself with that step that hardly wants to touch the ground, how if she treads more heavily it would eventually harm others. Now I am pale, my lips unpainted, my face is thin and I wear that missionary hat.

When I land I'll probably already have that air of suffering-transcended-by-peace-at-having-a-mission. And stamped across my face will be the sweetness of moral hope. Because above all I have become utterly moral. Yet when I first boarded the plane I was so robustly amoral. I was, no, I am! I cry in revolt against the missionary's prejudices. It's no use: all my strength is directed toward managing to be fragile. I pretend to read a magazine, while she reads the Bible.

We're going to make a quick descent before landing. The steward passes out chewing gum. And she blushes at the young man's approach.

Back on solid ground I'm a missionary in the airport wind, I secure my imaginary long, gray skirt against the wind's impropriety. I understand, I understand. I understand her, oh, how I understand her and the propriety with which she exists when not on duty carrying out her mission. I denounce, as the good little missionary, those women's short skirts, temptation to men. And, when I don't understand, it's with the same purified fanaticism of that pale woman who easily blushes when the young man approaches to inform us we must proceed on our journey.

I already know that it will be several days before I can finally resume my own life. Which, who knows, might never have been my own, except at the moment of birth, and all the rest has been incarnations. But no: I am a person. And when my own ghost claims me—then it's such a joyful encounter, such a celebration, that in a manner of speaking we cry on each other's shoulders. Afterward we dry our happy tears, my ghost becomes fully embodied in me, and we venture somewhat haughtily into that outside world.

Once, also while traveling, I met a heavily perfumed prostitute who smoked with her eyes half closed, while also staring fixedly at a man who was already getting hypnotized. I immediately, to better understand, started smoking with my eyes half closed toward the only man in my line of sight. But the fat man I'd been looking at in order to experience and have the prostitute's soul, that fatso was absorbed in the *New York Times*. And my perfume was too discreet. It fell flat.

Two Stories My Way
("Duas histórias a meu modo")

ONCE, HAVING NOTHING TO DO, I DID A KIND OF WRIT-*ing exercise*, just for fun. And I had fun. I took a double story of Marcel Aymé's as a theme. I came across the exercise today, and here's how it goes:

A good story involving wine is the one about the man who didn't like it, and Félicien Guérillot, a wine-grower of all things, was his name—names, man and story invented by Marcel Aymé, and so well-invented that all they needed to be true was the truth.

Félicien would have lived—had he lived—in Arbois, a land in France, and been married to a woman who was neither prettier nor shapelier than necessary for an honest man's peace. He came from a good family, though he didn't like wine. Yet the best vines around were his. He didn't like any kind of wine, and searched in vain for the wine that would free him from the curse of not loving the excellence of something excellent. For even when he was thirsty, which is the very time to have wine, the best wine tasted awful to him. Leontina, the wife who was neither too much nor too little, helped him hide this shame from everyone.

The story, now completely rewritten by me, would have proceeded on quite all right—and even better if its nucleus belonged to us, from the good ideas I have about how to end it. Marcel Aymé, however, who began it, this far into describing the man who didn't love wine seems to have gotten sick of this very story. And he himself intervened to say: but suddenly it bores me, this story. And to escape it, like someone who drinks wine to forget, now the author starts talking about everything he could have invented about Félicien, but won't because he doesn't want to. He's very sorry, because he would even have made Félicien pretend to get the shakes in an attempt to hide from others how he didn't have the shakes. What a good author, this Marcel Aymé. So good that he spent several pages on what he himself would have invented if Félicien were someone who interested him. The truth is that Aymé, as he's talking about what he would have invented, takes the opportunity to actually tell it—only, we know that's not it, because even with invented things what might have been doesn't count.

And at this point Aymé moves on to another story. No longer wanting the sad story about wine, he switches to Paris, where he takes up a man named Duvilé.

And in Paris it's the opposite: Etienne Duvilé, here was a man who enjoyed wine but didn't have any. It was expensive, and Etienne was a clerk. He would have liked to be corrupt but selling out or betraying the State isn't an opportunity that comes along every day. What came along every day was a house full of children, and a father-in-law who lived to eat incessantly. The family dreaming about an abundant table, and Duvilé about wine.

And there comes a day when Etienne really does dream, by which we mean that this time, while he dreamed, he was asleep. But now that we're supposed to recount the dream—since Marcel Aymé does at great length—now we're the ones that *ça vraiment* bores. We veil whatever the author wished to narrate, just as what we wanted to hear about Félicien was veiled by the author.

Here it shall only be said that, after this dream on a Saturday, at night, Duvilé's thirst worsened substantially. And his hatred for his father-in-law seemed more like a thirst. And everything grew so complicated, its underlying cause always being his original lack of wine, that out of thirst he nearly kills the father of his wife, of whom Aymé fails to say whether she was shapely, apparently neither yes nor no, all that matters to the story is wine. From a sleeping dream he shifted to a waking dream, which is now an illness. And Duvilé wished to drink up the whole world, and at the police station expressed his desire to drink the commissioner.

To this day Duvilé remains in an asylum, with no hope of getting out, since the doctors, not understanding his spirit, treat him with excellent mineral water that staunches small thirsts but not the great one.

Meanwhile, Aymé, maybe possessed himself, by thirst and mercy, hopes that Duvilé's family will send him to the good land of Arbois, where that first man, Félicien Guérillot, after adventures that deserve to be recounted, has now acquired a taste for wine. And, since we're not told how, we must leave it at that, with two stories not well told, neither by Aymé nor by us, but when it comes to wine people want less talk and more wine.

The First Kiss
("O primeiro beijo")

THE TWO MURMURED MORE THAN TALKED: THEY HAD just started dating and were giddy, it was love. Love and what comes with it: jealousy.

"Okay, I'll believe I'm your first girlfriend, I'm happy about that. But tell me the truth, the whole truth: have you ever kissed a woman before me?"

He answered simply:

"Yes, I've kissed a woman before."

"Who was she?" she asked, hurt.

He tried to tell her haltingly, didn't know how to explain.

The field-trip bus was slowly climbing into the mountains. He, one of the boys among a boisterous bunch of girls, let the cool breeze hit his face and run its long, thin fingers through his hair with a mother's light touch. To sit still once in a while, almost without thinking, and just feel—was so good. Staying focused on feeling was hard with all the commotion from his buddies.

And in any case thirst had hit: joking with his classmates, talking really loud, louder than the noise from the motor, laughing, shouting, thinking, feeling, oh man! did it leave his throat dry.

410

And not the slightest hint of water. The thing to do was pool your saliva, and that's what he did. After gathering it in his burning mouth he swallowed it slowly, over and over. It was warm, though, his saliva, and failed to quench his thirst. An enormous thirst, bigger than he was, that now seized his whole body.

The delicate breeze, so pleasant before, had now in the midday sun become hot and arid, and going in through his nose further dried what little saliva he was patiently gathering.

And what if he shut his nostrils and breathed a bit less of that desert wind? He tried for a few seconds but immediately started suffocating. You just had to wait, wait. Maybe just a few minutes, maybe hours, whereas his thirst had been going on for years.

He didn't know how and why but he was now feeling closer to water, he had a premonition that it was getting close, and his eyes leaped through the window searching the highway, penetrating the underbrush, scanning, sniffing.

The animal instinct inside him hadn't been wrong: around the unexpected curve in the highway, amid the underbrush, was … the fountain from which sprang a rivulet of the dreamed-of water.

The bus stopped, everyone was thirsty but he managed to reach the stone fountain first, before everyone else.

Eyes closed, he parted his lips and put them fiercely to the orifice from which the water was streaming. The first cool sip of water went down, sliding through his chest down to his belly.

It was life coming back, and it completely soaked his sandy insides until they were quenched. Now he could open his eyes.

He opened them and saw right near his face the two eyes of a statue staring at him and saw it was the statue of a woman and that the water was flowing from the woman's mouth. He recalled that at the first sip his lips had actually felt an ice-cold touch, colder than the water.

And he realized then that he had put his mouth on the mouth of the stone statue of the woman. Life had streamed from that mouth, from one mouth to another.

Intuitively, confused in his innocence, he felt intrigued: but the life-giving liquid, the liquid seed of life doesn't come from a woman … He gazed at the naked statue.

He'd kissed her.

He was racked by a shudder not visible on the outside and that originated from deep within and seized his whole body, bursting onto his face in flames.

He took a step back or forward, he no longer knew what he was doing. Disconcerted, stunned, he noticed that one part of his body, always relaxed before, was now aggressively tense, and this had never happened to him.

He stood, sweetly aggressive, alone among the others, his heart beating deeply, at intervals, feeling the world transform. Life was brand new, something else, discovered with a shock. Bewildered, in a fragile balance.

Until, coming from the depth of his being, streaming from a hidden source inside him came the truth. Which filled him immediately with alarm and also immediately with a pride he had never felt before: he …

He had become a man.

WHERE WERE YOU AT NIGHT

(*"Onde estivestes de noite"*)

In Search of a Dignity
("A procura de uma dignidade")

SENHORA JORGE B. XAVIER SIMPLY COULDN'T SAY HOW she had come in. It hadn't been through a main gate. It seemed to her in a vaguely dreamy way that she had come in through some kind of narrow opening amid the rubble of a construction site, as if she'd slipped sideways through a hole made just for her. The fact is, by the time she noticed she was already inside.

And by the time she noticed, she realized that she was deep, deep inside. She was walking interminably through the underground tunnels of Maracanã Stadium or at least they seemed to her narrow caves that ended in closed rooms and when the rooms were opened they had just a single window facing the stadium. Which, at that scorchingly deserted hour, was shimmering in the extreme glare of an uncommon heat that was descending on that midwinter day.

Then the old woman went down a shadowy passage. It led her like the others to an even darker one. The tunnel ceilings seemed low to her.

And then that passage led to another that led in turn to another.

She went down the deserted passage. And then bumped into another corner. That led her to another passage that opened onto another corner.

So she kept automatically heading down passages that kept ending in other passages. Where could the classroom for the first session be? Because that's where she would find the people she'd planned to meet. The lecture might have already started. She was going to miss it, she who made every effort not to miss anything *cultural* because that's how she stayed young inside, though even from the outside no one ever guessed she was almost 70 years old, everyone assumed she was around 57.

But now, lost in the dark, inner twists and turns of Maracanã, the woman was now dragging the heavy feet of an old lady.

That's when suddenly in a passage she came upon a man who popped up out of nowhere and asked him about the lecture which the man said he knew nothing about. But that man asked a second man who had also popped suddenly from around the bend in the passage.

Then this second man told them he had seen, near the right-hand bleachers, out there in the stadium, "two ladies and a gentleman, one of the ladies in red." Senhora Xavier doubted these people were the group she was supposed to meet before the lecture, and in fact had already lost track of the reason she was walking around with no end in sight. In any case she followed the man out to the stadium, where she stopped, dazzled in the hollow space filled with broad daylight and open muteness, the naked stadium disemboweled, with neither ball nor match. Above all with no crowd. There was a crowd that existed through the void of its absolute absence.

Had the two ladies and gentleman already vanished down some passage?

Then the man declared with exaggerated defiance: "Well I'm going to search for you, ma'am, and I'll find those people no matter what, they can't have vanished into thin air."

And in fact from faraway they both spotted them. But a second later they disappeared again. It was like a child's game in which muffled peals of laughter were mocking Senhora Jorge B. Xavier.

Then she accompanied the man down further passages. Then this man too vanished around a corner.

The woman had already given up on the lecture which deep down didn't really matter to her. As long as she made it out of that tangle of endless paths. Wasn't there an exit? Then she felt like she was in an elevator stuck between floors. Wasn't there an exit?

And that's when she suddenly recalled the wording of her friend's directions on the phone: "it's more or less near Maracanã Stadium." In light of this memory she understood her mistake, made by a scatterbrained and distracted person who only heard half of things, the other half remaining submerged. Senhora Xavier was very inattentive. So, then, the meeting wasn't at Maracanã after all, it was just nearby. Yet that little destiny of hers had wanted her to be lost in the labyrinth.

All right, then the struggle started up again even worse: she was determined to get out and didn't know how or where. And again that man showed up in the passage who was searching for those people and who again assured her that he'd find them because they couldn't have vanished into thin air. That's exactly what he said:

"Those people can't have vanished into thin air!"

The woman informed him:

"You don't have to take the trouble to look for them, all

right? Thank you very much, all right? Because the place I'm supposed to meet those people isn't in Maracanã."

The man halted immediately to look at her in bewilderment: "So what exactly are you doing here, ma'am?"

She wanted to explain that her life was just like that, but since she didn't even know what she meant by "just like that" or even by "her life," she said nothing in reply. The man pressed the question, somewhere between suspicious and cautious: what exactly was she doing there? Nothing, the woman replied only in her mind, by that point about to collapse from exhaustion. But she didn't reply, she let him think she was crazy. Besides, she never explained herself. She knew the man decided she was crazy—and who ever said she wasn't? because didn't she feel that thing she called "that" out of shame? Even if she knew her so-called mental health was every bit as sound as her physical health. Physical health now failing because she'd been dragging her feet for years and years walking through that labyrinth. Her via crucis. She was dressed in very heavy wool and was stifled sweating in the unexpected heat that belonged to the peak of summer, that summer day that was a freak occurrence in winter. Her legs were aching, aching under the weight of that old cross. She'd already resigned herself in a way to never making it out of Maracanã and dying there from a heart bled dry.

Then, and as always, it was only after she had given up on the things she desired that they happened. What occurred to her suddenly was an idea: "oh I'm such a crazy old bat." Why, instead of continuing to ask about the people who weren't there, didn't she find the man and ask him how to get out of those passages? Because all she wanted was to get out and not run into anybody.

She finally found the man, while rounding a corner. And

she spoke to him in a voice slightly tremulous and hoarse from exhaustion and fear of hoping in vain. The wary man agreed in a flash that the best thing for her to do really was go home and told her cautiously: "Ma'am, you don't seem to be thinking straight, maybe it's this strange heat."

Having said this, the man then simply accompanied her down the next passage and at the corner they spotted the two broad gates standing open. Simple as that? easy as that?

Simple as that.

Then the woman thought without coming to any conclusions that it was just for her that the exit had become impossible to find. Senhora Xavier was only slightly taken aback and at the same time used to it. Surely everyone had a path to follow interminably, this being part of destiny, though she didn't know whether she believed in that or not.

And there was the taxi passing. She hailed it and said to him controlling her voice that was becoming increasingly old and tired:

"Young man, I don't know the exact address, I've forgotten. But what I do know is that the house is on a street—I-don't-remember-which-anymore but something with 'Gusmão' and the cross street if I'm not mistaken is Colonel-so-and-so."

The driver was patient as with a child: "All right now don't you get upset, let's calmly look for a street with 'Gusmão' in the middle and 'Colonel' at the end," he said turning around with a smile and then winked at her with a conspiratorial look that seemed indecent. They took off with a jerk that rattled her insides.

Then suddenly she recognized the people she was looking for and who were to be found on the sidewalk in front of a big house. Yet it was as if the goal had been to get there and not to listen to the lecture that by then was completely forgotten, since Senhora Xavier had lost track of her objective. And she didn't know in the name of what she had walked so far. Then she realized she'd worn herself out beyond her own strength and wanted to leave, the lecture was a nightmare. So she asked a distinguished lady she was semi-acquainted with and who had a car with a driver to take her home because she wasn't feeling well in that strange heat. The chauffeur would only arrive in an hour. So Senhora Xavier sat in a chair they'd placed in the hallway for her, she sat bolt upright in her tight girdle, outside the culture being dissected across the way in the closed room. From which not a sound could be heard. She didn't really care about culture. And there she was in those labyrinths of 60 seconds and 60 minutes that would lead her to an hour.

Then the distinguished lady came and said: that there was a car for her out front but she was letting her know that, since her driver had said he was going to take a while, considering that you, ma'am, aren't feeling well, she had hailed the first taxi she saw. Why hadn't Senhora Xavier herself thought to call a taxi, instead of readily subjecting herself to the twists and turns of time spent waiting? Then Senhora Jorge B. Xavier thanked her with the utmost refinement. The woman had always been very refined and polite. She got into the taxi and said:

"Leblon, if you please."

Her brain was hollow, it seemed like her head was fasting.

After a while she noticed they were driving around and around but that they kept ending up back at the same square. Why weren't they getting out of there? Was there once again no way out? The driver ended up admitting that he wasn't familiar with the Zona Sul, that he only worked in the Zona Norte. And she didn't know how to give him directions. The cross of the years weighed ever more heavily on her and yet another lack of an exit merely revived the black magic of the passages of Maracanã. There was no way for them to be freed from the square! Then the driver told her to take another taxi, and he even flagged down one that was passing by. She thanked him stiffly, she was formal with people, even those she knew. Moreover she was very kind. In the new taxi she said fearfully:

"If it's not too much trouble, sir, let's go to Leblon."

And they simply left the square at once and took different streets.

While unlocking the door to her apartment she had the urge, just in her head and fantasizing, to sob very loudly. But she wasn't the sort to sob or complain. In passing she told the maid she wouldn't be taking any phone calls. She went straight to her bedroom, took off all her clothes, swallowed a pill without water and then waited for it to take effect.

Meanwhile, she smoked. She remembered it was August and they say August brings bad luck. But September would arrive one day like an exit. And September was for some reason the month of May: a lighter and more transparent month. She vaguely pondered this until drowsiness finally set in and she fell asleep.

When she awoke hours later she saw then that a very fine, cool rain was coming down, it was cold as a knife blade. Naked in bed she was freezing. Then she thought that a naked old lady was a very curious thing. She remembered that she'd been planning to buy a wool scarf. She looked at the clock: the shops would still be open. She took a taxi and said:

"Ipanema, if you please."

The man said:

"Sorry? Jardim Botânico?"

"Ipanema, please," the woman repeated, quite surprised. It was the absurdity of total miscommunication: for, what did the words "Ipanema" and "Jardim Botânico" have in common? But once again she vaguely thought how "her life was just like that."

She quickly made her purchase and found herself on the already dark street with nothing to do. Because Senhor Jorge B. Xavier had traveled to São Paulo the day before and wouldn't be back until the next day.

Then, back home again, between taking another sleeping pill or doing something else, she opted for the second scenario, since she remembered she could now go back to looking for that misplaced bill of exchange. From what little she understood, that piece of paper represented money. Two days before she had exhaustively searched for it all over the house, even in the kitchen, but in vain. Now it occurred to her: and why not under the bed? Maybe. So she knelt on the floor. But she quickly got tired from putting all her weight on her knees and leaned on her two hands as well.

Then she realized she was on all fours.

She stayed that way awhile, perhaps meditative, perhaps not. Who knows, maybe Senhora Xavier was tired of being a human. She was being a bitch on all fours. Without the slightest nobility. Having shed her last bit of pride. On all fours, a little thoughtful perhaps. But all there was under the bed was dust.

She stood with concerted effort from her discombobulated joints and saw there was nothing else to do except realistically consider—and it was with a painstaking effort that she saw reality—realistically consider that the bill was lost for good and that keeping up the search would be never making it out of Maracanã.

And as always, since she'd given up the search, upon opening a little drawer of handkerchiefs to take one out—there was the bill of exchange.

Then the woman, tired from the effort of being on all fours, sat on the bed and completely out of nowhere started crying softly. It sounded more like some Arabic gibberish. She hadn't cried in 30 years, but now she was so tired. If crying was what that was. It wasn't. It was something. Finally she blew her nose. Then she had the following thought: that she would force the hand of "destiny" and have a greater destiny. With willpower you can accomplish everything, she thought without the least conviction. And all this about being bound to a destiny had occurred to her because she had already started, without meaning to, thinking about "that."

But then it so happened that the woman also had the following thought: it was too late to have a destiny. She thought she would readily trade places with another being. That's when it occurred to her that there wasn't anyone to trade places with: no matter what she was, she was she and couldn't be transformed into another unique individual. Everyone was unique. So was Senhora Jorge B. Xavier.

But everything that had happened to her was still preferable to feeling "that." And that came with its long passages without an exit. "That," now with no shame at all, was the gnawing hunger in her guts, hunger to be possessed by that unattainable television idol. She never missed a single show of his. So, since she hadn't been able to keep from thinking about him, the thing to do was let herself think and recall the ladylike girl face of Roberto Carlos, my love.

She went to wash her dusty hands and caught sight of herself in the mirror above the sink. Then Senhora Xavier had this thought: "If I really want it, really really want it, he'll be mine for at least one night." She vaguely believed in willpower. Once again she had become entangled in a desire that was twisted and strangled.

But, who knows? If she gave up on Roberto Carlos, that's when things might happen between him and her. Senhora Xavier reflected a bit on the matter. Then she slyly pretended that she was giving up on Roberto Carlos. But she was well aware that the magic of giving up only produced positive results when it was real, and not just a ploy to get her way. Reality demanded a lot from the woman. She examined herself in the mirror to see if her face would become bestial under the influence of her feelings. But it was a subdued face that had long since stopped showing what she felt. Besides, her face had never expressed anything but good manners. And now it was merely the mask of a seventy-year-old woman. Then her lightly made-up face looked to her like a clown's. The woman faked a smile to see if that might improve things. It didn't.

From the outside — she saw in the mirror — she was a dried up thing like a dried fig. But on the inside she wasn't shriveled. Quite the contrary. On the inside she was like moist gums, soft just like toothless gums.

Then she searched for a thought that would make her spiritual or shrivel her once and for all. But she'd never been spiritual. And because of Roberto Carlos the woman was enveloped in the shadows of that matter in which she was profoundly anonymous.

Standing in the bathroom she was as anonymous as a chicken.

For a fraction of a fleeting second, she almost unconsciously glimpsed that all people are anonymous. Because no one is the other and the other didn't know the other. So—so the person is anonymous. And now she was tangled in that deep and fatal well, in the revolution of the body. A body whose depths were unseen and that was the darkness of the malignant shadows of her instincts, alive like lizards and rats. And everything out of season, fruit out of season? Why hadn't other old women warned her that this could happen up till the end? In old men she'd certainly witnessed leering glances. But not in old women. Out of season. And she, alive as if she were still somebody, she who wasn't anybody.

Senhora Jorge B. Xavier was nobody.

Then she wished for nice and romantic feelings in relation to the delicacy of Roberto Carlos's face. But she couldn't manage it: his delicacy merely led her to a dark passage of sensuality. And her damnation was lasciviousness. It was base hunger: she wanted to devour Roberto Carlos's mouth. She wasn't romantic, she was crude in matters of love. There in the bathroom, in front of the mirror above the sink.

With her indelibly sullied age.

Without at least a sublime thought that might serve as her rudder and ennoble her existence.

Then she began taking her hair out of its bun and combing it slowly. It needed to be colored again, its white roots were already showing. Then the woman had the following thought: in all my life there's never been a climax like in the stories you read. The climax was Roberto Carlos. She reflected, concluded that she would die secretly as she had secretly lived. But she also knew that every death is secret.

From the depths of her future death she thought she saw in the mirror the coveted figure of Roberto Carlos, with that soft wavy hair of his. There she was, trapped in desire out of season like that summer day in midwinter. Trapped in the tangle of passages in Maracanã. Trapped in the fatal secret of old women. It was just that she wasn't used to being nearly 70, she lacked practice and hadn't the slightest experience.

Then she said out loud and all alone:

"Robertinho Carlinhos."

And to that she added: my love. She heard her voice in wonder as if making for the very first time, with no modesty or guilt whatsoever, the confession that all the same should have been shameful. The woman daydreamed that Robertinho might not want to accept her love because she herself was aware that this love was too sentimental, cloyingly voluptuous and greedy. And Roberto Carlos seemed so chaste, so asexual.

Were her lightly tinted lips still kissable? Or was it disgusting to kiss an old lady on the mouth? She studied her own lips up close and with no expression. And still with no expression she softly sang the chorus from Roberto Carlos's most famous song: "I want you to keep me warm this winter and to hell with all the rest."

That was when Senhora Jorge B. Xavier abruptly doubled over the sink as if about to vomit up her guts and interrupted her life with an earth-shattering silence: there! must! be! an! exiiiiiiit!

The Departure of the Train
("A partida do trem")

THE DEPARTURE WAS FROM CENTRAL STATION WITH
its enormous clock, the biggest in the world. It showed six
o'clock in the morning. Angela Pralini paid the taxi and took
her small suitcase. Dona Maria Rita Alvarenga Chagas Souza
Melo got out of her daughter's Opala and they headed toward
the tracks. The old woman was dressed up and wearing jewelry. Emerging from the wrinkles that disguised her was the
pure form of a nose lost in old age, and of a mouth that in
times past must have been full and sensitive. But no matter.
You reach a certain point—and it no longer matters what you
were. A new race begins. An old woman cannot be communicated. She received the icy kiss from her daughter who left
before the train departed. She used to help her board the train
car. Since there was no center, she'd placed herself on the side.
When the locomotive started moving, she was slightly taken
aback: she hadn't expected the train to move in that direction
and had sat facing backward.

Angela Pralini noticed her stirring and asked:

"Would you like to change places with me, ma'am?"

Dona Maria Rita gave a genteel start, said no, thank you, she

427

was fine where she was. But she seemed to have been shaken. She ran her hand over her gold filigree brooch, pinned to her breast, ran her hand over the clasp, took it off, raised it to her felt hat adorned with a fabric rose, took it off. Stern. Affronted? Finally she asked Angela Pralini:

"Is it on my account that you'd like to change places, miss?"

Angela Pralini said no, was surprised, the old woman surprised for the same reason: you don't accept favors from a little old lady. She smiled a bit too much and her powder-covered lips parted in dry furrows: she was charmed. And a bit worked up:

"How nice of you," she said, "how kind."

There was a moment of disturbance because Angela Pralini laughed too, and the old woman kept laughing, revealing her well-polished dentures. She tugged discreetly at the girdle that was a little too tight.

"How nice," she repeated.

She regained her composure somewhat quickly, crossed her hands over her purse that contained everything you could possibly imagine. Her wrinkles, as she'd been laughing, had taken on a meaning, thought Angela. Now they were once more incomprehensible, superimposed on a face that was once more unmalleable. But Angela had taken away her peace. She'd already seen lots of nervous girls telling themselves: if I laugh any more I'll ruin everything, it'll be ridiculous, I've got to stop — and it was impossible. The situation was very sad. With immense compassion, Angela saw the cruel wart on her chin, a wart with a sharp black hair poking out. But Angela had taken away her peace. You could tell she was about to smile any moment now: Angela had set the old woman on edge. Now she was one of those little old ladies who seem to think they're always late, that the appointed time has passed. A second later she couldn't contain herself, rose and peered out her window, as if it were impossible to stay seated.

"Do you want to open the window, ma'am?" said a young man listening to Handel on his transistor radio.

"Ah!" she exclaimed in terror.

Oh no! thought Angela, everything was getting ruined, the boy shouldn't have said that, it was too much, no one should have touched her again. Because the old woman, on the verge of losing the attitude which she lived off, on the verge of losing a certain bitterness, quivered like harpsichord music between smiling and being utterly charmed:

"No, no, no," she said with false authority, "not at all, thank you, I just wanted to look out."

She sat immediately as if the young man and woman's consideration were keeping watch over her. The old woman, before boarding the train, had crossed her heart three times, discreetly kissing her fingertips. She was wearing a black dress with a real lace collar and a solid gold brooch. On her dark left hand were a widow's two thick wedding bands, thick like they don't make them anymore. From the next car a group of girl scouts could be heard singing a hymn to Brazil in high voices. Fortunately, in the next car. The music from the boy's radio mingled with another boy's music: he was listening to Edith Piaf who was singing "J'attendrai."

That had been when the train suddenly lurched and its wheels sprang into motion. The departure had begun. The old woman said softly: Oh Jesus! She bathed in the waters of Jesus. Amen. From a lady's transistor radio she learned it was six-thirty in the morning, a frigid morning. The old woman thought: Brazil was improving the signs along its highways. Someone named Kissinger seemed to be in charge of the world.

Nobody knows where I am, thought Angela Pralini, and that scared her a little, she was a fugitive.

"My name is Maria Rita Alvarenga Chagas Souza Melo—Alvarenga Chagas was my father's last name," she added to beg pardon for having to utter so many words just to say her name. "Chagas," she added modestly, "refers to the Wounds of Christ. But you can call me Dona Maria Ritinha. And your name?, what's your Christian name?"

"My name is Angela Pralini. I'm going to spend six months on my aunt and uncle's farm. And you, ma'am?"

"Ah, I'm going to my son's farm, I'm going to spend the rest of my life there, my daughter brought me to the train and my son is waiting for me with the horse cart at the station. I'm like a package delivered from hand to hand."

Angela's aunt and uncle didn't have children and treated her like a daughter. Angela recalled the note she'd left Eduardo: "Don't try to find me. I'm going to disappear from you forever. I love you more than ever. Farewell. Your Angela stopped being yours because you didn't want her."

They sat in silence. Angela Pralini let the rhythmic sounds of the train wash over her. Dona Maria Rita gazed once again at the diamond-and-pearl ring on her finger, adjusted her gold brooch: "I'm old but I'm rich, richer than everyone in this car. I'm rich, I'm rich." She peered at her watch, more to see its heavy gold case than to check the time. "I'm very rich, I'm not just any old lady." But she knew, ah she very well knew that she was just some little old lady, a little old lady frightened by the smallest things. She recalled herself, alone all day long in her rocking chair, alone with the servants, while her "public relations" daughter spent all day out of the house, not coming home until eight at night, and without even giving her a kiss.

She'd awoken that day at five in the morning, everything still dark, it was cold.

In the wake of the young man's consideration she was extraordinarily worked up and smiling. She seemed weakened. Her laugh revealed her to be one of those little old ladies full of teeth. The misplaced cruelty of teeth. The boy had already moved off. She opened and closed her eyelids. Suddenly she slapped her fingers against Angela's leg, extremely quickly and lightly:

"Today everyone is truly, just truly nice! so kind, so kind."

Angela smiled. The old woman kept smiling without taking her deep, vacant eyes off the young woman's. Come on, come on they urged her all around, and she peered here and there as if to make a choice. Come on, come on! they pushed her laughing all around, and she shook with laughter, genteel.

"How nice everyone on this train is," she said.

Suddenly she tried to regain her composure, pretended to clear her throat, got ahold of herself. It must have been hard. She feared she had reached a point of not being able to stop herself. She reined herself in severely and trembling, closed her lips over her innumerable teeth. But she couldn't fool anyone: her face held such hope that it disturbed any eyes that saw it. She no longer depended on anyone: once they had touched her, she could be on her way—she radiated on her own, thin, tall. She still would have liked to say anything at all and was already preparing some sociable head movement, full of studied charm. Angela wondered whether she'd manage to express herself. She seemed to think, think, and tenderly find a fully formed thought that might adequately couch her feelings. She said carefully and with the wisdom of the elders, as if she needed to act the part in order to speak like an old woman:

"Youth. Darling youth."

Her laugh came out somewhat forced. Was she going to have a nervous breakdown? thought Angela Pralini. Because she was so marvelous. But she cleared her throat again austerely, drummed her fingertips on the seat as if urgently summoning the orchestra to prepare a new score. She opened her purse, pulled out a little square of newspaper, unfolded it, unfolded it, until she turned it into a large, regular newspaper, dating from three days before — Angela saw from the date. She began to read.

Angela had lost over fifteen pounds. On the farm she'd gorge herself: black bean mash and collard greens, to gain back those precious lost pounds. She was so skinny from having gone along with Eduardo's brilliant and uninterrupted reasoning: she'd drink coffee without sugar nonstop in order to stay awake. Angela Pralini had very pretty breasts, they were her best feature. She had pointy ears and a pretty, curved mouth, kissable. Deep dark circles under her eyes. She made use of the train's screaming whistle as her own scream. It was a piercing howl, hers, only turned inward. She was the woman who drank the most whiskey in Eduardo's group. She could take 6 or 7 in a row, maintaining a terror-stricken lucidity. On the farm she'd drink creamy cow's milk. One thing united the old woman with Angela: both would be met with open arms, but neither knew this about the other. Angela suddenly shivered: who would give the dog its final dose of deworming treatment. Ah, Ulisses, she told the dog in her head, I didn't abandon you willingly, it's because I had to escape Eduardo, before he ruined me completely with his lucidity: a lucidity that illuminated too much and singed everything. Angela knew that her aunt and uncle had antivenom for snake bites: she was planning to go straight into the heart of the dense and verdant forest, wearing tall boots and slathered in mosquito repellent. As if stepping off the Trans-Amazonian Highway, the explorer. What animals would she encounter? It was best to bring a rifle, food and water. And a compass. Ever since she'd discovered—but really discovered with a note of alarm—that she would die some day, then she no longer feared life, and, because of death, she had full rights: she'd risk everything. After having gone through two relationships that ended in nothing, this third was ending in love-adoration, cut off by the inevitability of the desire to survive. Eduardo had transformed her: he'd made her have eyes on the inside. But now she was looking outward. Through the window she saw the breasts of the land, in mountains. Little birds exist, Eduardo! clouds exist, Eduardo! a whole world of stallions and mares and cows exists, Eduardo, and when I was a little girl I would gallop on a bare horse, without a saddle! I'm fleeing my suicide, Eduardo. I'm sorry, Eduardo, but I don't want to die. I want to be fresh and rare like a pomegranate.

The old woman pretended to be reading the newspaper. But she was thinking: her world was a sigh. She didn't want others to think she'd been abandoned. God gave me health so I could travel alone. I'm also of sound mind, I don't talk to myself and I bathe by myself every day. She gave off the fragrance of wilted and crushed roses, it was her elderly, musty fragrance. To possess a breathing rhythm, Angela thought about the old woman, was the loveliest thing to have existed since Dona Maria Rita's birth. It was life.

Dona Maria Rita was thinking: once she got old she'd started to disappear to other people, they only glimpsed her. Old age: supreme moment. She was an outsider to the world's

433

general strategy and her own was paltry. She'd lost track of her more far-reaching goals. She was already the future.

Angela thought: I think that if I happened upon the truth, I wouldn't be able to think it. It would be mentally unpronounceable.

The old woman had always been slightly empty, well, ever so slightly. Death? it was odd, it played no part in her days. And even "not existing" didn't exist, not-existing was impossible. Not existing didn't fit into our daily life. Her daughter wasn't affectionate. In compensation her son was incredibly affectionate, good-natured, chubby. Her daughter was as brusque as her cursory kisses, the "public relations" one. The old woman didn't feel quite up to living. The monotony, however, was what kept her going.

Eduardo would listen to music to accompany his thinking. And he *understood* the dissonance of modern music, all he knew how to do was *understand*. His intelligence that smothered her. You're a temperamental person, Angela, he once told her. So what? What's wrong with that? I am what I am and not what you think I am. The proof that I am is in the departure of this train. My proof is also Dona Maria Rita, right there across from me. Proof of what? Yes. She'd already had plenitude. When she and Eduardo were so in love that while in the same bed, holding hands, they had felt life was complete. Few people have known plenitude. And, because plenitude is also an explosion, she and Eduardo had cowardly begun to live "normally." Because you can't prolong ecstasy without dying. They separated for a pointless, semi-invented reason: they didn't want to die of passion. Plenitude is one of those truths you happen upon. But the necessary split had been an amputation for her, just as there are women whose uterus and ovaries are removed. Empty inside.

Dona Maria Rita was so antique that people in her daughter's house were used to her like an old piece of furniture. She wasn't a novelty for anyone. But it had never crossed her mind that she was living in solitude. It was just that she didn't have anything to do. It was a forced leisure that at times became heartrending: she had nothing to do in the world. Except live like a cat, like a dog. Her ideal was to be a lady-in-waiting for some noble gentlewoman, but people didn't have them anymore and even so, no one would have believed in her hardy seventy-seven years, they'd have thought her feeble. She didn't do anything, all she did was this: be old. Sometimes she got depressed: she thought she was no good for anything, she was even no good for God. Dona Maria Ritinha didn't have hell inside her. Why did old people, even those who didn't tremble, evoke something delicately tremulous? Dona Maria Rita had a brittle tremor of accordion music.

But when it's a matter of life itself—who comes to our rescue? for each one stands alone. And each life must be rescued by that each-one's own life. Each one of us: that's what we count on. Since Dona Maria Rita had always been an average person, she thought dying wasn't a normal thing. Dying was surprising. It was as if she wasn't up to the act of death, for nothing extraordinary had ever happened to her in life up till now that could suddenly justify such an extraordinary fact. She talked and even thought about death, but deep down she was skeptical and suspicious. She thought you died when there was some disaster or someone killed someone else. The old woman had little experience. Sometimes she got palpitations: the heart's bacchanal. But that was it and even that dated back to girlhood. During her first kiss, for example, her heart had lost control. And it had been a good thing bordering on bad.

Something that recalled her past, not as facts but as life: a sensation of shadowy vegetation, caladiums, giant ferns, maidenhair ferns, green freshness. Whenever she felt this all over again, she smiled. One of the most erudite words she used was "picturesque." It was good. It was like listening to the murmur of a spring and not knowing where it came from.

A dialogue she carried on with herself:

"Are you doing anything?"

"Yes I am: I am being sad."

"Doesn't it bother you to be alone?"

"No, I think."

Sometimes she didn't think. Sometimes a person sat there being. She didn't have to do. Being was already doing. You could be slowly or a bit fast.

In the row behind them, two women were talking and talking nonstop. Their constant sounds fused with the noise of the train wheels on the tracks.

As much as Dona Maria Rita had been hoping her daughter would wait on the train platform to give her a little sendoff, it didn't happen. The train motionless. Until it had lurched forward.

"Angela," she said, "a woman never tells her age, that's why all I can say is it's a lot of years. No, with you, Angela—can I use your first name?—with you I'm going to let you in on a secret: I'm seventy-seven years old."

"I'm thirty-seven," Angela Pralini said.

It was seven in the morning.

"When I was a girl I was such a little liar. I'd lie for no reason."

Later, as if disenchanted with the magic of lying, she'd stopped.

Angela, looking at the elderly Dona Maria Rita, was afraid to grow old and die. Hold my hand, Eduardo, so I won't be afraid to die. But he didn't hold anything. All he did was: think, think and think. Ah, Eduardo, I want the sweetness of Schumann! Her life was a life undone, evanescent. She lacked a bone that was hard, tough and strong, that no one could cross. Who could be this essential bone? To distance herself from the sensation of overwhelming neediness, she thought: how did they get by in the Middle Ages without telephones or airplanes? Mystery. Middle Ages, I adore ye and thy black, laden clouds that opened onto the luminous and fresh Renaissance.

As for the old woman, she had checked out. She was gazing into the nothing.

Angela looked at herself in her compact. I look like I'm about to faint. Watch out for the abyss, I tell the woman who looks like she's about to faint. When I die I'll miss you so much, Eduardo! The declaration didn't stand up to logic yet possessed in itself an imponderable meaning. It was as if she wanted to express one thing and was expressing another.

The old woman was already the future. She seemed ashamed. Ashamed of being old? At some point in her life there certainly must have been a mistake, and the result was that strange state of life. Which nevertheless wasn't leading her to death. Death was always such a surprise for the person dying. Yet she took pride in not drooling or wetting the bed, as if that uncultivated form of health was the merited result of an act of her own will. The only reason she wasn't a grande dame, a distinguished older lady, was because she wasn't arrogant: she was a dignified little old lady who suddenly looked skittish. She—all right, she was praising herself, considered herself an old woman full of precociousness like a precocious child. But her life's true intention, she did not know.

Angela was dreaming about the farm: there you could hear shouts, barks and howls, at night. "Eduardo," she said to him in her head, "I was tired of trying to be what you thought I am. There's a bad side—the stronger one and the one that dominated though I tried to hide it because of you—on that strong side I'm a cow, I'm a free horse that stamps at the ground, I'm a streetwalker, I'm a whore—and not a 'woman of letters.' I know I'm intelligent and that sometimes I hide it so I won't offend others with my intelligence, I who am a subconscious. I fled you, Eduardo, because you were killing me with that genius head of yours that made me nearly clap both hands over my ears and nearly scream with horror and exhaustion. And now I'm going to spend six months on the farm, you don't know where I'll be, and every day I'll bathe in the river mixing its mud with my own blessed clay. I'm common, Eduardo! and you should know that I like reading comics, my love, oh my love! how I love you and how I love your terrible incantations, ah how I adore you, slave of yours that I am. But I am physical, my love, I am physical and I had to hide from you the glory of being physical. And you, who are the very radiance of reasoning, though you don't know it, were nourished by me. You, super-intellectual and brilliant and leaving everyone stunned and speechless."

"I think," the old woman said to herself very slowly, "I think that pretty girl isn't interested in chatting with me. I don't know why, but nobody chats with me anymore. And even when I'm with people, they don't seem to remember me. After all it's not my fault I'm old. But never mind, I keep myself company. And anyhow I've got Nandinho, my dear son who adores me."

"The agonizing pleasure of scratching one's itch!" thought Angela. "I, hmm, who never go in for this or that—I'm free!!!

I'm getting healthier, oh I feel like blurting something really loud to scare everyone. Would the old woman get it? I don't know, she must have given birth plenty of times. I'm not falling into the trap of thinking the right thing to do is be unhappy, Eduardo. I want to enjoy everything and then die and be damned! be damned! be damned! Though the old woman might be unhappy without knowing it. Passivity. I won't go in for that either, no passivity whatsoever, what I want to do is bathe naked in the muddy river that resembles me, naked and free! hooray! Hip hip hooray! I'm abandoning everything! everything! and that way I won't be abandoned, I don't want to depend on more than around three people and for the rest it's: Hello, how are you? fine. Edu, you know what? I'm abandoning you. You, at the core of your intellectualism, aren't worth the life of a dog. I'm abandoning you, then. And I'm abandoning that group of pseudo-intellectuals that used to demand from me a vain and nervous constant exercise of false and hasty intelligence. I needed God to abandon me so I could feel his presence. I need to kill someone inside me. You ruined my intelligence with yours, a genius's. And forced me to know, to know, to know. Ah, Eduardo, don't worry, I've brought along the books you gave me so I can 'follow a course of home study,' as you wanted. I'll study philosophy by the river, out of the love I have for you."

Angela Pralini had thoughts so deep there were no words to express them. It was a lie to say you could only have one thought at a time: she had many thoughts that intersected and were multiple. "Not to mention the 'subconscious' that explodes inside me, whether I want it to or you don't. I am a fount," thought Angela, thinking at the same time about where she'd put her head scarf, thinking about whether the dog had drunk the milk she'd left him, Eduardo's shirts, and her extreme physical and mental depletion. And about elderly Dona Maria Rita. "I'll never forget your face, Eduardo." His was a somewhat astonished face, astonished at his own intelligence. He was naive. And he loved without knowing he was loving. He'd be beside himself when he found out that she'd left, leaving the dog and him. Abandonment due to lack of nutrition, she thought. At the same time she was thinking about the old woman sitting across from her. It wasn't true that you only think one thought at a time. She was, for example, capable of writing a check perfectly, without a single error, while thinking about her life, for example. Which wasn't good but in the end was hers. Hers again. Coherence, I don't want it anymore. Coherence is mutilation. I want disorder. I can only guess at it through a vehement incoherence. To meditate, I took myself out of me first and I feel the void. It is in the void that one passes the time. She who adored a nice day at the beach, with sun, sand and sun. Man is abandoned, has lost contact with the earth, with the sky. He no longer lives, he exists. The atmosphere between her and Eduardo Gosme was filled with emergency. He had transformed her into an urgent woman. And one who, to keep her urgency awake, took stimulants that made her thinner and thinner and took away her hunger. I want to eat, Eduardo, I'm hungry, Eduardo, hungry for lots of food! I am organic!

"Discover today the supertrain of tomorrow." *Selections from the Reader's Digest* that she sometimes read in secret from Eduardo. It was like the *Selections* that said: discover today the supertrain of tomorrow. She positively wasn't discovering it today. But Eduardo was the supertrain. Super everything. She was discovering today the super of tomorrow. And she couldn't stand it. She couldn't stand the perpetual motion. You are the desert, and I am going to Oceania, to the South Seas, to the Isles of Tahiti. Though they're ruined by tourists. You're no more than a tourist, Eduardo. I'm headed for my own life, Edu. And I say like Fellini: in darkness and ignorance I create more. The life I had with Eduardo smelled like a freshly painted new pharmacy. She preferred the living smell of manure disgusting as it was. He was correct like a tennis court. Incidentally, he played tennis to stay in shape. Anyway, he was a bore she used to love and almost no longer did. She was recovering her mental health right there on the train. She was still in love with Eduardo. And he, without knowing it, was still in love with her. I who can't get anything right, except omelets. With just one hand she'd crack eggs with incredible speed, and she cracked them into the bowl without spilling a single drop. Eduardo was consumed with envy at such elegance and efficiency. He sometimes gave lectures at universities and they adored him. She attended them too, she adoring him too. How was it again that he'd begin? "I feel uncomfortable seeing people stand up when they hear I'm about to speak." Angela was always afraid they'd walk out and leave him there alone.

The old woman, as if she'd received a mental transmission, was thinking: don't let them leave me alone. How old am I exactly? Oh I don't even know anymore.

Right afterward she let the thought drain away. And she was peacefully nothing. She hardly existed. It was good that way, very good indeed. Plunges into the nothing.

Angela Pralini, to calm down, told herself a very calming, very peaceful story: once upon a time there was a man who liked jabuticaba fruit very much. So he went to an orchard where there were trees laden with black, smooth and lustrous globules, that dropped into his hands in complete surrender and dropped from his hands to his feet. There was such an abundance of jabuticaba fruit that he gave in to the luxury of stepping on them. And they made a very delicious sound. They went like this: pop-pop-pop etc. Angela grew calm like the jabuticaba man. There were jabuticabas on the farm and with her bare feet she'd make that soft, moist "pop-pop." She never knew whether or not you were supposed to swallow the pits. Who would answer that question? No one. Perhaps only a man who, like Ulisses, the dog, and unlike Eduardo, would answer: "*Mangia, bella, que te fa bene.*"* She knew a little Italian but was never sure whether she had it right. And, after what that man said, she'd swallow the pits. Another delicious tree was one whose scientific name she had forgotten but that in childhood everyone had known directly, without science, it was one that in the Rio Botanical Garden made a dry little "pop-pop." See? see how you're being reborn? The cat's seven breaths. The number seven followed her everywhere, it was her secret, her strength. She felt beautiful. She wasn't. But that's how she felt. She also felt kindhearted. With tenderness toward the elderly Maria Ritinha who had put on her glasses and was reading the newspaper. Everything about the elderly Maria Rita was meandering. Near the end? oh, how it hurts to die. In life you suffer but you're holding on to something: ineffable life. And as for the question of death? You mustn't be afraid: go forward, always.

Always.

Like the train.

Somewhere there's something written on the wall. And it's

* Italian: "Eat, pretty girl, it's good for you."

for me, thought Angela. From the flames of Hell a fresh telegram will arrive for me. And never again will my hope be disappointed. Never. Never again.

The old woman was anonymous as a chicken, as someone named Clarice had said talking about a shameless old woman, in love with Roberto Carlos. That Clarice made people uncomfortable. She made the old woman shout: there! must! be! an! exiiit! And there was. For example, the exit for that old woman was the husband who'd be home the next day, it was the people she knew, it was her maid, it was the intense and fruitful prayer in the face of despair. Angela told herself as if furiously biting herself: there must be an exit. As much for me as for Dona Maria Rita.

I couldn't stop time, thought Maria Rita Alvarenga Chagas Souza Melo. I've failed. I'm old. And she pretended to read the newspaper just to gain some composure.

I want shade, Angela moaned, I want shade and anonymity.

The old woman thought: her son was so kindhearted, so warm, so affectionate! He called her "dear little mother." Yes, maybe I'll spend the rest of my life on the farm, far from "public relations" who doesn't need me. And my life should be very long, judging by my parents and grandparents. I could easily, easily, make it to a hundred, she thought comfortably. And die suddenly so I won't have time to be afraid. She crossed herself discreetly and prayed to God for a good death.

Ulisses, if his face were viewed from a human perspective, would be monstrous and ugly. He was beautiful from a dog's perspective. He was vigorous like a white and free horse, only he was a soft brown, orangish, whiskey-colored. But his coat is beautiful like that of an energetic rearing horse. The muscles of his neck were vigorous and people could grasp those muscles in hands with knowing fingers. Ulisses was a man. Without the dog-eat-dog world. He was refined like a man. A woman should treat her man well.

The train entering the countryside: the crickets were calling, shrill and hoarse.

Eduardo, every once in a while, awkwardly like someone forced to fulfill a duty—gave her an ice-cold diamond as a present. She who was partial to sparkling gems. Anyhow, she sighed, things are the way they are. At times she felt, whenever she looked down from high in her apartment, the urge to commit suicide. Ah, not because of Eduardo but from a kind of fatal curiosity. She didn't tell anyone this, afraid of influencing a latent suicide. She wanted life, a level and full life, very laid-back, very much reading *Reader's Digest* in the open. She didn't want to die until she was ninety, in the midst of some act of life, without feeling anything. What are you doing? I'm waiting for the future.

When the train had finally started moving, Angela Pralini lit a cigarette in hallelujah: she'd been worried that, until the train departed, she wouldn't have the courage to go and would end up leaving the car. But right after, they were subjected to the deafening yet sudden jerking of the wheels. The train was chugging along. And old Maria Rita was sighing: she was that much closer to her beloved son. With him she could be a mother, she who was castrated by her daughter.

Once when Angela was suffering from menstrual cramps, Eduardo had tried, rather awkwardly, to be affectionate. And he'd said something horrifying to her: you have an ouchy, don't you? It was enough to make her flush with embarrassment.

The train sped along as fast as it could. The happy engineer: that's how I like it, and he blew the whistle at every curve in the rails. It was the long, hearty whistle of a moving train, making headway. The morning was cool and full of tall green grasses. That's it, yessir, come on, said the engineer to the engine. The engine responded with joy.

The old woman was nothing. And she was looking at the air as one looks at God. She was made of God. That is: all or nothing. The old woman, thought Angela, was vulnerable. Vulnerable to love, love for her son. The mother was Franciscan, the daughter was pollution.

God, Angela thought, if you exist, show yourself! Because it was time. It's this hour, this minute and this second.

And the result was that she had to hide the tears that sprang to her eyes. God had her. She was satisfied and stifled a muffled sob. How living hurt. Living was an open wound. Living is being like my dog. Ulisses has nothing to do with Joyce's Ulysses. I tried to read Joyce but stopped because he was boring, sorry, Eduardo. Still, a brilliant bore. Angela was loving the old woman who was nothing, the mother she lacked. A sweet, naive, long-suffering mother. Her mother who had died when she turned nine. Even sick but alive was good enough. Even paralyzed.

The air between Eduardo and her tasted like Saturday. And suddenly the two of them were rare, rarity in the air. They felt rare, not part of the thousand people wandering the streets. The two of them were sometimes conspiratorial, they had a secret life because no one would understand them. And also because the rare ones are persecuted by the people who don't tolerate the insulting offense of those who are different. They hid their love so as not to wound the eyes of others with envy. So as not to wound them with a spark too luminous for the eyes.

Bow, wow, wow, my dog had barked. My big dog.

The old woman thought: I'm an involuntary person. So much that, when she laughed—which was rare—you couldn't tell whether she was laughing or crying. Yes. She was involuntary.

Meanwhile there was Angela Pralini effervescing like the bubbles in Caxambu mineral water, she was one: all of a sudden. Just like that: suddenly. Suddenly what? Just suddenly. Zero. Nothing. She was thirty-seven and planning at any moment to start her life over. Like the little effervescent bubbles in Caxambu water. The seven letters in Pralini gave her strength. The seven letters in Angela made her anonymous.

With a long, howling whistle, they arrived at the little station where Angela Pralini would get off. She took her suitcase. In the space between a porter's cap and a young woman's nose, there was the old woman sleeping stiffly, her head erect beneath her felt hat, a fist closed on the newspaper.

Angela left the train.

Naturally this hadn't the slightest importance: there are people who are always led to regret, it's a trait of certain guilty natures. But what kept disturbing her was the vision of the old woman when she awoke, the image of her astonished face across from Angela's empty seat. After all who knew if she had fallen asleep out of trust in her.

Trust in the world.

Dry Sketch of Horses
("Seco estudo de cavalos")

STRIPPING

The horse is naked.

FALSE DOMESTICATION

What is a horse? It is freedom so indomitable that it becomes useless to imprison it to serve man: it lets itself be do-
mesticated but with a simple movement, a rebellious toss of
the head—shaking its mane like flowing locks—it shows that
its innermost nature is forever wild and limpid and free.

FORM

The form of the horse represents what is best in the human
being. I have a horse inside me that rarely manifests itself. But
when I see another horse then mine expresses itself. Its form
speaks.

SWEETNESS

What makes the horse that shining satin? It is the sweetness of one who has taken on life and its rainbow. That sweetness becomes concrete in the soft coat that suggests the supple muscles, agile and controlled.

THE EYES OF THE HORSE

I once saw a blind horse: nature had erred. It was painful to sense its restlessness, attuned to the slightest murmur provoked by the breeze in the grasses, its nerves ready to bristle in a shiver running the length of its alert body. What is it that a horse sees to the extent that not seeing its like renders it lost as if from itself? What happens is—when it does see—it sees outside itself whatever is inside itself. It is an animal expressed by its form. When it sees mountains, meadows, people, sky— it dominates men and nature itself.

SENSITIVITY

Every horse is wild and skittish when unsure hands touch it.

HE AND I

Attempting to put my most hidden and subtle sensation into sentences—and disobeying my strict need for truthfulness—I would say: if it had been up to me I would have wanted to be born a horse. But—who knows—perhaps the horse him-self doesn't sense the great symbol of free life that we sense in him. Should I then conclude that the horse exists above all to be sensed by me? Does the horse represent the beautiful and liberated animality of the human being? Does the human already contain the best of the horse? Then I renounce being a horse and in glory I'll go over to my humanity. The horse shows me what I am.

ADOLESCENCE OF THE COLT-GIRL

I have related perfectly to a horse before. I remember adolescent-me. Standing with the same pride as the horse and running my hand over its lustrous coat. Over its rustic aggressive mane. I felt as if something of mine were watching us from afar — Thus: "The Girl and the Horse."

THE FANFARE

On the farm the white horse — king of nature — launched high into the keenness of the air its prolonged neigh of splendor.

THE DANGEROUS HORSE

In the country town — which would one day become a small metropolis — horses still reigned as prominent inhabitants. Due to the increasingly urgent need for transport, teams of horses had invaded the village, and there stirred in the still-wild children the secret desire to gallop. A young bay had fatally kicked a boy trying to mount it. And the place where the daring child died was looked upon by the people with a disapproval that in fact they didn't know where to direct. With their market baskets on their arms, the women stopped and stared. A newspaper looked into the affair and people took a certain pride in reading an item entitled The Horse's Crime. It was the Crime of one of the town's sons. By then the village was already mingling its scent of stables with an awareness of the pent-up power of horses.

ON THE SUN-BAKED STREET

But suddenly—in the silence of the two o'clock sun and with almost no one on the street in those outskirts—a pair of horses emerged from around a corner. For a moment they froze with legs slightly raised. Their mouths flaring as if unbridled. There, like statues. The few pedestrians braving the heat of the sun stared, hard, separate, not understanding in words what they were seeing. They just understood. Once the blinding glare of the apparition faded—the horses bowed their necks, lowered their legs and continued on their way. The glimmering instant had passed. An instant frozen as by a camera that had captured something words will never say.

AT SUNSET

That day, as the sun was already setting, gold spread through the clouds and over the rocks. The inhabitants' faces were golden like armor and thus glowed their tousled hair. Dusty factories whistled continuously signaling the end of the workday, the wheel of a cart gained a golden nimbus. In that pale gold blowing in the breeze was the raising of an unsheathed sword. Because that was how the equestrian statue on the square stood in the sweetness of sundown.

IN THE COLD DAWN

You could see the warm moist breath—the radiant and tranquil breath that came from the trembling extremely alive and quivering nostrils of the stallions and mares on certain cold dawns.

IN THE MYSTERY OF NIGHT

But at night the horses released from their burdens and led to pasture would gallop exquisite and free in the dark. Colts, nags, sorrels, long mares, hard hooves—suddenly a cold, dark horse's head!—hooves pounding, foaming muzzles rising into the air in fury and murmurs. And at times a long exhalation would cool the trembling grasses. Then the bay would move ahead. He'd amble sideways, head bowed to his chest, at a steady cadence. The others watched without looking. Hearing the faint sound of horses, I'd imagine the dry hooves advancing until halting at the summit of the hill. And his head dominating the town, launching a prolonged neigh. Fear seized me in the shadows of my bedroom, the terror of a king, I wanted to answer, baring my gums in a neigh. In the envy of desire my face acquired the restless nobility of a horse's head. Tired, jubilant, listening to the somnambulant trotting. As soon as I left my bedroom my form would start expanding and refining itself, and, by the time I made it outside, I'd already be galloping on sensitive legs, hooves gliding down the last few steps of the house. On the deserted sidewalk I would look around: in one corner and the next. And I'd see things as a horse sees them. That was my desire. From my house I would try at least to listen for the hilly pasture where in the dark nameless horses galloped reverting to a state of hunting and war.

The beasts never abandoned their secret life that goes on in the night. And if in the midst of their wild roaming a white colt appeared—it was a ghost in the dark. All would halt. The extraordinary horse would *appear*, it was an apparition. It showed off rearing for an instant. The animals would wait motionless without watching one another. But one would stamp its hoof—and the brief blow shattered the vigil: riled up they'd spring into motion suddenly merry, crisscrossing without ever colliding and in their midst the white horse would be lost. Until a neigh of sudden rage alerted them—attentive for a second, they soon fanned out again trotting in a new formation, backs riderless, necks lowered until their muzzles grazed their chests. Manes bristling. Cadenced, ungoverned.

The deep of night—while men slept—found them motionless in the dark. Stable and weightless. There they were, invisible, breathing. Waiting with slow-witted intelligence. Below, in the sleeping town, a rooster was flapping and perching on a window sill. The chickens were watching. Beyond the railway, a rat ready to flee. Then the gray stamped its hoof. It had no mouth with which to speak but gave a little signal that resounded from space to space in the darkness. They were watching. Those animals that had one eye to see on either side—nothing needed to be seen head-on by them, and this was the great night. A swift contraction rippling over the flanks of a mare. In the silences of the night the mare gazed ahead as if surrounded by eternity. The most restless of the colts still bristled its mane in inward neighing. At last total silence reigned.

Until the fragile luminosity of dawn revealed them. They were separate, standing atop the hill. Exhausted, fresh. They had passed in the darkness through the mystery of the nature of beings.

452

Never again shall I find rest, for I stole the hunting horse of a King. I am now worse than myself! Never again shall I find rest: I stole the King's hunting horse on the enchanted Sabbath. If I fall asleep for an instant, the echo of neighing awakens me. And it is no use trying not to go. In the dark of night the panting makes me shudder. I pretend to be asleep but in the silence the stallion is breathing. Every day it will be the same thing: at dusk I begin to feel melancholy and pensive. I know that the first rumbling on the mountain of evil will make it night, I know that the third will have already enveloped me in its thunder. And by the fifth rumble I shall already covet the ghost horse. Until at dawn, at the final faintest rumblings, I shall find myself without knowing how by a cool brook, without ever knowing what I did, beside that enormous weary horse head.

But weary from what? What did we do, I and the horse, we, those that trot through the hell of the vampire's joy? He, the King's horse, calls to me. I have been resisting in a crisis of sweat and won't go. The last time I dismounted from his silver saddle, my human sadness was so great at having been what I should not have been, that I swore never again. The trotting nonetheless goes on inside me. I chat, clean the house, smile, but I know the trotting is inside me. I long for it like one dying.

No, I cannot stop going.

And I know that at night, when he calls to me, I shall go. I want once more for the horse to guide my thought. He was the one who taught me. If thought is what this hour between the barking is. I grow sad because I know with my eye—oh not on purpose! it's not my fault!—with my eye unintentionally already glinting with evil glee—I know I shall go.

When at night he calls me to the attraction of hell, I shall go. I descend like a cat down the rooftops. No one knows, no one sees. Only the dogs bark sensing the supernatural.

And I present myself in the dark to the horse that awaits me, royal horse, I present myself mute and flaring. Obedient to the Beast.

Fifty-three flutes chase after us. In front a clarinet lights our way, we, the shameless accomplices of the enigma. And nothing more is given me to know.

At dawn I shall see us exhausted by the brook, not knowing what crimes we committed before arriving at the innocent dawn.

On my mouth and on his hooves the mark of the great blood. What did we immolate?

At dawn I shall be standing beside the now-silent stallion, the remaining flutes still coursing through my hair. The first bells of a faraway church make us shudder and flee, we vanish before the cross.

The night is my life with the diabolical horse, I enchantress of the horror. The night is my life, it grows late, the sinfully happy night is the sad life that is my orgy—ah steal it, steal that stallion from me because with each theft until dawn I have already stolen for myself and my fantastical mate, and of the dawn I have made a premonition of terror of demoniacal unwholesome joy.

Relieve me, quick steal the stallion while there's still time, before dusk falls, while it is shawdowless day, if there really still is time, for in stealing the stallion I had to kill the King, and in murdering him I stole the death of the King. And the orgiastic joy of our murder consumes me with terrible pleasure. Quick steal the dangerous horse of the King, rob me before night falls and calls to me.

454

Where Were You at Night
("Onde estivestes de noite")

Stories have no conclusion. —Alberto Dines

The unknown is addictive. —Fauzi Arap

Sitting in an easy chair, mouth full of teeth, waiting for death.
—Raul Seixas

*What I shall present is so unheard of that I dread lest I have all
men as enemies, so much do preconceived notions and doctrines
take root in the world, once they are accepted.*
—William Harvey

THE NIGHT WAS AN EXCEPTIONAL POSSIBILITY. WELL
into a moonless night of a scorching summer a rooster crowed
at the wrong time and just once to announce the start of its
ascent of the mountain. The crowd below waited in silence.

He-she was already there atop the mountain, and she was
personalized in the he and he was personalized in the she. The
androgynous mixture created a being so terribly beautiful, so
horrifically stupefying that the participants couldn't take it all
in at once: as a person adjusts little by little to the dark and

gradually starts to discern things. Gradually they discerned the She-he and when the He-she appeared before them in a brightness that emanated from him-her, they paralyzed by the Beautiful would say: "Ah, Ah." It was an exclamation that was allowed in the silence of the night. They gazed upon the frightening beauty and its danger. But they had come precisely in order to suffer danger.

Vapors wafted from the swamps. A star of enormous density guided them. They were the contrary of the Good. They climbed the mountain mingling men, women, elves, gnomes and dwarves — like extinct gods. The golden bell tolled for the suicides. Besides the great star, not a single star. And there was no sea. What there was atop the mountain was darkness. A northwest wind blew. Was He-she a beacon? The worship of the damned was about to proceed.

The men wriggled on the ground like fat and spineless worms: climbing. Risking everything, since they were fated to die one day, perhaps in two months, perhaps seven years — this was what He-she was thinking inside them.

Look at the cat. Look at what the cat saw. Look at what the cat thought. Look at what it was. At last, at last, there was no symbol, the "thing" was! the orgiastic thing. Those climbing were on the verge of the truth. Nebuchadnezzar. They resembled 20 Nebuchadnezzars. And in the night they disbanded. They are awaiting us. It was an absence — a journey outside of time.

A dog howled with laughter in the dark. "I'm scared," said a child. "Scared of what?" asked the mother. "Of my dog." "But you don't have a dog." "Yes I do." But then the little child also laughed while crying, mingling tears of laughter and fright.

At last they arrived, the damned. And they gazed upon that

eternal Widow, the great Solitary Woman who fascinated everyone, and men and women couldn't resist and wanted to get closer so as to die loving her but she with a gesture kept them all at a distance. They wanted to love her with a strange love that vibrates in death. It didn't bother them to love her while dying. The cloak the She-he wore was an agonizing shade of violet. But the mercenary women of the feasting sex tried to imitate her in vain.

What time could it be? no one could live in time, time was indirect and by its very nature forever unattainable. Their joints were already swollen, their excesses rumbled in their earth-filled stomachs, their lips swelling yet cracked—they climbed the slope. The shadows were of a low and dark sound like the darkest note from a cello. They arrived. The Ill-fated, the He-she, before the worship of kings and vassals, gleamed like a gigantic illuminated eagle. The silence swarmed with panting breaths. The vision was of mouths parted in the sensuality that nearly paralyzed them, so crude was it. They felt saved from the Great Tedium.

The hill was a scrap heap. When the She-he stopped for an instant, men and women, surrendering to themselves for an instant, said to themselves fearfully: I don't know how to think. But the He-she was thinking inside them.

A mute herald proclaimed the news with a strident clarinet. What news? about bestiality? Though perhaps it was this: starting from the herald every one of them began to "feel himself," to feel his own self. And there was no repression: free!

Then they began to murmur but inwardly because the She-he was scathing when it came to not disturbing one another during their slow metamorphosis. "I am Jesus! I am a Jew!" the poor Jew cried in silence. The annals of astronomy have never recorded anything like this spectacular comet, recently discovered—its vaporous tail will drag millions of miles through space. Not to mention time.

A hunchbacked dwarf was hopping like a frog, from one crossroad to another—the place was full of crossroads. Suddenly the stars appeared and were gems and diamonds in the dark sky. And the dwarf-hunchback kept leaping, as high as he could to reach the diamonds that awakened his greedy desire. Crystals! Crystals! he cried in thoughts that bounded like his leaps.

Latency pulsated light, rhythmic, ceaseless. All were entirely latent. "There is no crime we have not committed in our thoughts": Goethe. A new and inauthentic Brazilian history was written abroad. Furthermore, domestic researchers complained about the lack of resources for their work.

The mountain had volcanic origins. And suddenly the sea: the crashing revolt of the Atlantic filled their ears. And the salt smell of the sea fertilized them and tripled them into little monsters.

Can the human body fly? Levitation. Saint Teresa of Avila: "It seemed as if a great force was lifting me into the air. This put a great fear in me." The dwarf levitated for a few seconds but enjoyed it and was not afraid.

"What's your name," the boy said mutely, "so I can call you for the rest of my life. I'll shout your name."

"I have no name down there. Here I have the name Xantipa."

"Ah, I want to shout Xantipa! Xantipa! Look, I'm shouting on the inside. And what's your name during the day?"

"I think it's ... it's ... it seems to be Maria Luísa."

And she shuddered as a horse bristles. Then fell bloodless to the ground. No one was killing anyone because they had already been killed. No one wanted to die and indeed no one died.

Meanwhile—delicately, delicately—the He-she was using a certain emblem. The color of the emblem. For I want to live in abundance and would betray my best friend in exchange for more life than one can have. That seeking, that ambition. I scorned the precepts of the wise men who counseled moderation and poverty of the soul—the simplification of the soul, in my experience, was saintly innocence. But I struggled against temptation.

Yes. Yes: to fall until hitting abjection. That is their ambition. The sound was the herald of the silence. Because none could let themselves be possessed by That-nameless-he-she.

They wanted to revel in the forbidden. They wanted to praise life and didn't want the pain that is required to live, to feel and to love. They wanted to feel dreadful immortality. Because the forbidden is always the best. They at the same time were not bothered by possibly falling into the enormous pit of death. And life was only precious to them while they were shouting and moaning. To feel the strength of hatred was what they most wanted. I call myself the people, they thought.

"What must I do to be a hero? Because only heroes can enter the temples."

And in the silence suddenly his howling cry, hard to say whether of love or mortal pain, the hero smelling of myrrh, frankincense and resin.

He-she covered his-her nudity with a cloak that was beautiful but like a shroud, a purple shroud, now cathedral-red. On moonless nights She-he became an owl. Thou shalt devour thy brother, she said in the thoughts of others, and at the savage hour there shall be a solar eclipse.

So they wouldn't betray themselves they ignored the fact that today was yesterday and there would be a tomorrow. A transparency wafted through the air the likes of which no man had ever breathed. But they sprinkled pepper on their own genital organs and writhed in ardor. And suddenly hatred. They weren't killing one another but felt such implacable hatred that it was like a dart launched at a body. And they rejoiced damned by what they felt. The hatred was a vomit that released them from a greater vomit, the vomit of the soul.

He-she with seven musical notes achieved the howl. Just as with the same seven notes one can create sacred music. They heard inside themselves the do-re-mi-fa-sol-la-ti, the "ti" soft and extremely high. They were independent and sovereign, despite being guided by the He-she. Death roaring in dark dungeons. Fire, scream, color, vice, cross. I remain vigilant in the world: by night I live and by day I sleep, elusive. I, with a dog's sense of smell, orgiastic.

As for them, they carried out rituals that the faithful execute without understanding their mysteries. The ceremonies. With a light gesture She-he touched a child striking it down and everyone said: amen. The mother let out a wolf howl: she, completely dead, she, too.

But it was in order to have super-sensations that people went up there. And it was a sensation so secret and so profound that jubilation sparkled in the air. They wanted the superior power that has reigned over the world through the centuries. Were they afraid? They were. Nothing could substitute the richness of the silent dread. Being afraid was the accursed glory of the darkness, silent like a Moon.

Gradually they adjusted to the dark and the Moon, previously hidden, all round and pale, had smoothed their ascent. It was pitch dark when one by one they had climbed "the mountain," as they called the somewhat elevated plain. They had leaned against the ground so as not to fall, treading on dry and rugged trees, treading on prickly cactuses. It was an irresistibly attractive fear, they would rather die than abandon it. The He-she was like their Lover. But if anyone was ambitious enough to dare touch her he was frozen in place.

He-she told them inside their brains—and everyone heard her inside themselves—what happened to a person when that person didn't heed the call of the night: what happened was that in the blinding light of day that person lived in open flesh and with eyes dazzled by the sin of the light—that person lived without anesthesia the terror of being alive. There is nothing to fear, when you have no fear. It was the eve of the apocalypse. Who was the king of the Earth? If you abuse the power you have conquered, the masters will punish you. Filled with terror of a fierce joy they prostrated themselves and amid shrieks of laughter ate poisonous weeds off the ground and the echoes of their laughter resounded from darkness to darkness. The air was heavy with the suffocating scent of roses, roses damned in their strength of nature gone mad, the same nature that invented snakes and rats and pearls and children—the mad nature that now was night in darkness, now bright day. This flesh that moves merely because it has a spirit.

From their mouths drooled saliva, thick, bitter and slick, and they urinated on themselves without feeling it. The women who had recently given birth violently squeezed their own breasts and from their nipples a thick black milk gushed. One woman spit hard in the face of a man and the harsh spittle slid down his cheek to his mouth—eagerly he licked his lips.

They were all unleashed. The joy was frenetic. They were the harem of the He-she. They had fallen at last into the impossible. Mysticism was the highest form of superstition.

The millionaire was shouting: I want power! power! I want

even objects to do my bidding! And I'll say: move, object! and it will move all by itself.

The old, disheveled woman said to the millionaire: want to see how you're not a millionaire? Well I'll tell you: you do not own the next second of your life, you could die without knowing it. Death will humiliate you. The millionaire: I want the truth, the absolute truth!

The journalist working on a magnificent story about raw life. I'm going to be internationally famous like the author of *The Exorcist* which I haven't read so it won't influence me. I'm looking directly at raw life, I'm living it.

I am a solitary person, said the masturbator to himself.

I'm waiting, and waiting, nothing ever happens to me, I've already given up on waiting. They were drinking the bitter liquor of the rough weeds.

"I am a prophet! I see the beyond!" a boy was shouting to himself.

Father Joaquim Jesus Jacinto—all J's because his mother liked the letter J.

It was December 31, 1973. Astronomical time would be harmed by atomic clocks, which are off by a mere second every three thousand three hundred years.

The other woman was prone to spitting, one glob after another, nonstop. But she liked it. The other woman was named J. B.

"My life is truly a novel!" cried the failed writer.

Ecstasy was reserved for the He-she. Who suddenly underwent a bodily exaltation, at length. She-he said: stop! Because she was falling under the demon's sway by feeling the ecstasy of Evil. All of them through her were coming: it was the celebration of the Great Law. The eunuchs were engaged in something it was forbidden to watch. The others, through She-he, were shudderingly receiving orgasms in waves—but only in waves because they weren't strong enough to, without destroying themselves, take it all. The women painted their mouths violet like fruit crushed by sharp teeth.

The She-he told them what happened when someone didn't become initiated into the prophesying of the night. State of shock. For example: the girl was a redhead and as if that weren't enough she was red on the inside and on top of that colorblind. Such that in her small apartment was a green cross on a red background: she mixed up the two colors. How had her terror begun? Listening to an album or the reigning silence or footsteps from upstairs—and there she was terrified. Afraid of the mirror that reflected her. Across from it was a wardrobe and she got the idea that the clothes were moving around inside it. Little by little she began shrinking the apartment. She was even afraid of getting out of bed. The feeling that they'd grab her foot from under the bed. She was emaciated. Her name was Psiu,* a red name. She was afraid of turning on the light in the dark and finding the cold gecko that lived with her. In agony she felt the gecko's clammy little white toes. She eagerly scanned the newspaper for the crime reports, news of what was going on. Frightful things were always happening to people, like her, who lived alone and were attacked at night. On her wall was a picture of a man who stared her right in the eyes, watching her. She imagined that figure following her through every corner of the house. She had a panicked fear of rats. She'd rather die than come into contact with them. Yet she heard their squeaking. She even felt them nibbling at

* "Hey you" or "Psst."

her feet. She'd always bolt awake, in a cold sweat. She was a
cornered animal. Normally she'd talk things over with herself.
She'd weigh the pros and cons and the one who lost was always
her. Her life was a constant subtraction of itself. All because
she didn't heed the siren's call.

The He-she only showed his-her androgynous face. And
from it radiated such a blind splendor of a madman that the
others reveled in their own madness. She was the prediction
and the dissolution and was born tattooed. All the air now
bore the scent of fatal jasmine and was so strong that some
vomited their own entrails. The Moon was full in the sky. Fifteen thousand adolescents awaited the kind of man or woman
they would be.

Then She-he said:

"I shall eat thy brother and there will be a total eclipse and
the end of the world."

Once in a while a prolonged neighing could be heard and
no horse was seen. All one knew was that with seven musical
notes one could make all the songs that exist and that existed
and that will exist. From the She-he emanated the strong scent
of crushed jasmine because it was the night of a full Moon.
Voodoo or witchcraft. Max Ernst as a child was mistaken for
the Baby Jesus during a procession. Later he provoked artistic
scandals. He had a limitless passion for men and an immense
and poetic freedom. But why am I speaking of this? I don't
know. "I don't know" is a fine answer.

What was Thomas Edison doing, so inventive and free,
among those who were commanded by He-she?

Griffonage, thought the perfect student, was the most difficult word in the language.

Hark! the herald angels sing!

The poor Jew was shouting mutely and no one heard him,

the whole world wasn't hearing him. He spoke thus: I am thirsty, sweat and tears! and to quench my thirst I drink my sweat and my own salt tears. I don't eat pork! I follow the Torah! but grant me relief, Jehovah, who looks too much like me!

Jubileu de Almeida was listening to his transistor radio, always. "The tastiest porridge is made from Cream of Wheat." And afterward they announced, from Strauss, a waltz that incredible as it might seem was called "The Free Thinker." It's true, it really exists, I've heard it. Jubileu was the owner of "The Golden Mandolin," a musical instrument shop on the verge of bankruptcy, and was mad about Strauss waltzes. A widower, he was, Jubileu that is. His rival was "The Bugle," his competitor on Rua Gomes Freire or Frei Caneca. Jubileu was also a piano tuner.

Everyone there was ready to fall in love. Sex. Pure sex. They reined themselves in. Romania was a dangerous country: gypsies.

The world had an oil shortage. And, without oil, there was a food shortage. Meat, especially. And without meat they were becoming terribly carnivorous.

"Here, Lord, I offer up my soul," Christopher Colombus had said upon dying, dressed in the Franciscan habit. He didn't eat meat. He became sanctified, Christopher Columbus, the discoverer of the waves, and who discovered St. Francis of Assisi. Hélas! he perished. Where are you now? where? for God's sake, answer!

Suddenly and ever so slightly—*fiat lux*.

There was a startled scattering as of sparrows.

All so fast that it rather seemed like they had dissolved.

At that same hour they were either lying in bed asleep, or already awake. What had existed was silence. They didn't know anything. The guardian angels—who had been resting since everyone was peacefully in bed—awoke refreshed, still yawning, but already protecting their wards.

Dawn: the egg came spinning very slowly from the horizon into space. It was morning: a blonde girl, married to a rich young man, gives birth to a black baby. Child of the demon of the night? No one knows. Troubles, shame.

Jubileu de Almeida awoke like day-old bread: stale. Since childhood he had been bland like that. He turned on the radio and heard: "Morena's Shoes where high prices are against the rules." He'd check it out, he needed shoes. Jubileu was an albino, a light-skinned black man whose eyelashes were an almost-white yellow. He cracked an egg into the frying pan. And thought: if one day I could hear "The Free Thinker," by Strauss, it would make up for my solitude. He'd only heard that waltz once, he couldn't remember when.

The powerful man wished to eat spoonfuls of Danish caviar at breakfast, popping the little balls between his sharp teeth. He was a member of the Rotary Club and the Freemasons and the Diners Club. He had enough class not to eat Russian caviar: it was a way of defeating mighty Russia.

The poor Jew awakes and drinks water thirstily right from the faucet. It was the only water there was at the back of the flophouse where he lived: once there was a cockroach swimming in the soupy beans. The prostitutes who lived there didn't even complain.

The perfect student, who didn't suspect he was a bore, thought: what was the most difficult word in existence? What was it? One that meant adornments, embellishments, finery? Ah, yes, griffonage. He memorized the word so as to write it on his next exam.

When the first rays of daylight began to shine everyone was

in bed yawning endlessly. As they awoke, one was a cobbler, one had been imprisoned for rape, one was a housewife, giving orders to the cook, who never arrived late, another was a banker, another was a secretary, etc. They awoke, then, a bit groggy, satisfied by a night of such deep sleep. Saturday had passed and today was Sunday. And many went to the mass celebrated by Father Jacinto who was the priest currently in fashion: but none went to confession, for they had nothing to confess.

The failed writer opened her red leather-bound diary and began to write this down: "July 7, 1974. Me, me, me, me, me, me, me! On this beautiful morning of Sunday sunshine, after having slept very badly, I, in spite of everything, appreciate the marvelous beauties of Mother Nature. I won't go to the beach because I'm too fat and that's unfortunate for someone who so appreciates the little green waves of the Sea! I find myself revolting! But I can't stick to a diet: I die of hunger. I like living dangerously. Thy viper's tongue shall be cut by the scissors of complacency."

In the morning: agnus dei. Golden calf? Vulture.

The poor Jew: free me from the pride of being a Jew!

The journalist called her friend first thing in the morning:

"Claudia, sorry to call at this hour on a Sunday! But I woke up with a fabulous inspiration: I'm going to write a book about Black Magic! No, I didn't read that one about the Exorcist, because I heard it's no good and I don't want everybody saying I copied it. Have you ever really thought about it? human beings have always tried to communicate with the supernatural, from ancient Egypt with the secret of the Pyramids, to Greece with its gods, to Shakespeare in *Hamlet*. Well, I'm going to do it too. And, by God, I'm going to do it best!"

The smell of coffee wafted through many Rio households. It was Sunday. And the boy still in bed, completely lethargic, still half-awake, said to himself: another boring Sunday. What exactly had he dreamed about? Who knows, he answered, if I dreamed, I dreamed about women.

At last, the air brightens. And the same old day begins. The brutal day. The light was wicked: the haunted daily day was settling in. A religion became a necessity: a religion unafraid of the morning. I want to be envied. I want rape, robbery, infanticide, and my challenge is forceful. I wanted gold and fame, I scorned even sex: I loved fast and I didn't know what love was. I want bad gold. Profanation. I'm going to my extreme. After the revelry—what revelry? at night?—after the revelry, desolation.

There was the observer who wrote this in his notebook: "Progress and all the phenomena surrounding it seem to participate intimately in this law of general, cosmic, and centrifugal acceleration that drags civilization toward 'maximum progress,' so that thereafter comes the fall. An uninterrupted fall or a quickly contained fall? That is the problem: we cannot know whether this society will destroy itself completely or if it will experience merely a brief interruption and then resume its onward march." And then: "The Sun's effects on the Earth would diminish and provoke the start of a new ice age that could last a minimum of ten thousand years." Ten thousand years was a lot and was frightening. That's what happens when someone chooses, from fear of the dark night, to live in the superficial light of day. Since the supernatural, divine or demonic, has been a temptation since Egypt, through the Middle Ages up to cheap mystery novels.

The butcher, who that day was working just from eight till eleven, opened the butcher shop: and halted drunk with pleasure at the smell of meat upon raw meat, raw and bloody. He was the only one who carried the night into day.

Father Jacinto was in fashion because no one lifted the chalice as limpidly as he and drank with holy unction and purity, saving everyone, the blood of Jesus, who was the Good. Delicately his pale hands in a gesture of offering.

The baker rose as usual at four o'clock and started kneading dough. At night did he knead the Devil?

An angel painted by Fra Angelico, fifteenth century, fluttered through the air: he was the annunciating clarinet of morning. The electric street lights had not yet been shut off and were glowing palely. Poles. Speed devours the poles when you're cruising by in a car.

The morning masturbator: my only loyal friend is my dog. He didn't trust anyone, especially women.

The woman who had been yawning all night and said: "I conjure thee, High Priestess!" started scratching herself and yawning. Oh hell, she said.

The powerful man—who grew orchids, cattleyas, laelias and oncidiums—rang the bell impatiently to summon the butler who would bring his already-late breakfast. The butler read his mind and knew when to bring the Danish greyhounds to be quickly caressed.

That woman who at night had screamed, "I'm waiting, waiting, waiting," in the morning, all disheveled said to the milk in the saucepan on the burner:

"I'm going to get you, you slob! Let's just see if you're going to drag your heels and boil over in my face, I spend my whole life waiting. Everyone knows that if I take my eyes off the milk for a single second, that good-for-nothing will take the chance to boil over. The way death comes when you don't expect it."

She waited, waited and the milk didn't boil. So, she turned off the gas.

In the sky the faintest of rainbows: it was the announcement. The morning like a white sheep. A white dove was the prophecy. Manger. Secret. The preordained morning. Ave Maria, gratia plena, dominus tecum. Benedicta tu in mulieribus et benedictum frutus ventri tui Jesus. Sancta Maria Mater Dei ora pro nobis pecatoribus. Nunca et ora nostrae morte Amen.

Father Jacinto used both hands to lift the crystal chalice that holds the scarlet blood of Christ. Wow, good wine. And a flower bloomed. A light, rosy flower, with the fragrance of God. He-she had long since vanished into thin air. The morning was clear like some freshly washed thing.

AMEN

The absentminded faithful made the sign of the Cross.

AMEN
GOD
THE END

Epilogue

All I have written is true and exists. A universal mind exists that guided me. Where were you at night? No one knows. Don't try to answer—for the love of God. I don't want to know the answer. Adieu. A-Dieu.

Report on the Thing
("O relatório da coisa")

THIS THING IS THE MOST DIFFICULT FOR A PERSON TO understand. Keep trying. Don't get discouraged. It will seem obvious. But it is extremely difficult to know about it. For it involves time.

We divide time when in reality it is not divisible. It is always immutable. But we need to divide it. And to that end a monstrous thing was created: the clock.

I am not going to speak of clocks. But of one particular clock. I'm showing my cards: I'll say up front what I have to say and without literature. This report is the antiliterature of the thing.

The clock of which I speak is electronic and has an alarm. The brand is Sveglia, which means "wake up." Wake up to what, my God? To time. To the hour. To the instant. This clock is not mine. But I took possession of its infernal tranquil soul.

It is not a wristwatch: therefore it is freestanding. It is less than an inch tall and stands on the surface of the table. I would like its actual name to be Sveglia. But the clock's owner wants its name to be Horácio. No matter. Because the main thing is that it is time.

Its mechanism is very simple. It does not have the complexity of a person but it is more people than people. Is it a superman? No, it comes straight from the planet Mars, so it seems. If that's where it is from then that's where it will one day return. It is silly to state that it does not need to be wound, since this is the case with other timepieces, as with mine that's a wristwatch, that's shock resistant, that can get wet as you like. Those are even more than people. But at least they are from Earth. The Sveglia is from God. Divine human brains were used to capture what this watch should be. I am writing about it but have yet to see it. It will be the Encounter. Sveglia: wake up, woman, wake up to see what must be seen. It is important to be awake in order to see. But it is also important to sleep in order to dream about the lack of time. Sveglia is the Object, it is the Thing, with a capital letter. I wonder, does the Sveglia see me? Yes, it does, as if I were another object. It recognizes that sometimes we too come from Mars.

Things have been happening to me, after I found out about the Sveglia, that seem like a dream. Wake me up, Sveglia, I want to see reality. But then, reality resembles a dream. I am melancholy because I am happy. It is not a paradox. After the act of love don't you feel a certain melancholy? That of plenitude. I feel like crying. Sveglia does not cry. Besides, it has no way to. Does its energy have any weight? Sleep, Sveglia, sleep a little, I can't stand your constant vigil. You never stop being. You never dream. It cannot be said that you "function": you are not the act of functioning, you just are.

You are just so thin. And nothing happens to you. But you are the one who makes things happen. Happen to me, Sveglia, happen to me. I am in need of a certain event of which I cannot speak. And bring back desire to me, which is the coil spring behind animal life. I do not want you for myself. I do not like being watched. And you are the only eye always open like an eye floating in space. You wish me no harm but neither do you wish me good. Could I be getting that way too, without the feeling of love? Am I a thing? I know that I have little capacity to love. My capacity to love has been trampled too much, my God. All I have left is a flicker of desire. I *need* this to be strengthened. Because it is not as you think, that only death matters. To live, something you don't know about because it is susceptible to rot—to live while rotting matters quite a bit. A harsh way to live: a way to live the essential.

If it breaks, do they think it died? No, it simply departed itself. But you have weaknesses, Sveglia. I learned from your owner that you need a leather case to protect you from humidity. I also learned, in secret, that you once stopped. Your owner didn't panic. She fiddled with it a little and you never stopped again. I understand you, I forgive you: you came from Europe and you need a little time to get acclimated, don't you? Does that mean that you die too, Sveglia? Are you the time that stops?

I once heard, over the phone, the Sveglia's alarm go off. It is like inside us: we wake up from the inside out. It seems its electronic-God communicates with our electronic-God brain: the sound is low, not the least bit shrill. Sveglia ambles like a white horse roaming free and saddleless.

I learned of a man who owned a Sveglia and to whom Sveglia happened. He was walking with his ten-year-old son, at night, and the son said: watch out, Father, there's voodoo out there. The father recoiled—but wouldn't you know he stepped right on a burning candle, snuffing it out? Nothing seemed to have happened, which is also very Sveglia. The man went to bed. When he awoke he saw that one of his feet was swollen and black. He called some doctor friends who saw no sign of injury: the foot was intact—only black and very swollen, the kind of swelling that stretches the skin completely taut. The doctors called more colleagues. And nine doctors decided it was gangrene. They had to amputate the foot. They made an appointment for the next day and an exact time. The man fell asleep.

And he had a terrible dream. A white horse was trying to attack him and he was fleeing like a madman. This all took place in the Campo de Santana. The white horse was beautiful and adorned with silver. But there was no escape. The horse got him right on the foot, trampling it. That's when the man awoke screaming. They thought it was nerves, explained that these things happened right before an operation, gave him a sedative, he went back to sleep. When he awoke, he immediately looked at his foot. Surprise: the foot was white and its normal size. The nine doctors came and couldn't explain it. They didn't know about the enigma of the Sveglia against which only a white horse can fight. There was no longer any reason to operate. Only, he can't put any weight on that foot: it was weakened. It was the sign of the horse harnessed with silver, of the snuffed candle, of the Sveglia. But Sveglia wanted to be victorious and something happened. That man's wife, in perfect health, at the dinner table, started feeling sharp pains in her intestines. She cut dinner short and went to lie down. The husband, worried sick, went to check on her. She was white, drained of blood. He took her pulse: there was none. The only sign of life was that her forehead was pearled with sweat. He called the doctor who said it might be a case of catalepsy. The husband didn't agree. He uncovered her stomach and made simple movements over her—the same he himself made when

474

Sveglia had stopped—movements he couldn't explain.

The wife opened her eyes. She was in perfect health. And she's alive, may God keep her.

This has to do with Sveglia. I don't know how. But that it does, no question. And what about the white horse of the Campo de Santana, which is a plaza full of little birds, pigeons and coatis? In full regalia, trimmed in silver, with a lofty and bristling mane. Running rhythmically in counterpoint to Sveglia's rhythm. Running without haste.

I am in perfect physical and mental health. But one night I was sleeping soundly and could be heard saying in a loud voice: I want to have a baby with Sveglia!

I believe in the Sveglia. It doesn't believe in me. It thinks I lie a lot. And I do. On Earth we lie a lot.

I went five years without catching the flu: that is Sveglia. And when I did it lasted three days. Afterward a dry cough lingered. But the doctor prescribed antibiotics and I got better. Antibiotics are Sveglia.

This is a report. Sveglia does not allow short stories or novels no matter what. It only permits transmission. It hardly allows me to call this a report. I call it a report on the mystery. And I do my best to write a report dry as extra-dry champagne. But sometimes—forgive me—it gets wet. A dry thing is sterling silver. Whereas gold is wet. May I speak of diamonds in relation to Sveglia?

No, it just is. And in fact Sveglia has no intimate name: it preserves its anonymity. Besides, God has no name: he preserves perfect anonymity: there is no language that utters his true name.

Sveglia is dumb: it acts covertly without premeditation. I am now going to say a very serious thing that will seem like heresy: God is dumb. Because he does not understand, he does not think, he just is. It is true that it's a kind of dumbness that executes itself. But He commits many errors. And knows it. Just look at us who are a grave error. Just look how we organize ourselves into society and intrinsically, from one to another. But there is one error He does not commit: He does not die.

Sveglia does not die either. I have still not seen the Sveglia, as I have mentioned. Perhaps seeing it is wet. I know everything about it. But its owner does not want me to see it. She is jealous. Jealousy eventually drips from being so wet. Anyhow, our Earth risks becoming wet with feelings. The rooster is Sveglia. The egg is pure Sveglia. But the egg only when whole, complete, white, its shell dry, completely oval. Inside it is life; wet life. But eating raw yolk is Sveglia.

Do you want to see who Sveglia is? A football match. Whereas Pelé is not. Why? Impossible to explain. Perhaps he didn't respect anonymity.

Fights are Sveglia. I just had one with the clock's owner. I said: since you don't want to let me see Sveglia, describe its gears to me. Then she lost her temper—and that is Sveglia—and said she had a lot of problems—having problems is not Sveglia. So I tried to calm her down and it was fine. I won't call her tomorrow. I'll let her rest.

It seems to me that I will write about the electronic thing without ever seeing it. It seems it will have to be that way. It is fated.

I am sleepy. Could that be permitted? I know that dreaming is not Sveglia. Numbers are permitted. Though six is not. Very few poems are permitted. Novels, then, forget it. I had a maid for seven days, named Severina, who had gone hungry as a child. I asked if she was sad. She said she was neither happy nor sad: she was just that way. She was Sveglia. But I was not and couldn't stand the absence of feeling.

Sweden is Sveglia.

But now I am going to sleep though I shouldn't dream.

Water, despite being wet *par excellence*, is. Writing is. But style is not. Having breasts is. The male organ is too much. Kindness is not. But not-kindness, giving oneself, is. Kindness is not the opposite of meanness.

Will my writing be wet? I think so. My last name is. Whereas my first name is too sweet, it is meant for love. Not having any secrets—and yet maintaining the enigma—is Sveglia. In terms of punctuation ellipses are not. If someone understands this undisclosed and precise report of mine, that someone is. It seems that I am not I, because I am so much I. The Sun is, not the Moon. My face is. Probably yours is too. Whiskey is. And, as incredible as it might seem, Coca-Cola is, while Pepsi never was. Am I giving free advertising? That's wrong, you hear, Coca-Cola?

Being faithful is. The act of love contains in itself a desperation that is.

Now I am going to tell a story. But first I would like to say that the person who told me this story was someone who, despite being incredibly kind, is Sveglia.

Now I am nearly dying of exhaustion. Sveglia—if we aren't careful—kills.

The story goes like this:

It takes place in a locale called Coelho Neto, in the State of Guanabara. The woman in the story was very unhappy because her leg was wounded and the wound wouldn't heal. She worked very hard and her husband was a postman. Being a postman is Sveglia. They had many children. Almost nothing

to eat. But that postman had been instilled with the responsibility of making his wife happy. Being happy is Sveglia. And
the postman resolved to resolve the situation. He pointed out
a neighbor who was barren and suffered greatly from this. She
just couldn't get pregnant. He pointed out to his wife how
happy she was because she had children. And she became
happy, even with so little food. The postman also pointed out
how another neighbor had children but her husband drank a
lot and beat her and the children. Whereas he didn't drink and
had never hit his wife or the children. Which made her happy.

Every night they felt sorry for their barren neighbor and for
the one whose husband beat her. Every night they were very
happy. And being happy is Sveglia. Every night.

I was hoping to reach page 9 on the typewriter. The number nine is nearly unattainable. The number 13 is God. The
typewriter is. The danger of its no longer being Sveglia comes
when it gets a little mixed up with the feelings of the person
who's writing.

I got sick of Consul cigarettes which are menthol and sweet.
Whereas Carlton cigarettes are dry, they're rough, they're
harsh, and do not cooperate with the smoker. Since everything
is or isn't, it doesn't bother me to give free advertising for Carlton. But, as for Coca-Cola, I don't excuse it.

I want to send this report to *Senhor* magazine and I want
them to pay me very well.

Since you are, why don't you judge whether my cook, who
cooks well and sings all day, is.

I think I'll conclude this report that is essential for explaining the energetic phenomena of matter. But I don't know what
to do. Ah, I'll go get dressed.

See you never, Sveglia. The deep blue sky is. The waves white
with sea foam are, more than the sea. (I have already bid fare-

well to Sveglia, but will keep speaking about it strictly because I can't help it, bear with me). The smell of the sea combines male and female and in the air a son is born that is.

The clock's owner told me today that it's the one that owns her. She told me that it has some tiny black holes from which a low sound comes out like an absence of words, the sound of satin. It has an internal gear that is golden. The external gear is silver, nearly colorless—like an aircraft in space, flying metal. Waiting, is it or isn't it? I don't know how to answer because I suffer from urgency and am rendered incapable of judging this item without getting emotionally involved. I don't like waiting.

A musical quartet is immensely more so than a symphony. The flute is. The harpsichord has an element of terror in it: the sounds come out rustling and brittle. Something from an otherworldly soul.

Sveglia, when will you finally leave me in peace? You aren't going to stalk me for the rest of my life transforming it into the brightness of everlasting insomnia, are you? Now I hate you. Now I would like to be able to write a story: a short story or a novel or a transmission. What will be my future step in literature? I suspect I won't write anymore. But it's true that at other times I have suspected this yet still wrote. What, however, must I write, my God? Was I contaminated by the mathematics of Sveglia and will I only be able to write reports?

And now I am going to end this report on the mystery. It so happens that I am very tired. I'll take a shower before going out and put on a perfume that is my secret. I'll say just one thing about it: it is rustic and a bit harsh, with hidden sweetness. It is.

Farewell, Sveglia. Farewell forever never. You already killed a part of me. I died and am rotting. Dying is.

And now—now farewell.

Manifesto of the City
("O manifesto da cidade")

WHY NOT TRY IN THIS MOMENT, WHICH ISN'T A GRAVE
one, to look out the window? This is the bridge. This is the river.
Here is the Penitentiary. Here is the clock. And Recife. Here is
the canal. Where is the stone that I'm sensing? the stone that
crushed the city. In the palpable form of things. For this is a realized city. Its last earthquake is lost in the annals. I reach out
my hand and without sadness trace from afar the curves of the
stone. Something still escapes the compass rose. Something has
hardened in the steel arrow that points toward—Another City.

This moment isn't grave. I take advantage of it and look out
the window. Here is a house. I feel my way along your stairs,
those I climbed in Recife. Then the short column. I am seeing
everything extraordinarily well. Nothing eludes me. The city
laid out. With such ingenuity. Masons, carpenters, engineers,
sculptors of saints, artisans—they bore death in mind. I am
seeing ever more clearly: this is the house, mine, the bridge, the
river, the Penitentiary, the square blocks of buildings, the steps
empty of me, the stone.

But here comes a Horse. Here is a horse with four legs and
hard hooves of stone, a powerful neck, and the head of Horse.
Here is a horse.

If this was a word echoing off the hard ground, what do you mean? How hollow this heart is in the center of the city. I am searching, searching. House, pavement, steps, monument, lamppost, your industry.

From the highest rampart—I am looking. I am searching. From the highest rampart I receive no signal. From here I cannot see, for your clarity is impenetrable. From here I cannot see but feel that something is written in charcoal on a wall. On a wall of this city.

THE WHITE ROSE

Petal up high: what an extreme surface. Cathedral of glass, surface of the surface, unreachable by voice. Through your stem two voices join a third and a fifth and a ninth—wise children open mouths in the morning and chant spirit, spirit, surface, spirit, untouchable surface of a rose.

I reach out my left hand which is the weaker, dark hand that I quickly withdraw smiling demurely. I cannot touch you. My crude thinking wants to sing your new understanding of ice and glory.

I try to recall the memory, to understand you as one sees the dawn, a chair, another flower. Have no fear, I do not wish to possess you. I rise toward your surface that now is perfume.

I rise until I reach my own appearance. I pale in that frightened and fragile region, I nearly reach your divine surface …

In the ridiculous fall I've broken the wings of an angel. I do not hang my head snarling: I want at least to suffer your victory with the angelic suffering of your harmony, of your joy. But my coarse heart aches as with love for a man.

And from such large hands emerges the embarrassed word.

The Conjurings of Dona Frozina
("As maniganças de Dona Frozina")

"EVEN ON THIS POCKET CHANGE ..."

That's what the widow Dona Frozina says about her monthly pension. But it's enough for her to afford Leite de Rosas and take real baths with the milky liquid. People say her skin is spectacular. She's been using the same product since she was a girl and she smells like a mother.

She is very Catholic and practically lives in churches. Smelling like Leite de Rosas the whole time. Like a little girl. She was widowed at twenty-nine. And from then on—not a man in sight. A widow in the old-fashioned way. Severe. Nothing low-cut and always in long sleeves.

"Dona Frozina, how did you get by without a man?" I want to ask her.

The answer would be:

"Conjurings, my girl, conjurings."

They say of her: plenty of young people don't have her spirit. She's in her seventies, the finest of ladies, Dona Frozina. She's a good mother-in-law and a fantastic grandmother. She was a good breeder. And kept on bearing fruit. I'd like to have a serious conversation with Dona Frozina.

"Dona Frozina, do you have anything to do with Dona Flor and her three husbands?"

"Good gracious, my dear, what a terrible sin! I'm a virgin widow, my child."

Her husband was named Epaminondas, nicknamed Buddy.

Look, Dona Frozina, there are worse names than yours. There's a woman named Flor de Lis—and since people thought it was an awful name, they gave her an even worse nickname: Minhora. It's almost *minhoca*, worm. And what about parents who name their kids Brazil, Argentina, Colombia, Belgium and France? You did escape being a country, ma'am. You and your conjurings. "Not much money in it," she says, "but it's amusing."

Amusing how, ma'am? So you haven't experienced pain? Have you been finding a way around pain all your life? Yes, ma'am, thanks to my conjurings I kept escaping.

Dona Frozina doesn't drink Coca-Cola. She thinks it's too modern.

"But everyone drinks it!"

"Not me, Heaven forbid! it even tastes like tapeworm medicine, God bless me and keep me!"

But if she thinks it tastes like medicine that means she's tried it.

Dona Frozina invokes the name of God more than she should. One shouldn't take God's name in vain. But with her this rule doesn't hold.

And she clings to the saints. The saints are already sick of her, she's pestered them so much. Not to mention "Our Lady"; the mother of Jesus gets no peace. And, since she's from the north, she's always saying: "Holy Mary!" whenever something astonishes her. And there's a lot to astonish an innocent widow.

Dona Frozina would pray every night. She'd say a prayer to every saint. Then disaster struck: she fell asleep halfway through.

"Dona Frozina, how awful, dozing off halfway through your prayers and leaving the saints on their own!"

She answered with a dismissive wave:

"Ah, my child, it's every man for himself."

She had the oddest dream: she dreamed she saw the Christ on Corcovado—and where were his outstretched arms? They were tightly crossed, and Christ looked fed up as if to say: deal with it yourselves, I've had it. It was a sin, that dream.

Dona Frozina, enough of conjurings. Keep your Leite de Rosas and "*io me ne vado*." (Is that how you say it in Italian when you want to leave?)

Dona Frozina, finest of ladies, I'm the one who's had it with you. Farewell, then. I dozed off halfway through the prayer.

P. S. Look up conjurings in the dictionary. But I'll do you the favor: conjuring—sleight of hand; mysterious trick, art of hocus-pocus. (From the *Shorter Brazilian Dictionary of the Portuguese Language*).

One detail before I'm done:

Dona Frozina, when she was a child, up in Sergipe, used to eat squatting behind the kitchen door. Nobody knows why.

That's Where I'm Going
("É para lá que eu vou")

BEYOND THE EAR THERE IS A SOUND, AT THE FAR END of sight a view, at the tips of the fingers an object—that's where I'm going.

At the tip of the pencil the line.

Where a thought expires is an idea, at the final breath of joy another joy, at the point of the sword magic—that's where I'm going.

At the tips of the toes the leap.

It's like the story of someone who went and didn't return—that's where I'm going.

Or am I? Yes, I'm going. And I'll return to see how things are. Whether they're still magic. Reality? I await you all. That's where I'm going.

At the tip of the word is the word. I want to use the word "soirée" and don't know where and when. At the edge of the soirée is the family. At the edge of the family am I. At the edge of I is me. To me is where I'm going. And from me I go out to see. See what? to see what exists. After I am dead to reality is where I'm going. For now it is a dream. A fateful dream. But later—later all is real. And the free soul seeks a place to get settled. Me is an I that I proclaim. I don't know what I'm talking about. I'm talking about the nothing. I am nothing. Once dead I shall expand and disperse, and someone will say my name with love.

To my poor name is where I'm going.

And from there I'll return to call the names of my beloved and my sons. They will answer me. At last I shall have an answer. What answer? that of love. Love: I love you all so much. I love love. Love is red. Jealousy is green. My eyes are green. But they're so dark a green that in photographs they look black. My secret is having green eyes and nobody knows it.

At the far end of me is I. I, imploring, I the one who needs, who begs, who cries, who laments. Yet who sings. Who speaks words. Words on the wind? who cares, the winds bring them back and I possess them.

I at the edge of the wind. The wuthering heights call to me. I go, witch that I am. And I am transmuted.

Oh, dog, where is your soul? is it at the edge of your body? I am at the edge of my body. And I waste away slowly.

What am I saying? I am saying love. And at the edge of love are we.

The Dead Man in the Sea at Urca

("O morto no mar da Urca")

I WAS AT THE APARTMENT OF DONA LOURDES, THE seamstress, trying on my dress painted by Olly—and Dona Lourdes said: a man died in the sea, look at all the lifeguards. I looked and all I saw was the sea that must have been very salty, blue sea, white houses. What about the dead man?

The dead man in brine. I don't want to die! I screamed mutely inside my dress. The dress is yellow and blue. What about me? dying of heat, not dead from the blue sea.

I'm going to tell a secret: my dress is lovely and I don't want to die. On Friday the dress will be at my house, and on Saturday I'll wear it. No death, just blue sea. Are there yellow clouds? There are golden ones. I don't have a story. Does the dead man? He does: he went to swim in the sea at Urca, the fool, and died, who gave the order? I swim in the sea with caution, I'm not an idiot, and I only go to Urca to try on dresses. And three blouses. S. came along. She's meticulous when it comes to fittings. What about the dead man? meticulously dead?

I'm going to tell a story: once upon a time there was a still-young man who enjoyed swimming in the sea. And then, one Wednesday morning he went to Urca. In Urca, on the rocks

487

of Urca, I don't go because it's full of rats. But the young man didn't care about the rats. Nor did the rats care about him. The white row houses in Urca. He cared about those. Then there was a woman trying on a dress and who got there too late: the young man was already dead. Salty. Were there piranhas in the sea? I pretended not to understand. I really don't understand death. A young man dead?

Dead from being the fool he was. You should only go to Urca to try on cheerful dresses. The woman, that's me, wants only cheerfulness. But I bow before death. Which shall come, shall come, shall come. When? that's the thing, it can come at any moment. But I, who was trying on the dress in the morning heat, asked for a proof of God. And I smelled the most intense thing, an overwhelmingly intense fragrance of roses. So I had fitting proof, the fitting and the proof; of the dress and of God.

One should only die of natural causes, never from disaster, never from drowning in the sea. I beg protection for my loved ones, who are many. And this protection, I am sure, shall come.

But what about the young man? and his story? He might have been a student. I'll never know. I just stood looking at the sea and the houses. Dona Lourdes unflappable, asking whether to take it in at the waist. I said yes, that waistlines are supposed to look tight. But I was stunned. Stunned in my lovely dress.

Silence
("Silêncio")

THE SILENCE OF THE NIGHT IN THE MOUNTAINS IS SO
vast. It is so desolate. You try in vain to work not to hear it, to
think quickly to cover it up. Or to invent some plans, a fragile
stitch that barely links us to the suddenly improbable day of tomorrow. How to surmount this peace that spies us. A silence so
great that despair is ashamed. Mountains so high that despair is
ashamed. The ears prick, the head tilts, the whole body listens:
not a murmur. Not a rooster. How to come within reach of this
deep meditation on the silence. On that silence without memory of words. If thou art death, how to reach thee.

It is a silence that does not sleep: it is insomniac: motionless
but insomniac; and without ghosts. It is terrible—not a single
ghost. It's no use wanting to people it with the possibility of
a door that creaks while opening, of a curtain that opens and
says something. It is empty and without promise. If only there
were the wind. Wind is fury, fury is life. Or snow. Which is silent but leaves tracks—everything turns white, children laugh,
footsteps crunch and leave a mark. There is a continuity that
is life. But this silence leaves no trace. You cannot speak of silence as you do of snow. You cannot say to anyone as you say

about snow: did you feel the silence last night? Those who did don't say.

Night descends with its little joys for those who light the lamps with the weariness that so justifies the day. The children of Bern drop off to sleep, the last doors are shut. The streets shine in the cobblestones and shine empty now. And finally the most distant lights go out.

But this first silence is still not the silence. Wait, for the leaves in the trees will settle down better, some belated step on the stairs may be heard with hope.

But there's a moment when from the rested body the spirit rises alert, and from the earth the moon up high. Then it, the silence, appears.

The heart beats upon recognizing it.

You could quickly think about the day that has passed. Or about friends who have passed and are forever lost. But there's no use avoiding it: there is the silence. Even the worst suffering, that of lost friendship, is just an escape. For if at first the silence seems to await an answer—how much do we burn to be called to answer—early on you discover that it demands nothing of you, perhaps only your silence. How many hours are wasted in the dark supposing that the silence is judging you—as we wait in vain to be judged by God. Justifications arise, tragic, forced justifications, excuses humble to the point of indignity. How pleasant it is for the human being to reveal at last his indignity and be forgiven on the argument that he is a human being brought low by birth.

Until you discover—it doesn't even want your indignity. It is the silence.

You can also try to fool it. You can drop, as if by accident, a book from your nightstand. But, the horror—the book falls into the silence and gets lost in its mute and frozen vortex. And if a deranged bird began to sing? A useless hope. The song would merely graze the silence like a faint flute.

So, if you are brave, you won't fight it. You enter it, go along with it, we the only ghosts on a night in Bern. You must enter. You mustn't wait for the remaining darkness while faced with it, only it alone. It will be as if we were on a ship so uncommonly enormous that we didn't realize we were on a ship. And it sailed so far and wide that we didn't realize we were moving. A man cannot do more than that. Living on the shores of death and of the stars is a tenser vibration than the veins can take. There is not even the son of a star and a woman to act as a pious intermediary. The heart must appear before the nothing alone and alone beat high in the darkness. The only thing sounding in your ears is your own heart. When it appears completely naked, it is not even communication, it is submission. For we were made for nothing but the small silence.

If you are not brave, you mustn't enter. Wait for the remaining darkness faced with the silence, only your feet wet from the foam of something that sprays from inside us. Wait. One unsolvable for the other. Side by side, two things that do not see each other in the dark. Wait. Not for the end of the silence but for the blessed help of a third element, the light of dawn.

Afterward you will never again forget. There's no use even fleeing to another city. For when you least expect to you may recognize it—suddenly. While crossing the street amid cars honking. Between one phantasmagoric burst of laughter and another. After a word uttered. Sometimes in the very heart of the word. The ears are haunted, the vision blurs—here it is. And this time it's a ghost.

A Full Afternoon
("Uma tarde plena")

THE MARMOSET IS AS SMALL AS A RAT, AND THE SAME color.

The woman, after sitting on the bus and casting a peaceful, proprietary glance over the seats, choked back a scream: beside her, in the fat man's hand, was something that looked like a fidgety rat and that in fact was the liveliest marmoset. The first seconds of woman *versus* marmoset were spent trying to feel that it was not a rat in disguise.

Once this was accomplished, some delightful and intense moments began: observing the animal. The whole bus, as it happened, was doing nothing else.

But the woman had the privilege of sitting right beside the main character. From where she could, for example, study the itty-bitty thing that is a marmoset's tongue: a stroke of a red pencil.

And there were its teeth too: you could almost count close to thousands of teeth inside that brushstroke of a mouth, and each tiny shard smaller than the next, and whiter. The marmoset didn't close its mouth a single moment.

Its eyes were round, hyperthyroid, complementing a slight

underbite—and this combination, though it lent a strangely shameless expression, formed the somewhat cheeky face of a street kid, the ones with a permanent cold and who sniffle while sucking on candy.

When the marmoset leaped onto the lady's lap, she held back a *frisson*, and the bashful pleasure of someone who'd been singled out.

But the other passengers looked at her in a friendly way, approving of the event, and, blushing a little, she accepted being the shy favorite. She didn't pet it because she didn't know if that was the right gesture to make.

And the animal didn't suffer from the lack of affection. In fact its owner, the fat man, bore it a solid and stern love, like a father's for his son, a master's for his wife. He was a man who, without smiling, had a so-called heart of gold. The expression on his face was tragic even, as if he had a mission. A mission to love? The marmoset was his dog in life.

The bus, whipped by the breeze, as if streaming with banners, drove on. The marmoset ate a cookie. The marmoset rapidly scratched at its round ear with its dainty hind leg. The marmoset squealed. It clung to the window, and peered out as fast as it could—startling faces in passing buses that looked astonished and had no time to verify whether they'd really seen what they'd seen.

Meanwhile, near the lady, another lady told another lady that she had a cat. Whoever had something to love, mentioned it.

It was in that happy familial atmosphere that a truck tried to cut off the bus, there was nearly a fatal collision, the screams. Everyone rushed off. The lady, running late, for an appointment, took a taxi.

It was only in the taxi that she recalled the marmoset.

And she regretted with an awkward smile that—the days so full of news in the papers and so little concerning her—that events should be so poorly distributed that a marmoset and a near-disaster could happen at the same time.

"I'll bet," she thought, "that nothing else will happen to me for a long time, I'll bet I'm in for a dry spell." Which was generally how things went for her.

But that same day other things did happen. All of which even fell under the category of goods to declare. They just weren't communicable. That woman was, moreover, a bit silent with herself and didn't understand herself very well.

But that's how it goes. And no one's ever heard of a marmoset that failed to be born, live and die—just because it didn't understand itself or wasn't understood.

In any case it had been an afternoon streaming with banners.

NOTE TO ERICO VERISSIMO

I don't agree when you say: "Sorry, but I am not profound."

You are *profoundly* human—and what more can you want from a person? You have a greatness of spirit. A kiss to you, Érico.

Such Gentleness
("Tanta mansidão")

SO THE DARK HOUR, PERHAPS THE DARKEST, IN BROAD daylight, preceded that thing that I don't even want to attempt to define. In broad daylight it was night, and that thing I still don't want to define is a peaceful light inside me, and they call it joy, gentle joy. I am a bit disoriented as if a heart had been torn from me, and in its place were now the sudden absence, an almost palpable absence of what before was an organ bathed in the darkness of pain. I am not feeling a thing. But it's the opposite of a torpor. It's a lighter and more silent way of existing.

But I am also uneasy. I was prepared to console my anguish and my pain. But how do I deal with this simple and peaceful joy. I'm just not used to not needing my own comfort. The word comfort occurred without my sensing it, and I didn't notice, and when I went to seek it, it had already transformed into flesh and spirit, it now no longer existed as thought.

I'll go to the window then, it's raining hard. Out of habit I'm searching the rain for something that at another time would have served as comfort for me. But I have no pain to be comforted.

Ah, I know. I'm now searching the rain for a joy so great that it becomes acute, and which puts me in contact with an acuteness akin to the acuteness of pain. But the search is no use. I am at the window and this is all that happens: I see the rain with benevolent eyes, and the rain sees me in harmony with me. We are both busy flowing. How long will this state of mine last? I realize that, with this question, I am taking my pulse to feel where that painful throbbing from before will be. And I see that there is no throbbing of pain.

Only this: it is raining and I am watching the rain. What simplicity. I never thought that the world and I would reach this point of wheat. The rain falls not because it needs me, and I watch the rain not because I need it. But we are as united as rainwater is to rain. And I am not giving thanks for anything. If I, just after being born, hadn't involuntarily and forcibly taken the path I did—and I would always have been what I truly am now: a peasant in a field where it is raining. Not even thanking God or nature. The rain doesn't give thanks for anything either. I am not a thing that gives thanks for being transformed into something else. I am a woman, I am a person, I am an awareness, I am a body looking out the window. As the rain isn't grateful for not being a rock. It is rain. Perhaps that is what we could call being alive. No more than this, but this: alive. And just alive with a gentle joy.

Soul Storm
("Tempestade de almas")

AH, FOR ALL I KNOW, I WASN'T BORN, AH, FOR ALL I know, I wasn't born. Madness is neighbor to the cruelest prudence. I swallow the madness because it calmly makes me hallucinate. The ring you gave me was made of glass and broke and love didn't end, but in its place, hatred of those who love. The chair for me is an object. Useless while I'm looking at it. Tell me please what time it is so I can know that I'm living at this time. Creativity is unleashed by a germ and I don't have that germ today but I have the incipient madness that in itself is a valid creation. I have nothing more to do with the validity of things. I am freed or lost. I'm going to tell you all a secret: life is fatal. We keep this secret in muteness each faced with ourselves because it's convenient, otherwise we would make every instant fatal. The chair object has always interested me. I look at this one which is old, bought at an antique shop, Empire style; you couldn't imagine a greater simplicity of line, contrasting with the red felt seat. I love objects all the more when they don't love me. But if I don't understand what I write the fault is not my own. I must speak because speaking saves. But I don't have a single word to say. The words already spoken gag my mouth. What exactly does one person say to another? Besides "how's it going?" If they allowed the madness of candor, what would people say to one another? And the worst is what a person would say to himself, but that would be salvation, though candor is determined on a conscious level and the terror of candor comes from the part that exists in the utterly vast unconsciousness that joins me to the world and to the creative unconsciousness of the world. Today is a day with many stars in the sky, at least that's what is promised by this sad afternoon that a human word would save.

I open my eyes wide, and it's no use: I merely see. But the secret, this I neither see nor sense. The record player is broken and not to live with music is to betray the human condition that is surrounded by music. Besides, music is an abstraction of thought, I'm speaking of Bach, Vivaldi, Handel. I can only write if I am free, and free from censure, otherwise I succumb. I look at the Empire chair and this time it's as if it too had looked and seen me. The future is mine while I live. In the future they'll have more time to live, and, to haphazardly write. In the future, they say: as far as I know, I wasn't born. Marly de Oliveira, I don't write you letters because I only know how to be intimate. Besides I only know how to be intimate whatever the circumstance: that's why I tend to be quiet. Will everything that's never been done, be done one day? The future of technology threatens to destroy all that is human in mankind, but technology doesn't reach madness; and so that's where the human part of mankind has sought refuge. I see the flowers in the vase: they are wildflowers, born without being planted, they are beautiful and yellow. But my cook said: what ugly flowers. Just because it's hard to understand and love something spontaneous and Franciscan. Understanding something hard is no advantage, but loving something easy to love is a great step up the human ladder. I am forced to tell so many lies. But I'd like not to have to lie to myself. Otherwise what do I have left? Truth is the final residue of all things, and in my unconscious is the truth that is the same as the world's. The Moon is, as Paul Éluard would say, *éclatante de silence.** Today I don't know whether we'll be able to see the Moon because it's already getting late and I don't see it in the sky. Once, I looked up at the night sky, circumscribing it with my head leaning back, and I got dizzy from all the stars you see in the countryside, since the sky in the countryside is clear. There is no logic, if you think about it a little, to the perfectly balanced illogic of nature. Of human nature too. What would become of the world, of the cosmos, if mankind didn't exist? If I could always write the way I'm writing right now I'd be in the middle of that *tempestade de cerebro* that means brainstorm. Who invented the chair? Someone with love for himself. So he invented a greater comfort for his body. Then centuries passed and never again did anyone really pay attention to a chair, since using it is merely automatic. You need courage for a brainstorm: you never know what might come frighten us. The sacred monster has died: in its place was born a little girl who was alone. I am well aware that I'll have to stop, not for lack of words, but because these things, and above all those I only thought and didn't write, don't normally get published in newspapers.

* French: "exploding with silence."

Natural Life
("Vida ao natural")

SO IN RIO THERE WAS A PLACE WITH A HEARTH. AND when she realized that, besides the cold, it was raining in the trees, she couldn't believe that so much had been given her. The harmony of the world with whatever it was she didn't even realize she needed as in a hunger. It was raining, raining. The crackling fire winks at her and at the man. He, the man, takes care of things she doesn't even thank him for; he stokes the fire in the hearth, which for him is no more than a duty he was born with. And she—constantly restless, doer of things and seeker of novelties—well she doesn't even remember to stoke the fire: that's not her role, since that's what your man is for. Since she's no damsel, let the man carry out his mission. The most she does is sometimes goad him: "that log," she tells him, "that one hasn't caught yet." And he, an instant before she finishes the sentence that would clarify things, he's already noticed the log on his own, being her man, and is already stoking the log. Not at her command, she who's the wife of a man and who'd lose her status if she gave him orders. His other hand, the free one, is within her reach. She knows, and doesn't take it. She wants his hand, she knows she does, and doesn't take it. She has exactly what she needs: she could do it if she wanted.

Ah, and to say this will end, that on its own it cannot last. No, she doesn't mean the fire, she means what she feels. What she feels never lasts, what she feels always ends, and might never return. So she pounces on the moment, devours its fire, and the sweet fire burns, burns, blazes. Then, she who knows that all will end, takes the man's free hand, and as she clasps it in hers, she sweetly burns, burns, blazes.

THE VIA CRUCIS
OF THE BODY
("A via crucis do corpo")

My soul breaketh for your desire.

(Psalms 119:12)

I, who understand the body. And its cruel demands. I have always known the body. Its dizzying vortex. The grave body.

(A still-unnamed character of mine)

For these things I weep. Mine eye runneth down with water.

(Lamentations of Jeremiah)

And let all flesh bless his holy name for ever and ever.

(Psalm of David)

Who has ever seen a love life and not seen it drowned in tears of disaster or regret?

(I don't know who said this.)

Explanation
("Explicação")

THE POET ÁLVARO PACHECO, MY PUBLISHER AT AR-
tenova, commissioned three stories from me about things that,
he said, really happened. The facts I had, what I lacked was
imagination. And it was a dangerous subject. I replied that I
didn't know how to make up stories on commission. Yet—as he
was talking to me on the phone—I was already feeling inspiration strike. The phone conversation was on Friday. I started on
Saturday. On Sunday morning three stories were ready: "Miss
Algrave," "The Body," and "Via Crucis." I myself was amazed.
All the stories in this book hit hard. And I myself suffered the
most. I was shocked by reality. If there are indecencies in the
stories it's not my fault. Needless to say they didn't happen to
me, my family and friends. How do I know? Knowing. Artists
know things. I just want to say that I write not for money but
on impulse. They'll throw stones at me. Big deal. I don't play
games, I'm a serious woman. Anyway it was a challenge.

Today is May twelfth, Mother's Day. It didn't make sense to
write stories on this day that I wouldn't want my sons to read
because I'd be ashamed. So I said to my editor: I'll only publish under a pseudonym. I'd even chosen a pretty nice name:

Cláudio Lemos. But he wouldn't have it. He said I should be free to write whatever I wanted. I gave in. What could I do? except be my own victim. I only beg God that no one commissions anything else from me. Because, apparently, I just might rebelliously obey, I the unfree.

Someone read my stories and said that's not literature, it's trash. I agree. But there's a time for everything. There's also the time for trash. This book is a bit sad because I discovered, like a silly child, that this is a dog-eat-dog world.

This is a book of thirteen (13) stories. But it could have been fourteen. I don't want that. Because I'd be betraying the trust of a simple man who told me his life story. He drives a cart on a farm. And he told me: "To avoid bloodshed, I split from my wife, she went astray and led my sixteen-year-old daughter astray." He has an eighteen-year-old son who doesn't even want to hear his own mother's name spoken. And that's how things are.

C. L.

P. S. — "The Man Who Showed Up" and "For the Time Being" were also written that same accursed Sunday. Today, May 13, Monday, the day the slaves were freed—and therefore me too—I wrote "Blue Danube," "Pig Latin," and "Praça Mauá." "The Sound of Footsteps" was written days later on a farm, in the darkness of the vast night.

I once tried to look at a person's face up close—a girl selling tickets at the movies. To learn the secret of her life. In vain. The other person is an enigma. And with the eyes of a statue: blind.

Miss Algrave

SHE WAS LIABLE TO BE JUDGED. THAT'S WHY SHE
didn't tell anyone anything. If she did, people wouldn't believe
her because they didn't believe in reality. But she, who lived in
London, where ghosts exist down dark alleys, knew the truth.

Her day, Friday, had been like all the rest. It didn't happen
until Saturday night. But on Friday she did everything as usual.
Though an awful memory tormented her: when she was little,
about seven, she'd play house with her cousin Jack, in Granny's
big bed. And they'd do everything to make babies, without success. She had never seen Jack again nor did she wish to. If she
was guilty, so was he.

Single, of course, a virgin, of course. She lived alone in a top
floor flat in Soho. That day she'd gone grocery shopping: vegetables and fruit. Because she thought eating meat was a sin.

As she was passing through Piccadilly Circus and saw the
women waiting for men on street corners, she practically vomited. And for money! It was too much to bear. And that statue
of Eros, over there, indecent.

After lunch she went to work: she was the perfect typist.

Her boss never looked at her and treated her, fortunately, with respect, addressing her as Miss Algrave. Her first name was Ruth. And she was of Irish stock. She was a redhead, wore her hair twisted into a severe bun at her nape. She had loads of freckles and her skin was so fair and delicate that it resembled white silk. Her eyelashes were red too. She was a pretty woman.

She took great pride in her figure: buxom and tall. But never had anyone touched her breasts.

She usually dined at a cheap restaurant right in Soho. She'd have pasta with tomato sauce. And she had never set foot in a pub: the smell of alcohol nauseated her, whenever she passed one. She felt offended by humanity.

She grew red geraniums that were a glory in spring. Her father had been a Protestant vicar and her mother still lived in Dublin with her married son. Her brother was married to a real bitch named Tootzi.

Once in a while Miss Algrave would write a letter of protest to *The Times*. And they'd publish it. She took great pleasure in seeing her name: sincerely Ruth Algrave.

She bathed just once a week, on Saturdays. In order not to see her naked body, she wouldn't even take off her knickers or bra.

The day it happened was Saturday so she didn't have work. She awoke very early and had some jasmine tea. Then she prayed. Then she went out for some fresh air.

Near the Savoy Hotel she was nearly run over. If that had happened and she had died, it would have been awful because nothing would have happened to her that night.

She went to choir practice. She had an expressive voice. Yes, she was a privileged individual.

Then she went to lunch and permitted herself to eat prawns: they were so good it even seemed like a sin.

Then she headed for Hyde Park and sat on the grass. She'd brought a Bible to read. But—God forgive her—the sun was so fierce, so good, so hot, that she didn't read a thing, she just sat on the ground lacking the courage to lie down. She did her best not to look at the couples who were kissing and fondling one another without the least bit of shame.

Then she went home, watered the begonias and took a bath. Then she paid a visit to Mrs. Cabot who was ninety-seven. She brought her a slice of raisin cake and they had tea. Miss Algrave felt very happy, even though ... Well, even though.

At seven she went home. There was nothing to do. So she knit a winter sweater. In a magnificent color: yellow as the sun.

Before going to sleep she had more jasmine tea with biscuits, brushed her teeth, changed her clothes and got into bed. She herself had made her gauzy curtains and hung them.

It was May. The curtains billowed in the breeze on that most singular of nights. Why singular? She didn't know.

She read a bit of the morning paper and turned off the bedside lamp. Through the open window she could see the moonlight. There was a full moon.

She sighed deeply because living alone was hard. Loneliness was crushing her. It was terrible not having a single person to talk to. She was the loneliest creature she knew. Even Mrs. Cabot had a cat. Ruth Algrave didn't have any pets: they were too bestial for her taste. She didn't have a television either. For two reasons: she couldn't afford it and she didn't want to sit there watching all that immorality flashing across the screen. On Mrs. Cabot's television she'd seen a man kissing a woman on the lips. And not to mention the danger of spreading germs.

Ah, if she could she'd write a letter of protest to *The Times* every day. But it was no use protesting, apparently. Shamelessness was in the air. She once even saw a dog with a bitch. It shocked her. But if that was how God wanted things, so be it. But no one would ever touch her, she thought. She went on coping with her loneliness.

Even children were immoral. She avoided them. And she deeply regretted having been born from her father and mother's lack of self-restraint. She was ashamed of their shamelessness.

Since she left uncooked rice on the windowsill, pigeons came to visit her. Sometimes they came into her bedroom. They were sent by God. So innocent. Cooing. But their cooing was somewhat immoral, though less so than seeing a half-naked woman on television. Tomorrow without fail she'd write a letter protesting the wicked ways of that accursed city of London. She even once saw addicts queuing outside a pharmacy, waiting their turn for an injection. How could the Queen allow it? A mystery. She'd write another letter denouncing the Queen herself. She wrote well, without grammatical errors and typed the letters on the office typewriter whenever she had a moment's pause. Mr. Clairson, her boss, showered her published letters with praise. He'd even said she might one day become a writer. She'd felt proud and thanked him profusely.

There she was lying in bed with her loneliness. The even though.

That's when it happened.

She sensed something coming through the window that wasn't a pigeon. She was frightened. She said loudly:

"Who's there?"

And the answer came in the form of wind:

"I am an I."

"Who are you?" she asked trembling.

"I came from Saturn to love you."

"But I don't see anyone!" she cried.

"What matters is that you can sense me."

And indeed she sensed him. She felt an electric frisson.

"What's your name?" she asked fearfully.

"It doesn't really matter."

"But I want to call your name!"

"Call me Ixtlan."

They understood one another in Sanskrit. His touch felt cold like a lizard's, he made her shiver. On his head Ixtlan had a crown of intertwining snakes, tame from the terror of possible death. The cloak that covered his body was the most agonizing shade of violet, it was bad gold and coagulated purple.

He said:

"Take off your clothes."

She took off her nightgown. The moon was enormous inside the bedroom. Ixtlan was white and small. He lay down beside her on the wrought-iron bed. And ran his hands over her breasts. Black roses.

Never before had she felt what she felt. It was too good. She was afraid it might end. It was as if a cripple were tossing his cane in the air.

She began to sigh and said to Ixtlan:

"I love you, my love! my great love!"

And—yes, indeed. It happened. She never wanted it to end. How good it was, my God. She craved more, more and more.

She thought: take me! Or rather: "I offer myself to thee." It was the realm of the "here and now."

She asked him: "when are you coming back?"

Ixtlan replied:

"At the next full moon."

"But I can't wait that long!"

"That's how it is," he said, coldly even.

"Am I going to have a baby?"

"No."

"But I'll die of longing for you! how will I manage?"

"Use yourself."

He rose, kissed her chastely on the forehead. And left through the window.

She began weeping softly. She seemed like a sad violin without a bow. The proof that it all really happened was the blood-stained sheet. She put it away without washing it and could show it to whoever didn't believe her.

She watched dawn arrive in a burst of pink. In the fog the first little birds began to chirp sweetly, not yet frenzied.

God was illuminating her body.

Yet, like a Baroness Von Blich nostalgically reclining beneath the satin canopy above her bed, she pretended to ring the bell to summon the butler who would bring her coffee that was hot and strong, strong.

She loved him and would wait ardently for the next full moon. She didn't want to bathe so as not to wash off the taste of Ixtlan. With him it hadn't been a sin but a delight. She no longer wished to write letters of protest: she no longer protested.

And she didn't go to church. She was a fulfilled woman. She had a husband.

Then, on Sunday, at lunchtime, she ate filet mignon with mashed potatoes. The bloody meat was great. And she had Italian red wine. She was privileged indeed. She had been chosen by a being from Saturn.

She'd asked him why he chose her. He'd said it was because

she was a redhead and a virgin. She felt bestial. Animals no longer nauseated her. Let them love one another, it was the best thing in the world. And she'd wait for Ixtlan. He'd return: I know it, I know it, I know it, she thought. And she no longer felt revulsion at the couples in Hyde Park. She knew how they felt.

How good it was to live. How good it was to eat bloody meat. How good it was to drink a really astringent Italian wine, somewhat bitter on the tongue and making it shrink.

She was now unsuitable for those eighteen and under. And she delighted in it, she drooled with pleasure at it.

Since it was Sunday, she went to choir practice. She sang better than ever and wasn't surprised when she was chosen to be a soloist. She sang her hallelujah. Thus: Hallelujah! Hallelujah! Hallelujah!

Then she went to Hyde Park and lay down in the warm grass, parting her legs slightly to let the sun in. Being a woman was a fine thing. Only a woman could know. But she thought: what if there's a high price to pay for my happiness? It didn't bother her. She'd pay whatever she had to. She had always paid and always been unhappy. And now her unhappiness was over. Ixtlan! Come back soon! I can't wait any longer! Come! Come! Come!

She thought: what if he liked me because I'm a bit cross-eyed? At the next full moon she'd ask. If that was the reason, there was no doubt: she'd take it even further and go completely cross-eyed. Ixtlan, anything you want me to do, I'll do it. Only, she was dying of longing. Come back, my love.

Yes. But she did something that counted as cheating. Ixtlan would understand and forgive her. At the end of the day, you had to take care of it, right?

Here's what happened: unable to bear it any longer, she

headed for Piccadilly Circus and sidled up to a hairy man. She took him back to her bedroom. She told him he didn't have to pay. But he insisted and before going left a whole one-pound note on her bedside table! Though she did need the money. She was furious, however, when he didn't care to believe her story. She showed him, almost waving it under his nose, the blood-stained sheet. He laughed at her.

On Monday morning she made up her mind: she'd no longer work as a typist, she had other talents. Mr. Clairson could go to hell. She'd walk the streets and take men back to her bedroom. Since she was good in bed, they'd pay her handsomely. She could drink Italian wine every day. She felt like buying a bright red dress with the money the hairy chap had left her. She'd let down her thick hair that was the most beautiful shade of red. She resembled a howl.

She had learned that she was quite valuable. If Mr. Clairson, that phoney, wanted her to work for him, it would have to be in some other capacity.

First she'd buy that low-cut red dress and then she'd go to the office, arriving on purpose, for the first time in her life, very late. And here's what she'd say to her boss:

"I've had it with typing! Don't play dumb with me! Want to know something? come to bed with me, you bastard! and another thing: pay me a high salary every month, you cheapskate!"

She was sure he'd go for it. He was married to a pale and insignificant woman, Joan, and had an anemic daughter, Lucy. He'll live it up with me, that son of a bitch.

And when the full moon came—she would take a bath to purify herself of all those men to be ready for the feast with Ixtlan.

The Body
("O corpo")

XAVIER WAS A BELLIGERENT AND RED-BLOODED MAN.
Mighty strong, that man. He loved tangos. He went to see
Last Tango in Paris and got awfully turned on. He didn't get
the movie: he thought it was a sex film. He didn't realize it was
the story of a desperate man.

On the night he saw *Last Tango in Paris* the three of them
went to bed together: Xavier, Carmem and Beatriz. Everyone
knew that Xavier was a bigamist: he lived with two women.

Every night it was one of them. Sometimes twice the same
night. The odd one out would watch. Neither was jealous of
the other.

Beatriz ate like a pig: she was fat and greasy. Whereas Carmem was tall and thin.

The night of the last tango in Paris was memorable for all
three. By dawn they were exhausted. But Carmem got up in
the morning, made a most sumptuous breakfast—with fat
spoonfuls of thick cream—and brought it to Beatriz and
Xavier. She felt groggy. She had to take a cold shower to pull
herself together.

That day—Sunday—they had lunch at three in the afternoon. The one who cooked was Beatriz, the fat one. Xavier drank French wine. And he ate a whole chicken all by himself. The two women ate the other chicken. The chickens were stuffed with raisins and prunes tossed in manioc flour, all moist and good.

At six in the evening the three went to church. They resembled a bolero. Ravel's bolero.

And at night they stayed home watching television and eating. That night nothing happened: all three were very tired.

And that's how it went, day after day.

Xavier worked hard to support the two women and himself, their lavish meals. And sometimes he cheated on them both with a fantastic prostitute. But he didn't mention it at home because he wasn't crazy.

Days passed, months, years. No one died. Xavier was forty-seven years old. Carmem was thirty-nine. And Beatriz had just turned fifty.

Life was good to them. Sometimes Carmem and Beatriz would go shopping for super sexy nighties. And perfume. Carmem was more elegant. Beatriz, with her fat rolls, would pick out some little panties and a skimpy bra for those enormous breasts of hers.

One night Xavier didn't come home until very late: the two women distraught. Little did they know he'd been with his prostitute. The three were in fact four, like the three musketeers.

Xavier came home with a bottomless hunger. And popped open a bottle of champagne. He was flush with vigor. He chatted enthusiastically with the two women, telling them that the pharmaceutical business he owned was making good money.

And he suggested all three take a trip down to Montevideo, to a luxury hotel.

What a frenzy, packing the three bags.

Carmem brought all her complicated makeup. Beatriz went out and bought a miniskirt. They caught a plane. They sat in a row with three seats: he between the two women.

In Montevideo they bought whatever they wanted. Including a sewing machine for Beatriz and a typewriter Carmem wanted to learn how to use. She didn't actually need anything, she was a poor wretch. She kept a diary: she'd write in the pages of her thick red notebook the dates Xavier sought her out. She'd let Beatriz read the diary.

In Montevideo they bought a cookbook. Except it was in French and they couldn't understand a thing. The words looked more like dirty words.

Then they bought a recipe book in Spanish. And perfected their sauces and soups. They learned how to make roast beef. Xavier gained over six pounds and his bullish strength increased.

Sometimes the two women slept together. The day was long. And, though they weren't homosexuals, they'd turn each other on and make love. Sad love.

One day they told Xavier about it.

Xavier quivered. And he wanted the two women to make love in front of him that night. But, on command like that, it all came to nothing. The two women cried and Xavier flew into a rage.

For three days he didn't say a word to either.

However, during that time, and not on command, the two women went to bed together and it worked.

The three never went to the theater. They preferred television. Or going to dinner.

Xavier had bad table manners: he'd pick food up with his hands, make a lot of noise while chewing, besides eating with his mouth open. Carmem, who was more refined, felt disgusted and ashamed. The really shameless one was Beatriz who even went around the house naked.

No one knows how it began. But it began.

One day Xavier came home from work with lipstick stains on his shirt. He couldn't deny that he'd been with his favorite prostitute. Carmem and Beatriz each grabbed a stick and chased Xavier all over the house. He ran in frantic desperation, shouting: sorry! sorry! sorry!

The two women, also worn out, finally stopped chasing him.

At three in the morning Xavier got the urge for a woman. He called Beatriz because she held less of a grudge. Beatriz, weak and tired, gave in to the desires of the man who was like a superman.

But the next day they informed him that they weren't going to cook for him anymore. Let him work it out with the third woman.

The two would burst into tears every so often and Beatriz made them some potato salad with mayonnaise.

That afternoon the women went to the movies. They went to dinner and didn't come home until midnight. To find Xavier despondent, sad and hungry. He tried to explain:

"It's because sometimes I want it in the middle of the day!"

"Well," said Carmem, "well why don't you come home then?"

He promised he would. And cried. When he cried, it broke Carmem and Beatriz's hearts. That night the two women made love in front of him and he was consumed with envy.

How did the desire for revenge begin? With the two women getting closer and despising him.

He didn't keep his promise and sought out the prostitute. She turned him on because she talked dirty a lot. And she called him a son of a bitch. He took it all.

Until one fine day.

Or rather, one night. Xavier was sleeping peacefully like the good citizen he was. The two women were sitting at a table, pensive. Each was thinking about her lost childhood. And they thought about death. Carmem said:

"Someday all three of us will die."

Beatriz answered:

"And for no reason."

They had to wait patiently for the day they'd close their eyes forever. And Xavier? What would they do with Xavier? He looked like a sleeping child.

"Should we wait till Xavier dies of natural causes?" asked Beatriz.

Carmem thought and thought and said:

"I think the two of us should take care of it."

"How?"

"I don't know yet."

"But we've got to figure it out."

"Just leave it to me, I know what to do."

And doing nothing was out of the question. Soon it would be dawn and nothing would have happened. Carmem made them some very strong coffee. And they ate chocolate until it made them sick. And nothing, nothing at all.

They turned on the transistor radio and listened to a heart-rending piece by Schubert. It was a piano solo. Carmem said:

"It has to be today."

Carmem led and Beatriz followed. It was a special night: full of stars watching them, sparkling and tranquil. What silence. Oh what silence. They went up to Xavier to see if they might get inspired. Xavier was snoring. Carmem really did get inspired.

She said to Beatriz:

"In the kitchen are two big knives."

"So?"

"So there are two of us and we've got two big knives."

"So?"

"So, dummy, the two of us have weapons and we can do what we have to do. God commands it."

"Isn't it better not to talk about God at a time like this?"

"You want me to talk about the Devil? No, I'm talking about God, the lord of everything. Of space and time."

So they went to the kitchen. The two big knives were sharpened, made of fine, polished steel. Would they have the strength?

Yes, they would.

They were armed. The bedroom was dark. They stabbed in the wrong places, piercing the heavy blanket. It was a cold night. Then they managed to distinguish Xavier's sleeping body.

Xavier's rich blood flowed all over the bed, onto the floor, a waste.

Carmem and Beatriz sat at the dining room table, under the yellow glare of the bare bulb, they were exhausted. Killing requires strength. Human strength. Divine strength. They were sweaty, mute, despondent. If they could have helped it, they wouldn't have killed their great love.

Now what? Now they had to get rid of the body. The body was big. The body was heavy.

So the two went out to the garden and with the help of two shovels, dug a grave in the ground.

And, in the dark of night—they carried the body out to the garden. It was hard because, Xavier dead seemed to weigh more than when he was alive, since his spirit had left him. As they carried him, they groaned with exhaustion and pain. Beatriz was crying.

They laid the big body in the grave, covered it with the damp, fragrant soil from the garden, good soil for planting. Then they went back inside, made more coffee, and were somewhat revived.

Beatriz, being a hopeless romantic—she was constantly reading pulp romances involving star-crossed or lost loves— Beatriz got the idea to plant roses in that fertile soil.

So they went back to the garden, took a cutting of red roses and planted it on the tomb of the late lamented Xavier. Day was breaking. The garden was kissed with dew. The dew was a blessing on the murder. That's what they thought, sitting out there on the white bench.

Days passed. They bought black dresses. And hardly ate. When night fell sadness overtook them. They no longer enjoyed cooking. Out of rage, Carmem, the hot-tempered one, tore up the cookbook in French. She kept the Spanish one: you never know when you might need it.

Beatriz eventually took over in the kitchen. Both ate and drank in silence. The red rose cutting seemed to have taken root. A nice green thumb, good thriving soil. It had all worked out.

And that took care of the problem.

But it so happened that Xavier's secretary wondered about his extended absence. There were urgent documents to sign. Since there was no phone at Xavier's house, he came over. The house seemed bathed in "*mala suerte.*"* The two women told him Xavier was on a trip, that he'd gone down to Montevideo. The secretary didn't entirely believe it but seemed to buy the story.

The next week the secretary went to the Police. You don't fool around with the Police. At first, the Police hadn't wanted to believe the story. But, confronted with the secretary's persistence, they lazily decided to search the polygamist's house. All in vain: no sign of Xavier.

Then Carmem spoke up:

"Xavier's in the garden."

"In the garden? doing what?"

"Only God knows."

"But we didn't see anything or anybody."

They went out to the garden: Carmem, Beatriz, the secretary whose name was Alberto, two police officers, and two other men nobody knew. Seven people. Then Beatriz, without a single tear in her eyes, showed them the flowering grave. Three men dug it up, destroying the rose bush that suffered human brutality for no reason.

And they saw Xavier. He looked horrible, deformed, already half-eaten, eyes open.

"Now what?" said one of the police officers.

"Now we arrest those two women."

"But," said Carmem, "let us be in the same cell."

* Spanish: "bad luck, an evil spell."

"Look," said one of the officers in front of the stunned secretary, "the best thing to do is pretend nothing happened or else it's gonna stir up a lot of noise, a lot of paperwork, a lot of chatter."

"You two," said the other officer, "pack your bags and go live in Montevideo. Don't give us any more trouble."

The two women said: thank you so much.

And Xavier didn't say a thing. There really wasn't anything to say.

Via Crucis

MARIA DAS DORES WAS SCARED. OH SHE REALLY WAS scared.

It began when she missed her period. That surprised her because she was very regular.

Two more months passed and nothing. She went to a gynecologist. The doctor diagnosed her as visibly pregnant.

"It can't be!" cried Maria das Dores.

"Why not? aren't you married, ma'am?"

"Yes, but I'm a virgin, my husband's never touched me. First because he's a patient man, second because he's kind of impotent."

The gynecologist tried to reason with her:

"Who knows, maybe one night you ..."

"Never! oh never ever!"

"Well then," the gynecologist concluded, "I can't explain it. You're already at the end of the third month."

Maria das Dores left the doctor's office completely in a daze. She had to stop at a restaurant and have some coffee. To try to understand.

What was happening to her? A surge of anguish seized her. But she left the restaurant feeling calmer.

On the street, on her way home, she bought a little jacket for the baby. Blue, since she was sure it was a boy. What would she name him? There was only one name she could give him: Jesus.

At home she found her husband reading the newspaper in his slippers. She told him what was going on. The man got scared:

"So that makes me St. Joseph?"

"Yep," came the laconic reply.

They both fell into deep contemplation.

Maria das Dores sent the maid out to buy the vitamins the gynecologist had prescribed. They were for her son's benefit.

Divine son. She had been chosen by God to give the world the new Messiah.

She bought a blue cradle. She started knitting little jackets and making cloth diapers.

Meanwhile her belly was growing. The fetus was energetic: it would kick her violently. Sometimes she called St. Joseph over to put his hand on her belly and feel how powerfully their son was alive.

St. Joseph would then get misty-eyed. This was a vigorous Jesus. She felt completely illuminated.

Maria das Dores told a close friend the breathtaking story. The friend got scared too:

"Maria das Dores, what a privileged destiny you have!"

"Privileged, indeed," sighed Maria das Dores. "But what can I do so my son doesn't follow the Via Crucis?"

"Pray," her friend counseled, "pray a lot."

And Maria das Dores started believing in miracles. Once she thought she saw the Virgin Mary standing by her side smiling at her. Another time she herself performed the miracle: there was an open wound on her husband's leg, Maria das Dores kissed the wound. The next day there wasn't so much as a trace.

It was cold, it was July. In October the child would be born.

But where to find a stable? Only if she went to a farm in the countryside of Minas Gerais. So she decided to go to Aunt Mininha's farm.

What worried her was that the child wouldn't be born on the twenty-fifth of December.

She went to Church every single day and, even with her big belly, would kneel for hours. As her son's godmother, she had chosen the Virgin Mary. And as his godfather, Christ.

And that's how the time passed. Maria das Dores had grown brutally fat and had strange cravings. Like eating frozen grapes. St. Joseph came along with her to the farm. And did his carpentry work there.

One day Maria das Dores overstuffed herself—she vomited a great deal and cried. And thought: it's beginning, my holy son's Via Crucis has begun.

But it seemed likely that if she named the child Jesus, he'd be, as an adult, crucified. It was better to name him Emmanuel. A simple name. A good name.

She waited for Emmanuel seated beneath a jabuticaba tree. And thinking:

When the time comes, I won't scream, I'll just say: oh Jesus!

And she kept eating jabuticabas. The mother of Jesus was stuffing herself.

The aunt—who knew everything—made up the bedroom with blue curtains. The stable was right there, with its good manure smell and its cows.

At night Maria das Dores would gaze at the starry sky in search of the guiding star. Who would be the three kings? Who would bring him incense and myrrh?

She took long strolls because the doctor had recommended

plenty of walking. St. Joseph had let his graying beard grow and his long hair reached his shoulders.

Waiting was hard. Time wasn't passing. Her aunt made them, for breakfast, cornmeal muffins that crumbled in their mouths. And the cold left their hands red and rough.

At night they'd light a fire in the hearth and sit warming themselves. St. Joseph had found himself a staff. And, because he never changed clothes, his stench was suffocating. His tunic was made of burlap. He'd sip wine by the hearth. Maria das Dores sipped creamy white milk, holding her rosary.

Very early in the morning she'd go peek at the cows in the stable. The cows would moo. Maria das Dores would smile at them. All humble: cows and woman. Maria das Dores about to cry. She'd smooth the straw on the ground, readying a place to lie down when the hour came. The hour of illumination.

St. Joseph, would set off with his staff to go meditate on the mountain. The aunt made roast pork and they'd all eat like crazy. And no sign of the child being born.

Until one night, at three in the morning, Maria das Dores felt the first pang. She lit the oil lamp, woke St. Joseph, woke her aunt. They got dressed. And with a torch illuminating their path, they headed through the trees to the stable. A dense star sparkled in the black sky.

The cows, now awake, grew uneasy, started mooing.

Soon another pang. Maria das Dores bit down on her own hand so she wouldn't scream. And day wasn't dawning.

St. Joseph shivered with cold. Maria das Dores, lying on the straw, under a blanket, waited.

Then came a pang too strong. Oh Jesus, moaned Maria das Dores. Oh Jesus, the cows seemed to moo.

The stars in the sky.

Then it happened.

Emmanuel was born.

And the stable seemed to be completely illuminated.

It was a strong and beautiful boy who bellowed at dawn.

St. Joseph cut the umbilical cord. And the mother was smiling. The aunt was weeping.

No one knows whether that child had to walk the Via Crucis. Everyone does.

The Man Who Showed Up
("O homem que apareceu")

IT WAS SATURDAY EVENING, AROUND SIX O'CLOCK. AL-
most seven. I went out to buy some Coca-Cola and cigarettes.
I crossed the street and headed for Portuguese Manuel's corner bar.

As I was waiting to be helped, a man playing a little harmonica came up, looked at me, played a little tune and said
my name. He said he'd met me at the Cultura Inglesa English school, where I'd actually only studied for two or three
months. He said to me:

"Don't be scared of me."

I replied:

"I'm not. What's your name?"

He replied with a sad smile, in English: "what's in a name?"

He said to Mr. Manuel:

"The only person here who's better than me is this woman
because she writes and I don't."

Mr. Manuel didn't so much as blink. And the man was completely drunk. I gathered my purchases and was leaving when
he said:

"May I have the honor of carrying your bottle and pack of
cigarettes?

I handed my purchases to him. At the entrance to my building, I took back the Coca-Cola and cigarettes. He was standing there in front of me. Then, thinking his face was so very familiar, I asked his name again.

"I'm Cláudio."

"Cláudio what?"

"Come on, what do you mean what? I used to be called Cláudio Brito …"

"Cláudio!" I cried. "Oh, my God, please come up to my place!"

"What floor?"

I told him the apartment number and floor. He said he'd pay his tab at the bar and come up after.

A friend of mine was over. I told her what happened to me, saying: "He might be too ashamed to come."

My friend said: "He won't come, drunks always forget the apartment number. And, if he does, he'll never leave. Warn me so I can go into the bedroom and leave you two alone."

I waited—and nothing. I was stunned by Cláudio Brito's collapse. I got discouraged and changed clothes.

Then the doorbell rang. I asked through the closed door who it was. He said: "Cláudio." I said: "Wait on the bench in the hall and I'll open the door in a second." I changed clothes. He was a good poet, Cláudio. What had he been up to all this time?

He came in and immediately started playing with my dog, saying that animals were the only ones that understood him. I asked if he'd like some coffee. He said: "All I drink is alcohol, I've been drinking for three days straight." I lied: I told him that unfortunately there was no alcohol in the house. And I offered coffee again. He looked at me solemnly and said:

"Don't boss me around."

I replied:

"I'm not bossing you around, I'm asking you to have some coffee, I've got a thermos full of good coffee in the pantry." He said he liked strong coffee. I brought him a full teacup, with just a little sugar.

And he made no move to drink it. And I insisted. Then he drank the coffee, saying to my dog:

"Break this teacup and you're gonna get it. See how he's looking at me, he understands me."

"I understand you too."

"You? all that matters to you is literature."

"Well you're mistaken. Children, families, friends, come first."

He eyed me warily, somewhat askance. And asked:

"You swear that literature doesn't matter?"

"I swear," I answered with the assuredness that comes from inner truth. And added: "Any cat, any dog is worth more than literature."

"Then," he said, deeply moved, "shake my hand. I believe you."

"Are you married?"

"About a thousand times, I can't remember anymore."

"Do you have children?"

"I have a five-year-old boy."

"I'll get you some more coffee."

I brought him the teacup, nearly full again. He drank it slowly. He said:

"You're a strange woman."

"No I'm not," I replied, "I'm very simple, not sophisticated at all."

He told me a story involving some guy nicknamed Francisquinho, I didn't really get who he was. I asked him:

"What do you do for work?"

"I don't work. I'm retired because I'm an alcoholic and mentally ill."

"You don't seem mentally ill at all. You just drink more than you should."

He told me he'd served in the Vietnam War. And that he'd spent two years as a sailor. That he got on very well with the sea. And his eyes filled with tears. I said:

"Be a man and cry, cry as much as you want; have the great courage to cry. You must have plenty of reasons to cry."

"And here I am, drinking coffee and crying..."

"It doesn't matter, cry and make believe I don't exist."

He cried a little. He was a very handsome man, in need of a shave and utterly defeated. You could see he was a failure. Like all of us. He asked if he could read me a poem. I said I'd like to hear it. He opened a bag, pulled a thick notebook out of it, burst into laughter, upon opening the pages.

Then he read the poem. It was simply lovely. It mixed dirty words with the most delicate sentiments. Oh Cláudio—I felt like crying out—we're all failures, we're all going to die some day! Who? but who can sincerely say they've realized their potential in life. Success is a lie.

I said:

"Your poem is so wonderful. Do you have any others?"

"I have another one, but you must be getting annoyed with me. You must want me to go."

"I don't want you to go just yet. I'll let you know when it's time for you to leave. Because I go to bed early."

He looked for the poem in the pages of his notebook, didn't find it, gave up. He said:

"I know a thing or two about you. And I've even met your ex-husband."

I kept silent.

"You're pretty."

I kept silent.

I was very sad. And at a loss for how to help him. It's a terrible powerlessness, not knowing how to help.

He said to me:

"If I commit suicide one day ..."

"There's no way you're committing suicide," I cut him off. "Because it's our duty to live. And living can be good. Believe me."

I was the one about to cry.

There was nothing I could do.

I asked where he lived. He said he had a tiny apartment in Botafogo. I said: "Go home and sleep."

"First I have to see my son, he's got a fever."

"What's your son's name?"

He told me. I replied: "I have a son with that name."

"I know."

"I'm going to give you a children's book that I once wrote for my sons. Read it aloud to yours."

I gave him the book, wrote a dedication. He put the book into a kind of valise. And I in despair.

"Do you want some Coca-Cola?"

"You're crazy about offering people coffee and Coca-Cola."

"It's because I have nothing else to offer."

At the door he kissed my hand. I walked him to the elevator, pushed the button for the ground floor and said to him: "Go with God, for God's sake."

The elevator went down. I went back in, turned off the lights, told my friend he was gone and she soon left, I changed clothes, took a sleeping pill—and sat in the dark living room smoking a cigarette. I recalled how Cláudio, a few minutes earlier, had asked for the cigarette I was smoking. I gave it to him. He smoked it. He also said: "one day I'm going to kill somebody."

"That's not true, I don't believe you."

He also told me how he'd once shot a dog to put it out of its misery. I asked if he'd ever seen a film that in English was called *They Shoot Horses, Don't They?* and in Portuguese *Night of the Desperate*. Yes, he'd seen it.

I sat there smoking. My dog was watching me in the dark.

That was yesterday, Saturday. Today is Sunday, May twelfth, Mother's Day. How can I be a mother to this man? I ask myself and there's no answer.

There's no answer for anything.

I went to bed. I had died.

He Drank Me Up
("Ele me bebeu")

YES. IT ACTUALLY HAPPENED.
Serjoca was a makeup artist. But he didn't want anything to do with women. He wanted men.
And he always did Aurélia Nascimento's makeup. Aurélia was pretty and, with makeup on, she was a knockout. She was blonde, wore a wig and false eyelashes. They became friends. They went out together, the kind of thing where you go out to dinner at a nightclub.
Whenever Aurélia wanted to look beautiful she called Serjoca. Serjoca was good-looking too. He was slim and tall.
And that's how things went. A phone call and they'd make a date. She'd get dressed up, she went all out. She wore contact lenses. And stuffed her bra. But her own breasts were beautiful, pointy. She only stuffed her bra because she was flat-chested. Her mouth was a rosy red bud. And her teeth large and white.
One day, at six in the evening, at the peak of rush hour, Aurélia and Serjoca were standing outside the Copacabana Palace Hotel and waiting in vain for a taxi. Serjoca, worn out, was leaning against a tree. Aurélia impatient. She suggested giving the doorman ten cruzeiros to hail them a taxi. Serjoca refused: he was cheap.

It was almost seven. Getting dark. What to do?

Nearby was Affonso Carvalho. Metals magnate. He was waiting for his Mercedes and chauffeur. It was hot, the car was air-conditioned, with a phone and a fridge. Affonso had turned forty the day before.

He saw Aurélia's impatience as she tapped her feet on the sidewalk. An attractive woman, thought Affonso. And in need of a ride. He turned to her:

"Having trouble finding a cab, miss?"

"I've been here since six o'clock and not one taxi has stopped to pick us up! I can't take it anymore."

"My chauffeur's coming soon," Affonso said. "Can I give you a lift somewhere?"

"I'd be so grateful, especially since my feet are hurting."

But she didn't say she had corns. She hid her flaw. She was heavily made-up and looked at the man with desire. Serjoca very quiet.

Finally the chauffeur pulled up, got out, opened the door. The three of them got in. She in front, next to the chauffeur, the two of them in the backseat. She took off her shoes discreetly and sighed in relief.

"Where do you want to go?"

"We don't exactly have a destination," Aurélia said, increasingly turned on by Affonso's manly face.

He said:

"What if we went to Number One for a drink?"

"I'd love to," Aurélia said. "Wouldn't you, Serjoca?"

"Sure. I could use a stiff drink."

So they went to the club, at this nearly deserted hour. And chatted. Affonso talked about metallurgy. The other two didn't understand a thing. But they pretended to. It was tedious. But Affonso got all worked up and, under the table, slid his foot against Aurélia's. The very foot that had corns. She reciprocated, aroused. Then Affonso said:

"What if we went back to my place for dinner? Today I've got escargot and chicken with truffles. How about it?"

"I'm famished."

And Serjoca silent. Affonso turned him on too.

The apartment was carpeted in white and there was a Bruno Giorgi sculpture. They sat down, had another drink and went into the dining room. A jacaranda table. A waiter serving from the left. Serjoca didn't know how to eat escargot and got all tripped up by the special utensils. He didn't like it. But Aurélia really liked it, though she was afraid of getting garlic breath. But they drank French champagne all through dinner. No one wanted dessert, all they wanted was coffee.

And they went into the living room. Then Serjoca came to life. And started talking nonstop. He cast bedroom eyes at the industrialist. Affonso was astounded by the handsome young man's eloquence. The next day he'd call Aurélia to tell her: Serjoca is the most charming person.

And they made another date. This time at a restaurant, the Albamar. To start, they had oysters. Once again, Serjoca had a hard time eating the oysters. I'm a loser, he thought.

But before they all met up, Aurélia had called Serjoca: she urgently needed her makeup done. He went over to her place.

Then, while she was getting her makeup done, she thought: Serjoca's taking off my face.

She got the feeling he was erasing her features: empty, a face made only of flesh. Dark flesh.

She felt distress. She excused herself and went to the bathroom to look at herself in the mirror. It was just as she'd imagined: Serjoca had annulled her face. Even her bones—and she had spectacular bone structure—even her bones had disappeared. He's drinking me up, she thought, he's going to destroy me. And all because of Affonso.

She returned out of sorts. At the restaurant she hardly spoke. Affonso talked more with Serjoca, barely glancing at Aurélia: he was interested in the young man.

Finally, finally lunch was over.

Serjoca made a date with Affonso for that evening. Aurélia said she couldn't make it, she was tired. It was a lie: she wasn't going because she had no face to show.

She got home, took a long bubble bath, lay there thinking: before you know it he'll take away my body too. What could she do to take back what had been hers? Her individuality?

She got out of the bathtub lost in thought. She dried off with a huge red towel. Lost in thought the whole time. She stepped onto the scale: she was at a good weight. Before you know it he'll take away my weight too, she thought.

She went over to the mirror. She looked at herself deeply. But she was no longer anything.

Then — then all of a sudden she slapped herself brutally on the left side of her face. To wake herself up. She stood still looking at herself. And, as if that weren't enough, she slapped her face twice more. To find herself.

And it really happened.

In the mirror she finally saw a human face, sad, delicate. She was Aurélia Nascimento. She had just been born. Nas-ci-men-to.*

---

* "Birth."

For the Time Being
("Por enquanto")

SINCE HE HAD NOTHING TO DO, HE WENT TO PEE. AND then he really hit zero.

These things come with living: once in a while you hit zero. And all this is for the time being. While you're alive.

Today a young woman called me in tears, saying her father had died. That's how it is: just because.

One of my sons is abroad, the other one came over for lunch with me. The meat was so tough you could hardly chew it. But we drank some chilled rosé. And chatted. I'd asked him not to give in to the commercial pressure that exploits Mother's Day. I he did what I asked: he didn't give me anything. Or rather he gave me everything: his presence.

I've been working all day, it's ten to six. The phone's not ringing. I am alone. Alone in the world and in space. And when I call someone, the phone rings and no one answers. Or someone does and says: they're sleeping.

You have to know how to take it. Because that's just how it is. Sometimes you have nothing to do and so you go pee.

But if that's how God made us, then let us be that way. Empty-handed. With nothing to say.

Friday night I went to a party, I didn't even know it was my friend's birthday, his wife hadn't told me. It was crowded. I noticed a lot of people there feeling uncomfortable.

What should I do? call myself? I'll get a sad busy signal, I know it, once I absentmindedly dialed my own number. How can I wake someone who's sleeping? how do I call the person I want to call? what can I do? Nothing: because it's Sunday and even God rested. But I've been working alone all day.

But now the person who was sleeping woke up and is coming to see me at eight. It's 6:05.

We're having the so-called Indian Summer: sweltering heat. My fingers hurt from typing so much. Your fingertips are not to be taken lightly. It's through the fingertips that we take in fluids.

Should I have offered to go to the funeral for the girl's father? Death would be too much for me today. I know what I'll do: I'll eat. Then I'll come back. I went to the kitchen, it so happens the cook's not off today and she'll warm up some food for me. My cook is tremendously fat: she weighs two hundred pounds. Two hundred pounds of insecurity, two hundred pounds of fear. I feel like kissing her smooth, black face but she wouldn't understand. I came back to the typewriter while she warmed up the food. I realized I'm dying of hunger. I can hardly wait for her to call me.

Ah, I know what I'll do: I'll change clothes. Then I'll eat, and then I'll come back to the typewriter. See you soon.

Now I've eaten. It was great. I had a little rosé. Now I'll have some coffee. And turn on the air conditioning in the living room: in Brazil air conditioning isn't a luxury, it's a necessity. Especially for someone who, like me, suffers terribly from the heat. It's six-thirty. I turned on my transistor radio. It's tuned in to the Ministry of Education program. Oh what sad music! you don't have to be sad to be refined. I'm going to invite Chico Buarque, Tom Jobim and Caetano Veloso over and ask them to bring their guitars. I want joy, melancholy is slowly killing me.

Whenever we start asking ourselves: what for? then things aren't going well. And I'm asking myself what for. But I am very well aware that it's only "for the time being." It's twenty to seven. What's it twenty to seven for?

Meanwhile I made a phone call and, to my utmost exultation, it's now ten to seven. Never in my life have I spoken the phrase "to my utmost exultation." It's very strange. Once in a while I get a bit Machadian. Speaking of Machado de Assis, I miss him. It seems like a lie but I don't have a single book of his on my shelf. As for José de Alencar, I don't even remember if I've ever read him.

I miss some things. I miss my sons, yes, flesh of my flesh. Weak flesh and I haven't read every single book. *La chair est triste.**

But we smoke and soon feel better. It's five to seven. If I let myself go, I'll die. It's very easy. It's a matter of the clock stopping. It's three to seven. Should I turn on the television or not? But it's so boring to watch television by yourself.

But I finally made up my mind and I'm going to turn on the television. We die sometimes.

* French: "The flesh is sad."

Day After Day
("Dia após dia")

TODO IS MAY THIRTEENTH. THE DAY THE SLAVES were freed. Monday. Market day. I turned on the transistor radio and the Blue Danube was playing. I was overjoyed. I got dressed, went out, bought flowers in honor of the man who died yesterday. Red and white carnations. As I've been repeating to exhaustion someday we die. And we die in red and white. The man who died was pure: he worked for the good of humanity, warning that the world's food supply would run out. His wife, Laura, remains. A strong woman, a clairvoyant woman, with black hair and black eyes. In a few days I'll visit her. Or at least talk to her on the phone.

Yesterday, May twelfth, Mother's Day, the people who said they were coming over didn't. But a couple that I'm friends with came and we went to dinner. It's better that way. I don't want to depend on anyone anymore. What I want is the Blue Danube. And not the "Valse Triste" by Sibellius, if that's how you spell his name.

I went out again, down to Mr. Manuel's corner bar to change out the batteries in my radio. Here's what I said to him:

"Sir, do you remember the man playing the harmonica on Saturday? He was a great writer."

"Sure, I remember. He's a sad case. It's shell shock. He drinks all over town."

I left.

When I got home someone called to say: think twice before you write a pornographic book, think about whether this will add anything to your oeuvre. I replied:

"I've already asked my son's permission, I told him not to read my book. I told him a little about the stories I wrote. He listened and said: it's fine with me. I told him my first story was called 'Miss Algrave.' He said: 'grave' means tomb in English. Then I told him about the call from the girl in tears whose father had died. My son said to console me: he lived a lot. I said: he lived well."

But the person who called got angry, I got angry, she hung up, I called back, she didn't want to talk and hung up again.

If this book gets published with "*mala suerte*," I'm lost. But we're lost anyhow. There's no escaping it. We all have shell shock.

I remembered something funny. A friend of mine came one day for the open-air market across from my house. But she was wearing shorts. And a vendor shouted at her:

"Check out those thighs! really in shape!"

My friend was furious and said to him:

"Your mom's got nice thighs, asshole."

The man laughed, that bastard.

Oh well. Who knows whether this book will add anything to my oeuvre. My oeuvre be damned. I don't know why people think literature is so important. And as for my good name? let it be damned too, I have other things to worry about.

I'm thinking, for example, about the friend who had a lump in her right breast and coped with her fear alone until, almost the night before the operation, she told me. We were terrified.

The forbidden word: cancer. I prayed a lot. She prayed. And luckily it was benign, her husband called to tell me. The next day she called to say it had been just a "fluid sac." I told her that next time she should make it a leather sack, that was more cheerful.

After buying the flowers and new batteries, I don't have a single cruzeiro in the house. But in a while I'll call the pharmacy, where they know me, and ask them to cash a check for a hundred cruzeiros. That way I can go over to the market.

But I'm Sagittarius and Scorpio, with Aquarius rising. And I hold grudges. One day a couple asked me to lunch on Sunday. And on Saturday afternoon, just like that, at the last minute, they called it off because they had to have lunch with a very important foreigner. Why didn't they invite me too? why did they leave me alone on Sunday? So I got my revenge. I'm no saint. I never contacted them again. And I stopped accepting their invitations. Plain and simple.

I remembered I had a hundred cruzeiros in a purse. So I don't have to call the pharmacy anymore. I hate asking favors. I don't call anyone anymore. Whoever wants to can get in touch with me. And I won't make it easy. No more playing games.

In a couple weeks I'm going to Brasília. To give a speech. But—when they call me to set the date—I'm going to make a request: that they not make a big deal of me. To keep it simple. I'll stay in a hotel because I feel more comfortable that way. The awful thing is, when I give a speech, I get so nervous that I read too fast and no one can understand me. Once I took a chartered flight to Campos and gave a speech at the University there. Beforehand, they showed me books of mine translated into Braille. I didn't know what to say. And there were blind people in the audience. I got nervous. Afterward there was a dinner in my honor. But I couldn't take it, I excused myself and went to bed. In the morning they offered me a sweet called *chuvisco* made of eggs and sugar. We ate *chuviscos* at home for several days. I like getting presents. And giving them. It's nice. Yolanda gave me chocolates. Marly gave me a lovely shopping bag. I gave Marly's daughter a small gold saint charm. She's a clever little girl and speaks French.

Now I'm going to tell some stories about a little girl named Nicole. Nicole said to her older brother, named Marco: your long hair makes you look like a woman. Marco responded with a violent kick since he's really a little man. Then Nicole quickly said:

"Don't get mad, 'cause God's a woman!"

And, softly, she whispered to her mother: "I know God's a man, but I don't want to get beat up!"

Nicole told her cousin, who was making a mess at their grandmother's house: "don't do that 'cause one time I did and Grandma punched me so hard I fainted." Nicole's mother found out, and scolded her. And she told the story to Marco. Marco said:

"That's nothing. One time Adriana made a mess at Grandma's house and I told her: 'don't do that 'cause one time I did and Grandma beat me up so bad I slept for a hundred years.'"

Didn't I mention today was the day of the Blue Danube? I'm happy, in spite of that good man's death, in spite of Cláudio Brito, in spite of that phone call about my miserable literary oeuvre. I'm going to have more coffee.

And Coca-Cola. Like Cláudio Brito said, I'm crazy about Coca-Cola and coffee.

My dog is scratching his ear and enjoying it so much he's starting to moan. I'm his mother.

And I need money. But how lovely the Blue Danube is, it really is.

Long live the open-air market! Long live Cláudio Brito! (I changed his name, of course. Any resemblance is mere coincidence.) Long live me! who's still alive.

And now I'm done.

The Sound of Footsteps
("Ruído de passos")

SHE WAS EIGHTY-ONE YEARS OLD. HER NAME WAS MRS. Cândida Raposo.

Life made this old woman dizzy. The dizziness got worse whenever she spent a few days on a farm: the altitude, the green of the trees, the rain, they all made it worse. Whenever she listened to Liszt she got goose bumps all over. She'd been a beauty in her youth. And she got dizzy whenever she deeply inhaled the scent of a rose.

It so happened that for Mrs. Cândida Raposo the desire for pleasure didn't go away.

She finally mustered the great courage to see a gynecologist. And she asked him, ashamed, eyes downcast:

"When will it go away?"

"When will what go away, ma'am?"

"The thing."

"What thing?"

"The thing," she repeated. "The desire for pleasure," she finally said.

"Ma'am, I'm sorry to say it never goes away."

She stared at him in shock.

"But I'm eighty-one years old!"

"It doesn't matter, ma'am. It lasts until we die."

"But that's hell!"

"That's life, Mrs. Raposo."

So that was life, then? this shamelessness?

"So what am I supposed to do? no one wants me anymore ..."

The doctor looked at her with compassion.

"There's no cure for it, ma'am."

"And what if I paid?"

"It wouldn't matter. You've got to remember, ma'am, you're eighty-one years old."

"And ... and what if I took care of it myself? do you know what I mean?"

"Yes," said the doctor. "That might be a remedy."

Then she left the doctor's office. Her daughter was waiting down below, in the car. Cândida Raposo had lost a son in World War II, he was a soldier. She had this unbearable pain in her heart: that of surviving someone she loved.

That same night she found a way to satisfy herself on her own. Mute fireworks.

Afterward she cried. She was ashamed. From then on she'd use the same method. Always sad. That's life, Mrs. Raposo, that's life. Until the blessing of death.

Death.

She thought she heard the sound of footsteps. The footsteps of her husband Antenor Raposo.

Before the Rio-Niterói Bridge
"Antes da ponte Rio-Niterói"

WELL THEN.
Whose father was the lover, with that tiepin of his, the
lover of the wife of the doctor who treated his daughter, that
is, the lover's daughter and everyone knew, and the doctor's
wife would hang a white towel in the window signaling that
her lover could come in. Or else it was a colored towel and in
which case he wouldn't.
But I'm getting all mixed up or maybe this whole affair is so
tangled that I'll try to untangle it. Its realities are invented. I
apologize because besides recounting the facts I'm also guessing and whatever I guess I write down here, scribe that I am
by fate. I guess at reality. But I didn't sow the seeds for this
story. The harvest is for someone more capable than I, insignificant as I am. So the daughter's leg got gangrene and they
had to amputate it. This Jandira, seventeen, fiery as a young
colt and with beautiful hair, was engaged. As soon as her fiancé saw that figure on crutches, brimming with joy, a joy that
he didn't realize was pathetic, you see, the fiancé had the nerve
to simply call off the engagement without remorse. Everyone, even the girl's long-suffering mother, begged the fiancé to

pretend he still loved her, which—they told him—wouldn't be so hard because it wouldn't last long: since his fiancée didn't have long to live.

And three months later—as if keeping the promise not to weigh heavily on the fiancé's fainthearted notions—three months later she died, beautiful, hair flowing, inconsolable, longing for her fiancé, and frightened of death the way a child is afraid of the dark: death is made of a great darkness. Or maybe not. I don't know what it's like, I haven't died yet, and I won't know even after I die. Maybe it's not all that dark. Maybe it's a blinding light. Death, I mean.

The fiancé, who went by his last name, Bastos, apparently lived, even while his fiancée was still alive, lived with a woman. And he stayed with her, not too worried about things.

Well. That passionate woman got jealous one day. And she was devious. I can't leave out the cruel details. But where was I, did I lose my train of thought? Let's start over, and on another line and another paragraph to get off to a better start.

Well. The woman got jealous and while Bastos was asleep poured boiling water from the spout of a teapot into his ear and all he had time to do was howl before fainting, a howl we might guess was the worst cry he had, the cry of an animal. Bastos was taken to the hospital and hanging between life and death, one locked in fierce combat with the other.

The virago, named Leontina, got just over a year in jail.

From which she got out to meet—guess who? well she went to meet Bastos. By then, a very gaunt Bastos who, of course, was deaf forevermore, the same guy who hadn't excused a physical defect.

What happened? Well they moved back in together, love forevermore.

Meanwhile the seventeen-year-old girl was long dead, her sole trace remaining in her wretched mother. And if I've thought of that girl out of the blue it's from the love I feel for Jandira.

So now her father turns up, as if by chance. He was still the lover of the wife of the doctor who had treated his daughter with devotion. The daughter, that is, of the lover. And everyone knew, the doctor and the dead ex-fiancée's mother. I think I've lost my train of thought again, it's all a bit jumbled, but what can I do?

The doctor, though he knew that the girl's father was his wife's lover, had taken good care of the little fiancée so terrified of the dark that I mentioned. The father's wife—hence the ex-fiancée's mother—knew all about the adulterous flourishes of her husband who wore a gold pocket watch in his vest and a jeweled ring, a diamond-studded tiepin. A well-to-do businessman, as they say, for folks respect and bow to the rich, the winners, don't they? He, the girl's father, dressed in a green suit with a pink pinstriped shirt. How do I know? Look, I just know, the way you do by imaginative guessing. I know, period.

There's one detail I can't forget. Which is: the lover had a little gold front tooth, purely out of luxury. And he smelled like garlic. His entire aura was pure garlic, and his lover didn't even care, all she wanted was a lover, give or take the smell of food. How do I know? Knowing.

I don't know what became of these people, I didn't hear any more news. Did they go their separate ways? you see, it's an old story and there may have been some deaths among them, these people. Dark, dark death. I don't want to die.

I'll add an important fact, and one that, I don't know why, explains the accursed source of the whole story: it happened in Niterói, with its wooden docks always damp and grimy, and its ferries coming and going. Niterói is a mysterious place and has old, dark houses. And could boiling water in a lover's ear happen there? I don't know.

What's to be done with this story that took place back when the Rio-Niterói bridge was no more than a dream? I don't know that either, I offer it as a gift to whoever wants it, because I'm sick of it. Nauseated, even. Sometimes I get sick of people. Then it passes and I become fully curious and attentive again.

And that's it.

Praça Mauá

THE CABARET ON THE PRAÇA MAUÁ WAS CALLED "ERÓ-tica." And Luísa's stage name was Carla.

Carla was a dancer at the "Erótica." She was married to Joa-quim who worked himself to death as a carpenter. And Carla "worked" in two ways: dancing half-naked and cheating on her husband.

Carla was beautiful. She had small teeth and a tiny waist. She was utterly fragile. She barely had any breasts but her hips were nice and curvy. It took her an hour to do her makeup: afterward she looked like a porcelain doll. She was thirty but looked a lot younger.

She didn't have children. She and Joaquim didn't have much to do with each other. He worked until ten at night. She started work right at ten. She slept all day.

Carla was a lazy Luísa. She'd show up at night, when it was time for her to perform, start yawning, feeling like being in her own bed in a nightie. It was also because she was shy. As incredible as it might seem, Carla was a shy Luísa. She'd strip, sure, but those first moments of dancing and gyrating were filled with shame. She only "warmed up" a few minutes later.

Then she pulled out all the stops, gyrating, giving it her all. The samba was her specialty. But a really romantic blues number also got her going.

She'd get called over for a drink with customers. She got a commission for every bottle. She'd pick the most expensive one. And pretend to drink: it wasn't alcohol. She'd let the customer get drunk and spend money. Chatting with them was a chore. They'd caress her, run their hands over her tiny breasts. And she'd be wearing a sparkly bikini. Gorgeous.

Once in a while she'd sleep with a customer. She'd take the money, tuck it safe and sound in her bra and the next day go shopping for clothes. Her closet was overflowing. She'd get blue jeans. And necklaces. Loads of necklaces. And bracelets, rings.

Sometimes, just to mix it up, she'd dance in blue jeans and no bra, her breasts swaying between her glittering necklaces. She'd have bangs and make a little beauty mark near her lips with black eyeliner. She was darling. She'd wear long, dangly earrings, sometimes pearls, sometimes fake gold.

Whenever she was feeling down she'd be saved by Celsinho, a man who wasn't a man. They really got each other. She'd vent bitterly to him, complaining about Joaquim, complaining about inflation. Celsinho, a popular transvestite, listened to it all and gave her advice. They weren't rivals. Each had their own partner.

Celsinho came from an upper-class family. He'd left everything behind to follow his calling. He didn't dance. But he wore lipstick and false eyelashes. The sailors on the Praça Mauá adored him. And he played hard to get. He only gave in at the last second. And he got paid in dollars. He invested the money he exchanged on the black market at Halles Bank. He was awfully afraid of growing old and helpless. Especially because an old tranny is a pitiful sight. To keep up his strength he took two packets of protein powder daily. He had wide hips and, from taking so many hormones, had acquired a facsimile of breasts. Celsinho's stage name was Moleirão.*

Moleirão and Carla made good money for the owner of the "Erótica." The smoky atmosphere reeked of alcohol. And there was the dance floor. It was rough being dragged out to dance by a drunk sailor. But what could you do. Everyone's got their "*métier.*"

Celsinho had adopted a four-year-old girl. He was a real mother to her. He didn't sleep much because he was taking care of his little girl. There was nothing she lacked: everything she had was the very best. And a Portuguese nanny. On Sundays, Celsinho would take Claretinha to the zoo, in the Quinta da Boa Vista. And they'd both eat popcorn. And feed the monkeys. Claretinha was afraid of the elephants. She'd ask:

"How come their noses are so big?"

Celsinho would then tell a whimsical story involving evil fairies and good fairies. Or then he'd take her to the circus. And they'd suck noisily on their candy, the two of them. Celsinho wanted a brilliant future for Claretinha: marriage to a wealthy man, children, jewels.

Carla had a Siamese cat that gazed at her with hard blue eyes. But Carla barely had time to take care of her pet: she was either sleeping, or dancing, or shopping. The cat's name was Leléu. And it lapped up milk with its delicate little red tongue.

Joaquim barely ever saw Luísa. He refused to call her Carla. Joaquim was fat and short, of Italian stock. He'd been given the name Joaquim by a Portuguese neighbor woman.

---

* Clumsy, lazy; a softy.

His name was Joaquim Fioriti. Fioriti? there was nothing flowery about him.

Joaquim and Luísa's maid was a cheeky black woman who stole as much as she could. Luísa hardly ate, to maintain her figure. Joaquim would drench himself with minestrone. The maid knew about everything but kept her mouth shut. And she was in charge of polishing Carla's jewelry with Brasso and Silvo. While Joaquim was sleeping and Carla was working, the maid, named Silvinha, would wear her mistress's jewelry. And she was a somewhat ashy black color.

Here's how what happened, happened.

Carla was telling secrets to Moleirão, when she was asked to dance by a tall man with broad shoulders. Celsinho lusted after him. And was consumed with envy. He was vindictive.

When the dance ended and Carla came back to sit with Moleirão, he could barely contain his anger. And there sat Carla, innocent. It wasn't her fault she was attractive. And she'd taken quite a liking to that big hunky man. She said to Celsinho:

"I'd sleep with that one without charging a cent."

Celsinho silent. It was nearly three in the morning. The "Erótica" was full of men and women. Lots of housewives went there for fun and to make a little extra cash.

Then Carla said:

"It's so nice to dance with a real man."

Celsinho jumped up:

"But you're not a real woman!"

"Me? what do you mean I'm not?" gasped the girl who that night was dressed in black, a full-length gown with long sleeves, she looked like a nun. She did it purposely to excite the men who wanted a pure woman.

"You," Celsinho sputtered, "aren't a woman at all! You don't even know how to fry an egg! And I do! I do! I do!"

Carla turned into Luísa. Pale, bewildered. She'd been stung in her innermost femininity. Bewildered, staring at Celsinho who looked like an old hag.

Carla didn't say a word. She rose, stubbed out her cigarette in the ashtray and, without a word of explanation, ditching the party at its peak, left.

There she stood, all in black, on the Praça Mauá, at three in the morning. Like the cheapest of whores. Alone. With nowhere to turn. It was true: she didn't know how to fry an egg. And Celsinho was more woman than she.

The square was dark. And Luísa took a deep breath. She looked at the lampposts. The empty square.

And in the sky the stars.

Pig Latin
("A língua do 'p'")

MARIA APARECIDA — CIDINHA, AS THEY CALLED HER
at home—was an English teacher. Neither rich nor poor: she
got by. But she dressed impeccably. She looked rich. Even her
suitcases were high quality.

She lived in Minas Gerais and was taking the train to Rio,
where she'd spend three days, and then catch a plane to New
York.

She was a highly sought-after teacher. She prized perfection
and was affectionate, yet strict. She wanted to perfect her skills
in the United States.

She took the seven a.m. train to Rio. It was cold out. There
she was in a suede jacket with three suitcases. The train car
was empty, just a little old lady asleep in a corner under her
shawl.

At the next station, two men boarded and sat in the row
across from Cidinha's. The train in motion. One of the men
was tall and skinny, with a thin mustache and a cold stare, the
other was short and bald, with a gut. They looked at Cidinha.
She averted her gaze, looked out the train window.

There was an unease in the car. As if it were too hot. The

girl nervous. The men watchful. My God, the girl thought, what do they want from me? There was no answer. And to top it all off, she was a virgin. Why, but why had she thought of her own virginity?

Then the two men started talking to each other. At first Cidinha didn't understand a word. It seemed like a game. They were talking too fast. And the language seemed vaguely familiar to her. What language was that?

It suddenly dawned on her: they were speaking flawless Pig Latin. Like this:

"Idday ouyay eckchay outway atthay ettypray irlgay?"

"Uresay idday. E'sshay away ockoutknay. Itsway inway ethay agbay."

They meant: did you check out that pretty girl? Sure did. She's a knockout. It's in the bag.

Cidinha pretended not to understand: understanding would be dangerous for her. That was the language she used, in childhood, to keep adults away. The men went on:

"Iway annaway angbay atthay irlgay. Owhay outbay ouyay?"

"Emay ootay. Onnagay appenhay inway ethay unneltay."

What they meant was that they were going to bang her in the tunnel ... What could she do? Cidinha didn't know and trembled in fear. She hardly knew herself. Moreover she'd never gotten to know herself on the inside. As for knowing others, well, that was even worse. Help me, Virgin Mary! help me! help me!

"Ifway eshay utspay upway away ightfay eway ancay illkay erhay."

If she put up a fight they could kill her. So that's how it was.

"Ithway away ifeknay. Andway obray erhay."

Kill her with a knife. And they could rob her.

How could she let them know she wasn't rich? that she was fragile, the slightest gesture would kill her. She took a cigarette from her purse to smoke and calm down. It didn't help. When was the next tunnel coming? She had to think fast, fast, fast.

Then she thought: if I pretend I'm a prostitute, they'll change their minds, they don't like whores.

So she hiked up her skirt, made sensual movements—she didn't even know she knew how, so little did she know herself—unbuttoned the top of her blouse, letting her cleavage show. The men suddenly shocked.

"E'sshay azycray."

She's crazy, they meant.

And there she was gyrating like a samba dancer from the slums. She took some lipstick from her purse and smeared it on. And started humming.

Then the men burst out laughing. They thought Cidinha's antics were funny. She herself feeling desperate. And the tunnel?

The conductor came. He saw the whole thing. Didn't say a word. But he went to the engineer and told him. The latter said:

"Let's take care of it, I'll turn her in to the cops at the first station."

And the next station came.

The engineer got off, spoke to a soldier by the name of José Lindalvo. José Lindalvo wasn't one to play games. He boarded the car, spotted Cidinha, grabbed her roughly by the arm, gathered her three suitcases as best he could, and they got off.

The two men roaring with laughter.

At the little blue and pink station was a young girl holding a suitcase. She looked at Cidinha with scorn. She boarded the train and it departed.

Cidinha didn't know how to explain herself to the police. There was no explanation for Pig Latin. She was taken to the jail and booked. They called her the worst names. And she was stuck in the cell for three days. They let her smoke. She smoked like a madwoman, taking long drags, stamping out her cigarettes on the concrete floor. There was a fat cockroach creeping along the floor.

Finally they let her go. She caught the next train to Rio. She'd washed her face, she was no longer a prostitute. What worried her was this: when the two men had talked about banging her, she'd wanted to be banged. She was utterly brazen. Andway I'mway away utslay. That's what she'd discovered. Eyes downcast.

She arrived in Rio exhausted. Went to a cheap hotel. Soon realized she'd missed the flight. At the airport she bought a ticket.

And she wandered the streets of Copacabana, she miserable, Copacabana miserable.

Then on the corner of the Rua Figueiredo Magalhães she saw a newsstand. And hanging there was the newspaper *O Dia*. She couldn't say why she bought it.

A bold headline read: "Girl Raped and Murdered on Train."

She trembled all over. So it had happened. And to the girl who had scorned her.

She started crying on the street. She threw away that damned newspaper. She didn't want the details. She thought: "Esyay. Atefay isway implacableway."

Fate is implacable.

Better Than to Burn
("Melhor do que arder")

SHE WAS TALL, STRONG, HAIRY. SISTER CLARA HAD dark hair on her upper lip and deep black eyes.

She had entered the convent at her family's insistence: they wanted her sheltered in God's embrace. She obeyed.

She carried out her duties without complaint. Her duties were manifold. And there were the prayers. She prayed fervently.

And she confessed every day. Every day the white host that crumbled in her mouth.

But she began to tire of living only among women. Women, women, women. She chose a friend as her confidante. She told her she couldn't bear it any longer. The friend counseled her:

"Mortify your body."

She began sleeping on the cold stone floor. And castigated herself by wearing sackcloth. It was no use. She got violent fevers and chills, had scratches all over.

She confessed to the priest. He ordered her to keep mortifying herself. She did.

But whenever the priest touched her mouth while giving her the host she'd have to stop herself from biting the priest's hand. He noticed, didn't say a word. There was a silent pact between them. Both mortified themselves.

She could no longer look at Christ's half-naked body.

Sister Clara was the daughter of Portuguese parents and, in secret, shaved her hairy legs. If anyone ever found out, she was in for it. She told the priest. He went pale. He imagined how strong her legs must be, how shapely.

One day, at lunchtime, she began to cry. She didn't tell anyone why. Not even she knew why she was crying.

And from then on she was always crying. Though she hardly ate, she was gaining weight. But there were purplish circles under her eyes. When she sang in church, she was a contralto.

Until she told the priest in the confessional:

"I can't bear it any longer, I swear I can't bear it any longer."

He said meditatively:

"It's better not to marry. But it's better to marry than to burn."

She requested an audience with the mother superior. The mother superior fiercely reprimanded her. But Sister Clara stood firm: she wanted to leave the convent, she wanted to find a man, she wanted to get married. The mother superior asked her to wait another year. She answered that she couldn't, that it had to be now.

She packed her few things and took off. She went to live in a boardinghouse for young women.

Her black hair grew abundantly. And she seemed in the clouds, dreamy. She paid for the boardinghouse with the money her northern family sent. Her family didn't approve. But they couldn't let her starve to death.

She made her own quaint dresses out of cheap fabric, on a

sewing machine lent by another girl at the boardinghouse. The dresses had long sleeves, high collars, went below the knee.

And nothing happened. She prayed often for something good to happen to her. In the form of a man.

And indeed it did.

She went down to the corner bar to buy a bottle of Caxambu mineral water. The owner was a handsome Portuguese man who was enchanted by Clara's demure manner. He didn't let her pay for the Caxambu water. She blushed.

But she went back the next day to buy some coconut sweets. She didn't pay for those either. The Portuguese, named Antônio, got up the nerve to ask her to the movies. She declined.

The next day she went back to have some coffee. Antônio promised he wouldn't touch her if they went to the movies. She accepted.

They went to see a movie and didn't pay any attention to it. By the end, they were holding hands.

They began meeting for long strolls. She, with her black hair. He in a suit and tie.

Then one night he said to her:

"I'm rich, the bar makes enough money for us to get married. How about it?"

"Yes," she answered solemnly.

They got married in church and at City Hall. In church the person who married them was the priest who had told her marrying was better than burning. They had a steamy honeymoon in Lisbon. Antônio left his brother in charge of the bar.

She came back pregnant, satisfied, happy.

They had four children, all boys, all hairy.

But It's Going to Rain
("Mas vai chover")

MARIA ANGÉLICA DE ANDRADE WAS SIXTY. AND HER lover, Alexandre, was nineteen.

Everyone knew the boy was taking advantage of Maria Angélica's money. Maria Angélica was the only one who didn't suspect.

Here's how it started: Alexandre was the pharmacy delivery boy and rang Maria Angélica's doorbell. She opened the door herself. And came face to face with a tall, strapping youth who was incredibly handsome. Instead of taking the medicine she'd ordered and paying for it, she asked him, half-startled by her own boldness, if he wanted to come in for some coffee.

Alexandre was taken aback and said no, thanks. But she insisted. She added that there was cake too.

The young man hesitated, visibly embarrassed. But he said: "If it's just for a minute, I'll come in, because I have to work."

He went in. Maria Angélica didn't realize she was already in love. She gave him a big slice of cake and coffee with milk. As he ate uncomfortably, she watched him enraptured. He was strength, youth, the sex long since left behind. The young man finished eating and drinking, and wiped his mouth on his sleeve. Maria Angélica didn't consider it bad manners: she was delighted, she found him natural, simple, enchanting.

"I have to go now 'cause I'll get in trouble with my boss if I take too long."

She was fascinated. She noted the scattering of pimples on his face. But that didn't affect his good looks or his masculinity: hormones were raging in there. That, yes, was a man. She gave him a huge tip, way too much, that surprised the young man. And she said in a sing-song voice and with the mannerisms of a romantic girl:

"I'll only let you go if you promise you'll come back! Today even! Because I'm going to order some vitamins from the pharmacy ..."

An hour later he was back with the vitamins. She'd changed clothes, and was wearing a sheer lace kimono. You could see the outline of her panties. She made him come in. She told him she was a widow. That was her way of letting him know she was available. But the young man didn't get it.

She invited him to tour her nicely decorated apartment leaving him speechless. She took him to her bedroom. She didn't know how to make him understand. So she said:

"Let me give you a little kiss!"

The young man was taken aback, he tilted his face toward her. But she quickly reached his mouth and nearly devoured it.

"Ma'am," said the boy nervously, "please control yourself! Ma'am, are you feeling all right?"

"I can't control myself! I love you! Go to bed with me!"

"Are you crazy?!"

"I'm not crazy! I mean: I'm crazy about you!" she shouted at him as she tore the purple covers off the big bed.

And seeing that he'd never understand, she said to him, dying of shame:

"Go to bed with me …"

"Me?!"

"I'll give you a big present! I'll give you a car!"

Car? The young man's eyes glittered with greed. A car! It was all he desired in life. He asked her suspiciously:

"A Karmann Ghia?"

"Yes, my love, whatever you want!"

What happened next was awful. You don't need to know. Maria Angélica—oh, dear God, have mercy on me, forgive me for having to write this!— Maria Angélica let out little shrieks during their lovemaking. And Alexandre had to stand it feeling nauseated, revolted. He became a rebel for the rest of his life. He had the feeling he'd never be able to sleep with a woman again. Which actually happened: at the age of twenty-seven he became impotent.

And they became lovers. He, on account of the neighbors, didn't live with her. He wanted to live in a luxury hotel: he had breakfast in bed. And soon quit his job. He bought wildly expensive shirts. He went to a dermatologist and his pimples cleared up.

Maria Angélica could hardly believe her luck. What did she care about the servants who practically laughed in her face.

A friend warned her:

"Maria Angélica, can't you see that boy's a gold-digger? that he's using you?"

"I won't let you call Alexandre a gold-digger! And he loves me!"

One day Alex did something bold. He told her:

"I'm going to spend a few days away from Rio with a girl I met. I need some money."

Those were awful days for Maria Angélica. She didn't leave the house, didn't bathe, hardly ate. Only out of stubbornness did she still believe in God. Because God had abandoned her. She was forced to be grievously herself.

Five days later he returned, full of swagger, full of joy. He brought her a tin of guava preserves as a present. She started eating it and broke a tooth. She had to go to the dentist to get a fake tooth put in.

And life went on. The bills were mounting. Alexandre demanding. Maria Angélica anguished. When she turned sixty-one he didn't show. She sat alone before her birthday cake.

Then—then it happened.

Alexandre said to her:

"I need a million cruzeiros."

"A million?" Maria Angélica gasped.

"Yes!" he answered annoyed, "a billion in old cruzeiros!"

"But ... but I don't have that kind of money ..."

"Sell your apartment, then, and sell your Mercedes, get rid of your driver."

"Even so, it wouldn't be enough, my love, have mercy on me!"

The young man lost his temper:

"You miserable old wretch! you slob, you whore! Without a billion, I won't go along with your indecency anymore!"

And in an impulse born of hatred, he left, slamming the door.

Maria Angélica stood there. Her body ached all over.

Then she slowly went to sit on the living-room sofa. She looked like a casualty of war. But there was no Red Cross to rescue her. She sat still, mute. Without a word to say.

"Looks like," she thought, "looks like it's going to rain."

VISION OF SPLENDOR
(*"Visão do esplendor"*)

Brasília

BRASÍLIA IS CONSTRUCTED ON THE LINE OF THE HORI-
zon. Brasília is artificial. As artificial as the world must have
been when it was created. When the world was created, a man
had to be created especially for that world. We are all deformed
by our adaptation to the freedom of God. We don't know how
we would be if we had been created first and the world were
deformed after according to our requirements. Brasília does
not yet have the Brasília man. If I said that Brasília is pretty
they would immediately see that I liked the city. But if I say
that Brasília is the image of my insomnia they would see this as
an accusation. But my insomnia is neither pretty nor ugly, my
insomnia is me myself, it is lived, it is my astonishment. It is a
semicolon. The two architects didn't think of building beauty,
that would be easy: they erected inexplicable astonishment.
Creation is not a comprehension, it is a new mystery. —When
I died, one day I opened my eyes and there was Brasília. I was
alone in the world. There was a parked taxi. Without a driver.
Oh how frightening. —Lúcio Costa and Oscar Niemeyer, two
solitary men. —I regard Brasília as I regard Rome: Brasília began with a final simplification of ruins. The ivy has yet to grow.

Besides the wind there is something else that blows. One can only recognize it by the supernatural rippling of the lake. —Wherever people stand, children might fall, and off the face of the world. Brasília lies at the edge. —If I lived here I would let my hair grow to the ground. —Brasília has a splendored past that now no longer exists. This type of civilization disappeared millennia ago. In the 4th century BC it was inhabited by extremely tall blond men and women who were neither Americans nor Swedes and who sparkled in the sun. They were all blind. That is why in Brasília there is nothing to stumble into. The Brasilianaires dressed in white gold. The race went extinct because few children were born. The more beautiful the Brasilianaires were, the blinder and purer and more sparkling, and the fewer children. The Brasilianaires lived for nearly three hundred years. There was nothing in the name of which to die. Millennia later it was discovered by a band of outcasts who would not have been welcomed anywhere else: they had nothing to lose. There they lit fires, pitched tents, gradually digging away at the sands that buried the city. These were men and women, smaller and dark, with darting and uneasy eyes, and who, being fugitives and desperate, had something in the name of which to live and die. They dwelled in ruined houses, multiplied, establishing a deeply contemplative race of humans. —I waited for nightfall like someone waiting for the shadows so as to steal out. When night fell I realized in horror that it was no use: no matter where I was I would be seen. What terrifies me is: seen by whom? —It was built with no place for rats. A whole part of us, the worst, precisely the one horrified by rats, that part has no place in Brasília. They wished to deny that we are worthless. A construction with space factored in for the clouds. Hell understands me better.

But the rats, all huge, are invading. That is an invisible headline in the newspapers. —Here I am afraid. —The construction of Brasília: that of a totalitarian State. —This great visual
silence that I love. My insomnia too would have created this
peace of the never. I too, like those two who are monks, would
meditate in this desert. Where there's no place for temptation.
But I see in the distance vultures hovering. What could be
dying, my God? —I didn't cry once in Brasília. There was no
place for it. —It is a beach without the sea. —In Brasília there
is no way in, and no way out. —Mama, it's lovely to see you
standing there in that fluttering white cape. (It's because I died,
my son). —An open-air prison. In any case there would be nowhere to escape. Because whoever escapes would probably go
to Brasília. —They imprisoned me in freedom. But freedom
is only what can be conquered. When they grant it to me, they
are ordering me to be free. —A whole side of human coldness
that I possess, I encounter in myself here in Brasília, and it
blossoms ice-cold, potent, ice-cold force of Nature. This is the
place where my crimes (not the worst, but those I won't ever
understand in myself), where my ice-cold crimes find space. I
am leaving. Here my crimes would not be those of love. I am
leaving on behalf of my other crimes, those that God and I
comprehend. But I know I shall return. I am drawn here by
whatever frightens me in myself. —I have never seen anything
like it in the world. But I recognize this city in the furthest
depths of my dream. The furthest depths of my dream is a
lucidity. —Well as I was saying, Flash Gordon ... —If they
took my picture standing in Brasília, when they developed
the photograph only the landscape would appear. —Where
are Brasília's giraffes? —A certain cringing of mine, certain silences, make my son say: gosh, grown-ups are the worst. —It's

urgent. If it doesn't get populated, or rather, overpopulated, it will be too late: there will be no place for people. They will feel tacitly expelled. —The soul here casts no shadow on the ground. —For the first couple of days I wasn't hungry. Everything looked to me like airplane food. —At night I reached my face toward the silence. I know there is a hidden hour when manna descends and moistens the lands of Brasília. —No matter how close one gets, everything here is seen from afar. I couldn't find a way to touch. But at least I had this in my favor: before I got here, I already knew how to touch from afar. I never got too discouraged: from afar, I would touch. I've had a lot, and not even what I touched, you know. That's how rich women are. Pure Brasília. —The city of Brasília lies beyond the city. —*Boys, boys, come here, will you, look who is coming on the street all dressed up in modernistic style. It ain't nobody but ... (Aunt Hagar's Blues, Ted Lewis and His Band, with Jimmy Dorsey on the clarinet.)* —That frightening beauty, this city, drawn up in the air. —For now no samba can spring up in Brasília. —Brasília doesn't let me get tired. It pursues a little. Feeling good, feeling good, feeling good, I'm in a good mood. And after all I have always cultivated my weariness, as my richest passivity. —All this is just today. Only God knows what will happen in Brasília. Because here chance is abrupt. —Brasília is haunted. It is the still profile of a thing. —In my insomnia I look out the hotel window at three in the morning. Brasília is the landscape of insomnia. It never falls asleep. —Here the organic being does not decompose. It is petrified. —I would like to see scattered through Brasília five hundred thousand eagles of the blackest onyx. —Brasília is asexual. —The First instant of seeing is like a certain instant of drunkenness: your feet don't touch the ground. —How deeply we breathe in Brasília. Whoever breathes starts to desire. And to desire is what one cannot do. There isn't any. Will there ever be? The thing is, I am not seeing where. —I wouldn't be shocked to run into Arabs in the street. Arabs, ancient and dead. —Here my passion dies. And I gain a lucidity that leaves me grandiose for no reason. I am fabulous and useless, I am made of pure gold. And almost psychic. —If there is any crime humanity has yet to commit, that new crime will be inaugurated here. And so hardly kept secret, so well-suited to the high plain, that no one would ever know. —Here is the place where space most resembles time. —I am sure this is my rightful place. But the thing is, I am too addicted to the land. I have bad life habits. —Erosion will strip Brasília to the bone. —The religious atmosphere I felt from the first instant, and that I denied. This city has been achieved through prayer. Two men beatified by solitude created me standing here, restless, alone, out in this wind. —Brasília badly needs roaming white horses. At night they would be green in the moonlight. —I know what the two wanted: slowness and silence, which is also my idea of eternity. The two created the picture of an eternal city. —There is something here that frightens me. When I figure out what it is that frightens me, I shall also know what I love here. Fear has always guided me toward what I desire. And because I desire, I fear. Often it was fear that took me by the hand and led me. Fear leads me to danger. And everything I love is risky. —In Brasília are the craters of the Moon. —The beauty of Brasília is its invisible statues.

I went to Brasília in 1962. What I wrote about it is what you have just read. And now I have returned twelve years later for two days. And I wrote about it too. So here is everything I vomited up.

Warning: I am about to begin.

This piece is accompanied by Strauss's "Vienna Blood" waltz. It's 11:20 on the morning of the 13th.

BRASÍLIA: SPLENDOR

Brasília is an abstract city. And there is no way to make it concrete. It is a rounded city with no corners. Neither does it have any neighborhood bars for people to get a cup of coffee. It's true, I swear I didn't see any corners. In Brasília the everyday does not exist. The cathedral begs God. It is two hands held open to receive. But Niemeyer is an ironic man: he has ironized life. It is sacred. Brasília does not allow the diminutive. Brasília is a joke, strictly perfect and without error. And the only thing that saves me is error.

The São Bosco church has such splendid stained glass that I fell silent seated on the pew, not believing it was real. Moreover the age we are passing through is fantastical, it is blue and yellow, and scarlet and emerald. My God, but what wealth. The stained glass holds light made of organ music. This church thus illuminated is nevertheless inviting. The only flaw is the unusual circular chandelier that looks like some nouveau riche thing. The church would have been pure without the chandelier. But what can you do? go at night, in the dark, and steal it?

Then I went to the National Library. A young Russian girl named Kira helped me. I saw young men and women studying and flirting: something totally compatible. And praiseworthy, of course.

I pause for a moment to say that Brasília is a tennis court.

There is a reinvigorating chill there. What hunger, but what hunger. I asked if the city had a lot of crime. I was told that in the suburb of Grama (is that its name?) there are about three homicides per week. (I interrupted the crimes to eat). The light of Brasília left me blind. I forgot my sunglasses at the hotel and was invaded by a terrible white light. But Brasília is red. And is completely naked. There is no way for people not to be exposed in that city. Although the air is unpolluted: you can breathe well, a little too well, your nose gets dry.

Naked Brasília leaves me beatified. And crazy. In Brasília I have to think in parentheses. Will they arrest me for living? That's exactly it.

I am no more than phrases overheard by chance. On the street, while crossing through traffic, I heard: "It was out of necessity." And at the Roxy Cinema, in Rio de Janeiro, I heard two fat women saying: "In the morning she slept and at night she woke up." "She has no stamina." In Brasília I have stamina, whereas in Rio I am sort of languid, sort of sweet. And I heard the following phrase from the same fat women who were short: "Just what does she have to go do over there?" And that, my dears, is how I got expelled.

Brasília has euphoria in the air. I said to the driver of the yellow cab: today seems like Monday, doesn't it? "Yep," he answered. And nothing more was said. I wanted so badly to tell him I had been to the utterly adored Brasília. But he didn't want to hear it. Sometimes I'm too much.

Then I went to the dentist, got that, Brasília? I take care of myself. Should I read odontology journals just became I'm in the dentist's waiting room? After I sat in the dentist's magnificent death chair, electric chair, and saw a machine looking at me, called "Atlas 200." It looked in vain, since I had no cavities. Brasília has no cavities. A powerful land, that one. And it doesn't mess around. It bets high and plays to win. Merquior and I burst into howls of laughter that are still echoing back to me in Rio. I have been irremediably impregnated by Brasília.

I prefer the Carioca entanglement. I was delicately pampered in Brasília but scared to death of reading my lecture. (Here I note an event that astonishes me: I am writing in the past, present and future. Am I being levitated? Brasília suffers from levitation.) I throw myself into each one, I'm telling you. But it is good because it is risky. Believe it or not: as I was reading the words, I was praying inwardly. But, again, it is good because it is risky. Now I wonder: if there are no corners, where do the prostitutes stand smoking? do they sit on the ground? And the beggars? do they have cars? because there you can only get around by car.

The light in Brasília sometimes leads to ecstasy and total plenitude. But it is also aggressive and harsh—ah, how I would like the shade of a tree. Brasília has trees. But they have yet to be convincing. They look plastic.

I am now going to write something of the utmost importance: Brasília is the failure of the most spectacular success in the world. Brasília is a splattered star. It takes my breath away. It is beautiful and it is naked. The lack of shame one has in solitude. At the same time I was embarrassed to undress for a shower. As if a gigantic green eye were staring at me, implacable. Moreover Brasília is implacable. I felt as if someone were pointing at me: as if they could arrest me or take away my papers, my identity, my veracity, my last private breath. Oh what if the Radio Patrol catches me and beats me up! then I'll say the worst word in the Portuguese language: *sovaco*, armpit. And they'll drop dead. But for you, my love, I am more delicate and softly say: *axilas*, underarms ...

Brasília smells like toothpaste. And whoever's not married,

loves without passion. They simply have sex. But I want to return, I want to try to decipher its enigma. I want especially to talk with university students. I want them to invite me to participate in this aridness, luminous and full of stars. Does anyone ever die in Brasília? No. Never. No one ever dies because there you cannot close your eyes. There they have hibernation: the air leaves a person in a stupor for years, who later comes back to life. The climate is challenging and whips people a bit. But Brasília needs magic, it needs voodoo. I don't want Brasília to put a curse on me: because it would work. I pray. I pray a lot. Oh what a good God. Everything there is out in the open and whoever wants it has to deal with it. Though the rats adore the city. I wonder what they eat? ah, I know: they eat human flesh. I escaped as best I could. And seemed to be remotely controlled.

I gave countless interviews. They changed what I said. I no longer give interviews. And if the whole business really is based on invading my privacy, then they should pay for it. They say that's how it's done in the United States. And another thing: there's one price just for me, but if my precious dog gets included, I charge extra. If they distort me, I charge a fine. Sorry, I have no wish to humiliate anyone but I have no wish to be humiliated. While there I said I might go to Colombia and they wrote that I was going to Bolivia. They switched the country for no reason. But there's no danger: all I concede about my own life is that I have two sons. I am not important, I am an average person who wants a little anonymity. I hate giving interviews. Come on, I am a woman who's simple and a tiny bit sophisticated. A mix of peasant and a star in the sky.

I adore Brasília. Is that contradictory? But what isn't contradictory? People only go down the deserted streets by car.

When I had a car and drove, I was always getting lost. I never knew where I was coming from and where I was going. I am disoriented in life, in art, in time and in space. Unbelievable, for God's sake.

There people have dinner and lunch together—it is to have people to populate them. This is good and very pleasant. It is the slow humanization of a city that for some hidden reason is arduous. I really enjoyed it, they pampered me so much in Brasília. But there were some people who wanted me gone in a flash. I was tripping up their routine. For those people I was an inconvenient novelty. Living is dramatic. But there is no escaping it: we are born.

What will a person born in Brasília be like when he grows up and becomes a man? Because the city is inhabited by nostalgic outsiders. Exiles. Those born there will be the future. A future sparkling like steel. If I am still alive, I shall applaud the strange and highly novel product that will emerge. Will smoking be banned? Will everything be banned, my God? Brasília seems like an inauguration. Every day it is inaugurated. Festivities, my dears, festivities. Let them raise the flags.

Who wants me in Brasília? So whoever wants me can call me. Not just yet, because I am still stunned. But in a while. At your service. Brasília is at your service. I want to speak with the hotel maid who said to me when she found out who I was: I wanted to write so badly! I said: go on, woman, and write. She answered: but I've already suffered too much. I said severely: so go ahead and write about what you've suffered.

Because there needs to be someone crying in Brasília. The eyes of its inhabitants are much too dry. In that case—in that case I am volunteering to cry. My maid and I, we, girlfriends. She told me: when I saw you ma'am, I got goose bumps on my arm. She told me she was a psychic.

Yes. I've got goose bumps. And I am shivering. God help me. I am mute like a moon.

Brasília is full-time. I have a panicked fear of it. It is the ideal place for taking a sauna. Sauna? Yes. Because there you don't know what to do with yourself. I look down, I look up, I look around—and the reply is a howl: noooooooo! Brasília stupefies us so much it's scary. Why do I feel so guilty there? what did I do wrong? and why haven't they erected right in the city center a great white Egg? It is because there is no center. But it needs the Egg.

What kind of clothes do people wear in Brasília? Metallic? Brasília is my martyrdom. And it has no nouns. It's all adjectives. And how it hurts. Ah, my dear little God, grant me just one little noun, for God's sake! Ah, you don't want to? then pretend I didn't say anything. I know how to lose.

Oh stewardess, try to give me a less numbered smile. Is that the sandwich we're supposed to eat? all dehydrated? But I'll do like Sérgio Porto: I heard that on a plane a stewardess once asked him: can I offer you some coffee, sir? And he answered: I'll take everything I have a right to.

In Brasília it is never night. It is always implacably day. Punishment? But what did I do wrong, my God? I don't want to hear it, He says, punishment is punishment.

In Brasília there is practically nowhere to drop dead. But there is one thing: Brasília is pure protein. Didn't I say that Brasília is a tennis court? Because Brasília is blood on a tennis court. And as for me? where am I? me? poor me, with my scarlet-stained handkerchief. Do I kill myself? No. I live in brute reply. I am right there for whoever wants me.

But Brasília is the opposite sound. And no one denies that Brasília is: goooooooooal! Though it slightly warps the samba. Who is that? who is that singing hallelujah and whom I hear with joy? Who is it that traverses, like the sharpest of swords, the future and always future city of Brasília? I repeat: pure protein, you are. You have fertilized me. Or am I the one singing? Listening to myself I am moved. There's Brasília in the air. In the air unfortunately lacking the indispensable support of corners for people to live. Have I already mentioned that nobody lives in Brasília? they reside. Brasília is bone dried out from pure astonishment under the merciless sun on the beach. Ah white horse but what a rustic mane. Oh, I can't wait any longer. A little airplane, please. And the ashen moonlight that enters the room and watches me, I, pale, white, cunning.

I don't have a corner. My transistor radio isn't picking up any music. What's wrong? Not that way either. Do I repeat myself? And does it hurt?

For the love of Cod, (I was so startled I even mixed up the word God) for the love of God, please forgive me those of you who reside in Brasília for saying what I am forced to say, I, a lowly slave to the truth. I do not mean to offend anyone. It is just that the light is too white. I have sensitive eyes, I am invaded by the stark brightness and all that red land.

Brasília is a future that happened in the past.

Eternal as a stone. The light of Brasília—am I repeating myself?—the light of Brasília wounds my feminine modesty. That is all, people, that is all.

Aside from that, long live Brasília! I will help hoist the flag. And I will forgive the slap I got in my poor face. Oh, poor little me. So motherless. It is our duty to have a mother. It is a thing of nature. I am in favor of Brasília.

In the year 2000 there will be a celebration there. If I am still alive, I want to join in the revelry. Brasília is an exaggerated general revelry. A little hysterical, it's true, but that's fine.

Bursts of laughter in the dark hallway. I laugh, you laugh, he laughs. Three.

In Brasília there are no lampposts for dogs to pee on. It badly needs a peepee-dog. But Brasília is a gem, dear sir. There everything works as it should. Brasília envelops me in gold. I'm off to the hairdresser. I'm talking about Rio. Hello, Rio! Hello! Hello! I really am frightened. God help me.

But there comes a time when I'll tell you, my friend, there comes a time when Brasília is a hair in your soup. I am very busy, Brasília, to hell with you and leave me alone. Brasília is located nowhere. Its atmosphere is indignation and you know why. Brasília: before being born it was already born, the premature, the unborn, the fetus, in a word me. Oh the nerve.

Not just anyone can enter Brasília, no. You need nobility, lots of shamelessness and lots of nobility. Brasília is not. It is merely the picture of itself. I love you, oh extragantic one! oh word I invented and do not know the meaning of. Oh furuncle! crystallized pus but whose? Warning: there's sperm in the air.

I, the scribe. I, fated to be the unfortunate definer. Brasília is the opposite of Bahia. Bahia is buttocks. Ah how I long for the soaked Place Vendôme. Ah, how I long for the Praça Maciel Pinheiro in Recife. So much poverty of soul. And you demand it of me. I, who can do nothing. Ah how I long for my dog. Such a dear friend. But a newspaper took his picture and he was standing at the end of the street. He and I. We, little brother and sister of St. Francis of Assisi. Let us be silent: it is better for us.

I'm going to get you, Brasília! And you'll suffer terrible torture at my hands! You annoy me, o ice-cold Brasília, pearl among swine. Oh apocalyptic one.

And suddenly the big disgrace. All that racket. Why? Nobody knows. Oh God, how did I not see it right away? because isn't Brasília "Women's Health"? Brasília can't figure out what it wants: it's a tease. Brasília is a chipped tooth right in front. And it is the summit too. There is one main reason. What is it? secrets, lots of secrets, murmurs, whispers and whisps. Rumors that never end.

Healthy, healthy. Here I am a physical education teacher. I go tumbling. That's right: I raise hell. Brasília is a heavenly hell. It is a typewriter: click-click-click. I want to sleep! leave me alone!!! I am ti-i-red. Of being in-com-pre-hen-si-ble. But I do not want to be understood because I will lose my sacred intimacy. It is very serious, what I am saying, very serious indeed: Brasília is the ghost of an old blind man with a cane going click-click-click. And with no dog, poor guy. And me? how can I help? Brasília helps itself. It is a high-high-high-pitched violin. It needs a cello. But what a racket. This was surely uncalled for. I guarantee it. Though Brasília has no guarantor.

I want to return to Brasília to Room 700. So I can dot the "i." But Brasília does not flow. It goes in the opposite direction. Like this: wolf (flow).

It is mad yet functional. How I hate the word "yet." I only use it because it's needed.

When night falls Brasília becomes Zebedee. Brasília is a round-the-clock pharmacy.

The girl frisked me all over at the airport. I asked: do I look like a subversive? She said laughing: actually you do. I have never been so thoroughly felt up, Holy Mary, it's practically a sin. Her hands patted me down so much I don't know how I could stand it.

Brasília is slim. And utterly elegant. It wears a wig and false eyelashes. It is a scroll inside a Pyramid. It does not age. It is Coca-Cola, my God, and will outlive me. Too bad. For Coca-

Cola, of course. Help! Help! *help me!* Do you know how Brasília answers my cry for help? It is formal: may I offer you some coffee? And what about me? don't I get any help? Treat me well, got it? like that ... like that ... nice and slow. That's it. That's it. What a relief. Happiness, my dear, is relief. Brasília is a kick in the rear. It is a place where the Portuguese get rich. And what about me, who plays the lottery and doesn't win?

Oh what a pretty nose Brasília has. So delicate.

Did you know that Brasília is etc.? Well now you know. Brasília is XPTR ... as many consonants as you like but not a single vowel to give you a break. And Brasília, well dear sir, sorry, but Brasília left off right there.

Look, Brasília, I'm not just anyone, not at all. Show more respect, do me the favor. I am a space traveler. I demand lots of respect. Lots of Shakespeare. Ah but I don't want to die! Oh, what a sigh. But Brasília is waiting. And I can't stand waiting. Blue phantom. Ah, how annoying. It's like trying to remember and not being able to. I want to forget Brasília but it won't let me. What a dried-up wound. Gold. Brasília is gold. A gem. Sparkling. There are things about Brasília that I know but can't say, they won't let me. Guess.

And may God help me.

Go ahead, woman, go and fulfill your destiny, woman. Being the woman I am is a duty. Right this instant-now I am hoisting the flags—but what a fierce southern wind!—and here I am saying hurrah!

Oh I am so tired.

In Brasília it is always Sunday. But now I am going to speak very softly. Like this: my love. My great love. Have I said it? You're the one who answers. I am going to end with the most beautiful word in the world. Nice and slow like this: my love how I have longed for you. L-o-v-e. I kiss you. Like a flower. Mouth to mouth. How bold. And now—now peace. Peace and life. I-am a-live. Maybe I don't deserve so much. I am afraid. But I don't want to end with fear. Ecstasy. *Yes, my love.* I surrender. Yes. *Pour toujours.* Everything—but everything is absolutely natural. *Yes.* I. But above all you are the guilty one, Brasília. However, I pardon you. It's not your fault you're so lovely and pitiful and poignant and mad. Yes, a wind of Justice is blowing. So I say to the Great Natural Law: yes. Hey cracked mirror: who is prettier than me? No one, the magic mirror replies. Yes, I am well aware, it's us two. Yes! yes! yes! I said yes.

I call humbly for help. They're robbing me. Am I the whole world? General astonishment. This isn't a high wind, sir, it's a tornado. I am in Rio. I finally got off the flying saucer. And a friend comes up saying—hello there Carmen Miranda!—telling me there's a song called "Tar Baby Doll" that goes more or less like this: here I come all pinched with my aching corns, almost choking in my tight collar, to see my baby.

I have landed. My voice is weak but I will say what Brasília wants me to: bravo! bravíssimo! And that is enough. Now I am going to live in Rio with my dog. Please do me the favor of remaining silent. Like this: si-lence. I am so sad.

Brasília is a wildly twinkling blue eye that burns in my heart.

Brasília is Malta. Where is Malta? It's in the day of the super-never. Hello! hello! Malta! Today it's Sunday in New York. In Brasília, the gleaming one, it's already Tuesday. Brasília just skips Monday. Monday is the day you go to the dentist, what can you do, boring things have to get done too, woe is me. In Brasília I bet they're still dancing, unbelievable. It's six-twenty in the evening, almost night. At 6:20 nothing happens. Hello! Hello! Brasília! I want an answer, I'm in a hurry, I have just come to terms with my death. I am sad. The stride is too big for my legs though they are long. Help me die in peace. As I may have said, I want a beloved hand to hold mine when it is time for me to go. I go under protest. I. The phantasmagoric one. My name does not exist. What exists is a picture faked from another picture of me. But the real one died already. I died on the ninth of June. Sunday. After lunch in the precious company of those I love. I had roast chicken. I am happy. But lack true death. I am in a hurry to see God. Pray for me. I died elegantly.

I have a virgin soul and therefore need protection. Who will help me? The paroxysm of Chopin. Only you can help me. Deep down I am alone. There are truths I haven't even told God. And not even myself. I am a secret under the lock of seven keys. Please spare me. I am so alone. I and my rituals. The phone doesn't ring. It hurts. But God is the one who spares me. Amen.

Did you know that I can speak the language of dogs and also of plants? Amen. But my word is not the last. There exists one I cannot utter. And my tale is gallant. I am an anonymous letter. I do not sign the things I write. Let other people sign. I do not have the credentials. Me? But me of all people? Never! I need a father. Who will volunteer? No, I do not need a father, I need my equal. I am waiting for death. Oh such wind, dear sir. Wind is a thing you cannot see. I ask Our Lord God Jehovah about his wrath in the form of wind. Only He can explain. Or can he? If He cannot, I am lost. Oh how I love you and I love so much that I die you.

Remember how I mentioned the tennis court with blood? Well the blood was mine, the scarlet, the clotting was mine.

Brasília is a horse race. No I am not a horse. Brasília can go to hell and run by itself without me.

Brasília is hyperbolic. I am suspended until the final order. I survive by being as stubborn as I am. I have landed indeed. *There is no place like home.* How good it is to be back. Leaving is good but coming back is more better. That's right: more better.

What is supplementary in Brasília? No I don't know, dear sir. All I know is that all is nothing and nothing is all. My dog is sleeping. I am my dog. I call myself Ulisses. We are both tired. So, so tired. Woe is me, woe is us. Silence. You should sleep too. Ah astonished city. It astonishes itself. I am feeling stale. What I'll do is complain like Chopin complained about the invasion of Poland. After all I have my rights. I am I, that's what other people say. And if they say so, why not believe it? Farewell. I'm fed up. I'm going to complain. I'm going to complain to God. And if He can, let him heed me. I am one of the needy. I left Brasília with a cane. Today is Sunday. Even God rested. God is a funny thing: He can do it all for Himself and needs Himself.

I came home, it is true, but wouldn't you know my cook writes literature? I asked her where the Coca-Cola in the fridge was. She answered, lovely black girl that she is: she was just so tired, so I made her go rest, poor thing. Once, ages ago I recounted to Paulo Mendes Campos a comment my maid at the time had made. And he wrote something like this: everyone gets the maid they deserve: My maid has a beautiful voice and sings to me when I ask her to: "Nobody Loves Me." She draws, she writes. I am so humbled. For I don't deserve this much.

I am nothing. I am a frustrated Sunday. Or am I being ungrateful? Much has been given me, much has been taken away. Who wins? Not me that's for sure. Someone hyperbolic does.

Brasília, be a little bit animal too. It's so nice. So very nice. Not having peepee-dogs is an affront to my dog who will never go to Brasília for obvious reasons. It's a quarter to six. No particular time. Even Kissinger is asleep. Or is he on a plane? There's no way to guess. Happy birthday, Kissinger. Happy birthday, Brasília. Brasília is a mass suicide. Brasília, are you scratching yourself? not me, I don't go in for that kind of thing because whoever starts won't stop from. You know the rest.

The rest is paroxysm.

No one knows it, but my dog not only smokes but also drinks coffee and eats flowers. And drinks beer. He also takes antidepressants. He resembles a little mulatto. What he needs is a girlfriend. He's middle class. I didn't let the newspaper in on everything. But now it's time for the truth. You too should have the courage to read. The only thing this dog doesn't do is write. He eats pens and shreds paper. Better than I do. He is my animal son. He was born of the instantaneous contact between the Moon and a mare. Mare of the Sun. He is a thing Brasília is not. He is: an animal. I am an animal. I really want to repeat myself, just to annoy people.

My God, I've gone back in time. It's exactly twenty to six. And I answer the typewriter: yes. The monstrous typewriter. It's a telescope. Such wind. Is it a tornado? It is.

Oh what a place to look pretty. Today is Monday, the tenth. As you can see, I didn't die. I am going to the dentist. A dangerous week, this one. I am telling the truth. Not the whole truth, as I said. And if God knows it, that's His business. Let him deal with it. I don't know how but I am going to deal as best I can. Like a cripple. Living for free is what you cannot do. Pay to live? I am living on borrowed time. Just like that mutt Ulisses. As for me, I think that.

How embarrassing. It is my case of public embarrassment. I have three bison in my life. One plus one plus one plus one plus one. The fourth kills me in Malta. In fact the seventh is the shiniest. Bison, if you didn't know, are cave-dwelling animals. I perform my stories. Human warmth. Fearless city, that one. God is the hour. I am going to last a while yet. No one is immortal. Just see if you can find someone who doesn't die.

I died. I died murdered by Brasília. I died to pursue research. Pray for me because I died on my back.

Look, Brasília, I left. And God help me. It's because I am slightly before. That's all. I swear to God. And I am slightly after too. What can you do. Brasília is broken glass on the street. Shards. Brasília is a dentist's metal tool. And very motorcycle too. Which doesn't stop it from being mullet roe, fried up with plenty of salt. I just happen to be so eager for life, I want so much from it and I take advantage of it so much and everything is so much—that I become immoral. That's right: I am immoral. How nice to be unsuitable for those eighteen and under.

Brasília exercises every day at 5 a.m. The Bahians there are the only ones who don't go in for that kind of thing. They write poetry.

Brasília is the mystery categorized in steel filing cabinets. Everything there is categorized. And me? who am I? how have they categorized me? Have they given me a number? I feel numbered, and constricted all over. I barely fit inside myself. I am just a little me, very unimportant. But with a certain class.

Being happy is such a great responsibility. Brasília is happy. It has the nerve. What will become of Brasília in the year, let us say, 3000? How big a pile of bones. No one remembers the future because it's not possible. The authorities won't allow it.

And me, who am I? Out of pure fear I obey the most insignificant soldier who stands before me and says: you're under arrest. Oh I'm going to cry. I am barely. *On the verge of.*

It's becoming clear that I don't know how to describe Brasília. It is Jupiter. It is a word well chosen. It is too grammatical for my taste. And the worst thing is it demands grammar *but I don't know, sir, I don't know the rules.*

Brasília is an airport. The loudspeakers coldly and courteously announce the departing flights.

What else? the thing is, no one knows what to do in Brasília. The only ones who do anything are the people who work like crazy, who make babies like crazy and get together like crazy to dine on the finest delicacies.

I stayed at the Hotel Nacional. Room 800. And drank Coca-Cola in my room. I am constantly—fool that I am—giving away free advertising.

At seven in the evening I will speak just superficially about avant-garde Brazilian literature, since I am not a critic. God spare me from critiquing. I have a morbid fear of facing people who are listening to me. Electrified. Speaking of which Brasília is electrified and a computer. I am definitely going to read too fast so I can get through it quickly. I will be introduced to the audience by José Guilherme Merquior. Merquior is much too wholesome. I feel honored and at the same time so humble. After all, who am I to face a demanding public? I'll do what I can. Once I gave a talk at the Catholic University and Affonso Romano de Sant'Anna, I don't know what got into that fabulous critic, asked me a question: does two plus two equal five? For a second I was speechless. But then a darkly humorous anecdote sprang to mind: It goes like this: the psychotic says that two plus two equals five. The neurotic says: two plus two equals four but I just can't take it. Then there was laughter and everyone relaxed.

Tomorrow I return to Rio, turbulent city of my loves. I like to fly: I love speed. With Vicente I got him to zip around Brasília very fast by car. I sat beside him and we talked a lot. See you later: I'm going to read while waiting to be picked up for the conference. In Brasília you feel like looking pretty. I felt like getting all done up. Brasília is risky and I love risk. It's an adventure: it brings me face to face with the unknown. I'm going to speak words. Words have nothing to do with sensations. Words are hard stones and sensations are ever so delicate, fleeting, extreme. Brasília became humanized. Only I can't stand those rounded streets, that vital lack of corners. There, even the sky, is rounded. The clouds are agnus dei. Brasília's air is so *dry* that the skin on your face gets dry, your hands rough.

The dentist's machine called "Atlas 200" says this to me: tchi! tchi! tchi! Today is the 14th. Fourteen leaves me suspended. Brasília is fifteen point one. Rio is one, but a tiny one. Doesn't Atlas 200 ever die? No, it doesn't. It is like me when I am hibernating in Brasília.

Brasília is an orange construction crane fishing out something very delicate: a small white egg. Is that white egg me or a little child born today?

I feel like people are working voodoo on me: who wants to steal my poor identity? All I'll do is this: I'll ask for help and have some coffee. Then I'll smoke. Oh how I smoked and smoked in Brasília! Brasília is a Hollywood-brand filtered cigarette. Brasília is like this: right now I am listening to the sound of the key in the front door lock. A mystery? A mystery, yes sir. I go open it and guess who it was? it was nobody. Brasília is somebody, red carpet, tails and a top hat.

Brasília is a pair of stainless steel scissors. I save what I can to make ends meet. And I have already drawn up my will. I say a bunch of things in it.

Brasília is the sound of ice cubes in a glass of whiskey, at six in the evening, the hour of nobody.

Do you want me to tell Brasília: here's to you? I say here's to you with the glass in my hand. In Rio, in my pantry, I killed a mosquito that was quivering in midair. Why this right to kill? It was merely a flying atom. Never will I forget that mosquito whose destiny I plotted, I, the one without a destiny.

I am tired, listening at dawn to the Ministry of Education that also comes from Brasília. Right now I am listening to the Blue Danube in whose waters I recline, serious and alert.

Brasília is science fiction. Brasília is Ceará turned inside out: both bruising and conquering.

And it is a chorus of children on an incredibly blue, super cold morning, the kids opening their little round mouths and intoning an utterly innocent Te Deum, accompanied by organ music. I wish this would happen in the stained glass church at 7 in the evening. Or 7 in the morning. I prefer morning, since twilight in Brasília is more beautiful than the involuntary sunset in Porto Alegre. Brasília is a first place on the university entrance exams. I'm happy with just a little ol' second place.

I see that I wrote seven as a numeral: 7. Well Brasília is 7. It's 3. It's four. It's eight, nine—I'm skipping the others, and at 13 I meet God.

The problem is that blank paper demands I write. I'll go ahead and write. Alone in the world, high on a hill. I would like to conduct an orchestra, but they say women can't because they don't have the physical stamina. Ah, Schubert, sweeten up Brasília a little. I'm so good to Brasília.

Right this instant-now it's ten to seven. *Me muero.* Make yourself at home, dear sir, and the service I offer is deluxe. Whoever wants to can live it up. Brasília is a five-hundred-cruzeiro bill that nobody wants to break. And the number 1 penny? that one I insist on keeping for myself. It's so rare. It brings good luck. And it brings privileges. Five hundred cruzeiros go down my throat.

Brasília is different. Brasília is inviting. And if invited, I'll attend. Brasília uses a diamond-studded cigarette holder.

But it is common for people to say: I want money and I want to die suddenly. Even me. But St. Francis took off all his clothes and went naked. He and my dog Ulisses ask for nothing. Brasília is a pact I made with God.

All I ask is one favor, Brasília, of you: don't take up speaking Esperanto. Don't you see that words get distorted in Esperanto as in a badly translated translation? *Yes, my Lord. I said yes, sir. I almost said: my love,* instead of *my Lord. But my love is my Lord. There is no answer? O.K., I can stand It.* But how it hurts. It hurts so much to be offended by not getting a reply. I can take it. But don't anyone step on my feet because that hurts. And I am on familiar terms, I go by my first name, don't stand on ceremony. It'll go like this: I address you as honorable sir and you use my first name. You are so gallant, Brasília.

Does Brasília have a botanical garden? and does it have a zoo? It needs them, because people cannot live on man alone. Having animals around is essential.

Where is your tragic opera, Brasília? I won't accept operettas, they are too nostalgic, lead soldiers are what I used to play with, despite being a girl. The blues gently shatters my heart that even so is as hot as the blues itself.

Brasília is Physical Law. Relax, ma'am, take off your girdle, don't get flustered, have a little sip of sugar water—and then see what it's like to be Natural Law a little. You'll love it, ma'am. Does there happen to exist a course of study called Course on the Existence of Time? Well it should.

Well didn't they pour bleach on the ground in Brasília. Well they did: to disinfect. But I am, thank God, thoroughly infected. But I had my lungs x-rayed and said to the doctor: my lungs must be black from smoke. He answered: well actually they aren't, they're nice and clear.

And so it goes on. I am suddenly silent and have nothing to say. Respect my silence. I don't paint, no ma'am, I write and do I ever.

In Brasília I didn't dream. Could it be my fault or does no one dream in Brasília? And that hotel maid? what became of her? I too have suffered, you hear, maid-woman? Suffering is the privilege of those who feel. But now I am sheer joy. It's almost six in the morning. I got up at four. I am wide awake. Brasília is wide awake. Pay attention to what I am saying: Brasília will never end. I die and Brasília remains. With new people, of course. Brasília is hot off the press.

Brasília is the Wedding March. The groom is a northeasterner who eats up the whole cake because he's gone hungry for several generations. The bride is a widowed old lady, rich and cranky. From this unusual wedding that I witnessed, forced by circumstances, I left defeated by the violence of the Wedding March that sounded like a Military March and commanded me to get married too and I don't want to. I left covered in Band-Aids, my ankle twisted, my neck aching and a big wound aching in my heart.

Everything I have said is true. Or it is symbolic. But what difficult syntax Brasília has! The fortuneteller said I would go to Brasília. She knows everything, Dona Nadir, from Méier.

Brasília is an eyelid fluttering like the yellow butterfly I saw a few days ago on the corner near my house. Yellow butterflies are a good omen. Geckos say neither yes nor no. But S. has a fear of geckos who are shedding their skin. What I am more afraid of are rats. At the Hotel Nacional they guaranteed they didn't have rats. So, in that case, I stayed. With a guarantee, I often stay.

Working is fate. Look, *Jornal de Brasília*, you better include astrology in your paper. After all, we need to know where we stand. I am completely magical and my aura is bright blue just like the sweet stained glass in the church I mentioned. Everything I touch, is born.

It is daybreak here in Rio. A lovely and cold dry morning. How nice that all nights have radiant mornings. Brasília's horoscope is dazzling. And whoever wants to, let them bear it.

It's a quarter to six. I write while listening to music. Anything will do, I'm not difficult. What I was hoping to hear right now was a really astringent fado sung by Amália Rodrigues in Lisbon. Ah how I long for Capri. I suffered so much in Capri. But I forgave it. It's all right: Capri, like Brasília, is beautiful. I do feel sorry for Brasília because it doesn't have the sea. But the salt wind is in the air. I detest swimming in a pool. Swimming in the sea breeds courage. A few days ago I went to the beach and entered the sea feeling moved. I drank seven gulps of saltwater from the sea. The water was chilly, gentle, with little waves that were also agnus dei. I am letting you know that I am going to buy an old-fashioned felt hat, with a small crown and upturned brim. And also a green crocheted shawl. Brasília isn't crochet, it is a knit made by special machines that don't make errors. But, as I said, I am pure error. And I have a left-handed soul. I get all tangled in emerald-green crochet, I get all tangled. To protect myself. Green is the color of hope. And Tuesday could be a disaster. On my last Tuesday I cried because I had been wronged. But in general Tuesdays are good. As for Thursday, it is sweet and a little bit sad. Laugh all you want, clown, as your house catches fire. *Mais tout va très bien, madame la Marquise.* Except.

Could there be fauns in Brasília? That settles it: what I'll do is buy a green hat to match my shawl. Or should I not buy one at all? I am so indecisive. Brasília is decision. Brasília is a man. And I, such a woman. I go bumbling along. I stumble into something here, I stumble into something there. And arrive at last.

The song I am listening to now is completely pure and free of guilt. Debussy. With cool little waves in the sea.

Does Brasília have gnomes?

My house in Rio is full of them. All fantastic. Try just one gnome and you'll be hooked. Elves also do the trick. Dwarves? I feel sorry for them.

I've settled it: I don't need a hat at all. Or do I? My God, what shall become of me? Brasília, save me for I am in need of it.

One day I was a child just like Brasília. And I so badly wanted a carrier pigeon. To send letters to Brasília. Does anyone get them? yes or no?

I am innocent and ignorant. And when I am in writing mode, I don't read. That would be too much for me, I don't have the strength.

I was on the plane with an older Portuguese gentleman, a businessman of some sort, but very genteel: he carried my heavy suitcase. On the way back from Brasília I sat next to an older gentleman who was such a good conversationalist, we had such a good conversation, that I said: it's incredible how fast the time went and now we're here. He said: the time went fast for me too. I'll see that man some day. He's going to teach me. He knows a lot of things.

I am so lost. But that is exactly how we live: lost in time and space.

I am scared to death of appearing before a Judge. Your Most Esteemed Honor, may I have permission to smoke? Yes, indeed ma'am, I myself smoke a pipe. Thank you, Your Eminence. I treat the Judge well, a Judge is Brasília. But I won't sue Brasília. It hasn't wronged me.

We are in the middle of the world cup. There is an African country that is poor and ignorant and lost to Yugoslavia 9 to zero. But their ignorance is different: I heard that in that country the black boys either win or they die. Such helplessness.

I know how to die. I have been dying since I was little. And it hurts but we pretend it doesn't. I miss God so badly.

And now I am going to die a little bit. I need to so much.

Yes. I accept, *my Lord.* Under protest.

But Brasília is splendor.

I am utterly afraid.

FINAL STORIES

Beauty and the Beast or The Enormous Wound

("A bela e a fera ou A ferida grande demais")

IT BEGINS:

Well, so she left the beauty salon by the elevator in the Copacabana Palace Hotel. Her driver wasn't there. She looked at her watch: it was four in the afternoon. And suddenly she remembered: she'd told "her" José to pick her up at five, not factoring in that she wouldn't get a manicure or pedicure, just a massage. What should she do? Take a taxi? But she had a five-hundred-cruzeiro bill on her and the cab driver wouldn't have change. She'd brought cash because her husband had told her you should never go out without cash. It crossed her mind to go back to the beauty salon and ask for change. But—but it was a May afternoon and the cool air was a flower blooming with its perfume. And so she thought it wonderful and unusual to be standing on the street—out in the wind that was ruffling her hair. She couldn't remember the last time she'd been alone with herself. Maybe never. It was always her—with others, and in these others she was reflected and the others were reflected in her. Nothing was—was pure, she thought without understanding what she meant. When she saw herself in the mirror—her skin, tawny from sunbathing, made the gold flowers in her black hair stand out against her face—, she held back from exclaiming "ah!"—for she was fifty million units of beautiful people. Never had there been—in all the world's history—anyone like her. And then, in three trillion trillion years—there wouldn't be a single girl exactly like her.

"I am a burning flame! And I shine and shine all that darkness!"

This moment was unique—and she would have in the course of her life thousands of unique moments. Her forehead even broke out in a cold sweat, because so much had been given her and eagerly taken by her.

"Beauty can lead to the kind of madness that is passion." She thought: "I am married, I have three children, I am safe."

She had a name to uphold: it was Carla de Sousa e Santos. The "de" and the "e" were important: they denoted class and a four-hundred-year-old Rio family. She lived among the herds of women and men who, yes, who simply "could." Could what? Look, they just could. And to top it off, they were slick because their "could" was just so greasy in the machines that ran without the sound of rusty metal. She, who was a powerful woman. A generator of electric energy. She, who made use of the vineyards on her country estate to relax. She possessed traditions in decay but still standing. And since there was no new criterion to sustain all those vague and grandiose hopes, the weighty tradition still held. Tradition of what? Of nothing, if you had to pry. The only argument in its favor was the fact that the inhabitants were backed by a long lineage, which, though plebeian, was enough to grant them a certain pose of dignity.

She thought, all tangled: She who, being a woman, which seemed to her a funny thing to be or not to be, knew that, if she were a man, she'd naturally be a banker, a normal thing that happens among "her" people, that is, those of her social class, which her husband, on the other hand, had attained after a lot of hard work and which classified him as a "self-made man" whereas she was not a "self-made woman." At the end of the long train of thought, it seemed to her that—that she hadn't been thinking about anything.

A man missing a leg, dragging himself along on a crutch, stopped before her and said:

"Miss, won't you give me some money so I can eat?"

"Help!!!" she screamed in her head upon seeing the enormous wound in the man's leg. "Help me, God," she said very softly.

She was exposed to that man. She was completely exposed. Had she told "her" José to come to the exit on the Avenida Atlântica, the hotel where the hairdresser's was wouldn't have allowed "those people" to come near. But on the Avenida Copacabana anything was possible: people of every sort. At least a different sort from hers. "Hers"? "What sort of she was she for it to be "hers"?

She—the others. But, but death doesn't separate us, she thought suddenly and her face took on the aspect of a mask of beauty and not human beauty: her face hardened for a moment.

The beggar's thoughts: "this lady with all that makeup and little gold stars on her forehead, either won't give me anything or just a little." It struck him then, a bit wearily: "or next to nothing."

She was alarmed: since she practically never walked down the street—she was chauffeured from door to door—she started thinking: is he going to kill me? She was distraught and asked:

"How much do people usually give?"

"However much they can and want to," answered the shocked beggar.

She, who never paid at the beauty salon, the manager there sent her monthly bill to her husband's secretary. "Husband." She thought: her husband, what would he do with the beggar? She knew what: nothing. They don't do anything. And she—she was "them" too. All that she could give? She could give her husband's bank, she might give him their apartment, her country house, her jewelry …

But something that was a greed in everyone, asked:

"Is five hundred cruzeiros enough? That's all I have."

The beggar stared at her in shock.

"Are you making fun of me, miss?"

"Me?? No I'm not, I really do have the five hundred in my purse …"

She opened it, pulled out the bill and humbly handed it to the man, nearly begging his pardon.

The man bewildered.

And then laughing, showing his nearly toothless gums:

"Look," he said, "either you're very kind, ma'am, or you're not right in the head … But, I'll take it, don't go saying later that I robbed you, no one's gonna believe me. It would've been better if you gave me some change."

"I don't have any change, all I have is that five hundred."

The man seemed to get scared, he said something nearly incomprehensible, garbled from his having so few teeth.

Meanwhile his head was thinking: food, food, good food, money, money.

Her head was full of parties, parties, parties. Celebrating what? Celebrating someone else's wound? One thing united them: both had a vocation for money. The beggar spent every cent he had, whereas Carla's husband, the banker, accumulated money. His bread and butter was the Stock Market, and inflation, and profit. The beggar's bread and butter was his round gaping wound. And to top it off, he was probably afraid of healing, she guessed, because, if it got better, he'd have nothing to eat, that much Carla knew: "if you don't have a good job by a certain age ..." If he were younger, he could paint walls. Since he wasn't, he invested in that big wound with living and pestilent flesh. No, life wasn't pretty.

She leaned against the wall and decided to think carefully. It was different because she wasn't in the habit and she didn't know thought was vision and comprehension and that no one could order herself to do it just like that: think! Fine. But it so happened that deciding to posed an obstacle. So then she started looking inside herself and they actually started happening. Only, she had the most ridiculous thoughts. Like: does that beggar speak English? Has that beggar ever eaten caviar, while drinking champagne? They were ridiculous thoughts because she clearly knew the beggar didn't speak English, nor had he ever tasted caviar or champagne. But she couldn't help watching another absurd thought arise in her: had he ever skied in Switzerland?

She grew desperate then. She grew so desperate that a thought came to her made of just two words: "Social Justice."

Death to the rich! That would solve things, she thought cheerfully. But—who would give money to the poor?

Suddenly—suddenly everything stopped. The buses stopped, the cars stopped, the clocks stopped, the people on the street froze—only her heart was beating, and for what?

She saw that she didn't know how to deal with the world.

She was an incompetent person, with her black hair and her long, red nails. She was: as if in a blurry color photograph. Every day she made a list of what she needed or wanted to do the next day—that was how she'd stayed connected to the empty hours. She simply had nothing to do. Everything was done for her. Even her two children—well, her husband was the one who had decided they'd have two ...

"You've got to make an effort to be a winner in life," her late grandfather had told her. Was she, by any chance, a "winner"? If winning meant standing on the street in the middle of the bright afternoon, her face smeared with makeup and gold spangles ... Was that winning? What patience she needed to have with herself. What patience she needed in order to save her own little life. Save it from what? Judgment? But who was judging? Her mouth felt completely dry and her throat on fire—just like whenever she had to take tests in school. And there was no water! Do you know what that's like—not having water?

She wanted to think about something else and forget the difficult present moment. Then she recalled lines from a posthumous book by Eça de Queirós that she'd studied in high school: "Lake TIBERIAS shimmered transparently, covered in silence, bluer than the heavens, ringed entirely by flowering meadows, dense groves, rocks of porphyry, and pristine white lands among the palms, beneath the doves in flight."

She knew it by heart because, as a teenager, she'd been very sensitive to words and because she'd desired for herself the same shimmering destiny as Lake TIBERIAS.

She felt an unexpectedly murderous urge: to kill all the beggars in the world! Just so she, after the massacre, could enjoy her extraordinary well-being in peace.

No. The world wasn't whispering.

The world was scre-am-ing!!! through that man's toothless mouth.

The banker's young wife thought she wasn't going to withstand the lack of softness being hurled in her impeccably made-up face.

And what about the party? How would she bring it up at the party, while dancing, how would she tell the partner who'd be in her arms ... This: look, the beggar has a sex too, he said he had eleven children. He doesn't go to social gatherings, he doesn't appear in Ibrahim's society columns, or in Zózimo's, he's hungry for bread not cake, actually all he should eat is porridge since he doesn't have any teeth for chewing meat ... "Meat?" She vaguely recalled that the cook had said the price of filet mignon had gone up. Yes. How could she dance? Only if it were a mad and macabre beggars' dance.

No, she wasn't the kind of woman prone to hysteria and nerves and fainting or feeling ill. Like some of her little society "colleagues." She smiled a little thinking in terms of her little "colleagues." Colleagues in what? in dressing up? in hosting dinners for thirty, forty people?

She herself taking advantage of the garden in late summer had thrown a reception for how many guests? No, she didn't want to think about that, she recalled (why without the same pleasure?) the tables dispersed over the lawn, candlelight ... "candlelight"? she thought, but am I out of my mind? have I fallen for a scam? Some rich people's scam?

"Before I got married I was middle class, secretary to the banker I married and now—now candlelight. What I'm doing is playing at living," she thought, "this isn't life."

"Beauty can be a great threat." Extreme grace got mixed up

with a bewilderment and a deep melancholy. "Beauty frightens." "If I weren't so pretty I'd have had a different fate," she thought arranging the gold flowers in her jet black hair.

She'd once seen a friend whose heart got all twisted up and hurt and mad with forceful passion. So she'd never wanted to experience it. She had always been frightened of things that were too beautiful or too horrible: because she didn't inherently know how to respond to them and whether she would respond if she were equally beautiful or equally horrible.

She was frightened as when she'd seen the Mona Lisa's smile, right there, up close at the Louvre. As she'd been frightened by the man with the wound or the man's wound.

She felt like screaming at the world: "I'm not awful! I'm a product of I don't even know what, how can I know anything about this misery of the soul."

To shift her feelings—since she couldn't bear them and now felt like, in despair, violently kicking the beggar's wound—, to shift her feelings she thought: this is my second marriage, I mean, my previous husband was alive.

Now she understood why she'd married the first time and was auctioned off: who'll bid higher? who'll bid higher? Sold, then. Yes, she'd married the first time to the man who "bid the highest," she accepted him because he was rich and slightly above her social class. She had sold herself. And as for her second husband? Her second marriage was on the rocks, he had two mistresses … and she putting up with it all because a separation would have been scandalous: her name was mentioned too often in the society pages. And would she go back to her maiden name? Even getting used to her maiden name, that would take a long time. Anyway, she thought laughing at herself, anyway, she tolerated this second one because he gave her great prestige. Had she sold herself to the society pages? Yes. She was discovering that now. If there were a third marriage in store for her—for she was pretty and rich—, if there were, whom would she marry? She started laughing a little hysterically because she had the thought: her third husband was the beggar.

Suddenly she asked the beggar:

"Sir, do you speak English?"

The man didn't have a clue what she'd asked. But, forced to answer since the woman had just bought him with all that money, he improvised:

"Yes I do. Well aren't I speaking with you right now, ma'am? Why? Are you deaf? Then I'll shout: YES."

Alarmed by the man's ear-splitting shouts, she broke into a cold sweat. She was becoming fully aware that up till now she'd pretended there were no starving people, no people who don't speak any foreign languages and that there were no anonymous masses begging in order to survive. She'd known it, yes, but she'd turned her head and covered her eyes. Everyone, but everyone—knows and pretends they don't. And even if they didn't they'd feel a certain distress. How could they not? No, they wouldn't even feel that.

She was ...

After all who was she?

No comment, especially since the question lasted a fraction of a second: question and answer hadn't been thoughts in her head, but in her body.

I am the Devil, she thought remembering what she'd learned in childhood. And the beggar is Jesus. But—what he wants isn't money, it's love, that man has lost his way from humanity just as I too have lost mine.

She wanted to force herself to understand the world and could only manage to remember snippets of remarks from her husband's friends: "those power plants won't be enough." What power plants, good Lord? the ones that belonged to Minister Galhardo? would he own power plants? "Electric energy … hydroelectric"?

And the essential magic of living—where was it now? In what corner of the world? in the man sitting on the corner?

Is money what makes the world go round? she asked herself. But she wanted to pretend it wasn't. She felt so, so rich that she felt a certain pang.

The beggar's thoughts: "Either that woman's crazy or she stole the money because there's no way she can be a millionaire," millionaire was just a word to him and even if he wanted to see a millionaire in this woman he wouldn't have been able to because: who's ever seen a millionaire just standing around on the street, people? So he thought: what if she's one of those high-class hookers who charges their customers a lot and must be keeping some kind of religious vow?

Then.

Then.

Silence.

But suddenly that screaming thought:

"How did I never realize I'm a beggar too? I've never asked for spare change but I beg for the love of my husband who has two mistresses, I beg for God's sake for people to think I'm pretty, cheerful and acceptable, and my soul's clothing is in tatters …"

"There are things that equalize us," she thought desperately seeking another point of equality. The answer suddenly came: they were equal because they'd been born and they both would die. They were, therefore, brother and sister.

She felt like saying: look, man, I'm a poor wretch too, the only difference is that I'm rich. I … she thought ferociously, I'm about to undermine money threatening my husband's credit in the market. I'm about to, any moment now, sit right on the curb. Being born was my worst disgrace. Now that I've paid for that accursed event, I feel I have a right to everything.

She was afraid. But suddenly she took the great leap of her life: courageously she sat on the ground.

"I bet she's a communist!" the beggar thought half believing it. "And if she's a communist I'd have a right to her jewels, her apartments, her money and even her perfumes."

Never again would she be the same person. Not that she'd never seen a beggar before. But—even this came at the wrong time, as if someone had jostled her and made her spill red wine all down a white lace dress. Suddenly she knew: that beggar was made of the same substance as she. Simple as that. The "why" was what made the difference. On a physical level they were equal. As for her, she had an average education, and he didn't seem to know anything, not even who the President of Brazil was. She, however, had a keen capacity for understanding. Could it be that till now she'd possessed a buried intelligence? But what if she had just recently, coming into contact with a wound begging for money in order to eat—started thinking only of money? Money, which had always been obvious for her. And the wound, she'd never seen it so close up …

"Are you feeling bad, ma'am?"

"Not bad … but not good, I don't know …"

She thought: the body is a thing that, when ill, we carry. The beggar carries himself by himself.

"Today at the party? you'll feel better and everything will go back to normal," said José.

Really at the party she'd refresh her attractiveness and everything would go back to normal.

She sat in the backseat of the air-conditioned car, casting before she left a final glance at that companion of an hour and a half. It seemed hard for her to say goodbye to him, he was now her alter ego "I," he was forever a part of her life. Farewell. She was dreamy, distracted, her lips parted as if a word were hanging there. For some reason she couldn't have explained— she was truly herself. And just like that, when the driver turned on the radio, she heard that codfish produced nine thousand eggs per year. She could deduce nothing from that statement, she who was in need of a destiny. She remembered how as a teenager she sought a destiny and chose to sing. As part of her upbringing, they easily found her a good teacher. But she sang badly, she herself knew it and her father, an opera lover, pretended not to notice that she sang badly. But there was a moment when she started to cry. Her perplexed teacher asked her what the matter was.

"It's just, it's just, I'm scared of, of, of, of singing well ..."

But you sing very badly, the teacher had told her.

"I'm also scared, I'm also scared of singing much, much, much worse. Baaaaad way too bad!" she wailed and never had another singing lesson. That stuff about seeking art in order to understand had only happened to her once—afterward she had plunged into a forgetting that only now, at the age of thirty-five, through that wound, she needed either to sing very badly or very well—she was disoriented. How long since she had listened to so-called classical music because it might pull her out of the automatic sleep in which she lived. I—I'm playing at living. Next month she was going to New York and she realized the trip was like a new lie, like a daze. Having a wound in your leg—that's a reality. And everything in her life, since she was born, everything in her life had been soft like the leap of a cat.

(In the moving car)
 Suddenly she thought: I didn't even think to ask his name.

One Day Less
("Um dia a menos")

I DOUBT THAT DEATH WILL COME. DEATH?

Could it be that the days, so long, will end?

That's how I daydream, calm, quiet. Could it be that death is a bluff? A trick of life? Is it persecution?

And that's how it is.

The day had begun at four in the morning, she'd always risen early, immediately finding the flask of coffee in the little pantry. She drank a lukewarm cup and was about to leave it for Augusta to wash, when she remembered that old Augusta had asked for a month off to see her son.

She wasn't feeling up to the long day ahead: no appointments, no chores, neither joys nor sorrows. She sat down, then, in her oldest bathrobe, since she never expected any visitors. But being so badly dressed—in a robe belonging to her late mother—didn't please her. She got up and put on some silk pajamas with blue and white polka dots that Augusta had given her on her last birthday. That was a big improvement. And things improved still more when she sat in the armchair that had been recently reupholstered in violet (Augusta's taste) and lit her first cigarette of the day. It was an expensive brand, with that blond tobacco, a long, slim cigarillo, meant for someone of a social class that happened not to be hers. For that matter, she just happened not to be a lot of things. And she just happened to have been born.

And then?

Then.

Then.

Well anyway.

That's how it is.

Isn't it?

Well, anyway well it suddenly became clear: well anyway well that's how it is. Augusta had told her things would get better later on. That's how it is had already arrived from that's how it was.

She remembered the newspaper that she got delivered to her front door. She went over there a bit excited, you never know what you're going to read, whether the minister of Indochina will kill himself or the lover threatened by his fiancée's father will end up getting married.

But the newspaper wasn't there: that rascal of a neighbor, her enemy, must have already taken it with him. It was a constant struggle to see who first got to the newspaper that, nonetheless, had her name clearly printed on it: Margarida Flores. Along with her address. Whenever she absentmindedly saw her name written, it recalled her primary-school nickname: Margarida Flores de Enterro.* Why didn't anyone think to call her Margarida Flores de Jardim?† Because things simply were not on her side. She had a silly thought: even her little face was on its side. At an angle. She didn't even wonder whether she was pretty or ugly. She was obvious.

* "Daisy Funeral Flowers."
† "Daisy Garden Flowers."

Then.

Then she didn't have money issues.

Then there was the phone. Would she call someone? But whenever she called someone she had the distinct impression that she was bothering them. For instance, interrupting a sexual embrace. Or else she was annoying because she had nothing to say.

And what if someone called her? She'd have to contain the joyful tremor in her voice at someone finally calling her. She imagined this:

"Ring-ring-ring."

"Hello? Yes?"

"Is this Margarida Flores de Jardim?"

Faced with such a suave male voice, she'd answer:

"Margarida Flores de Bosques Floridos!"*

And the melodious voice would ask her to afternoon tea at the Confeitaria Colombo. Just in time she remembered that men these days don't ask you to tea and toast but instead for a drink. Which would already complicate things: for a drink you definitely had to be dressed more boldly, more mysteriously, more distinctively, more ... She wasn't very distinctive. And she made people a little uncomfortable, not a lot.

And, besides, the phone didn't ring.

Then. She was what she saw when she saw herself in the mirror. She rarely ever saw herself in the mirror, as if she already knew herself too well. And she ate too much. She was fat and her fat was extremely pale and flabby.

Then she decided to arrange her underwear and bra drawer: she was just the sort who arranged underwear and bra drawers,

* "Daisy Flowers of the Flowering Woods."

616

the delicate task gave her a sense of well-being. And if she were married, her husband would have a row of ties perfectly in order, by color, or by ... By whatever. Since there's always something to guide you and your arranging. As for herself, she was guided by the fact that she wasn't married, that she'd had the same maid since birth, that she was a thirty-year-old woman, who wore just a touch of lipstick, drab clothing ... and what else? She quickly avoided the "what else" because that question would make her fall into a very self-centered and ungrateful feeling: she'd feel lonely, which was a sin because whoever has God is never alone. She had God, since wasn't that the only thing she had? Besides Augusta.

So she went to take a bath which gave her such pleasure that she couldn't help wondering what other bodily pleasures might be like. Being a virgin at the age of thirty, there was nothing for it, unless she got raped by a hoodlum. Once her bath and her thinking were over, talcum powder, talcum powder, lots of talcum powder. And tons and tons of deodorant: she doubted anyone in Rio de Janeiro smelled less than she did. She might be the most odorless of creatures. And she emerged from the bathroom, so to speak, in a light minuet.

Then.

Then she saw to her great satisfaction, on the kitchen clock, that it was already eleven ... How time had flown since four in the morning. What a gift for time to pass. As she was warming the pale, flabular chicken from dinner, she turned on the radio and caught a man in the middle of a thought: "flute and guitar" ... the man said and suddenly she couldn't stand it and turned the radio off. As if "flute and guitar" were in fact her secret, longed-for, and unattainable way of being. She mustered her courage and said very softly: flute and guitar.

Once the radio and above all her thinking were turned off, the rooms sank into a silence: as if someone somewhere had just died and … But fortunately there was the noise of the pan warming the pieces of chicken that, who knew, might be gaining some color and flavor. She started eating. But immediately she realized her mistake: because she'd taken the chicken out of the fridge and only warmed it slightly, there were parts where the fat was gelatinous and cold, and others where it was burnt and dried out.

Yes.

And for dessert? She reheated a little of her breakfast and seasoned it with bitter sweetener so she'd never gain weight. She would take great pride in being practically emaciated.

Then.

She remembered apropos of nothing that millions of people were starving, in her country and elsewhere. She felt distress every time she ate.

Then.

Then! How had she forgotten about television? Ah, without Augusta she forgot everything. She turned it on, full of hope. But at that hour they were only showing old Westerns constantly interrupted by commercials for onions, maxi pads, red-currant syrup that must be tasty but fattening. She sat there staring. She decided to light a cigarette. That would improve everything since it made her into a painting at an exhibition: *Woman Smoking in Front of Television*. It was only after a long while that she realized she wasn't even watching television and was just wasting electricity. She switched it off in relief.

Then.

Then?

Then she decided to read old magazines, something she

hadn't done in a while. They had been piled up in her mother's room, ever since her death. But they were a bit too dated, some from back when her mother had been single, the fashions were different, all the men had mustaches, ads for girdles to perfect your waistline. And in particular all the men had mustaches. She lost her enthusiasm, once more lacking the nerve to throw them out because they'd been her mother's.

Then.

Yes and then?

Then she went to boil some water for tea, still not forgetting that the phone wasn't ringing. If only she had coworkers, but she didn't have a job: the inheritance from her father and mother covered her few expenses. Anyway she didn't have nice handwriting and thought they didn't accept applicants without nice handwriting.

She drank the boiling-hot tea, chewing small pieces of dry toast that scratched her gums. They'd be better with a little butter. But, of course, butter was fattening, besides raising your cholesterol, whatever that modern term meant.

Just as her teeth were tearing into the third piece of toast— she usually counted things, due to a certain obsession with order, ultimately innocuous and even amusing—just as she was about to eat the third piece of toast ... IT HAPPENED! I swear, she said to herself, I swear I heard the phone ring. She spit out the bite from the third piece of toast onto the tablecloth and, so as not to give the impression that she was impatient or needy, she let it ring four times, and each time was a sharp pang in her heart because what if they hung up thinking no one was home! At this terrifying thought she suddenly lunged for that fourth ring and managed to say in a rather offhand voice:

"Hello ..."

"If you please," said the female voice that must have been over eighty judging by its drawn-out hoarseness, "could you please call Flávia to the receiver"—no one said *receiver* anymore—"for me? My name is Constança."

"Madame Constança, I regret to inform you that there's no one in this house by the name of Flávia, I know Flávia's a very romantic name, but the thing is, there aren't any here, so what can I do?" she said with a certain despair due to Madame Constança's commanding voice.

"But isn't this General Isidro Street?"

That made matters worse.

"Yes, it is, but which phone number did you ask the operator for? Which? Mine? But I assure you that I have lived here for exactly thirty years, since birth, and there's never been any young lady named Flávia!"

"Young lady, my foot, Flávia's a year older than me and if she's lying about her age that's her problem!"

"Maybe she's not lying about her age, who knows, Madame Constança."

"If she's lying about it, that's fine with me, but at least do me a favor and tell her I'm waiting on the receiver for her and hurry up!"

"I ... I ... I've been trying to tell you that our family was the first and only ever to live in this little house and I assure you, I swear to God, that no Senhora Flávia ever lived here, and I'm not saying that Senhora Flávia doesn't exist, but here, ma'am, here—she does not e-x-i-s-t ..."

"Now stop being rude, you hussy! By the way what's your name?"

"Margarida Flores do Jardim."

"Why? Are there flowers in your garden?"

"Ha, ha, ha, you've got a sense of humor, ma'am! No, there aren't any flowers in my garden but I just have a flowery name."

"And does that do you any good?"

Silence.

"Well, does it or doesn't it?"

"I don't know what to say because I've never thought about it before. I can only answer questions I've already thought about."

"Then make a little effort to imagine the name Flávia and I bet you'll find the answer."

"I'm imagining, I'm imagining ... Aha, I've got it! The name of my childhood nanny is Augusta!"

"But, sweet child of the Lord, I'm running out of patience, it's not your childhood nanny I want, it's Flá-vi-a!"

"I don't want to seem rude, but my mother always said that pushy people are impolite, sorry!"

"Impolite? Me? Brought up in Paris and London? Do you at least speak French or English, so we can practice a little?"

"I only speak the language of Brazil, ma'am, and I believe it's time for you to hang up because my tea must be cold by now."

"Tea at three in the afternoon? It's quite clear you don't have the least bit of class, and here I thought you might have studied in England and would at least know what time people have tea!"

"The tea is because I didn't have anything else to do ... Madame Constança. And now I beg you in the name of God not to torture me any longer, I'm begging you on my knees to hang up so I can finish having my Brazilian tea."

"All right, but there's no need to whine, Dona Flores, my sole and absolute intention was to speak to Flávia to invite her over for a little game of bridge. Ah! I've got an idea! Since Flávia's out, why don't you come over for a couple rounds of low-stakes cards? Hm? How about it? Aren't you tempted? And how about entertaining a lady of a certain age?"

"My God, I don't know how to play any games."

"But how can that be!?"

"I just don't. That's how."

"And to what do you owe this lapse in your upbringing?"

"My father was strict: in his house the vice of card-playing was never allowed."

"Your father, your mother and Augusta were very old-fashioned, if I may say so and I think that ..."

"No! You may not! And now I'm the one hanging up, beg your pardon, Madame."

Wiping her eyes, she felt relieved for a moment and had an idea so novel it didn't even seem like her own: it seemed demonic like the lady's ideas ... It was to take the phone off the hook so that, should Madame Constança be as constant as her name, she wouldn't call back for that miserable Flávia. She blew her nose. Ah, if it weren't for her manners, what she would have said to that Constança woman! She was already regretting everything she hadn't said because of her manners.

Yes. The tea was cold.

And tasting distinctly of sweetener. The third little piece of toast spit out onto the tablecloth. The afternoon ruined. Or the day ruined? Or her life ruined? Never had she stopped to consider whether or not she was happy. So, instead of tea, she ate a slightly tart banana.

Then.

Then. So then it was four o'clock.

Then five.

Six.

Seven: dinnertime!

She would have liked to eat something else and not yesterday's chicken but she'd been taught not to waste food. She ate a dried-out thigh along with the little toasts. Truth be told, she wasn't hungry. She only sometimes perked up with Augusta because they'd talk and talk and eat, ah, they'd break their diets and not even gain weight! But Augusta would be gone for a month. A month is a lifetime.

Eight o'clock. She could already go to bed. She brushed her teeth for a long while, pensive. She put on a tattered, somewhat threadbare cotton nightgown, one of those nice cozy ones that her mother had made. And got into bed, under the covers.

Eyes wide open.

Eyes wide open.

Eyes wide open.

That was when she remembered the vials of sleeping pills that had been her mother's. She remembered her father: careful, Leontina, with the dosage, one too many could be fatal. I, Leontina would answer, don't want to leave this good life behind so soon, and I'll take just two little pills, enough to sleep soundly and wake up all rosy for my little husband.

That's right, thought Margarida das Flores no Jardim,* to get some nice, sound sleep and wake up rosy. She went to her mother's room, opened a drawer to the left of the big double bed — and indeed found three vials full of tablets. She was going to take two pills to start the day rosy. She didn't have bad intentions. She went to get the pitcher and a glass. She opened one of the vials: took out two little pills. They tasted like mold and sugar. She didn't notice the slightest bad intention in herself. But no one in the world will know. And now no one will ever be

---

* "Daisy of the Flowers in the Garden."

able to tell whether it happened due to some sort of imbalance or ultimately due to a great balance: glassful after glassful she swallowed each and every pill from the three big vials. But on the second vial she thought for the first time in her life: "I." And it wasn't merely a rehearsal: it was in fact a debut. All of her was debuting at last. And even before they ran out, she was already feeling something in her legs, better than anything she'd ever felt. She didn't even know it was Sunday. She didn't have the strength to go to her own room: she let herself collapse on the bed where she'd been conceived. It was one day less. Vaguely she thought: if only Augusta had left me a raspberry tart.

Appendix: The Useless Explanation

*Clarice Lispector rarely commented on her own writing, or on any-
one else's. Here, presumably in response to a query, she describes
the genesis of* Family Ties. *This text appears in the "Back of the
Drawer" section of* The Foreign Legion.

IT IS NOT EASY TO REMEMBER HOW AND WHY I WROTE
a story or a novel. Once they detach from me, I too find them
unfamiliar. It's not a "trance," but the concentration during the
writing seems to take away the awareness of whatever isn't
writing itself. There is something, however, that I can try to
reconstruct, if it really matters, and if it answers what I have
been asked.

What I remember of the story "Happy Birthday," for example, is the impression of a party that was no different from other
birthdays; but it was a stifling summer day, and I don't think I
even put the idea of summer in the story. I had an "impression,"
from which a few vague lines resulted, set down just for the enjoyment and necessity of deepening a feeling. Years later, when
I came across these lines, the whole story was born, with the
speed of someone transcribing a previously witnessed scene—

yet none of what I wrote happened at that or any other party. Much later a friend asked me whose grandmother that was. I answered that she was someone else's grandmother. Two days later the true answer came to me spontaneously, and with surprise: I discovered that the grandmother was my very own, and all I had known of her, as a child, was a picture, nothing more.

"Mystery in São Cristóvão" is a mystery to me: I went on writing it calmly like someone unwinding a ball of yarn. I didn't encounter the least difficulty. I believe that the absence of difficulty arose from the very conception of the story: its atmosphere may have needed this detached attitude of mine, a certain non-participation. The lack of difficulty might have been an internal technique, an approach, delicateness, feigned distraction.

Of "Daydream and Drunkenness of a Young Lady" I know I had so much fun that it really was a pleasure to write. While the work lasted, I was always in a good mood unlike usual days and, though others never quite noticed, I would speak in the Portuguese style, making, it seems to me, an experiment with language. It was great to write about the Portuguese woman.

Of "Family Ties" I recall nothing.

Of the story "Love" I remember two things: one, while writing, the intensity with which I unexpectedly ended up with the character in an uncalculated Botanical Garden, and from which we nearly didn't manage to get out, from being so surrounded in vines, and half-hypnotized—to the point that I had to make my character call the guard to open the gates that were already shut, or else we would still be living there to this day. The second thing I remember is a friend reading the typed story to critique it, and I, upon hearing it in a human and familiar voice, having the sudden impression that only at that instant was it born, and born fully made, as a child is born. That was the best moment of all: the story was given to me there, and I received it, or there I gave it and it was received, or both things that are one.

Of "The Dinner" I know nothing.

"A Chicken" was written in about half an hour. Someone had commissioned a column from me, I was trying without exactly trying, and I ended up not turning it in; until one day I realized that it was a fully rounded story, and felt with what love I had written it. I also saw I had written a story, and that in it was the fondness I'd always had for animals, one of the accessible forms of people.

"Beginnings of a Fortune" was written more to see what would come of trying out a technique so light that it merely gets interspersed with the story. I dove right in and was guided only by curiosity. Another practice scale.

"Preciousness" is a little irritating, I ended up disliking the girl, and then asking her forgiveness for disliking her, and at the moment of asking forgiveness feeling like not asking after all. I ended up sorting out her life more to unburden my conscience and from responsibility than from love. Writing like that isn't worth it, it gets you caught up in the wrong way, tests the patience. I have the impression that, even if I could make this story into a good one, it intrinsically wouldn't be worthwhile.

"Imitation of the Rose" made use of several fathers and mothers to be born. There was the initial shock of the news that someone had fallen ill, without my understanding why. On that same day there were roses sent to me, and that I shared with a friend. There was that constant in everyone's life, which is the rose as flower. And there was all the rest that

I don't know, and that is the fertile ground of any story. "Imitation" gave me a chance to use a monotonous tone that satisfies me very much: repetition pleases me, and repetition happening in the same place ends up digging down bit by bit, the same old song ad nauseam says something.

"The Crime of the Mathematics Teacher" used to be called "The Crime," and was published. Years later I understood that the story simply hadn't been written. So I wrote it. I nevertheless have the lingering impression that it remains not written. I still don't understand the mathematics teacher, though I know that he is what I said.

"The Smallest Woman in the World" reminds me of Sunday, springtime in Washington, child falling asleep on my lap in the middle of an outing, the first heat of May—while the smallest woman in the world (an item read in the newspaper) was intensifying all this in a place that seems to me the birthplace of the world: Africa. I think this story too came from my love of animals; it seems to me that I feel animals as one of the things still very close to God, material that didn't invent itself, a thing still warm from its own birth; and, nonetheless, a thing already getting up on its feet, and already living fully, and in each minute living all at once, never just bit by bit, never sparing itself, never wasting itself.

"The Buffalo" reminds me very vaguely of a face that I saw on a woman or on several, or on men; and one of the thousand visits I've made to zoos. That time, a tiger looked at me, I looked at him, he held my gaze, I did not, and I got out of there until today. The story has nothing to do with all that, it was written and put aside. One day I reread it and felt a shock of distress and horror.

Translator's Note

READING CLARICE LISPECTOR IS A DISORIENTING EX-
perience. There are the startling faces and eyes that appear in
mirrors, in windows, in crowds, eyes peering out from animal
masks or resembling cockroaches fringed with cilia, faces exposed like the viscera of a body on an operating table. There
are the intense feelings that explode inside her characters in
shifting constellations—nausea, distress, shock, fright, rage,
joy. And the moments of grace punctured by jarring intrusions,
as when a rat shatters a woman's communion with the divine.

   Translating Clarice has meant growing attuned to the ways
her sly surrealism, which can veer into the absurdist or fantastical, is embedded in her style. The logic of a deceptively simple
narrative or series of declarations becomes distorted or ends
in non sequiturs. "The general law for us to stay alive: one can
say 'a pretty face,' but whoever says 'the face,' dies; for having
exhausted the topic." Or: "Brasília is slim. And utterly elegant.
It wears a wig and false eyelashes. It is a scroll inside a Pyramid. It does not age. It is Coca-Cola, my God, and will outlive me." The most dizzying feature in Clarice's writing are the
surprises on the level of the sentence. Certain combinations

seem contradictory or disproportionate like "delicate abyss," or "horribly marvelous." The usual expression takes a detour, as when an elderly matriarch scornfully calls her offspring "flesh of my knee" instead of "flesh of my flesh." A comma trips up the pace where it doesn't seem to belong, like a hair she's placed in your soup.

Over and over, these stories find their force in a pivotal encounter, one that forever changes a character, drastically or in the form of a subtle but lasting imprint—a single white hair or wrinkle #3. And the language ripples along the contours of these events, lyrical or hypnotic in a moment of rapture, fragmented or puzzling when a character apprehends something previously unseen. The story "Love" hinges on one such encounter. It occurs when the housewife Ana sees a blind man on the street as she's riding the tram home from errands. He's chewing gum in a way that seems to mock her, toppling her contentment with her seemingly picture-perfect domestic life. Just as Ana is thrown into a crisis, the words start revolting against common sense. Subject and object don't match up: "everything had gained strength and louder voices." The sentences become as choppy and jumbled as Ana's consciousness: "Next to her was a lady in blue, with a face. She averted her gaze, quickly. On the sidewalk, a woman shoved her son! Two lovers interlaced their fingers smiling … And the blind man? Ana had fallen into an excruciating benevolence."

Perhaps no one will be as distraught as the translator over what seem to be grammatical mishaps. Why all those commas, why that face? It's challenging to carry out these choices with the conviction the author is entitled to. A previous translator chose to smooth things over and interpret the face as an expression: "Beside her sat a woman in blue with an expression which made Ana avert her gaze rapidly. On the pavement a mother shook her little boy." Yet the original really does include these oddities: *"Junto dela havia uma senhora de azul, com um rosto. Desviou o olhar, depressa. Na calçada, uma mulher deu um empurrão no filho!"* The word *rosto* is almost always just a face, sometimes suggesting a look but in the sense that "face" also can. My advantage in translating the *Complete Stories* nearly forty years after their author's death, as her international fame and readership rise, is that a growing familiarity with her style enables its peculiarities to be understood as more than arbitrary. If my first instinct is to explain, rereading almost always reveals that Clarice's mysterious decisions maintain their power in English—as they do here, where the jittery phrasing and the riddle of the face frustrate ordinary comprehension in a way that evokes the unraveling of Ana's everyday life.

If Clarice's language were more stridently experimental, finding equivalents would be more straightforward. The departures from standard Portuguese would be more emphatically marked and allow more freedom in English. Instead, she produces a maddening effect (maddening if you're tasked with reproducing it) of bending known forms nearly to the breaking point, yet almost always making them sound *right* if not correct, as if they ought to exist, or somewhere already do. These unexpected choices often make you do a double-take or blur your reading even if you don't stumble. She shuffles words, leaves out parts of speech, invents new yet generally understandable words by giving them alternate suffixes or extra syllables. These touches sometimes lend a literary effect and sometimes come off as conversational in the flexible, playful mode of spoken Brazilian Portuguese.

Clarice's most head-tilting constructions are those involving basic words. "I knew that only a mother can resolve birth," seems to invoke a saying, yet "*só mãe resolve nascimento*" is just as ambiguous to Brazilians. In the multiple meanings of *resolver*, is birth a puzzle to solve, a decision to make, or a matter to resolve? Elsewhere, she turns *morrer*, to die, into a cryptic transitive verb in the phrase *te morro*, "I die you," as in, "Oh how I love you and I love so much that I die you." And it's difficult to conclude what a husband means when he reminisces of his sinning wife, "There was no jewel she did not covet, and for her the bareness of her neck did not choke," and describes her as "awaiting me in her empty necklaces." When there's no context to determine a more recognizable sense, the most transparent translation is often precisely the most opaquely literal.

Having all these stories in one volume for the first time in any language allows us to apprehend Clarice's tremendous range, and to become acclimated to her singular style as it develops over time. The stories share certain characteristics of the novels, such as mystical, philosophical musings, passages that read like fever dreams, a certain noir feel, and intense psychological drama. Yet the stories also offer a more Brazilian, down-to-earth side of Clarice. They give a fuller taste of everyday Brazil during her time, from bourgeois ladies in Rio and drunks at the local bar to children's adventures in Recife and the dramas of small-town life. She's also more mischievous and affectionate with her characters, taking pleasure in portraying human vanity, pettiness, and idiosyncratic fixations. This makes for a diverse, often colloquial range of dialects and voices, and language that's less consistently otherworldly than in the more abstract novels like *The Passion According to G. H.* and *Água*

Viva. Clarice's Portuguese, in fact, often sounds surprisingly normal in these stories, which can make the inevitable deviations hard to assimilate.

Even as Clarice's voice is distinctly her own from the start, the early stories show a young writer enamored of words and their creative possibilities, revealing a sophisticated knowledge of Portuguese and the ability to write fluid, beautiful prose when she so chooses. She takes up themes she will return to throughout her life—magnetic relationships that flame out, the passion that ideas inspire, questions of perfection versus error, and the trouble with masculine authority, with adult authority, with intellectual authority. *Family Ties* and *The Foreign Legion*, written in the period that bridges marriage, motherhood, and divorce, show a writer in full command of her literary powers. These collections contain her most tightly constructed stories; translating them required constant fine-tuning to follow her dense style. Clarice also becomes more comic during this period, especially in her family and animal portraits, mixing perverse or warm humor with a solemn, mystical tone in the same story, as in "Happy Birthday," "Temptation," and "The Foreign Legion."

In Clarice's last decade there is a rupture. The great writer is sick of literature and sick of life. She gravitates toward what she calls "antiliterature" and declares, "Any cat, any dog is worth more than literature." Her stories in *Where Were You At Night* and especially in *The Via Crucis of the Body* take on a certain rawness that goes against writerly restraint. Rejecting concern for reputation or literary refinement, in both technique and subject, she writes in a looser, more provocative mode. She dwells unflinchingly on the body's mortality and its desires, so often associated with discomfort and shame. Storylines take whimsical turns, as when a prudish secretary loses her virginity to a being from Saturn named Ixtlan. Sentences are bare and disjointed, as in the erotic and bloody story "The Body": "Sometimes the two women slept together. The day was long. And, though they weren't homosexuals, they'd turn each other on and make love. Sad love. One day they told Xavier about it. Xavier quivered." Accounts of the author's life break into the fiction—waiting for the phone to ring, having a glass of rosé, debating whether to watch television alone, thinking of death—a feature she excised from earlier work. "That Clarice made people uncomfortable," thinks one character, suddenly interrupting the narrative in "The Departure of the Train."

In keeping up with Clarice's shifting registers and translating nearly four decades of work in two years' time, I've often felt like a one-woman vaudeville act, shouting, laughing, crying, musing, singing, and tap-dancing my way breathlessly across the stage. Her language swings between elegant, formal, and poetic in her more conventionally literary stories, colloquial in her comic moods, stark and fragmented in her abstract, oracular pieces, and spontaneous, even delirious, in her later works. Beyond the technical difficulty of capturing these diverse voices and distinguishing the standard from the strange, what makes translating Clarice especially taxing is the emotional weight of inhabiting her characters, often moody, volatile individuals caught in an upheaval. She draws you into these worlds until their logic is yours. I found myself growing as restless and combative as Cristina and Daniel while working on "Obsession." And I knew I was deep inside "The Buffalo" when I matter-of-factly described it as "a story about a woman who goes to the zoo to learn how to hate," only realizing from my friend's confused look that this "plot" wasn't perfectly normal.

What remains constant is the intimate physicality of Clarice's voice—its strong rhythms and the way she seems to be whispering in your ear like a sister, mother, and lover, somehow touching you from far away. Part of her rhythm comes from a fondness for repetition: refrains that produce an incantatory feel or thematic crescendo, anaphoric structures that lend a biblical tone, the slapstick effect of a repeated catchphrase, or the compulsive reiterations of an obsessive mind, like Laura's in "The Imitation of the Rose." Her words hold onto a sensory coherence, even when their semantic logic threatens to come undone.

Clarice inspires big feelings. As with "the rare thing herself" from "The Smallest Woman in the World," those who love her want her for their very own. But no one can claim the key to her entirely, not even in the Portuguese. She haunts us each in different ways. I have presented to you the Clarice that I hear best.

KATRINA DODSON

Bibliographical Note

THE PRESENT VOLUME COLLECTS, FOR THE FIRST TIME, all of Clarice Lispector's stories. There are many reasons why this has not been done before, even in Brazil. These include a publishing history that created variants of her writings in her lifetime, thanks principally to the author's habit of recycling her older works for publication in new formats. The instability of the publishing industry and of her own "critical fortune" often forced her to change publishers. Her nine novels had eight different publishers, for example, a number that does not include the reprints of earlier works in her lifetime.

It is much the same with the stories. Stories published in one place show variants with the same story published elsewhere; financial concerns often forced her to recycle earlier material in magazines and newspapers. Other later publications were careless and published without her supervision or approval. For the sake of simplicity, we have generally opted to translate the first editions of these stories as they were published in book form.

This decision, despite its theoretical cleanness, has not always been easy in practice, particularly because many of these stories were never collected in her lifetime and only emerged years—even decades—after her death in 1977.

When she died, she was a cult favorite among artists and intellectuals. Her reputation as the greatest figure of modern Brazilian literature came posthumously. Her acolytes—the word "admirers" is unequal to her obsessive, lifelong enthusiasts—have scoured the archives, discovering much early work. Though more stories may yet emerge (especially from fresh examinations of the periodicals with which she collaborated as a young woman), none have appeared since the discovery of the short first part of "Letters to Hermengardo" several years ago. It is reasonable to expect that the list of works we present here will not be significantly expanded.

Clarice Lispector was no respecter of genres. Many of her writings were presented as journalism but are clearly fictional; many published as fictions might be more comfortably classified as memoirs or essays; and so on. In the interests of making as much of her work available in our language as we can, we have cast a broad net, excluding journalism, essays, and short miscellany.

For these stories in the context of her work and life, see *Why This World: A Biography of Clarice Lispector* by Benjamin Moser.

FIRST STORIES

The works we have called "First Stories" are the juvenilia of Clarice Lispector, published when she was a law student in Rio de Janeiro, before her marriage and subsequent departure from Brazil. They also predate the spectacular debut of *Near to the Wild Heart*.

These early works come from three sources. The first is Clarice's earliest known manuscript, which has a note on the first page in her late handwriting: "In 1942 I wrote *Near to the Wild*

Heart, published in 1944. This book of stories was written in 1940–41. Never published. Clarice." (In fact, the novel was published in December 1943, around Clarice's twenty-third birthday.)

These are: "Interrupted Story," dated October 1940; "Gertrudes Asks for Advice," September 1941; "Obsession," October 1941; "The Fever Dream," July 1940; "The Escape," bearing only the notation "Rio 1940"; and "Another Couple of Drunks," December 1941. They were published in that order in a posthumous volume entitled *Beauty and the Beast* (*A bela e a fera,* Nova Fronteira, Rio de Janeiro, 1979), edited by Olga Borelli, the friend and collaborator of Clarice's final years. The original manuscripts are kept in the Instituto Moreira Salles, Rio de Janeiro.

The second source for the "First Stories" is another posthumous volume called *Other Writings* (*Outros escritos,* Rocco, Rio de Janeiro, 2005), which preserves some of her early journalism as well as essays, speeches, and interviews. It includes her earliest known story, "The Triumph," published in the magazine *Pan* on May 25, 1940; "Jimmy and I," published in the *Folha de Minas,* Belo Horizonte, December 24, 1944, but probably dating from several years earlier; the second part of "Letters to Hermengardo," published in the newspaper *Dom Casmurro,* August 30, 1941; and "Excerpt," *Vamos Lêr!,* January 9, 1941.

The third source, for the first part of "Letters to Hermengardo," is a copy of *Dom Casmurro* from July 26, 1941, preserved in the Museum of Brazilian Literature, Fundação Casa de Rui Barbosa, Rio de Janeiro.

FAMILY TIES ("LAÇOS DE FAMÍLIA")

This work, famous in Brazil, did not appear until 1960, when it was published by Francisco Alves, São Paulo. Several of its stories had been published by the Ministry of Education and Health in 1952 in a now-rare pamphlet called *Some Stories* (*Alguns contos*). These were "Mystery in São Cristóvão," "Family Ties," "Beginnings of a Fortune," "Love," "A Chicken," "The Dinner." At the time, Clarice was living in the United States. Others appeared in the legendary magazine *Senhor*, around the time of her definitive return to Rio de Janeiro in 1959.

The collection is dedicated to Clarice's psychiatrist, Inês Besouchet. The story "Preciousness" is dedicated to her close friend Mafalda Verissimo, wife of the celebrated novelist Erico Verissimo. She mentions Erico in a stray note following "A Full Afternoon" in *Where Were You at Night*.

THE FOREIGN LEGION ("A LEGIÃO ESTRANGEIRA")

This work was published in 1964 by the Editora do Autor, Rio de Janeiro. It was divided into two parts: "Stories" and "Back of the Drawer" (*"Fundo de gaveta"*). Subsequent Brazilian editions have included just the 13 selections from "Stories," all of which we include here—from "The Disasters of Sofia" through "The Foreign Legion.'"Back of the Drawer" is a compilation of mainly occasional pieces, short fictional sketches, and essayistic fragments. Of the more substantial pieces, we have selected the versions more formally collected later in *Covert Joy*, and we also include four additional works here. Two of these illustrate the difficulties in making our selection: "The Burned Sinner and the Harmonious Angels" is Clarice's only play; and "Mineirinho" is *sensu stricto* journalistic, but its style brings it much closer to her stories. Many of these works, too, were originally published in *Senhor* magazine; many, too, would be recycled.

At the beginning of "Back of the Drawer," Clarice includes the following note:

This second part will be called, as the never sufficiently quoted Otto Lara Resende once suggested to me, "Back of the Drawer." But why get rid of things that pile up, as in every house, at the back of drawers? As Manuel Bandeira put it: so that it [death] will find me with "the house clean, the table set, with everything in its place." Why pull from the back of the drawer, for example, "the burned sinner," written just for fun while I was waiting for my first child to be born? Why publish things that aren't worthwhile? Because worthwhile things aren't worthwhile either. Besides, things that evidently aren't worthwhile always interested me very much. I have an affectionate fondness for the unfinished, the poorly made, whatever awkwardly attempts a little flight and falls clumsily to the ground.

COVERT JOY ("FELICIDADE CLANDESTINA")

This collection of twenty-five stories was first published by the Editora Sabiá in 1971. It includes many works that originally appeared in *The Foreign Legion*, two of which Clarice retitled: "Journey to Petrópolis" became "The Great Outing" ("*O grande passeio*") and "Evolution of a Myopia" became "Progressive Myopia" ("*Miopia progressiva*").

The thirteen we have included are those that had not been previously published or that appeared, sometimes in a less developed version and with different titles, in the second section of *The Foreign Legion*.

These include: "Eat up, My Son"; "Forgiving God," formerly "Vengeance and Grievous Reconciliation" ("*A vingança e a reconciliação penosa*"); "Boy in Pen and Ink," formerly "Sketching a Boy" ("*Desenhando um menino*"); "A Hope," formerly in a shorter variant as "Hope" ("*Esperança*"); and "Involuntary

Incarnation," which began as the fragment "The Missionary Woman's Turn" ("*A vez da missionária*").

WHERE WERE YOU AT NIGHT ("ONDE ESTIVESTES DE NOITE")

Published on April 5, 1974, one of the three original works Clarice Lispector published in that year—the others were *The Via Crucis of the Body* and *Água viva*—at Editora Artenova, Rio de Janeiro.

We have included all but three stories, featured in other collections: "Emptying Out" ("*Esvaziamento*") appears as "A Sincere Friendship" in *Covert Joy*, which also contains "Waters of the World." "A Complicated Case" ("*Um caso complicado*") is translated as "Before the Rio-Niterói Bridge" in *The Via Crucis of the Body* for reasons noted below.

"Report on the Thing" was originally published as "Object: antistory" ("*Objeto: anticonto*") and given its current title when published in the newspaper *Jornal do Brasil*. There, Clarice included this preface:

> Note: this report-mystery, this geometrical anti-story was published in São Paulo's *Senhor* magazine. In his introduction, Nélson Coelho says that I have killed the writer in me. He cites several writers who attempted suicide of the written word. None succeeded. "Just as Clarice shall not succeed," Nélson Coelho writes.
>
> What did I attempt with this type of report?
>
> I think that I wanted to write an anti-story, an anti-literature. As if that way I might demystify fiction. It was a worthwhile experience for me. It doesn't matter that I have failed. It is called: OBJECT.

THE VIA CRUCIS OF THE BODY ("A VIA CRUCIS DO CORPO")

Published in 1974, this work was composed over the course of a single weekend, as Clarice states in her "Explanation." The looseness of its style, as well as a certain fatigued defiance in its tone, reflect her frustration, as she neared the end of her life, with her own personal struggles. The reactions to the book reflected the increasingly conservative political mood in the most repressive years of the Brazilian dictatorship. At the time, it was considered pornographic and, as she indicates in the "Explanation," "trash."

The story she refers to as "Blue Danube" in the "Explanation" was ultimately published as "Day After Day."

Though Clarice wrote most of this collection on a weekend in May, she included "Before the Rio-Niterói Bridge," published the previous month in *Where Were You at Night* as "A Complicated Case." We have grouped it with these stories to preserve the continuity of Clarice Lispector's most deliberately arranged collection. In the "Explanation" she states, "This is a book of thirteen (13) stories. But it could have been fourteen."

VISION OF SPLENDOR: LIGHT IMPRESSIONS ("VISÃO DO ESPLENDOR: IMPRESSÕES LEVES")

This collection from 1975, the second to be published by Francisco Alves, includes mainly older short pieces. The exception is "Brasília." She wrote an initial version in 1962, after her first visit to the new capital, published in *The Foreign Legion* as "Brasília: Five Days" ("*Brasília: cinco dias*"). The version here is the expanded version she wrote following her return to Brasília in 1974.

These two stories, left incomplete at Clarice Lispector's death on December 9, 1977, were published, with the manuscript of her earliest stories, in *Beauty and the Beast*, 1979. They were edited by the great friend of Clarice Lispector's last years, Olga Borelli. The title for the collection was chosen by her son, Paulo Gurgel Valente. Their incomplete state is reflected by a few inconsistencies: Carla in "Beauty and the Beast," for example, has three children early in the story, two toward the end; at the beginning she is from a rich family, whereas later she is described as her husband's former secretary.

Acknowledgments

Katrina Dodson thanks the Brazilian friends who answered endless questions like "Does this sound strange in Portuguese?": Vanessa Barbara, Ricardo Ferreira, Regina Ponce, Victoria Saramago, and especially Beatriz Bastos, Paulo Henriques Britto, and Brenno Kenji Kaneyasu. Much gratitude goes to those who commented on the English and who generally kept me alive and well: Corey Byrnes, Kathryn Crim, Andrea Gadberry, Hilary Kaplan, Erin Klenow, Adam Morris, Lucy Reynell, Yael Segalovitz, Zohar Weiman-Kelman, Tristram Wolff, and Steve Fiduccia, as well as my family, especially Thao Dodson. And a big, exhausted *abraço* to the demanding, hilarious, and deeply committed Benjamin Moser, without whose energies this would never have been completed in less than a lifetime.

Benjamin Moser thanks Carlos Alberto Asfora, Schneider Carpeggiani, José Geraldo Couto, Cassiano Elek Machado, Eduardo Heck de Sá, and Paulo Gurgel Valente. My introduction is the fruit of long conversations with Honor Moore, to whom it is dedicated; the book in your hands is the fruit of the dedication of Katrina Dodson, *sine qua non*.

Both are grateful to the publishers in New York and London for their unremitting support. At Penguin, to Alexis Kirschbaum and Sam Voulters. At New Directions, to Michael Barron, Laurie Callahan, Mieke Chew, Helen Graves, Clarissa Kerner, Tynan Kogane, Declan Spring, and especially our beloved friend Barbara Epler.